PENGUIN  CLASSICS

OBLOMOV

IVAN ALEKSANDROVICH GONCHAROV (1812–91) was the son of a rich merchant family. He attended Moscow University for three years, graduating in 1831, and spent most of his life as a civil servant, eventually becoming a censor. Besides publishing three novels, *Obyknovennaya istoriya* (1847; tr. C. Garnett, *A Common Story*, 1917), *Oblomov* (1859; tr. D. Magarshack, 1954), and *Obryv* (1869; tr. anon., *The Precipice*, 1915), the main event in his otherwise monotonous life was a voyage to Japan (1852–5) as secretary to a Russian mission, described in *Fregat Pallada* (1858). Both in himself and in his environment, he saw the clash between dreamy traditionalism (which could be well-meaning and imaginative) and vigorous practicality (which could be prosaically limited). This conflict is worked out in *A Common Story* with ingenious artificiality and in *The Precipice* with uneven diffuseness; but in *Oblomov* it is the foundation of one of the most profound Russian novels.

DAVID MAGARSHACK was born in Riga, Russia, and educated at a Russian secondary school. He came to England in 1920 and was naturalized in 1931. After graduating in English literature and language at University College, London, he worked in Fleet Street and published a number of novels. For the Penguin Classics he translated Dostoyevsky's *Crime and Punishment*, *The Idiot*, *The Devils*, and *The Brothers Karamazov*; *Dead Souls* by Gogol; and *Lady with Lapdog and Other Tales* by Chekhov. He also wrote biographies of Chekhov, Dostoyevsky, Gogol, Pushkin, Turgenev and Stanislavsky; and he is the author of *Chekhov the Dramatist*, a critical study of Chekhov's plays, and a study of Stanislavsky's system of acting. His last books to be published before his death were *The Real Chekhov* and a translation of Chekhov's *Four Plays*.

IVAN GONCHAROV

OBLOMOV

TRANSLATED
AND WITH AN INTRODUCTION
BY DAVID MAGARSHACK

PENGUIN BOOKS

PENGUIN BOOKS

Published by the Penguin Group
Penguin Books Ltd, 27 Wrights Lane, London W8 5TZ, England
Penguin Books USA Inc., 375 Hudson Street, New York, New York 10014, USA
Penguin Books Australia Ltd, Ringwood, Victoria, Australia
Penguin Books Canada Ltd, 10 Alcorn Avenue, Toronto, Ontario, Canada M4V 3B2
Penguin Books (NZ) Ltd, 182–190 Wairau Road, Auckland 10, New Zealand

Penguin Books Ltd, Registered Offices: Harmondsworth, Middlesex, England

Oblomov was first published in 1859
This translation first published in 1954
11 13 15 17 19 20 18 16 14 12

Introduction and translation copyright 1954 by David Magarshack
All rights reserved

Printed in England by Clays Ltd, St Ives plc
Set in Monophoto Scotch Roman

CONTENTS

INTRODUCTION

OBLOMOV *occupies a unique place among the great Russian masterpieces of the nineteenth century. Goncharov's great novel lacks Dostoyevsky's violence, Turgenev's brilliance and compactness, and Tolstoy's monumental force. And yet Goncharov did something that none of these great creative writers was able to do: he transformed the humdrum life of his totally insignificant and uninteresting hero into a great tragi-comedy, and he did it not by any trick from the novelist's bag, but by a painstaking accumulation of seemingly insignificant details and by a completely detached and, at the same time, sympathetic analysis of his hero's character.*

In his reminiscences Goncharov pointed out that he created the character of Oblomov as a result both of his personal observations and self-analysis. Already as a very observant and impressionable little boy, he wrote, he was so deeply struck by the carefree existence and the idleness of the representatives of the nobility in his native town that a vague impression of Oblomov as a type of human being first arose in his mind. Later on, he declared, 'Oblomov's indolent image was constantly thrust before my eyes in myself and others'. In creating Oblomov, therefore, Goncharov had in mind the universal aspect of his hero, and indeed the greatness of his novel as a work of art lies in the universality of its hero. Oblomov can hardly be said to be a typically Russian *character: there are thousands of Oblomovs scattered all over the world.*

It is no less true, moreover, that it was by his deeply sympathetic attitude towards a hero with such negative qualities as Oblomov that Goncharov succeeded in creating a full-blooded human being. It is interesting that in his novel Goncharov himself condemned the so-called 'realistic' writers who wage 'bitter war on vice' and indulge in 'contemptuous laughter at fallen humanity' in the belief that 'to express ideas one does not need a heart'. The novel as a whole is, of course, a powerful condemnation of serfdom, but the exposure of its iniquities is all the more effective for being indirect and implicit.

Ivan Goncharov himself did not belong to the class of the Russian serf-owning nobility. His father was a well-to-do grain merchant of Simbirsk, a small provincial town on the Volga which, to quote Goncharov, 'presented a complete picture of sleep and stagnation'. He was born on 18 June 1812. His father died when he was a boy of seven. His mother, an intelligent and practical woman, was too occupied with the family business to devote herself to bringing up her four children. Goncharov's education became the chief concern of an intimate friend of the family, a retired naval captain, at whose insistence the young boy was sent to a local boarding-school for the sons of the landed gentry, where he first picked up his French and English. At the age of ten he was sent off to Moscow to receive a business training at the Moscow Commercial School. Goncharov's high opinion of successful business men no doubt derived from his memories of his mother and his school. He himself did not make a success of his commercial studies. His school certificate shows that his best results were obtained in Russian language and literature and in 'German and French syntax and English etymology[!]'. In 1831 he passed the Moscow university entrance examination, and spent the next three years as a student of the philological faculty. It was the time of the formation of the famous student 'circle' of the Moscow Hegelians, led by Nicholas Stankevich and Michael Bakunin, and of the more politically orientated 'circle' of Alexander Herzen. Goncharov took no part in either, having, according to his biographers, already at that early age shown his political 'indifferentism'. It is not unlikely, however, that, belonging to the despised merchant class, Goncharov found the atmosphere of the 'circles', consisting almost exclusively of members of the Russian aristocracy, highly uncongenial. It was as a student that Goncharov first appeared in print as the translator of a novel by Eugène Sue published in a Moscow periodical in 1832.

After completing his university studies, Goncharov returned to his native Simbirsk, where he obtained a post in the Civil Service as private secretary to the Governor of the Simbirsk province. After a few months he gave up this rather unrewarding job and migrated to Petersburg, where he obtained a position in the Ministry of Finance, first as a translator and later on as the head of a small department. This was the beginning of his career in the Civil Service, which lasted for over thirty years and which brought little honour.

It was during the first years of his life in Petersburg that Goncharov became friendly with the family of the painter Nicholas Maykov, whose two sons, Apollon, the future poet and close friend of Dostoyevsky's, and Valerian, the future critic, he coached in Latin and Russian literature. The Maykovs published their own home magazines, to which Goncharov contributed two stories. One of these contained a sketch of Oblomov in the character of Tyazhelen-ko, 'a man of unexampled and methodical laziness and heroic indifference to the bustle and turmoil of life'.

Goncharov began writing his first novel, An Ordinary Story, *in 1844. It was published three years later in the* Contemporary Review, *one of Petersburg's leading periodicals. Goncharov was thirty-five at the time. The novel deals with the conflict between the decaying class of the Russian landed aristocracy and the newly emerging class of the Russian bourgeoisie, whose defence Goncharov, naturally enough, took up. The exact date when Goncharov began working on his second novel – Oblomov – is not known, but two years after the publication of* An Ordinary Story *he had already written several chapters of it, and one of them, 'Oblomov's Dream', was published in a supplement of the* Contemporary Review *in 1849. In the same year Goncharov paid another visit to Simbirsk and, as a result of the impressions he received during that visit, he conceived the idea of his third and last novel,* The Precipice. *It would seem that for the next few years his work on Oblomov practically ceased. His interest in* The Precipice *might have had something to do with it. It is more likely, though, that the severity of the censorship during the last six years of the reign of Nicholas I made Goncharov, always an extremely loyal civil servant, reluctant to carry on his work on a novel whose social implications, namely the condemnation of serfdom, were so out of tune with Government policy as to make its prospects of publication extremely doubtful.*

In 1852 Goncharov went on a round-the-world voyage in the frigate Pallas *as private secretary to the vice-admiral commanding the expedition. His two-volume account of the voyage, published three years after his return to Petersburg via Siberia at the beginning of 1855, contains a detailed description of London and a number of very shrewd observations on English life and manners. A further delay in the completion of Oblomov was brought about by Goncharov's appointment as literary censor in 1856. The death of Nicholas I a year earlier and the more liberal régime of his successor Alexander II, which culminated in the emancipation of the serfs in 1861, brought about a change in the Russian Government's attitude towards the censorship. Goncharov's appointment was generally interpreted as an indication of the new Tsar's desire for a relaxation of his predecessor's reactionary policy, which (in the words of one of the more enlightened censors of that day) 'transformed the censorship department into a police station where ideas were treated like thieves and drunkards'. Goncharov did not quite live up to the expectations of the more progressive writers of his time, being extremely conscientious and careful as a censor and never swerving from his own conservative views. 'In many things', he wrote later, 'I shared their opinions' (i.e. the opinions of the progressive writers) 'about, for instance, the liberation of the peasants, the introduction of better measures for the enlightenment of society and the common people, the harm done by all sorts of constraints imposed on education, etc. But I was never carried away by the jejune social utopias propagating the ideals of equality and fraternity, etc., which exercised the minds of the younger generation so powerfully at the time. I never had any faith in materialism or in anything people like to deduce from it.'*

The change of the political régime in Russia and the prospect of the liberation of the peasants made Goncharov resume his work on Oblomov, which he completed in the summer of 1857 during his stay at his favourite foreign spa of Marienburg. It was published in the Petersburg periodical Home Annals *in 1859, ten years after the publication of 'Oblomov's Dream'.*

Oblomov *made Goncharov famous throughout Russia and ensured for him a foremost position among contemporary Russian novelists. What struck the first readers of the novel as well as its critics most was its truthful representation of life, the minute description of significant details which raised them into symbols, and the profound psychological insight with which its characters were drawn. The simplicity of the novel's plot and its natural and inevitable development was another striking characteristic of the general style of the novel which assured its success. To a non-Russian reader it is perhaps the remarkable synthesis of the social and human problems that forms its main attraction as a work of art. With the sole exception of Stolz, who is certainly too good to be true and whom Goncharov himself declared to be 'weak and pale – the idea peeping through him too nakedly', the main characters of the novel – Oblomov and his servant Zakhar as well as Olga and Mrs Pshenitzyn – remain vitally alive in spite of the fact that the world in which they lived is as dead as a doornail.*

Goncharov was not so successful with his last and longest novel, The Precipice, *published in 1869, two years after his resignation from the Civil Service. It is more tendentious than* Oblomov *and more overloaded with details, which makes it a much more cumbersome and, at times, drearily tiresome work.*

Already at the time of the publication of Oblomov, *Goncharov showed symptoms of the mental malady which made him spend the last years of his life as a recluse in his Petersburg flat. In 1860 he accused Turgenev of stealing his plots and, as his illness progressed, he began regarding Turgenev, who was so much more brilliant and successful than he, as his chief enemy and as the head of a gang who were constantly plotting against him and devising schemes for his undoing. It was no doubt due to his illness that, with the exception of a few sketches and critical essays, he wrote nothing during the last twenty-two years of his life. He died on 27 September 1891, surviving his 'enemy' Turgenev by eight years.*

D. M.

PART ONE

1

ILYA ILYICH OBLOMOV was lying in bed one morning in his flat in Gorokhovaya Street in one of those large houses which have as many inhabitants as a country town.

He was a man of about thirty-two or three, of medium height and pleasant appearance, with dark grey eyes, but with a total absence of any definite idea, any concentration, in his features. Thoughts promenaded freely all over his face, fluttered about in his eyes, reposed on his half-parted lips, concealed themselves in the furrows of his brow, and then vanished completely – and it was at such moments that an expression of serene unconcern spread all over his face. This unconcern passed from his face into the contours of his body and even into the folds of his dressing-gown.

Occasionally a sombre look of something like fatigue or boredom crept into his eyes; but neither fatigue nor boredom could banish for a moment the mildness which was the predominant and fundamental expression not only of his face but of his whole soul, so serenely and unashamedly reflected in his eyes, his smile and every movement of his head and hands. A cold and superficial observer, casting a passing glance at Oblomov, would have said: 'A good-natured fellow, I'll be bound, a simpleton!' A more thoughtful and sympathetic man, after a long scrutiny of his face, would have walked away with a smile, full of pleasant thoughts.

Oblomov's complexion was not ruddy, nor dark, nor particularly pale, but rather nondescript, or seemed to be so because he had grown so fat and flabby – which was unusual for a man of his age – whether because of lack of exercise, or fresh air, or both, it is difficult to say. Generally speaking, his body, if one were to judge by the dull and excessively white colour of his neck, his small, chubby hands, and his soft shoulders, seemed too effeminate for a man.

His movements, too, even when he was excited, were kept in check by a certain kind of mildness and laziness which was not without its own touch of gracefulness. If his mind was troubled, his eyes were clouded over, lines appeared on his forehead, and he was plunged into doubt, sadness, and fear; but his anxiety seldom took the form of any definite idea and still more seldom was it transformed into a decision. All his anxiety resolved itself into a sigh and dissolved into apathy or drowsiness.

How well Oblomov's indoor clothes went with the calm features of his countenance and his effeminate body! He wore a dressing-gown of Persian cloth – a real oriental dressing-gown, without the slightest hint of Europe, without tassels, without velvet trimmings, and so capacious that he could wrap it round him twice. The sleeves, in true Asiatic fashion, got wider and wider from the shoulders to the hands. Though this dressing-gown had lost its original freshness and here and there exchanged its natural sheen for one acquired by years of faithful service, it still preserved the brilliance of its oriental colour, and the material was as strong as ever.

The dressing-gown had a vast number of inestimable qualities in Oblomov's eyes: it was soft and flexible, it was so light that he did not feel its weight, and it obeyed the least movement of his body like a devoted slave.

Oblomov never wore a tie or a waistcoat at home because he liked to feel unhampered and free. He wore long, soft, wide slippers; when he put his feet on the floor as he got out of bed, he invariably stepped into them without looking.

Lying down was not for Oblomov a necessity, as it is for a sick man or for a man who is sleepy; or a matter of chance, as it is for a man who is tired; or a pleasure, as it is for a lazy man: it was his normal condition. When he was at home – and he was almost always at home – he lay down all the time, and always in the same room, the room in which we have found him and which served him as a bedroom, study, and reception-room. He had three more rooms, but he seldom looked into them, except perhaps in the morning, and that, too, not every day, but only when his man-servant swept his study – which did not happen every day. In those rooms the furniture was covered with dust sheets and the curtains were drawn.

The room in which Oblomov was lying seemed at first glance to be splendidly furnished. It had a mahogany bureau, two sofas, upholstered in a silk material, and a beautiful screen embroidered with birds and fruits never to be found in nature. It had silk curtains, rugs, a number of pictures, bronze, porcelain, and all sorts of pretty knick-knacks. But an experienced person of good taste casting a cursory glance round the room would at once detect a desire to keep up appearances somehow or other, since appearances had to be kept up. Oblomov, of course, had nothing else in mind when he furnished his study. A man of refined taste would never have been satisfied with those clumsy and heavy mahogany chairs and those rickety book-stands. The back of one of the sofas had dropped and the mahogany veneer had come unstuck in some places.

The pictures, vases, and knick-knacks were equally shoddy.

The owner himself, however, was so utterly indifferent to the furniture of his study that he seemed to be wondering who on earth could have dumped all that junk there. It was Oblomov's indifference to his own property, and perhaps even still more the utter indifference shown by his servant Zakhar, that made the study look, on closer inspection, so neglected and untidy.

Dust-covered cobwebs were festooned round the pictures on the walls; instead of reflecting the objects in the room, the mirrors were more like tablets which might be used for writing memoranda on in the dust. The rugs were covered in stains. A towel had been left on the sofa; almost every morning a dirty plate, with a salt-cellar and a bare bone from the previous night's supper, could be seen on the table, which was strewn with crumbs. If it had not been for this plate and a freshly smoked pipe by the bed, or the owner of the flat himself lying in it, one might have thought that no one lived there – everything was so dusty and faded and void of all living traces of human habitation. It is true there were two or three open books and a newspaper on the book-stands, an inkwell with pens on the bureau; but the open pages had turned yellow and were covered with dust – it was clear that they had been left like that for a long, long time; the newspaper bore last year's date, and if one were to dip a pen in the inkwell, a startled fly was as likely as not to come buzzing out of it.

Oblomov, contrary to his custom, had woken up very early – about eight o'clock. He looked very worried about something. The expression of his face kept changing continually from that of alarm to one of anguish and vexation. It was clear that he was in the throes of some inner struggle, and his reason had not yet come to his aid.

What had happened was that on the previous evening Oblomov had received a disagreeable letter from the bailiff of his estate. The sort of disagreeable news a bailiff usually sends can be easily imagined: bad harvest, arrears of taxes due from the peasants, falling income, and so on. Though the bailiff had written identical letters to his master the year before and the year before that, this last letter had the same strong effect as any other unpleasant and unexpected piece of news.

The whole thing was a great nuisance: he had to think of raising some money and of taking certain steps. Still, it is only fair to do justice to the care Oblomov bestowed on his affairs. Already, after receiving his bailiff's first unpleasant letter several years before, he had begun devising a plan for all sorts of changes and improvements in the management of his estate. According to his plan, various economic, administrative, and other measures would have to be introduced. But it was far from being thoroughly thought out, and the bailiff's disagreeable letters went on arriving every year, arousing in him the desire to do something and, consequently, disturbing his peace of mind. Oblomov, indeed, realized very well that he would have to do something decisive before his plan was worked out.

As soon as he woke he made up his mind to get up, wash, and, after he had had breakfast, think things over thoroughly, come to some sort of decision, put it down on paper and, generally, make a good job of it. He lay for half an hour, tormented by this decision; but afterwards it occurred to him that he would have plenty of time to do it after breakfast, which he could have in bed as usual, particularly as there was nothing to prevent him from thinking while lying down.

That was what he did. After breakfast he sat up and nearly got out of bed; glancing at his slippers, he even lowered one foot from the bed, but immediately put it back again. It struck half-past nine. Oblomov gave a start.

'What am I doing?' he said aloud in a vexed voice. 'This is awful! I must set to work! If I go on like this – –

'Zakhar!' he shouted.

From the room separated from Oblomov's study only by a narrow passage came what sounded like the growl of a watch-dog on a chain, followed by the noise of a pair of legs which had jumped off from somewhere. That was Zakhar, who had jumped off the stove where he usually sat dozing.

An elderly man, wearing a grey waistcoat with brass buttons and a grey coat with a hole under the arm from which a bit of his shirt protruded, came into the room; his head was bald as a billiard ball, but his side-whiskers, light brown and streaked with grey, were so enormous and so thick that each of them could have made three beards.

Zakhar had made no attempt to change either the appearance

16

which the good Lord had bestowed upon him or the clothes he had worn in the country. His clothes were made after the pattern he had brought from his village. He liked the grey coat and waistcoat, for they reminded him vaguely of the livery he used to wear in the good old days when he accompanied his late master and mistress to church or on some visit; and to his mind this livery was the only evidence of the dignity of the Oblomov family. There was nothing else to remind the old man of his prosperous and peaceful life in his old master's house in the wilds of the country. His old master and mistress were dead, the family portraits had been left behind in the old country house, where, no doubt, they were lying somewhere in the attic; the stories which told of the old way of life and the important position occupied by the family were no longer heard and only lived in the memory of a few old people who had remained on the estate. This was why his grey coat was so dear to Zakhar. He saw in it a faint reflection of past glory, of which he was also reminded by something in Oblomov's face and manner which recalled his parents, Zakhar's old master and mistress, and by his whims, at which the servant grumbled both to himself and aloud, but which he respected for all that as a manifestation of his master's will and his master's rights. Without these whims he would, somehow, not have felt that he had a master over him; without them nothing would have brought back to him the memory of his youth, the country they had left so long ago, and the tales of the ancient family seat, preserved in the memory of the old servants and nursemaids and passed on from one generation to another.

The Oblomov family had once been rich and famous in its part of the country, but afterwards, goodness only knows why, it had grown poorer, lost all its influence, and, at last, was imperceptibly lost among the newer families of the landed gentry. Only the grey-haired servants of the family kept alive and handed on the faithful memories of the past which they treasured as if they were something sacred.

That was why Zakhar was so fond of his grey coat. Perhaps he valued his side-whiskers, too, because as a child he had seen so many old servants who wore that ancient and aristocratic adornment.

Oblomov, absorbed in his thoughts, did not notice Zakhar for a long time. Zakhar stood before him in silence. At last he coughed.

'What do you want?' Oblomov asked.

'But you called me, sir, didn't you?'

'Called you? Whatever did I call you for? Can't remember!' he replied, stretching himself. 'You'd better go back to your room and I'll try and remember.'

Zakhar went out of the room, and Oblomov went on lying in bed and thinking of the cursed letter.

A quarter of an hour passed.

'Well, I've been lying long enough,' he said. 'I must get up. But wait – let me read the bailiff's letter carefully once more and then I'll get up. Zakhar!'

Again the same jump and louder growling. Zakhar came in, and Oblomov again sank into thought. Zakhar stood for a couple of minutes looking at his master disapprovingly and slightly sideways, and at last walked towards the door.

'Where are you off to?' Oblomov asked suddenly.

'You say nothing, sir, so why should I stand here for nothing?' Zakhar said in a hoarse whisper, having lost his voice, so he claimed, riding to hounds with the old master, when a strong gust of wind had blown into his throat.

He was standing in the middle of the room, half turned away from Oblomov, at whom he went on looking sideways.

'Have you lost the use of your legs, that you can't stand a little longer? You see I am worried – so just wait! Haven't you been lying down long enough in your room? Find the letter I received from the bailiff yesterday. Where did you put it?'

'What letter? I've seen no letter, sir,' Zakhar said.

'But you took it from the postman yourself – such a dirty letter!'

'How should I know where you put it?' said Zakhar, tapping the papers and the various articles on the table.

'You never know anything! Look there – in the waste-paper basket! Or perhaps it has dropped behind the sofa? Look at the back of that sofa – hasn't it been repaired yet? Why don't you send for the carpenter and have it repaired? It was you who broke it, wasn't it? You never think of anything!'

'It wasn't me that broke it, sir,' replied Zakhar. 'It broke by itself. Can't last for ever, can it? It's bound to get broken some day.'

Oblomov did not think it necessary to contest the point.

'Haven't you found it yet?' he merely asked.

'Here are some letters, sir.'

'That's not it.'

'Well, sir, there ain't no more,' Zakhar said.

'Very well, you can go,' Oblomov said impatiently. 'I'll look for it myself when I get up.'

Zakhar went back to his room, but he was just about to lay his hands on the stove in order to jump on to it, when he again heard a hurried call:

'Zakhar! Zakhar!'

'Oh Lord!' Zakhar growled, as he went into the study again. 'What a trial he is! I wish I was dead!

'What is it now, sir?' he asked, holding on to the door of the study with one hand, and, to show his extreme disapproval, looking at Oblomov at such an angle that he could see his master only out of the corner of his eye, while his master could only see one of his vast side-whiskers, out of which, it would seem, two or three birds might fly at any moment.

'My handkerchief, and be quick about it! You might have thought of it yourself – you never see anything!' Oblomov observed sternly.

Zakhar showed no sign of any particular displeasure or surprise at his master's command and reproach, no doubt finding both quite natural.

'How should I know where your handkerchief is?' he grumbled, walking round the room and feeling every chair with his hand, though one could see there was nothing lying there.

'You're always losing things,' he observed, opening the drawing-room door to see if the handkerchief was there.

'Where are you going? Look for it here! I haven't been there since the day before yesterday. And hurry up, will you?' Oblomov said.

'Where is that handkerchief? Can't see it anywhere!' said Zakhar, throwing up his hands and looking round the room. 'Why, there it is,' he suddenly hissed angrily. 'It's under you, sir! There's one end of it sticking out! You lie on your handkerchief and then you ask for it!'

And, without waiting for a reply, Zakhar was about to leave the room. Oblomov felt a little disconcerted by his own mistake. But he quickly found another reason for putting the blame on Zakhar.

'Is this the way you keep the place clean and tidy? Look at the dust, the dirt – good Lord! There – have a look in the corners – you don't do anything!'

'Don't I, sir?' Zakhar said in a hurt voice. 'As if I wasn't trying. Working my fingers to the bone, I am. Dusting and sweeping nearly every day.'

He pointed to the middle of the floor and the table at which Oblomov had dinner.

'Look there, sir, there,' he said; 'everything's swept up and tidy as for a wedding. What more do you want?'

'And what's this?' Oblomov interrupted him, pointing to the walls and the ceiling. 'And this! And this!'

He pointed to the towel left on the sofa since the day before and to a plate with a piece of bread on it, forgotten on the table.

'Well, sir, I daresay I might take this away,' said Zakhar, picking up the plate with a condescending air.

'Only that? And what about the dust on the walls – the cobwebs?' Oblomov said, pointing to the walls.

'I usually sweep the walls before Easter, sir. I clean the icons then, too, and take off the cobwebs.'

'And the books and pictures – when do you dust them?'

'The books and pictures, sir, I do before Christmas: Anisya and I turn out all the book-cases then. How do you expect me to clean the place now? You're at home all day, aren't you?'

'I sometimes go to the theatre or visit friends – that's when you ought to do it.'

'Can't do things at night, can I, sir?'

Oblomov gave him a reproachful look, shook his head, and sighed. Zakhar cast an indifferent glance out of the window and sighed, too. The master seemed to think: 'Well, my dear chap, you're even more of an Oblomov than I am.' And Zakhar, quite likely, thought to himself: 'Fiddlesticks! All you're good at is to use high-sounding and aggravating words – you don't care a fig for the dust and the cobwebs!'

'Don't you realize,' said Oblomov, 'that moths thrive on dust? And sometimes I can even see a bug on the wall!'

'I've got fleas as well, sir,' Zakhar remarked unconcernedly.

'You think that's all right, do you?' Oblomov said. 'Why, it's vermin!'

Zakhar grinned all over his face, so that his eyebrows and side-whiskers parted, and a red flush spread all over his face.

'Isn't my fault, sir, if there are bugs in the world,' he said with naïve surprise. 'I didn't invent them, did I?'

'It's because of the dirt,' Oblomov interrupted him. 'What nonsense you do talk!'

'I didn't invent dirt, either.'

'You've got mice running about in your room at night – I can hear them.'

'I didn't invent the mice, either. There are lots of these creatures everywhere, sir: mice and moths and bugs.'

'How is it other people have neither moths nor bugs?'

Zakhar's face expressed incredulity, or rather a calm certainty that this never happened.

'I've got lots of everything, sir,' he said obstinately. 'You can't expect me to see to every bug. I can't crawl into their cracks, can I?'

He seemed to be thinking to himself: 'And what would sleep be like without a bug?'

'Sweep up the dirt out of the corners – then there won't be any,' Oblomov instructed him.

'Sweep it up to-day and there'll be plenty of it to-morrow,' said Zakhar.

'No, there won't,' his master interrupted him. 'There shouldn't be.'

'There will be,' the servant insisted; 'I know, sir.'

'Well, if there is, you must sweep it up again.'

'What, sir? Sweep out all the corners every day?' Zakhar asked. 'Why, what sort of life would that be? I'd rather be dead!'

'But why are other people's rooms clean?' Oblomov retorted. 'Look at the piano-tuner's opposite: it's a pleasure to look at his place, and he has only one maid.'

'And where, sir, do you expect Germans to get dirt from?' Zakhar objected suddenly. 'See how they live! The whole family gnaw a bone all the week. A coat passes from the father to the son and from the son back again to the father. His wife and daughters wear short frocks: their legs stick out under them like geese. ... Where are they to get dirt from? They're not like us, with stacks of worn-out clothes lying in wardrobes for years. They don't get a whole corner full of crusts of bread during the winter. They don't waste a crust, they don't! They make them into rusks and have them with their beer!'

Zakhar spat through his teeth at the thought of such a niggardly existence.

'It's no good your talking!' replied Oblomov. 'You'd better tidy up the rooms.'

'Well, sir, I'd be glad to tidy up sometimes, but you won't let me.'

'There he goes again! It's I who won't let him, if you please!'

'Of course it's you, sir. You're always at home: how can I tidy the place with you here? Go out for a whole day and I'll get it nice and tidy.'

'Good Lord! what next? Go out indeed! You'd better go back to your room.'

'But really, sir,' Zakhar insisted. 'Why don't you go out to-day, and Anisya and me will get everything ship-shape. Though, mind you, sir, we shan't be able to do everything by ourselves – not the two of us: we should have to get some charwomen to come and wash. ...'

'Good Lord! what an idea – charwomen! Go on, back to your room,' said Oblomov.

He was sorry he had started the conversation with Zakhar. He kept forgetting that as soon as he touched on that delicate subject he got involved in endless trouble. Oblomov would have liked to have his rooms clean, but he could not help wishing that it would all happen somehow of itself, without any fuss; but the moment Zakhar was asked to dust, scrub, and so on, he always made a fuss. Every time it was mentioned he began proving that it would mean a tremendous lot of trouble, knowing very well that the very thought of it terrified his master.

Zakhar left the room and Oblomov sank into thought. A few minutes later it again struck the half-hour.

'Good heavens,' Oblomov said almost in dismay, 'it'll soon be eleven o'clock, and I haven't got up and washed! Zakhar! Zakhar!'

'Dear, oh dear! What now?' Zakhar's voice came from the passage followed by the familiar sound of a jump.

'Is my water ready?' Oblomov asked.

'Been ready for hours,' Zakhar replied. 'Why don't you get up, sir?'

'Why didn't you tell me it was ready? I'd have got up long ago. Go now, I'll follow you presently. I have some work to do. I'll sit down and write.'

Zakhar went out, but a minute later returned with a greasy notebook covered with writing and scraps of paper.

'If you're going to write, sir, you might as well check these accounts – they have to be paid.'

'What accounts? What has to be paid?' Oblomov asked, looking displeased.

'The butcher, the greengrocer, the laundress, and the baker, sir. They are all asking for money.'

'All they think of is money!' Oblomov grumbled. 'And why don't you give me a few bills at a time? Why do you produce them all at once?'

'But every time I do, sir, you tell me to go – it's always to-morrow, to-morrow.'

'Well, can't we put it off till to-morrow now?'

'No, sir. They keep on pestering me, sir. They won't give us any credit. To-day's the first of the month.'

'Oh dear!' said Oblomov dejectedly. 'A fresh worry! Well, what are you standing there for? Put them on the table. I'll get up presently, wash, and have a look at them. So my water is ready, is it?'

'It's ready, sir,' said Zakhar.

'All right, now – –' he groaned and was about to raise himself in his bed in order to get up.

'I forgot to tell you, sir,' Zakhar began. 'Just a few hours ago, while you were still asleep, the house agent sent the porter to say that we must move – they want the flat.'

'Well, what about it? If they want it, we shall of course move. What are you pestering me for? It's the third time you've told me.'

'They're pestering me too, sir.'

'Tell them we're going to move.'

'They say, sir, you've been promising to move for the last month but you still don't move. They're threatening to tell the police.'

'Let them!' Oblomov said resolutely. 'We'll move as soon as the weather gets warmer – in three weeks or so.'

'In three weeks, sir? Why, sir, the agent says the workmen are coming in in a fortnight's time. They're going to break the whole place down. You'll have to move to-morrow or the day after – that's what he says, sir!'

'Does he? He's in too much of a hurry! He wants us to move at once, does he? Don't you dare even to mention the flat to me again. I've told you once before and you're at it again. Take care!'

'But what am I to do, sir?' Zakhar asked.

'What are you to do? So that's the way you want to wriggle out of your responsibilities?' replied Oblomov. 'You're asking me! What do I care? So long as you don't bother me, you can make any arrangements you like, provided we haven't got to move out of this flat! You won't do anything for your master, will you?'

'But what can I do, sir?' Zakhar began, speaking in a soft, hoarse voice. 'It's not my house, is it? How can we refuse to go, if we're being chucked out? Now, if it was my house, sir, I'd have been only too glad – –'

'Can't you persuade them somehow? Tell them we've been living here for years, always paid the rent regularly – –'

23

'I told them that, sir.'

'Oh? Well, what did they say?'

'Why, sir, what do you think they said? They just keep on saying we must move because they have to do all sorts of alterations. You see, sir, they want to convert this flat and the doctor's next door into one big flat in time for the landlord's son's wedding.'

'Goodness me, how do you like that?' Oblomov said with vexation. 'To think that there are such donkeys who want to get married!'

He turned over on his back.

'Why don't you write to the landlord, sir?' said Zakhar. 'Perhaps he wouldn't bother you then, but tell the workmen to break down the flat next door first.'

Zakhar pointed somewhere to the right.

'Oh, very well, I'll write as soon as I get up. You'd better go back to your room now, and I'll think it over,' he added. 'It seems that you can't do anything and I shall have to arrange this stupid affair myself too.'

Zakhar went out of the room and Oblomov began thinking. But he could not make up his mind what he was to think of first: the bailiff's letter, or moving out of the flat, or looking through the accounts. He was lost in a flood of worldly cares, and remained lying in bed, turning over from side to side. At times sudden cries were heard in the room: 'Oh dear, oh dear! You can't run away from life – it gets at you everywhere!'

It is difficult to say how long he would have remained in this state of indecision, if there had not been a ring at the front door.

'There's someone at the door already,' said Oblomov, wrapping his dressing-gown round him, 'and I haven't got up yet. Oh, it's disgraceful! I wonder who it can be so early?'

And without attempting to get up, he looked curiously at the door.

2

A YOUNG MAN of twenty-five, looking the picture of health, with laughing cheeks, lips, and eyes, entered the room. It made one envious to look at him.

He was irreproachably groomed and dressed, and his countenance, linen, gloves, and frock-coat had a dazzling freshness.

An elegant chain with numberless tiny trinkets stretched across his waistcoat. He pulled out a handkerchief of the finest lawn, inhaled the perfumes of the Orient, then, passing it lightly across his face and his shiny hat, flicked his patent leather boots with it.

'Oh, Volkov, how are you?' said Oblomov.

'How are you, Oblomov?' the dazzling gentleman said, walking up to him.

'Don't come near me,' Oblomov cried, 'don't come near me; you're straight from the cold street!'

'Oh, you spoilt darling, you sybarite!' Volkov said, looking — for a place to put down his hat, but, seeing the dust everywhere, he decided to keep it in his hand. He parted the skirts of his frock-coat to sit down, but after a careful glance at the arm-chair, remained standing.

'You aren't up yet! What an old-fashioned dressing-gown you're wearing – I haven't seen one like it for ages!'

'It's a perfectly good dressing-gown,' said Oblomov, lovingly *again* wrapping the wide folds of the garment round him.

'Are you well?' asked Volkov.

'Well? Good Lord, no!' Oblomov answered, yawning. 'Couldn't feel worse. High blood pressure, you know. And how are you?'

'Me? I'm all right. In perfect health, and having a jolly good time,' the young man added with feeling.

'Where do you come from so early?' asked Oblomov.

'From my tailor's. How do you like my frock-coat? Splendid, isn't it?' he said, turning round before Oblomov.

'Splendid! In excellent taste,' said Oblomov. 'But why is it so wide at the back?'

'It's a riding-coat; for riding on horseback.'

'Oh, I see! But do you ride?'

'Of course I do! I had the coat specially made for to-day. It's the first of May to-day: Goryunov and I are going to Yekaterin-hof. Oh, you don't know, do you? Misha Goryunov has received his commission – so we're celebrating to-day,' Volkov added with enthusiasm.

'Oh, indeed,' said Oblomov.

'He has a chestnut horse,' Volkov went on. 'All the horses in his regiment are chestnut; and mine is a black one. How will you go – will you walk or drive?'

'Oh, I don't think I'll go at all,' said Oblomov.

'Not go to Yekaterinhof on the first of May? Good Lord,

Oblomov!' Volkov cried in surprise. 'Why, everyone will be there!'

'Not everyone, surely,' Oblomov observed lazily.

'Do come, my dear fellow! Sofya Nikolayevna and Lydia will be alone in the carriage, and the seat opposite is entirely at your disposal.'

'No, that seat is too small for me. And, besides, what on earth am I going to do there?'

'Very well, in that case Misha could hire another horse for you.'

'The things he thinks of!' Oblomov said, almost to himself. 'Why are you so interested in the Goryunovs?'

'Oh!' Volkov said, flushing crimson. 'Shall I tell you?'

'Do.'

'You won't tell anyone – on your word of honour?' Volkov went on, sitting down on the sofa beside him.

'I won't.'

'I – I'm in love with Lydia,' he whispered.

'Bravo! How long? – She's very charming, I believe.'

'For three weeks,' Volkov said with a deep sigh. 'And Misha is in love with Dashenka.'

'Which Dashenka?'

'Where have you been, Oblomov? You don't know Dashenka? Why, the whole town is crazy about her dancing. To-night I'm going to the ballet with him: he wants to throw a bouquet on to the stage. I must introduce him into society. He's so shy – a novice. Oh, good Lord, I have got to go and buy some camelias.'

'Whatever for? You'd better come and dine with me. We'd have a talk. I'm afraid two awful things have happened to me – –'

'Sorry, I can't. I'm dining at Prince Tyumenev's. The Goryunovs will be there and she – my darling Lydia,' he added in a whisper. 'Why have you given up the prince? It's such a gay house! So wealthy! And their country cottage! Buried in flowers! They've added a balcony to it – *gothique*. I understand they're going to have dances there in the summer – *tableaux vivants!* You'll be coming, won't you?'

'No, I don't think I will.'

'Oh, what a splendid house! On their Wednesday at homes last winter there were never fewer than fifty people there – sometimes, indeed, there were as many as a hundred!'

'Good heavens, I can imagine how horribly boring it must have been.'

'Boring! How can you say that? The more the merrier. Lydia, too, used to come, but I never noticed her there, then suddenly –

> *In vain to banish her from my mind I try,*
> *And by reason, my passion to tame – –'*

he sang, and without thinking sat down in the arm-chair, but jumped up immediately and began dusting his clothes.

'How awfully dusty your room is!' he said.

'It's all Zakhar's fault!' Oblomov complained.

'Well, I must be off,' said Volkov. 'Must get those camelias for Misha's bouquet. Au revoir.'

'Come and have tea with me in the evening, after the ballet, and tell me all about it,' Oblomov invited him.

'I'm sorry, I've promised to go to the Mussinskys'; it's their At Home to-day. Won't you come, too? I'll introduce you.'

'No, thank you. What should I do there?'

'At the Mussinskys'? Why, half the town is there! What should you do there? It's a house where they talk about everything.'

'That's what I find so boring – talking about everything,' said Oblomov.

'Well, why don't you go to the Mezdrovs'?' Volkov interrupted him. 'There they talk about one thing only – art. All you hear there is – the Venetian school, Bach and Beethoven, Leonardo da Vinci – –'

'Always the same thing – how boring!' said Oblomov with a yawn. 'Pedants, I suppose.'

'There's no pleasing you. Why, there are hundreds of houses you can go to. Everyone has definite visiting days now: the Savinovs have dinners on Thursdays, the Maklashins on Fridays, the Vyaznikovs on Sundays, Prince Tyumenev on Wednesdays. I'm engaged every day of the week,' Volkov concluded with shining eyes.

'And don't you find it exhausting to go rushing about day after day?'

'Exhausting? Good Lord, no! It's great fun!' Volkov said happily. 'In the morning I read the papers – one must be *au courant* with everything, know the news. Thank heavens my job in the Civil Service doesn't require my presence at the office. All I'm supposed to do is to have dinner twice a week with the head of my department. Then I go visiting people I haven't seen for some time – well, then – er – there's always a new actress in the Russian or in the French theatre. The opera season will be opening soon and I shall book seats for it. And now I'm in love – summer is coming – Misha has been promised leave – we'll go for a month to their estate for a change. We can do some shooting there. They have splendid neighbours who give *bals champêtres*. Lydia and I will go for walks in the woods, go boating, pick flowers – Oh!' and he spun round and round with delight. 'However, I must be off. Good-bye,' he said, trying in vain to have a good look at himself in the dusty mirror.

'Wait a moment,' Oblomov tried to stop him. 'I wanted to talk business with you.'

'Sorry – I'm in a hurry,' Volkov replied. 'Another time! But won't you come with me and have some oysters? You'll be able to tell me all about it then. Come, Misha is treating us.'

'No, thank you,' said Oblomov.

'Good-bye, then.'

He walked to the door and came back.

'Have you seen this?' he asked, showing him a hand in a marvellously fitting glove.

'What is it?' asked Oblomov, looking perplexed.

'The new *lacets*. You see how wonderfully they fit. You haven't got to wrestle for two hours trying to button your glove. You just pull the lace and it's done. It's just arrived from Paris. Would you like me to bring you a pair to try?'

'All right, bring me a pair,' said Oblomov.

'And have a look at this. Very charming, isn't it?' he asked, picking out one of his trinkets. 'A visiting-card with a corner turned down.'

'Can't make out the inscription.'

'Pr. Prince M. Michel,' Volkov said. 'There was no room for the surname Tyumenev. He gave this to me instead of an Easter egg. – But good-bye – au revoir. I've another ten calls to make. Oh, how gay life is!'

And he vanished.

'Ten visits in one day – the poor wretch!' thought Oblomov. 'And this is life!' he shrugged his shoulders. 'What's there left of the man? What is he wasting and frittering himself away for? No doubt it's nice to look in at the theatre, and fall in love with some Lydia – she's very charming! Pick flowers with her in the country, go shooting – there's nothing wrong with that. But make ten calls in one day – poor wretch!' he concluded, turning over on his back, glad that he had no such empty thoughts and desires, that he did not rush about, but lay in bed, preserving his peace and his human dignity.

Another ring at the door interrupted his thoughts. A new visitor came in.

It was a man in a dark green frock-coat, with brass embossed buttons, his cleanly-shaven, worn-out face framed evenly by a pair of dark side-whiskers; he had tired, but calm and thoughtful, eyes, and a pensive smile.

'Good morning, Sudbinsky,' Oblomov greeted him gaily. 'So you've come at last to see your old colleague! Don't come near – don't come near – you're straight from the cold street!'

'How are you, Oblomov? I've long been meaning to call on you,' said the visitor, 'but you know how devilishly busy I am. Look – I'm taking a caseful of official papers to the office to report on. And I've told the courier to come straight here if I should be asked for. I haven't a moment to myself.'

'You're going to your office at this hour? Why so late?' asked Oblomov. 'You used to be there at ten o'clock.'

'I used to – yes. But now it's different: I *drive* there at twelve.' He emphasized the word 'drive'.

'Oh, I see,' said Oblomov. 'You're head of a department! Since when?'

Sudbinsky nodded significantly.

'Since Easter,' he said. 'But the amount of work – it's dreadful! From eight to twelve at home, from twelve to five at the office, and more work in the evening. Never see anyone!'

'Well, well! Head of a department – so that's it!' said Oblomov. 'Congratulations! What a fellow! And we used to be office clerks together. I shouldn't be surprised if you were made a State Counsellor next year.'

'Good heavens, no. I should have been given the order of the Crown this year. I thought I'd receive an order for *distinguished services* – but now that I've been given my new post – you can't be promoted twice in two years.'

'Come and have dinner with me; we'll drink to your promotion,' said Oblomov.

'I'm sorry, but I'm dining with the vice-director to-day. I have to get my report ready for Thursday – hellish work! You can't rely on the provincial reports. You have to check the lists yourself. Our vice-director is so particular, he insists on doing everything himself. So we shall sit down to it together after dinner.'

'Not after dinner, surely?' asked Oblomov, incredulously.

'Why, what do you think? I'll be lucky to get off early – I'll have time to drive to Yekaterinhof. As a matter of fact, I came to ask if you wouldn't go with me. I'd call for you.'

'I'm afraid I'm not feeling very well,' said Oblomov, frowning. 'Besides, I've a lot to do – No, sorry, I can't!'

'A pity,' said Sudbinsky. 'It's a lovely day. To-day is my only chance of getting some fresh air.'

'Well, any news at the office?' asked Oblomov.

'Yes, all sorts of things. We don't sign letters now, "Your humble servant", but: "Accept our assurance of". We're no longer required to send in service lists in duplicate. Our department is to get three more sections and two more officials for special duties. Our committee has been closed. Lots of things!'

'Well, and what about our former colleagues?'

'Nothing special so far. Svinkin has lost a file of official documents.'

'No? What did the director do?' Oblomov asked in a trembling voice. In spite of himself, he felt frightened from force of habit.

'He ordered to withhold his promotion till the file turns up. It's an important case, concerning penalties. The director believes,' Sudbinsky added almost in a whisper, 'that he has lost it on purpose.'

'I don't believe it!'

'You're quite right,' Sudbinsky affirmed importantly, with an air of condescension. 'Svinkin is such a feather-brained fellow. He sometimes makes a mess of his figures and gets all his references muddled up. I've had such awful trouble with him, but I haven't noticed anything of that kind – I mean, he wouldn't do such a thing. He just wouldn't. He must have mislaid the documents. They'll turn up one day.'

'So that's how you spend your time,' said Oblomov. 'Always busy – working.'

'Oh, it's dreadful, dreadful! But of course with a man like the vice-director of our department it's a pleasure. He never fails to reward a good and conscientious official for faithful service, and he doesn't forget those who don't do any work, either. Those who have done their term of service he recommends for promotion; and for those who aren't due for promotion or the conferment of an order he'll try to get a bonus.'

'What salary do you get?'

'Oh, nothing much. One thousand two hundred salary, seven hundred and fifty for board, six hundred for lodgings, five hundred for travelling expenses, and up to a thousand in bonuses.'

'Good God!' Oblomov exclaimed, jumping off the bed. 'It isn't singing you're doing, is it? Why, you earn as much as an Italian opera singer!'

'Oh, that's nothing! Peresvetov receives additional remuneration, and he does less work than I – and he can't make head or tail of anything. But then of course he hasn't the same reputation. They think very highly of me,' he added modestly, lowering his eyes. 'The minister said the other day that I was a credit to the ministry.'

'Stout fellow!' said Oblomov. 'But working from eight to twelve, from twelve to five, and at home, too – well!' He shook his head.

'But what should I do if I were not in the service?' asked Sudbinsky.

'Lots of things! You could read, write ...' said Oblomov.

'But I do nothing but read and write now.'

'I don't mean that. You could publish your writings.'

'Not everyone can be a writer. Look at you. You don't write, do you?' replied Sudbinsky.

'Ah, but I have an estate on my hands,' said Oblomov with a sigh. 'I'm devising a new scheme, introducing all sorts of improvements. Worrying myself to death. But you're doing other people's work – not your own.'

'Well, that can't be helped. One has to work, if one is paid. I'll have a rest in the summer. My chief has promised to get me some special work which will take me out into the country. I'll get travelling expenses to hire five horses, three roubles a day for my other expenses, and then promotion. ...'

'They have money to burn!' Oblomov said enviously; then he sighed and fell into thought.

'I need money,' added Sudbinsky. 'I'm getting married in the autumn.'

'Good Lord! Really? To whom?' Oblomov cried sympathetically.

'Yes, indeed, to Miss Murashin. You remember they were staying next to me in the country during my summer holidays and had tea at my place? I believe you met her.'

'No, I don't remember. Is she pretty?' asked Oblomov.

'Yes, she's a charming girl. If you like, we can go and have dinner with them.'

Oblomov looked embarrassed. 'All right – only – –'

'Next week,' said Sudbinsky.

'Yes, yes, next week,' Oblomov agreed, feeling relieved. 'My new suit isn't ready yet. Tell me, is it a good match?'

'Oh yes, her father is a high-grade civil servant. He's giving her ten thousand, and he has free Government quarters. He's letting us have twelve rooms; furniture, heating, and lighting provided free. Not so bad.'

'Not so bad, indeed! You're a lucky chap, Sudbinsky,' Oblomov added, not without envy.

'You must be my best man, Oblomov! Don't forget.'

'Why, of course,' said Oblomov. 'Well, and what about Kuznetzov, Vassilyev, Makhov?'

'Kuznetzov has been married for years, Makhov is now in my place, and Vassilyev has been transferred to Poland. Ivan Petrovich has received the Order of St Vladimir, and Oleshkin is "His Excellency" now.'

'He's a nice fellow,' said Oblomov.

'Yes, yes. He deserves it.'

'A very nice fellow indeed. Good-natured and even-tempered.'

'So obliging,' Sudbinsky added. 'And, you know, never tries to curry favour, to make mischief, trip one up, get ahead of anyone – he does all he can for people.'

'An excellent fellow! I remember if I made a mess of some official report, left something out, expressed a wrong opinion, or quoted the wrong law in a memorandum, he didn't mind; he'd merely tell someone else to put it right. An excellent fellow!' Oblomov concluded.

'But our Semyon Semyonovich is incorrigible,' said Sudbinsky. 'All he's good for is to throw dust in people's eyes. What do you think he did the other day? We received a demand from the provinces for putting up dog kennels near the buildings of our ministry, to guard against the depredation of Government property; our architect, a capable, experienced, and honest man, drew up a very moderate estimate; but Semyon Semyonovich thought it was too high and began making inquiries to find out how much the kennels would cost to build. He discovered someone who agreed to do it at thirty copecks less and at once sent in a memorandum about it. ...'

There was another ring at the front door.

'Good-bye,' said the civil servant. 'I'm afraid I've been chatting too long to you. I may be wanted at the office. ...'

'Do stay a little longer,' Oblomov said, trying to detain him. 'Besides, I'd like to ask your advice – two awful things have happened to me.'

'No, no, I'm sorry, old man, I'd better look you up again in a couple of days,' Sudbinsky said, leaving the room.

'My dear fellow, you're up to your neck in it,' thought Oblomov, as he watched him go. 'Blind, deaf, and dumb to everything else in the world. But he'll be a big man one day, be put in charge of all sorts of important things, and reach a high rank in the service. This is what they call making a career, I suppose! But how little of the real man is wanted for such a career – intelligence, will, feelings are not wanted. What for? They're a luxury! And so he'll go on till he dies, and he'll go through life without being aware of lots of things. And there he goes on working from twelve till five at his office and from eight till twelve at home – poor fellow!'

He felt a quiet satisfaction at the thought that he could stay in bed from nine till three and from eight till nine, and was proud that he had no reports to make nor papers to write and that there was ample scope both for his feelings and his imagination.

Oblomov was absorbed in his thoughts and did not notice a very thin dark man standing by his bed, a man whose face was practically invisible behind his whiskers, moustache, and imperial. He was dressed with studied negligence. ✗

'Good morning, Oblomov!'

'Good morning, Penkin,' said Oblomov. 'Don't come near, don't come near, you're straight from the cold!'

'Oh, you funny fellow,' Penkin said. 'Still the same incorrigible, care-free idler!'

'Yes, care-free!' said Oblomov. 'Let me show you the letter I received from my bailiff last night: I am racking my brains and you say: care-free! Where do you come from?'

'From a bookshop: I went to find out if the magazines were out. Have you read my article?'

'No.'

'I'll send it to you. Read it.'

'What is it about?' asked Oblomov, yawning heartily.

'About trade, the emancipation of women, the beautiful April weather we've been having, and about a newly invented fire extinguisher. How is it you don't read the papers? Why, you find all about our daily life there. But most of all I'm agitating for the realistic movement in literature.'

'Have you plenty of work?' asked Oblomov.

'Oh, quite a lot. Two articles a week for my paper, reviewing novels, and I've just written a short story.'

'What about?'

'About the mayor of a provincial town who boxes the ears of the local tradespeople.'

'Yes, that's realism all right,' said Oblomov.

'Isn't it?' the literary gentleman said, looking pleased. 'This is the main idea of my story and, mind you, I know it is new and daring. A traveller happened to see the beating and he went and complained to the Governor about it. The Governor ordered a civil servant, who was going to the town on official business, to look into the matter and, generally, find out all he could about the mayor's conduct and personality. The official called a meeting of the local tradespeople on the pretext of discussing their trade with them, and began questioning them about that, too. Well, what do you think those shopkeepers did? Why, they bowed and scraped and praised the mayor up to the skies. The official made some private inquiries and found that the trades-men were awful rogues, sold rotten goods, gave short measure, cheated the Government, were utterly immoral, so that the beating was a well-deserved punishment!'

'So the mayor's blows play the part of Fate in the ancient tragedies?' said Oblomov.

'Yes, indeed,' Penkin was quick to agree. 'You have a fine appreciation of literature, Oblomov. You ought to be a writer. You see, I've succeeded in showing up the mayor's arbitrary disregard of the laws and the common people's corrupt morals, the bad methods adopted by the subordinate officials, and the need for stern but legal measures. Don't you think this idea of mine is – er – rather new?'

'Yes, especially to me,' said Oblomov. 'I read so little, you see.'

'As a matter of fact,' said Penkin, 'one doesn't see many books in your room, does one? But you must read one thing, a most excellent poem will be published shortly – *A Corrupt Official's Love for a Fallen Woman* – I can't tell you who the author is. It is still a secret.'

'What is it about?'

'The whole mechanism of our social life is shown up, and all in a highly poetic vein. All the hidden wires are exposed, all the rungs of the social ladder are carefully examined. The author summons, as though for trial, the weak but vicious statesman and a whole swarm of corrupt officials who deceive him; and every type of fallen woman is closely scrutinized – French-women, German, Finnish – and everything, everything is so remarkably, so thrillingly true to life. ... I've heard extracts from it – the author is a great man! He reminds one of Dante and Shakespeare. ...'

'Good Lord!' cried Oblomov in surprise, sitting up. 'Going a bit too far, aren't you?'

Penkin suddenly fell silent, realizing that he had really gone too far.

'Read it and judge for yourself,' he said, but with no enthusiasm this time.

'No, Penkin, I won't read it.'

'Why not? It's creating a sensation, people are talking about it.'

'Let them! Some people have nothing to do but talk. It is their vocation in life, you know.'

'But why not read it, just out of curiosity?'

'Oh, what is there to be curious about?' said Oblomov. 'I don't know why they keep on writing – just to amuse themselves, I suppose.'

'To amuse themselves! Why, it's all so true to life! So laughably true! Just like living portraits. Whoever it is – a merchant, a civil servant, an army officer, a policeman – it's as if the writers caught them alive!'

'But in that case why all this bother? Just for the fun of picking up some man and presenting him as true to life? As a matter of fact, there is no life in anything they do – no true understanding of it, no true sympathy, nothing of what one can call real humanity. Mere vanity – that's what it is. They describe thieves and fallen women just as though they had caught them in the street and taken them to prison. What you feel in their stories is not "invisible tears", but visible, coarse laughter and spitefulness.'

'What more do you want? That's excellent. You've said it yourself. Burning spite, bitter war on vice, contemptuous laughter at fallen human beings – everything's there!'

'No, no, not everything,' Oblomov cried, suddenly working himself up into a passion. 'Depict a thief, a prostitute, a defrauded fool, but don't forget that they, too, are human beings. Where's your feeling of humanity? You want to write with your head only!' Oblomov almost hissed. 'Do you think that to express ideas one doesn't need a heart? One does need it – they are rendered fruitful by love; stretch out a helping hand to the fallen man to raise him, or shed bitter tears over him, if he faces ruin, but do not jeer at him. Love him, remember that

35

he is a man like you, and deal with him as if he were yourself, then I shall read you and acknowledge you,' he said, lying down again comfortably on the couch. 'They describe a thief or a prostitute,' he went on, 'but forget the human being or are incapable of depicting him – what art and what poetic vein do you find in that? Expose vice and filth, but please don't pretend that your exposures have anything to do with poetry.'

'According to you, then, all we have to do is to describe nature – roses, nightingales, frosty mornings – while everything around us is in a continuous state of turmoil and movement? All we want is the bare physiology of society – we have no time for songs nowadays.'

'Give me man – man!' Oblomov said. 'Love him!'

'Love the money-lender, the hypocrite, the thieving or dull-witted official? Surely you can't mean that? One can see at once that you're not a literary person!' Penkin said heatedly. 'No, sir, they must be punished, cast out from civil life, from society.'

'Cast out from society?' Oblomov suddenly cried, as though inspired, jumping to his feet and facing Penkin. 'That means forgetting that there was a living spirit in this unworthy vessel; that he is a depraved man, but a man none the less like yourself. Cast him out! And how do you propose to cast him out from human society, from nature, from the mercy of God!' he almost shouted, his eyes blazing.

'Going a bit too far, aren't you?' Penkin said in his turn with surprise.

Oblomov realized, too, that he had overstepped the mark. He fell silent suddenly, stood still for a moment, yawned, and slowly lay down on the couch.

Both lapsed into silence.

'What do you read then?' asked Penkin.

'Me? Oh, books of travel mostly.'

Again silence.

'But you will read the poem when it comes out, won't you?' Penkin asked. 'I'd bring it to you ...'

Oblomov shook his head.

'Well, shall I send you my story?'

Oblomov nodded.

'I'm afraid I must really be off to the printers,' said Penkin. 'Do you know why I called? I came to ask you to go to Yekaterinhof with me. I have a carriage. I have to write an article to-morrow about the festival, and we could watch it together.

You could point out to me what I failed to notice. It would be more jolly. Let's go!'

'No, thank you, I don't feel well,' said Oblomov, frowning and pulling the blankets over himself. 'I'm afraid of the damp. The ground hasn't dried up yet. But why not come and have dinner with me to-day? We could have a talk. Two awful things have happened to me ...'

'I'm sorry but the whole of our editorial staff dine at St George's to-day. We shall go to the festival from there. And I must get my article ready during the night and send it off to the printers before the morning. Good-bye.'

'Good-bye, Penkin.'

'Writes articles at night,' Oblomov mused. 'When does he sleep? And yet he probably earns five thousand a year. It's his bread and butter. But to keep on writing, wasting his mind and soul on trifles, to change his convictions, sell his intelligence and imagination, do violence to his nature, be in a perpetual state of excitement and turmoil, knowing no rest, always rushing about. ... And write and write, like a wheel or a machine – write to-morrow, write the day after – the holidays, summer will come – always writing, writing! When is he to stop and have a rest? Poor wretch!'

He turned his head towards the table, where everything was so bare, the ink dried up, and no pen to be seen, and he was glad that he lay as free of care as a new-born babe, without trying to do too many things at once, without selling anything.

'And the bailiff's letter? And the flat?' he remembered suddenly, and sank into thought again.

But presently there was another ring at the front door.

'I seem to be holding a regular reception to-day,' said Oblomov and waited to see who his new visitor was.

A man of indefinite age and of an indefinite appearance came into the room; he had reached the age when it was difficult to say how old he was; he was neither ugly nor handsome, neither tall nor short, neither fair nor dark; nature had not bestowed on him a single striking or outstanding characteristic, neither good nor bad. Some called him Ivan Ivanich, others Ivan Vassilyevich, and still others Ivan Mikhaylovich. People were also uncertain about his surname: some said it was Ivanov, some called him Vassilyev or Andreyev, and others thought he was Alexeyev. A stranger, meeting him for the first time and being told his name, immediately forgot it, as he forgot his face, and never noticed what he said. His presence added nothing to society and

37

his absence took nothing away from it. His mind possessed no wit or originality or other peculiarities, just as his body possessed no peculiarities. He might have been able to tell everything he had seen or heard, and entertain people at least in that way, but he never went anywhere; he had been born in Petersburg and never left it, so that he merely saw and heard what others knew already. Is such a man attractive? Does he love or hate or suffer? It would seem that he ought to love and hate and suffer, for no one is exempt from that. But somehow or other he managed to love everyone. There are people in whom, however hard you try, you cannot arouse any feeling of hostility, revenge, etc. Whatever you do to them, they go on being nice to you. To do them justice, however, it is only fair to say that if you were to measure their love by degrees, it would never reach boiling point. Although such people are said to love everybody and are therefore supposed to be good-natured, they do not really love anybody and are good-natured simply because they are not ill-natured. If people were to give alms to a beggar in the presence of such a man, he, too, would give him a penny, and if they should scold the beggar or drive him away and laugh at him, he, too, would scold him or laugh at him. He cannot be .called wealthy, because he is rather poor than rich; but he cannot be called poor either, if only because there are many people poorer than he. He has a private income of about 300 roubles a year, and, besides, has some unimportant post in the Civil Service, for which he receives a small salary; he is never in need, nor does he ever borrow money, nor, needless to say, would it ever occur to anyone to borrow money from him. He has no special or regular job in the service, because neither his superiors nor his colleagues could ever discover if there were any one thing he did better or worse in order to decide what he was particularly fit for. If he were told to do one thing or another, he did it in such a way that his superior was unable to say whether he had done it badly or well. He would just look at his work, read it through a few times and say: 'Leave it, I'll look it through later, and, anyway, it seems to be perfectly all right.' No trace of worry or strong desire could be detected on his face, nor anything that would show that he was at that moment thinking of something; nor would you ever see him examining anything closely to show that he took a particular interest in it. If he happened to meet an acquaintance in the street and was asked where he was going, he would reply that he was going to his office or to a shop or to see some friend. But if his acquaintance asked him to go with him instead to the post office or to his tailor or just for a walk, he would go with him to the post office, the tailor, or for a walk, though it might mean going in the opposite direction.

It is doubtful if anyone except his mother noticed his advent into the world, and indeed very few people are aware of him while he lives, and it is quite certain that no one will miss him when he is gone. No one will inquire after him, no one will pity him, no one rejoice at his death. He has neither friends nor enemies, but lots of acquaintances. Quite likely only his funeral procession will attract the attention of a passer-by, who will for the first time honour this obscure individual by a show of respect, namely a low bow; and perhaps some curious fellow will run in front of the procession to find out the dead man's name, and immediately forget it.

This Alexeyev, Andreyev, Vassilyev, or whatever his name is, seems to be a sort of incomplete and impersonal reminder of the human crowd, its dull echo, its pale reflection.

Even Zakhar, who in his candid talks with his cronies at the gate or in the shops gave all sorts of characterizations of his master's visitors, always felt perplexed when they came to talk of this – let us say, Alexeyev. He would reflect a long time, trying to catch some prominent feature in the face, the looks or the manners or the character of this man, to which he might be able to hold on, and at last had to give it up with the words: 'Oh, that one is neither fish, flesh, nor good red herring.'

'Oh, that's you, Alexeyev?' Oblomov greeted him. 'Good morning. Where do you come from? Don't come near – don't come near, I won't shake hands – you're straight from the cold street!'

'Good Lord, it isn't cold at all!' said Alexeyev. 'I hadn't intended to call on you to-day, but I met Ovchinin and he carried me off to his place. I've come to fetch you, Oblomov.'

'Where to?'

'Why, to Ovchinin's, of course. Matvey Andreyich Alyanov, Kasimir Albertovich Pkhailo, and Vassily Sevastyanych Kolymyagin are there.'

'What are they doing there and what do they want me for?'

'Ovchinin invites you to dinner.'

'Oh, to dinner,' Oblomov repeated without enthusiasm.

'And then we're all going to Yekaterinhof; they told me to ask you to hire a carriage.'

'And what are we going to do there?'

'What do you mean? There's a fête there to-day. Don't you know? It's the first of May.'

'Sit down, please; we'll think about it,' said Oblomov.

'Do get up! It's time you were dressed.'

'Wait a little; we've plenty of time.'

'Plenty of time! They are expecting us at twelve, we'll have dinner early, at two o'clock, and go to the festival. Do hurry up! Shall I ask Zakhar to help you to dress?'

'Dress? I haven't washed yet!'

'Well, wash, then!'

Alexeyev began pacing the room, then he stopped before a picture he had seen a thousand times before, cast a quick glance out of the window, picked up some knick-knack from the bookcase, turned it round in his hand, examined it thoroughly, put it back, and began pacing the room again, whistling to himself – so as not to interfere with Oblomov's getting up and washing. Ten minutes passed in this way.

'What on earth are you doing?' Alexeyev suddenly asked Oblomov.

'Why?'

'But you're still lying down!'

'Should I have got up, then?'

'Why, of course! They're waiting for us. You wanted to go, didn't you?'

'Go? Where? I didn't want to go anywhere.'

'But, my dear fellow, you've just been saying that we were going to dine at Ovchinin's and then go to the festival.'

'Go there in this damp weather?' Oblomov said lazily. 'What do you expect to see there? It's going to rain, too, it's so dull outside.'

'There's not a cloud in the sky and you talk of rain! It looks so dull because your windows haven't been cleaned for ages! Look at the dirt on them! You can't see a thing here, and one curtain is almost closed.'

'I daresay, but just try to say a word about it to Zakhar and he'll at once suggest engaging charwomen and driving me out of the house for a whole day!'

Oblomov sank into thought, and Alexeyev sat at the table drumming on it with his finger-tips and gazing absent-mindedly at the walls and the ceiling.

'So what are we going to do?' he asked a few minutes later. 'Are you going to dress or do you stay as you are?'

'Why?'

'What about Yekaterinhof?'

'What on earth are you so anxious about Yekaterinhof for – really!' Oblomov cried vexatiously. 'Can't you stay here? Are you cold here or is there a bad smell in the room that you're so anxious to get out?'

'Why, no,' said Alexeyev; 'I'm not complaining. I'm always very happy here.'

'Well, if you are, why are you so anxious to be somewhere else? Why not stay here with me for the day? We'll have dinner and in the evening you may go where you like. Oh dear, I've forgotten: I can't possibly go out! Tarantyev is coming to dinner: it's Saturday.'

'Well, of course, I don't mind. I'll do as you wish,' said Alexeyev.

'I haven't told you anything about my affairs, have I?' Oblomov asked quickly.

'What affairs? I don't know anything,' said Alexeyev, staring at him in surprise.

'Why do you think I haven't got up all this time? You see, I've been lying here trying to find some way out of my troubles.'

'What's the matter?' asked Alexeyev, trying to look alarmed.

'Two misfortunes! I don't know what to do.'

'What misfortunes?'

'They're driving me out of my flat. Just imagine it – I must move: the upset, the breakages – the mere thought of it frightens me – I have lived here for eight years, you know. My landlord has played a dirty trick on me. Hurry up and move, he says.'

'Hurry up! That means he wants your flat badly. Moving is a great nuisance – a very troublesome business,' said Alexeyev. 'They're sure to lose and break things – such an infernal nuisance! And you have such a nice flat. ... What rent do you pay?'

'Where am I to find another such flat?' Oblomov went on; 'and in a hurry, too? Dry and warm; a nice quiet house; we've had only one burglary here. The ceiling, it is true, doesn't look quite safe – the plaster is bulging – but it hasn't come down yet.'

'Fancy that!' said Alexeyev, shaking his head.

'I wonder if there is anything I could do so that I – needn't move?' Oblomov remarked pensively, as though speaking to himself.

'Have you got your flat on a lease?' Alexeyev asked, examining the room from floor to ceiling.

'Yes, but the lease has expired: I've been paying the rent monthly for some time – don't remember for how long.'

'Well, what do you intend to do?' Alexeyev asked after a short pause. 'Are you going to move or not?'

'I don't intend to do anything,' said Oblomov. 'I don't want even to think of it. Let Zakhar think of something.'

'But, you know, some people like moving,' said Alexeyev. 'Changing flats seems to be their only pleasure in life.'

'Well, let them move, then,' Oblomov retorted. 'For my part, I can't stand any changes! But the flat's nothing – you'd better have a look at what my bailiff writes to me! Here, I'll show you his letter – where the devil is it? Zakhar! Zakhar!'

'Mother of God!' Zakhar wheezed to himself, jumping off his stove. 'When will the good Lord put an end to my troubles?' He came in and looked dully at his master.

'Why haven't you found the letter?'

'Where am I to find it, sir? I don't even know which letter you want. I can't read, can I?'

'Never mind, look for it,' said Oblomov.

'You were reading some letter last night, sir,' said Zakhar, 'but I haven't seen it since.'

'Where is it then?' Oblomov asked with vexation. 'I haven't swallowed it, have I? I remember very well that you took it from me and put it somewhere. There it is – look!'

He shook the blanket and the letter fell on the floor out of its folds.

'Aye, I'm always the one what gets the blame for everything!'

'All right, all right,' Oblomov and Zakhar shouted at each other at the same time. 'Go – go!'

Zakhar went out, and Oblomov began reading the letter, which seemed to have been written in *kvas* on grey paper and sealed with brownish sealing-wax. Enormous pale letters followed in solemn procession, without touching each other, along an oblique line from the top to the bottom corner of the page. The procession was occasionally interrupted by a huge pale blot.

'Dear Sir,' Oblomov began, 'our father and benefactor – –' Here he omitted several greetings and good wishes and went on from the middle: 'I am glad to inform you, Sir, that everything on your estate is in good order. There has been no rain for five weeks and I daresay, Sir, the good Lord must be angry with us not to send us rain. The old men don't remember such a drought, Sir. The spring crops have all been burnt up as if by a devouring fire; the winter crops have been ruined, some by the worm and some by early frost; we have ploughed it over for spring crops, but we can't be sure if it will be any good. Let us

42

hope, Sir, that merciful heaven will spare you; we do not care what happens to us – let us all starve to death. On St John's Eve three more peasants ran away: Laptev, Balochov, and Vasska, the blacksmith's son, who ran off by himself. I sent the women after their husbands, but they never came back, and are living at Cholki, I am told. A relative of mine went to Cholki from Verkhlyovo, the estate manager sent him there to inspect a foreign plough. I told him about the runaway peasants. He said he had been to see the police inspector who told him to send in a written statement, after which everything would be done to send the peasants back to their places of domicile. He said nothing except that, and I fell at his feet and begged him with tears in my eyes, but he bawled at me at the top of his voice: "Be off! Be off with you! I've told you it will be done if you send in your signed statement!" But I never did send in the statement. There is no one I can hire here; all have gone to the Volga, to work on the barges – the people here have all become so stupid, Sir. There will be no linen of ours at the fair this year: I have locked up the drying and the bleaching sheds and put Sychuga to watch them day and night; he never touches a drop, and to make sure he don't steal any of his master's goods, I watch over him day and night. The other peasants drink a lot and they are all anxious to pay rent for their land instead of working on your land without any payment. Many of them have not paid up their arrears. This year, Sir, we will send you about two thousand less than last year, unless the drought ruins us completely, otherwise we shall send you the money as promised.'

There followed expressions of loyalty and the signature: 'Your bailiff and most humble slave, Sir, Prokofy Vytyagush-kin, has put his hand to it with his own hand.' Being illiterate he put a cross under the letter. 'Written from the words of the said bailiff by his brother-in-law, Dyomka the One-Eyed.'

Oblomov glanced at the end of the letter. 'No month or year,' he said. 'I suppose the letter must have been lying about at the bailiff's since last year – St John's Eve and the drought! Just woken up to it!' He sank into thought. 'Well?' he went on. 'What do you make of it? He offers to send me about two thousand less – how much will that leave? How much do you think I received last year?' he asked, looking at Alexeyev. 'I didn't mention it to you at the time, did I?'

Alexeyev raised his eyes to the ceiling and pondered.

'I must ask Stolz when he comes,' Oblomov continued. 'Seven or eight thousand, I believe – I should have made a note of it!

So now he puts me down to six! Why, I shall starve! How can I live on it?'

'Why worry?' said Alexeyev. 'A man must never give way to despair. It will all come right in the end.'

'But did you hear what he said? He doesn't send me the money – oh no! He doesn't say anything to put my mind at rest. All he is thinking of is to cause me unpleasantness, and he does it deliberately! Every year the same story! I simply don't know what to do! Two thousand less!'

'Yes, it's a great loss!' said Alexeyev. 'Two thousand is no joke! Alexey Login, I understand, also got twelve instead of seventeen thousand this year.'

'Twelve thousand isn't six thousand,' Oblomov interrupted him. 'The bailiff has thoroughly upset me! If all this is really true – I mean, the bad harvest and the drought, then why has he to worry me before the proper time?'

'Well, of course,' Alexeyev began, 'he shouldn't have done that. But you can't expect a peasant to have nice feelings, can you? That sort of man doesn't understand anything.'

'But what would you do in my place?' asked Oblomov, looking questioningly at Alexeyev in the vain hope that he might think of something to allay his fears.

'This requires careful thought,' said Alexeyev. 'It's impossible to decide at once.'

'Ought I to write to the Governor, I wonder?' Oblomov said, musingly.

'Who is your Governor?' asked Alexeyev.

Oblomov did not reply and sank into thought. Alexeyev fell silent and also pondered.

Crumpling the letter in his hands, Oblomov propped up his head on them and, resting his elbows on his knees, sat like that for some time, tormented by an onrush of profitless thoughts.

'I wish Stolz would hurry up and come,' he said. 'He writes to say he's coming soon, meanwhile he's rushing about goodness only knows where. He'd settle it all!'

He again stared sadly about him. They were both silent a long time. Oblomov was the first to rouse himself at last.

'That's what has to be done,' he said resolutely and almost got out of bed. 'And it must be done as soon as possible. No use wasting any more time. First – –'

At that moment there was a desperate ring at the front door, so that Oblomov and Alexeyev both gave a start and Zakhar at once jumped off the stove.

3

A T H O M E?' someone in the hall asked loudly and gruffly.

'Where would he go at this hour?' Zakhar replied, more gruffly still.

A man of about forty came into the room. He was of massive build, tall, broad-shouldered, bulky, with a large head and big features, a short, thick neck, large protruding eyes, and full lips. A glance at him made one think of something coarse and untidy. It was clear that he made no attempt at dressing elegantly. It was not often that one saw him clean-shaven. But he did not seem to care; he was not ashamed of his clothes, and wore them with a kind of cynical dignity.

It was Mikhey Andreyich Tarantyev, a country neighbour of Oblomov.

Tarantyev looked at everything morosely, with ill-disguised contempt and open hostility towards the world at large; he was ready to abuse everyone and everything as though he had suffered some injustice or had been offended in his dignity, or like a man of strong character persecuted by destiny and submitting to it under protest and unwillingly. His gestures were bold and sweeping; he spoke in a loud voice, glibly and almost always angrily; listening to him from a distance one got the impression of three empty carts going over a bridge. He was never put out by anyone's presence, was never at a loss for a word, and was generally rude to everyone, including his friends, as though making it clear that he bestowed a great honour on a person by talking to him or having dinner or supper at his place.

Tarantyev was a man of quick and cunning intelligence; no one could solve some practical question or some complicated legal problem better than he; he would at once devise his own theory of how it was best to act in the circumstances and would adduce very subtle arguments in favour of it, and in conclusion almost always be rude to the person who had asked his advice.

And yet, having obtained the job of a clerk in some government office twenty-five years before, he remained there in the same post till his hair began to turn grey. It never occurred to him or to anyone else that he might get higher up in the service.

The trouble was that Tarantyev was good only at talking; in words he settled everything simply and easily, especially where other people were concerned; but as soon as he had to move a finger or stir from his place – in short, apply his own theory in practice and show efficiency and expedition – he became an entirely different person; he was unable to rise to the occasion, he suddenly became dejected or unwell or awkward, or he found he had something else to do, which he did not do, either; or if he did, he made an unholy mess of it. He behaved just like a child: he overlooked something, or showed himself to be ignorant of the merest trifles, or was late for an appointment, or threw up the business half-way, or began at the wrong end and bungled it in such a way that it was quite impossible to put it right – and finally he would blame everybody but himself for his own incompetence.

His father, an old-fashioned provincial lawyer, had meant his son to inherit his skill and experience of looking after other people's affairs and his professional ability at the Bar; but fate decided otherwise. The father, who was too poor to pay for a good education, did not want his son to lag behind the times and wished him to learn something besides the tricky business of legal practice. He sent him for three years to a priest to learn Latin.

The boy was gifted by nature, and in three years he mastered Latin grammar and syntax and had just begun to construe Cornelius Nepos when his father decided that he had already acquired enough knowledge to give him an enormous advantage over the older generation and that, indeed, any further studies might interfere with his practice in court.

Not knowing what to do with his Latin, the sixteen-year-old Mikhey began to forget it in his father's house, but in the meantime, while waiting for the honour of attending the rural or the district court, he went to all his father's merry parties, and in this school, amid the frank exchanges of opinions, the young man's mind developed most thoroughly. He listened with the impressionability of youth to the stories told by his father and his cronies of various civil and criminal actions and of curious cases which passed through the hands of these old-fashioned lawyers. But all this led to nothing. Mikhey did not become a business man and a pettifogging lawyer in spite of his father's efforts, which would of course have been successful had not fate ruined all his well-laid plans. Mikhey certainly mastered the whole theory on which his father's talks were based; he had merely to put it into practice, but his father's death prevented him from qualifying for the Bar and he was taken to Petersburg by some benefactor who found him a clerk's job in a government office and then forgot all about him.

So Tarantyev remained a mere theoretician all his life. In his Petersburg office he had no use for Latin, or for his clever theory of twisting all cases, whether fairly or unfairly, as he liked; and yet he was conscious of a dormant force inside him, locked up through hostile circumstances without hope of ever breaking out, as the evil spirits in fairy-tales were deprived of their powers of doing harm by being imprisoned in enchanted dungeons. Quite likely it was this consciousness of the powers wasted within him which made Tarantyev so rude, malevolent, perpetually angry and abusive. He looked on his present occupation – the copying of papers, the filing of documents, etc. – with bitterness and contempt. He had only one last hope of improving his position in the distant future: to get a job in the spirit monopoly. This seemed to him the only profitable change from the occupation bequeathed to him by his father that he never succeeded in obtaining. And in expectation of this happy turn in his career, the ready-made theory of life and work created by his father, the theory of bribery and dishonest dealing, having failed to find its chief and worthy outlet in the provinces, was applied by him to all the trivial details of his paltry existence in Petersburg and, for lack of any official application, crept into his relations with his friends.

He was a bribe-taker at heart, on principle, and not having any official business with people, he contrived to take bribes from his colleagues and friends, goodness only knows for what services; he forced them either by bullying or cunning to entertain him whenever and wherever they could; he demanded to be treated with undeserved respect and constantly found fault with everybody. He was never ashamed of his threadbare clothes, but he could not help being worried if in the course of the day he could not look forward to an enormous dinner with a proper quantity of wines and spirits.

That was why among his friends he played the part of a big watchdog, which barks at everybody and allows no one to stir, but at the same time catches a piece of meat in the air, from whatever direction it may come.

Such were Oblomov's two most assiduous visitors. Why did these two Russian proletarians come to him? They knew very well why: to eat, to drink, to smoke good cigars. They found a warm and comfortable place of refuge at his flat and met always with the same, if not cordial, then indifferent, reception.

But why did Oblomov let them come? That he could hardly tell himself. Quite possibly it was for the same reason that even to this day, in our remote Oblomovkas, every well-to-do house is crowded with the same sort of men and women, penniless, without a trade, with no abilities for any productive work, but with hungry mouths and almost always of some rank and standing.

There are still sybarites who need such accessories to life: they are bored without superfluous people. Who would hand them the snuff-box they had mislaid or pick up their handkerchief from the floor? To whom complain of their headache and from whom expect sympathy as a right, or tell a bad dream and demand an interpretation of it? Who would read a book to them at bedtime and help them go to sleep? And sometimes such a proletarian would be sent to the nearest town on an errand or put to help in the household – they could not be expected to bother with such tasks themselves, could they?

Tarantyev made a lot of noise and got Oblomov out of his immobility and boredom. He shouted, argued, and formed a sort of one-man show, making it unnecessary for his lazy host to speak or act. Into the room where sleep and peace reigned, Tarantyev brought life and movement and sometimes news from the outside world. Oblomov could listen and look, without lifting a finger, at something that was alive, moving and talking in front of him. Besides, he was still simple-minded enough to believe that Tarantyev could really give him some good piece of advice.

Oblomov put up with Alexeyev's visits for another, no less important, reason. If he wanted to live in his own way – that is to say, lie without uttering a word, doze or pace the room – Alexeyev did not seem to be there at all; he, too, was silent, dozed or pretended to read a book, or looked lazily at the pictures and knick-knacks, yawning till tears came into his eyes. He could go on like that for three days on end. If, on the other hand, Oblomov tired of being by himself and felt the need for expressing his thoughts, for talking, reading, arguing, showing emotion – he had always at his side an obedient and ready listener who shared with equal willingness his silence, his conversation, his excitement, and his trend of thoughts, whatever it might be.

Other visitors came seldom and only for a short time, as the first three visitors had done; with all of them he was getting more and more out of touch. Sometimes Oblomov was interested in some piece of news, in a conversation lasting about five minutes, then, his curiosity satisfied, he fell silent. But they had to be entertained in turn – they expected him to take part in what interested them. They enjoyed being among a crowd of people; every one of them understood life in his own way, not as Oblomov understood it, and they kept dragging him into it: he resented it all, disliked it, and was antagonized by it.

There was one man only whom he was fond of; he, too, gave him no peace; he liked the latest news, and society, and learning, and life as a whole, but, somehow, more deeply and sincerely – and though Oblomov was kind to everyone, he loved only him and trusted him alone, perhaps because they were brought up, educated, and had lived together. This man was Andrey Karlovich Stolz. He was away, but Oblomov was expecting him back any moment.

4

'MORNING, old man,' said Tarantyev abruptly, holding out a hirsute hand to Oblomov. 'Why are you lying like a log at this hour?'

'Don't come near, don't come near, you're straight from the cold street,' said Oblomov, covering himself up with a blanket.

'Good Lord, from the cold street!' Tarantyev roared. 'There, take my hand, if I give it to you! It'll soon be twelve o'clock and he's still lounging about!'

He was going to drag Oblomov from the bed, but Oblomov forestalled him by putting his feet quickly on the floor and getting into both his slippers at once.

'I was just about to get up myself,' he said, yawning.

'I know how you get up! You'd have lain there till dinner. Hey, there, Zakhar! Where are you, you old fool? Help your master to dress and be quick about it!'

'You'd better get a Zakhar of your own first, sir, and then start calling him names!' said Zakhar, coming into the room and looking spitefully at Tarantyev. 'Look at the mess you've made on the floor – just like a hawker,' he added.

'No backchat from you, my lad,' said Tarantyev, lifting his foot to kick Zakhar as he walked past him; but Zakhar stopped, turned round, and scowled.

'Just try to touch me,' he wheezed furiously. 'What do you

think you're doing? I'll go back,' he said, walking back to the door.

'Good heavens, Tarantyev, what a cantankerous fellow you are! Why can't you leave him alone?' said Oblomov. 'Give me my clothes, Zakhar.'

Zakhar came back and, looking askance at Tarantyev, darted past him.

Leaning on Zakhar, Oblomov reluctantly rose from his bed like a man who was very tired and as reluctantly walked to an arm-chair, sank into it, and sat still. Zakhar took the pomatum, a comb and brushes from a small table, greased Oblomov's hair, parted it, and then brushed it.

'Will you wash now, sir?' he asked.

'I'll wait a little,' Oblomov replied. 'You can go now.'

'Oh, you're here too, are you?' Tarantyev said suddenly to Alexeyev while Zakhar was brushing Oblomov's hair. 'I never saw you. Why are you here? What a swine that relative of yours is! I've been meaning to tell you – –'

'What relative? I have no relative,' Alexeyev said timidly, staring in surprise at Tarantyev.

'Why, that fellow – what do you call him? The fellow who's in the Civil Service – Afanasyev. You don't mean to say he's no relative of yours? Of course he is!'

'But I'm not Afanasyev – I'm Alexeyev,' said Alexeyev. 'I have no relatives.'

'What do you mean – no relative? Why, he's just as poor a specimen as you are – and his name's also Vassily Nikolayevich.'

'I swear he's no relation of mine. My name is Ivan Alexeyich.'

'Makes no difference. He looks like you. But he's a swine. You tell him so when you see him.'

'I don't know him,' said Alexeyev, opening his snuff-box. 'Never seen him.'

'Let's have a pinch of your snuff,' said Tarantyev. 'Why, yours is ordinary snuff, not French! Yes, so it is,' he said, taking a pinch. 'Why isn't it French?' he added sternly. 'I've never met a swine like that relative of yours,' he went on. 'I borrowed fifty roubles from him about two years ago. Fifty roubles – not such a big sum, is it? You might have expected him to forget it. But not at all – he remembered. A month later he began pestering me, asking me every time he met me: "What about that loan?" I got sick and tired of the sight of him. And as if that wasn't enough, he barged into my office yesterday. "I expect," he said, "you've got your salary to-day and can repay me now."

My salary, indeed! I told him off properly in front of everybody and he was glad to get out, I can tell you. "I'm a poor man," he said, "I need the money!" As if I didn't need it! Who does he take me for? A rich man, to give him fifty roubles every time he asks for it? Let's have a cigar, old man!'

'You'll find the cigars in the box there,' replied Oblomov, pointing to a bookcase.

He was sitting pensively in the arm-chair in his customary picturesquely lazy pose, not noticing what was happening round him or listening to what was being said. He was examining his small white hands and stroking them lovingly.

'I say, they're still the same!' Tarantyev observed sternly, taking out a cigar and looking at Oblomov.

'Yes, they're the same,' Oblomov replied absent-mindedly.

'But didn't I tell you to buy the others – foreign ones? So that's how you remember what is said to you! Mind you get some by next Saturday or you won't see me here for a long time. Good Lord, what horrible stuff!' he went on, lighting a cigar, and letting out one cloud of smoke into the room, he inhaled another. 'Can't smoke it.'

'You've come early to-day, Tarantyev,' said Oblomov, yawning.

'Why? You're not getting tired of me, are you?'

'No, I just mentioned it. You usually come in time for dinner, and now it's only just gone twelve.'

'I've come earlier on purpose to find out what there is for dinner. Your food is so awful as a rule that I thought I'd better find out what you've ordered for to-day.'

'You'd better ask in the kitchen,' said Oblomov.

Tarantyev went out.

'Good heavens!' he said, returning. 'Beef and veal! The trouble with you, old man, is that you don't know how to live – a landowner, forsooth! What sort of a gentleman are you? You look like a shopkeeper – you've no idea how to treat a friend! Have you bought any Madeira at least?'

'Don't know, you'd better ask Zakhar,' said Oblomov, hardly listening to him. 'I expect they must have some wine there.'

'You mean the same wine as before – from the German? Really, my dear fellow, you ought to buy some in the English shop.'

'Oh, it'll have to do,' said Oblomov. 'Don't want to send out for it.'

'But look here, give me the money and I'll fetch it. I have to go past the shop anyway. I've still to make another call.'

Oblomov rummaged in the drawer and produced a red ten-rouble note.

'Madeira costs seven roubles, and this is ten,' said Oblomov.

'Let's have it all. Don't be afraid – they'll give me the change at the shop.'

He snatched the note from Oblomov's hand and quickly hid it in his pocket.

'Well,' said Tarantyev, putting on his hat. 'I'll be back by five o'clock. I have a call to make: I've been promised a job in a spirits depot and they asked me to look in. By the way, my dear fellow, won't you hire a carriage to go to Yekaterinhof to-day? You might take me with you.'

Oblomov shook his head.

'Why not? Are you too lazy, or do you grudge the money? Oh, you sluggard!' he said. 'Well, good-bye for the present.'

'Wait, Tarantyev,' Oblomov interrupted him. 'I want to ask your advice.'

'What is it? Come on, out with it! I'm in a hurry.'

'Well, two misfortunes have befallen me, all at once. I have to move ...'

'Serves you right. Why don't you pay your rent?' said Tarantyev, turning to go.

'Good Lord, no! I always pay in advance. No, they're going to convert this flat. Wait a moment. Where are you off to? Tell me what I am to do. They rush me. They want me to move within a week.'

'What sort of advice do you expect me to give you? You needn't imagine – –'

'I don't imagine anything,' said Oblomov. 'Don't shout. Better think what I am to do. You're a practical man – –'

But Tarantyev was no longer listening to him. He was thinking of something.

'Well,' he said, taking off his hat and sitting down. 'All right, you may thank me and order champagne for dinner. Your business is settled.'

'What do you mean?' asked Oblomov.

'Will there be champagne?'

'Perhaps, if your advice is worth it.'

'Aye, but you're not worth the advice. You don't imagine I'll give you advice for nothing, do you? There, you can ask him,' he added, pointing to Alexeyev, 'or his relative.'

'All right, all right, tell me,' Oblomov begged.

'Now, listen: you must move to-morrow.'

'Good Lord, what an idea! I knew that myself.'

'Wait, don't interrupt,' Tarantyev shouted. 'To-morrow you will move to the flat of a good friend of mine in Vyborg.'

'What nonsense is that! Vyborg! Why, they say wolves roam the streets there in winter!'

'Oh, well, they do come there sometimes from the islands, but what has that got to do with you?'

'But it's such a dull place – a wilderness, no one lives there.'

'Nonsense! A good friend of mine lives there. She has a house of her own with big kitchen gardens. She is a gentlewoman, a widow with two children. Her unmarried brother lives with her. He's a clever fellow, not like that chap in the corner there,' he said, pointing to Alexeyev. 'He's a damn sight more intelligent than you or I.'

'What has that got to do with me?' Oblomov said impatiently. 'I'm not going to move there.'

'We shall see about that. No, sir, if you ask for my advice, you have to do as I tell you.'

'I'm not going there,' Oblomov said firmly.

'To hell with you, then,' replied Tarantyev, and, pulling his hat over his eyes, walked to the door.

'You funny fellow,' Tarantyev said, coming back. 'Do you find it so pleasant here?'

'Pleasant? Why it's so near to everything,' Oblomov said. 'To the shops, the theatre, my friends – it's the centre of the city, everything – –'

'Wha-at?' Tarantyev interrupted him. 'And how long is it since you went out? Tell me that. How long is it since you went to a theatre? Who are the friends you visit? Why the hell do you want to live in the centre of the city, pray?'

'What do you mean, why? For lots of reasons.'

'You see, you don't know yourself. But there – why, think of it: you'll live in the house of a gentlewoman, a good friend of mine, in peace and quiet. No one to disturb you – no noise, clean and tidy. Why, you live here just as at an inn – you, a gentleman, a landowner! But there everything is clean and quiet, and there's always someone to talk to if you're bored. Except me, no one will come to visit you there. Two children – play about with them to your heart's content. What more do you want? And think what you will save! What do you pay here?'

'Fifteen hundred.'

'Well, there you'd pay a thousand for almost a whole house! And such lovely bright rooms! She's long been wanting a quiet, tidy lodger – so there you are!'

Oblomov shook his head absent-mindedly.

'Nonsense, you'll move all right!' said Tarantyev. 'Just consider: it'll cost you half of what you're spending here: you'll save five hundred in rent alone. Your food will be twice as good and as clean; your cook and Zakhar won't be able to steal – –'

A growl was heard from the entrance hall.

'– and there'll be more order too,' Tarantyev went on. 'Why, it's dreadful to sit down to dinner at your place now. You want the pepper – it isn't there; vinegar – they've forgotten to buy any, the knives have not been cleaned; you say you keep losing your linen – dust everywhere – it's disgusting! And there a woman will be keeping house – neither you, nor that fool Zakhar – –'

The growling in the entrance hall grew louder.

'– that old dog won't have to bother about anything,' Tarantyev went on. 'You will be provided with board and lodgings. Why hesitate? Move – and that's the end of it.'

'But how could I – for no rhyme or reason – suddenly move to Vyborg?'

'What's the use of talking to you?' Tarantyev said, wiping the perspiration from his face. 'It's summer time now: why, it's as good as living in a country house. Why rot here in Gorokhovaya Street? There you would have the Bezbarodkin Gardens, Okhta is next door, the Neva within a few yards, your own kitchen garden – no dust, no stuffiness! Why waste time thinking? I'll nip over to her now before dinner – you'll let me have the cab fares – and to-morrow you can move – –'

'What a man!' said Oblomov. 'Suddenly he gets a crazy idea into his head and I have to move to Vyborg. I mean, it's not difficult to think of such a plan. No, sir, you'd better think of something that would make it possible for me to stay here. I've lived here for eight years and I don't want to change.'

'It's settled: you're going to move. I'll go and see my friend at once and call about my job another time.'

He was about to go, but Oblomov stopped him.

'Wait, wait! Where are you off to? I've a much more important business to settle. Have a look at the letter I've received from my bailiff and tell me what to do about it.'

'Dear me, you are a queer fish and no mistake,' Tarantyev replied. 'You can't do anything by yourself. It's always I who have to do things for you. Of what use is a man like you? But, then, you're not a man: you're just a stuffed dummy.'

'Where's that letter? Zakhar, Zakhar! He's put it away somewhere again!' Oblomov said.

'Here's the bailiff's letter,' said Alexeyev, picking up the crumpled letter.

'Yes, here it is,' Oblomov repeated and began to read it aloud. 'What do you say?' he asked when he had finished reading the letter. 'What am I to do? Droughts, arrears – –'

'You're hopeless – hopeless!' said Tarantyev.

'But why am I hopeless?'

'Why, aren't you hopeless?'

'Well, if I am, tell me what to do.'

'And what will I get out of it?'

'I've promised you champagne – what more do you want?'

'Champagne was for finding you a flat. Why, I've done you a favour, and you don't appreciate it – you argue about it – you're ungrateful. Well, try and find a flat by yourself! And what a flat! The main thing is you'll have absolute peace, just as if you were living at your own sister's. Two children, an unmarried brother, I shall be calling every day – –'

'All right, all right,' Oblomov interrupted. 'You'd better tell me now what I am to do about the bailiff.'

'No, sir, not unless you add beer for dinner. I'll tell you then.'

'He wants beer now! Haven't you had enough – –'

'Good-bye, then,' said Tarantyev, again putting on his hat.

'Good heavens! here the bailiff writes that my income will be two thousand less, and he wants beer, too! All right, buy some beer.'

'Let's have some more money,' said Tarantyev.

'But what about the change from the ten-rouble note?'

'And what about the cab fares to Vyborg?'

Oblomov took out another rouble and thrust it into his hand crossly.

'Your bailiff is a rogue – that's what I think,' Tarantyev began, putting the rouble in his pocket, 'and you stand there with your mouth open and believe him. You see the sort of tall story he tells you! Drought, bad harvest, arrears, runaway peasants – it's all a pack of lies! I've heard that in our district, on the Shumilov estate, the harvest last year was so good that they paid off all their debts. And Shumilov is only thirty-five miles from you: why haven't the crops there been burnt up? Then there is something else he has invented – arrears! But what was he doing? Why did he neglect them? Why should there be arrears? Is there no work to be had in our district – no market for a peasant's produce? Why, the thief – I'd teach him a lesson! And I daresay the peasants ran away because he got some money from them and then let them go, and he never complained to the police at all.'

'I don't believe it,' said Oblomov. 'Why, he actually quotes the police inspector's answer in the letter and so authentically, too.'

'Oh, you simpleton! You don't know anything. All rogues write authentically – take my word for it. Here, for instance,' he went on, pointing to Alexeyev, 'sits an honest fellow who won't hurt a fly – well, will he write an authentic letter? Never. But his relation, though a rogue and a swine, will. And you won't write such a letter, either. Your bailiff therefore is a rascal just because he has written such a clever and authentic-sounding letter. You see how carefully he chose his words: "to send them back to their place of domicile." '

'What am I to do with him?' asked Oblomov.

'Sack him at once.'

'But whom shall I appoint in his place? What do I know about the peasants? Another one might be worse. I haven't been there for twelve years.'

'Go to your estate yourself : that must be done. Spend the summer there and in the autumn come straight to the new flat. I'll see that it's all ready for you.'

'Move to a new flat – go to the country – and all by myself ! What desperate measures you suggest!' Oblomov said, looking displeased. 'Nothing about avoiding extremes and suggesting some sort of compromise.'

'Well, my dear fellow, you're as good as done for. Why, in your place I'd have mortgaged the estate long ago and bought another or a house here in a good residential part of the town; that's a damn sight better than that country place of yours. And then I'd have mortgaged the house and bought another. Let me have your estate and I'd soon make them sit up.'

'Stop boasting and think of something so that I need not leave this flat or go to the country and so that everything should be settled satisfactorily,' Oblomov remarked.

'But will you ever do anything?' said Tarantyev. 'Have a good look at yourself. Why, you're not good for anything. Of what use are you to your country? You can't even go to your estate!'

'It's a bit too soon for me to go there,' replied Oblomov. 'I must first finish my plan of the changes I intend to introduce on my estate. ... But, look here, Tarantyev,' Oblomov said suddenly, 'why shouldn't you go instead? You know what the business is and you have a pretty good idea what the country-side is like in those parts – I would pay your expenses – –'

'I'm not your manager, am I?' Tarantyev said haughtily. 'Besides, I've lost the knack of dealing with peasants.'

'What am I to do?' said Oblomov, pensively. 'I'm hanged if I know.'

'Well, write to the police inspector. Ask him if the bailiff has spoken to him about runaway peasants,' Tarantyev advised, 'and ask him to visit your estates too; then write to the Governor to order the police inspector to report on the bailiff's conduct. "Will your Excellency be so good as to take a fatherly interest in me and cast a merciful eye upon the terrible and inevitable misfortune that threatens to overwhelm me as a result of my bailiff's outrageous behaviour and the utter ruin which is bound to overtake me together with my wife and twelve little children who will be left unprovided for and starving" – –'

Oblomov laughed.

'Where am I to get so many children if I am asked to produce them?' he said.

'Nonsense, man! Write: "Twelve children". No one will pay any attention to it and no one will make inquiries, but it will sound "authentic". The Governor will pass on the letter to his secretary, and you will write to the secretary at the same time – with an enclosure, of course – and he will give the necessary order. And ask your neighbours, too: whom have you got there?'

'Dobrynin lives near,' said Oblomov. 'I used to see him often here; he is in the country now.'

'Well, write to him, too. Ask him nicely: "You will be doing me a great favour and oblige me as a Christian, a neighbour, and a friend." And add some Petersburg present to the letter – a box of cigars, for instance. That is what you should do, but you don't seem to have any sense at all. You're hopeless! I'd have made that bailiff sit up; I'd have shown him! When does the post go?'

'The day after to-morrow,' said Oblomov.

'Very well. Sit down and write at once.'

'But if it's the day after to-morrow, why should I write now?' Oblomov remarked. 'To-morrow will do. And, look here, old man,' he added. 'You may as well crown your "act of charity", and I will add a fish or some bird for dinner.'

'What now?'

'Sit down and write – it won't take you long to scribble three letters. You put everything so "authentically",' he added, trying to conceal a smile, 'and Alexeyev could copy it out.'

'Good Lord, how do you like that!' Tarantyev replied. 'Me write your letters? I haven't written anything at the office for the last two days: the moment I sit down, my left eye begins to run. Must have caught a chill in it, and my head, too, begins to swim if I bend down. You're lazy, my dear fellow, lazy. Hopeless, hopeless ...'

'Oh, if only Andrey would hurry up and come!' said Oblomov. 'He'd put everything straight!'

'Some good Samaritan you've found, I must say!' Tarantyev interrupted. 'A damned German – a crafty rascal!'

Tarantyev had a sort of instinctive aversion to foreigners. To him a Frenchman, a German, or an Englishman were synonymous with swindler, impostor, rogue, or bandit. He made no distinction between nations: they were all alike in his eyes.

'Look here, Tarantyev,' Oblomov said sternly, 'I'd be glad if you would control your language, especially when speaking of an intimate friend of mine. ...'

'An intimate friend!' Tarantyev replied with hatred. 'What sort of connexion is he of yours? A German – we all know what that is.'

'He's closer than any relation. I was brought up with him and we were educated together, and I shan't allow any impertinence – –'

Tarantyev turned purple with rage.

'Well,' he said, 'if you prefer the German to me, I shan't set foot in your house again.'

He put on his hat and walked to the door. Oblomov at once felt sorry.

'You ought to respect him as my friend and speak more carefully about him – that is all I ask,' he said. 'It isn't much of a favour, is it?'

'To respect a German?' Tarantyev said with the utmost contempt. 'Why should I?'

'But I've just told you – if for nothing else then because we grew up and went to the same school together.'

'What does that matter? We all go to school with someone or other!'

'Well, if he'd been here,' said Oblomov, 'he'd long ago have solved my problems without asking for beer or champagne.'

'Ah, so you blame me, do you? Well, to hell with you and with your beer and champagne! Here, take back your money! Where did I put it? Can't remember what I did with the damned note!'

He pulled out a greasy scrap of paper covered with writing.

'No, that's not it!' he said. 'Where did I put it?'

He rummaged in his pockets.

'Don't bother to look for it,' said Oblomov. 'I'm not blaming you, but merely ask you to speak with more respect of a man who is a close friend of mine and who has done so much for me.'

'So much!' Tarantyev said spitefully. 'You wait, he'll do even more for you – you do as he says!'

'Why do you say this to me?' asked Oblomov.

'I'm saying this so that you should know when that German of yours robs you of your last penny what it means to give up a neighbour of yours, a true Russian, for some tramp – –'

'Listen, Tarantyev – –' Oblomov began.

'I'm not going to listen, I've listened enough, you've given me enough trouble as it is. God knows the insults I've had to bear – I suppose in Germany his father was starving and he comes here and turns up his nose at us!'

'Leave the dead alone! How is his father to blame?'

'They are both to blame: father and son,' Tarantyev said gloomily with a wave of his hand. 'It's not for nothing my father warned me to beware of the Germans – and he knew all sorts of people in his time!'

'But what have you against his father, pray?' asked Oblomov.

'What I have against him is that he came to our province in September with nothing but the clothes he had on and then left a fortune to his son – what does that mean?'

'He only left his son some forty thousand roubles. Some of it was his wife's dowry and he made the rest by giving lessons and managing an estate: he received a good salary. You must admit the father didn't do anything wrong. Now what about the son? What wrong has he done?'

'A nice fellow! All of a sudden he makes three hundred thousand out of his father's forty and then becomes a Court Councillor, a man of learning – and now he is away travelling! The rogue has a finger in every pie! Would a good Russian, a real Russian, do all that? A Russian would choose one thing, and that, too, without rush or hurry, in his own good time, and carry on somehow or other – but this one – Good Lord! If he'd become a Government contractor, then at least one could understand how he had grown rich, but he did nothing of the kind – just got rich by some knavery! There's certainly something wrong there! I'd prosecute a fellow like that! And now he's knocking about goodness knows where!' Tarantyev went on. 'What does he go knocking about in foreign parts for?'

'He wants to study, to see everything, to know!'

'To study! Hasn't he been taught enough? What does he want to learn? He's telling you lies, don't believe him: he deceives you to your face like a small child. Do grown-up people study anything? Hear what he says! Would a Court Councillor want to study? You studied at school, but are you studying now? And does he,' Tarantyev pointed to Alexeyev, 'study? Does that relative of his study? Can you think of any decent man who is studying? Do you imagine he is sitting in a German school and doing his lessons? Rubbish! I've heard he's gone to look at some machine and order one like it: I suppose it is a press for printing Russian money! I'd put him in jail. Some sort of shares – – Oh, these shares – they make me sick!'

Oblomov burst out laughing.

'What are you laughing at?' said Tarantyev. 'Isn't it true what I say?'

'Let's drop the subject,' Oblomov interrupted him. 'You'd better go about your business, and I'll write the letters with Alexeyev and try to put down my plan on paper as quickly as possible – may as well do it all at once.'

Tarantyev went out, but came back immediately.

'I've quite forgotten!' he began, not at all as brusquely as before. 'I came to you on business this morning. I am invited to a wedding to-morrow: Rokotov is getting married. Lend me your frock-coat, old man. Mine, you can see, is rather shabby.'

'But,' said Oblomov, frowning at this new demand, 'how can I? My coat won't fit you.'

'It will, of course it will!' Tarantyev interrupted. 'You remember I tried it on once: it might have been made for me! Zakhar! Zakhar! Come here, you old brute!'

Zakhar growled like a bear, but did not come.

'Call him, old man,' Tarantyev pleaded. 'What a funny chap he is!'

'Zakhar!' Oblomov called.

'Oh, the devil take you!' Zakhar could be heard saying from his room as he jumped off the stove.

'Well, what do you want?' he asked, addressing Tarantyev.

'Fetch my black frock-coat,' Oblomov ordered. 'Mr Tarantyev wants to see if it fits him: he has to go to a wedding tomorrow.'

'I won't bring the coat, sir,' Zakhar said firmly.

'How dare you, when your master orders you to?' Tarantyev shouted. 'Why don't you send him to the house of correction, old man?'

'That would be a nice thing to do: send an old man to the house of correction!' said Oblomov. 'Don't be obstinate, Zakhar, bring the coat.'

'I won't!' Zakhar answered coldly. 'Let him first return your waistcoat and shirt: he's had them for five months. He borrowed them to go to a birthday party and we've never seen them since. A velvet waistcoat, too, and a fine cambric shirt; cost twenty-five roubles. I won't give him the coat.'

'Well, good-bye and to hell with both of you!' Tarantyev said angrily, turning to go and shaking his fist at Zakhar. 'Remember, old man, I'll take the flat for you – do you hear?' he added.

'All right, all right,' Oblomov said impatiently, just to get rid of him.

'And you write what I told you,' Tarantyev went on, 'and don't forget to tell the Governor that you have twelve little children. And, mind, the soup is to be on the table at five sharp. Why haven't you ordered a pie?'

But Oblomov did not reply; he had not been listening and, closing his eyes, was thinking of something else.

With Tarantyev's departure a dead silence reigned in the room for about ten minutes. Oblomov was worried by the bailiff's letter and the prospect of moving to another flat, and partly tired by Tarantyev's loud chatter. At last he sighed.

'Why don't you write?' Alexeyev asked quietly. 'I'll sharpen a pen for you.'

'Do, and then please go away,' said Oblomov. 'I'll do it myself and you can copy it out after dinner.'

'Very good, sir,' Alexeyev replied. 'I was afraid I might be disturbing you. I'll go now and tell them not to expect you in Yekaterinhof. Good-bye, Mr Oblomov.'

But Oblomov was not listening to him; he almost lay down in the arm-chair, with his feet tucked under him, looking very dispirited, lost in thought or perhaps dozing.

5

OBLOMOV, a gentleman by birth and a collegiate secretary by rank, had lived in Petersburg without a break for the last twelve years.

At first, while his parents were still alive, he had lived more modestly, occupying two rooms, and was satisfied with the services of Zakhar, whom he had brought with him from the country; but after the death of his father and mother he became the sole owner of 350 serfs, whom he had inherited in one of the remote provinces almost on the borders of Asia. Instead of 5,000 he had received from 7,000 to 10,000 roubles a year, and it was then that the manner of his life became different and much grander. He took a bigger flat, added a cook to his domestic staff, and even kept a carriage and pair. He was still young then, and while it could not be said that he was lively, he was at all events livelier than now; he was still full of all sorts of aspirations, still hoped for something, and expected a great deal from the future and from himself; he was still preparing himself for a career, for the part he was going to play in life, and, above all, of course for the Civil Service, which was the main reason for his arrival in Petersburg. Later he also thought of the part he was going to play in society; finally, in the distant future, at the turning point of youth and mature age, the thought of family happiness filled his imagination with agreeable expectations.

But days and years passed – the soft down on his chin turned into a tough, stubbly growth, his eyes lost their brightness, his waist expanded, his hair had begun to thin out relentlessly, he turned thirty, and he had not advanced a step, but was still standing on the threshold of his career, just where he had been ten years before. Yet he was still hoping to start his life, he was still tracing in his mind the pattern of his future, but with every year that passed he had to change and rub out something in that pattern.

In his opinion, life was divided into two halves: one consisted of work and boredom – those words were synonymous for him – and the other of rest and quiet enjoyment. This was why his chief pursuit in life – his career as a civil servant – proved to be an unpleasant surprise to him from the outset.

Brought up in the wilds of the country, amid the gentle and kindly manners and customs of his native province, and passing for twenty years from the embraces of his parents to those of his friends and relations, he had become so imbued with the idea of family life, that his career in the Civil Service appeared to him as a sort of family occupation, such as, for instance, the unhurried writing down of income and expenditure in a note-book, which his father used to do. He thought that the civil servants employed in one department were one big, happy family, unremittingly concerned about one another's peace and pleasure; that going to the office was not by any means a duty that must be performed day in and day out, and that rainy weather, heat, or a mere disinclination could always be given as a legitimate and sufficient excuse for not going to the office. One can easily imagine his disappointment when he discovered that nothing short of an earthquake could prevent a civil servant who was in good health from turning up at his office, and unfortunately there were no earthquakes in Petersburg; to be sure, a flood could also serve as an excuse, but even floods were rare occurrences. Oblomov grew still more worried when documents inscribed 'Important' and 'Very Important' began to flash before his eyes, when he was asked to make various inquiries, extracts from official documents, look through papers, write reports two inches thick, which were called, as though in jest, *notes*, and, what was even worse, everything had to be done in a hurry – everyone seemed to be rushing about without stopping to take breath; as soon as one case was finished, they threw themselves furiously upon another, as though that was the only thing that mattered, and when they had finished that, they forgot it and pounced upon a third – and so it went on and on! Twice he had been roused at night and made to write 'notes'; a few times he was dragged out by a courier from visits to friends – always because of those notes. All this appalled him and bored him terribly. 'But when am I going to live? When am I to live?' he kept repeating.

He had heard at home that the head of a department was a father to his subordinates and had therefore formed a most fanciful and homely idea of such a person. He imagined him to be something like a second father whose only concern was to reward his subordinates whether they deserved it or not, and to provide not only for their needs but also for their pleasures. Oblomov had thought that a superior was so eager to put himself in the place of his subordinate that he would inquire carefully how he had slept, why he was bleary-eyed, and whether he had a headache. But he was bitterly disappointed on his very first day at the office. With the arrival of the head of the department the office was in a turmoil; they began rushing about, they looked harassed, they ran into one another, some pulling their uniforms straight for fear that they were not tidy enough to appear before their chief. This happened, as Oblomov observed afterwards, because certain heads of departments were apt to regard the stupidly frightened face of a subordinate rushing out to meet them as a sign not only of his respect for them, but also of his zeal and sometimes of his ability for the service. Oblomov had no need to be afraid of his chief, a kindly and agreeable person, who had never done any harm to anyone and whose subordinates were highly satisfied and wished for nothing better. No one had ever heard him utter an unpleasant word or raise his voice; he never demanded, but always asked. If it was a question of doing some work, he asked one of his subordinates to do it; if he wanted to invite one to his house, he asked him; if he wanted to put him under arrest, he asked him. He was never familiar with anyone; he treated all individually and collectively with the utmost respect. But somehow all his subordinates quailed before him; they answered his kind questions in a voice that was different from their own, such as they never used in speaking to other people. Oblomov, too, suddenly quailed, without himself knowing why, when his chief entered his office and he, too, began to lose his voice and to speak in a different tone – a high, horrible falsetto – as soon as his chief addressed him.

Oblomov was worn out with fear and anguish serving under a good and lenient chief; goodness only knows what would have become of him if he had had a stern and exacting one! He somehow or other managed to stay in the service for two years; he might have endured for a third and obtained a higher rank had not a particular incident forced him to send in his resignation. One day he sent an important paper to Arkhangelsk instead of to Astrakhan. The mistake was discovered and a search was made for the culprit. They all waited with interest for the chief to summon Oblomov and ask him coldly and calmly whether he had sent the paper to Arkhangelsk, and they all wondered in what kind of voice Oblomov would reply. Some surmised that he would not reply at all, that he would not be able to. Watching his colleagues, Oblomov became frightened himself, though like the others he knew that his chief would merely reprimand him; but his own conscience was much sterner than any reprimand. Oblomov did not wait for the punishment he deserved, but went home and sent in a medical certificate.

The certificate was as follows: 'I, the undersigned, certify, and affix my seal hereto, that the collegiate secretary Ilya Oblomov suffers from an enlarged heart and a dilation of its left ventricle ((*Hypertrophia cordis cum dilatatione ejus ventriculi sinistri*) and from a chronic pain in the liver (*hetitis*) which may endanger the patient's health and life, the attacks, it may be presumed, being caused by his daily attendance at the office. Therefore, to prevent a repetition and an intensification of these morbid attacks, I consider it necessary that Mr Oblomov should stop going to the office for a time and, generally, prescribe an abstention from mental and any other activity.'

But this helped for a time only; he had to become well again sooner or later, and then he would have to go to the office again every day. Oblomov could not stand it, and he sent in his resignation. That was the end of his work for the State, and it was never resumed again.

His social career seemed to be more successful at first. During his early years in Petersburg the tranquil features of his face were more frequently animated, his eyes used to glow for hours with the fire of life, they shone with light, hope, and strength. He was as animated as other people, was full of hope, rejoiced at trifles, and also suffered from the same trifles. But that was long ago, when he was still at the tender age when a man regards every other man as his best friend and falls in love with almost every woman, ready to offer her his hand and heart – which some indeed succeed in doing, often to their profound regret for the rest of their lives. In those blissful days Oblomov, too, had his share of not a few tender, soft, and even passionate glances from the crowd of beauties, a lot of promising smiles, two or three stolen kisses, and many more friendly handshakes, that made him suffer and brought tears to his eyes. Still, he never surrendered entirely to a pretty woman and never became her slave, or even a faithful admirer, if only because intimacy with a woman involves a great deal of trouble. Oblomov confined himself mostly to expressing his admiration from afar, from a respectable distance.

Very seldom did fate throw him together with a woman so closely that he could catch fire for a few days and imagine himself to be in love. That was why his love adventures never developed into love affairs; they stopped short at the very beginning, and in their simplicity, innocence, and purity equalled the love-stories of a schoolgirl. He particularly avoided the pale, melancholy maidens, mostly with black eyes which reflected 'tormenting days and iniquitous nights', maidens with secret joys and sorrows, who always have something to confide, something to tell, and when they tell it, shudder, burst into tears, then suddenly throw their arms around their friend's neck, gaze into his eyes, then at the sky, and declare that there is a curse on their life, and sometimes fall down in a faint. He avoided them fearfully. His soul was still pure and virginal; it was perhaps waiting for real love, for support, for overpowering passion, and then, as the years passed, seemed to have despaired of waiting.

Oblomov parted still more coldly from his many friends. Immediately after receiving his first letter from the bailiff with news of arrears and failure of crops, he replaced his best friend, the chef, by a woman cook, then sold his horses and, finally, dismissed his other 'friends'. There was hardly anything that attracted him in the town and he became more and more firmly attached to his flat. At first he found it a bit hard to remain dressed all day, then he felt too lazy to dine out except with intimate friends, mostly bachelors, who did not object to his divesting himself of his tie or unbuttoning his waistcoat, and even, if possible, lying down to have an hour's sleep. Soon he got tired of parties, too: one had to put on a dress-suit and shave every day. He read somewhere that only morning mists were good for one and evening mists were bad, and he began to fear the damp. In spite of these eccentricities, his friend Stolz succeeded in making him go out and call on people; but Stolz often left Petersburg for Moscow, Nizhny-Novgorod, the Crimea, and latterly abroad, too, and without him Oblomov was plunged up to the neck in solitude and seclusion, from which he could be dragged only by something unusual, something out of the ordinary events of life; but nothing of the sort ever happened or was likely to happen.

Besides, as Oblomov grew older, he reverted to a sort of childish timidity, an expectation of danger and evil from everything that was outside the sphere of his daily experience, the result of getting out of touch with life. He was not afraid, for example, of the crack in his bedroom ceiling, he was used to it; nor did it ever occur to him that the stuffy atmosphere in the room and his constant sitting indoors was almost more perilous for his health than night dampness, that his daily over-indulgence at a meal was a kind of slow suicide, for he was used to it and felt no fear. He was not used to movement, to life, to crowds, and to bustle. He felt stifled in a crowd; he got into a boat fearing that he would not reach the other bank in safety; he drove in a carriage expecting the horse to bolt and smash it. Sometimes he had an attack of nerves; he was afraid of the stillness around him or for a reason he did not understand a cold shiver ran down his spine. Sometimes he looked apprehensively at a dark corner, dreading lest his imagination should trick him into seeing a ghost there.

That was what his social life had come to. He lazily dismissed all the youthful hopes that had betrayed him or been betrayed by him, all the bitter-sweet, bright memories that sometimes make even an old man's heart beat faster.

6

WHAT did he do at home, then? Did he read or write or study? Yes, if he chanced to pick up a book or a newspaper, he read it. If he heard of some remarkable work, he would feel an urge to become acquainted with it. He tried to get the book, asked for it, and if it was brought to him soon, he began it and formed some idea of what it was about; another step and he would have mastered it, but instead he lay looking apathetically at the ceiling, with the book lying beside him unfinished and not properly understood. He grew indifferent much faster than he had grown interested: he never went back to a book he had abandoned. And yet he had been educated like other people, like everyone, in fact – that is to say, till the age of fifteen he had been in a boarding-school, then his old parents had decided, after a long struggle, to send their darling boy to Moscow, where willy-nilly he had to follow the course of his studies to the end. His timid, apathetic nature prevented him from giving full play to his laziness and caprices among strangers at school, where no exceptions were made for spoiled children. He had to sit straight in his schoolroom and listen to what the teachers were saying, because there was nothing else he could do, and he learned his lessons with much labour, with sighs, in the sweat of his brow. All that he regarded as a punishment sent by heaven for our sins.

He never looked beyond the line which the teacher marked with his nail in setting the lesson; he never asked any questions and never required any explanations. He was quite satisfied with what was written in his note-book and showed no tiresome curiosity even when he failed to understand all that he heard and learned. If he managed somehow or other to master a book on statecraft, history, or political economy, he was perfectly satisfied. When Stolz brought him books, which he had to read in addition to what he had learned, he used to look at him in silence for a long time.

'So you, too, Brutus, are against me?' he said with a sigh, as he sat down to read them.

Such immoderate reading seemed hard and unnatural to him. Of what use were all those note-books which had taken up so much time, paper, and ink? What is the use of text-books? And, last but not least, why waste six or seven years of your life being cooped up in a school? Why put up with all the strict discipline, the reprimands, the boredom of sitting over lessons, the bans on running about, playing, and amusing yourself, when life is still ahead of him?

'When am I to live?' he asked himself again. 'When am I at last to put into circulation all this capital of knowledge, most of which will be of no use to me in life anyway? Political economy, for instance, algebra, geometry – what am I going to do with them in Oblomovka?'

History, too, depressed him terribly: you learn and read that at a certain date the people were overtaken by all sorts of calamities and were unhappy, then they summoned up their strength, worked, took infinite care, endured great hardships, laboured in preparation for better days. At last they came – one would think history might take a rest, but no, clouds gathered again, the edifice crashed down, and again the people had to toil and labour. ... The bright days do not remain, they fly, and life flows on, one crisis follows upon another.

Serious reading tired him. Philosophers did not succeed in awakening in him a passion for speculative thought. The poets, on the other hand, touched him to the quick: like everyone else, he became young again. He, too, reached the happy time of life, which never fails anyone and which smiles upon all, the time when one's powers are at their height, when one is conscious of life and full of hope and desire to do good, to show one's prowess, to work, when one's heart beats faster and the pulses quicken, when one thrills with emotion, makes enthusiastic speeches, and sheds sweet tears. His heart and mind grew clear: he shook off his drowsiness and longed for activity. Stolz helped him to prolong that moment as long as was possible for such a nature as his friend's. He took advantage of Oblomov's love of the poets and kept him for sixteen months under the spell of thought and learning. He made use of the ecstatic flight of his young friend's fancy to introduce aims other than pure delight in the reading of poetry, pointed out the distant goals of his own and his friend's life, and carried him off into the future. Both grew excited, wept, and exchanged solemn promises to follow the path of reason and light. Oblomov was infected by the youthful ardour of Stolz, and he was aflame with the desire to work and to reach his distant, but fascinating goal.

But the flower of life opened up and bore no fruit. Oblomov sobered down, and only occasionally, on Stolz's advice, read one book or another, though not at once, and without hurry or eagerness, lazily scanning the lines. However absorbing the passage that engaged his attention might be, if it was time to have dinner or to go to bed, he put the book face downwards and went to have dinner or blew out the candle and went to sleep. If he was given the first volume of some work, he did not, after finishing it, ask for the second, but if it were brought to him, he read it through slowly. Later on he found even the first volume too much for him and spent most of his leisure with his elbow on the table and his head on his elbow; sometimes, instead of his elbow, he used the book Stolz insisted that he should read.

So ended Oblomov's career as a student. The date on which he heard his last lecture was the utmost limit of his learning. The principal's signature on his certificate, like his teacher's nail-mark on his book in the old days, was the line beyond which our hero did not think it necessary to extend the field of his knowledge. His head was a complicated depository of past deeds, persons, epochs, figures, religions, disconnected political, economic, mathematical and other truths, problems, principles, and so on. It was like a library composed entirely of odd volumes of various branches of knowledge. His studies had a strange effect on Oblomov; there was for him a gulf between life and learning which he never attempted to cross. To him life was one thing and learning another. He had studied all the existing and the no longer existing systems of law, he had been through the course of practical jurisprudence, but when after a burglary in his house he had to write to the police, he took a sheet of paper and pen, spent a long time thinking over it, and in the end sent for a clerk. His estate accounts were kept by the bailiff. 'What has learning to do with it?' he asked himself in perplexity.

He returned to his seclusion without any store of knowledge which might have given a direction to his roving and idly slumbering thoughts. What did he do? Why, he went on drawing the pattern of his own life. He found in it, not without reason, so much wisdom and poetry that it provided him with an inexhaustible source of occupation even without any books and learning. Having given up the service and society, he began to solve the problem of existence in a different way; he began to ponder about the purpose of his life, and at last discovered that it was in himself that he had to look for its secret. He understood that family happiness and the care of the estate were his sole business in life. Till then he had no idea of the position of his affairs: Stolz sometimes looked after them for him. He did not know exactly what his income and expenditure were, he never drew up any budget – he did nothing.

Oblomov's father left the estate to his son as he had received it from his father. Though he had spent all his life in the country, he never tried to be clever or racked his brains over different improvements as landowners do nowadays: how to discover new sources of productivity of the land or to enlarge and increase the old sources, and so on. The fields were cultivated in the same way as in his grandfather's time, and the methods of marketing the agricultural produce were the same. The old man, to be sure, was very pleased if a good harvest or a rise in prices provided him with a larger income than the year before: he called it a divine blessing. He had merely an aversion to making money in all sorts of new-fangled and devious ways.

'Our fathers and forefathers were no stupider than we,' he used to say in answer to what he regarded as harmful advice, 'and yet they lived happily, and so shall we: God willing, we shall not starve.'

Receiving, without various cunning shifts, an income from the estate that was sufficient to provide a good dinner and supper for his family and guests, he thanked God and thought it a sin to try to get more than that. If his steward brought him 2,000 roubles, having put another 1,000 in his own pocket, and tearfully blamed the hail, drought, or bad harvest for it, old Oblomov crossed himself and said also with tears:

'God's will be done. I shall not argue with God. We must thank God for what there is.'

Since the death of Oblomov's parents the affairs on the estate had not improved; on the contrary, as was evident from the bailiff's letter, they had grown worse. It was obvious that Oblomov had to go there himself and find out on the spot the reason for the gradual decline in his income. He intended to do so, but kept delaying, partly because such a journey meant almost a new and unknown feat for him. In all his life he had made only one journey – in a big, old-fashioned coach, amidst featherbeds, chests, trunks, hams, loaves, all sorts of roasted and cooked beef and poultry, and accompanied by several servants. That was how he had made his only journey from the estate to Moscow, and this journey he took as the standard for all journeys. And now, he was told, one no longer journeyed like that: one travelled at breakneck speed. Again, Oblomov put off his journey because he was not yet ready to put his affairs in order. He was certainly not like his father and grandfather. He had studied and lived in the world: all that suggested all sorts of ideas that were new to him. He understood that acquisition was not a sin, but that it was the duty of every citizen to help to raise the general welfare by honest labour. That was why the greatest part of the pattern of life which he drew in his seclusion was devoted to a fresh plan for re-organization of the estate and dealing with the peasants in accordance with the needs of the times. The fundamental idea of the plan, its arrangement and its main parts had long been ready in his head; only the details, the estimates and the figures remained. He worked untiringly on the plan for several years, thinking it over continually as he was pacing his room or lying down or visiting friends; he kept adding to it or changing various items, recalling what he had thought of the day before and forgotten during the night; and sometimes a new, unexpected idea would flash like lightning through his mind and set it simmering – and the work would start all over again. He was not some petty executor of somebody else's ready-made notions; he had himself created his own ideas and he was going to carry them out.

As soon as he got up in the morning and had taken his breakfast, he lay down at once on the sofa, propped up his head on his hand and plunged into thought without sparing himself till at last his head grew weary from the hard work and his conscience told him that he had done enough for the common welfare. Only then did he permit himself to rest from his labours and change his thoughtful pose for another less stern and business-like and a more comfortable one for languorous day-dreaming. Having done with the cares of business, Oblomov liked to withdraw into himself and live in the world of his own creation. He was not unacquainted with the joys of lofty thoughts; he was not unfamiliar with human sorrows. Sometimes he wept bitterly in his heart of hearts over the calamities of mankind and experienced secret and nameless sufferings and anguish and a yearning for something far away, for the world, perhaps, where Stolz used to carry him away. ... Sweet tears flowed from his eyes.

It would also happen that sometimes he would be filled with contempt for human vice, lies, and slanders, for the evil that was rife in the world, and he was consumed by a desire to point out to man his sores, and suddenly thoughts were kindled in him, sweeping through his head like waves of the sea, growing into intentions, setting his blood on fire, flexing his muscles, and swelling his veins; then his intentions turned to strivings; moved by a spiritual force, he would change his position two or three times in one minute, and half-rising on his couch with blazing eyes, stretch forth his hand and look around him like one inspired. ... In another moment the striving would turn into an heroic act – and then, heavens! What wonders, what beneficent results might one not expect from such a lofty effort!

But the morning passed, the day was drawing to its close, and with it Oblomov's exhausted energies were crying out for a rest: the storms and emotions died down, his head recovered from the spell of his reverie, and his blood flowed more slowly in his veins. Oblomov turned on his back quietly and wistfully and, fixing a sorrowful gaze at the window and the sky, mournfully watched the sun setting gorgeously behind a four-storied house. How many times had he watched the sun set like that!

Next morning there was life once more, new excitements and dreams! He liked to imagine himself sometimes as some invincible general, compared with whom not only Napoleon, but also Yeruslau Lazarevich dwindled into insignificance; he invented a war and a cause for it, such as, for instance, an invasion of Europe by the peoples of Africa, or he organized new crusades, and fought to settle the fate of nations, devastating cities, showing mercy, putting to death, performing deeds of goodness and magnanimity. Or he would choose to be a thinker or a great artist: everyone worshipped him, he was crowned with laurels, the crowd ran after him, shouting: 'Look, look, here comes Oblomov, our famous Ilya Ilyich!' At bitter moments he suffered greatly, tossed from side to side, lay face downwards, and sometimes lost heart completely; then he rose from his bed, knelt down and began to pray ardently, zealously, imploring heaven to avert the storm that threatened him. After entrusting the care of his future to Providence, he grew calm and indifferent to everything in the world – let the storm do its worst!

This was how he used his spiritual powers, after spending days in a state of agitation and only recovering with a deep sigh from an enchanting dream or an agonizing anxiety when the day was drawing to a close and the sun began to set gorgeously in an enormous ball behind the four-storied house. Then he once more watched it with a wistful look and a sorrowful smile and rested peacefully from his emotional exertions.

No one saw or knew this inner life of Oblomov; they all thought that there was nothing special about him, that he just lay about and enjoyed his meals, and that that was all one could expect from him; that it was doubtful whether he was able to form any coherent thoughts in his head. That was what the people who knew him said about him. Only Stolz knew and could testify as to his abilities and the volcanic work that was going on inside his ardent head and humane heart; but Stolz was hardly ever in Petersburg.

Only Zakhar, whose whole life centred round his master, knew his inner life even better than Stolz; but he was convinced that both he and his master were doing useful work and living a normal life, as they should, and that they could not possibly live otherwise.

7

ZAKHAR was over fifty. He no longer belonged to the direct descendants of those Russian Calebs, the knights of the servants' hall without fear and without reproach, who were full of selfless loyalty to their masters and who had all the virtues and no vices. This knight was with fear and with reproach. He belonged to two different epochs, and each of them had left its mark on him. From one he had inherited his boundless loyalty to the Oblomov family, and from the other, the later one, refinement and corrupt morals. Passionately devoted to his master, not a day passed without his telling him a lie. In the old days a servant would have restrained his master from extravagance and intemperance, but Zakhar was himself fond of having a drink with his cronies at his master's expense; an old-fashioned servant was chaste as a eunuch, but this one kept running to a lady friend of doubtful character. The one guarded his master's money better than any safe, but Zakhar always tried to cheat his master of ten copecks over some purchase and never failed to appropriate any coppers that were left lying on the table. In the same way, if Oblomov forgot to ask Zakhar for the change, he would never see it again. He did not steal bigger sums because he measured his needs in coppers and ten-copeck pieces, or because he was afraid of being found out – certainly it was not because he was too honest. An old-fashioned Caleb, like a well-trained gun-dog, would rather die than touch the food entrusted to his care; but Zakhar was always watching out for an opportunity to eat and drink something he had been told not to touch; the one was anxious that his master should eat as much as possible and felt upset when he did not eat; the other felt upset if his master ate up all that had been put on his plate.

Moreover, Zakhar was a gossip. In the kitchen, in the shop, and at all the meetings at the gate he complained every day of his hard life. He claimed that there had never been a worse master, that Oblomov was capricious, stingy, and bad-tempered, that there was no pleasing him – that, in short, he would rather be dead than go on living with him. Zakhar did these things not out of malice and not out of a desire to injure his master, but just because he had inherited from his father and grandfather the habit of abusing the master at every favourable opportunity.

Sometimes he told some cock-and-bull story about Oblomov out of sheer boredom or lack of a subject for conversation or out of a desire to impress his listeners.

'My master,' he wheezed quietly in a confidential whisper, 'has taken to visiting that widow. Wrote a note to her yesterday, he did.' Or he would declare that his master was the greatest gambler and drunkard in the world, that he played cards and drank all night long. There was not a word of truth in it: Oblomov paid no visits to the widow, he spent his nights sleeping peacefully and did not touch cards.

Zakhar was slovenly. He seldom shaved and though he washed his hands and face, it was more for show; besides, no soap could wash off the dirt. After a visit to the bath-house his hands turned red instead of black for a couple of hours, and then became black again. He was very clumsy; when he opened the doors or the gates, one half would shut while he was opening the other, and as he ran to the second half, the first one would shut. He could never pick up a handkerchief or anything else from the floor at once, but always bent down about three times, as though he were trying to catch it, and only got hold of it at the fourth attempt, and even then he was liable to drop it again. If he carried a number of plates or some other crockery across the room, those on the top began to decamp to the floor at the first step he took. First one fell off; he suddenly made a belated and useless attempt to stop it, and dropped another two. As he stood gaping with surprise at the falling plates, paying no attention to those he still held in his hands and holding the tray aslant, the plates continued to drop on the floor; by the time he reached the other end of the room there was sometimes only one plate or wine-glass left on the tray, and, cursing and swearing, he very often deliberately flung down the last things that still remained in his hands. Walking across the room he invariably caught his side or his feet against a table or a chair; he rarely passed through the open half of the door without knocking his shoulder against the other half, swearing at both, at the landlord, and at the carpenter who made them. In Oblomov's study almost all articles, especially the small ones which required careful handling, were either broken or damaged, and all thanks to Zakhar. This talent for handling things he applied equally to all articles, making no distinction in his method of treating them. He was, for instance, told to snuff a candle or pour out a glass of water: to do that he used as much force as was needed to open the gates. But the real danger came when Zakhar, inspired by a sudden zeal to please his master, took it into his head to tidy everything, clean and put everything in its proper place quickly, at once! There was no end of trouble and breakages; an enemy soldier, rushing into the house, could not have done so much mischief. Things fell down and broke, crockery was smashed, chairs turned over. In the end he had to be driven out of the room, or he went away, swearing and cursing, of his own accord. Fortunately, he was rarely inspired with such zeal.

All that, of course, happened because Zakhar had been brought up and acquired his manners not in the dark and narrow, but fastidiously furnished, drawing-rooms and studies, cluttered up with all sorts of fancy articles, but in the country, where there was plenty of room to move about. There he was accustomed to work without being cramped and to handle things of solid dimensions and massive weight, such as a spade, a crowbar, iron door clamps, and chairs of such size that he could shift them only with difficulty.

Some article, such as a candlestick, a lamp, a transparency, a paper-weight, remained undamaged for three or four years, but as soon as Zakhar picked it up, it broke.

'Oh,' he sometimes used to say to Oblomov when this happened, 'look, sir, what an extraordinary thing: I just picked it up and it came to pieces in my hands.'

Or he said nothing at all, but would put it back secretly and afterwards assured his master that he had broken it himself; and sometimes he excused himself by saying that even an iron article must get broken sooner or later since it could not possibly last for ever. In the first two instances one could still argue with him, but when, driven into a corner, he armed himself with the last argument, every objection was useless and nothing in the world could convince him that he was wrong.

Zakhar had drawn up a definite programme of activity which he never varied, if he could help it. In the morning he set the *samovar*, cleaned the boots and clothes his master asked for, but not those he did not ask for, though they might be hanging in the wardrobe for ten years. Then he swept – not every day, though – the middle of the room without touching the corners and dusted only the table that had nothing on it, to save himself the trouble of moving anything. After this he considered that he had a right to snooze on the stove or chatter with Anisya in the kitchen or with the servants at the gates. If he was ordered to do something else besides, he did it only reluctantly after long arguments to show that what was asked of him was useless or impossible. It was quite impossible to make him introduce any permanent new item into his programme of daily tasks. If he was told to clean or wash some article, or fetch something or take something away, he carried out the order with his usual growling, but Oblomov could never make him do that regularly and without being told. The next day or the day after he had to be told to do it again with a resumption of the same unpleasant arguments.

In spite of the fact that Zakhar liked to drink and gossip, took Oblomov's coppers and silver ten-copeck pieces, smashed the crockery and damaged the furniture, and shirked his work, he was nevertheless deeply devoted to his master. He would gladly have jumped into fire or water for him without a moment's hesitation and without thinking it heroic or worthy of any admiration or reward. He thought it a natural thing, as something that could not be otherwise, or rather he did not think at all, but acted without any reflection. He had no theories on the subject. It never occurred to him to analyse his feelings towards Oblomov; he had not invented them; they had descended to him from his father, his grandfather, his brothers, and the servants among whom he was brought up, and had become part of his flesh and blood. Zakhar would have died instead of his master, since he considered it as his bounden duty, and even without thinking about it he would have rushed to his death just as a dog rushes at a wild beast in the forest, without thinking why it, and not its master, should rush upon it. But if, on the other hand, he had had to keep awake by his master's bedside all night because his master's health and even life depended on it, Zakhar would most certainly have fallen asleep.

Outwardly he did not show any servility to his master, he even treated him familiarly and rudely, was angry with him in good earnest over every trifle and even, as already said, told tales about him at the gate; but all this merely pushed into the background for a time, but not by any means diminished, his inborn and intimate feeling of devotion not to Oblomov as such, but to everything that bore the name of Oblomov and that was close, dear, and precious to him. It is possible even that this feeling was opposed to Zakhar's own opinion of Oblomov personally; it is possible that a close study of his master's character gave Zakhar a far from flattering opinion of him. Quite probably Zakhar would have objected if the degree of his devotion to Oblomov had been explained to him.

Zakhar loved Oblomovka as a cat loves its attic, a horse its stable, and a dog the kennel in which it has been born and grown up. Within the sphere of this attachment he developed certain personal impressions. For instance, he liked the Oblomov coachman better than the cook, the dairy-maid Varvara better than either of them, and Oblomov himself least of all; but still, the Oblomovka cook was in his eyes better than any other cook in the world, and Oblomov better than all other landowners. He could not stand Taras the butler, but he would not exchange even him for the best man in the world simply because Taras was an Oblomov servant. He treated Oblomov familiarly and rudely just as a medicine-man treats his idol: he dusts it, drops it, sometimes even strikes it in vexation, but nevertheless at heart he is always conscious of the idol's superiority to himself. The slightest occasion was sufficient to call forth this feeling from the very depths of Zakhar's soul and make him look at his master with reverence, and sometimes even burst into tears with emotion. He would never dream of regarding any other gentleman as being in any way better than his master – or even equal to his master. And God help any man who dared compare his master to his disadvantage with anyone else!

Zakhar could not help looking down on the gentlemen who came to visit Oblomov; he served them, handed them tea and so on, with a kind of condescension, as though making them feel the honour his master bestowed on them by receiving them. He turned them away rather rudely: 'Master's asleep,' he would say, looking the visitor up and down haughtily. Sometimes, instead of telling tales about Oblomov and abusing him, he would extol him immoderately at the shops and the meetings at the gate, and there was no end to his enthusiasm. He would suddenly begin to enumerate his master's virtues, his intelligence, dexterity, generosity, good nature; and if his master's fine qualities were not sufficient to merit his panegyrics, he borrowed them from others and declared Oblomov to be a person of high rank, wealth, and extraordinary influence. If he had to put the fear of God into the caretaker, the landlord's agent, or even the landlord himself, he always threatened them with Oblomov. 'You wait,' he would say menacingly, 'I'll tell my master and then you'll catch it.' He did not expect there could be a higher authority in the whole world.

Outwardly, however, Oblomov's relations with Zakhar were always rather hostile. Living together, they got on each other's nerves. A close, daily intimacy between two people has to be paid for: it requires a great deal of experience of life, logic, and warmth of heart on both sides to enjoy each other's good qualities without being irritated by each other's shortcomings and blaming each other for them. Oblomov knew at least one inestimable virtue in Zakhar – his devotion to himself – and was used to it, believing, too, that it couldn't and shouldn't be otherwise; but having grown used to the virtue once and for all, he could no longer enjoy it; at the same time, however, he could not, in spite of his indifference to everything, patiently put up with Zakhar's innumerable shortcomings. If Zakhar, while being greatly devoted to his master, differed from the old-fashioned servants by his modern shortcomings, Oblomov, too, much as he appreciated his servant's loyalty, differed from the masters of former times in not cherishing the same friendly and almost affectionate feelings towards Zakhar that they had had for their servants. Occasionally, indeed, he had rows with Zakhar.

Zakhar, too, was often tired of his master. Having served his term as a footman in his youth, Zakhar had been appointed to look after the young master; from that day he began to regard himself as an article of luxury, an aristocratic accessory of the house, whose duty it was to keep up the prestige and splendour of an old family and not to be of any real use. That was why, having dressed the young master in the morning and undressed him in the evening, he spent the rest of the day doing nothing at all. Lazy by nature, he became even more so by his upbringing as a flunkey. He gave himself airs before the servants, did not take the trouble to set the *samovar* or sweep the floors. He either dozed in the hall or went to have a chat in the servants' hall or the kitchen; or he did neither, but just stood for hours at the gates, his arms crossed, and looked dreamily about him. And after such a life, he was suddenly burdened with the heavy task of doing the work of a whole household single-handed! He had to look after his master, sweep and clean, and run errands! No wonder he became morose, bad-tempered, and rude; no wonder he growled every time his master's voice forced him to leave the stove. In spite, however, of his outward sullenness and unsociableness, Zakhar possessed a soft and kind heart. He even liked to spend his time with children. He was often seen with a crowd of children in the courtyard or by the gate. He settled their quarrels, teased them, organized games, or simply sat with one child on each knee, while another little rascal would throw his arms round his neck from behind or pull at his whiskers.

And so Oblomov interfered with Zakhar's life by constantly demanding his services and his presence, while Zakhar's heart, his talkative nature, his love of idleness, and a perpetual, never-ceasing need for munching something drew him to the gate, or to his lady-friend, to the shop, or to the kitchen.

They had known each other and lived together for a very long time. Zakhar had dandled little Oblomov in his arms, and Oblomov remembered him as a quick and sly young man with a prodigious appetite. Nothing in the world could sever the old ties between them. Just as Oblomov could not get up or go to bed, brush his hair, put on his shoes, or have his dinner without Zakhar, so Zakhar could imagine no other master than Oblomov and no other existence than that of dressing him, feeding him, being rude to him, cheating him, lying to him and, at the same time, inwardly revering him.

8

HAVING closed the door behind Tarantyev and Alexeyev, Zakhar did not sit down on the stove, but waited for his master to call him any minute, for he had heard that Oblomov was going to write letters. But everything in Oblomov's study was as silent as the grave.

Zakhar peeped through the chink in the wall – and what did

he see? Oblomov was lying quietly on the sofa, his head propped on his hand; a book lay open in front of him. Zakhar opened the door.

'Why are you lying down again, sir?' he asked.

'Don't disturb me, you see I am reading,' Oblomov said curtly.

'It's time to wash and to write,' Zakhar said mercilessly.

'Yes,' Oblomov said, coming to himself. 'As a matter of fact it is. I'll be ready directly. You go now. I'll think.'

'How did he manage to lie down again?' Zakhar growled, jumping on the stove. 'He's not half quick!'

Oblomov, however, managed to read the page which had turned yellow during the month since he had last read the book. He put the book down, yawned, and then began thinking of 'the two misfortunes'.

'What a bore!' he whispered, stretching his legs and tucking them under him again. He felt like lying like that in comfort and dreaming. He gazed at the sky, looking for the sun that he loved so much, but it was right overhead, shining dazzlingly on the whitewashed wall of the house behind which Oblomov watched it set in the evening.

'No,' he said to himself sternly, 'first to business and then——'

In the country the morning would long have been over, but in Petersburg it was just drawing to a close. From the courtyard a mingled sound of human and animal noises reached Oblomov's ears: the singing of some strolling street musicians, accompanied by the barking of dogs. A sea monster was being brought for show, hawkers shouted their wares in all sorts of voices.

He lay on his back and put both hands under his head. Oblomov was busy with his plan for reorganizing his estate. He rapidly ran through several important, vital points about the rent he was going to charge for leasing his land, the fields that had to be ploughed, thought of a new and sterner measure against laziness and vagrancy among the peasants, and went over to the subject of arranging his own life in the country. He was preoccupied with the problem of building his new country house; he dwelt pleasurably for a few minutes on the arrangement of the rooms, made up his mind about the size of the dining-room and billiard-room, thought on which side the windows of his study would look, and even remembered the furniture and carpets. After that he decided where to erect the outbuildings, taking into account the number of guests he intended to entertain, and allotted the space for the stables, barns, servants' quarters, and so on. At last he turned his attention to the garden: he decided to leave all the old lime trees and oaks, to cut down the apple and pear trees and plant acacias in their place; he thought of having a park, but making a rough estimate of the expenses, found that it would cost too much and, leaving it for the time being, passed on to the flower-beds and hot-houses. At this point the tempting thought of the fruit he would gather flashed through his mind so vividly that he suddenly transferred himself to the country as it would be several years hence when his estate was already reorganized according to his plan and when he lived there permanently.

He imagined himself sitting one summer evening at the tea-table on the veranda under an impenetrable canopy of trees, lazily inhaling the smoke from a long pipe, dreamily enjoying the view from behind the trees, the cool air, the stillness; in the distance the corn in the fields was turning yellow, the sun was setting behind the familiar birch-wood and spreading a red glow over the mirror-like surface of the pond; a mist was rising from the fields; it was getting cool, dusk was falling; the peasants were returning home in crowds. The idle servants were sitting at the gate; cheerful voices came from there, laughter, the sound of a balalaika; girls were playing a game of catch; his own little children were playing round him, climbing on his knees, putting their arms about his neck; at the *samovar* sat – the queen of it all – his divinity – a woman – his wife! Meanwhile, in the dining-room, furnished with elegant simplicity, bright, friendly lights were lighted, and the big, round table was being laid; Zakhar, promoted to butler, his whiskers perfectly white by now, was setting the table, placing the glasses and the silver on it with a pleasant ringing sound, every moment dropping a glass or a fork on the floor; they sat down to an abundant supper; Stolz, the comrade of his childhood and his faithful friend, was sitting next to him, as well as other familiar faces; then they went to bed. ...

Oblomov's face suddenly flushed with happiness: his dream was so vivid, so distinct, and so poetical that he at once buried his face in the pillow. He suddenly felt a vague longing for love and peaceful happiness, a keen desire for his native fields and hills, for a home with a wife and children of his own. ... After lying for five minutes with his face in the pillow, Oblomov slowly turned over on his back again. His face shone with tender, warm emotion; he was happy. He stretched out his legs slowly and with delight, which made his trousers roll up a little, but he did not notice this slight disorder. His obliging imagination carried him lightly and freely into the far-away future. Now he became absorbed in his favourite idea: he was thinking of a small group of friends settling in villages and farms within ten or fifteen miles of his estate, who would visit each other daily in turn, and dine, sup, and dance together; he saw nothing but bright days and bright, laughing people, without a care or a wrinkle, with round faces and rosy cheeks, double chins and insatiable appetites; it was going to be a perpetual summer, everlasting gaiety, lovely food, and sweet leisure. ...

'Oh Lord, oh Lord!' he murmured, overflowing with happiness, and came back to reality. He heard five people shouting their wares in the courtyard: 'Potatoes! Who wants sand – sand? Coals! Coals! Spare a few coppers for building a temple of God, ladies and gentlemen!' And from the house that was being built next door came the sound of axes and the shouts of workmen.

'Oh dear!' Oblomov sighed mournfully aloud. 'What a life! How horrible these town noises are! When will the heavenly life I long for come? When shall I return to my native woods and fields? Oh,' he thought, 'if only I were lying under a tree on the grass now, looking at the sun through the branches and counting the birds on them. Some rosy-cheeked maid-servant with soft, round bare arms and a sunburnt neck would bring me my lunch or dinner, lowering her eyes, the pretty rogue, and smiling. ... Oh, when will this time come at last?'

'And what about my plan, the bailiff, the flat?' he suddenly heard a voice inside him say.

'Yes, yes!' Oblomov said hurriedly. 'At once! At once!'

He quickly rose and sat up on the sofa, then he lowered his feet to the floor, got into both his slippers at once, and sat like that for several minutes; then he got up and stood thinking for a minute or two.

'Zakhar! Zakhar!' he called loudly, looking at the table and the inkstand.

'Oh, what is it now?' Zakhar muttered as he jumped off the stove. 'I wonder I've still strength left to drag my feet about,' he added in a hoarse whisper.

'Zakhar!' Oblomov repeated thoughtfully, without taking his eyes off the table. 'Look here, old fellow,' he began, pointing to the inkstand, but sank into thought again, without finishing the sentence.

Then he raised his arms slowly, his knees gave way, as he began stretching himself and yawning.

'We've still got some cheese left,' he said slowly, still stretching himself, 'and – er – yes, bring me some Madeira; dinner won't be for some time yet, so I think I'll have a little lunch. ...'

'Where was it left, sir?' Zakhar said. 'There was nothing left.'

'What do you mean?' Oblomov interrupted him. 'I remember very well – it was a piece as big as that.'

'No, sir,' Zakhar insisted stubbornly. 'There wasn't any piece left at all.'

'There was!' said Oblomov.

'There wasn't,' replied Zakhar.

'Well, go and buy some.'

'Give me the money, please, sir.'

'There's some change on the table, take it.'

'There's only one rouble forty copecks, sir, and the cheese costs one rouble sixty copecks.'

'There were some coppers there too.'

'I never saw them, sir,' said Zakhar, shifting from one foot to another. 'There was some silver and it's still there, but there were no coppers.'

'There were – the pedlar gave them to me himself yesterday.'

'Yes, sir, I saw him give you your change,' said Zakhar, 'but I never saw no coppers.'

'I wonder if Tarantyev took it,' Oblomov thought irresolutely. 'But no, he would have taken all the change.'

'What else is there left?' he asked.

'Nothing, sir. There may be some ham left over from yesterday,' said Zakhar. 'I'll go and ask Anisya. Shall I bring it?'

'Bring what there is. But how is it there's no cheese left?'

'Well, there isn't,' said Zakhar, and went out.

Oblomov slowly and thoughtfully paced about the study.

'Yes,' he said softly, 'there's plenty to do. Take the plan alone – lots of work still to be done on it! I'm sure there was some cheese left,' he added thoughtfully. 'It's that Zakhar who's eaten it and he's just saying there wasn't any. And where could the coppers have gone to?' he went on, rummaging on the table.

A quarter of an hour later Zakhar opened the door with the tray, which he carried in both hands. As he came into the room, he wanted to shut the door with his foot, but missed it and nearly fell over; a wine-glass, the stopper of the decanter, and a roll dropped to the floor.

'You can't take a step without dropping something,' said Oblomov. 'Well, pick up what you've dropped! Look at him, standing there and admiring his handiwork!'

Zakhar, still holding the tray, bent down to pick up the roll, but as he squatted down, he realized that both his hands were still occupied and he could not possibly do so.

'Well, sir, pick it up!' Oblomov said sarcastically. 'Why don't you? What's wrong?'

'Oh, damn you all!' Zakhar burst out furiously, addressing himself to the articles on the floor. 'Who ever heard of having lunch before dinner?'

And, putting down the tray, he picked up the things from the floor; taking the roll, he blew on it and then put it on the table.

Oblomov began his lunch, and Zakhar remained standing at some distance from him, glancing at him sideways and evidently intending to say something. But Oblomov went on eating without taking the slightest notice of him. Zakhar coughed once or twice. Oblomov still paid no attention.

'The landlord's agent, sir, has just called again,' Zakhar at last began timidly. 'The builder has been to see him and asked if he could have a look at our flat. It's all about the conversion, sir. ...'

Oblomov went on eating without answering a word.

'Sir,' Zakhar said after a pause, more quietly than ever.

Oblomov pretended not to hear.

'They say we must move next week, sir,' Zakhar wheezed.

Oblomov drank a glass of wine and said nothing.

'What are we going to do, sir?' Zakhar asked almost in a whisper.

'I told you not to mention it to me again,' Oblomov said sternly and, getting up, went up to Zakhar.

Zakhar drew back from him.

'What a venomous creature you are, Zakhar!' Oblomov added with feeling.

Zakhar was hurt.

'Me, sir?' he said. 'Me venomous? I haven't killed nobody.'

'Why, of course you are venomous,' Oblomov repeated. 'You poison my life.'

'No, sir,' Zakhar insisted. 'I'm not venomous, sir!'

'Why, then, do you pester me about the flat?'

'But what can I do, sir?'

'What can *I* do?'

'But you were going to write to the landlord, weren't you, sir?'

'Well, of course, I will write. But you must have patience. One can't do it all at once.'

'You ought to write to him now, sir.'

'Now, now! I have much more important business to attend to. You think it's just like chopping wood? Bang – and it's done? Look,' Oblomov said, turning a dry pen in the inkwell, 'there no ink in the inkwell, either. How can I write?'

'I'll dilute it with *kvas* at once,' said Zakhar, picking up the inkstand, and he walked quickly out of the room, while Oblomov began looking for note-paper.

'I don't think we have any note-paper in the house,' he said, rummaging in a drawer and running his fingers over the table. 'No, there isn't! Oh, that Zakhar – what a damn nuisance the fellow is!'

'Well,' said Oblomov to Zakhar as he came back, 'aren't you a venomous creature? You never look after anything! Why isn't there any note-paper in the house?'

'But really, sir, how can you say that? I am a Christian, I am. Why do you call me venomous? Venomous, indeed! I was born and grew up in the old master's time. He'd call me a puppy, and box my ears, but I never heard him call me that! He'd never have thought of such a word, he wouldn't! There is no telling what you might do next! Here's the paper, sir.'

He picked up half a sheet of grey note-paper from the bookcase and gave it to Oblomov.

'You don't suppose I can write a letter on this, do you?' Oblomov asked, throwing down the paper. 'I've been using it to cover my glass at night so that nothing – venomous might drop into it!'

Zakhar turned away and looked at the wall.

'Oh, never mind, give it to me and I'll write a rough draft and Alexeyev will copy it.'

Oblomov sat down at the table and quickly wrote: 'Dear Sir ...'

'What awful ink!' said Oblomov. 'Next time you'd better look out, Zakhar, and see everything's done properly.'

He thought a little and began writing.

'The flat which I occupy on the second floor of the house in which you propose to make some alterations, entirely conforms to my mode of life and habits acquired by my long residence in this house. Having been informed by my serf, Zakhar Trofimov, that you had asked him to tell me that the flat I occupy ...'

Oblomov paused and read what he had written.

'It's awkward,' he said. 'There are two *whichs* at the beginning and two *thats* at the end.'

He read it through in a whisper and transposed the words: *which* now seemed to refer to the floor – again awkward. He corrected it somehow and began thinking how he could avoid using *that* twice. He crossed out a word and then put it in again. He transposed *that* three times, but it either made nonsense or was too near the other *that*.

'Can't get rid of the second *that*!' he said impatiently. 'Oh, to hell with the letter! Rack my brains over such trifles! I've lost the knack of writing business letters. Good Lord, it's almost three o'clock!'

'Well, Zakhar, here you are!'

He tore the letter into four and threw it on the floor.

'Did you see that?' he asked.

'I saw it,' replied Zakhar, picking up the bits of paper.

'So don't pester me any more about the flat, there's a good fellow. And what have you got there?'

'The bills, sir.'

'Oh, good heavens, you'll be the death of me! Well, how much is it? Tell me quickly?'

'Eighty-six roubles and fifty-four copecks – to the butcher, sir.'

Oblomov threw up his hands in dismay.

'Have you gone mad? Such a lot of money for the butcher only?'

'If you don't pay for three months, sir, it's liable to mount up. It's all written down here. No one has stolen it!'

'And you still say you're not venomous, do you?' said Oblomov. 'Spent a million on beef! And what good does it do you? None at all as far as I can see.'

'I didn't eat it,' Zakhar muttered angrily.

'You didn't, didn't you?'

'So you begrudge me my food now, do you, sir? Here, have a look at it yourself!' And he shoved the bills to Oblomov.

'Well, who else is there?' said Oblomov, pushing away the greasy little books with vexation.

'There's another one hundred and twenty-one roubles and eighteen copecks owing to the baker and greengrocer.'

'This is sheer ruin! It's just madness!' Oblomov said, losing his temper. 'Are you a cow that you have munched so much greenstuff?'

'No, sir, I'm a venomous creature!' Zakhar observed bitterly, turning almost entirely away from his master. 'If you didn't let Mr Tarantyev come, you wouldn't have to pay so much,' he added.

'Well, how much does it come to altogether? Count!' said Oblomov and began counting himself.

Zakhar was calculating on his fingers.

'Goodness only knows how much it comes to: every time it's different,' said Oblomov. 'Well, what do you make it? Two hundred, isn't it?'

'Half a minute, sir! Give me time!' said Zakhar, screwing up his eyes and muttering. 'Eight tens and ten tens – eighteen and two more tens – –'

'Oh, you'll never finish it,' said Oblomov. 'You'd better go back to your room and let me have the bills to-morrow, and see about the paper and ink too. ... What a lot of money! I told you to pay a little at a time, but no! he prefers to pay all at once – what people!'

'Two hundred and five roubles and seventy-two copecks,' said Zakhar, having added it up. 'Won't you give me the money, sir?'

'You want it at once, do you? I'm afraid you'll have to wait a little longer. I'll check it to-morrow.'

'Just as you like, sir, only they're asking for it – –'

'All right, all right! Leave me alone, will you? I said to-morrow, and to-morrow you will have it. You go back to your room, and I'll do a bit of work. I've something more important to worry about.'

Oblomov settled in his chair and tucked his feet under him, but before he had time to start thinking, the doorbell rang.

A shortish man with a small paunch, a fair complexion, red cheeks, and a bald head, covered at the back by a thick fringe of black hair, came into the room. The bald patch on his head was round, clean, and so shiny that it seemed to have been carved out of ivory. The visitor's face was remarkable for the carefully attentive look with which he regarded everything he saw; there was an expression of reserve in his eyes and of discretion in his smile; his behaviour was distinguished by a modestly official decorum. He was wearing a comfortable frock-coat which opened widely and easily like a gate at a single touch. His linen was dazzlingly white, as though to match his bald head. On the forefinger of his right hand he wore a massive ring with some dark stone in it.

'Doctor, how nice to see you!' Oblomov cried, holding out one hand to the visitor and pulling up a chair for him with the other.

'I've got tired of your being well all the time and not calling me in, so I called without being asked,' the doctor replied jestingly. 'Well, no,' he added seriously afterwards. 'I have been upstairs with your neighbour and have called in to see how you are.'

'Thank you. And how's the patient?'

'Not so good, I'm afraid. He may last for three or four weeks or perhaps till the autumn, and then – it's a dropsy in the chest; I'm afraid there's no hope. Well, and how are you?'

Oblomov shook his head sadly.

'I'm not feeling at all well, doctor. I've been thinking of calling you in. I don't know what to do. My digestion is awful; I've such a feeling of heaviness in the pit of the stomach, terrible heartburn, and attacks of breathlessness,' Oblomov said, looking miserable.

'Give me your hand,' said the doctor, closing his eyes for a minute and feeling Oblomov's pulse.

'Any cough?' he asked.

'At night, especially after supper.'

'I see. Any palpitations? Headache?'

The doctor asked several more questions of the same kind, then he bent his bald head and thought deeply. After two minutes he suddenly raised his head and said in a firm voice:

'If you spend another two or three years in this climate, and go on lying about and eating rich, heavy food, you'll die of a stroke.'

Oblomov gave a start.

'What am I to do? Tell me, for heaven's sake!' he cried.

'What everyone else does – go abroad.'

'Abroad?' Oblomov repeated in surprise.

'Yes, why not?'

'But! Good Lord, doctor – abroad! How can I?'

'Why can't you?'

Oblomov looked silently at himself, at his study, and repeated mechanically:

'Abroad!'

'What is there to prevent you?'

'Why, everything.'

'Everything? Have you no money?'

'Well, as a matter of fact, I haven't any money at all,' Oblomov said quickly, glad of this perfectly natural excuse. 'Just have a look what my bailiff writes me. Where's the letter? Where have I put it? Zakhar!'

'All right, all right,' said the doctor. 'That isn't my business. It is my duty to tell you that you must change the manner of your life, the place, air, occupation – everything, everything.'

'Very well, I'll think about it,' said Oblomov. 'Where ought I to go and what must I do?'

'Go to Kissingen or Ems,' the doctor began. 'Spend June and July there, drink the waters, then go to Switzerland or the Tyrol for a grape cure. Spend September and October there – –'

'Good Lord, the Tyrol!' Oblomov whispered in a barely audible voice.

'... then to some dry place, say, to Egypt – –'

'Good Lord!' thought Oblomov.

'Avoid worry and vexation – –'

'It's all very well for you to talk,' said Oblomov. 'You don't get such letters from the bailiff.'

'You must also avoid thinking,' the doctor went on.

'Thinking?'

'Yes, mental strain.'

'And what about my plan for reorganizing my estate? Good heavens, doctor, I'm not a piece of wood, am I?'

'Well, do as you like. It's my duty to warn you. That's all. You must also avoid passionate entanglements; they interfere with the cure. You must try and divert yourself by riding, dancing, moderate exercise in the fresh air, pleasant conversation, especially with ladies, so that your heart should be stirred lightly and only by pleasant sensations.'

Oblomov listened to him dejectedly.

'And then?' he asked.

'And then keep away from reading and writing – that's very important! Hire a villa with a southern aspect, with lots of flowers, and see there are women about you and music – –'

'What sort of food ought I to have?'

'Avoid meat and animal food in general, also starchy food and meat jellies. You may have thin soup and vegetables, only remember there's cholera about, so you must be careful. You may walk for about eight hours a day. Get yourself a shotgun – –'

'Good heavens!' Oblomov groaned.

'– and, finally,' the doctor concluded, 'go to Paris for the winter and amuse yourself there – in the whirl of life – and try not to think; from the theatre to a dance, a fancy-dress ball, pay visits to friends in the country, see that you have friends, noise, laughter around you.'

'Anything else?' asked Oblomov with ill-disguised vexation.

The doctor pondered.

'Perhaps you could try the sea air; get on a steamer in England and take a trip to America.'

He got up to leave.

'If you carry it all out exactly – –' he said.

'Very well, very well,' Oblomov replied sarcastically, as he saw him off, 'I shall certainly carry it out.'

The doctor went away, leaving Oblomov in a most pitiful condition. He closed his eyes, put both hands behind his head, huddled himself up in the chair and sat like that, seeing and feeling nothing.

A timid voice called behind him:

'Sir!'

'Well?' he replied.

'And what shall I tell the landlord's agent?'

'What about?'

'About our moving?'

'You're at it again?' Oblomov asked in surprise.

'But, sir, what am I to do? You must admit that my life's not easy as it is. I'm worried to death – –'

'Oh no, it's me you're worrying to death by your talk of moving,' said Oblomov. 'You'd better hear what the doctor has just told me!'

Zakhar did not know what to say to that and merely fetched so deep a sigh that the ends of the kerchief round his neck shook on his breast.

'You've made up your mind to kill me, have you?' Oblomov asked again. 'You're sick of me, are you? Well, speak!'

'Good Lord, sir, live as long as you like! I'm sure no one wishes you ill, sir,' Zakhar growled, completely put out by the tragic turn the conversation was taking.

'You do!' said Oblomov. 'I've forbidden you to mention moving to me, and you remind me of it half a dozen times a day. It upsets me – don't you realize that? I'm in a bad way as it is.'

'I thought, sir, that – I thought why shouldn't we move?' Zakhar said in a voice trembling with emotion.

'Why shouldn't we move?' Oblomov said, turning together

with his chair towards Zakhar. 'You think it's so easy, don't you? But, my dear fellow, have you considered carefully what moving means? You haven't, have you?'

'I don't think I have, sir,' Zakhar answered humbly, ready to agree with his master about everything so long as there were no pathetic scenes, which he could not endure.

'If you haven't,' said Oblomov, 'then listen and see for yourself whether we can move or not. What does moving mean? It means that your master will have to leave the house for a whole day and walk about dressed from early morning.'

'Well, sir, why not leave the house?' Zakhar remarked. 'Why not go away for a whole day? It's unhealthy to sit at home. You do look bad, sir! Before, you looked the picture of health, but now that you always sit at home you look like nothing on earth. If you only took a walk in the streets, had a look at the people or something – –'

'Don't talk nonsense and listen!' said Oblomov. 'Take a walk in the streets!'

'Why not, sir?' Zakhar went on warmly. 'I'm told, sir, there's a terrible monster on show. Why not go and have a look at it? Or you might go to a theatre or a mask ball, and we'd do the moving without you.'

'Don't talk rubbish! So that's how you look after your master's comfort! You don't care if I tramp about the streets all day long, do you? What would it matter to you if I had dinner in some poky little hole and couldn't lie down after it? They'll do the moving without me! If I'm not here to keep an eye on things, you'd be moving – bits and pieces. I know,' Oblomov went on with growing conviction, 'what moving furniture means! It means breakages, noise, everything will be piled together on the floor: trunks, the back of the sofa, pictures, books, pipes, all sorts of bottles one never sees at any other time which suddenly turn up goodness knows from where! And you have to look after it all so that nothing gets broken or lost – one half here, another on the cart, or in the new flat! You want to smoke, you pick up your pipe, but the tobacco's already gone – you want to sit down, but there's nothing to sit on, you can't touch anything without getting dirty and covered with dust – nothing to wash with and you have to go about with hands as filthy as yours – –'

'My hands are clean,' Zakhar remarked, showing what looked more like two soles than a pair of hands.

'Oh, you'd better not show them to me,' said Oblomov,

turning away. 'And should you want to have a drink, the decanter's there, but there's no glass.'

'You can drink from the decanter just as well,' Zakhar observed good-naturedly.

'That's just like you: one can just as well not sweep the floor, not dust, and not beat the carpets. And at the new flat,' Oblomov went on, carried away by the vivid picture of the moving he had conjured up, 'things won't be put straight for at least three days – everything is sure to be in the wrong place: the pictures on the floor by the walls, the goloshes on the bed, the boots in the same bundle as the tea and the pomatum. There's a chair with a broken leg, a picture with a smashed glass, a sofa covered in stains. Whatever you ask for is not to be found, no one knows where it is – been lost or left at the old flat – go and run back for it.'

'Aye,' Zakhar interrupted, 'sometimes one has to run there and back a dozen times.'

'There you are!' Oblomov went on. 'And getting up in the morning in a new flat – what a bore! No water, no charcoal for the *samovar*, and in the winter you're sure to freeze to death, the rooms are cold and there's no firewood; you have to run and borrow some.'

'That depends on the kind of neighbours you get,' Zakhar observed again. 'Some wouldn't lend you a jug of water, let alone a bundle of firewood.'

'Yes, indeed!' said Oblomov. 'You move and you'd suppose that by the evening everything would be over, but not at all, you won't be settled for another fortnight at least. Everything seems to be in its place, but there are still heaps of things to do: hang up the curtains, put up the pictures – you'd be sick and tired of it all, you'd wish you were dead. And the expense!'

'Last time we moved, eight years ago,' Zakhar confirmed, 'it cost us two hundred roubles – I remember it as if it was to-day.'

'Well, that's no joke, is it?' said Oblomov. 'And how strange life is in a new flat at first! How soon will you get used to it? Why, I shan't be able to sleep for at least a week in the new place. I'll be eaten up with misery when I get up and don't see the wood-turner's signboard opposite; if that old woman with the short hair doesn't look out of the window before dinner, I feel miserable. So you see now what you're trying to let your master in for, don't you?' Oblomov asked reproachfully.

'I see, sir,' Zakhar whispered humbly.

'Then why did you try to persuade me to move?' said Oblomov. 'Do you think I'm strong enough to stand it?'

'I thought, sir, that other people are no better than us, and if they move, why can't we?'

'What? What?' Oblomov asked in surprise, rising from his chair. 'What did you say?'

Zakhar was utterly confused, not knowing what he could have said to cause his master's pathetic words and gestures. He was silent.

'Other people are no better!' Oblomov repeated in dismay. 'So that's what you've been leading up to! Now I shall know that I'm the same as "other people" to you!'

Oblomov bowed to Zakhar ironically, and looked highly offended.

'Good Lord, sir, I never said that you were the same as anyone else, did I?'

'Get out of my sight, sir!' Oblomov cried imperiously, pointing to the door. 'I can't bear to look at you! "Other people!" That's nice!'

Zakhar heaved a deep sigh and withdrew to his room.

'What a life!' he growled, sitting down on the stove.

'Good Lord,' Oblomov, too, groaned. 'Here I was going to devote the morning to some decent work, and now I'm upset for the whole day. And who's done it? My own tried and devoted servant. And the things he has said! How could he have said it?'

Oblomov could not compose himself for a long time; he lay down, he got up, paced the room, and again lay down. In Zakhar's attempt to reduce him to the level of *other people* he saw a violation of his rights to Zakhar's exclusive preference of his own master. He tried to grasp the whole meaning of that comparison and analyse what *the others* were and what he was, and to what an extent a parallel between him and other people was justified, and how gravely Zakhar had insulted him. Finally, he wondered whether Zakhar had insulted him consciously, that is to say, whether he was convinced that he, Oblomov, was the same as 'another', or whether the words had escaped him without thinking. All this hurt Oblomov's vanity and he decided to show Zakhar the difference between himself and those 'others' and make him feel the whole baseness of his action.

'Zakhar!' he called solemnly in a drawn-out voice.

Hearing this call, Zakhar did not growl or jump off the stove as usual, making a noise with his feet, but got down slowly and, brushing against everything with his arms and sides, walked out of his room quietly and reluctantly like a dog which knows by the sound of its master's voice that its trick has been discovered and that it is being called to receive punishment. Zakhar half opened the door, but did not venture to go in.

'Come in!' said Oblomov.

Though the door could be opened easily, Zakhar opened it only an inch and stuck in the doorway instead of walking in.

Oblomov was sitting on the edge of his couch.

'Come here!' Oblomov ordered.

Zakhar disentangled himself from the door with difficulty, but at once closed it behind him and leant against it firmly with his back.

'Here!' said Oblomov, pointing to a place beside him.

Zakhar took half a step and stopped five yards from the place indicated.

'Nearer!' said Oblomov.

Zakhar pretended to take another step, but merely swayed forward, stamped his foot, and remained where he was. Seeing that this time he could not make Zakhar come nearer, Oblomov let him stay where he was and looked at him for some time reproachfully and in silence. Embarrassed by this silent contemplation of his person, Zakhar pretended not to notice his master and stood turning away from him more than usual and did not even at that moment look at Oblomov out of the corner of his eye. He looked stubbornly to the left, where he saw a long-familiar sight: the fringe of the spider's web round the pictures and the spider – a living reproach to his remissness.

'Zakhar!' Oblomov said quietly and with dignity.

Zakhar made no answer.

'Well,' he seemed to be thinking, 'what do you want? Some other Zakhar? Can't you see that I'm here?' He transferred his gaze from the left to the right, past his master; there, too, he was reminded of himself by the looking-glass covered with a thick layer of dust as with muslin – his own gloomy and unattractive face looked at him sullenly and wildly from there as through a mist. He turned away with displeasure from that melancholy and all-too-familiar object and made up his mind to glance for a moment at Oblomov. Their eyes met.

Zakhar could not bear the reproach in his master's eyes, and lowered his own eyes: there again, in the carpet, impregnated with dust and covered with stains, he read the sad testimony to his zeal in his master's service.

'Zakhar!' Oblomov repeated with feeling.

'What is it, sir?' Zakhar asked in a barely audible whisper and gave a slight shudder, anticipating a pathetic speech.

'Give me some *kvas*,' said Oblomov.

Zakhar breathed freely; he felt so happy that he rushed like a boy to the sideboard and brought some *kvas*.

'Well, how do you feel?' Oblomov asked gently, taking a sip from the glass and holding it in his hands. 'You're sorry, aren't you?'

The crestfallen expression on Zakhar's face was immediately softened by a ray of repentance that appeared on his features. Zakhar felt the first symptoms of awakening reverence for his master and he suddenly began to look straight in his eyes.

'Are you sorry for your misdemeanour?' asked Oblomov.

'Why, what "misdemeanour" is this?' Zakhar thought bitterly. 'Something awful, I'll be bound. I shall burst into tears if he goes on lecturing me like this.'

'Well, sir,' Zakhar began on the lowest note of his register, 'I haven't said nothing except that – –'

'No, wait!' Oblomov interrupted. 'Do you realize what you've done? Here, put the glass on the table and tell me.'

Zakhar said nothing, being completely at a loss to understand what he had done, but that did not prevent him from looking with reverence at his master; he even hung his head a little, conscious of his guilt.

'Well, aren't you a venomous creature?' Oblomov said.

Zakhar still said nothing, and only blinked slowly a few times.

'You've grieved your master!' Oblomov declared slowly, looking fixedly at Zakhar and enjoying his embarrassment.

Zakhar felt so miserable that he wished he could sink through the floor.

'You have grieved him, haven't you?' asked Oblomov.

'Grieved!' Zakhar whispered, utterly bewildered by that new, pathetic word. He glanced wildly from the right to the left, looking in vain for some deliverance, and again all he saw was the spider's web, the dust, and his own and his master's reflections in the looking-glass.

'Oh, I wish I could sink through the ground! Oh, why aren't I dead?' he thought, seeing that, try as he might, he could not avoid a pathetic scene. He felt that he was blinking more and more and that any moment tears would start in his eyes. At last he regaled his master with his familiar song, except that it was in prose.

'How have I grieved you, sir?' he asked, almost in tears.

'How?' Oblomov repeated. 'Why, did it occur to you to think what *other people* are?'

He stopped, still looking at Zakhar.

'Shall I tell you what they are?'

Zakhar turned like a bear in its lair and heaved a loud sigh.

'The *other people* you're thinking of are poor wretches, rough, uncivilized people who live in dirt and poverty in some attic; they can sleep comfortably on a felt mat somewhere in the yard. What can happen to such people? Nothing. They guzzle potatoes and salt herrings. Poverty drives them from one place to another, and so they rush about all day long. They, I'm sure, wouldn't mind moving to a new flat. Lyagayev, for instance. He would put his ruler under his arm, tie up his two shirts in a handkerchief, and go off. "Where are you going?" "I'm moving," he would say. That's what *other people* are like. Aren't they?'

Zakhar glanced at his master, shifted from foot to foot, and said nothing.

'What are *other people*?' Oblomov went on. 'They are people who do not mind cleaning their boots and dressing themselves, and though they sometimes look like gentlemen, it's all a put-up show; they don't know what a servant looks like. If they have no one to send out on an errand, they run out themselves. They don't mind stirring the fire in the stove or dusting their furniture. ...'

'There are many Germans who are like that,' Zakhar said gloomily.

'No doubt there are! And I? What do you think? Am I like them?'

'You're quite different, sir,' Zakhar said piteously, still at a loss to know what his master was driving at. 'What has come over you, sir?'

'I'm quite different, am I? Wait, think carefully what you're saying. Just consider how the "others" live. The "others" work hard, they rush about, they're always busy,' Oblomov went on. 'If they don't work, they don't eat. The "others" bow and scrape, beg, grovel. And I? Well, tell me, what do you think: am I like "other people"?'

'Please, sir, don't go on torturing me with pathetic words,' Zakhar implored. 'Oh dear, oh dear!'

'I am like the "others", am I? Do I rush about? Do I work? Have I not enough to eat? Do I look thin and wretched? Do I go short of things? It seems to me I have someone to wait on me and do things for me! Never in my life, thank God, have I had to pull a sock on my foot myself! Why should I worry? Whatever for? And who am I saying this to? Haven't you looked after me since I was a child? You know all this; you've seen how tenderly I've been brought up; you know that I've never suffered from hunger or cold, that I've never lacked anything, that I haven't had to earn my living and never done any heavy work. So how did you have the heart to compare me to "others"? Do you think I am as strong as those "others"? Can I do and endure what they can?'

Zakhar was no longer capable of understanding what Oblomov was talking about. But his lips were blown up with emotion: the pathetic scene was raging like a storm-cloud over his head. He was silent.

'Zakhar!' Oblomov repeated.

'Yes, sir?' Zakhar hissed in a barely audible whisper.

'Give me some more *kvas*.'

Zakhar brought the *kvas*, and when Oblomov had drunk it and handed him back the glass, he made a dash for the door.

'No, no, wait!' said Oblomov. 'I'm asking you how you could so terribly insult your master whom you carried in your arms as a baby, whom you have served all your life, and who has been your benefactor?'

Zakhar could not bear it any more. The word 'benefactor' finished him! He began blinking more and more. The less he understood what Oblomov was saying to him in his pathetic speech, the sadder he became.

'I'm very sorry, sir,' he began to wheeze penitently. 'It was out of foolishness, sir, out of foolishness that I – –'

Not understanding what he had done, Zakhar did not know what verb to use at the end of his speech.

'And I,' went on Oblomov in the voice of a man who had been insulted and whose merits had not been sufficiently appreciated, 'and I go on working and worrying day and night, sometimes with a burning head and a sinking heart. I lie awake at night, toss about, always thinking how to improve things – and for whom? Who is it I'm worrying about? All for you, for the peasants, and that means you, too ... I daresay when you see me pull my blankets over my head you think I lie there asleep like a log. But no, I don't sleep, I keep thinking all the time what I can do that my peasants should not suffer any hardships, that they should not envy the peasants belonging to other people, that they should not complain against me to God on the Day of

Judgement, but should pray for me and remember me for the good I had done them. Ungrateful ones!' Oblomov concluded bitterly.

Zakhar was completely overcome by the last *pathetic* words. He began to whimper quietly.

'Please, sir,' he implored, 'don't carry on like that! What are you saying, sir? Oh, Blessed Virgin, Mother of God, what a terrible calamity has befallen us!'

'And you,' Oblomov went on, without listening to him – 'you ought to be ashamed to say such things. That's the sort of snake I've warmed in my bosom!'

'Snake!' Zakhar repeated, throwing up his hands and bursting out sobbing so loudly that it sounded as though two dozen beetles had flown into the room and begun buzzing. 'When have I mentioned a snake?' he said amidst his sobs. 'Why, I never even dream of the cursed things!'

Each had ceased to understand the other and, at last, they no longer understood themselves.

'How could you have brought yourself to say a thing like that?' Oblomov went on. 'And in my plan I had assigned you a house of your own, a kitchen garden, a quantity of corn, and a regular wage! I had appointed you my steward, my butler, and my business manager! The peasants would bow low to you, they would all call you Zakhar Trofimych, Zakhar Trofimych! And you're still dissatisfied, you put me on the same level as the "others"! That's how you reward me! That's how you abuse your master!'

Zakhar continued to sob, and Oblomov himself was moved. While admonishing Zakhar, he was filled with the consciousness of the benefits he had conferred on his peasants, and he uttered his last reproaches in a trembling voice and with tears in his eyes.

'Well, you can go now,' he said to Zakhar in a conciliatory tone of voice. 'Wait, give me some more *kvas*! My throat is parched. You might have thought of it yourself – can't you hear your master is hoarse? That's what you have brought me to! I hope,' he went on when Zakhar had brought him the *kvas*, 'you've understood your misdemeanour and that you won't ever again compare your master to "other people"! To atone for your guilt, you must make some arrangement with the landlord so that we have not got to move. This is how much you care for your master's peace of mind: you have thoroughly upset me and made it impossible for me to think of any new and useful idea. And who will suffer from it? You will. It is to my peasants that I have devoted all my life, it is for all of you that I have resigned from the service and sit shut up in my room. Well, never mind! There, it's striking three. Only two hours left before dinner, and what can one do in two hours? Nothing. And there's lots to be done. Oh well, I shall have to put off my letter till the next post and jot down the plan to-morrow. And now I'll lie down for an hour: I'm worn out. Draw the blinds, shut the door, and be sure I'm not disturbed. Wake me at half-past four.'

Zakhar began to seal up his master in the study; first he covered him up and tucked the blanket under him, then he drew the blinds, closed the doors tightly, and retired to his own room.

'May you never get up again, you devil,' he growled, wiping away the traces of tears and climbing on the stove. 'A devil he is, and no mistake! A house of your own, a kitchen garden, wages!' Zakhar, who had understood only the last words, muttered. 'He knows how to talk, he does, just like cutting your heart with a knife! This is my house and my kitchen garden, and this is where I'll peg out!' he said, hitting the stove furiously. 'Wages! If I didn't pick up a few coppers now and then, I shouldn't have anything to buy tobacco with or to treat my friend. Curse you! ... I wish I was dead and buried!'

Oblomov lay on his back, but he did not fall asleep at once. He kept thinking and thinking, and got more and more agitated.

'Two misfortunes at once!' he said, pulling the blanket over his head. 'How is one to stand up to it?'

But actually those two *misfortunes* – that is, the bailiff's ominous letter and the moving – no longer worried Oblomov and were already becoming mere disturbing memories.

'The troubles the bailiff is threatening me with are still far off,' he thought. 'All sorts of things can happen before that: the rains may save the crops, the bailiff may make good the arrears, the runaway peasants may be returned to their "place of domicile" as he writes. ... And where could those peasants have gone to?' he thought, getting more and more absorbed in an artistic examination of that circumstance. 'They could not have gone off at night, in the damp and without provisions. Where would they sleep? Not in the woods, surely? They just can't stay there! There may be a bad smell in a peasant's cottage but at least it's warm. ... And what am I so worried about?' he thought. 'Soon my plan will be ready – why be frightened before I need to? Oh, you – –'

He was a little more troubled by the thought of moving. That was the new and the latest *misfortune*. But in his present hopeful mood that fact, too, was already pushed into the background. Though he vaguely realized that he would have to move, particularly as Tarantyev had taken a hand in this business, he postponed it in his mind for at least a week, and thus gained a whole week of peace! 'And *perhaps* Zakhar will succeed in coming to some arrangement so that it will not be necessary to move at all. Perhaps it could be arranged *somehow*! They might agree to put it off till next summer or give up the idea of conversion altogether; well, arrange it *in one way or another*! After all, I really can't – move!'

So he kept agitating and composing himself in turn, and, as always, found in the soothing and comforting words *perhaps*, *somehow*, *in one way or another*, a whole ark of hope and consolation as in the old ark of the Covenant, and succeeded with their help in warding off the two misfortunes for the time being. Already a slight, pleasant numbness spread over his body and began to cast a mist over his senses with sleep, just as the surface of the water is misted over with the first, timid frosts; another moment and his consciousness would have slipped away heaven only knows where, when suddenly he came to and opened his eyes.

'But, good Lord, I haven't washed! I haven't done a thing!' he whispered. 'I was going to put down my plan on paper, and I haven't done so. I haven't written to the police inspector or the Governor. I began a letter to the landlord, but haven't finished it. I haven't checked the bills – or given Zakhar the money – a whole morning wasted!'

He sank into thought. 'What's the matter with me? And would the "others" have done that?' flashed through his mind. ' "Others, others" – who are they?'

He became absorbed in a comparison of himself with those 'others'. He thought and thought, and presently an idea quite different from the one he had been expounding to Zakhar was formed in his mind. He had to admit that another one would have managed to write all the letters so that *which* and *that* would never have clashed with one another, that another would have moved to a new flat, carried out the plan, gone to the country. ...

'Why, I, too, could have done it,' he reflected. 'I can write well enough. I have written more complicated things than ordinary letters in my time! What has become of it all? And what is there so terrible about moving? It's only a question of making up one's mind! The "others",' he added a further characteristic of those other people, 'never wear a dressing-gown' – here he yawned – 'they hardly ever sleep, they enjoy life, they go everywhere, see everything, are interested in everything. . . . And I – I am not like them!' he added sadly and sank into deep thought. He even put his head out from under the blanket.

It was one of the most clear-sighted and courageous moments of Oblomov's life. Oh, how dreadful he felt when there arose in his mind a clear and vivid idea of human destiny and the purpose of a man's life, and when he compared this purpose with his own life, and when various vital problems wakened one after another in his mind and began whirling about confusedly, like frightened birds awakened suddenly by a ray of sunlight in some dark ruin. He felt sad and sorry at the thought of his own lack of education, at the arrested development of his spiritual powers, at the feeling of heaviness which interfered with everything he planned to do; and was overcome by envy of those whose lives were rich and full, while a huge rock seemed to have been thrown across the narrow and pitiful path of his own existence. Slowly there arose in his mind the painful realization that many sides of his nature had never been awakened, that others were barely touched, that none had developed fully. And yet he was painfully aware that something good and fine lay buried in him as in a grave, that it was perhaps already dead or lay hidden like gold in the heart of a mountain, and that it was high time that gold was put into circulation. But the treasure was deeply buried under a heap of rubbish and silt. It was as though he himself had stolen and buried in his own soul the treasures bestowed on him as a gift by the world and life. Something prevented him from launching out into the ocean of life and devoting all the powers of his mind and will to flying across it under full sail. Some secret enemy seemed to have laid a heavy hand upon him at the very start of his journey and cast him a long way off from the direct purpose of human existence. And it seemed that he would never find his way to the straight path from the wild and impenetrable jungle. The forest grew thicker and darker in his soul and around him; the path was getting more and more overgrown; clear consciousness awakened more and more seldom, and roused the slumbering powers only for a moment. His mind and will had long been paralysed and, it seemed, irretrievably. The events of his life had dwindled to microscopic dimensions, but even so he could not cope with them; he did not pass from one to another, but was tossed to and fro by them as by waves; he was powerless to oppose one by the resilience of his will or to follow another by the force of his reason. He felt bitter at having to confess it all to himself in secret. Fruitless regrets for the past, burning reproaches of his conscience pricked him like needles, and he tried hard to throw off the burden of those reproaches, to find someone else to blame and turn their sting against. But who?

'It's all – Zakhar's fault,' he whispered.

He recalled the details of the scene with Zakhar, and his face burned with shame. 'What if someone had overheard it?' he wondered, turning cold at the thought. 'Thank goodness Zakhar won't be able to repeat it to anyone, and no one would believe him, either.'

He sighed, cursed himself, turned from side to side, looked for someone to blame and could not find anyone. His moans and groans even reached Zakhar's ears.

'It's that *kvas* that's given him wind,' Zakhar muttered angrily.

'Why am I like this?' Oblomov asked himself almost with tears, hiding his head under the blanket again. 'Why?'

After seeking in vain for the hostile source that prevented him from living as he should, as the 'others' lived, he sighed, closed his eyes, and a few minutes later drowsiness began once again to benumb his senses.

'I, too, would have liked – liked,' he murmured, blinking with difficulty, 'something like that – has nature treated me so badly – no, thank God – I've nothing to complain of – –' There followed a resigned sigh. He was passing from agitation to his normal state of calm and apathy. 'It's fate, I suppose – can't do anything about it,' he was hardly able to whisper, overcome by sleep. 'Some two thousand less than last year,' he said suddenly in a loud voice, as though in a delirium. 'Wait – wait a moment – –' And he half awoke. 'Still,' he whispered again, 'it would be interesting – to know why – I am like that!' His eyelids closed tightly. 'Yes – why? Perhaps it's – because – –' He tried to utter the words but could not.

So he never arrived at the cause, after all; his tongue and lips stopped in the middle of the sentence and remained half open. Instead of a word, another sigh was heard, followed by the sound of the even snoring of a man who was peacefully asleep.

Sleep stopped the slow and lazy flow of his thoughts and

instantly transferred him to another age and other people, to another place, where we, too, gentle reader, will follow him in the next chapter.

OBLOMOV'S DREAM

WHERE ARE WE? In what blessed little corner of the earth has Oblomov's dream transferred us? What a lovely spot!

It is true there is no sea there, no high mountains, cliffs or precipices, no virgin forests – nothing grand, gloomy, and wild. But what is the good of the grand and the wild? The sea, for instance? Let it stay where it is! It merely makes you melancholy: looking at it, you feel like crying. The heart quails at the sight of the boundless expanse of water, and the eyes grow tired of the endless monotony of the scene. The roaring and the wild pounding of the waves do not caress your feeble ears; they go on repeating their old, old song, gloomy and mysterious, the same since the world began; and the same old moaning is heard in it, the same complaints as though of a monster condemned to torture, and piercing, sinister voices. No birds twitter around; only silent sea-gulls like doomed creatures, mournfully fly to and fro near the coast and circle over the water.

The roar of a beast is powerless beside these lamentations of nature, the human voice, too, is insignificant, and man himself is so little and weak, so lost among the small details of the vast picture! Perhaps it is because of this that he feels so depressed when he looks at the sea. Yes, the sea can stay where it is! Its very calm and stillness bring no comfort to a man's heart; in the barely perceptible swell of the mass of waters man still sees the same boundless, though slumbering, force which can so cruelly mock his proud will and bury so deeply his brave schemes, and all his labour and toil.

Mountains and precipices, too, have not been created for man's enjoyment. They are as terrifying and menacing as the teeth and claws of a wild beast rushing upon him; they remind us too vividly of our frailty and keep us continually in fear of our lives. And the sky over the peaks and the precipices seems so far and unattainable, as though it had recoiled from men.

The peaceful spot where our hero suddenly found himself was

not like that. The sky there seems to hug the earth, not in order to fling its thunderbolts at it, but to embrace it more tightly and lovingly; it hangs as low overhead as the trustworthy roof of the parental house, to preserve, it would seem, the chosen spot from all calamities. The sun there shines brightly and warmly for about six months of the year and withdraws gradually, as though reluctantly, as though turning back to take another look at the place it loves and to give it a warm, clear day in the autumn, amid the rain and slush.

The mountains there seem to be only small-scale models of the terrifying mountains far away that frighten the imagination. They form a chain of gently sloping hillocks, down which it is pleasant to slide on one's back in play, or to sit on watching the sunset dreamily.

The river runs gaily, sporting and playing; sometimes it spreads into a wide pond, and sometimes it rushes along in a swift stream, or grows quiet, as though lost in meditation, and creeps slowly along the pebbles, breaking up into lively streams on all sides, whose rippling lulls you pleasantly to sleep.

The whole place, for ten or fifteen miles around, consists of a series of picturesque, smiling, gay landscapes. The sandy, sloping banks of the clear stream, the small bushes that steal down to the water from the hills, the twisting ravine with a brook running at the bottom, and the birch copse – all seem to have been carefully chosen and composed with the hand of a master. A heart worn out by tribulations or wholly unacquainted with them cries out to hide itself in that secluded spot and live there happily and undisturbed. Everything there promises a calm, long life, till the hair turns white with age and death comes unawares, like sleep.

The year follows a regular and imperturbable course there. Spring arrives in March, according to the calendar, muddy streams run down the hills, the ground thaws, and a warm mist rises from it; the peasant throws off his sheepskin, comes out into the open only in his shirt and, shielding his eyes with a hand, stands there enjoying the sunshine and shakes his shoulders with pleasure; then he pulls the overturned cart first by one shaft, then by the other, or examines and kicks with his foot at the plough that lies idle in the shed, getting ready for his usual labours. No sudden blizzards return in the spring, covering the fields or breaking down the trees with snow. Like a cold and unapproachable beauty, winter remains true to its character till the lawfully appointed time for warmth; it does not tease with sudden thaws or bend one double with unheard of frosts; everything goes on in the usual way prescribed by nature. In November snow and frost begin, and by Twelfth-day it grows so cold that a peasant leaving his cottage for a minute returns with hoar-frost on his beard; and in February a sensitive nose already feels the soft breath of approaching spring in the air. But the summer – the summer is especially enchanting in that part of the country. The air there is fresh and dry; it is not filled with the fragrance of lemons and laurels, but only with the scent of wormwood, pine, and wild cherry; the days are bright with slightly burning but not scorching sunshine, and for almost three months there is not a cloud in the sky. As soon as clear days come, they go on for three or four weeks; the evenings are warm and the nights are close. The stars twinkle in such a kindly and friendly way from the sky. If rain comes, it is such a beneficent summer rain! It falls briskly, abundantly, splashing along merrily like the big, warm tears of a man overcome with sudden joy; and as soon as it stops the sun once more looks down with a bright smile of love on the hills and fields and dries them; and the whole countryside responds to the sun with a happy smile. The peasant welcomes the rain joyfully. 'The rain will wet me and the sun will dry me,' he says, holding up delightedly his face, shoulders, and back to the warm shower. Thunderstorms are not a menace but a blessing there; they always occur at the appointed times, hardly ever missing St Elijah's day on the second of August, as though to confirm the well-known legend among the people. The strength and number of thunder-claps also seem to be the same each year, as though a definite amount of electricity had been allotted annually for the whole place. Terrible storms, bringing devastation in their wake, are unheard-of in those parts, and no report of them has ever appeared in the newspapers. And nothing would ever have been published about that thrice-blessed spot had not a twenty-eight-year-old peasant widow, Marina Kulkov, given birth to quadruplets, an event the Press could not possibly have ignored.

The Lord has never visited those parts either by Egyptian or ordinary plagues. No one of the inhabitants has ever seen or remembered any terrible heavenly signs, fiery balls, or sudden darkness; there are no poisonous snakes there; locusts do not come; there are no roaring lions, nor growling tigers, nor even bears nor wolves, because there are no forests. Only ruminating cows, bleating sheep, and cackling hens walk about the villages and fields in vast numbers.

It is hard to say whether a poet or a dreamer would have been pleased with nature in this peaceful spot. These gentlemen, as everyone knows, love to gaze at the moon and listen to the song of the nightingale. They love the coquette-moon when she dresses up in amber clouds and peeps mysteriously through the branches or flings sheaves of silvery beams into the eyes of her admirers. But in that country no one has even heard of the moon being anything but an ordinary moon. It stares very good-naturedly at the villages and the fields, looking very like a polished brass basin. The poet would have looked at her in vain with eyes of rapture; she gazes as good-naturedly at a poet as does a round-faced village beauty in response to the eloquent and passionate glances of a city philanderer.

There are no nightingales in those parts, either – perhaps because there are no shady nooks and roses there. But what an abundance of quail! At harvest time in the summer boys catch them with their hands. Do not imagine, however, that quail are regarded there as a gastronomic luxury – no, the morals of the inhabitants had not been corrupted to that extent: a quail is a bird which is not mentioned in the dietary rules. In that part of the country it delights the ear with its singing; that is why almost every house has a quail in a string cage under the roof.

The poet and dreamer would have remained dissatisfied by the general appearance of that modest and unpretentious district. They would never have succeeded in seeing an evening in the Swiss or Scottish style, when the whole of nature – the woods, the river, the cottage walls, and the sandy hills – is suffused by the red glow of the sunset, against which is set off a cavalcade of gentlemen, riding on a twisting, sandy road after having escorted a lady on a trip to some gloomy ruin and now returning at a smart pace to a strong castle, where an ancient native would tell them a story about the Wars of the Roses and where, after a supper of wild goat's meat, a young girl would sing them a ballad to the accompaniment of a lute – scenes with which the pen of Walter Scott has so richly filled our imagination. No, there is nothing like that in our part of the country.

How quiet and sleepy everything is in the three or four villages which compose this little plot of land! They lie close to one another and look as though they had been flung down accidentally by a giant's hand and scattered about in different directions, where they had remained to this day. One cottage, dropped on the edge of a ravine, has remained hanging there since time immemorial, half of it suspended in the air and propped up by three poles. People have lived quietly and happily there for three or four generations. One would think that a hen would be afraid to go into it, and yet Onisim Suslov, a steady man, who is too big to stand up in his own cottage, lives there with his wife. Not everyone would be able to enter Onisim's cottage, unless, indeed, the visitor persuaded it to stand *with its back to the forest and its front to him*. For its front steps hang over the ravine, and in order to enter it one has to hold on to the grass with one hand and its roof with the other, and then lift one's foot and place it firmly on the steps.

Another cottage clings precariously to the hillside like a swallow's nest; three other cottages have been thrown together accidentally not far away, and two more stand at the very bottom of the ravine.

Everything in the village is quiet and sleepy: the doors of the silent cottages are wide open; not a soul is to be seen; only the flies swarm in clouds and buzz in the stuffy air. On entering a cottage, you will call in vain in a loud voice: dead silence will be your answer; very seldom will some old woman, who is spending her remaining years on the stove, reply with a painful sigh or a sepulchral cough; or a three-year-old child, long-haired, barefoot, and with only a torn shirt on, will appear from behind a partition, stare at you in silence, and hide himself again.

In the fields, too, peace and a profound silence reign; only here and there a ploughman can be seen stirring like an ant on the black earth – and, scorched by the heat and bathed in perspiration, pitching his plough forward. The same imperturbable peace and quiet prevail among the people of that locality. No robberies, murders, or fatal accidents ever happened there; no strong passions or daring enterprises ever agitated them. And, indeed, what passions or daring enterprises could have agitated them? Everyone there knew what he was capable of. The inhabitants of those villages lived far from other people. The nearest villages and the district town were twenty and twenty-five miles away. At a certain time the peasants carted their corn to the nearest landing-stage of the Volga, which was their Colchis or Pillars of Hercules, and some of them went to the market once a year, and that was all the intercourse they had with the outside world. Their interests were centred upon themselves and they never came into contact with or ran foul of any one else's. They knew that the administrative city of the province was sixty miles away, but very few of them ever went there; they also knew that farther away in the same direction was Saratov or

Nizhny-Novgorod; they had heard of Petersburg and Moscow, and that French and Germans lived beyond Petersburg, and the world farther away was for them as mysterious as it was for the ancients – unknown countries, inhabited by monsters, people with two heads, giants; farther away still there was darkness, and at the end of it all was the fish which held the world on its back. And as their part of the country was hardly ever visited by travellers, they had no opportunity of learning the latest news of what was going on in the world: the peasants who supplied them with their wooden vessels lived within fifteen miles of their villages and were as ignorant as they. There was nothing even with which they could compare their way of living and find out in this way whether they lived well or no, whether they were rich or poor, or whether there was anything others had that they, too, would like.

These lucky people imagined that everything was as it should be and were convinced that everyone else lived like them and to live otherwise was a sin. They would not believe it if someone told them that there were people who had other ways of ploughing, sowing, harvesting, and selling. What passions and excitements could they possibly have? Like everyone else, they had their worries and weaknesses, rent and taxes, idleness and sleep; but all this did not amount to a great deal and did not stir their blood. For the last five years not one of the several hundred peasants of that locality had died a natural, let alone a violent, death. And when someone had gone to his eternal sleep either from old age or from some chronic illness, the people there had gone on marvelling at such an extraordinary event for months. And yet it did not surprise them at all that, for instance, Taras the blacksmith had nearly steamed himself to death in his mud hut so that he had to be revived with cold water. The only crime that was greatly prevalent was the theft of peas, carrots, and turnips from the kitchen gardens, and on one occasion two sucking pigs and a chicken had suddenly disappeared – an event which outraged the whole neighbourhood and was unanimously attributed to the fact that carts with wooden wares had passed through the village on their way to the fair. But, generally speaking, accidents of any kind were extremely rare.

Once, however, a man had been found lying in a ditch by the bridge outside a village, evidently a member of a co-operative group of workmen who had passed by on their way to the town. The boys were the first to discover him, and they ran back terrified to the village with the news that some terrible serpent or werewolf was lying in a ditch, adding that he had chased them and nearly eaten Kuzka. The braver souls among the peasants armed themselves with pitchforks and axes and went in a crowd to the ditch.

'Where are you off to?' The old men tried to stop them. 'Think yourselves stout fellows, do you? What do you want there? Leave it alone, no one's driving you.'

But the peasants went, and about a hundred yards from the spot began calling to the monster in different voices, and as there was no reply, they stopped, then moved on again. A peasant lay in the ditch, leaning his head against its side; a bundle and a stick with two pairs of bast-shoes tied on it, lay beside him. They did not venture near him or touch him.

'Hey you, there!' they shouted in turn, scratching their heads or their backs. 'What's your name? Hey, you! What do you want here?'

The stranger tried to raise his head but could not; evidently he was either ill or very tired. One peasant nearly brought himself to touch him with his pitchfork.

'Don't touch him! Don't touch him!' many of the others cried. 'How do we know what sort of a man he is? He hasn't said a word. He may be one of them – don't touch him, lads!'

'Let's go,' some said. 'Come on now: he isn't one of ours, is he? He'll only bring us trouble!'

And they all went back to the village, telling the old men that a stranger was lying there who would not speak and goodness only knows what he was up to.

'Don't have anything to do with him if he is a stranger,' the old men said, sitting on the mound of earth beside their cottages, with their elbows on their knees. 'Let him do as he likes! You shouldn't have gone at all!'

Such was the spot where Oblomov suddenly found himself in his dream. Of the three or four villages scattered there, one was Sosnovka and another Vavilovka, about a mile from each other. Sosnovka and Vavilovka were the hereditary property of the Oblomov family and were therefore known under the general name of Oblomovka. The Oblomov country seat was in Sosnovka. About three and a half miles from Sosnovka lay the little village of Verkhlyovo, which had once belonged to the Oblomov family but which had long since passed into other hands, and a few more scattered cottages which went with it. This village belonged to a rich landowner who was never to be seen on his estate, which was managed by a German steward.

Such was the whole geography of the place.

Oblomov woke up in the morning in his small bed. He was only seven. He felt light-hearted and gay. What a pretty, red-cheeked, and plump boy he was! He had such sweet, round cheeks that were the envy of many a little rogue who would blow up his own on purpose, but could never get cheeks like that. His nurse was waiting for him to wake up. She began putting on his stockings, but he did not let her; he played about, dangling his legs. His nurse caught him, and they both laughed. At last she succeeded in making him get up. She washed his face, combed his hair, and took him to his mother. Seeing his mother, who had been dead for years, Oblomov even in his sleep thrilled with joy and his ardent love for her; two warm tears slowly appeared from under his eyelashes and remained motionless. His mother covered him with passionate kisses, then looked at him anxiously to see if his eyes were clear, if anything hurt him, asked the nurse if he had slept well, if he had waked in the night, if he had tossed in his sleep, if he had a temperature. Then she took him by the hand and led him to the ikon. Kneeling down and putting her arm round him, she made him repeat the words of a prayer. The boy repeated them after her absent-mindedly, gazing at the window, through which the cool of the morning and the scent of lilac poured into the room.

'Are we going for a walk to-day, Mummy?' he suddenly asked in the middle of the prayer.

'Yes, darling,' she replied hurriedly, without taking her eyes off the ikon and hastening to finish the holy words.

The boy repeated them listlessly, but his mother put her whole soul into them. Then they went to see his father, and then they had breakfast.

At the breakfast table Oblomov saw their aunt, an old lady of eighty; she was constantly grumbling at her maid, who stood behind her chair waiting on her and whose head shook with age. Three elderly spinsters, his father's distant relations, were also there, as well as his father's slightly mad brother, and a poor landowner by the name of Chekmenev, the owner of seven serfs, who was staying with them, and several old ladies and old gentlemen. All these members of the Oblomov retinue and establishment picked up the little boy and began showering caresses and praises on him; he had hardly time to wipe away the traces of the unbidden kisses. After that they began stuffing him with rolls, biscuits, and cream. Then his mother hugged and kissed him again and sent him for a walk in the garden, the yard, and the meadow, with strict instructions to his nurse not to leave the child alone, not to let him go near the horses, the dogs, and the goat or wander too far from the house, and, above all, not to let him go to the ravine, which had a bad name as the most terrible place in the neighbourhood. Once they found a dog there which was reputed to be mad only because it ran away and disappeared behind the hills when attacked with pitchforks and axes; carcasses were thrown into the ravine, and wolves and robbers and other creatures which did not exist in those parts or anywhere else in the world were supposed to live there.

The child did not wait for his mother to finish her warnings: he was already out in the yard. He examined his father's house and ran round it with joyful surprise, as though he had never seen it before: the gates which leaned to one side; the wooden roof which had settled in the middle and was overgrown with tender green moss; the rickety front steps; the various out-buildings and additions built on to it, and the neglected garden. He was dying to climb on to the projecting gallery which went all round the house and to have a look at the stream from there; but the gallery was very old and unsafe, and only the servants were allowed to go there – nobody else used it. He didn't heed his mother's prohibition and was already running to the inviting steps when his nurse appeared and succeeded in catching him. He rushed away from her to the hay-loft, intending to climb up the steep ladder leading to it, and she had no sooner reached the hay-loft than she had to stop him climbing up the dovecote, getting into the cattle yard and – Lord forbid – the ravine.

'Dear me, what an awful child – what a fidget, to be sure!' his nurse said. 'Can't you sit still for a minute, sir? Fie, for shame!'

The nurse's days – and nights – were one continuous scurrying and dashing about: one moment in agony, another full of joy, afraid that he might fall and hurt himself, deeply moved by his unfeigned childish affection, or vaguely apprehensive about his distant future – this was all she lived for, these agitations warmed the old woman's blood and sustained her sluggish existence which might otherwise have come to an end long before.

The child, however, was not always so playful; sometimes he suddenly grew quiet and gazed intently at everything as he sat beside his nurse. His childish mind was observing closely all that was going on around him; these impressions sank deeply into his soul, and grew and matured with him.

It was a glorious morning; the air was cool; the sun was still low. Long shadows fell from the house, the trees, the dovecote, and the gallery. The garden and the yard were full of cool places, inviting sleep and day-dreaming. Only the rye-fields in the distance blazed and shimmered, and the stream sparkled and glittered in the sun so that it hurt one's eyes to look at it.

'Why, Nanny, is it so dark here and so light there, and why will it be light here soon as well?'

'Because the sun is going to meet the moon, my dear, and frowns when it can't find it, but as soon as it sees it in the distance it grows brighter.'

The little boy grew thoughtful and went on looking all about him: he saw Antip going to get water and another Antip, ten times bigger than the real one, walking beside him along the ground, and the water-barrel looked as big as a house, and the horse's shadow covered the whole of the meadow, and after taking only two steps across the meadow, it suddenly moved across the hill, and Antip had had no time to leave the yard. The child, too, took two steps – another step and he would be on the other side of the hill. He would like to have gone there to see where the horse had disappeared to. He ran to the gate, but his mother's voice could be heard from the window:

'Nurse, don't you see that the child has run out in the sun! Take him where it's cool. If his head gets hot, he'll be sick and lose his appetite. If you're not careful, he'll run to the ravine.'

'Oh, you naughty boy!' the nurse grumbled softly as she took him back to the house.

The boy watched with his keen and sensitive eyes what the grown-ups were doing and how they were spending the morning. Not a single detail, however trifling, escaped the child's inquisitive attention; the picture of his home-life was indelibly engraved on his memory; his malleable mind absorbed the living examples before him and unconsciously drew up the programme of his life in accordance with the life around him.

The morning could not be said to be wasted in the Oblomov house. The clatter of knives chopping meat and vegetables in the kitchen could be heard as far as the village. From the servants' hall came the hum of the spindle and the soft, thin voice of a woman: it was difficult to say whether she was crying or improvising a melancholy song without words. As soon as Antip returned to the yard with the barrel of water, the women and the coachmen came trudging towards it from every direction with pails, troughs, and jugs. Then an old woman carried a basinful of flour and a large number of eggs from the store-house to the kitchen; the cook suddenly threw some water out through the window and splashed Arapka, which sat all morning with its eyes fixed on the window, wagging its tail and licking its chops.

Oblomov's father was not idle, either. He sat at the window all morning, keeping a wary eye on all that was going on in the yard.

'Hey, Ignashka, what are you carrying there, you fool?' he would ask a servant walking across the yard.

'I'm taking the knives to be sharpened, sir,' the man would answer, without looking at his master.

'Very well, and mind you sharpen them properly.'

Then he would stop a peasant woman.

'Hey, my good woman, where have you been?'

'To the cellar, sir,' she would stop and reply, shielding her eyes and gazing at the window. 'Been to fetch some milk for dinner.'

'All right, go, go,' her master would reply. 'And mind you don't spill the milk. And you, Zakharka, where are you off to again, you rogue?' he shouted later. 'I'll show you how to run! It's the third time I've seen you. Back to the hall with you!'

And Zakharka went back to the hall to doze.

If the cows came back from the fields, Oblomov's father would be the first to see that they were watered; if he saw from the window that the dog was chasing a hen, he would at once take stern measures to restore order.

His wife, too, was very busy: she spent three hours explaining to Averka, the tailor, how to make a tunic for Oblomov out of her husband's jacket, drawing the pattern in chalk and watching that Averka did not steal any cloth; then she went to the maids' room to tell each girl what her daily task of lace-making was; then she called Nastasya Ivanovna, or Stepanida Agapovna, or someone else from her retinue for a walk in the garden with the practical purpose of seeing how ripe the apples were, if the one that was ripe the day before had fallen off the tree, to do some grafting or pruning, and so on. Her chief concern, however, was the kitchen and the dinner. The whole household was consulted about the dinner: the aged aunt, too, was invited to the council. Everyone suggested a dish: giblet soup, noodles, brawn, tripe, red or white sauce. Every advice was taken into consideration, thoroughly discussed, and then accepted or rejected in accordance with the final decision of the mistress of the house. Nastasya Petrovna or Stepanida Ivanovna was constantly being sent to the kitchen to remind the cook of something or other, to add one dish or cancel another, to take sugar, honey, wine for the cooking, and see whether the cook had used all that he had been given.

Food was the first and foremost concern at Oblomovka. What calves were fattened there every year for the festival days! What birds were reared there! What deep understanding, what hard work, what care were needed in looking after them! Turkeys and chickens for name-days and other solemn occasions were fattened on nuts. Geese were deprived of exercise and hung up motionless in a sack a few days before a festival so that they should get covered with fat. What stores of jams, pickles, and biscuits! What meads, what *kvases*, were brewed, what pies baked at Oblomovka!

And so up to midday everyone was busy, everyone was living a full, conspicuous, ant-like life. These industrious ants were not idle on Sundays and holidays, either: on those days the clatter of knives in the kitchen was louder than ever; the kitchen-maid journeyed a few times from the barn to the kitchen with a double quantity of flour and eggs; in the poultry yard there was a greater uproar and more bloodshed than ever. An enormous pie was baked, which was served cold for dinner on the following day; on the third and fourth day its remnants were sent to the maids' room, where it lasted till Friday, when one stale end of it without stuffing descended by special favour to Antip, who, crossing himself, proudly and fearlessly demolished this interesting fossil, enjoying the consciousness that it was his master's pie more than the pie itself, like an archaeologist who will enjoy drinking some wretched wine out of what remains of some vessel a thousand years old.

The child kept observing and watching it all with his childish mind, which did not miss anything. He saw how often a usefully and busily spent morning was followed by midday and dinner.

At midday it was hot; not a cloud in the sky. The sun stood motionless overhead scorching the grass. There was not the faintest breeze in the motionless air. Neither tree nor water stirred; an imperturbable stillness fell over the village and the fields, as though everything were dead. The human voice sounded loud and clear in the empty air. The flight and the buzzing of a beetle could be heard a hundred yards away, and from the thick grass there came the sound of snoring, as if someone were fast asleep there. In the house, too, dead silence reigned. It was the hour of after-dinner sleep. The child saw that everyone – father, mother, the old aunt, and their retinue – had retired to their rooms; and those who had no rooms of their own went to the hay-loft, the garden, or sought coolness in the hall, while some, covering their faces from the flies with a handkerchief, dropped off to sleep where the heat and the heavy dinner had overcome them. The gardener stretched himself out under a bush in the garden beside his mattock, and the coachman was asleep in the stables. Oblomov looked into the servants' quarters: there everyone was lying stretched out side by side on the floor, on the benches, and in the passage, and the children, left to their own devices, were crawling about and playing in the sand. The dogs, too, stole into their kennels, there being no one to bark at. One could walk through the house from one end to the other without meeting a soul; it would have been easy to steal everything and take it away in carts, if there were any thieves in those parts, for no one would have interfered with them. It was a sort of all-absorbing and invincible sleep, a true semblance of death. Everything was dead, except for the snoring that came in all sorts of tones and variations from every corner of the house. Occasionally someone would raise his head, look round senselessly, in surprise, and turn over, or spit without opening his eyes, and munching his lips or muttering something under his breath, fall asleep again. Another would suddenly, without any preliminary preparations, jump up from his couch, as though afraid of losing a precious moment, seize a mug of *kvas*, and blowing away the flies that floated in it, which made the hitherto motionless flies begin to move about in the hope of improving their position, have a drink, and then fall back on the bed as though shot dead.

The child went on watching and watching. He ran out into the open with his nurse again after dinner. But in spite of the strict injunctions of her mistress and her own determination, the nurse could not resist the fascination of sleep. She, too, was infected by the epidemic that raged in Oblomovka. At first she looked sedulously after the child, did not let him go far from her, scolded him for being naughty; then, feeling the symptoms of the infection, she begged him not to go out of the gate, not to tease the goat, and not to climb on the dovecote or the gallery. She herself sat down in some shady nook – on the front steps, at the entrance to the cellar, or simply on the grass, with the apparent intention of knitting a sock and looking after the child.

But soon her admonitions grew more sluggish and she began nodding. 'Oh dear,' she thought, falling asleep, 'that fidget is sure to climb on the gallery or – run off to – the ravine. ...' At this point the old woman's head dropped forward and the sock fell out of her hands; she lost sight of the child and, opening her mouth slightly, began to snore softly.

The child had been waiting impatiently for that moment, with which his independent life began. He seemed to be alone in the whole world; he tiptoed past his nurse and ran off to see where everybody was asleep; he stopped and watched intently if someone woke for a minute, spat and mumbled in his sleep, then, with a sinking heart, ran up on the gallery, raced round it on the creaking boards, climbed the dovecote, penetrated into the remotest corners of the garden, where he listened to the buzzing of a beetle and watched its flight in the air for a long time; he listened to the chirring in the grass and tried to catch the disturbers of peace; caught a dragon-fly, tore off its wings to see what it would do, or stuck a straw through it and watched it fly with that appendage; observed with delight, holding his breath, a spider sucking a fly and the poor victim struggling and buzzing in its clutches. In the end the child killed both the victim and its torturer. Then he went to a ditch, dug up some roots, peeled them, and enjoyed eating them more than the jams and apples his mother gave him. He ran out of the gate, too: he would like to go to the birch-wood, which seemed to him so near that he was sure he would get there in five minutes, not by the road, but straight across the ditch, the wattle fences, and the pits; but he was afraid, for he had been told that there were wood demons and robbers and terrible beasts there. He wanted to go to the ravine, too, for it was only about a hundred yards from the garden; he ran to the very edge of it, to peer into it as into the crater of a volcano, when suddenly all the stories and legends about the ravine rose before his mind's eye; he was thrown into a panic, and rushed more dead than alive back to his nurse trembling with fear, and woke the old woman. She awoke with a start, straightened the kerchief on her head, pushed back the wisps of grey hair under it with a finger, and, pretending not to have been asleep at all, glanced suspiciously at Oblomov and at the windows of her master's house and, with trembling fingers, began clicking with the knitting-needles of the sock that lay on her lap.

Meanwhile the heat had begun to abate a little; everything in nature was getting more animated; the sun had moved towards the woods. In the house, too, the silence was little by little broken; a door creaked somewhere; someone could be heard walking in the yard; someone else sneezed in the hay-loft. Soon a servant hurriedly brought an enormous *samovar* from the kitchen, bending under its weight. The company began to assemble for tea; one had a crumpled face and swollen eyelids; another had a red spot on the cheek and on the temple; a third was still too sleepy to speak in his natural voice. They wheezed, groaned, yawned, scratched their heads, stretched themselves, still barely awake. The dinner and the sleep had made them terribly thirsty. Their throats were parched; they drank about twelve cups of tea each, but this did not help; they moaned and groaned; they tried cranberry water, pear water, *kvas*, and some medicinal drinks to quench their thirst. All sought deliverance from it as though it were some punishment inflicted on them by God; all rushed about, panting for a drink, like a caravan of travellers in the Arabian desert looking in vain for a spring of water.

The little boy was there beside his mother, watching the strange faces around him and listening to their languid and sleepy conversation. He enjoyed looking at them, and thought every stupid remark they made interesting. After tea they all found something to do: one went down to the river and walked slowly along the bank, kicking the pebbles into the water; another sat by the window watching everything that went on outside; if a cat ran across the yard or a magpie flew by, he followed it with his eyes and the tip of his nose, turning his head to right and left. So dogs sometimes like to sit for a whole day on the window-sill, basking in the sun and carefully examining every passer-by. Oblomov's mother would put his head on her lap and slowly comb his hair, admiring its softness and making Nastasya Ivanovna and Stepanida Tikhonovna admire it too. She talked to them of his future, conjuring up a vision of him as the hero of some brilliant exploit, while they predicted great riches for him.

But presently it was getting dark, again a fire crackled in the kitchen and again there was a loud clatter of knives; supper was being prepared. The servants had gathered at the gates; sounds of the balalaika and of laughter were heard there. They were playing catch.

The sun was setting behind the woods; its last few warm rays cut straight across the woods like shafts of fire, brightly gilding the tops of the pines. Then the rays were extinguished one by one, the last one lingering for a long time and piercing the thicket of branches like a thin quill; but it, too, was extinguished. Objects lost their shapes: at first everything was merged into a grey, and then into a black, mass. The birds gradually stopped singing; soon they fell silent altogether, except one, which, as though in defiance of the rest, went on chirping monotonously amid the general silence and at intervals which were getting longer and longer till, finally, it gave one last low whistle, slightly rustled the leaves round it, and fell asleep. All was silent. Only the grasshoppers chirped louder than ever. White mists rose from the ground and spread over the meadows and the river. The river, too, grew quieter; a few more moments and something splashed in it for the last time, and it grew motionless. There was a smell of damp in the air. It grew darker and darker. The trees began to look like groups of monsters; the woods were full of nameless terrors; someone suddenly moved about there with a creaking noise, as though one of the monsters shifted from one place to another, a dead twig cracking under its foot. The first star, like a living eye, gleamed brightly in the sky, and lights appeared in the windows of the house.

It was the time of solemn and universal stillness in nature, a time when the creative mind is most active, when poetic thoughts are fanned into flames, when passion burns more brightly or anguish is felt more acutely in the heart, when the seed of a criminal design ripens more imperturbably and more strongly in the cruel heart, and when everybody in Oblomovka is once more peacefully and soundly asleep.

'Let's go for a walk, Mummy,' said Oblomov.

'Good heavens, child,' she replied, 'go for a walk at this hour! It's damp, you'll get your feet wet, and it's so frightening: the wood-demon is walking about in the woods now, carrying off little children.'

'Where to? What is he like? Where does he live?' the little boy asked.

And his mother gave full rein to her unbridled fancy. The boy listened to her, opening and closing his eyes, till at last he was overcome by sleep. The nurse came and, taking him from his mother's lap, carried him off to bed asleep, his head hanging over her shoulder.

'Well, thank goodness, another day gone,' the Oblomovka inhabitants said, getting into bed, groaning, and crossing themselves. 'We've lived through it safely, God grant it may be the same to-morrow! Praise be unto thee, O Lord!'

Then Oblomov dreamt of another occasion: one endless winter

evening he was timidly pressing closely to his nurse, who was whispering a fairy-story to him about some wonderful country where there was no night and no cold, where all sorts of miracles happened, where the rivers flowed with milk and honey, where no one did a stroke of work all the year round, and fine fellows, like Oblomov, and maidens more beautiful than words can tell did nothing but enjoy themselves all day long. A fairy godmother lived there, who sometimes took the shape of a pike and who chose for her favourite some quiet and harmless man – in other words, some loafer, ill-treated by everyone, and for no reason in the world, bestowed all sorts of treasures on him, while he did nothing but eat and drink and dressed in costly clothes, and then married some indescribable beauty, Militrissa Kirbit-yevna. The little boy listened breathlessly to the story, pricking up his ears, and his eyes glued to his nurse's face. The nurse or the traditional tale so artfully avoided every reference to reality that the child's imagination and intellect, having absorbed the fiction, remained enslaved by it all his life. The nurse told him good-humouredly the story of Yemelya-the-Fool, that wickedly insidious satire on our forefathers and, perhaps, on ourselves too. Though when he grew up Oblomov discovered that there were no rivers flowing with milk and honey, nor fairy godmothers, and though he smiled at his nurse's tales, his smile was not sincere, and it was accompanied by a secret sigh: the fairy-tale had become mixed up with real life in his mind, and sometimes he was sorry that fairy-tale was not life and life was not fairy-tale. He could not help dreaming of Militrissa Kirbit-yevna; he was always drawn to the land where people do nothing but have a good time and where there are no worries or sorrows; he preserved for the rest of his life a predisposition for doing no work, walking about in clothes that had been provided for him, and eating at the fairy godmother's expense.

Oblomov's father and grandfather, too, had heard as children the same fairy stories, handed down for centuries and generations in their stereotyped form by their nurses.

In the meantime the nurse was drawing another picture for the little boy's imagination. She was telling him about the heroic exploits of our Achilles and Ulysses, about the great bravery of Ilya Muromets, Dobryna Nikitich, Alyosha Popovich, Polkan the Giant, Kolechishche the Traveller, about how they had journeyed all over Russia, defeating numberless hosts of infidels, how they vied with each other in drinking big goblets of wine at one gulp without uttering a sound; she then told him of wicked robbers, sleeping princesses, towns and people turned to stone; finally, she passed on to our demonology, dead men, monsters, and werewolves.

With Homer's simplicity and good humour and his eye for vivid detail and concrete imagery, she filled the boy's memory and imagination with the Iliad of Russian life, created by our Homers in the far-off days when man was not yet able to stand up to the dangers and mysteries of life and nature, when he trembled at the thought of werewolves and wood-demons and sought Alyosha Popovich's help against the adversities threatening him on all sides, and when the air, water, forests, and plains were full of marvels. Man's life in those days was insecure and terrible; it was dangerous for him to go beyond his own threshold; a wild beast might fall upon him any moment, or a robber might kill him, or a wicked Tartar rob him of all his possessions, or he might disappear without a trace. Or else signs from heaven might appear, pillars or balls of fire; or a light might glimmer above a new grave; or some creature might walk about in the forest as though swinging a lantern, laughing terribly and flashing its eyes in the dark. And so many mysterious things happened to people, too: a man might live for years happily without mishap, and all of a sudden he would begin to talk strangely or scream in a wild voice, or walk in his sleep; another would for no reason at all begin to writhe on the ground in convulsions. And before it happened, a hen had crowed like a cock or a raven had croaked over the roof. Man, weak creature that he is, felt bewildered, and tried to find in his imagination the key to his own being and to the mysteries that encompassed him. And perhaps it was the everlasting quiet of a sleepy and stagnant life and the absence of movement and of any real terrors, adventures, and dangers that made man create amidst the real life another fantastic one where he might find amusement and true scope for his idle imagination or an explanation of ordinary events and the causes of the events outside the events themselves. Our poor ancestors groped their way through life, they neither controlled their will nor let it be inspired, and then marvelled naïvely or were horrified at the discomforts and evils of life, and sought for an explanation of them in the mute and obscure hieroglyphics of nature. A death, they thought, was caused by the fact that, shortly before, a corpse had been carried out of the house head and not feet foremost, and a fire because a dog had howled for three nights under the window; and they took great care that a corpse should be carried out feet foremost, but went on eating the same food and sleeping on the bare grass as before; a barking dog was beaten or driven away, but still they shook the sparks from a burning splinter down the cracks of the rotten floor. And to this day the Russian people, amid the stark and commonplace realities of life, prefer to believe in seductive legends of the old days, and it may be a long, long time before they give up this belief.

Listening to his nurse's stories of our Golden Fleece – the Fire Bird – of the obstacles and secret passages in the enchanted castle, the little boy plucked up courage, imagining himself the hero of some great exploit – and a shiver ran down his back, or he grieved over the misfortunes of the brave hero of the tale. One story followed another. The nurse told her stories picturesquely, with fervour and enthusiasm, sometimes with inspiration, because she half-believed them herself. Her eyes sparkled, her head shook with excitement, her voice rose to unaccustomed notes. Overcome by a mysterious terror, the boy clung to her with tears in his eyes. Whether she spoke of dead men rising from their graves at midnight, or of the victims of some monster, pining away in captivity, or of the bear with the wooden leg walking through large and small villages in search of the leg that had been cut off – the boy's hair stood on end with horror; his childish imagination was paralysed and then worked feverishly; he was going through an agonizing, sweet, and painful experience; his nerves were taut like chords. When his nurse repeated the bear's words grimly: 'Creak, creak, limewood leg; I've walked through large villages, I've walked though a small village, all the women are fast asleep, but one woman does not sleep, she is sitting on my skin, she is cooking my flesh, she is spinning my own fur,' and so on, when the bear entered the cottage and was about to seize the woman who had robbed him of his leg, the little boy could stand it no longer: he flung himself shrieking into his nurse's arms, trembling all over; he cried with fright and laughed with joy because he was not in the wild beast's claws, but on the stove beside his nurse. The little boy's imagination was peopled with strange phantoms; fear and anguish struck root in his soul for years, perhaps for ever. He looked sadly about him, and seeing only evil and misfortune everywhere in life, dreamt constantly of that magic country where there were no evils, troubles, or sorrows, where Militrissa Kirbityevna lived, where such excellent food and such fine clothes could be had for nothing. ...

Fairy-tales held sway not only over the children in Oblomovka, but also over the grown-ups to the end of their lives. Everyone in the house and the village, from the master and mistress down to the burly blacksmith Taras, was afraid of something on a dark night: every tree was transformed into a giant and every bush into a den of brigands. The rattling of a shutter and the howling of the wind in the chimney made men, women and children turn pale. At Epiphany no one went out of the gate by himself at ten o'clock at night; on Easter night no one ventured into the stables, afraid of meeting the house-demon there. They believed in everything at Oblomovka: in ghosts and were-wolves. If they were told that a stack of hay walked about the field, they believed it implicitly; if someone spread a rumour that a certain ram was not really a ram but something else, or that a certain Marfa or Stepanida was a witch, they were afraid of both the ram and Marfa; it never occurred to them to ask why the ram was not a ram or why Marfa had become a witch, and, indeed, they would attack anyone who dared to doubt it – so strong was their belief in the miraculous at Oblomovka!

Oblomov realized afterwards that the world was a very simple affair, that dead men did not rise from their graves, that as soon as there were any giants about, they were put in a sideshow, and robbers were clapped into jail; but if his belief in phantoms disappeared, there remained a sort of sediment of fear and a vague feeling of anguish. Oblomov discovered that no misfortunes were caused by monsters, and he scarcely knew what misfortunes there were, and yet he expected something dreadful to happen any moment and he could not help being afraid. Even now, if he were left in a dark room or if he saw a corpse, he would still be frightened because of the sinister feeling of anguish sown in his mind as a child; laughing at his fears in the morning, he could not help turning pale again in the evening.

Then Oblomov saw himself as a boy of thirteen or fourteen. He was going to school at Verkhlyovo, about three miles from Oblomovka. The steward of the estate, a German by the name of Stolz, had started a small boarding-school for the children of the local gentry. He had a son, Andrey, who was almost of the same age as Oblomov, and there was another boy, who hardly ever worked at all. He was scrofulous and spent all his childhood with his eyes or ears in bandages, and was always weeping surreptitiously because he lived with wicked strangers and not with his grandmother and had no one to fondle him and make him his favourite pasty. So far there were no other children at the school.

There was nothing for it: Oblomov's father and mother decided to send their darling child to school. The boy protested violently at first, shrieking, crying, and being as unreasonable about it as he possibly could, but in the end he was sent off to Verkhlyovo. The German was a strict and business-like man like most Germans. Oblomov might have learnt something from him had Oblomovka been 300 miles from Verkhlyovo. But in the circumstances, how could he have learnt anything? The fascination of the Oblomovka atmosphere, way of life, and habits extended to Verkhlyovo, which had also once belonged to the Oblomovs; except for Stolz's house, everything there was imbued with the same primitive laziness, simplicity of customs, peace, and inertia. The child's heart and mind had been filled with the scenes, pictures, and habits of that life long before he set eyes on his first book. And who can tell when the development of a child's intellect begins? How can one trace the birth of the first ideas and impressions in a child's mind? Perhaps when a child begins to talk, or even before it can talk or walk, but only gazes at everything with that dumb, intent look that seems blank to grown-ups, it already catches and perceives the meaning and the connexions of the events of his life, but is not able to tell it to himself or to others. Perhaps Oblomov had observed and understood long ago what was being said and done in his presence: that his father, dressed in velveteen trousers and a brown quilted cotton coat, did nothing but walk up and down the room all day with his hands behind his back, take snuff, and blow his nose, while his mother passed on from coffee to tea, from tea to dinner; that it never entered his father's head to check how many stacks of hay or corn had been mown or reaped, and call to account those who were guilty of neglecting their duties, but if his handkerchief was not handed to him soon enough, he would make a scene and turn the whole house upside down. Perhaps his childish mind had decided long ago that the only way to live was how the grown-ups round him lived. What other decision could he possibly have reached? And how did the grown-ups live at Oblomovka? Did they ever ask themselves why life had been given them? Goodness only knows. And how did they answer it? Most probably they did not answer it at all: everything seemed so clear and simple to them. They had never heard of the so-called hard life, of people who were constantly worried, who rushed about from place to place, or who devoted their lives to everlasting, never-ending work. They did not really believe in mental worries, either; they did not think that life existed so that man should constantly strive for some barely apprehended aims; they were terribly afraid of strong passions, and just as with other people bodies might be consumed by the volcanic action of inner, spiritual fire, so their souls wallowed peacefully and undisturbed in their soft bodies. Life did not mark them, as it did other people, with premature wrinkles, devastating moral blows and diseases. The good people conceived life merely as an ideal of peace and inactivity, disturbed from time to time by all sorts of unpleasant accidents, such as illness, loss of money, quarrels, and, incidentally, work. They suffered work as a punishment imposed upon our forefathers, but they could not love it and avoided it wherever and whenever they could, believing it both right and necessary to do so. They never troubled themselves about any vague moral and intellectual problems, and that was why they were always so well and happy and lived so long. Men of forty looked like boys; old men did not struggle with a hard, painful death, but, having lived to an unbelievably old age, died as if by stealth, quietly growing cold and imperceptibly breathing their last. This is why it is said that in the old days people were stronger. Yes, indeed they were: in those days they were in no hurry to explain to a boy the meaning of life and prepare him for it as though it were some complicated and serious business; they did not worry him with books which arouse all sorts of questions, which corrode your heart and mind and shorten life. Their way of life was ready-made and was taught to them by their parents, who in turn received it ready-made from their grandparents, and their grandparents from their great-grandparents, being enjoined to keep it whole and undefiled like Vesta's fire. Whatever was done in the time of Oblomov's father, had been done in the times of his grandfather and great-grandfather and, perhaps, is still being done at Oblomovka.

What, then, had they to worry or get excited about, or to learn? What aims had they to pursue? They wanted nothing: life, like a quiet river, flowed past them, and all that remained for them was to sit on the bank of that river and watch the inevitable events which presented themselves uncalled for to every one of them in turn. And so, too, like living pictures, there unrolled themselves in turn before the imagination of Oblomov in his sleep the three main events of life, as they happened in his family and among his relations and friends: births, marriages, and funerals. Then there followed a motley procession of their gay and mournful sub-divisions: christenings, name-days, family celebrations, fast and feast days, noisy dinner-parties, assemblies of relatives, greetings, congratulations, conventional tears and smiles. Everything was done with the utmost precision, gravity, and solemnity. He even saw the familiar faces and their expression on these different occasions, their preoccupied looks and the fuss they made. Present them with any ticklish problem of match-making, any solemn wedding or name-day you like, and they would arrange it according to all the accepted rules and without the least omission. No one in Oblomovka made the slightest mistake about the right place for a guest at the table, what dishes were to be served, who were to drive together on a ceremonial occasion, what observances were to be kept. Did they not know how to rear a child? Why, you had only to look at the rosy and well-fed darlings that their mothers carried or led by the hand! It was their ambition that their children should be plump, white-skinned, and healthy. They would do without spring altogether rather than fail to bake a cake in the shape of a lark at its beginning. They did not belong to those who did not know how important that was and did not do it. All their life and learning, all their joys and sorrows were in these things, and that was the main reason why they banished all other griefs and worries and knew no other joys. Their life was full of these fundamental and inevitable events which provided endless food for their hearts and minds. They waited with beating hearts for some ceremony, rite, or feast, and then, having christened, married, or buried a man, they forgot him completely and sank into their usual apathy, from which some similar event – a name-day, a wedding, etc. – roused them once again. As soon as a baby was born, the first concern of his parents was to carry out as precisely as possible and without any omissions all the customary rites that decorum demanded, that is to say, to have a feast after the christening; then the careful rearing of the baby began. Its mother set herself and the nurse the task of rearing a healthy child, guarding it from colds, the evil eye, and other hostile influences. They took great care that the child should always be happy and eat a lot. As soon as the boy was firmly on his feet – that is to say, when he no longer needed a nurse – the mother was already secretly cherishing the desire to find him a mate – also as rosy and as healthy as possible. Again the time came for rites, feasts, and, at last, weddings: that was all they lived for. Then came the repetitions: the birth of children, rites, and feasts, until a funeral brought about a change of scenery, but not for long: one set of people made way for another, the children grew up into young men and in due course married and had children of their own – and so life, according to this programme, went on in an uninterrupted and monotonous sequence of events, breaking off imperceptibly at the very edge of the grave.

Sometimes, it is true, other cares were thrust upon them, but the inhabitants of Oblomovka met them for the most part with stoic impassivity, and after circling over their heads, the troubles flew past them like birds which, coming to a smooth wall and finding no shelter there, flutter their wings in vain near the hard stones and fly away. Thus, for instance, a part of the gallery round the house suddenly collapsed one day, burying under its ruins a hen with its chicks; Aksinya, Antip's wife, who had sat down under the gallery with her spinning, would have been badly injured had she not gone to fetch some more flax. There was a great commotion in the house: everyone, big and small, rushed to the spot and expressed dismay at the thought that instead of the hen and chicks the mistress herself might have been walking under the gallery with Oblomov. They all gasped with horror and began reproaching one another that it had never occurred to them before to remind each other to order someone to repair the gallery. They were all astonished that it should have collapsed, although only the day before they were surprised at its having stood so long! They began discussing how to repair the damage; they expressed regret about the hen and her chicks and then slowly dispersed to where they had come from, having first been strictly forbidden to take Oblomov anywhere near the gallery. Three weeks later, orders were given to Andrushka, Petrushka, and Vaska to take the fallen planks and banisters out of the way and put them near the barn, where they remained till the spring. Every time Oblomov's father caught sight of them out of the window, he would think of having the gallery repaired: he would call for the carpenter and consult him as to whether it would be better to build a new gallery or break down what remained of the old, then he would let him go home, saying, 'You can go now and I'll think it over.' That went on till Vaska or Motka told his master that, having climbed on to what remained of the gallery that morning, he noticed that the corners had broken away from the walls and might collapse any moment. Then the carpenter was called for a final consultation, as a result of which it was decided to prop up the part of the gallery that was still standing with the fragments of the old, which was actually done at the end of the month.

'Why,' said Oblomov's father to his wife, 'the gallery is as good as new. Look how beautifully Fyodor has fixed the planks, just like the pillars of the Marshal's house! It's perfectly all right now: it will last for years!'

Someone reminded him that it would be a good opportunity for repairing the gate and the front steps, for the holes between them were so big that pigs, let alone cats, got through them into the cellar.

'Yes, yes, to be sure,' Oblomov's father replied, looking worried, and went at once to inspect the front steps.

'Yes, indeed, look how rickety they are,' he said, rocking the steps with his foot like a cradle.

'But it rocked like that when it was made,' someone observed.

'Well, what about it?' Oblomov's father replied. 'They haven't fallen down, though they have stood there for sixteen years without any repairs. Luka made a good job of it. He was a real carpenter, Luka was! He's dead, may his soul rest in peace. They've got spoilt now – no carpenter could do such a job now!'

He turned his eyes away and, they say, the steps still rock but have not fallen to pieces yet. Luka, it would seem, was indeed an excellent carpenter!

One must do the Oblomovs justice, though: sometimes when things went wrong, they would take a great deal of trouble and even flew into a temper and grew angry. How could one thing or another have been neglected for so long? Something must be done about it at once! And they went on talking interminably about repairing the little bridge across the ditch or fencing off part of the garden to prevent the cattle from spoiling the trees because the wattle fence had collapsed in one place.

One day, while taking a walk in the garden, Oblomov's father had even gone so far as to lift, groaning and moaning, the fence off the ground with his own hands and told the gardener to prop it up at once with two poles; thanks to his promptness, the fence remained standing like that all through the summer, and it was only in winter that the snow brought it down again. At last even the bridge had three new planks laid across it after Antip had fallen through it with his horse and water-barrel. He had not had time to recover from his injuries before the bridge was as good as new. Nor did the cows and goats profit much from the fresh fall of the wattle fence in the garden: they had only had time to eat the currant bushes and to start stripping the bark off the tenth lime-tree, and never reached the apple-

127

trees, when an order was given to put the fence right and even to dig a ditch round it. The two cows and a goat which were caught in the act had received a good beating!

Oblomov also dreamt of the big, dark drawing-room in his parents' house, with its ancient ashwood arm-chairs, which were always covered, a huge, clumsy and hard sofa, upholstered in faded and stained blue barracan and one large leather arm-chair. A long winter evening; his mother sat on the sofa with her feet tucked under her, lazily knitting a child's stocking, yawning, and occasionally scratching her head with a knitting-needle. Nastasya Ivanovna and Pelageya Ignatyevna sat beside her and, bending low over their work, were diligently sewing something for Oblomov for the holidays or for his father or for themselves. His father paced the room with his hands behind his back, looking very pleased with himself, or sat down in the arm-chair, and after a time once more walked up and down the room, listening attentively to the sound of his own footsteps. Then he took a pinch of snuff, blew his nose and took another pinch. One tallow candle burned dimly in the room, and even this was permitted only on autumn and winter evenings. In the summer months everyone tried to get up and go to bed by day-light. This was done partly out of habit and partly out of eco-nomy. Oblomov's parents were extremely sparing with any ar-ticle which was not produced at home but had to be bought. They gladly killed an excellent turkey or a dozen chickens to entertain a guest, but they never put an extra raisin in a dish, and turned pale when their guest ventured to pour himself out another glass of wine. Such depravity, however, was a rare oc-currence at Oblomovka: that sort of thing would be done only by some desperate character, a social outcast, who would never be invited to the house again. No, they had quite a different code of behaviour there: a visitor would never dream of touch-ing anything before he had been asked at least three times. He knew very well that if he was asked only once to savour some dish or drink some wine, he was really expected to refuse it. It was not for every visitor, either, that two candles were lit: candles were bought in town for money and, like all purchased articles, were kept under lock and key by the mistress herself. Candle-ends were carefully counted and safely put away. Gener-ally speaking, they did not like spending money at Oblomovka, and however necessary a purchase might be, money for it was issued with the greatest regret and that, too, only if the sum was insignificant. Any considerable expense was accompanied by moans, shrieks, and abuse. At Oblomovka they preferred to put up with all sorts of inconveniences, and even stopped regarding them as such, rather than spend money. That was why the sofa in the drawing-room had for years been covered in stains ; that was why the leather arm-chair of Oblomov's father was leather only in name, being all rope, a piece of leather remaining only on the back, the rest having all peeled off five years before; and that was perhaps why the gate was lopsided and the front steps rickety. To pay 200, 300, or 500 roubles all at once for something, however necessary it might be, seemed almost suicidal to them. Hearing that a young local landowner had been to Moscow and bought a dozen shirts for 300 roubles, a pair of boots for twenty-five roubles, and a waistcoat for his wedding for forty roubles, Oblomov's father crossed himself and said, with a look of horror on his face, that 'such a scamp must be locked up'. They were, generally speaking, impervious to economic truths about the desirability of a quick turnover of capital, increased production, and exchange of goods. In the simplicity of their souls they understood and put into practice only one way of using capital – keeping it under lock and key – in a chest.

The other inhabitants of the house and the usual visitors sat in the arm-chairs in the drawing-room in different positions, breathing hard. As a rule, deep silence reigned among them: they saw each other every day, and had long ago explored and exhausted all their intellectual treasures, and there was little news from the outside world. All was quiet; only the sound of the heavy, home-made boots of Oblomov's father, the muffled ticking of a clock in its case on the wall, and the snapping of a thread by the teeth or the hands of Pelageya Ignatyevna or Nastasya Ivanovna broke the dead silence from time to time. Half an hour sometimes passed like that, unless of course someone yawned aloud and muttered, as he made the sign of the cross over his mouth, 'Lord, have mercy upon us!' His neighbour yawned after him, then the next person, as though at a word of command, opened his mouth slowly, and so the infectious play of the air and lungs spread among them all, moving some of them to tears.

Oblomov's father would go up to the window, look out, and say with mild surprise:

'Good Lord, it's only five o'clock, and how dark it is outside!'

'Yes,' someone would reply, 'it is always dark at this time of the year: the evenings are drawing in.'

And in the spring they would be surprised and happy that the days were drawing out. But if asked what they wanted the long days for, they did not know what to say.

And again they were silent. Then someone snuffed the candle and suddenly extinguished it, and they all gave a start.

'An unexpected guest!' someone was sure to say. Sometimes this would serve as topic for conversation.

'Who would that be?' the mistress would ask. 'Not Nastasya Faddeyevna? I wish it was! But no, she won't come before the holiday. That would have been nice! How we should embrace each other and have a good cry! And we should have gone to morning and afternoon Mass together. ... But I'm afraid I couldn't keep up with her! I may be the younger one, but I can't stand as long as she can!'

'When was it she left here?' Oblomov's father asked. 'After St Elijah's Day, I believe.'

'You always get the dates mixed up,' his wife corrected him. 'She left before Whitsun.'

'I think she was here on the eve of St Peter's Fast,' retorted Oblomov's father.

'You're always like that,' his wife said reprovingly. 'You will argue and make yourself ridiculous.'

'Of course she was here. Don't you remember we had mushroom pies because she liked them?'

'That's Maria Onisimovna: she likes mushroom pies – I do remember that! And Maria Onisimovna did not stop till St Elijah's Day, but only till St Prokhov's and Nikanor's.'

They reckoned the time by holy-days, by the seasons of the years, by different family and domestic occurrences, and never referred to dates or months. That was perhaps partly because, except for Oblomov's father, they all got mixed up with the dates and the months. Defeated, Oblomov's father made no answer, and again the whole company sank into drowsiness. Oblomov, snuggled up behind his mother's back, was also drowsing and occasionally dropped off to sleep.

'Aye,' some visitor would then say with a deep sigh, 'Maria Onisimovna's husband, the late Vassily Fomich, seemed a healthy chap, if ever there was one, and yet he died! Before he was fifty, too! He should have lived to be a hundred!'

'We shall all die at the appointed time – it's God's will,' Pelageya Ignatyevna replied with a sigh. 'Some people die, but the Khlopovs have one christening after another – I am told Anna Andreyevna has just had another baby – her sixth!'

'It isn't only Anna Andreyevna,' said the lady of the house. 'Wait till her brother gets married – there'll be one child after another – there's going to be plenty of trouble in that family! The young boys are growing up and will soon be old enough to marry; then the daughters will have to get married, and where is one to find husbands for them? To-day everyone is asking for a dowry, and in cash, too.'

'What are you saying?' asked Oblomov's father, going up to them.

'Well, we're saying that – –'

And they told him what they were talking about.

'Yes,' Oblomov's father said sententiously, 'that's life for you! One dies, another one is born, a third one marries, and we just go on getting older. There are no two days that are alike, let alone two years. Why should it be so? Wouldn't it have been nice if one day were just like the day before, and yesterday were just like to-morrow? It's sad, when you come to think of it.'

'The old are ageing and the young are growing up,' someone muttered sleepily in a corner of the room.

'One has to pray more and try not to think of anything,' the lady of the house said sternly.

'True, true,' Oblomov's father, who had meant to indulge in a bit of philosophy, remarked apprehensively and began pacing the room again.

There was another long silence; only the faint sound made by the wool as it was pulled through the material by the needles could be heard. Sometimes the lady of the house broke the silence.

'Yes,' she said, 'it is dark outside. At Christmas time, when our people come to stay, it will be merrier and we shan't notice the evenings pass. If Malanya Petrovna comes, there will be no end of fun! The things she does! Telling fortunes by melting down tin or wax, or running out of the gate; my maids don't know where they are when she's here. She'd organize all sorts of games – she is a rare one!'

'Yes,' someone observed, 'a society lady! Two years ago she took it into her head to go tobogganing – that was when Luka Savich injured his forehead.'

They all suddenly came to life and burst out laughing as they looked at Luka Savich.

'How did you manage to do that, Luka Savich?' said Oblomov's father, dying with laughter. 'Come on, tell us!'

And they all went on laughing, and Oblomov woke up, and he, too, laughed.

'Well, what is there to tell?' Luka Savich said, looking put out. 'Alexey Naumich has invented it all: there was nothing of the kind at all.'

'Oh!' they shouted in chorus. 'What do you mean – nothing happened at all? We're not dead, are we? And what about that scar on your forehead? You can still see it.'

And they shook with laughter.

'What are you laughing at?' Luka Savich tried to put in a word between the outbursts of laughter. 'I – I'd have been all right if that rascal Vaska had not given me that old toboggan – it came to pieces under me – I – –'

His voice was drowned in the general laughter. In vain did he try to finish the story of his fall: the laughter spread to the hall and the maids' room, till the whole house was full of it; they all recalled the amusing incident, they all laughed and laughed in unison, *ineffably*, like the Olympian gods. When the laughter began to die down, someone would start it anew and – off they went again.

At last they managed somehow to compose themselves.

'Will you go tobogganing this Christmas?' Luka Savich asked Oblomov's father after a pause.

Another general outburst of laughter which lasted for about ten minutes.

'Shall I ask Antip to get the hill ready before the holidays?' Oblomov's father said suddenly. 'Luka Savich is dying to have another go – he can't bear to wait – –'

The laughter of the whole company interrupted him.

'But is that toboggan still in working order?' one of them asked, choking with laughter.

There was more laughter.

They all went on laughing for a long time, then gradually began quieting down: one was wiping his tears, another blowing his nose, a third coughing violently and clearing his throat, saying with difficulty: 'Oh dear, oh dear, this will be the death of me! Dear me, the way he rolled over on his back with the skirts of his coat flying – –'

This was followed by another outburst of laughter, the last and the longest of all, and then all was quiet. One man sighed, another yawned aloud, muttering something under his breath, and everyone fell silent.

As before, the only sounds that could be heard were the ticking of the clock, Oblomov's father's footfalls, and the sharp snapping of a thread broken off by one of the ladies. Suddenly

Oblomov's father stopped in the middle of the room, looking dismayed and touching the tip of his nose.

'Good heavens,' he said, 'what can this mean? Someone's going to die: the tip of my nose keeps itching.'

'Goodness,' his wife cried, throwing up her hands, 'no one's going to die if it's the tip of the nose that's itching. Someone's going to die when the bridge of the nose is itching. Really, my dear, you never can remember anything! You'll say something like this when strangers or visitors are in the house, and you will disgrace yourself!'

'But what does it mean when the tip of your nose is itching?' Oblomov's father asked, looking embarrassed.

'Looking into a wine-glass! How could you say a thing like that! Someone's going to die, indeed!'

'I'm always mixing things up!' said Oblomov's father. 'How is one to remember – the nose itching at the side, or at the tip, or the eyebrows – –'

'At the side means news,' Pelageya Ivanovna chimed in. 'If the eyebrows are itching, it means tears; the forehead, bowing, if it's on the right – to a man, and if it's on the left side – to a woman; if the ears are itching, it means that it's going to rain; lips – kissing; moustache – eating sweets; elbow – sleeping in a new place; soles of the feet – a journey – –'

'Well done, Pelageya Ivanovna!' said Oblomov's father. 'And I suppose when butter is going to be cheap, your neck will be itching – –'

The ladies began to laugh and whisper to one another; some of the men smiled; it seemed as though they would burst out laughing again, but at that moment there came a sound like a dog growling and a cat hissing when they are about to throw themselves upon each other. That was the clock striking.

'Good Lord, it's nine o'clock already!' Oblomov's father cried with joyful surprise. 'Dear me, I never noticed how the time was passing. Hey, there! Vaska! Vanka! Motka!'

Three sleepy faces appeared at the door.

'Why don't you lay the table?' Oblomov's father asked with surprise and vexation. 'You never think of your masters! Well, what are you standing there for? Come on, vodka!'

'That's why the tip of your nose was itching,' Pelageya Ivanovna said quickly. 'When you drink vodka, you'll be looking into your glass.'

After supper, having kissed and made the sign of the cross over each other, they all went to bed, and sleep descended over their untroubled heads. In his dream Oblomov saw not one or two such evenings, but weeks, months, and years of days and evenings spent in this way. Nothing interfered with the monotony of their life, and the inhabitants of Oblomovka were not tired of it because they could not imagine any other kind of existence; and if they could, they would have recoiled from it in horror. They did not want any other life, and they would have hated it. They would have been sorry if circumstances had brought any change in their mode of living, whatever its nature. They would have been miserable if to-morrow were not like yesterday and if the day after to-morrow were not like to-morrow. What did they want with variety, change, or unforeseen contingencies, which other people were so keen on? Let others make the best of them if they could; at Oblomovka they did not want to have anything to do with it. Let others live as they liked. For unforeseen contingencies, though they might turn out well in the end, were disturbing: they involved constant worry and trouble, running about, restlessness, buying and selling or writing – in a word, doing something in a hurry, and that was no joking matter: they went on for years snuffling and yawning, or laughing good-humouredly at country jokes or, gathering in a circle, telling each other their dreams. If a dream happened to be frightening, they all looked depressed and were afraid in good earnest; if it were prophetic, they were all unfeignedly glad or sad, according to whether the dream was comforting or ominous. If the dream required the observance of some rite, they took the necessary steps at once. Or they played cards – ordinary games on weekdays, and Boston with their visitors on holy-days – or they played patience, told fortunes for a king of hearts or a queen of clubs, foretelling a marriage. Sometimes Natalya Faddeyevna came to stay for a week or a fortnight. To begin with, the two elderly ladies would tell each other all the latest news in the neighbourhood, what everyone did or how everyone lived; they discussed not only all the details of their family life and what was going on behind the scenes, but also everyone's most secret thoughts and intentions, prying into their very souls, criticizing and condemning the unworthy, especially the unfaithful husbands, and then they would go over all the important events: name-days, christenings, births, who invited or did not invite whom and how those who had been invited were entertained. Tired of this, they began showing each other their new clothes, dresses, coats, even skirts and stockings. The lady of the house boasted of her linen, yarn and lace of home manufacture. But that topic, too, would be exhausted. Then they would content themselves with coffee, tea, jam. Only after that would they fall silent. They sat for some time looking at each other and from time to time sighing deeply. Occasionally one of them would burst out crying.

'What's the matter, my dear?' the other one asked anxiously.

'Oh, I feel so sad, my dear,' the visitor replied with a heavy sigh. 'We've angered the good Lord, sinners that we are. No good will come of it.'

'Oh, don't frighten me, dear, don't scare me,' the lady of the house interrupted.

'Oh, yes, yes,' Natalya Faddeyevna went on, 'the day of judgement is coming: nation will rise against nation and kingdom against kingdom – the end of the world is near!' she exclaimed at last, and the two ladies burst out crying bitterly.

Natalya Faddeyevna had no grounds at all for her final conclusion, no one having risen against anyone and there not having been even a comet that year, but old ladies sometimes have dark forebodings.

Only very seldom was this way of passing the time interrupted by some unexpected event, such as, for instance, the whole household being overcome by the fumes from the stoves. Other sicknesses were practically unknown in the house and the village, except when a man would accidentally stumble in the dark against the sharp end of a stake, or fall off the hay-loft, or be hit on the head by a plank dropping from the roof. But this happened only seldom, and against such accidents there was a score of well-tried domestic remedies: the bruise would be rubbed with a fresh-water sponge or with daphne, the injured man was given holy water to drink or had some spell whispered over him – and he would be well again. But poisoning by charcoal fumes was a fairly frequent occurrence. If that happened, they all took to their beds, moaning and groaning were heard all over the house, some tied pickled cucumbers round their heads, some stuffed cranberries into their ears and sniffed horse-radish, some went out into the frost with nothing but their shirts on, and some simply lay unconscious on the floor. This happened periodically once or twice a month, because they did not like to waste the heat in the chimney and shut the flues while flames like those in *Robert the Devil* still flickered in the stoves. It was impossible to touch a single stove without blistering one's hand.

Only once was the monotony of their existence broken by a really unexpected event. Having rested after a heavy dinner, they had all gathered round the tea-table, when an Oblomov peasant, who had just returned from town, came suddenly into the room and after a great deal of trouble pulled out from the inside of his coat a crumpled letter addressed to Oblomov's father. They all looked dumbfounded; Mrs Oblomov even turned slightly pale; they all craned their necks towards the letter and fixed their eyes upon it.

'How extraordinary! Who could it be from?' Mrs Oblomov said at last, having recovered from her surprise.

Mr Oblomov took the letter and turned it about in bewilderment, not knowing what to do with it.

'Where did you get it?' he asked the peasant. 'Who gave it you?'

'Why, sir, at the inn where I stopped in town,' replied the peasant. 'A soldier came twice from the post office, sir, to ask if there was any peasant there from Oblomovka. He'd got a letter for the master, it seems.'

'Well?'

'Well, sir, at first I hid myself, so the soldier, sir, he went away with this here letter. But the sexton from Verkhlyovo had seen me and he told them. So he comes a second time, the soldier, sir. And as he comes the second time, he starts swearing at me and gives me the letter. Charged me five copecks for it, he did. I asks him what I was to do with the letter, and he told me to give it to you, sir.'

'You shouldn't have taken it,' Mrs Oblomov observed vexedly.

'I didn't take it, ma'am. I said to him, I said, "What do we want your letter for – we don't want no letters," I said. "I wasn't told to take letters and I durstn't," I said. "Take your letter and go away," I said. But he started cursing me something awful, he did, threatening to go to the police, so I took it.'

'Fool!' said Mrs Oblomov.

'Who could it be from?' Mr Oblomov said wonderingly, examining the address. 'The writing seems familiar!'

He passed the letter round and they all began discussing who it could be from and what it was about. They were all completely at a loss. Mr Oblomov asked for his glasses and they spent an hour and a half looking for them. He put them on and was already about to open the letter when his wife stopped him.

'Don't open it,' she said apprehensively. 'Who knows, it might be something dreadful – some awful trouble. You know what people are nowadays. There's plenty of time: you can open it to-morrow or the day after: it won't run away.'

The letter was locked up in a drawer with the glasses. They all sat down to tea, and the letter might have lain in the drawer for years had they not all been so greatly excited by the extraordinary event. At tea and all next day they talked of nothing but the letter. At last they could not stand it any longer, and on the fourth day, having all gathered in a crowd, they opened it nervously. Mr Oblomov glanced at the signature.

'Radishchev,' he read. 'Why, that's Filip Matveich.'

'Oh, so that's who it is from!' they cried from all sides. 'Is he still alive? Good Lord, fancy he's not dead! Well, thank God! What does he say?'

Mr Oblomov began reading the letter aloud. It seemed that Radishchev was asking for a recipe of beer that was brewed particularly well at Oblomovka.

'Send it him! Send it him!' they all shouted. 'You must write him a letter!'

A fortnight passed.

'Yes, I must write to him,' Mr Oblomov kept saying to his wife. 'Where's the recipe?'

'Where is it?' his wife replied. 'I must try and find it. But why all this hurry? Wait till the holy-days; the fast will be over, and then you can write to him. There's plenty of time. ...'

'Yes, indeed, I'd better write during the holy-days,' said Mr Oblomov.

The question of the letter was raised again during the holy-days. Mr Oblomov made up his mind to write the letter. He withdrew to his study, put on his glasses, and sat down at the table. Dead silence reigned in the house; the servants were told not to stamp their feet or make a noise. 'The master's writing,' everyone said, speaking in a timid and respectful voice as though someone was lying dead in the house. He had just time to write, 'Dear Sir,' in a trembling hand, slowly, crookedly, and as carefully as though performing some dangerous operation, when his wife came into the room.

'I'm very sorry,' she said, 'but I can't find the recipe. I must have a look in the bedroom cupboard. It may be there. But how are you going to send the letter?'

'By post, I suppose,' replied Mr Oblomov.

'And what will the postage be?'

Mr Oblomov produced an old calendar.

'Forty copecks,' he said.

'Waste forty copecks on such nonsense!' she observed. 'Let's rather wait till we can send it by someone. Tell the peasants to find out.'

'Yes,' said Mr Oblomov, 'it would certainly be better to send it by hand.' And tapping the pen on the table a few times, he put it back in the inkstand and took off his glasses.

'Yes, indeed,' he concluded. 'It won't run away; there's plenty of time.'

It is doubtful whether Filip Matveich ever received the recipe.

Sometimes Oblomov's father picked up a book. It made no difference to him what book it was. He did not feel any need for reading, but regarded it as a luxury, as something that one could easily do without, just as one could do without a picture on the wall or without taking a walk. That was why he did not mind what book he picked up: he looked upon it as something that was meant as an entertainment, something that would help to distract him when he was bored or had nothing better to do.

'I haven't read a book for ages,' he would say, or sometimes he would change the phrase to, 'Now, then, let's read a book.' Or he would simply happen to see the small pile of books that was left him by his brother and pick one up at random. Whether it happened to be Golikov, or the latest *Dream Book*, or Kheraskov's *Rossiade*, or Sumarokov's tragedies, or the *Moscow News* of two years ago, he read it all with equal pleasure, remarking at times: 'Whatever will he think of next! What a rascal! Damn the fellow!' These exclamations referred to the authors, for whose calling he had no respect whatever; he had even adopted the attitude of semi-indulgent contempt for a writer which is so characteristic of old-fashioned people. He, like many other people of his day, thought that an author must be a jovial fellow, a rake, a drunkard, and a mountebank, something like a clown. Sometimes he read the two-year-old papers aloud for the edification of everybody or just told them a piece of news from them. 'They write from The Hague,' he would say, 'that his Majesty the King has safely returned to his palace after a short journey,' and as he spoke he glanced at his listeners over his glasses. Or: 'The ambassador of such and such a country has presented his credentials in Vienna. And here they write,' he went on, 'that the works of Madame Genlis have been translated into Russian.'

'I suppose,' remarked one of his listeners, a small landowner, 'they do all these translations to extract some money from us gentry.'

Meanwhile poor Oblomov had still to go for his lessons to Stolz. As soon as he woke up on Monday morning, he felt terribly depressed. He heard Vaska's raucous voice shouting from the front steps:

'Antip, harness the piebald one to take the young master to the German!'

His heart sank. Sadly he went to his mother. She knew what was the matter with him and began gilding the pill, secretly sighing herself at the thought of parting with him for a whole week.

Nothing was good enough for him to eat that morning. They baked rolls of different shapes for him, loaded him with pickles, biscuits, jams, all sorts of sweetmeats, cooked and uncooked dainties, and even provisions. He was given it all on the supposition that he did not get enough to eat at the German's house.

'You won't get anything decent to eat there,' they said at Oblomovka. 'For dinner they'll give you nothing but soup, roast meat, and potatoes, and bread and butter for tea. As for supper – not a crumb, old man!'

Oblomov, however, dreamt mostly of Mondays on which he did not hear Vaska's voice shouting for the piebald to be harnessed, but his mother greeting him at breakfast with a smile and pleasant news.

'You're not going to-day, dear; Thursday is a great holy-day, and it isn't worth travelling there and back for three days.'

Or sometimes she would announce to him suddenly:

'To-day is commemoration week – it's no time for lessons: we shall be baking pancakes.'

Or his mother would look at him intently on a Monday morning and say:

'Your eyes look tired this morning, darling. Are you well?' and shake her head.

The sly little boy was perfectly well, but he said nothing.

'You'd better stay at home this week,' she said, 'and we shall see how you feel.'

And they were all convinced in the house that lessons and Commemoration Saturday must never be allowed to interfere with each other and that a holy-day on a Thursday was an insurmountable obstacle to lessons during the whole of the week. Only from time to time would a servant or a maid, who had been punished because of the young master, grumble:

'Oh, you spoilt little brat! When will you clear out to your German?'

At other times Antip would suddenly turn up at the German's on the familiar piebald in the middle or at the beginning of the week to fetch Oblomov.

'Maria Savishna or Natalya Faddeyevna or the Kuzovkovs with all their children have come on a visit and you're wanted back home!'

And Oblomov stayed at home for three weeks, and then Holy Week was not far off, followed by Easter; or someone in the house decided that for some reason or other one did not study in the week after Easter; there would be only a fortnight left till summer, and it was not worth going back to school, for the German himself had a rest in summer, so that it was best to put the lessons off till the autumn. Oblomov spent a most enjoyable six months. How tall he grew during that time! And how fat he grew! How soundly he slept! They could not admire him enough at home, nor could they help observing that when the dear child returned home from the German on Saturdays, he looked pale and thin.

'He can easily come to harm,' his mother would remark. 'He'll have plenty of time to study, but you cannot buy health for money: health is the most precious thing in life. The poor boy comes back from school as from a hospital: all his fat is gone, he looks so thin – and such a naughty boy, too: always running about!'

'Yes,' his father observed, 'learning is no joke: it will take it out of anyone!'

And the fond parents went on finding excuses for keeping their son at home. There was no difficulty in finding excuses besides holy-days. In winter they thought it was too cold, in summer it was too hot to drive to the next village, and sometimes it rained; in the autumn the roads were too muddy. Sometimes Antip aroused their doubts: he did not seem to be drunk, but he had a sort of wild look in his eyes – there might be trouble, he might get stuck in the mud or fall into a ditch. The Oblomovs, however, tried to make their excuses as legitimate as possible in their own eyes, and particularly in the eyes of Stolz, who did not spare *Donnerwetters* to their faces and behind their backs for pampering the child.

The days of the heroes of Fonvisin's comedy *The Minor* – the Prostakovs and Skotinins – had gone long before. The proverb 'Knowledge is light and ignorance is darkness' was already penetrating into the big and small villages together with the books sold by book pedlars. Oblomov's parents understood the advantages of education, but only its material advantages. They saw that it was only education that made it possible for people to make a career, that is, to acquire rank, decorations, and money; that old-fashioned lawyers, case-hardened and corrupt officials, who had grown old in their pettifogging ways and chicaneries, were having a bad time. Ominous rumours were abroad that not only reading and writing but all sorts of hither-to unheard-of subjects were required. A gulf opened up between the higher and the lower grades of civil servants which could be bridged only by something called a diploma. Officials of the old school, children of habit and nurslings of bribes, began to dis-appear. Many of those who had survived were dismissed as un-reliable, and others were put on trial; the luckiest were those who, giving up the new order of things as a bad job, retired to their well-feathered nests while the going was good. Oblomov's parents grasped all this and understood the advantages of edu-cation, but only these obvious advantages. They had only the vaguest and remotest idea of the intrinsic need of education, and that was why they wanted to obtain for their son some of its brilliant advantages. They dreamed of a gold-embroidered uniform for him; they imagined him as a Councillor at Court, and his mother even imagined him as a Governor of a province. But they wanted to obtain all this as cheaply as possible, by all sorts of tricks, by secretly dodging the rocks and obstacles scat-tered on the path of learning and honours, without bothering to jump over them – that is, for instance, by working a little, not by physical exhaustion or the loss of the blessed plumpness ac-quired in childhood. All they wanted was that their son should merely comply with the prescribed rules and regulations and ob-tain in some way or other a certificate which said that their dar-ling Ilya *had mastered all the arts and sciences*. The whole of this Oblomov system of education met with strong opposition in Stolz's system. Each fought stubbornly for his own ideas. Stolz struck at his opponents directly, openly, and persistently, and they parried his blows by all sorts of cunning devices, including those already described. Neither side won; German pertinacity might have overcome the stubbornness and obduracy of the Ob-lomovs, had not the German met opposition in his own camp. The fact was that Stolz's own son spoiled Oblomov, prompting him at lessons and doing his translations for him.

Oblomov clearly saw his life at home and at Stolz's. As soon as he woke up at home, he saw Zakhar, later his famous valet, Zakhar Trofimych, standing by his bed. Zakhar, like his old nurse, pulled on his stockings and put on his shoes, while Oblomov, a boy of fourteen, merely stretched out to him first one leg, then the other, as he lay on the bed; and if something seemed to him amiss, he hit Zakhar on the nose with a foot. If Zakhar resented it and had the impudence to complain, he would get a hiding from the grown-ups as well. Then Zakhar combed his hair, helped him on with his coat, forcing his arms carefully through the sleeves so as not to disturb him unduly, and reminded him of the things he had to do, washing as soon as he got up, and so on. If Oblomov wanted something, he had only to wink and three or four servants rushed to carry out his wish; if he dropped something, or if he had to get something, someone else would pick it up or get it for him; if he wanted to fetch something or run out of the house for something and, being a lively boy, would like to run out and do it all himself, his father, mother, and three aunts shouted all at once: 'What for? Where are you off to? And what are Vaska, Vanka, and Zakharka for? Hey, Vaska! Vanka! Zakharka! What are you gaping at, you idiots! I'll show you!'

And try as he might, Oblomov could never do anything for himself. Later he found that it was much less trouble and learned to shout himself:

'Hey, Vaska! Vanka! Bring me this! Bring me that! I don't want this, I want that! Run and fetch it!'

At times he got tired of the tender solicitude of his parents. If he ran down the stairs or across the yard, a dozen desperate voices shouted after him: 'Oh, hold him by the hand! Stop him! He'll fall down and hurt himself! Stop!' If he tried to run out into the hall in winter, or to open a window, there were again shouts: 'Where are you off to? You can't do that! Don't run, don't go, don't open it: you'll hurt yourself, you'll catch a cold ...!' And sadly Oblomov remained indoors, cherished like an exotic flower in a hot-house, and like it he grew slowly and languidly. His energies, finding no outlet, turned inwards and withered, drooping. Sometimes he woke up feeling so bright and cheerful, so fresh and gay; he felt as though something inside him were full of life and movement, just as if some imp had taken up its quarters there, daring him to climb on the roof, or mount the grey mare and gallop to the meadows where they were haymaking, or sit astride on the fence, or tease the village dogs; or he suddenly wanted to run like mad through the village, then

across the field and the gullies into the birch wood, and down
to the bottom of the ravine in three jumps, or getting the vil-
age boys to play a game of snowball with him and trying out
his strength. The little imp egged him on; he resisted as long as
he could, and at last jumped down the front steps into the yard
in winter, without his cap, ran through the gate, seized a ball
of snow in each hand and flew towards a group of boys. The
fresh wind cut into his face, the frost pinched his ears, the cold
air entered his mouth and throat, his chest expanded with joy –
he ran along faster and faster, laughing and screaming. There
were the boys; he flung a snowball at them but missed; he
was not used to it. He was about to pick up another when
his face was smothered by a huge lump of snow: he fell; his
face hurt from the new sensation; he was enjoying it all, he was
laughing, and there were tears in his eyes.

Meanwhile there was an uproar at home: darling Ilya had
vanished! A noise, shouts. Zakhar rushed into the yard, followed by Vaska, Mitka, Vanka – all running about in confusion.
Two dogs ran madly after them, catching them by the heels, for,
as everyone knows, dogs cannot bear to see a running man.
Shouting and yelling, the servants raced through the village, followed by the barking dogs. At last they came across the boys
and began meting out justice: pulled them by the hair and ears,
hit them across the back, and told off their fathers. Then they
got hold of the young master, wrapped him in the sheepskin
they had brought, then in his father's fur coat and two blankets,
and carried him home in triumph. At home they had despaired
of seeing him again, giving him up for lost; but the joy of his
parents at seeing him alive and unhurt was indescribable. They
offered up thanks to the Lord, then gave him mint and elder-
berry tea to drink, followed by raspberry tea in the evening,
and kept him three days in bed – yet only one thing could have
done him good – playing snowball again. ...

10

As soon as Oblomov's snoring reached Zakhar's ears, he jumped quietly and cautiously off the stove, tiptoed into the passage,
locked his master in, and went to the gate.

'Oh, Zakhar Trofimych, how are you? Haven't seen you for

ages!' coachmen, valets, women, and errand boys by the gate cried in various voices.

'What's your master doing? Gone out, has he?' the caretaker asked.

'Asleep as usual,' Zakhar said gloomily.

'Is he now?' a coachman asked. 'A bit too early, isn't it? Is he ill?'

'Ill, indeed! Drunk as a lord!' said Zakhar with such conviction that he might really have known it for a fact. 'Would you believe it? Drank a bottle and a half of Madeira by himself and two quarts of *kvas*, so he's sleeping it off now.'

'Go on!' the coachman said enviously.

'What made him have so much to drink to-day?' one of the women asked.

'It isn't only to-day, Tatyana Ivanovna,' Zakhar replied, casting his sidelong glance at her. 'He's gone off the rails, that he has – makes me sick to talk of it!'

'Just like my mistress,' she remarked with a sigh.

'Is she going out anywhere to-day, Tatyana Ivanovna?' inquired the coachman. 'I'd like to go to a place not far from here.'

'Not her!' replied Tatyana. 'She's sitting there with her sweetheart, and they can't take their eyes off each other.'

'He's been coming to you pretty often lately,' said the caretaker. 'A damned nuisance he is at nights, I must say. Everyone's come in, all the visitors have left, but he is always the last to go, and he makes a row if the main entrance is closed. Catch me guarding the front door for him!'

'What a fool he is, my dears,' said Tatyana. 'You won't find another one like him, I'm sure! The presents he gives her! She dresses up in all her finery like a peacock, and struts about so importantly, but if you'd only seen the petticoats and stockings she wears! Doesn't wash her neck for a fortnight, but paints her face. Sometimes I can't help thinking to myself, "Oh you poor creature, you ought to put a kerchief on your head and go to a monastery to pray for your sins, you ought to."'

All laughed, except Zakhar.

'She never misses, Tatyana Ivanovna doesn't,' approving voices said.

'But, really, how could gentlemen have anything to do with a woman like that?' Tatyana went on.

'Where are you going to?' someone asked her. 'What have you in that bundle?'

'I'm taking a dress to the dressmaker's. My fine lady has sent me. Too big, if you please! But when Dunyasha and I start lacing her into her corsets, we can't do anything with our hands for three days afterwards – everything snaps in them! But I must go – good-bye for the present.'

'Good-bye, good-bye,' said some.

'Good-bye, Tatyana Ivanovna,' said the coachman. 'Come along and see me in the evening.'

'Well, I don't know, I'm sure. I may and I mayn't. Good-bye.'

'Well, good-bye,' they all said.

'Good-bye, good luck to you,' she replied, going away.

'Good-bye, Tatyana Ivanovna,' the coachman called after her.

'Good-bye!' she cried loudly in the distance.

When she had gone, Zakhar seemed to have been waiting his turn to speak. He sat down on the iron post by the gate and began swinging his legs, watching the passers-by and the people in the carriages gloomily and absent-mindedly.

'Well, how is your master to-day, Zakhar Trofimych?' asked the caretaker.

'Just as ever,' said Zakhar. 'Doesn't know what he wants. And it was all because of you that I had so much trouble to-day: all about the flat! He's furious – don't want to move.'

'It's not my fault, is it?' said the caretaker. 'I don't mind if he stays there for ever, I'm sure. I'm not the landlord, am I? Of course, if I were the landlord – but then I'm not. ...'

'He doesn't swear at you, does he?' someone's coachman asked.

'He swears something awful! I don't know how I can stand it!'

'Well, I shouldn't worry! It means he's a good master if he swears all the time!' a valet said, opening a round snuff-box slowly and noisily, and all the hands except Zakhar's stretched out for a pinch.

There was general sniffing, sneezing, and spitting.

'If he swears, it's all the better,' the valet went on. 'The more he swears, the better it is: at least he won't strike you if he swears. Now, I had a master who grabbed you by the hair before you knew what was wrong.'

Zakhar waited contemptuously for him to finish his tirade and then went on, addressing the coachmen.

'So, you see,' he said, 'he's quite likely to disgrace a fellow for nothing at all without turning a hair!'

'Difficult to please, is he?' asked the caretaker.

145

'Dear me,' Zakhar wheezed meaningfully, screwing up his eyes. 'I can't tell you how difficult he is to please! One thing's wrong, and another thing's not right, and I don't know how to walk, or how to serve, and I break everything, and I don't clean the place, and I steal things and I eat everything up – damn him! He was going on at me to-day something awful! And what about? There was a little bit of cheese left over from last week – you would be ashamed to throw it to a dog, but no, a servant mustn't touch it! He asked for it and I said there was nothing left of it, so off he went! "You ought to be hanged," he says, "you ought to be boiled in pitch," he says, "and torn limb from limb with red-hot pincers! You ought to have an ashen stake driven through you," he says. And on he goes, on and on and on. What do you think? The other day I scalded his foot – I'm hanged if I know how it happened – and he screamed something awful! If I hadn't jumped back, he'd have hit me in the chest with his fist – I could see he wanted to – knocked me down, he would have!'

The coachman shook his head.

'A smart gentleman and no mistake,' said the caretaker. 'Don't give you much rope, he don't.'

'What I says is,' the same valet said phlegmatically, 'that if he swears at you, he's a good chap. One who doesn't swear is a hundred times worse: he looks and looks at you and before you know what's wrong, he's grabbed you by the hair!'

'It didn't do him no good,' said Zakhar, without paying any attention to the valet who had interrupted him. 'His foot hasn't healed up yet. He still keeps putting ointment on it – let him!'

'A high-spirited gentleman,' said the caretaker.

'Oh, terrible!' Zakhar went on. 'One day he's sure to kill someone, you'll see if he don't. And for every little thing he calls me "bald-headed —" – I'd rather not say the rest. To-day he thought of something new: "venomous", he said! How could he say a thing like that!'

'Well, that's nothing,' the valet went on. 'If he swears, you ought to be pleased – God bless him. But if he says nothing, but just looks and looks, and when you happen to go near him, grabs you by the hair, like the master I worked for ...! If he swears, it's nothing. ...'

'And it served you right,' observed Zakhar, angered by his unasked-for interference. 'I'd have treated you worse, I would.'

'What is it he calls you, Zakhar Trofimych, a "bald-headed devil"?' asked a boy-servant of fifteen.

Zakhar turned his head slowly and fixed him with a malignant glance.

'Look out, my lad,' he said sharply, 'you're too clever by half! You may belong to a general, but I'll pull your hair, for all that! Back to your place with you!'

The boy walked away a few yards and stopped, looking at Zakhar with a smile.

'What are you grinning at?' Zakhar growled furiously. 'Wait till I lay my hands on you. I'll box your ears, I will. I'll teach you how to grin at me!'

At that moment a huge footman in gaiters and shoulder-knots and with his livery coat unbuttoned ran out of the main entrance of the house. He went up to the page-boy, slapped his face, and called him a fool.

'What's the matter, Matvey Moiseich?' asked the ashamed and bewildered boy, holding his cheek and blinking convulsively. 'What's this for?'

'Oh, so you're talking, are you?' replied the footman. 'I'm looking all over the house for you, and you are here!'

He grabbed him by the hair, bent down his head, and hit him methodically three times with his fist across the neck.

'The master's rung five times,' he added by way of a moral, 'and I'm blamed because of you, you puppy! Off you go!'

And he pointed imperiously to the staircase. The boy stood still for a moment in a kind of stupor, blinked twice, glanced at the footman, and, seeing that he could not expect anything from him except a repetition of the same punishment, tossed his hair and ran briskly up the stairs.

What a triumph for Zakhar!

'Give it him good and proper, Matvey Moiseich! Give him some more, some more!' he said, beaming maliciously. 'That wasn't enough! Well done, Matvey Moiseich! Thank you! He's too clever by half! That's for calling me a "bald-headed devil"! You won't be jeering at me again, will you now?'

The servants laughed, sympathizing with the footman, who had beaten the boy, and with Zakhar, who rejoiced maliciously at it. No one sympathized with the page-boy.

'That's exactly how my old master used to go on,' the valet, who had kept interrupting Zakhar, began again. 'You'd be thinking of having some fun and he'd seem to guess your thoughts and grab you just as Matvey Moiseich grabbed Andrey. What does it matter if he does call you a "bald-headed devil"?'

'I daresay his master, too, would have grabbed you,' the coachman replied, pointing at Zakhar. 'Look at the growth on your head! But how is he to grab Zakhar Trofimych? His head's like a pumpkin. Unless, of course, he caught him by the two beards on his jaws – aye, he could do that and all!'

They all burst out laughing, but Zakhar was thunderstruck by this sally of the coachman, who was the only one among them he talked to as a friend.

'You wait till I tell my master,' he began wheezing furiously at the coachman, 'he'll find something to grab you by: he'll iron out that beard for you – look, it's covered in icicles!'

'Your master must be a terror, to iron out the beards of other people's coachmen! No, sir: you get your own coachmen first and then stroke their beards for them, but I'm afraid you're talking a bit too soon now!'

'You don't want us to engage a rogue like you for our coachman, do you?' Zakhar wheezed. 'You're not good enough to draw my master's carriage, you aren't!'

'Some master!' the coachman observed sarcastically. 'Where did you dig him up?'

He burst out laughing, followed by the caretaker, the barber, the footman, and the defender of the system of swearing.

'You may laugh,' Zakhar wheezed, 'but wait till I tell my master! As for you,' he added, turning to the caretaker, 'you ought to restrain these scoundrels, instead of laughing. What are you here for? To keep order. And what do you do? I'm going to tell my master. You wait, sir: you'll catch it!'

'Come, come, Zakhar Trofimych,' said the caretaker, trying to calm him. 'What has he done to you?'

'How dare he talk like that about my master?' Zakhar replied warmly, pointing at the coachman. 'Does he know who my master is?' he asked in a reverential voice. 'Why,' he said, addressing the coachman, 'you wouldn't see a master like that in your dreams! Such a kindly, clever, handsome gentleman! And yours is just like an underfed nag! It's disgraceful to see you driving out with your brown mare – just like beggars! All you eat is turnips and *kvas*. Look at that shabby coat of yours – all in holes!'

It should be observed here that the coachman's coat had not a single hole in it.

'Why, I couldn't find one like yours if I tried,' the coachman interrupted, quickly pulling out the piece of shirt that was showing under Zakhar's arm.

'Now, now, that will do,' the caretaker repeated, trying to keep them apart.

'Oh, so you're tearing my clothes, are you?' Zakhar cried, pulling out some more of his own shirt. 'You wait, I'll show it to my master! Look what he's done – he has torn my coat!'

'Me torn your coat!' said the coachman, somewhat alarmed. 'I suppose your master gave you a good thrashing. ...'

'My master?' Zakhar said. 'Why, he's the soul of kindness – he wouldn't hurt a fly, he would not, bless him! Living with him is like heaven – I have never wanted for anything and he never as much as called me a fool. I live in comfort and peace, I eat the same food as he, I can go out when I like – that's the sort of way I live! And in the country I have a house of my own, a kitchen garden, as much corn as I like, and all the peasants bow low to me! I'm the steward and the butler! And you with your master – –'

He was so enraged that his voice failed him, so that he could not finally annihilate his adversary. He paused for a minute to gather strength and think of some really venomous word, but he was too furious to do so.

'You wait and see what happens to you for tearing my clothes,' he said at last. 'They'll teach you to tear them!'

In attacking his master, they hurt him to the quick, too. His ambition and vanity were roused, his loyalty was awakened, and expressed itself with all its force. He was ready to pour out the vials of his wrath not only on his adversary, but also on his adversary's master and the master's friends and relations, though he did not know whether he had any. He repeated with amazing precision all the slanderous stories about their masters he had gathered from his previous talks with the coachman.

'And you and your master,' he said, 'are damned paupers. Jews, worse than Germans. I know who his grandfather was: a stall-holder in the flea-market. When your visitors left last night I wondered if they were not burglars who had got into the house: I felt sorry for them! His mother, too, used to sell stolen and threadbare clothes in the flea-market.'

'Come, come, now!' the caretaker tried to calm him.

'Oh yes,' Zakhar said, 'my master is a born gentleman, thank God. All his friends are generals, counts, and princes. It isn't every count he'll invite to dinner, either; some of them come and have to wait in the hall. ... All sorts of writers keep coming, too. ...'

'What sort of writers are they?' asked the caretaker, intent on stopping the quarrel. 'Are they civil servants or what?'

'No,' explained Zakhar, 'they are gentlemen who invent everything they want themselves.'

'What are they doing at your place?' asked the caretaker.

'Why, one of them will ask for a pipe of tobacco, another for a glass of sherry,' said Zakhar, and paused, noticing that almost everyone was smiling sarcastically.

'And you're a lot of scoundrels, every one of you!' he said hurriedly, casting a sidelong glance at them. 'You'll catch it for tearing other people's clothes. I'll go and tell my master!' he added and walked home quickly.

'Wait, wait! What's the hurry?' the caretaker cried. 'Zakhar Trofimych! Let's go and have a drink – come on!'

Zakhar stopped, turned back quickly, and, without looking at the other servants, rushed out into the street. He reached the door of the inn opposite the gate without paying heed to any of them, then he turned round, cast a sombre glance at the company, and motioning them even more sombrely to follow him, disappeared inside.

The others dispersed, too: some went into the inn, others went home: only the valet remained.

'Well,' he said thoughtfully and phlegmatically to himself, slowly opening his snuff-box, 'what if he tells his master? You can see from everything that his master is a kind man – he'd only swear! There's no harm in that, is there? Now, another one will just stare at you and then grab you by the hair. ...'

11

SOON AFTER FOUR Zakhar carefully and noiselessly opened the front door of his master's flat and tiptoed to his room; then he walked up to the door of his master's study, put his ear to it and, bending down, peeped through the key-hole.

From the study came the sound of regular snoring.

'Asleep,' he whispered. 'I must wake him – it'll be half-past four soon.'

He cleared his throat and went into the study.

'Sir! sir!' he began quietly, standing at the head of the bed.
The snoring continued.

'Oh, he's fast asleep!' said Zakhar. 'Like a regular brick-layer! Sir!'

Zakhar touched Oblomov's sleeve lightly.

'Get up, sir! It's half-past four!'

Oblomov just mumbled something, but did not wake.

'Get up, sir! It's disgraceful!' Zakhar said, raising his voice. No answer.

'Sir!' Zakhar repeated, touching his master on the sleeve.

Oblomov turned his head a little, with difficulty opened one eye and looked at Zakhar as though he had been stricken with paralysis.

'Who's that?' he asked hoarsely.

'It's me, sir. Get up, please.'

'Go away!' Oblomov muttered and sank into heavy sleep again. Instead of snoring, he began whistling through the nose. Zakhar pulled him by his dressing-gown.

'What do you want?' Oblomov asked sternly, opening both eyes suddenly.

'You told me to wake you, sir.'

'I know. You've done your duty and now clear out! Leave the rest to me. ...'

'I won't go,' Zakhar said, touching him again by the sleeve.

'There now,' Oblomov said gently, 'leave me alone.' And burying his face in the pillow, he was about to start snoring again.

'You mustn't, sir,' said Zakhar. 'I'd gladly leave you be, but I can't.'

And he touched his master once more.

'Now, do me a favour and don't disturb me,' Oblomov said earnestly, opening his eyes.

'Aye, and if I did you the favour, you'd be angry with me for not waking you.'

'Oh dear, what a man!' said Oblomov. 'Just let me sleep for one more minute – just one minute! I know myself – –'

Oblomov suddenly fell silent, overcome by sleep.

'You know how to sleep all right!' said Zakhar, convinced that his master did not hear him. 'Look at him – sleeping like a log! What's the good of a man like you? Get up, I tell you!' Zakhar roared.

'What's that? What's that?' Oblomov said menacingly, raising his head.

'Why don't you get up, sir?' Zakhar answered gently.

'Yes, but what did you say, eh? How dare you talk to me like this – eh?'

'Dare what, sir?'

'Speak so rudely.'

'You must have dreamt it, sir. I swear, you dreamt it.'

'You thought I was asleep, did you? Well, I wasn't. I heard everything.'

And he dropped off again.

'Well,' Zakhar said in despair, 'what is one to do? What are you lying about like a log for? It makes one sick to look at you. Just look at him! Damn!

'Get up! Get up!' he suddenly said in a frightened voice. 'Sir, look what's happening!'

Oblomov quickly raised his head, looked about him, and lay down again with a deep sigh.

'Leave me alone!' he said gravely. 'I told you to wake me and now I cancel my order – you hear? I'll wake when I like.'

Sometimes Zakhar left him alone, saying: 'Oh, sleep if you like, damn you!' But sometimes he insisted on having his way, and he did that this time.

'Get up, get up!' he roared at the top of his voice, seizing Oblomov with both hands by the skirt of his dressing-gown and by the sleeve.

Oblomov suddenly jumped out of bed and rushed at Zakhar.

'You wait,' he said, 'I'll teach you how to disturb your master when he wants to sleep!'

Zakhar took to his heels, but at the third step Oblomov shook off his sleep and began stretching and yawning.

'Give me – some *kvas*,' he said, between his yawns.

At this moment someone behind Zakhar's back burst into a peal of laughter. Both looked round.

'Stolz! Stolz!' Oblomov shouted joyfully, rushing towards his visitor.

'Andrey Ivanich!' Zakhar said with a grin. Stolz went on roaring with laughter; he had witnessed the whole scene.

PART TWO

1

STOLZ was only half German; on his father's side. His mother was Russian; he was of the Eastern Orthodox faith; his native tongue was Russian; he learnt it from his mother and from books, in the University lecture-rooms, in his games with the village children, in conversations with their fathers and in the Moscow markets. The German language he inherited from his father and learnt from books.

Stolz had been brought up in the village of Verkhlyovo, where his father was steward. Ever since he was a boy of eight he had sat with his father over maps, spelt out the verses of Herder, Wieland, and the Bible, cast up the badly written accounts of the peasants, artisans, and factory hands, and read with his mother the stories from the sacred books, learnt by heart Krylov's fables, and spelt out the verses of *Télémaque*. When his lessons were over he went bird-nesting with the village boys, and quite often the squeaking of young jackdaws came from his pocket during a lesson or at prayers. Sometimes when his father was sitting under a tree in the garden in the afternoon, smoking a pipe, and his mother was knitting a jersey or embroidering, a noise and shouts were heard from the street and a whole crowd of people would break into the house.

'What's the matter?' his mother asked in alarm.

'I expect they have brought Andrey again,' his father replied calmly.

The doors burst open, and a crowd of peasants, women and boys, rushed into the garden. And, indeed, they had brought Andrey, but in what a state! Without his boots, his clothes torn, and his nose bleeding – or the nose of some other boy. His mother was always worried when Andrey disappeared for a day, and had not her husband positively forbidden her to interfere with the boy, she would have always kept him at her side. She washed him, changed his clothes, and for a whole day Andrey walked about looking such a clean and well-behaved little boy, but in the evening and sometimes in the morning someone again brought him home dirty, dishevelled, and unrecognizable, or the peasants would bring him back on the top of a hay-cart, or he would return with the fishermen, asleep on a net in their boat.

His mother cried, but his father did not mind at all – he actually laughed.

'He'll be a good *Bursch* – a good *Bursch*,' he said sometimes.

'But really, dear,' his mother complained, 'not a day passes without his coming home with a bruise, and the other day he came back with his nose bleeding.'

'What kind of a child would he be if he never made his nose bleed – or someone else's?' his father said with a laugh.

His mother would burst into tears, but after a little while she would sit down at the piano and forget her troubles over Herz, her tears dropping on the keys. But soon Andrey came back or was brought home, and he began recounting his adventures so vividly and with such animation that he would make her laugh; and he was so quick too! Soon he was able to read *Télémaque* as well as she, and to play duets with her. Once he disappeared for a whole week. His mother cried her eyes out; his father did not seem to mind at all – he just walked in the garden smoking his pipe.

'Now if Oblomov's son had disappeared,' he said in reply to his wife's suggestion to go and look for him, 'I'd have roused the whole village and the rural police, but Andrey will come back. He's a good *Bursch*.'

Next morning Andrey was discovered sleeping peacefully in his bed. Under the bed lay a gun and a pound of powder and shot.

'Where have you been?' His mother began firing questions at him. 'Where did you get the gun? Why don't you speak?'

'Oh, nowhere!' was all he would say.

His father asked whether he had prepared the translation of Cornelius Nepos into German. 'No,' he replied.

His father took him by the collar, led him out of the gate, put his cap on his head and gave him such a kick from behind that he fell down.

'Go back to where you've come from,' he added, 'and come back with a translation of two chapters instead of one, and learn the part from the French comedy for your mother – don't show yourself until you have done it.' Andrey returned in a week, bringing the translation and having learnt the part.

When he grew older, his father took him in the trap with him, gave him the reins, and told him to drive to the factory, then to the fields, and to the town, to the shops and to the Government offices, or to have a look at some special clay which he took in his fingers, sniffed, sometimes licked, and gave to his son to sniff,

154

explaining what kind of clay it was and what it was good for. Or they would go to see how potash or tar was made or how lard was refined.

At fourteen or fifteen the boy went by himself in a trap or on horseback with a bag strapped to the saddle to carry out some commission for his father in the town, and he never forgot, or misinterpreted, or overlooked or missed anything.

'*Recht gut, mein lieber Junge!*' his father said, after hearing his report, patting him on the shoulder with his large hand, and gave him two or three roubles, according to the importance of the commission.

His mother spent a long time afterwards washing the soot, dirt, clay, and oil off her darling. She was not altogether pleased with this business-like, practical education. She was afraid that her son would become the same kind of middle-class business man as his father's people. She regarded the whole German nation as a crowd of patented middle-class tradesmen, and she disliked the coarseness, independence, and self-conceit with which the German masses everywhere asserted the civic rights they had acquired in the course of centuries, just like a cow that always carries her horns about with her and does not know where to hide them. In her opinion there was not and there could not be a single gentleman in the whole German nation. She could not discover any softness, delicacy, or true understanding in the German character, nothing that makes life so agreeable in good society, which makes it possible to infringe some rule, violate some generally accepted custom, or refuse to obey some regulation. No, those boorish fellows insisted on carrying out whatever had been assigned to them or what they happened to take into their heads – they were determined to act according to the rules if they had to knock through a wall with their heads.

She had been a governess in a rich family and had had an opportunity of going abroad, travelled all over Germany, and gained the impression that all Germans were just one mass of shop assistants, artisans, and store-keepers, smoking short pipes and spitting through their teeth; army officers straight as sticks with faces of common soldiers; and ordinary-looking officials – men who were capable only of hard work, of earning a living by the sweat of their brows, of keeping commonplace order, living dull lives and fulfilling their duties in a pedantic manner – all of them middle-class citizens with angular manners, large, coarse hands, plebeian freshness of complexion, and coarse speech. 'However well you dress a German,' she thought, 'even if he wears the finest and whitest shirt, patent-leather boots and even yellow gloves, he still looks as though he had been made of boot leather; his rough, red hands would protrude from the white cuffs, and however elegant the clothes he wears, he looks always, if not like a baker, then like a barman. His rough hands seem to be asking for an awl or at least for a fiddle in an orchestra.' In her son she hoped to see an ideal gentleman, for though he was the son of a middle-class German and a parvenu, his mother was a Russian lady, and he was a fair-skinned, well-built boy, with small hands and feet, a clear face and bright, alert eyes, such as she had often seen in rich Russian families and abroad, too, though not of course among the Germans. And this son of hers would be turning the mill-stones in the flour-mill, return home from the factory and the fields, like his father, covered in oil and manure, with rough, red, filthy hands and a wolfish appetite! She began cutting her son's nails, curling his hair, making him elegant collars and cuffs, ordering his coats in the town; she taught him to listen to the wistful melodies of Herz, sang to him about flowers, about the poetry of life, whispered to him about the brilliant calling of a soldier or a writer, and dreamed with him of the exalted part some men are destined to play. And all these prospects were to be ruined by the clicking of an abacus, the sorting out of the greasy receipts of the peasants, his dealings with factory workers! She grew to hate even the trap in which her darling Andrey drove to the town, and the oilskin cap his father had given him, and the green chamois-leather gloves – all of them coarse attributes of a life of labour. Unfortunately, Andrey was a good scholar, and his father made him coach the other boys in his small boarding-school. But this perhaps would not have mattered so much if he did not pay him a salary, just like a German, as if he were some artisan, of ten roubles a month, and made him sign a receipt for it.

Be comforted, good mother: your son has grown up on Russian soil and not in a crowd of humdrum people with middle-class bovine horns and hands turning mill-stones. Oblomovka was nearby: there it was a perpetual holiday! There they looked upon work as a heavy burden; there the master did not get up at dawn and go to factories and spend his time near oily wheels and springs. In Verkhlyovo itself there was a big mansion, shut up for most of the year, and the high-spirited boy often found his way in, and there he saw large halls and galleries hung with dark portraits of people who did not have fresh, plebeian complexions and big, rough hands – he saw languid, light-blue eyes, powdered hair, delicate faces, full bosoms, lovely, blue-veined hands in lace cuffs, resting proudly on the hilt of a sword; he saw a whole succession of generations that had lived uselessly-noble lives in luxury, clad in brocades, velvet, and lace. These portraits told him the story of glorious days, battles and famous names, a story of old times which was very different from the one his father had told him a hundred times, spitting and smoking his pipe, of his life in Saxony spent between turnips and potatoes, between the market and the kitchen garden.

Once in three years this big mansion suddenly filled with people and overflowed with life – fêtes and balls followed each other, and in the long galleries lights burned at nights. The prince and the princess arrived with their family: the prince – a grey-haired old man, with a faded, parchment-like face, dull, protruding eyes and a large, bald head; he had three stars on his coat, wore velvet boots, and carried a gold snuff-box and a cane with a sapphire top; the princess was a handsome woman of majestic size and height, whom no one, not even the prince himself, it would appear, had ever approached closely or embraced or kissed, though she had five children. She seemed to be above the world into which she descended once in three years; she did not speak to anyone or go anywhere, but spent her time in the green corner room with three old ladies, and walked to church under an awning across the garden and sat there on a chair behind a screen.

In addition to the prince and the princess, there was a whole gay and lively world in the house, so that little Andrey looked with his childish green eyes at three or four different social sets, and eagerly and unconsciously absorbed with his quick mind the different types of this motley crowd as one does the gaily-dressed people at a fancy-dress ball. There were the young princes, Pierre and Michel, the first of whom at once showed Andrey how they sound the reveille in the cavalry and the infantry, what sabres and spurs the hussars and the dragoons wear, what the colour of the horses of the different regiments is, and what regiment one has to join on leaving school so as not to disgrace oneself.

As soon as Michel made the acquaintance of little Andrey, he put him in position and began performing wonderful tricks with his fists, hitting Andrey on the nose or in the stomach, and telling him afterwards that it was English boxing. Three days later Andrey, without any special training, smashed his nose for him both in the English and the Russian fashion, merely with the aid of a pair of muscular arms and rude country health, and gained the respect of both young princes. Then there were the two princesses, tall and slender girls of eleven and twelve, who were smartly dressed, who spoke and bowed to no one, and who were afraid of peasants. Their governess, Mademoiselle Ernestine, who used to take coffee with Andrey's mother, and who taught her how to curl his hair, would sometimes put his head on her lap, twisting his hair in paper curlers till it hurt, then take his cheeks in her white hands and kiss him affectionately! Then there was their German tutor who made snuff-boxes and buttons on a turner's wheel; their teacher of music, who was drunk from one Sunday to another; and a whole bevy of maids and, finally, a pack of big and little dogs. All this filled the house and the village with noise, uproar, clatter, shouts, and music.

Oblomovka, on the one hand, and the prince's mansion with its life of ease and luxury, on the other, clashed with the German element, and Andrey grew up to be neither a good *Bursch* nor a philistine.

Andrey's father was an agronomist, a technologist, and a teacher. He had received his training in agronomy on his father's farm, he had studied technology in Saxon factories, and in the neighbouring university, where there were about forty professors, he had received his calling for teaching what the forty wise men had succeeded in expounding to him. He did not go any farther, but turned back stubbornly, having made up his mind to do something practical. He returned to his father, who gave him a hundred thalers and a new knapsack and sent him out into the world. Since that day he had never seen his father or his native country. For six years he had wandered about in Switzerland and Austria, and for twenty years he had lived in Russia, blessing his lucky stars. He had been to a university and made up his mind that his son should go to a university, although it could not be a German university, although a Russian university was bound to revolutionize his son's life and take him a long way off the track his father had mentally marked out for him. And he had done it all so simply: he drew a straight line from his grandfather to his future grandson and did not worry any more, and it never occurred to him that Herz's variations, his wife's stories and dreams, the galleries and drawing-rooms in the prince's mansion would transform the narrow German track into a road wider than his grandfather, his father, and himself ever dreamed of. However, he was no pedant, and in this instance he would not have insisted on his own plan; he merely could not conceive of any other road in his son's life. It did not worry him, either. When his son returned from the university and spent three months at home, he told Andrey that he had nothing more to do at Verkhlyovo, that even Oblomov had been sent to Petersburg, and that it was therefore time for him to go too. He did not ask himself why his son had to go to Petersburg and why he could not stay in Verkhlyovo and help with the management of the estate: he merely remembered that when he had finished his course at the university, his own father had sent him away; so he, too, sent away his son – such was the custom in Germany. His wife was dead and there was no one to oppose him.

On the day of Andrey's departure his father gave him a hundred roubles in notes.

'You'll ride to the town,' he said, 'and there Kalinnikov will give you three hundred and fifty roubles. You can leave the horse with him. If he isn't in town, you can sell the horse. There is going to be a fair there soon and you'll easily get four hundred roubles for it from anyone. Your fares to Moscow will be about forty roubles and from there to Petersburg, seventy-five. You will have enough left. After that you can do as you like. You have been in business with me and so you know that I have a small capital, but don't count on getting any of it before my death. I'll probably live for another twenty years, unless a stone falls on my head. The lamp still burns brightly and there is plenty of oil in it. You have received a good education and all careers are open to you. You can enter the Civil Service, or become a business man, or even a writer, if you like – I don't know the one you will choose, which you feel most attracted to. ...'

'I'll see whether I can't do all at once,' said Andrey.

His father burst out laughing with all his might and began patting his son's shoulders so vigorously that a horse would not have stood it, but Andrey did not mind.

'Well, and if your ability should not be equal to the task, and if you should find it difficult to strike the right road all at once and would like to ask someone's advice, go and see Reinhold – he'll tell you. Oh,' he added, rubbing his hands and shaking his head, 'he is – he is – –' he wanted to say something in Reinhold's praise, but could not find the right words; 'We came together from Saxony. He owns a house of four stories. I'll give you his address – –'

'Don't bother, I don't want it,' said Andrey. 'I'll go and see him when I have a house of four stories, and at present I shall do without him.'

There was more patting on the shoulder.

Andrey jumped on to his horse. Two bags were tied to the saddle: one had an oilskın cape, a pair of thick, nail-studded boots, and a few shirts made of Verkhlyovo linen – things he had bought and taken at his father's insistent request; in the other was an elegant dress-coat of fine cloth, a thick overcoat, a dozen fine shirts, and shoes that had been ordered from Moscow, in memory of his mother's admonitions.

'Well?' said the father.

'Well?' said the son.

'Is that all?' asked the father.

'All!' replied the son.

They looked at each other in silence, as though trying to pierce each other with their eyes.

Meanwhile, a small group of curious neighbours had collected and were gazing open-mouthed at the way the steward was taking leave of his son.

Father and son shook hands. Andrey rode off at a gallop.

'How do you like the young puppy?' the neighbours were saying to one another. 'He hasn't shed a tear! Those two crows on the fence are cawing as though their throats would burst. Mark my words, that bodes no good – he'd better look out!'

'What are crows to him? He's not afraid of walking in the woods alone on St John's Eve. All that means nothing to Germans. A Russian would have paid dearly for it!'

'And the old infidel is a fine fellow, too!' a mother observed. 'He threw him out into the street like a kitten: never embraced or wailed over him.'

'Stop, stop, Andrey!' the old man shouted.

Andrey stopped his horse.

'Oh, so his heart misgave him, after all,' people in the crowd said with approval.

'Well?' asked Andrey.

'The saddle-strap is loose – let me tighten it.'

'I'll tighten it myself when I get to Shamshevka. It's no use wasting time; I want to be there before dark.'

'All right,' said the father with a wave of the hand.

'All right,' the son repeated with a nod and, bending down a little, he was about to spur his horse.

'Just like dogs – the two of them,' said the neighbours. 'They might be strangers!'

Suddenly a loud wail was heard in the crowd: some woman could bear it no longer.

'Oh, you poor darling,' she said, wiping her tears with a corner of her kerchief. 'Poor little orphan! You have no mother, you have no one to bless you. ... Let me at least make the sign of the cross over you!'

Andrey rode up to her and jumped off his horse. He embraced the old woman and was about to ride on – when suddenly he burst out crying while she was kissing him and making the sign of the cross over him. In her fervent words he seemed to have heard the voice of his mother, and for a moment his mother's tender image rose before his mind. He embraced the woman once more with great tenderness, hastily wiped his tears, and jumped on to his horse. He struck it with his crop and disappeared in a cloud of dust; three dogs rushed after him desperately from two sides, barking at the top of their voices.

2

STOLZ was the same age as Oblomov: he, too, was over thirty. He had been a civil servant, retired, gone into business, and had actually acquired a house and capital. He was on the board of some company trading with foreign countries. He was continually on the move: if his company had to send an agent to Belgium or England, they sent him; if some new scheme had to be drafted or a new idea put into practice, he was chosen to do it. At the same time he kept up his social connexions and his reading; goodness only knows how he found time to do it.

He was made of bone, muscle, and nerve, like an English racehorse. He was spare: he had practically no cheeks, that is to say, there was bone and muscle but no sign of fat; his complexion was clear, darkish, and without a sign of red in it; his eyes were expressive, though slightly green. He made no superfluous gestures. If he was sitting, he sat quietly; if he was doing something, he used as few gestures as were necessary. Just as there was nothing excessive in his organism, so in his moral outlook he aimed at a balance between the practical side of life and the finer requirements of the spirit. The two sides ran parallel to each other, twisting and turning on the way, but never getting entangled in heavy, inextricable knots. He went along on his way firmly and cheerfully, lived within his income, and spent every day as he spent every rouble, keeping a firm and unremitting control over his time, his labour, and his mental and emotional powers. He seemed to be able to control his joys and sorrows like the movements of his hands and feet, and treated them as he did good or bad weather. When it rained, he put up an umbrella – that is to say, he suffered while the sorrow lasted, and even then with vexation and pride rather than timid submission – and bore patiently with it only because he blamed himself for his troubles and did not lay them at other people's doors. He enjoyed his pleasures as one enjoys a flower plucked by the wayside, until it begins to wilt in your hands, and never drained the cup to the last bitter drop which lies at the bottom of every pleasure. He constantly aimed at a simple, that is, a direct and true view of life, and as he gradually came to achieve it, he understood how difficult it was, and he was proud and happy every time he happened to notice a deviation from his path and put it right. 'Living simply is a hard and tricky business,' he often said to himself, and tried to see at once where he went wrong, where the thread of life was beginning to coil up into an irregular, complicated knot. Above everything else he feared imagination, that double-faced companion, friendly on one side and hostile on the other, your friend – the less you believe him, your foe – when you fall trustfully asleep to the sound of his sweet murmur. He was afraid of every dream, and if he ventured to enter the land of dreams, he did so as one enters a grotto inscribed: *ma solitude, mon ermitage, mon repos*, knowing exactly the hour and the minute when one should leave it. There was no room in his soul for a dream, for anything that was enigmatic and mysterious. He regarded everything that would not stand up to the analysis of reason and objective truth as an optical illusion, a particular reflection of the rays and colours on the retina or, at most, as a fact that had not yet been tested by experiment.

He had none of the dilettante's love for exploring the sphere of the supernatural and indulging in wild guesses about the discoveries of a thousand years hence. He obstinately halted at the threshold of a mystery without showing either a child's faith or a man of the world's doubts, but waited for the formulation of a law that would provide a key to it.

He kept as careful and keen a watch over his heart as over his imagination. But he had to admit after frequent retreats that the sphere of emotions was still *terra incognita* to him. He warmly thanked his lucky stars if he managed to distinguish in good time between the painted lie and the pale truth; he did not complain when a lie artfully concealed in flowers caused him to stumble but not fall, and he was overjoyed if his heart was merely beating fast and feverishly but did not bleed, if his brow did not break out in a cold sweat, and a long shadow was not cast over his life for many years. He thought himself fortunate because he could always keep at a certain height, and while carried along by his emotions, never overstepped the thin line that divides the world of feeling from the world of lies and sentimentality, the world of truth from the world of the ridiculous, or, when going in the opposite direction, he was not swept away to the sandy desert of rigid ideas, pettiness, mistrust, sophistication, and callousness.

Even when carried away, he was never swept off his feet, and always felt strong enough to wrench himself free if absolutely necessary. He was never blinded by beauty, and therefore never forgot or lowered his dignity as a man; he was never a slave, nor 'lay at the feet' of beautiful women, though he never experienced fiery joys, either. He had no idols, and that was why he preserved the powers of his soul and the strength of his body, that was why he was both chaste and proud; he exuded freshness and strength, which made even the least modest woman feel embarrassed. He knew the value of these rare and precious qualities and was so niggardly in their use that he was called an unfeeling egoist. He was blamed for his ability to control his impulses, keep within the bounds of rational behaviour, and preserve his spiritual freedom, while someone else who rushed headlong into disaster and ruined his own and another human being's life was excused and sometimes even envied and admired.

'Passion,' people round him said – 'passion justifies everything, and you in your egoism are taking care only of yourself : we shall see who you are doing it for.'

'Well, it must be for someone,' he said thoughtfully, as though gazing into the distance, and continued to disbelieve in the poesy of passions, refusing to admire their stormy manifestations and devastating consequences, but, as always, regarding an austere conception of life and its functions as the ideal aim of man's existence. The more people argued with him, the more obstinate he became, and lapsed, in discussions at any rate, into puritanical fanaticism. He used to say that 'the normal purpose of a man's life is to live through his four "ages" without sudden jumps and carry the vessel of life to the very end without spilling a single drop, and that a slowly and evenly burning fire is better than a blazing conflagration, however poetical it might be'. In conclusion, he added that he would have been happy if he could prove his conviction in his own case, but that he could not hope to do so because it was most difficult. As for himself, he steadily followed the path he had chosen. No one ever saw him brooding over anything painfully and morbidly; he was not apparently tormented by pricks of conscience; his heart did not ache, he never lost his presence of mind in new, difficult, or complicated situations, but tackled them as old acquaintances, as though he were living his life over again – as though he were visiting old familiar places once more. He always applied the right method in any emergency as a housekeeper chooses the right key for every door from the bunch hanging at her waist. Persistence in the pursuit of a certain aim was a quality he valued most; it was a mark of character in his eyes, and he never denied respect to people who possessed it, however insignificant their aims might be. 'These are *men*,' he used to say. Needless to say, he pursued his aims fearlessly, stepping over every obstacle in his way, and only relinquishing them when a brick wall rose before him or an unbridgeable abyss opened at his feet. He was incapable of the kind of courage which makes a man jump across an abyss or fling himself at a wall with his eyes shut, just on the off chance that he may succeed. He first measured the wall or the abyss, and if there were no certain way of overcoming the obstacle, he turned back, regardless of what people might say about him. Such a character could perhaps not be formed without the mixed elements of which Stolz's character was composed. Our statesmen have always conformed to five or six stereotyped models; they look lazily and with half-closed eyes about them, put their hand to the engine of State, and drowsily move it along the beaten track, following in their predecessors' footsteps. But soon their eyes awaken from their sleep, firm striding steps and lively voices were to be heard. ... How many Stolzes have still to appear under Russian names!

How could such a man be intimate with Oblomov, whose whole existence, every feature, every step was a flagrant protest against everything Stolz stood for? It seems, however, to be an established fact that while extremes do not necessarily, as it was formerly believed, give rise to a feeling of mutual sympathy, they do not prevent it. Besides, they had spent their childhood and schooldays together – two strong ties; then there was the typically Russian, big-hearted affection lavished in Oblomov's family on the German boy, the fact that Stolz had always played the part of the stronger, both physically and morally, and, finally and above all, there was in Oblomov's nature some-

164

thing good, pure, and irreproachable, which was deeply in sympathy with everything that was good and that responded to the call of his simple, unsophisticated, and eternally trustful nature. Anyone who once looked, whether by accident or design, into his pure and childlike soul – however gloomy and bitter he might be – could not help sympathizing with him and, if circumstances prevented them from becoming friends, retaining a good and lasting memory of him.

Andrey often tore himself away from his business affairs or from a fashionable crowd, a party or a ball, and went to sit on Oblomov's wide sofa and unburden his weary heart and find relief for his agitated spirits in a lazy conversation, and he always experienced the soothing feeling a man experiences on coming from magnificent halls to his own humble home or returning from the beautiful South to the birch wood where he used to walk as a child.

3

'GOOD MORNING, Ilya, I'm so glad to see you! Well, how are you? All right?' asked Stolz.

'Oh dear, no, Andrey, old man,' Oblomov said with a sigh. 'I'm not at all well.'

'Why, you're not ill, are you?' Stolz asked solicitously.

'Styes have got me down: last week I got rid of one on my right eye and now I'm getting one on the left.'

Stolz laughed.

'Is that all?' he asked. 'You've got them from sleeping too much.'

'All? Good heavens – no! I've awful heartburn. You should have heard what the doctor said this morning. He told me to go abroad or it would be the worse for me: I might have a stroke.'

'Well, are you going?'

'No.'

'Why not?'

'Good Lord, you should have heard all he told me! I have to live somewhere on a mountain, go to Egypt, or to America. ...'

'Well, what about it?' Stolz said coolly. 'You can be in Egypt in a fortnight and in America in three weeks.'

'You, too, old man? You were the only sensible man I knew and you, too, have gone off your head. Who goes to America and

Egypt? The English – but they have been made like that by the good Lord and, besides, they have not enough room at home. But who in Russia would dream of going? Some desperate fellow, perhaps, who doesn't value his own life.'

'But, good heavens, it's nothing: you get into a carriage or go on board ship, breathe pure air, look at foreign countries, cities, customs, at all the marvels. ... Oh, you funny fellow! Well, tell me how you are getting on? How are things at Oblomovka?'

'Oh!' Oblomov said with a despairing wave of the hand.

'What's happened?'

'Why, life doesn't leave me alone.'

'Thank goodness it doesn't!' said Stolz.

'Thank goodness indeed! if it just went on patting me on the head, but it keeps pestering me just as naughty boys pester a quiet boy at school, pinching him on the sly or rushing up to him and throwing sand in his face – I can't stand it any more!'

'You're much too quiet. What's happened?' asked Stolz.

'Two misfortunes.'

'Oh?'

'I'm utterly ruined.'

'How's that?'

'Let me read to you what my bailiff writes – where's the letter? Zakhar, Zakhar!'

Zakhar found the letter. Stolz read it and laughed, probably at the bailiff's style.

'What a rogue that bailiff is!' he said. 'He has let the peasants go and now he complains! He might as well have given them passports and let them go where they like.'

'Good Lord, if he did that, they might all want to go,' Oblomov retorted.

'Let them!' Stolz said with complete unconcern. 'Those who are happy and find it to their advantage to stay, will not go, and those who do not want to stay are of no use to you, anyway. Why keep them in that case?'

'What an idea!' said Oblomov. 'The Oblomovka peasants are quiet people who like to stay at home. What do they want to roam about for?'

'I don't suppose you know,' Stolz interrupted, 'they're going to build a landing-stage at Verkhlyovo and they also plan to make a highroad there, so that Oblomovka will be within a mile of it, and they're going to hold an annual fair in the town, too.'

'Dear me,' said Oblomov, 'that would be the last straw! Oblomovka used to be in a backwater, away from everything, and now there's going to be a fair, a highroad! The peasants will start going regularly to the town, merchants will be coming to us – it's the end! What a nuisance!'

Stolz laughed.

'Of course it's a nuisance!' Oblomov went on. 'The peasants were behaving nicely, you heard nothing, neither good nor bad, from them, they went about their business and asked for nothing, but now they'll be corrupted! They'll start drinking tea and coffee, wearing velvet trousers and blacked boots, playing accordions – no good will come of it!'

'Well, of course, if they do that, it will certainly not be much good,' observed Stolz. 'But why shouldn't you open a school in your village?'

'Isn't it a bit too soon?' said Oblomov. 'Literacy is harmful to the peasant: educate him and for all you know he may not want to plough any more.'

'But the peasants will be able to read how to plough their fields – you funny man! But, look here, you really ought to go to your estate this year.'

'Yes, that's true, but, you see, my plan isn't quite ready yet. . . .' Oblomov observed timidly.

'You don't want any plan!' said Stolz. 'All you have to do is to go there – you'll see on the spot what has to be done. You've been working on this plan for years: isn't it finished yet? What do you do?'

'My dear fellow, as though I have only the estate to worry about! What about my other misfortune?'

'What's that?'

'They're driving me out of my flat.'

'Driving you out?'

'Yes, they just told me to clear out, and they seem to mean it.'

'Well, what about it?'

'What about it? I've worn myself to a shadow worrying about it. I'm all alone, and there's this and that to be seen to, check the accounts, pay the bills, and then there's the moving! I'm spending a terrible amount of money and I'm hanged if I know what on! Before I know where I am, I shall be left penniless!'

'What a pampered fellow you are – can't bring yourself to move to a new flat!' Stolz said in surprise. 'Talking of money – how much money have you got on you? Let me have five hundred roubles, please. I must send it off at once. I'll get it from our office to-morrow – –'

'Wait, let me think! I received a thousand roubles from the estate the other day, and now there's left – wait a minute – –'

Oblomov began rummaging in the drawers.

'Here – ten, twenty, two hundred roubles – and here's another twenty. There were some coppers here – Zakhar! Zakhar!'

Zakhar, as usual, jumped off the stove and came in.

'Where are the twenty copecks I put on the table yesterday?'

'You keep on harping on the twenty copecks, sir! I've already told you that there were no twenty copecks on the table.'

'Of course there were! The change from the oranges.'

'You must have given it to somebody and forgotten all about it, sir,' said Zakhar, turning to the door.

Stolz laughed.

'Oh, you Oblomovs!' he upbraided them. 'Don't know how much money you have in your pockets!'

'And didn't you give some money to Mr Tarantyev, sir?' Zakhar reminded Oblomov.

'Yes, yes, of course,' Oblomov said, turning to Stolz. 'Tarantyev took ten roubles. I forgot all about it.'

'Why do you receive that brute?' Stolz observed.

'Receive him, sir?' Zakhar intervened. 'Why, he comes here as if it was his own house or a pub. Took the master's shirt and waistcoat, he did, and we never saw 'em again! This morning he came for a dress-coat, if you please. Wanted to put it on at once, he did! I wish, sir, you'd speak to him about it!'

'It's not your business, Zakhar!' Oblomov said sternly. 'Go back to your room.'

'Let's have a sheet of note-paper,' Stolz said. 'I must write a note to someone.'

'Zakhar, Mr Stolz wants paper; give him some,' said Oblomov.

'But there isn't any, sir,' Zakhar replied from the passage. 'You looked for it yourself this morning,' he added, without bothering to come in.

'Just a scrap of paper!' Stolz persisted.

Oblomov searched on the table; there wasn't a scrap.

'Give me your visiting card at least.'

'I haven't had any for ages,' said Oblomov.

'What is the matter with you?' Stolz asked ironically. 'And you're about to do something – you're writing a plan. Tell me, do you go out anywhere? Whom do you see?'

'Going out? Good Lord, no! I'm always at home. My plan does worry me, you know, and then there's the business of getting a new flat – thank goodness, Tarantyev promised to find something for me.'

'Does anyone come to see you?'

'Oh yes – Tarantyev, Alexeyev ... the doctor looked in this morning. Penkin, too, Sudbinsky, Volkov – –'

'I don't see any books in your room,' said Stolz.

'Here's one!' Oblomov observed, pointing to a book that lay on the table.

'What's this?' asked Stolz, glancing at the book. '*A Journey to Africa*. And the page you've stopped at has grown mouldy. Not a newspaper to be seen. Do you read the papers?'

'No, the print's too small – bad for the eyes, and there isn't really any need for it: if anything new happens, it's drummed into your ears all day long.'

'Good heavens, Ilya!' said Stolz, casting a surprised glance at Oblomov. 'What *do* you do? You just roll up and lie about like a piece of dough.'

'That's true enough, Andrey,' Oblomov answered sadly, 'just like a piece of dough.'

'But to be conscious of something does not excuse it, does it?'

'No, but I merely answered your question; I'm not justifying myself,' Oblomov replied with a sigh.

'But you must rouse yourself from your sleep.'

'I've tried, but failed, and now – what for? There is nothing to rouse me, my heart is at rest, my mind is peacefully asleep!' he concluded with a touch of bitterness. 'Don't let us talk about it. ... Better tell me where you have come from.'

'Kiev. In another fortnight I'll be going abroad. Come with me.'

'Very well – perhaps I will,' Oblomov decided.

'Well then, sit down and write the application for your passport and to-morrow you can hand it in.'

'To-morrow!' Oblomov cried, startled. 'You people are always in such a hurry, as though someone were driving you! We'll think it over and discuss it and then we shall see. Perhaps it would be best to go to the estate first and abroad – afterwards.'

'But why afterwards? Didn't the doctor tell you to? First of all you must get rid of your fat, of your bodily heaviness, then your spirit won't be sleepy, either. You need both physical and mental gymnastics.'

'No, Andrey, all that is sure to tire me: my health is bad. No, you'd better leave me and go alone.'

Stolz looked at the recumbent Oblomov, and Oblomov looked at him. Stolz shook his head, and Oblomov sighed.

'I suppose you're too lazy to live,' Stolz said.

'Well, I suppose I am, Andrey.'

Andrey was trying hard to think how he could touch him to the quick, if indeed anything could affect him any more, and meanwhile he scrutinized him in silence and suddenly burst out laughing.

'Why have you one woollen stocking and one cotton stocking on?' he suddenly remarked, pointing to Oblomov's feet. 'And your shirt is inside out, too!'

Oblomov looked at his feet, then at his shirt.

'So they are,' he confessed, looking put out. 'That Zakhar is the limit! You wouldn't believe how he tires me out! He argues, he is rude, and he never attends to his business.'

'Oh, Ilya, Ilya!' said Stolz. 'No, I can't leave you like that. In another week you won't know yourself. I'll tell you what I am going to do with you and myself this evening, and now get dressed! You wait; I'll shake you up! Zakhar!' he shouted, 'Mr Oblomov's clothes!'

'But where are we going – good Lord! Tarantyev and Alexeyev are coming to dine with me, and then we wanted to – –'

'Zakhar,' Stolz went on, without listening to him, 'fetch the clothes.'

'Yes, sir, but let me clean the boots, first,' Zakhar said readily.

'What? Don't you clean the boots before five o'clock?'

'They're cleaned all right, sir. I've cleaned them last week, but Master hasn't been out so they've lost their shine again.'

'Never mind, fetch them as they are. Take my trunk into the drawing-room; I'll stay here. I'm going to dress now and you, Ilya, get ready, too. We'll have dinner somewhere on the way, and then we'll call at two or three places and – –'

'But, look here, don't be in such a rush – wait a minute – let's think it over first – I haven't shaved – –'

'There's no need to think and scratch your head. ... You'll shave on the way: I'll take you to a hairdresser's.'

'But where are we going to?' Oblomov cried mournfully. 'Do I know the people? What an idea! I'd better call on Ivan Gerasimovich. I haven't seen him for three days.'

'Who is this Ivan Gerasimovich?'

'He was at the same office as I.'

'Oh, the grey-headed administrative official. What do you see in him? What makes you wish to waste your time with a block-head like that?'

'How harshly you speak of people sometimes, Andrey. Really! He's a nice man, though he doesn't wear shirts of Dutch linen!'

'What do you do there? What do you talk to him about?' asked Stolz.

'Well, you know, everything at his place is so nice and cosy. The rooms are small, the sofas so deep that you sink into them and can't be seen. The windows are covered with ivy and cactus, there are more than a dozen canaries, three dogs – such affec-tionate creatures! There is always some snack on the table. The prints on the walls are all of family scenes. You come and you don't want to go away. You sit without thinking or worrying about anything, you know there is a man beside you who – though perhaps far from intelligent, for it would be a waste of time to exchange ideas with him – is unsophisticated, kind-hearted, hospitable, without pretensions, a man who would never dream of insulting you behind your back!'

'But what do you do there?'

'What do we do? Well, you see, as soon as I come we sit down on sofas opposite each other with our feet up – he smokes – –'

'And you?'

'I also smoke and listen to the song of the canaries. Then Marfa brings in the *samovar*.'

'Tarantyev, Ivan Gerasimovich!' said Stolz, shrugging his shoulders. 'Well, come on and dress quickly,' he hurried him.

'Tell Tarantyev when he comes,' he added, addressing Zak-har, 'that we are dining out and that Mr Oblomov will be dining out all summer, and he will be too busy in the autumn to see him.'

'I'll tell him that, sir. Don't worry, I shan't forget,' replied Zakhar. 'And what shall I do with the dinner, sir?'

'Eat it with anyone you like.'

'Yes, sir.'

Ten minutes later Stolz came out of the drawing-room dressed, shaven, and with his hair brushed. Oblomov was sitting on his bed, looking melancholy and slowly buttoning his shirt and struggling with the buttonholes. Zakhar knelt before him on one knee, holding an unpolished boot in his hand as if it were some dish and waiting for his master to finish buttoning his shirt.

'You haven't put your boots on yet!' Stolz said in surprise. 'Well, come on, Ilya, hurry up!'

'But where are we going? And whatever for?' Oblomov cried miserably. 'I have seen it all before! I'm afraid I'm no longer interested – I don't want to – –'

'Come on! Come on!' Stolz hurried him.

4

ALTHOUGH it was already late, they managed to make a business call, then Stolz took an owner of some gold-mines to dinner, then they went to the latter's country house for tea. There they found a large company, and after his complete seclusion Oblomov found himself in a crowd. They returned home late at night.

The next day and the day after, the same thing happened, and a whole week passed by in a flash. Oblomov protested, complained, argued, but he was overborne and followed his friend everywhere. One morning, when they came home late, he protested especially against this sort of life.

'All day long,' Oblomov muttered, putting on his dressing-gown, 'you don't take off your boots: my feet are throbbing! I dislike this Petersburg life of yours!' he went on, lying down on the sofa.

'What sort of life do you like?' asked Stolz.

'Not this sort.'

'What is it you dislike particularly?'

'Everything – this constant rushing about, this eternal interplay of petty passions, greed especially, the eagerness with which they try to get the better of one another, the scandalmongering, the gossip, the way they look you up and down; listening to their talk makes your head swim and you go silly. They look so dignified and intelligent, but all you hear them say is, "This one has been given something and that one has got a big Government contract. ..." "Heavens above, what for?" someone cries. "So-and-so lost all his money at cards at the club last night; so-and-so takes three hundred thousand for his dowry!" The whole thing is boring, boring, boring! Where is the real man here? Where is his integrity? Where has he disappeared? How has he managed to squander his great gifts on trifles?'

'But society has to be occupied by something or other,' said Stolz. 'Everyone has his own interests. That's life. ...'

'Society! I suppose, Andrey, you are sending me into society on purpose so as to discourage me from going there. Life! A fine

172

life! What is one to look for there? Intellectual interests? True feeling? Just see whether you can find the centre round which all this revolves; there is no such centre, there is nothing deep, nothing vital. All these society people are dead, they are all asleep, they are worse than I! What is their aim in life? They do not lie about, they scurry to and fro every day like flies, but to what purpose? You come into a drawing-room and you cannot help admiring the symmetrical way in which the visitors are seated – at the card tables! It is indeed an excellent purpose in life! A wonderful example for a mind looking for something exciting. Aren't they all dead men? Aren't they asleep all their life sitting there like that? Why am I more to blame because I lie about at home and do not infect the minds of others with my talk of aces and knaves?'

'This is all old stuff,' Stolz remarked. 'It's been said a thousand times before. You've nothing newer, have you?'

'Well, and what about the best representatives of our younger generation? What do they do? Aren't they asleep even while walking or driving along the Nevsky, or dancing? What a continual, futile shuffling and reshuffling of days! But observe the pride and wonderful dignity, the supercilious look with which they regard everyone who is not dressed or of the same rank and social position as they. And the poor wretches imagine that they are above the common people! "We," they say, "occupy the best posts in the Civil Service, we sit in the front row of the stalls, we go to Prince N.'s balls where no other people are invited." And when they come together, they get drunk and fight like savages. Why, are these alive, wide-awake people? And it isn't just the young people, either. Take a look at the older people. They meet, entertain each other at meals, but there is no real good-fellowship, no real hospitality, no mutual sympathy. If they meet at a dinner or a party, it is just the same as at their office – coldly, without a spark of gaiety, to boast of their chef or their drawing-room, and then to jeer at each other in a discreet aside, to trip one another up. The other day at dinner I honestly did not know where to look and wished I could hide under the table, when they began tearing to shreds the reputations of those who did not happen to be there: so-and-so is an ass, so-and-so is a mean scoundrel; that one is a thief, and another one is ridiculous – a regular massacre! And as they said it, they looked at each other as if to say, "Just go out of the door, my dear fellow, and we'll do the same to you." Why, then, do they meet if they are like that? Why do they press each other's hands so warmly?

173

No genuine laughter, no glimmer of sympathy! They are all out to get someone of high rank, someone with a name, to come to their place. "So-and-so has called on me," they boast afterwards. "I've been to see so-and-so." What kind of life is that? I don't want it. What can I get out of it? What will I learn there?'

'Do you know, Ilya,' said Stolz, 'you talk like the ancients: they all used to write like that in old books. However, that, too, is a good thing: at least you talk and don't sleep. Well, what else? Go on.'

'Why go on? You have a good look: not a single person here looks fresh and healthy.'

'It's the climate,' Stolz interrupted. 'Your face, too, looks puffy and you're not running about – you lie in bed all day.'

'Not one of them has clear, calm eyes,' Oblomov went on. 'They all infect each other by a sort of tormenting anxiety and melancholy; they are all painfully searching for something. And if only it were for truth or their own and other people's welfare – but no, they turn pale when they learn of a friend's success. One man's only worry in the world is to be present in court to-morrow; his case has been dragging on for five years, the other side is winning, and for five years he has had only one desire, one thought in his head: to trip up the other man and erect his own welfare on his ruin. To go regularly to court for five years and to sit and wait in the corridor – that is the aim and the ideal of his life! One man is depressed because he has to go to his office every day and stay there for five hours, and another man is sighing deeply because such bliss has not fallen to his lot – –'

'You're a philosopher, Ilya,' said Stolz. 'Everyone is worrying, you alone want nothing.'

'That sallow-faced gentleman in glasses,' Oblomov went on, 'kept asking me if I had read the speech of some French deputy, and glared at me when I told him that I did not read the papers. And he kept talking and talking about Louis-Philippe as though he were his own father. Then he kept pestering me to tell him why the French ambassador had left Rome. Do you expect me to load myself every day with a fresh supply of world news and then to shout about it all week till it runs out? To-day Mahomet-Ali dispatched a ship to Constantinople and he is racking his brains wondering why. To-morrow Don Carlos has a setback and he is terribly worried. Here they are digging a canal, there a detachment of troops has been sent to the East: good Lord, it's war! He looks terribly upset, he runs, he shouts, as though an army was marching against him personally. They argue, they discuss everything from every possible point of view, but they are bored, they are not really interested in the whole thing: you can see they are fast asleep in spite of their shouts! The whole thing does not concern them; it is as if they walked about in borrowed hats. They have nothing to do, so they squander their energies all over the place without trying to aim at anything in particular. The universality of their interests merely conceals emptiness and a complete absence of sympathy with everything! To choose the modest path of hard work and follow it, to dig a deep channel – is dull and unostentatious, and knowing everything would be of no use there, and there would be no one to impress!'

'Well, Ilya,' said Stolz, 'you and I have not scattered our energies in all directions, have we? Where is our modest path of hard work?'

Oblomov suddenly fell silent.

'Oh, I've only to finish – er – my plan,' he said. 'Anyway, why should I worry about them?' he added with vexation after a pause. 'I'm not interfering with them. I'm not after anything. All I say is that I can't see that their life is normal. No, that is not life, but a distortion of the norm, of the ideal of life, which nature demands that man should regard as his aim.'

'What is this ideal, this norm of life?'

Oblomov made no answer.

'Now, tell me,' Stolz went on, 'what sort of life would you have planned for yourself?'

'I have already planned it.'

'Oh? Tell me, what is it?'

'What is it?' said Oblomov, turning over on his back and staring at the ceiling. 'Well, I'd go to the country.'

'Why don't you?'

'My plan isn't ready. Besides, I wouldn't have gone by myself, but with my wife.'

'Oh, I see! Well, why not? What are you waiting for? In another three or four years nobody will marry you.'

'Well, it can't be helped,' said Oblomov, sighing. 'I'm too poor to marry.'

'Good heavens, and what about Oblomovka? Three hundred serfs!'

'What about it? That isn't enough to live on with a wife.'

'Not enough for two people to live on?'

'But what about the children?'

'If you give them a decent education, they'll be able to earn their own living. You must know how to start them in the right direction – –'

'No, sir, it's no use making workmen out of gentlemen,' Oblomov interrupted dryly. 'Besides, even if we disregard the question of children, we shouldn't be just by ourselves. Alone with your wife is only a manner of speaking. Actually, hundreds of women will invade your house as soon as you are married. Look at any family you like: female relatives, housekeepers, and if they don't live in the house, they come every day to coffee and to dinner. How is one to keep such an establishment with three hundred serfs?'

'All right. Now, suppose you were given another three hundred thousand – what would you have done then?' Stolz asked, his curiosity aroused.

'I'd mortgage it at once and live on the interest.'

'But you wouldn't get a high enough interest. Why not invest your money in some company – ours, for instance?'

'No, sir, you won't catch me doing that.'

'Why not? Wouldn't you trust even me?'

'Certainly not. It isn't a question of not trusting you, but anything might happen: suppose your company went bankrupt and I was left without a penny! A bank is a different matter.'

'Very well. What would you do then?'

'I'd move into a comfortable new house. There would be good neighbours living in the vicinity – you, for instance. But no, you couldn't stay in one place long, could you?'

'Could you? Wouldn't you go on a journey at all?'

'Never.'

'Why, then, are they taking so much trouble building railways, steamers, if the ideal of life is to stay in the same place? Let's send in a proposal for them to stop, Ilya. We aren't going anywhere, are we?'

'There are lots of people who are – all sorts of agents, managers, merchants, civil servants, travellers with no home of their own. Let them travel as much as they like.'

'But who are you?'

Oblomov made no answer.

'To what category of people do you think you belong?'

'Ask Zakhar,' said Oblomov.

Stolz carried out Oblomov's wish literally.

'Zakhar!' he shouted.

Zakhar came in, looking sleepy.

176

'Who is it lying there?' asked Stolz.

Zakhar woke up suddenly and cast a suspicious, sidelong glance at Stolz, then at Oblomov.

'Who is it, sir? Why, don't you see?'

'I don't,' said Stolz.

'Good gracious! Why, it's the master, Ilya Ilyich.'

He grinned.

'All right, you can go.'

'The master!' Stolz repeated and burst out laughing.

'Oh, well,' Oblomov corrected with vexation, 'a gentleman, then.'

'No, no! You're a master!' Stolz continued, laughing.

'What's the difference?' said Oblomov. 'Gentleman is the same as master.'

'A gentleman,' Stolz defined, 'is the sort of master who puts on his socks and takes off his boots himself.'

'Yes, an Englishman does it himself because in England they haven't got many servants, but a Russian – –'

'Go on painting the ideal of your life for me. Well, you have your good friends around you: what next? How would you spend your days?'

'Well, I'd get up in the morning,' began Oblomov, putting his hands behind his neck, and his face assuming an expression of repose (in his thoughts he was already in the country). 'The weather is lovely, the sky is as blue as blue can be, not a cloud,' he said. 'The balcony on one side of the house in my plan faces east towards the garden and the fields, and the other side towards the village. While waiting for my wife to waken, I'd put on my dressing-gown and go for a walk in the garden, for a breath of fresh morning air. There I'd already find the gardener and we'd water the flowers together and prune the bushes and trees. I'd make a bouquet for my wife. Then I'd have my bath or go for a swim in the river. On my return, I'd find the balcony door open. My wife is wearing her morning dress and a light cap which looks as if it might be blown off any moment. ... She is waiting for me. "Tea's ready," she says. What a kiss! What tea! What an easy-chair! I sit down at the table: rusks, cream, fresh butter. ...'

'Well?'

'Well, then, having put on a loose coat or some sort of tunic and with my arm round my wife's waist, we walk down an endless dark avenue of trees; we walk along quietly, dreamily, in silence or thinking aloud, day-dreaming, counting the moments of happiness as the beating of one's pulse; we listen to the throbbing of our heart, we look for sympathy in nature and – imperceptibly – we come to the river, to the fields. ... There is scarcely a ripple on the river, the ears of corn wave in the light breeze – it is hot – we get into a boat, my wife steers, scarcely raising an oar. ...'

'Why, you're a poet, Ilya!' Stolz interrupted.

'Yes, a poet in life, because life is poetry. People are free to distort it, if they like! ... Then we might go into a hot-house,' Oblomov went on, carried away by the ideal of happiness he was depicting.

He was extracting from his imagination ready-made scenes, which he had drawn long ago, and that was why he spoke with such animation and without stopping.

'... to have a look at the peaches and grapes, to tell them what we want for the table, then to go back, have a light lunch and wait for visitors. ... Meanwhile there would be a note for my wife from Maria Petrovna, with a book and music, or somebody would send us a pineapple as a present, or a huge watermelon would ripen in my hot-house and I would send it to a dear friend for next day's dinner, and go there myself. ... In the meantime things are humming in the kitchen, the chef, in a snow-white cap and apron, is terribly busy, putting one saucepan on the stove, taking off another, stirring something in a third, making pastry, throwing away some water. ... A clatter of knives – the vegetables are being chopped – ice-cream is being made. ... I like to look into the kitchen before dinner, take the lid off a saucepan and have a sniff, to see them rolling up pasties, whipping cream. Then lie down on the sofa; my wife is reading something new aloud – we stop and discuss it. ... But the visitors arrive, you and your wife, for instance.'

'Oh, so you've married me, too, have you?'

'Certainly! Two or three friends more, all familiar faces. We resume the conversation where we had left off the day before – we crack jokes or there is an interval of eloquent silence – of reverie, not because we are worried by some High Court case, but because all our desires have been fully satisfied and we are plunged into a mood of thoughtful enjoyment. ... You will not hear someone delivering a violent philippic against an absent friend, you will not catch a glance that promises the same to you the moment you leave the house. You will not sit down to dinner with anyone you do not like. The eyes of your companions are full of sympathy, their jokes are full of sincere and kindly

laughter. ... Everything is sincere! Everyone looks and says
what he feels! After dinner there is mocha coffee, a Havana
cigar on the verandah. ...'

'You are describing to me the same sort of thing our fathers
and grandfathers used to do.'

'No, I'm not,' Oblomov replied, almost offended. 'How can
you say it's the same thing? Would my wife be making jams or
pickling mushrooms? Would she be measuring yarn and sorting
out home-spun linen? Would she box her maids' ears? You heard
what I said, didn't you? Music, books, piano, elegant furniture?'

'Well, and you?'

'I should not be reading last year's papers, travelling in an
unwieldy old carriage, or eating noodle soup and roast goose,
but I should have trained my chef in the English Club or at a
foreign embassy,'

'And then?'

'Then, when the heat abated, I'd send a cart with the *samovar* and dessert to the birch copse or else to the hay-field, spread
rugs on the newly mown grass between the ricks, and be bliss-
fully happy there till it was time for the cold soup and beefsteak.
The peasants are returning from the fields with scythes on their
shoulders, a hay-cart crawls past loaded so high that it conceals
the cart and the horse from view, a peasant's cap with flowers
and a child's head sticking out from the hay on top; and there
comes a crowd of women, barefoot and with sickles, singing at
the top of their voices. ... Suddenly they catch sight of their
master and his guests, grow quiet, and bow low. One of them,
a young girl with a sunburnt neck, bare arms, and timidly lowered, sly eyes, pretends to avoid her master's caress, but is really
happy – hush! my wife mustn't see it!'

Oblomov and Stolz burst out laughing.

'It is damp in the fields,' Oblomov concluded. 'it's dark; a
mist, like an inverted sea, hangs over the rye; a shiver passes
over the flanks of the horses and they paw the ground; it is time
to go home. In the house lights are already burning; knives are
clattering in the kitchen; a frying-pan full of mushrooms, cutlets, berries – music in the drawing-room – *Casta diva, Casta
diva!* ...' Oblomov burst into song. 'I can't think of *Casta diva*
without wishing to sing it,' he said, singing the beginning of the
cavatina. 'How that woman cried her heart out! How full of
sadness those sounds are! And no one around her knows anything. ... She is alone. ... Her secret oppresses her; she en-
trusts it to the moon. ...'

'You are fond of that aria? That's fine! Olga Ilyinsky sings it beautifully. I'll introduce you to her. She has a lovely voice and she sings wonderfully. And she herself is such a charming child! But I'm afraid I may be a little partial: I have a soft spot in my heart for her. ... However,' he added, 'go on, please.'

'Well,' Oblomov went on, 'what else is there? That is all. The visitors go to their rooms in the cottages and pavilions, and on the following day they disperse in different directions; some go fishing, some shooting, and some simply sit still.'

'Simply? Have they nothing in their hands?' asked Stolz.

'What would you like them to have? A handkerchief, maybe. Now, wouldn't you like to live like that?' asked Oblomov. 'It is real life, isn't it?'

'Always like that?' asked Stolz.

'Yes, till old age – till the grave. That is life!'

'No, that isn't life!'

'No? Why not? Did I leave anything out? Just think, you wouldn't see a single pale, worried face, no troubles, no questions about the high court, the stock exchange, shares, reports, the minister's reception, ranks, larger allowances for expenses. Instead, everything you heard people say would be sincere! You would never have to move to a new flat – that alone is worth something! And that isn't life?'

'No, it isn't!' Stolz repeated obstinately.

'What, then, is this life in your opinion?'

'It is – –' Stolz pondered for a while, trying to find a name for this sort of life – 'it is a sort of – Oblomovitis!' he said at last.

'Oblomovitis!' Oblomov repeated slowly, surprised at this strange definition and scanning it syllable by syllable. 'Oblomovitis – ob-lo-mo-vi-tis!'

He gave Stolz a strange and intent look.

'And what is the ideal of life, in your opinion, then? What is not Oblomovitis?' he asked timidly and without enthusiasm. 'Doesn't everybody strive to achieve the very thing I dream of? Why,' he added, 'isn't the whole purpose of all your rushing about, all your passions, wars, trade, and politics to attain rest – reach this ideal of a lost paradise?'

'Your utopia, too, is a typical Oblomov utopia,' replied Stolz.

'But everyone seeks peace and rest!' Oblomov defended himself.

'No, not all. Ten years ago you, too, were looking for something different.'

180

'What was I looking for?' Oblomov asked in perplexity, lost in thoughts of his past.

'Think! Try to remember! Where are your books, your translations?'

'Zakhar put them away somewhere,' replied Oblomov. 'In one of the corners of this room, I suppose.'

'In a corner!' Stolz said, reproachfully. 'In the same corner, I suppose, as your plan to serve Russia so long as you have any strength left, because Russia needs hands and brains for the exploitation of her inexhaustible resources (your own words!); to work so that rest should be the sweeter, and to rest means to live a different and more artistic, more elegant kind of life, the life of poets and artists! Has Zakhar put away all those plans in a corner too? Do you remember telling me that after you had finished with your studies you wanted to visit foreign countries so as to be able to appreciate and love your own country the more? "All life is work and thought," you used to repeat then, "obscure, unknown but incessant work – to die in the consciousness that you have performed your task." Didn't you say that? In what corner have you put that away?'

'Yes, yes,' Oblomov said, following anxiously every word of Stolz's. 'I remember I did actually – I believe – of course,' he went on, suddenly remembering the past, 'you and I, Andrey, were planning first to travel all over Europe, walk through Switzerland, scorch our feet on Vesuvius, go down to Herculaneum. We nearly went off our heads! Oh, the stupidities – –'

'Stupidities!' Stolz repeated reproachfully. 'Wasn't it you who said with tears in your eyes, as you looked at the prints of Raphael's Madonnas, Correggio's Night, Apollo Belvedere: "Good Lord, shall I never be able to see the originals and be struck dumb with awe at the thought that I am standing before the works of Michelangelo and Titian, and treading the soil of Rome? Shall I never in all my life see those myrtles, cypresses, and citrons in their native land instead of in hot-houses? Shall I never breathe the air of Italy and feast my eyes on her azure skies?" And what magnificent intellectual fireworks you used to let off in those days! Stupidities!'

'Yes, yes, I remember,' Oblomov said, going over the past in his mind. 'You took me by the hand and said, "Let us vow to see it all before we die." '

'I remember,' Stolz went on, 'how once you brought me a translation from a book by Jean-Baptiste Say which you dedicated to me on my name-day. I have it still. And how you used

181

to closet yourself with the teacher of mathematics because you were determined to find out why you had to know all about circles and squares, but threw it up half-way and never found out! You began to learn English and – never did learn it! And when I drew up a plan for a journey abroad and asked you to take a course at the German universities with me, you jumped to your feet, embraced me, and solemnly held out your hand to me: "I'm yours, Andrey, and I will go with you everywhere " – those were your very words. You always were a bit of an actor. Well, Ilya? I've been abroad twice, and after all the things I learned at our universities, I humbly sat on the students' benches in Bonn, Jena, and Erlangen, and then got to know Europe like my own estate. But after all a journey abroad is a luxury and not everybody can afford it – but Russia? I have travelled all over Russia. I work – –'

'But one day you will stop working, won't you?' Oblomov remarked.

'I shall never stop. Why should I?'

'When you have doubled your capital,' said Oblomov.

'I won't stop even when I have quadrupled it.'

'So why,' said Oblomov after a pause, 'do you work so hard if it is not your intention to get enough money to last you your lifetime and then retire to the country for a well-earned rest?'

'Oblomovitis in the country!' said Stolz.

'Or achieve a high position in society by your work as a civil servant and then enjoy a well-earned rest in honourable in-activity. ...'

'Oblomovitis in Petersburg!' Stolz retorted.

'In that case when are you going to live?' Oblomov replied, vexed by Stolz's remarks. 'Why work hard all your life?'

'For the sake of the work itself and nothing else. Work means everything to me, it is the very breath of life – of my life, at any rate. You have banished work from your life, and what is it like? I'll try to raise you up, perhaps for the last time. If after this you still go on sitting here with the Tarantyevs and Alexe-yevs, you will be done for and become a burden even to your-self. Now or never!' he concluded.

Oblomov listened, looking at him with anxious eyes. His friend seemed to have held out a mirror to him, and he was frightened when he recognized himself.

'Don't scold me, Andrey,' he began with a sigh, 'but help me rather! I'm worried to death about it myself, and had you seen me to-day and heard me bewailing my fate digging my own

182

grave, you would not have had the heart to reproach me. I know and understand everything, but I have no strength and no will of my own. Give me some of your will and your intelligence and lead me where you like. I may perhaps follow you, but alone I shall not stir from the place. You are right: it is now or never. In another year it will be too late.'

'Is this you, Ilya?' Andrey said. 'I remember you such a slim, lively boy, walking every day from Prechistenka to Kudrino – in the garden there – You have not forgotten the two sisters, have you? You have not forgotten Rousseau, Schiller, Goethe, Byron, whose works you used to take them, taking away from them the novels of Genlis and Cottin – how you used to give yourself airs before them and how you wanted to improve their taste?'

Oblomov jumped off the sofa.

'Do you remember that, too, Andrey? Of course, I dreamed with them, whispered hopes of the future, made plans, developed ideas and – feelings, too, without your knowledge so that you should not make fun of me. It all died there, and was never repeated again! And where did it all disappear to? Why has it become extinguished? I can't understand it! There were no storms or shocks in my life; I never lost anything; there is no load on my conscience: it is clear as glass; no blow has killed ambition in me, and goodness only knows why everything has been utterly wasted!'

He sighed.

'You see, Andrey, the trouble is that no devastating or redeeming fires have ever burnt in my life. It never was like a morning which gradually fills with light and colour and then turns, like other people's, into a blazing, hot day, when everything seethes and shimmers in the bright noonday sun, and then gradually grows paler and more subdued, fading naturally into the evening twilight. No! My life began by flickering out. It may sound strange but it is so. From the very first moment I became conscious of myself, I felt that I was already flickering out. I began to flicker out over the writing of official papers at the office; I went on flickering out when I read truths in books which I did not know how to apply in life, when I sat with friends listening to rumours, gossip, jeering, spiteful, cold, and empty chatter, and watching friendships kept up by meetings that were without aim or affection; I was flickering out and wasting my energies with Minna on whom I spent more than half of my income, imagining that I loved her; I was flickering out when I walked idly and dejectedly along Nevsky Avenue among people in raccoon coats and beaver collars – at parties, on reception days, where I was welcomed with open arms as a fairly eligible young man; I was flickering out and wasting my life and mind on trifles moving from town to some country house, and from the country house to Gorokhovaya, fixing the arrival of spring by the fact that lobsters and oysters had appeared in the shops, of autumn and winter by the special visiting days, of summer by the fêtes, and life in general by lazy and comfortable somnolence like the rest. ... Even ambition – what was it wasted on? To order clothes at a famous tailor's? To get an invitation to a famous house? To shake hands with Prince P.? And ambition is the salt of life! Where has it gone to? Either I have not understood this sort of life or it is utterly worthless; but I did not know of a better one. No one showed it to me. You appeared and disappeared like a bright and swiftly moving comet, and I forgot it all and went on flickering out. ...'

Stolz no longer replied to Oblomov with light mockery. He listened in gloomy silence.

'You said just now that my face had lost its freshness and was flabby,' Oblomov continued. 'Yes, I am an old shabby, worn-out coat, but not because of the climate or hard work, but because for twelve years the light has been shut up within me and, unable to find an outlet, it merely consumed itself inside its prison house and was extinguished without breaking out into the open. And so twelve years have passed, my dear Andrey: I did not want to wake up any more.'

'But why didn't you break out? Why didn't you run away somewhere, but preferred to perish in silence?' Stolz asked impatiently.

'Where to?'

'Where to? Why not to the Volga with your peasants? There is more life there, you could have found all sorts of interests there, a purpose, work! I'd have gone to Siberia, to Sitkha.'

'Well,' Oblomov observed dejectedly, 'the remedies you prescribe are rather drastic, aren't they? Besides, I'm not the only one. There's Mikhailov, Petrov, Semyonov, Alexeyev, Stepanov ... too many to count: our name is legion!'

Stolz was still under the influence of Oblomov's confession and said nothing. Then he sighed.

'Yes, much water has flowed past,' he said. 'I shan't leave you like that. I'll take you away from here, first abroad, then to the country. You will grow slimmer, you will recover from your depression, and then, we will find something for you to do. ...'

'Yes, let's go away somewhere!' Oblomov cried.

'To-morrow we will apply for a passport and then we'll start packing. I won't leave you alone – do you hear, Ilya?'

'It's always to-morrow with you!' Oblomov replied, as though coming down from the clouds.

'And you would like "not to put off till to-morrow what can be done to-day", would you? What energy! It is too late to-day,' Stolz added, 'but in a fortnight's time we shall be far from here.'

'Good Lord, man, what's your hurry?' Oblomov said. 'In a fortnight's time! A bit sudden, isn't it? Let me think it over carefully and get everything ready. We shall have to get a carriage of some sort – in three months perhaps.'

'A carriage! What will you be thinking of next! As far as the frontier we shall travel in a post-chaise or by steamer to Lubeck, whichever is more convenient; and abroad there are railways in many places.'

'And my flat, and Zakhar, and Oblomovka?' Oblomov defended himself. 'I must see to it all.'

'Oblomovitis! Oblomovitis!' said Stolz, laughing, and he took his candle and, bidding Oblomov good night, went to his room. 'Now or never, remember!' he added, turning to Oblomov before shutting the door behind him.

5

'NOW OR NEVER!' the stern words appeared before Oblomov as soon as he woke in the morning. He got up, walked up and down the room a few times, and glanced into the drawing-room; Stolz sat writing.

'Zakhar!' he called.

He heard no sound of Zakhar jumping off the stove. Zakhar did not come: Stolz had sent him to the post-office.

Oblomov went up to his dusty table, sat down, picked up a pen, dipped it in the inkwell, but there was no ink; he looked for paper, there was none, either. He sank into thought and began absent-mindedly writing in the dust with a finger, then he looked at what he had written – it was *Oblomovitis*. He quickly wiped it off with his sleeve. He had dreamt of that word at night written in letters of fire on the walls as at Belshazzar's feast. Zakhar came back and glared dully at his master, astonished

that he should have got out of bed. In this vacant look of astonishment he read: 'Oblomovitis.'

'A single word,' Oblomov reflected, 'but how – venomous it is!'

Zakhar, as was his wont, took up the comb, brush, and towel
and went up to do his master's hair.

'Go to hell!' Oblomov said angrily, knocking the brush out
of Zakhar's hand, while Zakhar dropped the comb himself.

'Aren't you going to lie down again, sir?' Zakhar asked. 'I
could make the bed.'

'Fetch me some paper and ink,' replied Oblomov.

He was pondering over the words 'Now or never!' As he listened intently to this desperate appeal of reason and energy, he
realized and carefully weighed up the amount of will-power he
still had left and where he could apply and what use he could
make of that meagre remnant. After thinking it over painfully,
he seized the pen and pulled a book out of the corner, wishing to
read, write, and think over in one hour what he had not read,
written, and thought over in ten years. What was he to do now?
Go forward or stay where he was? This typically Oblomov question was of deeper significance to him than Hamlet's. To go forward meant to throw the capacious dressing-gown not only off
his shoulders but also from his heart and mind, to sweep the
dust and cobwebs from his eyes as well as from the walls, and to
recover his sight!

What was the first step towards it? What had he to start
with? 'I·don't know, I can't – no! – I'm trying to deceive myself, I do know and – besides, Stolz is here and he will tell me at
once.' But what would he say? 'He would say that during the
week I should write detailed instructions to my agent and send
him to the country, mortgage Oblomovka, buy some more land,
send down a plan of the buildings to be erected, give up my flat,
take out a passport and go abroad for six months, get rid of my
superfluous fat, throw off my heaviness, refresh my soul with the
air of which I once dreamed with my friend, live without a dressing-gown, without Zakhar and Tarantyev, put on my socks and
take off my boots myself, sleep at night only, travel where everyone else is travelling, by rail or steamer, then – then – go to live
in Oblomovka, learn what sowing and harvesting means, why a
peasant is rich or poor; go out into the fields, journey to the district town for the elections, visit the factory, the mill, the landing
stage. And at the same time read the newspapers, books, and
worry about why the English have sent a man-of-war to the Far
East. … That's what he would say! That is what going forward

means. And so all my life! Good-bye, poetic ideal of life! That is a sort of smithy, and not life; it's continuous flame, heat, noise, clatter – When is one to live? Had one not better stay? To stay meant to wear your shirt inside out, to listen to Zakhar jumping off the stove, to dine with Tarantyev, to think as little as possible about everything, not to finish *The Journey to Africa*, to grow peacefully old in the house of Tarantyev's friend. ...

'Now or never!' 'To be or not to be!' – Oblomov raised himself from his chair a little, but failing to find his slippers with his feet at once, sat down again.

About a fortnight later Stolz left for England, having made Oblomov promise to come straight to Paris. Oblomov had even got his passport ready, he had even ordered a coat for travelling and bought a cap. That was how far things had advanced. Zakhar had been arguing with a wise air that it was enough to order one pair of boots and have the other re-soled. Oblomov had bought a blanket, a jersey, a travelling-bag, and was about to buy a bag for provisions when about a dozen people told him that one did not carry provisions abroad. Zakhar had been rushing about from one workshop and shop to another, perspiring copiously, and though he pocketed a good many five- and ten-copeck pieces out of the change in the shops, he cursed Stolz and all those who had invented travel.

'And what will he do there by himself?' he said in the shop. 'I hear that in them parts it's girls what attend on gentlemen. How can a girl pull off a gentleman's boots? And how is she going to put socks on the master's bare feet?'

He grinned so that his whiskers moved sideways, and shook his head. Oblomov was not too lazy to write down what he had to take with him and what had to be left at home. He asked Tarantyev to take the furniture and other things to his friend's house in Vyborg, to lock them up in three rooms and keep them there till his return from abroad. Oblomov's acquaintances were already saying – some incredulously, some laughingly, and some with a kind of alarm: 'He's going. Just fancy, Oblomov has actually budged from his place!'

But Oblomov did not go either after a month or after three months.

On the eve of his departure his lip became swollen during the night. 'A fly has bitten me,' he said. 'I can't possibly go on board ship with a lip like that!' and he decided to wait for the next ship.

It was already August. Stolz had been in Paris for some time,

187

writing furious letters to Oblomov, who did not reply. Why? Was it because the ink had gone dry in the inkwell and there was no paper? Or was it perhaps because *that* and *which* jostled each other too frequently in Oblomov's style? Or was it because, hearing the stern call: Now or never, Oblomov decided in favour of never and had relapsed into his recumbent position, and Zakhar was trying in vain to wake him?

No. His inkwell was full of ink: letters, papers, and even stamped paper, covered with his own handwriting, lay on his table. Having written several pages, he never once put *which* twice in the same sentence, he wrote freely and occasionally expressively and eloquently as 'in the days of yore' when he had dreamed with Stolz of a life of labour and travelling. He got up at seven, read, took books to a certain place. He did not look sleepy, tired, or bored. There was even a touch of colour in his face and a sparkle in his eyes – something like courage, or at any rate self-confidence. He never wore his dressing-gown: Tarantyev had taken it with him with the other things to his friend's. He read a book or wrote dressed in an ordinary coat, a light kerchief round his neck, his shirt-collar showed over his tie, and was white as snow. He went out in an excellently made frock-coat and an elegant hat. He looked cheerful. He hummed to himself. What was the matter? Now he was sitting at the window of his country villa (he was staying at a villa in the country a few miles from the town), a bunch of flowers lying by him. He was quickly finishing writing something, glancing continually over the top of the bushes at the path, and again writing hurriedly.

Suddenly the sand on the path crunched under light footsteps; Oblomov threw down the pen, grabbed the bunch of flowers, and rushed to the window.

'Is it you, Olga Sergeyevna?' he asked. 'I shan't be a minute!'

He seized his cap and cane, ran out through the gate, offered his arm to a beautiful woman, and disappeared with her in the woods, in the shade of enormous fir-trees.

Zakhar came out from some corner, followed him with his eyes, shut the door of the room, and went to the kitchen.

'Gone!' he said to Anisya.

'Will he be in to dinner?'

'I don't know, I'm sure,' Zakhar replied sleepily.

Zakhar was the same as ever: the same enormous side-whiskers, the same unshaven chin, the same grey waistcoat and tear in his coat, but he was married to Anisya, either because of a break with his lady-friend or just from conviction that a man ought to marry; he was married and, regardless of the proverb, he had not changed.

Stolz had introduced Oblomov to Olga and her aunt. When he brought Oblomov to her aunt's house for the first time, there were other visitors there. Oblomov felt depressed and ill at ease as usual. 'I wish I could take off my gloves,' he thought; 'it's so warm in the room. How I've grown out of it all!'

Stolz sat down beside Olga, who was sitting by herself under the lamp at some distance from the tea-table, leaning back in an arm-chair and showing little interest in what was going on around her. She was very glad to see Stolz; though her eyes did not glow, her cheeks were not flushed, an even, calm light spread over her face, and she smiled. She called him her friend; she liked him because he always made her laugh and did not let her be bored, but she was also a little afraid of him because she felt too much of a child in his company. When some question arose in her mind, or when she was puzzled by something, she did not at once decide to confide in him; he was too far ahead of her, too much above her, so that her vanity sometimes suffered from the realization of her immaturity and the difference in their ages and intelligence. Stolz, too, admired her disinterestedly as a lovely creature with a fragrant freshness of mind and feelings. He looked on her as on a charming child of great promise. Stolz, however, talked to her oftener and more readily than to other women, because, though unaware of it herself, her life was distinguished by the utmost simplicity and naturalness and, owing to her happy nature and her sensible and unsophisticated education, she did not shrink from expressing her thoughts, feelings, and desires without any trace of affectation, even in the tiniest movement of her eyes, her lips, and her hands. Quite likely she walked so confidently through life because she heard at times beside her the still more confident footsteps of her 'friend' whom she trusted and with whom she tried to keep in step. Be that as it may, there were few girls who possessed such a simplicity and spontaneity of opinions, words, and actions. You never read in her eyes: 'Now I will purse up my lips a little and try to look thoughtful – I look pretty like that. I'll glance over there and utter a little scream as though I were frightened, and they'll all run up to me at once. I'll sit down at the piano and show the tips of my feet.' There was not a trace of affectation, coquetry, falsity, tawdriness, or calculation about her! That was why hardly anyone but Stolz appreciated her and that was why she had sat through more than one mazurka alone without concealing her boredom; that was why the most gallant of the young men was silent in her presence, being at a loss what to say to her and how to say it. Some thought her simple, not very bright and not particularly profound because she did not overwhelm them with wise maxims about life and love or rapid, bold, and unexpected repartees or opinions on music and literature borrowed from books or overheard; she spoke little, and whatever she said was her own and not very important – so that the clever and dashing partners avoided her; on the other hand, those who were shy thought her too clever and were a little afraid of her. Stolz alone talked to her without stopping and never failed to make her laugh.

She was fond of music, but preferred to sing mostly to herself or to Stolz or to some schoolfriend; and, according to Stolz, she sang better than any professional singer. As soon as Stolz sat down beside her, she began laughing and her laughter was so melodious, so sincere, and so infectious that whoever heard it was sure to laugh too, without knowing why. But Stolz did not make her laugh all the time; half an hour later she listened to him with interest, and occasionally gazed at Oblomov with redoubled interest – and Oblomov felt like sinking through the ground because of her glances.

'What are they saying about me?' he thought, looking at them anxiously out of the corner of his eye.

He was on the point of leaving when Olga's aunt called him to the table and made him sit down beside her, under the cross-fire of the glances of all the other visitors. He turned round to Stolz apprehensively, but Stolz had gone; he glanced at Olga, and met the same interested gaze fixed upon him.

'She is still looking at me!' he thought, glancing in confusion at his clothes.

He even wiped his face with his handkerchief, wondering if his nose was smudged, and touched his tie to see if it had come undone, for that sometimes happened to him; but no, everything seemed to be in order, and she was still looking at him! The footman brought him a cup of tea and a tray with cakes. He wanted to suppress his feeling of embarrassment and to be free and easy – and picked up such a pile of rusks and biscuits that a little girl who sat next to him giggled. Others eyed the pile curiously.

'Good heavens, she too is looking!' thought Oblomov. 'What am I going to do with this pile?'

He could see without looking that Olga had got up from her

seat and walked to another end of the room. He felt greatly relieved. But the little girl gazed intently at him, waiting to see what he would do with the biscuits. 'I must hurry up and eat them,' he thought, and started putting them away quickly; luckily they seemed to melt in his mouth. Only two biscuits remained; he breathed freely and plucked up courage to look where Olga had gone. Oh dear, she was standing by a bust, leaning against the pedestal and watching him! She had apparently left her old place in order to be able to watch him more freely; she had noticed his *gaucherie* with the biscuits. At supper she sat at the other end of the table and she was talking and eating without apparently paying any attention to him. But no sooner did Oblomov turn apprehensively in her direction in the hope that she was not looking at him than he met her eyes, full of curiosity and at the same time so kind, too. ...

After supper Oblomov hastily took leave of Olga's aunt: she invited him to dinner the next day and asked him to convey the invitation to Stolz as well. Oblomov bowed and walked across the whole length of the room without raising his eyes. Behind the piano was the screen and the door – he looked up: Olga sat at the piano and looked at him with great interest. He thought she smiled. 'I expect,' he decided, 'Andrey must have told her that I had odd socks on yesterday or that my shirt was inside out!' He drove home, out of spirits, both because of this suspicion and still more because of the invitation to dine which he had answered with a bow – that is to say, he had accepted it.

From that moment Olga's persistent gaze haunted Oblomov. In vain did he stretch out full length on his back, in vain did he assume the laziest and most comfortable positions – he simply could not go to sleep. His dressing-gown seemed hateful to him, Zakhar stupid and unbearable, and the dust and cobwebs intolerable. He told Zakhar to take out of the room several worthless pictures some patron of poor artists had forced upon him; he himself put right the blind which had not functioned for months, called Anisya and told her to clean the windows, brushed away the cobwebs, and then lay down on his side and spent an hour thinking of – Olga. At first he tried hard to recall what she looked like, drawing her portrait from memory. Strictly speaking, Olga was no beauty – that is, her cheeks were not of a vivid colour, and her eyes did not burn with an inward fire; her lips were not corals nor her teeth pearls, nor were her hands as tiny as those of a child of five nor her fingernails shaped like grapes. But if she were made into a statue, she would have been a model of grace and harmony. She was rather tall, and the size of her head was in strict proportion to her height, and the oval of her face to the size of her head; all this, in turn, was in perfect harmony with her shoulders and waist. Anyone who met her, even if he were absent-minded, could not help stopping for a moment before a creature so carefully and artistically made. Her exquisite nose was slightly aquiline; her lips were thin and for the most part tightly closed; a sign of concentrated thought. Her keen, bright, and wide-awake blue-grey eyes, which never missed anything, shone, too, with the same light and thought. The brows lent a peculiar beauty to her eyes: they were not arched, they had not been plucked into two thin lines above the eyes – no, they were two brown, fluffy, almost straight streaks, which seldom lay symmetrically: one was a little higher than the other, forming a tiny wrinkle above it which seemed to say something, as if some idea was hidden there. When she walked, her head, which was so gracefully and nobly poised on her slender, proud neck, was slightly inclined; her whole body moved evenly, striding along with so light a step that it was almost imperceptible.

'Why did she look so intently at me yesterday?' Oblomov thought. 'Andrey swears that he never mentioned my socks and shirt to her, but spoke of his friendship for me, of how we had grown up and gone to school together – about all the good things we had experienced together, and he also told her how unhappy I was, how everything that is fine in me perishes for lack of sympathy and activity, how feebly life flickers in me and how – – But what was there to smile at?' Oblomov continued to muse. 'If she had a heart it ought to have throbbed or bled with pity, but instead – oh well, what does it matter what she did! I'd better stop thinking about her! I'll go and dine there to-day – and then I shall never cross the threshold of her house!'

Day followed day, and he never left Olga's house. One fine morning Tarantyev moved all his belongings to his friend's in Vyborg, and Oblomov spent three days as he had not done for years: without a bed, or a sofa, dining at Olga's aunt's. Then suddenly it appeared that the summer villa opposite to theirs was vacant. Oblomov rented it without inspecting it and settled there. He was with Olga from morning till night; he read to her, sent her flowers, went with her on the lake, on the hills – he, Oblomov! All sorts of strange things happen in the world, but how could this have come to pass? Well, it was like this:

When Stolz and he dined at Olga's, Oblomov suffered the

same agonies at dinner as on the previous day: he ate and talked knowing that she was looking at him, feeling that her gaze rested on him like sunshine, burning him, exciting him, stirring his nerves and blood. It was only after smoking a cigar on the balcony that he succeeded in hiding for a moment from her silent, persistent gaze. 'What is it all about?' he asked himself, fidgeting nervously. 'It's sheer agony! Have I come here to be laughed at by her? She does not look at anyone else like that – she dare not. I'm quieter than the others – so she – I'll talk to her,' he decided. 'I'd rather myself say in words what she's trying to drag out of me with her eyes.'

Suddenly she appeared before him at the balcony door; he offered her a chair and she sat down beside him.

'Is it true that you're awfully bored?' she asked him.

'It's true, but not awfully,' he replied. 'I have some work to do.'

'Mr Stolz told me that you were drawing up some scheme. Are you?'

'Yes. I want to go and live in the country, so I'm gradually preparing myself for it.'

'But aren't you going abroad?'

'Yes, certainly, as soon as Mr Stolz is ready.'

'Are you glad you're going?' she asked.

'Yes, I'm very glad. ...'

He looked at her: a smile crept all over her face, gleaming in her eyes or spreading over her cheeks; only her lips were tightly closed as always.

He could not bring himself to lie to her calmly.

'I'm a little – er – lazy,' he said, 'but – –'

He could not help feeling at the same time rather annoyed that she should so easily, almost without saying a word, have extracted from him a confession of laziness. 'What is she to me? I'm not afraid of her, am I?' he thought.

'Lazy?' she retorted, with hardly perceptible slyness. 'Is it possible? A man and lazy – I don't understand it.'

'What is there not to understand?' he thought. 'It seems simple enough.'

'I sit at home most of the time,' he said. 'That is why Andrey thinks that I – –'

'But,' she said, 'I expect you write and read a lot. Have you read – –' She looked intently at him.

'No, I haven't!' he suddenly blurted out, afraid that she might try to cross-examine him.

'What?' she asked, laughing.

He, too, laughed.

'I thought you were going to ask me about some novel. I don't read fiction.'

'You're wrong. I was going to ask you about books of travel. ...'

He looked keenly at her: her whole face was laughing, but not her lips.

'Oh, but she's – one must be careful with her,' Oblomov thought.

'What do you read?' she asked curiously.

'As a matter of fact, I do like books of travel mostly.'

'To Africa?' she asked softly and slyly.

He blushed, guessing not without good reason that she knew not only what he read, but also how he read it.

'Are you a musician?' she asked, to help him to recover from his embarrassment.

At that moment Stolz came up.

'Ilya, I've told Olga that you're passionately fond of music and asked her to sing something – *Casta diva*.'

'Why have you been telling stories about me?' Oblomov replied. 'I'm not at all passionately fond of music.'

'How do you like that?' Stolz interrupted. 'He seems offended! I recommend him to you as a decent chap and he hastens to disillusion you.'

'I merely decline the part of a lover of music: it's a doubtful and difficult part!'

'What music do you like best?' asked Olga.

'It's a difficult question to answer. Any music. I sometimes listen with pleasure to a hoarse barrel-organ, some tune I can't get out of my mind, and at other times I'll leave in the middle of an opera; Meyerbeer may move me, or even a bargeman's song: it all depends on what mood I'm in, I'm afraid! Sometimes I feel like stopping my ears to Mozart.'

'That means that you are really fond of music.'

'Sing something, Olga Sergeyevna,' Stolz asked.

'But if Mr Oblomov is in such a mood that he feels like stopping his ears?' she said, addressing Oblomov.

'I suppose I ought to pay some compliment at this point,' replied Oblomov. 'I'm afraid I'm not good at it, and even if I were, I shouldn't have dared to. ...'

'Why not?'

'Well,' Oblomov observed ingenuously, 'what if you sing badly? I'd feel awful afterwards.'

'As with the biscuits yesterday,' she suddenly blurted out, and blushed – she would have given anything not to have said it. 'I'm awfully sorry,' she said.

Oblomov did not expect that and he was utterly confused.

'It's wicked treachery!' he said in a low voice.

'No, perhaps just a little revenge and that, too, quite unpremeditated, I assure you – because you hadn't even a compliment for me.'

'Maybe I shall have when I hear you.'

'Do you want me to sing?' she asked.

'It's he who wants you to,' Oblomov replied, pointing to Stolz.

'And you?'

Oblomov shook his head.

'I can't want what I don't know.'

'You're rude, Ilya,' Stolz observed. 'That's what comes of lying about at home and putting on socks that – –'

'But, my dear fellow,' Oblomov interrupted him quickly, not letting him finish, 'I could easily have said, "Oh, I shall be very glad, very happy, you sing so wonderfully, of course," ' he went on, addressing Olga, ' "it will give me," etcetera. You didn't really want me to say that, did you?'

'But you might, I think, have expressed a wish that I should sing – oh, just out of curiosity.'

'I daren't,' Oblomov replied. 'You're not an actress.'

'Very well,' she said to Stolz, 'I'll sing for you.'

'Ilya,' said Stolz, 'have your compliment ready.'

Meanwhile it grew dark. The lamp was lit, and it looked like the moon through the ivy-covered trellis. The dusk had hidden the outlines of Olga's face and figure and had thrown, as it were, a crêpe veil over her; her face was in the shadow; only her mellow but powerful voice with the nervous tremor of feeling in it could be heard. She sang many love-songs and arias at Stolz's request; some of them expressed suffering with a vague premonition of happiness, and others joy with an undercurrent of sorrow already discernible in it. The words, the sounds, the pure, strong girlish voice made the heart throb, the nerves tremble, the eyes shine and fill with tears. One wanted to die listening to the sounds and at the same time one's heart was eager for more life.

Oblomov was enchanted, overcome; he could hardly hold back his tears or stifle the shout of joy that was ready to escape from his breast. He had not for many years felt so alive and strong – his strength seemed to be welling out from the depths of his soul ready for any heroic deed. He would have gone abroad that very moment if all he had to do was to step into a carriage and go off.

In conclusion she sang *Casta diva*: his transports, the thoughts that flashed like lightning through his head, the cold shiver that ran through his body – all this crushed him; he felt completely shattered.

'Are you satisfied with me to-day?' Olga asked Stolz suddenly as she finished singing.

'Ask Oblomov what he thinks,' said Stolz.

'Oh!' Oblomov cried, snatching Olga's hand suddenly and letting it go at once in confusion. 'I'm sorry,' he murmured.

'Do you hear?' Stolz said to her. 'Tell me honestly, Ilya, how long is it since this sort of thing happened to you?'

'It could have happened this morning if a hoarse barrel-organ had passed by Mr Oblomov's windows,' Olga interposed, but she spoke so kindly and gently that she took the sting out of the sarcasm.

He gave her a reproachful look.

'He hasn't yet taken out the double windows, so he can't hear what's happening outside,' Stolz added.

Oblomov gave Stolz a reproachful look.

Stolz took Olga's hand.

'I don't know why, but you sang to-day as you have never sung before, Olga Sergeyevna – at any rate, I've not heard you sing like that for a long time. This is my compliment,' he said, kissing every finger of her hand.

Stolz was about to say good-bye. Oblomov, too, wanted to go, but Stolz and Olga insisted that he should stay.

'I have some business to attend to,' Stolz observed, 'but you'd merely go to lie down – and it's still too early.'

'Andrey! Andrey!' Oblomov said imploringly. 'No,' he added, 'I'm afraid I can't stay – I must go!' And he went.

He did not sleep all night; sad and thoughtful, he walked up and down the room; he went out at daybreak, walked along the Neva and then along the streets, and goodness only knows what he was feeling and thinking. Three days later he was there again, and in the evening, when the other visitors had sat down to play cards, he found himself at the piano alone with Olga. Her aunt had a headache and she was sitting in her study sniffing smelling-salts.

'Would you like me to show you the collection of drawings

Mr Stolz brought me from Odessa?' Olga asked. 'He didn't show it to you, did he?'

'You're not trying to entertain me like a hostess, are you?' asked Oblomov. 'You needn't trouble.'

'Why not? I don't want you to be bored. I want you to feel at home here. I want you to be comfortable, free, and at your ease, so that you shouldn't go away – to lie down.'

'She's a spiteful, sarcastic creature,' Oblomov thought, admiring, in spite of himself, her every movement.

'You want me to be free and at ease and not be bored, do you?' he repeated.

'Yes,' she answered, looking at him as she had done before, but with an expression of still greater curiosity and kindness.

'If you do,' Oblomov said, 'you must, to begin with, not look at me as you are looking now and as you did the other day – –'

She looked at him with redoubled curiosity.

'For it is this look that makes me feel uncomfortable. ... Where's my hat?'

'Why does it make you feel uncomfortable?' she asked gently, and her look lost its expression of curiosity, becoming just kind and affectionate.

'I don't know. Only I can't help feeling that with that look you are trying to extract from me everything that I don't want other people to know – you, in particular.'

'But why not? You are a friend of Mr Stolz and he is my friend, therefore – –'

'– therefore,' he finished the sentence for her, 'there is no reason why you should know all that Mr Stolz knows about me.'

'There is no reason, but there is a chance.'

'Thanks to my friend's frankness – a bad service on his part.'

'You haven't any secrets, have you?' she asked. 'Crimes, perhaps?' she added, laughing and moving away from him.

'Perhaps,' he answered, with a sigh.

'Oh, it is a great crime,' she said softly and timidly, 'to put on odd socks.'

Oblomov grabbed his hat.

'I can't stand it!' he said. 'And you want me to be comfortable? I'll fall out with Andrey. Did he tell you that too?'

'He did make me laugh terribly at it to-day,' Olga added. 'He always makes me laugh. I'm sorry, I won't, I won't, and I'll try to look at you differently. ...' She looked at him with a mock-serious expression.

'All this is to begin with,' she went on. 'Very well, I'm not looking at you as I did the other day, so that you ought to feel comfortable and at ease now. Now, what must I do secondly so that you shouldn't be bored?'

He looked straight into her grey-blue, tender eyes.

'Now you, too, are looking strangely at me,' she said.

He really was looking at her not so much with his eyes as with his mind, with all his will, like a magnetizer, but involuntarily, being quite incapable of not looking.

'Heavens, how pretty she is!' he thought, looking at her almost with terrified eyes. 'And to think that such wonderful girls actually exist! This white skin, these eyes which are as dark as deep pools and yet there is something gleaming in them – her soul, no doubt! Her smile can be read like a book, disclosing her beautiful teeth and – and her whole head – how tenderly it rests on her shoulders, swaying, like a flower, breathing with fragrance. ... Yes,' he thought, 'I am extracting something from her – something is passing from her into me. Here – close to my heart – something is beginning to stir and flutter – I feel a new sensation there – something that was not there before. ... Oh dear, what a joy it is to look at her! It takes my breath away!'

His thoughts went whirling through his mind and he was looking at her as into an endless distance, a bottomless abyss, with self-oblivion and delight.

'Really, Mr Oblomov, see how you are looking at me now yourself,' she said, turning her head away shyly, but her curiosity got the better of her and she could not take her eyes off him.

He heard nothing. He really did look at her without hearing her words, and silently listened to what was happening inside him: he touched his head – there, too, something was stirring uneasily, rushing about with unimaginable swiftness. He could not catch his thoughts: they seemed to scurry away like a flock of birds, and there seemed to be a pain in his left side, by the heart.

'Don't look at me so strangely,' she said. 'It makes me, too, uncomfortable. I expect you also want to extract something from my soul.'

'What can I get from you?' he asked mechanically.

'I, too, have *plans*, begun and unfinished,' she replied.

He recovered his senses at this hint at his unfinished plan.

'Strange,' he said, 'you're spiteful, but you have kind eyes. It's not for nothing people say that one must never believe women: they lie intentionally with their tongue and unintentionally with their eyes, smile, blushes, and even fainting fits.'

She did not let this impression get stronger, took his hat from him quietly and sat down on a chair herself.

'I won't, I won't,' she repeated quickly. 'Oh, I'm so sorry. I shouldn't have said that! But I swear I wasn't trying to be sarcastic at all!' She almost sang, and in the singing of those words emotion stirred.

Oblomov calmed down.

'Oh that Andrey!' he said reproachfully.

'Well, secondly, tell me what I have to do so that you shouldn't be bored?' she asked.

'Sing!' he said.

'There, that's the compliment I was waiting for,' she said joyfully, flushing. 'Do you know,' she went on with animation, 'if you hadn't cried "Oh!" after my singing that night, I don't think I could have slept – I should have cried, perhaps.'

'Why?' Oblomov asked in surprise.

She pondered. 'I don't know myself,' she said, after a pause.

'You're vain. That's why.'

'Yes, of course,' she said, musing and touching the keys with one hand, 'but everyone is vain, and very much so. Mr Stolz claims that vanity is almost the only thing that controls a man's will. I expect you haven't any, and that is why you're – –'

She did not finish.

'I'm what?' he asked.

'Oh, nothing,' she said, changing the subject. 'I'm fond of Mr Stolz,' she went on, 'not only because he makes me laugh – sometimes his words make me cry – and not because he likes me, but I believe because – he likes me more than he likes other people: you see, my vanity betrays me!'

'You are fond of Mr Stolz?' Oblomov asked, looking intently and searchingly into her eyes.

'Why, of course, if he likes me more than he likes other people, then it's only fair that I should be,' she replied seriously.

Oblomov looked at her in silence: she answered him with a frank, silent look.

'He likes Anna Vassilyevna, too, and Zinaida Mikhailovna, but not as much as me,' she went on. 'He won't sit with them for two hours, or make them laugh, or talk frankly to them; he talks about business, about the theatre, the news, but he talks to me as to a sister – no,' she corrected herself quickly, 'as to a daughter. Sometimes he even scolds me if I am too slow to understand something, or if I refuse to do as he wishes, or if I do not agree with him. But he never scolds them, and I think I

199

like him all the more because of it. Vanity!' she added, pensively. 'But I don't know how it could have got into my singing. People have often praised it, but you wouldn't even listen to me – you had almost to be forced to. And if you had gone away without saying a word to me, if I hadn't noticed anything in your face – I think I'd have fallen ill. Yes, I must admit, that is vanity all right!' she concluded decisively.

'Why, did you notice something in my face?' he asked.

'Tears, though you did conceal them; it's a bad habit with men to be ashamed of their feelings. That, too, is vanity, only false vanity. They had better sometimes be ashamed of their intellect: it leads them more often astray. Even Mr Stolz is ashamed of his feelings. I told him that, and he agreed with me. And you?'

'Looking at you, one would agree with anything!' he said.

'Another compliment – and such a – –' she could not find the right word.

'– vulgar one,' Oblomov finished, without taking his eyes off her.

She assented with a smile.

'That was exactly what I was afraid of when I refused to ask you to sing. What can one say after a first hearing? And yet one has to say something. It is difficult to be clever and sincere at the same time, especially about one's feelings, when one is as greatly impressed as I was then.'

'I really did sing then as I had not done for ages, perhaps as I had never done. ... Don't ask me to sing, I shall not be able to sing so again. ... Wait, I'll sing one more thing,' she said, and her face seemed to flush, her eyes blazed. She sat down, struck two or three loud chords and began to sing.

Dear Lord, what did he not hear in her singing! Hopes, vague fear of storms, the storms themselves, transports of happiness – all this could be heard, not in the song, but in her voice. She sang a long time, turning to him now and again to ask like a child: 'Have you had enough? No? Well, just this, then,' and she went on singing. Her cheeks and ears were burning with agitation; sometimes her young face lit up with the sudden flash of emotion or with a ray of such mature passion as though she were re-living in her heart some great experience of the distant past, and then this momentary ray was suddenly extinguished and her voice once more sounded fresh and silvery. Oblomov, too, experienced the same sort of feeling: it seemed to him as though he had been living through it all not for one hour or two, but for years. ... Both of them, though outwardly motionless, were rent by an inward fire, shaken by the same agitation; the tears in their eyes were called forth by the same mood. These were all the symptoms of the passions which were evidently destined to arise in her young heart, now subject only to brief and fleeting outbursts of the still slumbering forces of life. She finished on a long-drawn-out note, and her voice died away in it. She stopped, put her hands in her lap, and, deeply moved and excited herself, glanced at Oblomov to see what he was feeling. His face was radiant with happiness that welled up from the depths of his being; he looked at her with eyes brimming with tears.

Now it was she who grasped his hand involuntarily.

'What's the matter?' she asked. 'Why do you look like that? Why?'

But she knew why he looked like that, and inwardly she modestly triumphed, enjoying this manifestation of her powers.

'Look in the glass,' she went on, pointing with a smile to the reflection of his face in the mirror. 'Your eyes are shining! Goodness, there are tears in them! How deeply you feel music!'

'No,' said Oblomov quietly, 'it isn't music I feel, it's – love!'

She at once dropped his hand and changed colour. Their eyes met: his gaze was fixed, almost deranged; it was not Oblomov, but passion that looked at her.

Olga realized that his words had escaped him against his will and that he was powerless to suppress them, for he merely spoke the truth.

He came to himself, took his hat, and ran out of the room without turning round. She did not follow him with curious eyes, but stood motionless like a statue at the piano for a long time, her eyes fixed on the ground; only her bosom rose and fell agitatedly.

6

WHENEVER Oblomov lay about indolently at home or was sunk into a dull slumber or indulged in flights of inspired fancies, there was always a woman in the foreground of his dreams, a woman who was his wife and sometimes – his mistress. The woman he saw in his dreams was tall and well-shaped, with her arms serenely folded on her breast, her eyes gentle yet proud, sitting leisurely under a clump of trees overhung with ivy, or stepping lightly on a carpet or a sandy path, her hips swaying, her head gracefully poised on her shoulders, and her eyes looking dreamily ahead; she was his ideal, the embodiment of a life full of enchantment and grave repose, she was the personification of rest itself. He dreamed of her first, smothered in flowers, standing at the altar wearing a long veil, then at the head of the marriage-bed with bashfully lowered eyes, and, finally, as a mother among a group of children. He dreamed of the smile on her lips, a smile that was not passionate, but sympathetic to him as her husband and indulgent to others; he dreamed of her eyes which were not moist with desire, but yielding only to him, and shy, even severe, to others. He never wanted to see her in a state of agitation, to hear of ardent dreams, sudden tears, languorous longings, exhaustion, followed by a frenzied burst of joy. He wanted neither moonlight nor sadness. She must not turn pale suddenly, faint, or experience shattering outbursts of emotion. 'Women like that,' he used to say, 'have lovers, and they give you no end of trouble: doctors, wateringplaces, and all sorts of fancies. You will not be able to sleep in peace!' But beside a wife who was proud, shy, and serene a man could sleep care-free. He goes to sleep confident that when he wakes he will meet the same gentle and kind gaze; and twenty or thirty years later, in response to his affectionate look, he would meet the same gentle and softly gleaming ray of sympathy in her eyes. And so to their dying day! 'Why, isn't it the secret aim of every man and woman to find in his or her friend unfailing repose, an even and everlasting flow of feeling? That is the norm of love, and the moment we deviate from it, change or grow cold, we suffer; so that my ideal must be the common ideal of everybody, mustn't it?' he thought. 'Is not that the crowning achievement, the final solution of the relations of the sexes?' To give passion a legitimate outlet, to show the direction in which it should flow, like a river, for the benefit of a whole country is the common problem of mankind, it is the very pinnacle of progress to which all advanced people like George Sand are striving but invariably go astray. Once it is solved, there can be no more unfaithfulness, nor coolness, but an even-beating, calm, and contented heart and, therefore, a full and happy life and everlasting moral health. There are cases of such a state of blessedness, but they are rare; they are pointed out as phenomenal. One has to be born for it, people say. But perhaps one ought to be educated for it, try to achieve it consciously. Passion! All this is very well in poetry or on the stage, where actors strut about in cloaks and with daggers and then – the murderers and the murdered – go and have supper together. It would be a good thing if passions, too, ended like that, but they leave nothing but smoke and stench behind, and no happiness! And the memories are nothing but shame and tearing of hair.

Finally, if such a misfortune, if passion, should overtake you, it would be like finding yourself on a terribly rough and hilly road where horses slip and the rider is exhausted, but your native village can already be seen in the distance: you must not lose sight of it and must do all you can to get out of the dangerous spot as quickly as possible. ... Yes, passion must be curbed, stifled, and destroyed by marriage. ... He would have run away in horror from a woman who suddenly scorched him with her gaze, or uttered a moan and fell on his shoulder with her eyes closed, then came to and threw her arms about his neck in a tight embrace. That could be like a firework, like an explosion of a barrel of gunpowder; and afterwards? Deafness, blindness, and singed hair!

But let us see what sort of a woman Olga was.

For many days after his sudden avowal they did not see each other alone. He hid like a schoolboy as soon as he caught sight of Olga. She had changed towards him, but did not avoid him and was not cold to him, but had merely grown more thoughtful. He could not help feeling that she was sorry something had happened that prevented her from tormenting him with her inquisitive glances and teasing him good-humouredly for his lying about, his laziness, and his clumsiness. She would have liked to make fun of him, but it was the sort of fun enjoyed by a mother who cannot help smiling at her son's comic get-up. Stolz had gone away, and she was bored to have no one to sing to; her piano was closed – in short, both felt constrained and awkward. And how wonderfully it had all gone at first! How simply had they come to know each other! How easily they had become friends! Oblomov was much more simple than Stolz, and more kind, too, though he did not amuse her so well – or rather he amused her by being what he was, and forgave her mockery so easily. Besides, before leaving, Stolz put Oblomov in her charge; he asked her to keep an eye on him and prevent him from stopping at home. In her clever, pretty little head she had devised a detailed plan of how she would break Oblomov of his habit of sleeping after dinner – and not only of sleeping but also of lying down on the sofa in the daytime; she would make him promise her. She dreamed of how she would 'tell him' to read the books Stolz had left behind, to read the newspapers every day and tell her the news, to write letters to his estate, to finish his plan of estate management, to get ready to go abroad – in a word, she would not let him drowse; she would show him his aim in life, make him love once more the things he cared for no longer, and Stolz, when he returned, would not recognize him. And she – the silent, shy Olga – would perform this miracle, she, who had not yet begun to live and whom no one had even obeyed so far! She would be the cause of this transformation! It had begun already; the moment she began singing, Oblomov was a different person. ... He would live, work, and bless life and her. To restore a man to life – why, think of the glory a doctor won when he restored a hopeless invalid to health! And what about saving a man whose mind and soul were facing moral ruin? The very thought of it made her tremble with pride and joy; she looked upon it as a task assigned to her from above. In her mind she made him her secretary, her librarian. And suddenly all that had come to an end! She did not know what she ought to do and that was why she was silent when she met Oblomov.

Oblomov was tortured by the thought that he had shocked and offended her and he was expecting annihilating glances and cold severity, and he trembled when he caught sight of her, hastening to turn aside. In the meanwhile he had already moved to the country villa, and for three days walked alone over marshy ground to the forest, or went to the village and sat idly by the gates of some peasant's cottage watching the children and the calves run about and the ducks swimming around in the pond. There was a lake and a huge park near his house: he did not go there because he was afraid of meeting Olga by herself. 'What did I want to blurt it out for?' he thought, without even asking himself whether the words he had uttered were true, or were due to the momentary action of the music on his nerves. The feeling of awkwardness, shame, or 'disgrace', as he called it, which he had brought on himself, prevented him from examining the nature of that outburst and, generally, what Olga meant to him. He no longer analysed the new thing that had entered his heart – a sort of lump that had not been there before. All his feelings coiled up into a huge ball of shame. And when she appeared for a moment before his imagination, there rose simultaneously that image, too, that ideal of incarnate peace, happiness, life: this ideal was the exact copy of – Olga. The two images were identical and merged into one another.

'Oh, what have I done!' he murmured. 'I've ruined everything! Thank God, Stolz has gone: she has not had time to tell him, or I should have sunk through the ground! Love, tears – it doesn't become me! Olga's aunt hasn't asked me to call again: I expect *she* must have told her. Oh, Lord!'

This was what he thought as he got farther and farther into the park, walking down a side avenue.

One thing that worried Olga was how she would meet him and how this encounter would go off : ought she to say something or ought she to pass it over in silence as if nothing had happened? But what could she say? Should she assume a stern expression, look at him proudly, or not look at all, but remark haughtily and dryly that she never expected him to behave like that: who does he think she is, to allow himself such an impertinence? That was what Sonia during a mazurka said to a second lieutenant, though she had taken a great deal of trouble to turn his head. 'But,' she asked herself, 'has he been impertinent? If he really feels it, why shouldn't he say it? But it was a bit sudden, all the same. He hardly knows me. No one would have said such a thing after seeing a woman for the second or third time, and no one would have fallen in love so quickly. Only Oblomov could ...' But she remembered having read and heard that love came suddenly sometimes. 'He acted on an impulse, he was carried away,' she thought. 'Now he doesn't show himself. He is ashamed. It can't be impertinence, then. But whose fault is it? Stolz's, of course, because he made me sing.' Oblomov did not want to listen at first – she resented it and – she tried. ... She blushed crimson. ... Yes, she had done all she could to rouse him. Stolz had said that he was apathetic, that nothing interested him, that all was dead within him. So she wanted to find out whether everything was dead, and she sang, she sang as never before. ... 'Good heavens, then it is my fault: I must ask him to forgive me. ... But whatever for?' she asked herself a moment later. 'What am I to tell him? "Mr Oblomov, I'm awfully sorry, I tried to seduce you!" ... Oh, how disgraceful! It's not true!' she said, flushing and stamping her foot. 'Who'd dare to think such a thing? I did not know what was going to happen, did I? And if it hadn't happened, if he had not said it – what then?' she asked. 'I don't know,' she thought. Ever since that evening she had felt so strange – she must have been very much offended – she felt positively feverish, her cheeks glowed. ...

'Nervous irritation – a slight fever,' the doctor told her.

'It is all Oblomov's doing!' she thought as she walked in the park. 'Oh, he must be taught a lesson so that it doesn't happen again! I'll ask auntie not to invite him to our house: he mustn't forget himself. .. How did he dare?' Her eyes blazed. Suddenly she heard someone coming.

'Someone's coming!' thought Oblomov.

And they met face to face.

'Olga Sergeyevna,' he said, shaking like an aspen leaf.

'Ilya Ilyich,' she said, timidly, and they both stopped.

'Good morning,' he said.

'Good morning,' she replied.

'Where are you going?' he asked.

'Nowhere in particular,' she said without raising her eyes.

'I'm not in your way?'

'Oh, not at all,' she replied, glancing at him quickly and curiously.

'May I come with you?' he asked suddenly, with a searching look.

They walked silently along the path. Neither the teacher's ruler nor the headmaster's eyebrows had ever made Oblomov's heart thump as it was doing at that moment. He tried to make an effort and say something, but the words would not come; only his heart was pounding away as though in anticipation of some calamity.

'Have you had a letter from Mr Stolz?' she asked.

'Yes, I have,' Oblomov replied.

'What does he say?'

'He wants me to join him in Paris.'

'And what are you going to do?'

'I'll go.'

'When?'

'Oh – some time – no, to-morrow – as soon as I get ready.'

'Why so soon?' she asked.

He made no answer.

'Don't you like your house or – tell me, why do you want to go?'

'The impudent wretch!' she thought. 'He wants to go abroad, does he?'

'I don't know,' Oblomov murmured, without looking at her, 'I – I feel awful – awkward – something's choking me.'

She said nothing, picked a spray of lilac and sniffed it, burying her face in it.

'Smell it,' she said, covering his face with it, too. 'Doesn't it smell lovely?'

'And here are some lilies of the valley,' he said, bending down to the grass. 'Wait, I'll pick you some. They smell better: of fields and woods; there is more of nature about them. Lilac always grows close to houses, the branches thrust themselves in at the windows, the smell is so cloying. Look, the lilies of the valley are still wet with dew!'

He gave her a few lilies of the valley.

'And do you like mignonette?' she asked.

'I'm afraid not; the smell is too strong. I don't like mignonette or roses. I don't care for flowers; they're all right in the fields, but they're such a trouble indoors – they make such a mess when they drop ...'

'You like it to be tidy indoors, don't you?' she asked, looking slyly at him. 'You don't like a mess, do you?'

'No, I don't,' he murmured, 'but my servant is such a – – Oh, you're wicked!' he added under his breath.

'Are you going straight to Paris?' she asked.

'Yes, Stolz has been expecting me for some time.'

'Take a letter from me: I'll write one to him,' she said.

'Let me have it to-day: I'll be going back to town to-morrow.'

'To-morrow?' she asked. 'Why so soon? There's no one driving you out of here, is there?'

'Well, I'm afraid there is. ...'

'Who?'

'Shame ...' he whispered.

'Shame!' she repeated mechanically. 'Now I'll tell him,' she added to herself, 'Mr Oblomov, I never expected – –'

'Yes, Olga Sergeyevna,' he brought himself to say at last, 'I believe you're surprised – you're angry – –'

'Now – now is the right moment to say it,' she thought, her heart beating fast. 'Oh dear, I can't, I can't!'

He tried to look into her face, to find out what she thought, but she was smelling the lilac and the lilies of the valley and did not know herself what she was thinking – what she ought to say or do.

'Oh,' she thought, 'Sonia would have thought of something at once, but I'm so silly – I never can do anything – it's awful!'

'I had quite forgotten,' she said.

'Please believe me, the whole thing – I mean, I don't know what made me say it – I couldn't help it,' he began, gradually growing bolder. 'I'd have said it if a thunderbolt had struck me or a stone had crashed on top of me. Nothing in the world could have stopped me. Please, please don't think that I wanted – I'd have given anything a moment later to take back the rash word. ...'

She walked with her head bowed, sniffing the flowers.

'Please forget it,' he went on, 'forget it, particularly as it wasn't true. ...'

'Not true?' she suddenly repeated, drawing herself up and dropping the flowers.

Her eyes opened wide and flashed with surprise.

'How do you mean – not true?' she repeated.

'I mean – well – for God's sake don't be angry with me and forget it. Please, believe me, I was just carried away for a moment – because of the music.'

'Only because of the music?'

She turned pale and her eyes grew dim.

'Well,' she thought, 'everything's all right now. He took back his rash words and there's no need for me to be angry any more! That's excellent – now I needn't worry any more. ... We can talk and joke as before.'

She broke off a twig from a tree absent-mindedly, bit off a leaf, and then at once threw down the twig and the leaf on the path.

'You're not angry with me, are you? You have forgotten, haven't you?' Oblomov said, bending forward to her.

'What was that? What did you ask?' she said nervously, almost with vexation, turning away from him. 'I've forgotten everything – I've such a bad memory!'

He fell silent and did not know what to do. He saw her sudden vexation but did not see the cause of it.

'Goodness,' she thought, 'now everything is all right again. It's just as if that scene had never taken place, thank heaven! Well, all the better. ... Oh dear, what does it all mean? Oh, Sonia, Sonia, how lucky you are!'

'I'm going home,' she said suddenly, quickening her steps and turning into another avenue.

There was a lump in her throat. She was afraid she might cry.

'Not that way,' Oblomov said. 'It's nearer, here!'

'You ass,' he said to himself gloomily. 'What did you want to explain for? Now you've offended her more than ever. You should not have reminded her: it would have passed off by itself and been forgotten. Now you'll jolly well have to ask her to forgive you.'

'I expect,' she thought to herself, 'I'm feeling so vexed because I've had no time to say to him, "Mr Oblomov, I never expected you to presume ..." But he forestalled me. "It wasn't

208

true!" How do you like that! So he was lying to me! How did he dare?'

'Have you really forgotten?' he asked softly.

'Yes, I've forgotten everything!' she said hurriedly, anxious to get home.

'Give me your hand to show you're not angry.'

Without looking at him, she gave him the tips of her fingers, and no sooner did he touch them than she snatched them away.

'No, you are angry!' he said with a sigh. 'How can I convince you that I was just carried away for a moment, that I should never have forgotten myself to such an extent? Of course, I shan't listen to your singing again!'

'Don't try to convince me,' she said quickly. 'I don't need your assurances. I shouldn't dream of singing to you anyhow!'

'All right, I shan't say another word,' he said. 'Only for heaven's sake don't go away like this, or there will be such a heavy load on my heart. ...'

She walked more slowly and listened intently to his words.

'If it's true that you would have burst into tears if I hadn't cried out in admiration of your singing, then – I mean – if you go away now without a smile and without holding out your hand to me like a friend and – have pity on me, Olga Sergeyevna! I shall be ill – my knees tremble – I can hardly stand. ...'

'Why?' she asked suddenly, glancing at him.

'I'm afraid I don't know myself,' he said. 'I feel no longer ashamed: I am not ashamed of my words – I think they were – –'

Again his heart missed a beat, again there seemed to be a lump there; again her kind and curious gaze began to burn him. She had turned to him so gracefully, and was awaiting his answer so anxiously.

'They were – what?' she asked impatiently.

'I'm sorry, I'm afraid to say it: you'll be angry again.'

'Say it!' she said imperiously.

He was silent.

'Well?'

'I again feel like crying as I look at you. ... You see I'm not vain, I'm not ashamed of my feelings.'

'Why do you feel like crying?' she asked, flushing again.

'I keep hearing your voice – I feel again – –'

'What?' she said, breathing freely again: she was waiting tensely.

They came up to the front steps of her house.

'I feel – –' Oblomov was in a hurry to finish, but stopped short.

She was mounting the steps slowly, as though with an effort.

'The same music – the same – excitement – the same feel – ... I'm sorry – I'm sorry – I can't control my – –'

'Sir,' she began severely, but suddenly her face lit up with a smile, 'I'm not angry and I forgive you,' she added gently, 'only in future – –'

Without turning round, she stretched out a hand to him; he seized it and kissed her palm; she softly pressed it against his lips and instantly disappeared behind the glass door, while he remained rooted to the spot.

7

FOR A LONG TIME he gazed after her open-mouthed and with wide-open eyes, and then stared blankly at the bushes. ... Some people he did not know passed by. A bird flew past. A peasant woman asked him in passing if he would like some strawberries – but the stupor continued. Then he walked very slowly down the same avenue and, half-way, came across the lilies of the valley Olga had dropped and the sprig of lilac she had torn off and thrown down in vexation. 'Why had she done it?' he wondered, calling it back to mind. 'You fool! You fool!' he cried suddenly aloud, picking up the lilies of the valley and the sprig of lilac, and almost running down the avenue. 'I asked her to forgive me, and she – oh, can it be true? ... What an idea!'

He came home, looking happy and radiant, 'With the moon on his forehead,' as his nurse used to say, sat down in the corner of the sofa and quickly wrote in large letters on the dust-covered table: 'Olga.'

'Oh, what dust!' he exclaimed, recovering from his ecstatic state. 'Zakhar! Zakhar!'

He shouted again and again, because Zakhar was sitting with some coachmen at the gate that faced the lane.

'Go on,' Anisya said in a stern whisper, pulling him by the sleeve, 'the master has been calling for you for a long time.'

'Have a look, Zakhar, what's this?' Oblomov said, but in a gentle and kind voice, for he could not be angry just then. 'You want everything to be in a mess here too, do you? Dust, cobwebs! No, my dear fellow, I shall not permit it! As it is, Olga Sergeyevna doesn't give me a moment's rest: "You like dirt," she says.'

'It's all very well for them to talk like that, sir,' Zakhar remarked, turning to the door. 'They have five servants, they have.'

'Where are you going? Will you sweep the room at once, please? It's impossible to sit down here, or lean on the table. Why, this is horrible – it's – it's Oblomovitis!'

Zakhar looked hurt and glanced sideways at his master.

'There he goes again!' he thought. 'He's invented another pathetic word, a familiar one, too!'

'Well,' said Oblomov, 'why don't you get on with the sweeping?'

'There's nothing to sweep here, sir,' Zakhar observed stubbornly. 'I've already swept the room to-day.'

'Where's the dust come from, if you've swept it? Look at it! There and there! I will not put up with it! Sweep it all up at once!'

'I did sweep it,' Zakhar repeated. 'You don't expect me to sweep the rooms ten times a day, do you? The dust comes from the road – we're in the country here, sir: there's a lot of dust on the road.'

'You shouldn't sweep the floor first and dust the furniture afterwards,' Anisya said, suddenly peeping out of the other room. 'The room is bound to be covered in dust again. You ought first to – –'

'Who asked you to come here and teach me what to do?' Zakhar wheezed furiously. 'Go back to your place!'

'Who ever heard of sweeping the floor first and dusting the furniture afterwards? That's why the master is angry. ...'

'Now then, now then!' he shouted, pushing out his elbow as though intending to aim it at her breast.

She grinned and disappeared. Oblomov waved him out of the room too. He put his head on the embroidered cushion, put his hand to his heart, and began listening to its beating.

'This is bad for me,' he said to himself. 'What's to be done? If I ask the doctor's advice, he will probably send me to Abyssinia!'

Before Zakhar and Anisya were married, they did their own work in the house without interference – that is to say, Anisya did the shopping and the cooking and helped with the tidying of the rooms only once a year, when she scrubbed the floors. But after their marriage, she found freer access to the master's rooms. She helped Zakhar, and the rooms were cleaner, and, besides, she took some of her husband's duties upon herself, partly of her own accord and partly because Zakhar despotically laid them upon her.

'Here, beat the carpet, will you?' he wheezed authoritatively. Or: 'You'd better sort out the things in that corner there and take what isn't wanted to the kitchen.'

He spent a month in this blissful state: the rooms were clean, his master did not grumble, or use 'pathetic words', and he, Zakhar, had nothing to do. But the state of bliss came to an end – and for the following reason. As soon as he and Anisya began to look after Oblomov's rooms together, everything Zakhar did turned out to be stupid. Whatever he did was wrong. For fifty-five years he had lived in the world in the conviction that whatever he did could not be done better or differently. And now, suddenly, Anisya proved to him that he was a wash-out, and she did it with such an offensive condescension, so quietly, as though he were a child or a perfect fool, and to make matters worse, she could not help smiling as she looked at him.

'You shouldn't open the windows and then shut the flues, dear,' she said affectionately. 'You'll chill the rooms again.'

'Well, and how would you do it?' he asked with the rudeness of a husband. 'When would you open the windows?'

'Why, dear, when lighting the stove,' she answered gently. 'The air will be drawn out and the room will get warm again.'

'What a silly fool!' he said. 'I've been doing it like that for twenty years and I'm not going to change it for you.'

On the same shelf in the cupboard he kept tea, sugar, lemons, silver, and, next to it, shoe-polish, brushes, and soap. One day he came home and found the soap on the wash-stand, the brushes and shoe-polish on the kitchen window-ledge, and the tea and sugar in a separate drawer.

'What do you mean by turning everything upside-down just as you please?' he asked sternly. 'I've put it all together on purpose to have it handy, and now you've come and put it all in different places!'

'But I did it, dear, so that the tea shouldn't smell of soap,' she remarked gently.

Another time she pointed out to Zakhar two or three moth holes in Oblomov's clothes and told him that he ought to shake and brush them at least once a week.

'Let me give them a brush, dear,' she concluded affectionately.

He snatched the brush and Oblomov's frock-coat out of her hands and put the coat back in the wardrobe. When on another occasion he began, as usual, to blame his master for scolding him without reason for the blackbeetles though he had not 'invented them', Anisya, without saying a word, removed all the pieces and crumbs of black bread which had been lying on the shelves from time immemorial and swept out and washed all the cupboards and crockery – and the blackbeetles disappeared almost completely. Zakhar still did not properly understand what it was all about, and merely attributed it to her zeal. But one day, when he took a tray with cups and glasses to his master's room and, dropping two glasses on the floor, began swearing as usual and was about to throw the whole tray down on the floor, Anisya took the tray from him, replaced the broken glasses and put the bread and the sugar-basin on the tray, arranging everything in such a way that not a cup moved, and then demonstrated to him how to pick up the tray with one hand and hold it firmly with the other; then she walked up and down the room twice, turning the tray to left and to right, and not a single spoon moved – it suddenly dawned on Zakhar that Anisya was cleverer than he. He snatched the tray from her, dropping the glasses, and could never forgive her for it.

'You see how it's done,' she added quietly.

He gave her a look of dull-witted superciliousness, but she only grinned.

'Oh, you silly peasant woman; you're trying to be clever, are you? You don't know the sort of a house we had in Oblomovka, do you now? Why, everything depended on me there. I had fifteen footmen and page-boys under me, not to mention other servants! And as for women like you, there were so many of them that I couldn't remember all their names. And you're trying to teach me, are you? Oh, you – –'

'But I mean well,' she began.

'All right, all right!' he wheezed, raising his elbow menacingly. 'Get out of the master's room. To the kitchen with you – and mind your woman's business!'

She grinned and went out, while he looked at her gloomily out of the corner of his eye. His pride was hurt, and he treated Anisya dismally. When, however, Oblomov asked for something, and it could not be found or had been broken, or when there was confusion in the house and a storm, accompanied by 'pathetic words', gathered over Zakhar's head, Zakhar winked at Anisya, motioned towards his master's study, and pointing to it with his thumb, said in an imperious whisper: 'Go and see what the master wants, will you?' Anisya went, and the storm was always averted by a simple explanation. Indeed, Zakhar himself suggested calling in Anisya as soon as Oblomov began using 'pathetic words'. But for Anisya, therefore, everything in Oblomov's rooms would have fallen into neglect again; she had already attached herself to Oblomov's household and quite unconsciously shared her husband's unshakeable connexion with Oblomov's house, life, and person; her woman's eyes kept careful watch over the neglected rooms. Zakhar had only to go out for a moment for Anisya to dust the tables and sofas, open a window, set the blinds right, put away the boots left in the middle of the room and the trousers thrown over an arm-chair, carefully examine all the clothes and even the papers, pencils, penknife, and pens on the table – and put it all in order; beat up the crumpled pillows and remake the bed – and all in no time at all; then she glanced round the room, moved a chair, closed a half-open drawer, took a napkin off the table, and quickly slipped into the kitchen the moment she heard Zakhar's squeaking boots. She was a quick and lively woman of about forty-seven with a solicitous smile, eyes that never missed anything, a strong neck and chest, and a pair of red, tenacious, untiring hands. She had hardly any face at all; the nose was the only thing that stood out on it; though small, it did not seem to belong to it at all or to have been clumsily attached, and, besides, the end of it was turned up, which made the rest of the face unnoticeable: it was so drawn and faded that one gained a clear impression of the nose long before noticing the rest of her face.

There are many husbands like Zakhar in the world. A diplomat will sometimes listen carelessly to his wife's advice, shrug, and – secretly write as she has advised him. A high official will whistle contemptuously while listening to his wife's chatter about some important affair of state and reply to her with a pitying grimace – and the next day he will solemnly repeat her chatter to the Minister. These gentlemen treat their wives as grimly or as lightly as Zakhar and barely vouchsafe to speak to them, regarding them, if not, like Zakhar, as silly women, then as a delightful relaxation from serious business affairs.

The bright noonday sun had long been burning the paths of the park. Everyone was sitting in the shade of the canvas awnings; only nursemaids and children walked about boldly in groups or sat on the grass in the noonday sun. Oblomov still lay on the sofa, believing and disbelieving the meaning of his conversation with Olga that morning. 'She loves me, she has set her affections on me. Is it possible? She dreams of me; it was for me

214

she sang so passionately, and the music awakened the same feelings in us for one another.' His pride was aroused, life shone brightly, its magic vistas opened before him, it was all aglow with light and colour, as it had not been so recently. He already saw himself travelling abroad with her, in Switzerland, on the lakes, in Italy, walking among the ruins in Rome, sailing in a gondola, then lost in a crowd in Paris and London, then – then in his earthly paradise, Oblomovka. She was divine with that charming prattle of hers, her exquisite, fair-skinned face, her lovely, slender neck. ... The peasants had never seen anything like her and they prostrated themselves before this angel. She was treading so softly on the grass; she walked with him in the shade of the young birch-trees; she sang to him. ... And he became conscious of life, of its gentle flow, of the splashing of its sweet stream – he sank into thought, his desires satisfied, his happiness full to overflowing. ... Suddenly his face clouded over.

'No,' he cried aloud, getting up from the sofa and pacing the room. 'This cannot be ! To love a ridiculous fellow like me, with sleepy eyes and flabby cheeks. ... She is just laughing at me. ...'

He stopped before the looking-glass and examined himself for a long time, first disapprovingly, then his eyes suddenly cleared ; he even smiled.

'I seem to look better, fresher than I did in town,' he said. 'My eyes are not dull – I was starting a stye, but it has disappeared. Must be because of the air here – I walk a lot, don't drink, don't lie about. ... No need for me to go to Egypt.'

A servant from Olga's aunt came with an invitation to dinner.

'I'm coming, I'm coming!' said Oblomov.

The servant turned to go.

'Wait! Here's something for you.' He gave him some money.

He felt gay and light-hearted. It was such a bright, sunny day. The people were so kind, everybody was enjoying himself, everybody looked happy. Zakhar alone was gloomy and kept looking sideways at his master; Anisya, on the other hand, was grinning so good-humouredly.

'I'll get myself a dog,' Oblomov decided, 'or a cat: cats are affectionate creatures – they purr.'

He rushed off to Olga's.

'But then – Olga loves me!' he thought on the way. 'She who is so young and so fresh! She, whose imagination should be wideawake to the poetic side of life, ought to be dreaming of black-haired, curly-headed youths, tall and slender, with

215

thoughtful, hidden power, with courage in their faces, a proud smile, with that melting and trembling light in the eye that touches the heart so easily, and with a gentle fresh voice that sounds like a harp-string. It is true there are women who do not care for youth, courage, good dancing, clever riding. ... Olga, I daresay, is no ordinary girl whose heart can be won by a handsome moustache or whose ears can be charmed by the rattle of a sword; but then something else is needed – intelligence, for instance, so that a woman should yield and bow her head to it as the rest of the world does. ... Or a famous artist. ... But what am I? Oblomov – and nothing more. Stolz, now, is a different matter: Stolz has intelligence, force, he knows how to control himself, others, and life. Wherever he goes and whoever he meets, he immediately gets the upper hand, playing on people as on an instrument. And I? Why, I can't get the better of Zakhar even – or of myself – I – Oblomov! Stolz – good Lord, she loves him,' he thought with horror. 'She said so herself. Like a friend, she said. But that's a lie, an unconscious lie perhaps. There can be no friendship between man and woman. ...' He walked slower and slower, overcome with doubts. 'And what if she is just flirting with me? If only – –' He stopped altogether, rooted to the spot for a moment. 'What if it is treachery, a plot? ... And whatever made me think that she loves me? She did not say so: it is just the satanic whispering of my vanity! Andrey! Can it be? No, it can't: she's so – so – – That is what she's like!' he suddenly cried joyfully, seeing Olga coming to meet him.

Olga held out her hand to him with a gay smile.

'No,' he decided, 'she is not like that, she is not like that, she is not a deceiver. Deceivers don't look so kind, they don't laugh so candidly – they titter. But, all the same, she never said she loved me!' he suddenly thought again in terror: that was how he had interpreted it. 'But, then, why should she have been vexed? Goodness, what a bog I am in!'

'What have you got there?'

'A twig.'

'What sort of twig?'

'As you see: it's lilac.'

'Where did you get it? There is no lilac here. Which way did you come?'

'It's the same sprig you plucked and threw away.'

'Why did you pick it up?'

'Oh, I don't know. I suppose I was glad that – that you threw it away in vexation.'

'You're glad I was vexed! That's something new. Why?'

'I won't tell you!'

'Please, do, I beg you.'

'Never! Not for anything in the world!'

'I implore you!'

He shook his head.

'And if I sing?'

'Then – perhaps.'

'So it's only music that has any effect on you, is it?' she said, frowning. 'That's true, isn't it?'

'Yes, music interpreted by you.'

'Very well, I'll sing. *Casta diva, Casta di – –*' she sang Norma's invocation and stopped.

'Well, tell me now!' she said.

For some time he struggled with himself.

'No, no!' he concluded even more decisively than before. 'Not for anything in the world! Never! Suppose it isn't true, and I've just imagined it? Never, never!'

'What's the matter? Is it something dreadful?' she said, her whole mind concentrated on the question, glancing searchingly at him.

Then gradually realization came to her: the ray of thought and surmise spread to every feature of her face and, suddenly, her whole face lit up with the consciousness of the truth. . . . Just like the sun which, emerging from behind a cloud, sometimes first lights up one bush, then another, then the roof of a house and, suddenly, floods a whole landscape with light. She knew what Oblomov's thought was.

'No, no,' Oblomov kept repeating. 'I could never say it. It's no use your asking.'

'I'm not asking you,' she replied indifferently.

'Aren't you? But just now – –'

'Let's go home,' she said seriously, without listening to him. 'Auntie is waiting.'

She walked in front of him and, leaving him with her aunt, went straight to her room.

8

THE whole of that day was a day of gradual disillusionment to Oblomov. He spent it with Olga's aunt, a very intelligent, estimable, and well-dressed woman; she always wore a new, well-made silk dress with an elegant lace collar; her cap, too, was tastefully made and the ribbons matched her face coquettishly, her complexion was fresh, although she was nearly fifty. A golden lorgnette hung on a chain round her neck. Her postures and gestures were full of dignity; she draped herself very skilfully in an expensive shawl, leaned her elbow very becomingly on an embroidered cushion, and reclined majestically on the sofa. You would never find her at work: bending down, sewing, occupying herself with trifles did not suit her face or her imposing figure. She even gave orders to her servants in a curt, dry, casual tone of voice. She sometimes read but never wrote; she spoke well, though mostly in French. However, noticing at once that Oblomov was not very fluent in French, she spoke to him in Russian after his first visit. She never indulged in reveries or tried to be clever in her conversation; she seemed to have drawn a line in her mind beyond which she never went. It was quite obvious that feelings, every kind of relationship, including love, entered into her life on equal terms with everything else, while in the case of other women love quite manifestly takes part, if not in deeds, then in words, in all the problems of life, and everything else is allowed in only in so far as love leaves room for it. The thing this woman esteemed most was the art of living, of being able to control oneself, of keeping a balance between thought and intention, intention and realization. You could never take her unawares, by surprise, but she was like a watchful enemy whose expectant gaze would always be fixed on you, however hard you tried to lie in wait for him. High society was her element, and therefore tact and caution prompted her every thought, word, and movement. She never opened her heart or confided her inmost secrets to anyone. You never saw her whispering to some old lady over a cup of coffee. It was only with Baron von Landwagen that she often remained alone. The baron sometimes stayed with her till midnight, but Olga was almost always there as well; most of the time they were silent anyway, but, somehow, significantly and intelligently silent, just as if they knew something that no one else did, but that was all. They evidently liked to be in each other's company – that was the only conclusion one could draw; she treated him exactly as she did everyone else – graciously and kindly, but also calmly and with absolute equanimity. Evil tongues made the best they could of it and hinted at some old friendship and a visit abroad together; but there was nothing in her attitude to him that betrayed any trace of some special, hidden sympathy, for that

218

would surely have come out sooner or later. He was, incidentally, trustee of Olga's small estate, which had been mortgaged as a result of some contract as security and never redeemed. The baron was engaged in a lawsuit about it, that is, he made some government clerk write papers, read them through his lorgnette, signed them, and sent the same official to the law-courts with them, while he himself made use of his connexions to bring about a satisfactory issue to the legal proceedings. He thought there was good reason to hope that everything would soon end happily. This put an end to the malicious gossip, and people grew accustomed to look upon the baron as a member of the family. He was nearly fifty, but he looked younger than his age, except that he dyed his moustache and had a slight limp. He was exquisitely polite, never smoked in the presence of ladies, never crossed his legs, and severely criticized the young men when during a visit they allowed themselves to lean back in an arm-chair or raise their knees and boots on a level with their noses. He kept his gloves on even indoors, removing them only when he sat down to dinner. He dressed in the latest fashion and wore several ribbons in his buttonhole. He always drove in a carriage and pair and took great care of his horses: before stepping into the carriage, he first walked round it, examined the harness and even the horses' hoofs, and sometimes took out a white handkerchief and rubbed their flanks and backs to see whether they had been well groomed. He greeted acquaintances with a polite and affable smile, and strangers coldly at first, but his coldness was replaced by a smile as soon as they had been introduced to him, and his new acquaintance could always count on it in future. He discussed everything: virtue, high cost of living, science and society – and with equal precision; he expressed his views in clear-cut and well-balanced sentences, as though speaking in ready-made maxims written down in some textbook and circulated among society people for general guidance.

Olga's relations with her aunt had so far been very simple and calm; they never transgressed against the limits of moderation in their expressions of affection for each other and there was never a shadow of displeasure between them. This was partly due to the character of Maria Mikhailovna, Olga's aunt, and partly to the absence of any reason for them to behave differently. It never occurred to the aunt to demand anything to which Olga would have strongly objected; Olga would never have dreamt of refusing to comply with her aunt's preferences or to follow her advice. And what was the nature of those preferences?

They concerned the choice of her clothes, the style of arranging her hair, or whether they should go to the French theatre or the opera. Olga obeyed in so far as her aunt expressed a preference or gave advice, but no more than that – and her aunt always expressed her wishes with a moderation that amounted to dryness, never exceeding her rights as an aunt. Their relations were so colourless that it was quite impossible to say whether her aunt made any claims on Olga's obedience or demanded any special tenderness, and whether Olga would dream of disobeying her aunt or felt any tenderness towards her. On the other hand, one could tell at once that they were aunt and niece and not mother and daughter.

'I'm going shopping; is there anything you want?' the aunt asked.

'Yes, Auntie, I have to change my lilac dress,' Olga said, and they went together. Or: 'No, Auntie,' Olga said, 'I went there the other day.'

The aunt touched her cheek with two fingers, kissed her on the forehead, and she kissed her aunt's hand, and one went and the other one stayed behind.

'Shall we take the same country cottage again?' the aunt would say, neither affirmatively nor questioningly, but just as though she were debating the question with herself and could not make up her mind.

'Yes,' Olga replied, 'it's very nice there.'

And the country cottage was taken.

And if Olga said, 'Goodness, Auntie, aren't you tired of that forest and sand? Hadn't we better go somewhere else?'

'Very well,' said the aunt, 'let us.'

'Shall we go to the theatre, Olga?' the aunt said. 'Everybody has been talking about this play for weeks.'

'With pleasure,' answered Olga, but without any particular desire to please her aunt or any expression of obedience.

Sometimes they had a slight argument.

'My dear child,' the aunt said, 'green ribbons do not suit you at all. Why not take straw-coloured ones?'

'But, Auntie dear, I've worn straw-coloured ones six times already: people will get tired of it.'

'Well, take *pensée*.'

'And do you like these?'

The aunt looked at them carefully and shook her head slowly.

'As you like, my dear, but if I were you I'd take straw-coloured or *pensée*.'

'No, Auntie, I'd rather take these,' Olga said gently, and took what she wanted.

Olga asked her aunt's advice not because she regarded her as an authority whose word was law, but as she would have asked any woman more experienced than she.

'You've read this book, Auntie,' she used to say. 'What is it like?'

'Oh, it's horrible!' said the aunt, pushing the book away, but not hiding it or taking any other measures to prevent Olga from reading it.

And it would never have occurred to Olga to read it. If neither knew what the book was like, they asked Baron von Landwagen or Stolz, if he was available, and the book was read or not, according to their verdict.

'My dear,' the aunt might say sometimes, 'I was told something yesterday about the young man who often talks to you at the Zavadskys' – a rather silly story.'

And that was all. She left it to Olga to decide whether to talk to him or not.

Oblomov's appearance in the house gave rise to no questions and attracted no particular attention on the part of the aunt, the baron, or Stolz himself. Stolz wanted to introduce his friend to a house where a certain decorum was observed, where people were not only not supposed to have a nap after their dinner, but where it was not considered proper to cross one's legs, where one was expected to change for dinner and remember what one was talking about – in short, where one could not doze off or sink idly into a chair and where there was always lively conversation on some topic of general interest. Stolz, besides, thought that the presence of a sympathetic, intelligent, lively, and a little ironical young woman in Oblomov's somnolent life would be like bringing into a gloomy, dark room a lamp that would shed an even light into all corners, raise its temperature by a few degrees and make it much more cheerful. That was all he tried to achieve in introducing his friend to Olga. He did not foresee that he was introducing a bomb that was liable to explode – neither did Olga, nor Oblomov.

Oblomov spent two hours with Olga's aunt, taking care to be on his best behaviour, without crossing his legs once and talking with the utmost decorum about everything; he even succeeded in twice pushing the footstool under her feet very dexterously. The baron arrived, smiled politely, and shook hands affably. Oblomov behaved still more decorously, and all three were extremely pleased with one another. Olga's aunt had considered Olga's walks and private talks with Oblomov as – or rather, she did not consider them at all. To go out for walks with a young man, a dandy, would have been quite a different matter: she would not have said anything even then, but with her usual tact would have imperceptibly arranged things differently: she would have accompanied them herself once or twice, sent someone else to chaperon her niece another time, and the walks would have come to an end by themselves. But to go out for a walk with 'Mr Oblomov', to sit with him in the corner of the large drawing-room or on the balcony – what did that matter? He was over thirty, and he was the last person in the world to talk sweet nothings to her or give her any improper books to read. Such a thing never occurred to any of them. Besides, the aunt had heard Stolz ask Olga on the eve of his departure not to let Oblomov doze, not to allow him to sleep in the daytime, but to worry him, make him do things, give him all sorts of commissions – in short, to take charge of him. And she, too, was asked not to lose sight of Oblomov, to invite him as often as possible, to see that he joined them in their walks and excursions, to rouse him in every possible way, if he did not go abroad.

While Oblomov sat with her aunt, Olga did not show herself, and time dragged on slowly. Oblomov was again getting hot and cold in turns. Now he guessed the reason for this change in Olga and somehow this change worried him more than the first. His first blunder had made him ashamed and frightened, but now he was feeling worried, awkward, chilled, and miserable, as in damp, rainy weather. He had made it clear to her that he had guessed she loved him, and perhaps he had guessed it at an inopportune moment. That was indeed an insult that could scarcely be put right. And even if the moment had been opportune, how clumsy he had been! He was simply a brainless coxcomb! He might have frightened away the feeling that was timidly knocking at her young, virginal heart, to settle there lightly and warily like a bird on a branch: let there be the slightest sound, the faintest rustle – and away it flies. He waited nervously and with trepidation for Olga to come down to dinner, wondering what she would say, how she would speak, and how she would look at him. ...

She came down – and he could not help admiring her; he hardly recognized her. Her face was different, even her voice was not the same. The young, naïve, almost childish smile not once appeared on her lips; she did not once look at him with

222

wide-open eyes questioningly or puzzled or with good-natured curiosity, as though she had nothing more to ask, find out, or be surprised at. Her eyes did not follow him as before. She looked at him as though she had known him for years and had studied him thoroughly, and, finally, as though he were nothing to her, no more than the baron – in short, he felt as though he had not seen her for a whole year during which she had grown into a woman. There was no trace of sternness or of the vexation of the day before; she joked and even laughed, and replied in detail to the questions she would have left unanswered before. It was obvious that she had made up her mind to force herself to behave as other people, which she had never done before. The freedom, the naturalness, which made it possible for her to say what was in her mind, was no longer there. Where had it all gone?

After dinner he went up to ask her if she would care to go for a walk. Without answering him, she turned to her aunt and asked:

'Shall we all go for a walk?'

'Yes, if we don't go too far,' said the aunt. 'Ask for my parasol, please.'

And they all went. They walked without enthusiasm, looked at Petersburg in the distance, went as far as the woods, and returned to the balcony.

'I don't expect you feel like singing to-day, do you?' asked Oblomov. 'I'm afraid to ask you,' he added, wondering whether her restraint would come to an end, her former cheerfulness return, and whether there was a chance of recapturing even for a moment, in a word, a smile or at least in her singing, her former sincerity, naïvety, and trustfulness.

'It's too hot!' the aunt observed.

'It doesn't matter,' said Olga, 'I'll try,' and she sang one song.

He listened and could not believe his ears. It was not she: where was the old passionate note? She sang so clearly, so correctly, and at the same time so – so like all young girls who were asked to sing in company: without passion. She had taken her soul out of her singing, and not a single nerve stirred in her listener. Was she playing a deep game, pretending or angry? It was impossible to tell: she looked at him kindly, she spoke readily, but she spoke as she sang, like everyone else. ... What did it mean?

Without waiting for tea, Oblomov took his hat and said goodbye.

'Do come more often,' said the aunt. 'We're always alone on week-days, if you're not afraid to be bored, and on Sundays there's always someone coming to see us, so you will certainly not be bored then.'

The baron got up politely and bowed to him.

Olga nodded to him as to an old friend, and when he was going out she turned to the window and looked out, listening with indifference to Oblomov's retreating steps.

These two hours and the next three or four days, or at most a week, had a profound effect on her and moved her a long way forward. Only women are capable of such a rapid expansion of all their powers and development of all sides of their nature. She seemed to be going through the course of life by hours rather than by days. And every hour the smallest and barely perceptible experience or incident that flashes past a man's nose like a bird, is seized with inexpressible quickness by a young girl: she follows its flight in the distance, and the curve it describes remains indelibly engraved on her memory as a sign or a lesson. Where a man needs a signpost with an inscription, a girl is satisfied with a faint rustle of the wind or a hardly audible tremor of the air. Why does a girl, whose face was so care-free and so ridiculously naïve, suddenly look so grave? What is she thinking of? It seems everything is contained in this thought of hers, the whole of man's logic, of his speculative and experimental philosophy, the whole system of life! The cousin who not so long ago left her a little girl has finished his course, put on his epaulettes, runs up to her gaily, intending to pat her as before on the shoulder, to spin her round by the hands, to jump with her over chairs and sofas – but after one intent look at her face, he suddenly grows timid, walks away confused, realizing that he is still a boy while she is already a woman! Why? What has happened? A drama? Some great event? Some news that the whole town knows? Nothing has happened – mother, uncle, aunt, nurse, maid know nothing about it. Nor has there been time for anything to happen: she has danced two mazurkas and a few quadrilles and she had a headache for some reason: she spent a sleepless night. ... And then it all passed off, except that there was something new in her face: she looked differently, she stopped laughing aloud, she did not eat a whole pear at one go, or tell how 'at school they used to – –'. She, too, had finished her course.

The next day, and the day after, Oblomov, like the cousin, hardly recognized Olga, and looked at her timidly, while she

224

looked at him simply, just as at other people, without her former curiosity or kindliness.

'What is the matter with her? What is she thinking or feeling now?' he tormented himself with questions. 'I'm hanged if I can make head or tail of it.' And how indeed could he grasp the fact that what had happened to her, happens to a man of twenty-five with the help of twenty-five professors and libraries, after roaming about the world, and sometimes even at the cost of the loss of some of his moral freshness and physical and intellectual fitness – that is, that she had become a fully conscious human being. This she had achieved easily and practically at no cost at all.

'No,' Oblomov decided, 'this is awfully boring. I'll move to Vyborg, I'll work, read, then go to Oblomovka – alone!' he added with profound dejection. 'Without her! Farewell, my paradise, my bright and peaceful ideal of life!'

He did not go to Olga's on the fourth or the fifth day; he did not read or write; he tried to go for a walk, but on coming out on to the dusty road going uphill, he said to himself : 'Why should I drag myself out in such a heat?' He yawned, went back home, lay down on the sofa, and sank into a heavy sleep as he used to in Gorokhovaya Street, in his dusty room, with the curtains drawn. His dreams were confused. Waking up, he saw the table set for dinner: cold fish and vegetable soup, Vienna steak. Zakhar stood looking sleepily out of the window; in the next room Anisya was rattling the plates. He had his dinner and sat down by the window. It was so boring, so absurd – always alone! Again he did not want to do anything or go out anywhere.

'Have a look, sir, at the kitten our neighbours have given us,' Anisya said, hoping to distract him and putting the kitten on his knee. 'Would you like it? You asked for one yesterday.'

He began stroking the kitten, but that, too, was boring.

'Zakhar!' he said.

'Yes, sir?' Zakhar responded listlessly.

'I'm thinking of moving to town.'

'To town, sir? But we have no flat.'

'Why, we have one in Vyborg.'

'But, sir, that'll only mean moving from one summer cottage to another,' Zakhar said. 'Who do you want to see there? Not Mr Tarantyev, sir?'

'But it's not comfortable here.'

'So it's moving again, is it, sir? Good Lord, haven't we had enough trouble as it is? Can't find two cups and the broom, and I daresay they're lost unless Mr Tarantyev has taken them off.'

Oblomov said nothing. Zakhar went out and came back at once, dragging a trunk and a travelling bag.

'And what are we to do with this, sir?' he asked, kicking the trunk. 'We might as well sell it.'

'Have you gone off your head, man?' Oblomov interrupted angrily. 'I shall be going abroad in a few days.'

'Abroad, sir?' Zakhar said with a sudden grin. 'You've been talking about it, that's true enough, but going abroad, sir, is a different matter.'

'Why do you think it so strange? I'm going, and that's that. My passport is ready.'

'And who'll take your boots off there?' Zakhar remarked ironically. 'Not the maid-servants by any chance? Why, sir, you'll be lost without me there!'

He grinned again, his whiskers and eyebrows moving in opposite directions.

'You're talking a lot of nonsense!' Oblomov said with vexation. 'Take this out and go!'

Next morning, as soon as Oblomov woke up at about nine o'clock, Zakhar, who had brought him his breakfast, told him that he had met the young lady on his way to the baker's.

'What young lady?' asked Oblomov.

'What young lady? Why, the Ilyinsky young lady, Olga Sergeyevna.'

'Well?' Oblomov asked impatiently.

'Well, sir, she sent you her greetings, and asked how you were and what you were doing.'

'What did you say?'

'Me, sir? I said you were all right – what could be wrong with you?'

'Why do you add your idiotic reflections?' Oblomov remarked. 'What could be wrong with him! How do you know what's wrong with me? Well, what else?'

'She asked where you had dinner yesterday.'

'Well?'

'I said, sir, you had dinner at home, and supper at home, too. Why, the young lady asked, does he have supper? Well, sir, I told her you only had two chickens for supper.'

'Id-i-ot!' Oblomov said with feeling.

'Why idiot, sir?' said Zakhar. 'Isn't it true? I can show you the bones if you like.'

'You *are* an idiot!' Oblomov repeated. 'Well, what did she say?'

'She smiled, sir. Why so little? she asked.'

'Oh dear, what an idiot!' Oblomov repeated. 'You might as well have told her that you put on my shirt inside out.'

'She didn't ask, so I didn't tell her,' Zakhar replied.

'What else did she ask you?'

'She asked me what you'd been doing all these days.'

'Well, what did you say?'

'I said you did nothing but just lay about.'

'Oh Lord!' Oblomov cried in great vexation, raising his fists to his temples. 'Get out!' he added sternly. 'If ever again you dare to tell such stories about me you'll see what I shall do to you! What a venomous creature this man is!'

'You don't expect me to go about telling lies at my age, do you, sir?' Zakhar tried to justify himself.

'Get out!' Oblomov repeated.

Zakhar did not mind abuse so long as his master did not use 'pathetic words'.

'I told her that you thought of moving to Vyborg,' Zakhar concluded.

'Go!' Oblomov cried imperiously.

Zakhar went out, heaving a loud sigh that could be heard all over the passage, and Oblomov began drinking tea. He drank his tea, and out of the large supply of rolls of different shapes he ate only one, fearful of some new indiscretion on Zakhar's part. Then he lit a cigar, sat down at the table, opened a book, read a page, and was about to turn it over when he discovered that the pages had not been cut. He tore the pages with his finger, which left festoons round the edges. It was not his book but Stolz's, and Stolz was so absurdly fussy about things, and especially about his books! Every little thing – papers, pencils, and so on – had to remain exactly as he had put them down. He should have taken a paper-knife, but it was not there; he could of course have asked for a paper-knife, but he preferred instead to replace the book and go to the sofa; he had no sooner put his head on the embroidered cushion so as to lie down more comfortably than Zakhar came into the room.

'The young lady, sir, asked you to come to – oh dear, what do you call it?' he announced.

'Why didn't you tell me about it two hours ago?' Oblomov asked hastily.

'You ordered me out of the room, sir,' Zakhar replied. 'You never let me finish. ...'

'Oh, you'll be the death of me, Zakhar,' Oblomov cried pathetically.

'Oh dear, he's starting again,' Zakhar thought, turning his left whisker towards his master and gazing at the wall. 'Just as he did the other day – sure to say something horrible.'

'Where am I supposed to go?' asked Oblomov.

'Well, sir, that what-d'you-call-it – the garden, is it?'

'The park?' asked Oblomov.

'Yes, sir, the park. She said to me, sir, would your master like to go for a walk, she said. I'll be there, she said.'

'Help me to dress!'

Oblomov ran all over the park, looked round all the flower-beds, glanced into the summer-houses – not a sign of Olga. He walked along the avenue where they had had their talk, and found her there on a seat near the place where she had plucked and thrown away the sprig of lilac.

'I thought you would never come,' she said in a kindly voice.

'I've been looking for you all over the park,' he replied.

'I knew you would be looking for me and sat down in this avenue on purpose. I thought you would be quite sure to walk through it.'

He was about to ask her what made her think so, but glancing at her, he said nothing. She looked different, not as she had been when they walked here, but as he had left her last time, when her expression had so greatly alarmed him. Even her kindness seemed somehow restrained, and her expression so concentrated and so definite; he saw that she would no longer be put off with guesses, hints, and naïve questions, that she had left that gay and childish moment behind her. Much of what had remained unsaid between them, and that might have been approached with a sly question, had been settled without words or explanations, goodness knows how, and there was no going back on it.

'Why haven't you been to see us all this time?' she asked.

He made no answer. He would have liked to make her feel somehow or other that the secret charm of their relations had gone, that he was oppressed by the air of concentration which seemed to envelop her like a cloud. She seemed to have withdrawn within herself and he did not know how to behave towards her. But he felt that the slightest hint of this would make her look surprised and grow still colder towards him, and perhaps even altogether extinguish the spark of sympathy that he had so carelessly damped at the very beginning. He had to blow it into a flame again, slowly and carefully, but he had not the slightest idea how it was to be done. He felt vaguely that she had grown up and was almost superior to him, that henceforth there could be no question of a return to child-like confidence, that a Rubicon lay between them and that his lost happiness had been left on the opposite bank: he simply had to cross over to it. But how? And what if he crossed over alone? She understood better than he what was passing in his mind, and she had therefore the advantage over him. His soul lay wide open to her and she could see how feeling was born in it, how it stirred within him and at last revealed itself; she saw that feminine guile, cunning, and coquetry – Sonia's weapons – were of no avail with him because there would be no struggle. She even realized that in spite of her youth it was she who had to play the chief role in their relations, for all she could possibly expect from him was that he would be deeply impressed, passionately but languidly devoted, in perpetual harmony with every beat of her pulse, but show no will of his own, nor any active thought. In an instant the power she wielded over him became clear to her and she liked her role of a guiding star, the ray of light she would shed over the stagnant pool and that would be reflected in it. She was already exulting over her supremacy in this duel in various ways. In this comedy, or perhaps tragedy, the protagonists almost invariably appear in the characters of tormentor and victim. Like every woman in the leading part – that is, in the part of tormentor – Olga could not deny herself the pleasure of playing cat and mouse with Oblomov, though perhaps unconsciously and not as much as other women: sometimes she would reveal her feeling in a momentary and unexpectedly capricious outburst, but would then immediately withdraw into herself again; mostly, though, she drove it farther and farther forward, knowing that he would not take a single step by himself and remain motionless where she left him.

'Have you been busy?' she asked, embroidering some piece of canvas.

'I'd have said I was busy but for that Zakhar,' thought Oblomov, groaning inwardly.

'Yes,' he said casually. 'I've been reading a book.'

'A novel?' she asked, raising her eyes to see his expression when telling a lie.

'No, I hardly ever read novels,' he replied very calmly. 'I've been reading *The History of Inventions and Discoveries*.'

'Thank goodness,' he thought, 'I've read through a page of the book to-day.'

'In Russian?' she asked.

'No, in English.'

'So you read English?'

'I do, though with difficulty. And you haven't been to town at all?' he asked chiefly in order to change the subject.

'No, I was at home all the time. I usually do my work here – in this avenue.'

'Always here?'

'Yes, I like this avenue very much. I'm very grateful to you for having shown it to me. No one ever comes here – –'

'I did not show it to you,' he interrupted. 'You remember we met here accidentally.'

'Yes, of course.'

Both were silent.

'Your stye has quite gone, hasn't it?' she asked, looking straight at his right eye.

He flushed.

'Yes, thank goodness,' he said.

'When your eye begins to itch bathe it with vodka and you won't get a stye,' she went on. 'My nurse taught me that.'

'Why does she keep on talking about styes?' Oblomov thought.

'And don't have any supper,' she added seriously.

'Zakhar!' he thought furiously, a silent imprecation rising to his lips.

'You've only to take a heavy supper,' she went on without raising her eyes from her work, 'and spend two or three days lying on your back, and you're sure to get a stye.'

'Id-i-ot!' Oblomov swore inwardly at Zakhar.

'What are you embroidering?' he asked, to change the subject.

'A bell-pull for the baron,' she said, unfolding the roll of canvas, and showing him the pattern. 'Nice?'

'Yes, very nice. The pattern is very charming. This is a sprig of lilac, isn't it?'

'Yes – I believe so,' she answered casually. 'I chose it at random. The first that turned up.'

And, blushing a little, she quickly rolled up the canvas.

'It's awfully boring if it goes on like this and I can't get anything out of her,' he thought. 'Another man – Stolz, for instance – could, but I cannot.'

He frowned and looked sleepily around him. She glanced at him and put her work into a basket.

'Let's walk as far as the road,' she said, and letting him carry the basket, she straightened her dress, opened her parasol, and walked on. 'Why are you so gloomy?' she asked.

'I don't know, Olga Sergeyevna. And why should I be happy? And how?'

'Find something to do and spend more time with other people.'

'Find something to do! I could do that if I had some aim in life. But what is my aim? I haven't one.'

'The aim is to live.'

'When you don't know what to live for, you live anyhow – from one day to another. You are glad the day is over, that the night has come, and in your sleep you can expunge from your mind the wearisome question why you have lived this day and are going to live the next.'

She listened in silence, with a stern look: severity was hidden in her knit brows and incredulity, or scorn, coiled like a serpent in the line of her lips.

'Why you have lived!' she repeated. 'Why, can anyone's life be useless?'

'It can. Mine, for instance,' he said.

'You don't yet know what the aim of your life is, do you?' she asked, stopping. 'I don't believe it: you're maligning yourself; if not, you are not worthy of life.'

'I have already passed the place where it can be found, and there is nothing more ahead of me.'

He sighed, and she smiled.

'Nothing more?' she repeated questioningly, but gaily and laughingly, as though she did not believe him and foresaw that there was something before him.

'You may laugh,' he went on, 'but it is so.'

She walked on slowly with a lowered head.

'What am I to live for?' he said, walking after her. 'Who for? What am I to seek? What am I to turn to? What am I to strive for? The flowers of life have fallen and only the thorns remain.'

They walked along slowly; she listened absent-mindedly and, in passing, tore off a sprig of lilac and gave it to him without looking.

'What's this?' he asked, taken aback.

'You see, it's a twig.'

'What kind of a twig?' he asked her, looking at her open-eyed.

'Lilac.'

'I know. But what does it mean?'

'The flower of life and – –'

He stopped and she stopped too.

231

'And?' he repeated questioningly.

'My vexation,' she said, looking straight at him with a concentrated gaze, and her smile told him that she knew what she was doing.

The cloud of impenetrability round her had dispersed. The look in her eyes was clear and intelligible. She seemed to have opened a certain page of a book on purpose and let him read the secret passage.

'Then I may hope for − −' he said suddenly, flushing with joy.

'Everything! But − −'

She fell silent. He suddenly came to life. She, too, hardly recognized Oblomov: his sleepy, misty face was transformed in a moment, his eyes opened, colour came into his cheeks; thoughts stirred in his mind, desires and resolution sparkled in his glance. She, too, read clearly in the mute play of his features that Oblomov had instantly acquired an aim in life.

'Life, life is opening to me once more,' he said, speaking as though in a delirium. 'It is there − in your eyes, your smile, in this sprig of lilac, in *Casta diva* − it's all there.'

She shook her head.

'No, not all − half.'

'The best.'

'Perhaps,' she said.

'But where is the other half? What else is there after this?'

'Look for it.'

'Why?'

'So as not to lose the first,' she replied, taking his arm, and they went home.

He kept glancing, sometimes with delight and sometimes stealthily, at her pretty head, her figure, her curls, clasping the lilac twig in his hand.

'It is all mine! Mine!' he kept repeating musingly, unable to believe his own words.

'You won't be moving to Vyborg, will you?' she asked when he was going home.

He laughed, and did not even call Zakhar a fool.

9

AFTER THAT there were no sudden changes in Olga. She was even-tempered and calm with her aunt and in company, but lived and felt that she was alive only with Oblomov. She no longer asked anyone what she ought to do or how she ought to behave, and did not appeal in her mind to Sonia's authority. As the different phases in life – that is to say, feelings – opened before her, she keenly observed all that happened around her, listened intently to the voice of her instinct, checking her feelings by the few observations she had made, and moved forward cautiously, trying with her foot the ground on which she was going to tread. She had no one she could ask for advice. Her aunt? But she skimmed over such problems so lightly and dexterously that Olga never succeeded in reducing any opinion of hers to a maxim and in fixing it in her memory. Stolz was away. Oblomov? But he was a kind of Galatea whose Pygmalion she herself had to be. Her life was filled so quietly and imperceptibly that no one noticed it, and she lived in her new sphere without arousing attention and without any visible outbursts of passion and anxieties. She did the same things for the others as before, but she did them differently. She went to the French theatre, but the play seemed to have some sort of connexion with her life; she read a book, and there were invariably lines in it which struck sparks in her own mind, passages which blazed with her own feelings, words which she had uttered the day before, as though the author had overheard her heart beating. There were the same trees in the woods, but their rustle had a special meaning for her; there was a living concord between her and them. The birds were not just chirping and twittering, but saying something to one another; and everything around her was speaking, everything responded to her mood; if a flower opened, she seemed to hear it breathe. Her dreams, too, had a life of their own: they were filled with visions and images to which she sometimes spoke aloud – they seemed to be telling her something, but so indistinctly that she could not understand; she made an effort to speak to them and ask them some question, but she, too, said something incomprehensible. It was her maid Katya who told her in the morning that she had been talking in her sleep. She remembered Stolz's words: he often told her that she had not begun to live, and she was sometimes offended that he should regard her as a child when she was twenty. But now she realized that he had been right, that she had only now begun to live.

'When all the powers of your organism awaken,' Stolz used to say to her, 'then life around you will also awaken, and you will see what you do not notice now, you will hear what you do not hear now: your nerves will become attuned to the music of the

233

spheres and you will listen to the grass growing. Wait, don't be in a hurry. It will come of itself!' he used to threaten her.

It had come.

'This is, I suppose, my powers asserting themselves, my organism awakening,' she repeated his words, listening intently to the unfamiliar tremor within her and watching keenly and timidly each new manifestation of the awakening force.

She did not give way to day-dreaming, she did not succumb to the sudden rustle of the leaves, the nightly visions, to the mysterious whispers, when someone seemed to bend over her and say something indistinct and incomprehensible in her ear.

'Nerves!' she would sometimes say with a smile, through tears, scarcely able to overcome her fear and bear the strain of the struggle between the awakening forces within her and her weak nerves. She got out of bed, drank a glass of water, opened the window, fanned her face with her handkerchief, and recovered from the visions that haunted her asleep and awake.

As soon as Oblomov awakened in the morning, the first image that arose before him was the image of Olga with a sprig of lilac in her hand. He thought of her when he went to sleep, and she was beside him when he went for a walk or when he read. He carried on an endless conversation with her in his mind by day and by night. He kept adding to the *History of Discoveries and Inventions* some fresh discoveries in Olga's appearance or character, invented occasions for meeting her accidentally or sending her a book or arranging some pleasant surprise for her. After talking to her at one of their meetings, he would continue the conversation at home, so that when Zakhar happened to come in he said to him in the very soft and tender voice in which he had been mentally addressing Olga: 'You've again forgotten to polish my boots, you bald-headed devil! Take care, or you'll catch it good and proper one day!'

But from the moment she had first sung to him, he was no longer care-free. He no longer lived his old life when it did not make any difference to him whether he was lying on his back or staring at a wall, whether Alexeyev was sitting in his drawing-room or he himself was at Ivan Gerasimovich's, in those days when he expected nothing and no one either by day or by night. Now day and night, every hour of the morning and the evening had its own shape and form, and was either filled with rainbow radiance or colourless and gloomy, according to whether he spent it in the presence of Olga or passed it dully and listlessly without her. All this had a great effect on him: his head was a regular network of daily and hourly considerations, conjectures, anticipations, agonies of uncertainty – all revolving round the questions whether he would see her or not, what she would say and do, how she would look, what commission she would give him, what she would ask him, would she be pleased or not. All these considerations had become questions of life and death to him. 'Oh, if one could experience only this warmth of love without its anxieties!' he mused. 'No, life does not leave you alone. You get burnt wherever you go! How many fresh emotions and occupations have suddenly been crowded into it! Love is a most difficult school of life!' He had read several books. Olga asked him to tell her what they were about, and listened to him with incredible patience. He wrote several letters to his estate, replaced his bailiff and got in touch with one of his neighbours through the good offices of Stolz. He would even have gone to Oblomovka if he had thought it possible to be away from Olga. He had no supper, and for the last fortnight he had not known what it meant to lie down in the daytime. In two or three weeks they had visited all the places round Petersburg. Olga and her aunt, the baron and Oblomov appeared at suburban concerts and fêtes. They talked of going to Imatra in Finland.

So far as Oblomov was concerned, he would not have stirred anywhere farther than the park, but Olga kept planning it all, and if he showed the slightest hesitation in accepting an invitation to go somewhere, the excursion was sure to take place. Then there was no end to Olga's smiles. There was not a hill within a radius of five miles from his summer cottage that he had not climbed several times.

Meanwhile their attachment grew and developed and expressed itself in accordance with the immutable laws. Olga blossomed out as her feeling grew stronger. Her eyes were brighter, her movements more graceful, her bosom filled out so gorgeously and rose and fell so evenly.

'You've grown prettier in the country, Olga,' her aunt said.

The baron's smile expressed the same compliment. Blushing, Olga put her head on her aunt's shoulders, and her aunt patted her affectionately on the cheek.

'Olga! Olga!' Oblomov called cautiously, almost in a whisper, standing at the foot of a hill, where she had asked him to meet her to go for a walk.

There was no answer. He looked at his watch.

'Olga Sergeyevna,' he added in a loud voice.

Silence.

Olga was sitting on the top of the hill. She had heard him call, but she suppressed her laughter and said nothing.

'Olga Sergeyevna!' he called, looking up to the top after having clambered half-way up between the bushes. 'She told me to come at half-past five,' he said to himself.

She could no longer refrain from laughing.

'Olga! Olga! Why, you're there!' he said, and continued to climb up. 'Ugh! What do you want to hide on a hill for?' he said, sitting down beside her.

'I suppose it's because you want to make me suffer, but you make yourself suffer too, don't you?'

'Where do you come from? Straight from home?' she asked.

'No, I went to your place first. They told me you had gone out.'

'What have you been doing to-day?' she asked.

'To-day – –'

'Had a row with Zakhar?' she finished for him.

He laughed as though it had been something utterly impossible.

'No, I read the *Revue*. Listen, Olga,' but he said nothing more and, sitting down beside her, sank into contemplation of her profile, her head, the up-and-down movement of her hand as she pulled the needle through the canvas. He fixed her with his eyes and was unable to take them off her. He did not move, only his glance moved to right and to left, following the movement of her hand. Everything within him was in a state of tremendous activity: his blood was racing through his veins, his pulse was beating twice as fast, his heart was seething – all this had such an effect on him that he breathed slowly and painfully, as people do before their execution or at the moment of the highest spiritual joy. He could not bring himself to speak or even to move; only his eyes, moist with deep-felt emotion, were fixed on her irresistibly.

From time to time she threw a deep glance at him, read the all-too-obvious meaning written on his face, and thought: 'Dear God, how he loves me! How tender he is to me, how tender!' and she felt proud and looked with admiration at the man brought to her feet by her own power. The time of symbolic hints, meaningful smiles, and sprigs of lilac had irrevocably passed. Love had become severer, more exacting, and was beginning to be transformed into a sort of duty; they felt that they possessed rights over each other. Both revealed more and more of themselves: misunderstandings and doubts disappeared or gave way to more positive and clearer questions. At first she taunted him with slightly sarcastic remarks for the years he had wasted in idleness; she passed a severe sentence on him and condemned his apathy more deeply and effectively than Stolz; then, as she grew more intimate with him, she gave up taunting him for his flabby and listless existence and began to manifest her despotic will over him, reminding him courageously of the purpose and the duties of life and sternly demanded a change in his state of mind, constantly arousing it from its torpor either by involving him in a subtle discussion of some vital problem that was familiar to her or by approaching him with a problem that was not clear to her and that she could not grasp. He struggled, racked his brains, did his best not to lower himself in her estimation and to help explain some knotty problem to her, or else boldly set it aside. All her feminine tactics were pervaded by tender sympathy; all his attempts to keep in step with the workings of her mind were inspired by passion. But more often he lay down at her feet exhausted, put his hand to his heart and listened to its beating without taking his wide-open, amazed, rapturous eyes from her. 'How he loves me!' she kept saying at those moments, looking admiringly at him. If she sometimes noticed some of Oblomov's old traits still lurking in his soul – and she could look deep into it – such as the least weariness or barely perceptible inertness of spirit, she overwhelmed him with reproaches, in which there was occasionally a touch of bitter regret and fear of having made a mistake. Sometimes, just when he was about to open his mouth in a yawn, he was struck by her look of astonishment and he immediately shut his mouth with a snap. She would not permit the faintest shadow of somnolence on his face. She asked him not only what he had been doing, but also what he was going to do. What made him sit up even more than her reproaches was the realization that his weariness made her weary too, and she became cold and indifferent. Then he became full of life, strength, and activity, and the shadow disappeared once more, and their feeling for one another was again full of strength and vigour. But all these troubles did not so far go beyond the magic circle of love. His activity was of a purely negative character: he did not sleep, he read, he sometimes thought about writing his plan for managing his estate, he walked and drove a lot. But what he was to make of his life, what he was to do with himself – that was still a matter of mere intentions.

'What other sort of life and activity does Andrey want?'

Oblomov said, opening his eyes wide after dinner so as not to fall asleep. 'Isn't this life? Isn't love service? Let him try it! Every day means a good seven-mile walk! I spent last night in a wretched inn in town without undressing, only took off my boots, and Zakhar was not there to help me, either – and all because I had to carry out some commissions for her!'

What he dreaded most was when Olga put some abstruse questions to him and demanded a fully satisfactory answer, as though he were some professor: and that happened often with her, not out of pedantry, but out of a desire to know what it was all about. She sometimes even forgot her aims with regard to Oblomov and was entirely carried away by the question itself.

'Why aren't we taught that?' she said with thoughtful vexation, as she listened eagerly to some desultory talk of a subject that was not considered necessary to women. One day she began worrying Oblomov with questions about double stars: he was unwise enough to refer to Herschel, and was at once sent to town for a book which he had to read and then tell her about till she was satisfied. Another time, in a conversation with the baron, he again unwisely said something about schools of painting – and again he had a whole week's work: reading books and telling Olga about what he had read; then they went to the Hermitage, and there he had once more to illustrate to her what he had read. If he said anything at random, she would see through it at once and start pestering him. Then he spent a week going to different shops in search of engravings of the best pictures. Poor Oblomov had to look up again what he had once learnt, or rush to bookshops for new works, and sometimes spent a sleepless night rummaging among books and reading something up so as to be able to reply with a casual air to a question she had asked him the day before. She put her questions not with feminine want of thought and not because the idea came suddenly into her head, but insistently and impatiently, and if Oblomov did not answer, she punished him by a long, searching glance. How he used to tremble under that glance!

'Why don't you say something?' she said. 'Why are you silent? One might think you were bored.'

'Oh,' he said, as though coming to after a fainting fit, 'how I love you!'

'Really? If you hadn't said so, I should never have thought so.'

'But don't you feel what is going on inside me?' he began.

'You know, I find it difficult to speak. Here – give me your hand – here something doesn't let me, first as if something heavy – some heavy stone–lay there, as though I were in deep sorrow, and yet – strange to say – the same kind of process occurs in one's organism both in joy and in sorrow: one finds it hard, almost painful, to breathe and one feels like crying! If I cried, I'd feel just as if I had been unhappy: tears would make me feel easier. ...'

She looked at him silently, as though checking the truth of his words, comparing it with what was written on his face, and smiled: she was satisfied with the result. Her face was full of the breath of happiness, peaceful happiness which nothing apparently could disturb. It was clear that her heart was not heavy, but tranquil as everything in nature on that peaceful morning.

'What is the matter with me?' Oblomov asked hesitantly, as though speaking to himself.

'Shall I tell you?'

'Yes, do.'

'You're in love.'

'Yes, of course,' he replied, snatching her hand away from her embroidery and not kissing it, but just pressing her fingers to his lips and apparently intending to keep them there for ever.

She tried to take her hand away gently, but he held it firmly.

'Let me go,' she said. 'There, that's enough.'

'And you?' he asked. 'Aren't you in love?'

'In love – no, I don't like that expression: I love you!' she said and gazed at him for some time as though making sure that she really loved him.

'L-love!' Oblomov said. 'But one may love one's mother, father, nurse, and even one's dog: all this is covered by the general, collective term "I love" as by an old – –'

'– dressing-gown?' she asked ironically. 'By the way, where is your dressing-gown?'

'What dressing-gown? I never had one.'

She looked at him with a reproachful smile.

'There you go again, Olga,' he said. 'My dressing-gown! I am waiting, I am all of a quiver to hear you tell me about the deepest experience of your life and what name you will give it and you – good Lord, Olga! Yes, I am in love with you and I assert that without it there is no true love: one does not fall in love with one's father, mother, or nurse, but loves them.'

'I don't know,' she said reflectively, as though listening to what was going on deep inside her, 'I don't know whether I am in love with you. If I'm not, then perhaps the right moment has not come yet; all I know is that I never loved my father, my mother, or my nurse like this.'

'What is the difference?' he tried to get her to answer. 'Do you feel anything special?'

'Do you want to know?' she asked slyly.

'Yes, yes, yes! Have you no desire to talk about it?'

'But why do you want to know?'

'So as to be able to live by it every minute: to-day, all night, to-morrow – till I meet you again. This is the only thing I live for.'

'Well, you see, you have to renew the supply of your tenderness every day! This is the difference between the person who is in love and the person who loves. I – –'

'Yes?' He waited impatiently.

'I love differently,' she said, leaning back on the seat and gazing vacantly at the moving clouds. 'I am bored without you, I feel sorry to part from you for a short time, and it would grieve me if I were to part from you for a long time. I know and believe, once and for all, that you love me, and I am happy, though you may never tell me again that you love me. I cannot love more or better than this.'

'It might be – Cordelia speaking,' thought Oblomov, looking passionately at Olga.

'If you – died,' she went on hesitantly, 'I'd wear mourning for you all my life and I'd never smile again. If you fell in love with another, I should not blame or curse you, but wish you happiness in my heart. ... For me this love is the same as – life, and life – –'

She was looking for a word.

'Well, what is life, do you think?'

'Life is duty, obligation, and hence love is duty, too: I feel as though God has sent it me,' she concluded, raising her eyes to the sky, 'and commanded me to love.'

'Cordelia!' Oblomov cried aloud. 'And she is twenty-one! So that is love in your opinion!' he added thoughtfully.

'Yes, and I think I shall have enough strength to live and love all my life.'

'Who could have suggested such an idea to her?' Oblomov thought, gazing at her almost with veneration. 'She could not have reached this clear and simple understanding of love and life through experience, torture, fire, and smoke.'

'But have you no intense joys – have you no passions?' he asked.

'I don't know,' she said. 'I have not experienced them and I don't understand them.'

'Oh, how I understand it now!'

'Perhaps I, too, will feel it in time, perhaps I, too, will feel the same powerful emotions as you, and I shall look at you as you do at me, as though I did not believe that it was really you. ... That must be awfully funny, I expect!' she added gaily. 'How you look at me sometimes! I'm sure Auntie notices it.'

'Then what happiness do you find in love if you don't feel the intense joy I feel?'

'What happiness! Why, this!' she said, pointing to him, to herself, and to the solitude around them. 'Isn't that happiness? Have I ever lived like that? Before I should not have sat here among these trees for a quarter of an hour alone without a book or without music. ... Talking to any man except Mr Stolz used to bore me. I had nothing to say to them. All I wanted was to be left alone. But now – why, I am happy even if we never say a word to each other.'

She looked round at the trees and the grass, then fixed her gaze on him, smiled and held out her hand to him.

'Won't I feel awful when you go away?' she added. 'Won't I be glad to hurry off to bed and go to sleep so as not to see the tedious night? Won't I send a message to you in the morning? Won't I – –'

With every 'won't I' Oblomov's face beamed more and more and his eyes shone more brightly.

'Yes, yes,' he echoed; 'I, too, wait for the morning, and the night is tedious to me, and I, too, will send a message to you to-morrow not because I have anything to tell you, but just for the sake of uttering your name another time and hearing the sound of it, of learning something about you from the servants and envying them for having seen you already. We think, live, and hope in the same way. I'm sorry I doubted you, Olga. I am quite convinced that you love me as you never loved your father or your mother or – –'

'– my lapdog,' she said with a laugh. 'You must trust me, then,' she concluded, 'as I trust you, and don't have any doubts, do not disturb this happiness by empty doubts or it will fly away. I shall never give back what I have once called my own, unless it is taken away from me. I know this: I may be young, but – – Do you know,' she said with confidence in her voice, 'for the month during which I have known you I have thought and felt a great deal. It is as though I had read a big book all by

241

myself a little at a time....So, please, don't have any doubts....'

'I can't help having doubts,' he interrupted. 'Don't ask me that. Now, while I am with you I am certain of everything: your eyes, your voice – everything tells me not to doubt. You look at me as though you wished to say: I do not need words, I can read everything in your eyes. But when you are not with me I am plunged into such agonizing doubts and questions that I have to run to you again just to have a look at you, for otherwise I do not believe. Why is that?'

'And I believe you: how is that?'

'I should think so! You have a lunatic before you who has been infected by passion. I expect you can see yourself in my eyes as in a mirror. Besides, you are twenty. Have a good look at yourself: what man could fail to pay you the meed of admiration, though only by a glance? To know you, to listen to you, to look at you for hours, to love you – – Oh, that's enough to drive one mad! And you are so calm, so placid, and if two or three days pass and I don't hear you say "I love you," I feel awful here,' he pointed to his heart.

'I love you, I love you, I love you – there's a three-days' supply for you!' she said, getting up from the seat.

'You're always joking,' he said with a sigh, walking down the hill with her, 'but it's no joking matter to me.'

So the same *motif* was played by them in different variations. Their meetings, their conversations – it was all one song, one light which burnt brightly; only its rays were broken up into rose, amber, and green, shimmering in the surrounding atmosphere. Every day and every hour brought new sounds and new colours, but the light and the tune were the same. Both he and she listened to these sounds and, having caught them, hastened to sing to each other what they heard without suspecting that next day new sounds would be heard, new rays would appear, and forgetting the next day that the song was different from that of the day before. She clothed the outpourings of her heart in the colours with which her imagination glowed at the moment, and firmly believed that they were true to nature, and hastened with innocent and unconscious coquetry to appear before her friend in that beautiful guise. He had even greater faith in those magic sounds and the entrancing light, and hastened to appear before her in the full armour of passion, to show her all the splendour and power of the fire that was consuming his soul. They did not lie to themselves or to each other: they were merely expressing what the heart dictated, and its voice was

242

coloured by the imagination. It did not really matter to Oblomov whether Olga appeared as Cordelia and remained true to that image or followed a new path and was transformed into another vision, so long as she appeared in the same colours as those in which she was enshrined in his heart and so long as he was happy. Neither did Olga inquire whether her passionate friend would pick up her glove if she threw it into the mouth of a lion or would jump into an abyss for her, so long as she could see the symptoms of his passion and so long as he remained true to her ideal of a man – and one who awakened to life through her: so long as the light of her eyes and her smile kept alive the flame of courage in him and he did not cease to regard her as the sole purpose of his life. That is why the fleeting image of Cordelia, the fire of Oblomov's passion reflected only one moment, one ephemeral breath of their love, only one of its fanciful patterns. And to-morrow – to-morrow will glow with a different light, a light as beautiful, perhaps, but a different one for all that. ...

10

OBLOMOV was like a man who has just been watching a summer sunset and enjoying its crimson afterglow, unable to tear his eyes away from the sky and turn back to see the approaching night, thinking all the time of the return of light and warmth next day. He lay on his back enjoying the afterglow of his last meeting with Olga. 'I love you, I love you, I love you,' Olga's words still rang in his ears, sweeter than anything she had ever sung; the last rays of the intent look she gave him still rested upon him. He was trying to get to the bottom of its meaning, to determine how much she loved him, and was about to fall asleep when suddenly – –

Next morning Oblomov got up looking pale and gloomy; his face bore the traces of a sleepless night, his forehead was furrowed, his eyes dull and phlegmatic. His pride, his gay and cheerful look, the deliberate, sober movements of a busy man had all gone. He drank his tea listlessly, and without opening a single book or sitting down to his desk, he thoughtfully lit a cigar and sat down on the sofa. Formerly he would have lain down, but he had lost the habit of that now and he felt no compulsion to put his head on a pillow. He did, however, lean his elbow on it – a symptom of his former inclination. He was in a dismal mood. From time to time he sighed, shrugged his shoulders suddenly, or shook his head bitterly. Something was agitating him violently, but it was not love. Olga's image was before him, but it seemed to be far away, in a haze, without radiance, a stranger to him; he gave it a sickly look and sighed.

'Live as God commands and not as you would like is a wise rule, but – –' And he sank into thought. 'No, you can't live as you like, that's clear,' some morose, cantankerous voice began speaking within him. 'You will fall into a chaos of contradictions which no human intellect, however profound and daring, can unravel! One day you desire something, next day you get what you have so passionately desired, and the day after you blush at the thought of having desired it, and then you curse life because it has been fulfilled – that is what comes from your arrogant and independent striding into life, from your wilful *I want to*. A man has to grope his way through life; he must close his eyes to many things and not dream of happiness or dare to murmur if it escapes him – that is life! Whose idea was it that it was happiness or enjoyment? The madmen! "Life is life, it is duty," Olga says – an obligation, and an obligation may be hard. Let us, then, do our duty. ...' He sighed. 'I'm not going to see Olga again – Lord, you have opened my eyes and shown me my duty,' he said, looking up at the sky, 'but where am I to get the necessary strength for it? To part! I can still do it now, though it may hurt. I shall not curse myself afterwards for not having parted from her. And one of her servants may come at any moment, for she said she would send me a message. ... She doesn't expect – –'

What was the cause of all this? What ill wind had suddenly blown on Oblomov? What clouds had it brought? And why did he assume so sorrowful a burden? The day before he seemed to have looked into Olga's soul and seen a bright world and a bright future there, had read his horoscope and hers. What had happened then?

He must have had supper or lain on his back, and his poetic mood gave way to horrors. It often happens that one goes to sleep on a quiet, cloudless summer evening under the twinkling stars, thinking how lovely the fields will be in the bright morning sunshine! How refreshing it will be to take a walk deep into the forest to escape from the heat! And suddenly one awakens to the patter of the rain, to grey, melancholy clouds; it is cold and damp. ... In the evening Oblomov had been listening to the beating of his heart as usual, felt with his hand to make sure that it had not grown larger or had hardened, then, finally, he started analysing his happiness and suddenly came upon a drop of bitterness which poisoned him. The poison acted quickly and violently. He ran through his whole life in his mind: for the hundredth time repentance and belated regret for the past filled his heart. He imagined what he would have been now if he had gone boldly forward, how much fuller and more varied his life would have been if he had been active, and then passed over to the question of what he was now, and how Olga could possibly love him. What could she love him for? Was it not a mistake? The thought suddenly flashed through his mind like lightning, and the lightning struck him right in the heart and shattered it. He groaned. 'A mistake! Yes – that's what it is!' he could not help thinking.

'I love you, I love you, I love you,' it came back to him, and his heart began to grow warmer, but was suddenly chilled again. Olga's thrice-repeated 'I love you' – what did it mean? Did her eyes deceive her? Did her heart beguile her? It was not love, but merely a presentiment of love! That voice would sound one day, and so powerfully, with such a tremendous crash of chords, that the whole world would be startled! The aunt and the baron would know of it, and the echo of that voice would resound far and wide! That feeling would not meander as gently as a brook concealed in the grass with hardly an audible murmur. She loved now just as she embroidered: the pattern came to light slowly, and she unfolded it even more lazily and, after admiring it for a moment, put it down and forgot all about it. Yes, that was only a preparation for love, it was only an experiment, and he chanced to have turned up as the first fairly tolerable subject for the experiment. ... For was it not chance that had brought them together? She would not have noticed him otherwise. Stolz had pointed him out to her and infected her young, impressionable heart with his own sympathy; she was sorry for him, was fired with the ambition to rouse him from his sleep, and then she would leave him. 'That's what it is!' he muttered in horror, getting out of bed and lighting a candle with a trembling hand. 'There has never been anything more than that! She was ready for love, her heart was waiting for it eagerly, and she met me accidentally, by chance. ... Let another man appear – and she will recognize her mistake with horror! How she will look at me then! How she will turn away! Awful! I'm taking what doesn't belong to me! I'm a thief! What am I doing? How blind I have been – my God!'

He looked at himself in the mirror: he was pale, yellow, his eyes were lustreless. He thought of those lucky young men whose eyes were moist and dreaming but, like Olga's, had a deep and forceful look in them and sparkled tremulously, whose smile was confident of victory, whose step was bold, and whose voice was strong and ringing. And one day one of them might come: she would flush suddenly, look at him and Oblomov and – burst out laughing!

He looked at himself in the glass again.

'Women don't love men like me!' he said.

Then he lay down and buried his face in the pillow.

'Good-bye, Olga,' he concluded. 'Be happy.'

'Zakhar!' he called in the morning. 'If a servant comes from the Ilyinskys for me, say I am not at home, that I've gone to town.'

'Very good, sir.'

'Yes – no, I'd better write to her,' he said to himself, 'or she'll think it strange that I've suddenly disappeared. I have to offer some explanation.'

He sat down to the table and began writing quickly, eagerly, with feverish haste, quite differently from the way he had written to his landlord at the beginning of May. Not once was there an unpleasant collision between two *whichs* and two *thats*.

'You may find it strange, Olga Sergeyevna,' (he wrote) 'to get this letter instead of seeing me, when we meet each other so often. Read it to the end and you will see that I could not have done otherwise. I ought to have begun by writing it, then we should have both been saved a great deal of self-reproach in the future; but it is not too late even now. We fell in love with one another so suddenly and so quickly, as though we both had fallen ill, and this prevented me from coming to my senses sooner. Besides, looking at you and listening to you for hours on end, who would willingly have undertaken the hard task of recovering from the enchantment? How could one have sufficient caution or will-power to be able to stop at any moment at every slope instead of sliding down it? Every day I thought: "I am not going to let myself be carried away any further – I am going to stop here and now – it all depends on me," and I was carried away, and now comes the struggle in which I must ask you to help me. It is only to-day, or rather last night, that I realized how fast I was sliding down: it was only yesterday that I succeeded in looking deeper into the abyss into which I am falling, and I decided to stop.

'I am speaking only of myself – not out of egoism, but because when I am lying at the bottom of this abyss you will still be soaring high above it like a pure angel, and I doubt whether you will want to cast a glance into it. Listen, let me put it plainly and frankly and without circumlocution: you do not love me and you cannot love me. Trust my experience and believe me absolutely. For my heart began beating long ago; it may have been beating wrongly and out of tune, but that is what taught me to distinguish its regular from its irregular beat. You cannot but I can and should know how to recognize truth from error, and I am in duty bound to warn one who has not had time to recognize it. And so I am warning you: you are in error, turn back!

'So long as our love took the form of a light, smiling vision, so long as it sounded in the *Casta diva*, came to us in the scent of a sprig of lilac, in unexpressed sympathy, in a shy glance, I did not trust it, taking it for a mere play of the imagination and the whisper of vanity. But the time for innocent play has passed; I have fallen ill with love, I have felt the symptoms of passion; you have grown thoughtful and serious; you have devoted your leisure to me, you are in a state of nerves, you have grown restless, and it was then – I mean, it is now, that I am frightened and feel that it is my duty to stop and tell you what it is.

'I have told you that I love you, and you said the same to me – don't you hear how discordant this sounds? You don't? Well, you will hear it later when I am already in the abyss. Look at me, think carefully of what my life is like: is it possible for you to love me? Do you love me? "I love you, I love you, I love you" – you said yesterday. "No, no, no!" I answer firmly.

'You do not love me, but – I hasten to add – you are not lying, nor are you deceiving me; you cannot say *yes*, when everything in you is saying *no*. I only want to prove to you that your present "I love you" is not real love, but only the expectation of love in the future; it is merely an unconscious need of love which, for lack of proper food, for lack of fire, burns with a false flame, without warmth, which with some women finds expression in fondling a child and with others simply in fits of crying or hysterics. From the very beginning I ought to have said to you sternly: "You have made a mistake. The man you have longed for and dreamed of is not before you. Wait, he will come, and then you will come to yourself and you will be vexed and ashamed of your mistake, and your shame and vexation will hurt me." That's what I should have said to you, had I been

247

more perceptive and more courageous and, last but not least, more sincere. ... I have, as a matter of fact, said it, but – you remember? – fearful that you might believe me, that it should really happen; I told you beforehand everything people might say later, so as to prepare you not to listen to them and not to believe them, while I hastened to meet you, thinking that I might as well be happy before the right man came. Such is the logic of infatuation and passion.

'Now I think differently. What will happen when I grow deeply attached to her, when seeing her is no longer a luxury but a necessity, when love digs deep into my heart (it's not for nothing that I feel a lump there)? How shall I be able to tear myself away then? Shall I be able to survive the pain? I shall have a bad time then. Even now I cannot think of it without horror. If you were older and more experienced, I should have blessed my happiness and given you my hand for ever. But now – –

'Why, then, do I write? Why haven't I come to tell you straight that my desire to see you grows stronger every day and yet I ought not to see you. But, I'm afraid, I have not the courage to say it to your face. You know that yourself! Sometimes I feel like saying something of the kind, but I say something quite different. Perhaps you would look sad (if it is true that you haven't been bored with me), or, having misunderstood my good intentions, you would be offended: I could not bear either, I would again say something different, and my honourable intentions would crumble into dust and end in an arrangement to meet next day. Now, away from you, it is quite different: your gentle eyes, your kind, pretty face is not before me; the paper is silent and does not mind, and I write calmly (this isn't true): *we shall never see each other again* (this is true).

'Another man might have added: *I write this in a flood of tears*, but I am not trying to show off before you, I do not parade my grief, because I do not want to make the pain worse, to aggravate regret and sorrow. All such showing off generally conceals the intention of making the feeling strike deeper roots, and I want to destroy its seeds in both you and me. Besides, tears are suitable either to seducers who try to capture a woman's imprudent vanity by phrases, or to languid dreamers. I am saying this, parting from you as one parts from a good friend who sets out on a long journey. In another three weeks or in another month it would be too late: love makes incredible progress, it is a kind of gangrene of the soul. Now I am in as bad a state as can be, I don't count time by hours and minutes, I know nothing of sunrise and sunset, but only by whether I have seen you or have not seen you, whether I shall or shall not see you, whether you have been or not, whether you will come. ... All this is all right for youth, which bears easily pleasant and unpleasant sensations; what I want is peace and quiet, however dull and somnolent, for it is familiar to me; for I cannot weather storms.

'Many people would be surprised at my action. "Why is he running away?" some will say, and others will laugh at me. Well, I can put up with this, too. If I can put up with not seeing you, I can put up with anything.

'I am comforted a little in my deep anguish by the thought that this brief episode of our lives will for ever leave so pure and fragrant a memory in my mind that it alone will be sufficient to prevent me from sinking into my former state of torpor, and without harming you, will serve you as a guiding principle for your normal life in future. Good-bye, my angel; make haste and fly away as a frightened bird flies from a branch on which it has alighted by mistake, and do it as lightly, cheerfully, and gaily!'

Oblomov was writing with inspiration; his pen was flying over the pages. His eyes shone and his cheeks were flushed. The letter turned out to be long, like all love-letters: lovers are terribly long-winded.

'Funny! I don't feel bored or depressed any more!' Oblomov thought. 'I am almost happy. Why is that? Probably because I've got a load off my mind by writing the letter.'

He read the letter over, folded and sealed it.

'Zakhar,' he said, 'when the servant comes give him this letter for the young lady.'

'Very good, sir,' said Zakhar.

Oblomov really felt almost cheerful. He sat down on the sofa with his feet tucked under him and even asked if there was anything for lunch. He ate two eggs and lighted a cigar. His heart and his mind felt at ease: he was living. He imagined how Olga would receive his letter, how she would be surprised, what she would look like reading it! What would happen afterwards? He was enjoying the prospects of the day and the newness of the position. He listened with a sinking heart for a knock at the door, wondering if the servant had been, if Olga was already reading his letter. No, all was quiet in the entrance hall.

'What can it mean?' he thought anxiously. 'No one has called. Why is that?'

249

A secret voice whispered to him: 'What are you so worried about? You want to break off all relations with her, don't you?' But he stifled that voice.

Half an hour later he at last succeeded in calling in Zakhar, who had been sitting in the yard with the coachman.

'Hasn't anyone been?' he asked. 'Hasn't the servant called?'

'He has called, sir,' Zakhar replied.

'Well, what did you do?'

'I said you were not at home – you had gone to town.' Oblomov glared at him.

'Why did you say that?' he asked. 'What did I tell you to do when the man came?'

'But it was a maid, sir, not a man,' Zakhar answered with unruffled calmness.

'Did you give her the letter?'

'No, sir. You told me first to say you were not at home and then give the letter. When the man-servant comes, I'll give it to him.'

'Why, you – you're a murderer! Where's the letter? Give it me!'

Zakhar brought the letter, which was considerably soiled by then.

'Why don't you wash your hands?' Oblomov cried angrily, pointing to a stain. 'Look at it!'

'My hands are clean, sir,' Zakhar replied, looking away.

'Anisya! Anisya!' cried Oblomov.

Anisya thrust her head and shoulders in at the door.

'Look what Zakhar has done!' he complained to her. 'Take this letter and give it to the maid or the man-servant who calls from the Ilyinskys, for the young lady. Do you hear?'

'Yes, sir. Let me have it, I'll see that it's delivered.'

But as soon as she left the room Zakhar snatched the letter out of her hands.

'Go along,' he shouted, 'and mind your own business.'

Soon the maid came again. Zakhar was opening the door to her, and when Anisya was about to go up to it, he glared furiously at her.

'What do you want here?' he asked hoarsely.

'I've just come to hear what you – –'

'All right, all right,' he thundered, threatening her with his elbow. 'Out you go!'

She smiled and went out, but watched through a crack in the door to see if Zakhar was carrying out his master's orders.

Hearing the noise, Oblomov himself rushed out into the hall.

'What is it, Katya?' he asked.

'My mistress, sir, sent me to ask where you have gone but it seems you haven't gone anywhere. You're at home. I'll run and tell her,' she said, turning to go.

'Of course I'm at home,' said Oblomov. 'Zakhar is always talking nonsense. Here, give this letter to your mistress.'

'Yes, sir, I will.'

'Where is she now?'

'She's gone for a walk in the village, sir. She asked me to tell you, sir, if you'd finished the book, to come to the park at two o'clock.'

Katya went away.

'I won't go,' Oblomov thought, walking towards the village. 'Why exacerbate one's feelings when all should be over?'

From a distance he saw Olga walking up the hill; he watched Katya overtaking her and giving her the letter; he saw Olga stop for a moment, glance at the letter, think it over, then nod to Katya and turn into the avenue leading to the park.

Oblomov made a detour, and walking past the hill, entered the same avenue from the other end and, half-way down it, sat down on the grass among the bushes and waited.

'She's bound to pass here,' he thought. 'I'll just peep at her unobserved, see how she is, and then go away for ever.'

He listened for the sound of her footsteps with a sinking heart. No – all was quiet. Nature carried on with her never-ceasing work: all around him unseen, tiny creatures were busy while everything seemed to be enjoying a solemn rest. In the grass everything was moving, creeping, bustling. Ants were running in different directions, looking very busy and engrossed in their work, running into one another, scampering about, hurrying – it was just like looking from a height at a busy market-place: the same small crowds, the same crush, the same bustle. Here a bumble-bee was buzzing about a flower and crawling into its calyx; here hundreds of flies were clustering round a drop of resin running out of a small crack in a lime-tree; and somewhere in the thicket a bird had long been repeating one and the same note, perhaps calling to its mate. Two butterflies, flying round and round one another, danced off precipitately as in a waltz among the tree trunks. The grass exuded a strong fragrance; an unceasing din rose from it.

'What a row is going on here,' he thought, watching intently all this bustle and listening to the faint noises of nature. 'And outside everything is so still, so quiet.'

But there was no sound of footsteps. At last – yes! 'Oh,' Oblomov sighed, quietly parting the branches, 'it is she – she ... But what's this? She's crying! Good heavens!'

Olga walked slowly along, wiping her tears with a handkerchief; but no sooner had she wiped them, than fresh tears came. She was ashamed of them, she tried to swallow them, to hide them from the very trees, but she could not. Oblomov had never seen Olga cry; he did not expect it, and her tears seemed to burn him, but in a way that made him feel warm, not hot. He walked quickly after her.

'Olga, Olga!' he called tenderly, as he followed her.

She gave a start, looked round, gazed at him in surprise, then turned away and walked on.

He walked beside her.

'You're crying?' he said.

Her tears flowed faster than ever. She could no longer keep them back and, pressing her handkerchief to her face, she burst into sobs and sat down on the nearest seat.

'What have I done!' he whispered in dismay, taking her hand and trying to draw it away from her face.

'Leave me, please!' she said. 'Go away. Why are you here? I know I ought not to cry. For what is there to cry about? You are right: yes, anything might happen!'

'What can I do to make you stop crying?' he asked, going down on his knees before her. 'Tell me, command me. I am ready for anything.'

'You've made me cry, but it's not in your power to stop my tears. You're not so strong as all that! Let me go, sir!' she said, fanning her face with her handkerchief.

He looked at her and cursed himself inwardly.

'The stupid letter!' he said penitently.

She opened her work-basket, took out the letter and gave it him.

'Take it,' she said, 'and carry it away with you so that I don't cry any longer looking at it.'

He put it in his pocket silently and sat beside her, hanging his head.

'At any rate you will do justice to my intention, Olga, won't you?' he said softly. 'It proves how dear your happiness is to me.'

'Yes, it does,' she said, sighing. 'I'm afraid, Mr Oblomov, you must have begrudged me my peaceful happiness and you hastened to destroy it.'

'Destroy it! So you haven't read my letter? I'll repeat it to you ...'

'I haven't read it to the end because I could not see it for tears: I'm still so silly. But I guessed the rest. Please, don't repeat it, for you will only make me cry again.'

Her tears began to flow again.

'But,' he began, 'am I not giving you up because of your future happiness? Am I not sacrificing myself? Do you think I am doing this cold-bloodedly? Am I not weeping inwardly? Why do you think I am doing it?'

'Why?' she repeated, turning to him and leaving off crying suddenly. 'For the same reason that you hid in the bushes to see whether I would cry and how I would cry – that's why! Had you sincerely meant what you have written, had you been convinced that we ought to part, you would have gone abroad without seeing me.'

'What an idea! ...' he said reproachfully, and fell silent.

He was struck by her suggestion because he suddenly realized that it was true.

'Yes,' she confirmed, 'yesterday you wanted me to say "I love you," to-day you wanted to see me cry, and to-morrow you may want to see me die.'

'Olga, how can you say a thing like that! Surely, you must know that I'd gladly give half my life now to hear you laugh and not to see your tears.'

'Yes, perhaps now when you have already seen a woman weeping for you, No,' she added, 'you have no pity. You say you didn't want my tears. Well, if you really meant it, you wouldn't have made me cry.'

'But I didn't know, did I?' he cried, pressing both his hands to his chest.

'A loving heart has its own way of reasoning,' she replied. 'It knows what it wants, and knows what is going to happen. Yesterday I shouldn't have come here because we had some visitors who arrived suddenly, but I knew how upset you would have been waiting for me and that you might have slept badly: so I came because I did not want you to suffer. ... And you – you are glad because I am crying. Well, look at me and be happy!'

And she began to cry again.

'I have slept badly as it is, Olga. I had an awful night. ...'

'So you were sorry that I slept well, that I didn't have an

253

awful night, were you?' she interrupted. 'Had I not been crying now, you would have slept badly to-night, wouldn't you?'

'What am I to do now?' he said with submissive tenderness. 'Say I am sorry?'

'Only children do that, or people who tread on a person's toes in a crowd – it's no good your being sorry,' she said, fanning her face with her handkerchief again.

'But what if it's true, Olga? I mean, what if I am right and our love is a mistake? What if you fall in love with another and blush when you look at me?'

'Well, what if I do?' she asked, looking at him with such deep, piercing, ironical eyes that he felt embarrassed.

'She is out to get something from me!' he thought. 'Take care, Oblomov!'

'What do you mean – "if I do?"' he repeated mechanically, looking at her anxiously and at a loss to know what was at the back of her mind and how she would explain her question, since it was obvious that it was impossible to justify their love if it was a mistake.

She looked at him with such conscious deliberation and confidence that it was clear that she knew what she was talking about.

'You are afraid,' she replied bitingly, 'of falling "to the bottom of the abyss". You are afraid of being made a fool of if I should cease loving you. "It will go badly with me," you write.'

He still did not quite understand her.

'But don't you see if I fell in love with another man, I should be happy, shouldn't I? And don't you say that you know I shall be happy in future and that you are ready to sacrifice everything, even your life, for me?'

He looked intently at her, blinking from time to time.

'So that's her logic!' he whispered. 'I must say I didn't expect that. ...'

And she looked him up and down with such annihilating irony.

'And what about the happiness that is driving you mad?' she went on. 'And these mornings and evenings, this park, my "I love you" – isn't this all worth something, some sacrifice, some pain?'

'Oh, I wish I could sink through the ground!' he thought, feeling miserable, as he grasped Olga's meaning more and more.

'And what if you grew tired of this love,' she began warmly with another question, 'as you have grown tired of books, of your work at the Civil Service, of society? What if in due course, even if I have no rival, if you don't fall in love with some other woman, you just drop asleep beside me as on your sofa, and even my voice won't waken you? If that lump in your heart disappears, if not even another woman, but your dressing-gown becomes dearer to you than I?'

'Olga, that's impossible!' he interrupted, displeased, and drew away from her.

'Why is it impossible?' she asked, 'You say that I am mistaken, that I will fall in love with somebody else, and I can't help feeling sometimes that you will simply fall out of love with me. And what then? How shall I justify myself for what I am doing now? What shall I say to myself, let alone to other people or society? I, too, sometimes spend sleepless nights because of this, but I do not torture you with conjectures about the future because I believe that everything will be for the best. With me happiness overcomes fear. I think it is something if your eyes begin to shine because of me, when you climb hills in search of me, when you forget your indolence and rush off in the heat to town for some flowers or a book for me, when I see that I make you smile and wish to live. ... I am waiting and searching for one thing – happiness, and I believe I have found it. If I am making a mistake, if it is true that I shall weep over it, at any rate I feel here' (she put her hand to her heart) 'that I am not to blame for it; it will mean that it was not to be, that it was not God's will. But I am not afraid of having to shed tears in the future; I shall not be weeping for nothing: I still have bought something for them. ... I was so happy – till now!' she added.

'Do go on being happy!' Oblomov besought her.

'And you see nothing but gloom ahead; happiness is nothing to you. This,' she went on, 'is ingratitude. It isn't love, it is – –'

'– egoism!' Oblomov finished the sentence for her, not daring to look at Olga or to speak or to ask her forgiveness.

'Go,' she said softly, 'where you wanted to go to.'

He looked at her. Her eyes were dry. She was looking down thoughtfully and drawing in the sand with her parasol.

'Lie down on your back again,' she added, 'You won't be making a mistake then, you won't "fall into an abyss".'

'I've poisoned myself and poisoned you instead of being happy simply and openly,' he murmured penitently.

'Drink *kvas*: it won't poison you,' she taunted him.

'Olga, that's not fair!' he said. 'After I've been punishing myself with the consciousness of – –'

'Yes, in words you punish yourself, throw yourself into an

255

abyss, give half your life, but when you are overwhelmed by doubt and spend sleepless nights how tender you become with yourself, how careful and solicitous, how far-seeing!'

'How true and simple it is!' thought Oblomov, but he was ashamed to say it aloud. Why had he not understood it himself, but had to wait for a woman who had scarcely begun to live to explain it to him? And how quickly she had grown up! Only a short time ago she had seemed such a child!

'We've nothing more to say to each other,' she concluded, getting up. 'Good-bye, and keep your peace of mind. That's your idea of happiness, isn't it?'

'Olga, no, for God's sake, no! Don't drive me away now everything has become clear again,' he said, taking her hand.

'But what do you want of me? You are not sure whether my love for you is a mistake and I cannot dispel your doubts. Perhaps it is a mistake – I don't know.'

He let go her hand. Again the knife was raised over him.

'You don't know? But don't you feel?' he asked, looking doubtful once more. 'Do you think – –'

'I don't think anything. I told you yesterday what I felt, but I don't know what's going to happen in a year's time. And do you really think that one happiness is followed by another and then by a third just like it?' she asked, looking open-eyed at him. 'Tell me, you've had more experience than I.'

But he was no longer anxious to confirm her in the idea, and he was silent, shaking an acacia branch with one hand.

'No,' he said, like a schoolboy repeating a lesson, 'one only loves once!'

'There, you see: I believe it too,' she added. 'But if it is not so, then perhaps I shall fall out of love with you, perhaps I shall suffer from my mistake and you too, perhaps we shall part! ... To love two or three times – no. ... I don't want to believe it!'

He sighed. The *perhaps* damped his spirits and he walked slowly and thoughtfully after her. But he felt more lighthearted at every step; the *mistake* he had invented at night seemed so far away. 'Why,' it occurred to him, 'it is not only love, all life is like this. And if every opportunity is to be rejected as a mistake, when is one to be sure that one is not making a mistake? What was I thinking of? I seem to have gone blind. ...'

'Olga,' he said, barely touching her waist with two fingers (she stopped), 'you're wiser than I am.'

She shook her head.

'No,' she said, 'I'm simpler and more courageous. What are

256

you afraid of? Do you seriously think one may fall out of love?' she asked, with proud confidence.

'Now I'm not afraid, either!' he said cheerfully. 'With you I do not fear the future.'

'I've read that phrase somewhere recently – in Sue, I think,' she suddenly said, with irony, turning towards him, 'only there, it's a woman who says it to a man. ...'

Oblomov flushed.

'Olga,' he implored, 'let everything be as yesterday. I'll never be afraid of *mistakes*.'

She said nothing.

'Well?' he asked timidly.

She said nothing.

'Well, if you don't want to say it, give me some sign – a sprig of lilac. ...'

'The lilac – is over!' she replied. 'You can see for yourself – it's all withered.'

'It's over – withered!' he repeated, looking at the lilac. 'It's all over with the letter, too!' he said suddenly.

She shook her head. He walked after her, thinking about the letter, yesterday's happiness, the withered lilac.

'The lilac is certainly withered!' he thought. 'Why did I send that letter? Why didn't I sleep all night and why did I write it in the morning? Now that my mind is at rest again' (he yawned) '... I feel awfully sleepy. If I hadn't written the letter, nothing of this would have happened: she wouldn't have cried, everything would have been as yesterday, we should have sat quietly in this avenue, looking at each other and talking of happiness. And it would have been the same to-day, and to-morrow ...' he gave a big yawn.

Then he suddenly began to wonder what would have happened if his letter had achieved its object, if she had agreed with him, if she had been afraid of mistakes and future distant storms, if she had listened to his so-called experience and common sense and agreed that they should part and forget each other. Heaven forbid! To say good-bye, to return to town, to a new flat! To be followed by an interminable night, a dull to-morrow, an unbearable day after to-morrow, and a long succession of days, each more colourless than the last. ... He could not allow that to happen! That was death! And it would most certainly have happened! He would have fallen ill. He had never wanted to part from her, he could not have endured it, he would have come and implored her to see him.

'Why, then, did I write that letter?' he asked himself.

'Olga Sergeyevna,' he said.

'What do you want?'

'I must add one more confession – –'

'What?'

'Why, there was no need for that letter at all!'

'Oh yes, there was,' she decided.

She looked round and laughed when she saw the face he made, how his drowsiness had suddenly vanished, and how he opened his eyes wide with astonishment.

'Was there?' he repeated, slowly fixing his gaze at her back, with surprise.

But all he could see were the two tassels of her cloak. What, then, was the meaning of her tears and reproaches? It was not cunning, was it? But Olga was not cunning – he saw that clearly. It was only women of comparatively low mentality who were cunning or subsisted on cunning. Possessing no real intelligence, they set the springs of their petty, everyday lives in motion by means of cunning, and wove, like lace, their domestic policies without suspecting the existence of the main currents of life, their points of intersection and their direction. Cunning was like a small coin with which one could not buy a great deal. Just as a small coin could keep one going for an hour or two, so cunning might help to conceal or distort something or to deceive someone, but it was not sufficient to enable one to scan a far horizon or to survey a big event from beginning to end. Cunning was short-sighted: it saw well only what was happening under its nose, but not at a distance, and that was why it was often caught in the trap it had set for others. Olga was simply intelligent: how easily and clearly she had solved the problem to-day, and, indeed, any problem! She grasped the true meaning of events at once and she reached it by a direct road. While cunning was like a mouse, running round and round everything and hiding. ... Besides, Olga's character was different. So what was the meaning of it? What was it all about?

'Why was the letter necessary?' he asked.

'Why?' she repeated, turning round to him quickly with a gay face, delighted that she could nonplus him at every step. 'Because,' she began slowly, 'you did not sleep all night and wrote it all for me. I too am an egoist! This is in the first place – –'

'Then why did you reproach me just now, if you now agree with me?' Oblomov interrupted.

'Because you invented these torments. I did not invent them,

258

they simply came, and I am glad that they have gone, but you prepared them and enjoyed it all beforehand. You're wicked! That is why I reproached you. Then – your letter shows feeling and thought – last night and this morning you lived not in your usual way, but as your friend and I wanted you to live – that's in the second place; thirdly – –'

She walked up so close to him that the blood rushed to his heart and his head; he began to breathe hard, with excitement. She looked him straight in the eyes.

'Thirdly, because in this letter is reflected as in a mirror your tenderness, your solicitude, your care for me, your fear for my happiness, your pure conscience – everything Mr Stolz pointed out to me in you, that made me love you and forget your laziness – your apathy. You revealed yourself in your letter without wishing to do so. You're not an egoist, you didn't write it because you wanted to part from me – you did not want that, but because you were afraid to deceive me. It was your honesty that spoke in it, otherwise your letter would have offended me and I should not have cried – from pride! You see, I know why I love you, and I am not afraid of a mistake: I am not mistaken in you!'

She looked radiant and magnificent as she said this. Her eyes shone with the triumph of love, with the consciousness of her power; her cheeks were flushed. And he – he was the cause of it! It was an impulse of his honest heart that had kindled this fire in her soul, inspired this outburst of feeling, this brilliance.

'Olga, you're better than any woman in the world, you're one of the best!' he said, ecstatically, and, beside himself, put out his arms and bent over her. 'For God's sake – one kiss as a pledge of ineffable happiness,' he whispered as in a delirium.

She instantly drew back a step; the triumphant radiance, the colour left her face, and her gentle eyes blazed sternly.

'Never! Never! Don't come near me!' she said in alarm, almost in horror, stretching out both arms and her parasol to keep him at a distance and standing motionless, as though rooted to the spot, without breathing, in a stern attitude, and looking sternly at him, her head half turned.

He sobered down suddenly: it was not the gentle Olga who stood before him, but an offended goddess of pride and anger with compressed lips and lightning in her eyes.

'I'm sorry!' he muttered in confusion, feeling utterly crushed.

She turned slowly and walked on, glancing fearfully over her shoulder to see what he was doing. But he was doing nothing: he was walking slowly like a dog that had been scolded and that was walking with its tail between its legs. She had quickened her pace, but seeing his face, suppressed a smile, and walked on more calmly, though still shuddering from time to time. The colour came and went in her cheeks. As she walked, her face cleared, her breathing became more even and quieter, and once more she proceeded on her way with measured steps. She saw how sacred her 'never' was to Oblomov, and her fit of anger subsided gradually and gave way to pity. She walked slower and slower. She wanted to soften her outburst and she was trying to find some excuse for speaking.

'I've made a mess of everything! That was my real mistake. "Never!" Good God! The lilac has withered,' he thought, looking at the flowers on the tree. 'Yesterday has withered, too, and the letter has withered, and this moment, the best in my life, when a woman has told me for the first time, like a voice from heaven, what good there is in me, has also withered!'

He looked at Olga – she stood, waiting for him, with lowered eyes.

'Please, give me the letter,' she said softly.

'It has withered!' he replied sadly, giving her the letter.

She drew close to him once more and bent down her head; her eyes were closed. She was almost trembling. He gave her the letter; she did not raise her head or move away.

'You frightened me,' she added softly.

'I'm sorry, Olga,' he murmured.

She said nothing.

'This stern "never!" ...' he said sadly and sighed.

'It will wither!' she said in a barely audible whisper, and blushed.

She cast a shy, tender glance at him, took both his hands, pressed them warmly in hers, and then put them to her heart.

'Do you hear how fast it is beating?' she said. 'You frightened me! Let me go!'

And without looking at him, she turned round and ran along the path, lifting the hem of her skirt lightly.

'Where are you off to?' he cried. 'I'm tired, I can't keep up with you.'

'Leave me,' she repeated with burning cheeks. 'I'm running to sing, sing, sing! There's such a tightness in my chest that it almost hurts me!'

He remained standing and gazed after her a long time, as if she were an angel that was flying away.

'Will the moment wither too?' he thought almost sadly, and he did not seem to know whether he was walking or standing.

'The lilacs are over,' he thought again. 'Yesterday is over, and the night with its phantoms and its stifling horrors is over too. . . . Yes, and this moment will also be gone like the lilac. But while last night was drawing to a close, this morning was beginning to dawn.'

'What is it, then?' he said aloud in a daze. 'And love too – love? And I had thought that like a hot noonday sun it would hang over lovers and that nothing would stir or breathe in its atmosphere; but there is no rest in love, either, and it moves on and on like all life, Stolz says. And the Joshua has not yet been born who could tell it: "Stand still and do not move!" What will happen to-morrow?' he asked himself anxiously and wistfully, and walked home slowly.

Passing under Olga's windows he heard the strains of Schubert in which her tightened chest found relief and seemed to be sobbing with happiness.

Oh, how wonderful life was!

11

AT HOME Oblomov found another letter from Stolz, which began and ended with the words: 'Now or never!' It was full of reproaches for his immobility and included an invitation to come to Switzerland, where Stolz himself was going, and then to Italy. If Oblomov could not manage it, Stolz suggested that he should go to the country to see to his affairs, rouse his peasants to work, find out the exact amount of his income, and give the necessary orders for the building of the new house. 'Remember our agreement: now or never,' he concluded. 'Now, now, now!' Oblomov repeated. 'Andrey does not know what a wonderful thing has happened in my life. What more does he want from me? Could I possibly be as busy as I am now? Let him try it! You read about the French and the English being always busy working, just as if they had nothing but business in mind. They travel all over Europe, and even in Asia and Africa, and not on business, either: some draw or paint, some excavate antiquities, some shoot lions or catch snakes. If they don't do that, they sit at home in honourable idleness, have lunches and dinners with friends and ladies – that is what all their business amounts to! Why should I be expected to work hard? All Andrey thinks of is work and work, like a horse! Whatever for? I have plenty to eat and I'm decently dressed. Still, Olga did ask me again if I meant to go to Oblomovka. ...'

He threw himself into work. He wrote, made plans, even paid a visit to an architect. Soon the plan of the house and the garden lay on his little table. It was a large, roomy house with two balconies. 'Here is my room, here is Olga's, there's the bedroom, the nursery ...' he thought with a smile. 'But, dear me, the peasants, the peasants ...' and the smile disappeared and he frowned. 'My neighbour writes to me, goes into all sorts of details, talks of land to be put under the plough, the yield of grain per acre. ... What a bore! And he proposes that we should share the expense of making a road to a big trading village, and a bridge over a stream, asks for three thousand roubles and wants me to mortgage Oblomovka. ... How do I know it is really necessary? If any good will come of it? He isn't trying to cheat me, is he? I daresay he is an honest man – Stolz knows him – but he may be mistaken, and my money will be lost! Three thousand – it's a lot of money! Where am I to get it? No, it's too risky! He also writes that some of the peasants ought to be settled on the waste-land, and demands an answer at once – everything, it seems, must be done at once. He undertakes to send me all the documents for the mortgage of the estate. Send him a deed of trust and go to the courts to have it witnessed – what next! And I have no idea where the courts are and which door to try when I get there.'

Oblomov did not answer his neighbour's letter for a fortnight, and in the meantime even Olga asked him if he had been to the courts. A few days earlier Stolz sent a letter to him and one to Olga, asking what he was doing. Olga, no doubt, could keep only a superficial watch over her friend's doings, and that, too, only in her own sphere. She could tell whether he looked happy, went everywhere readily, came to the woods at the appointed hour, was interested in the latest news or general conversation. She kept a particularly anxious watch that he did not lose sight of his main purpose in life. If she did ask him about the courts, it was only because she had to answer Stolz's questions about the affairs of their friend.

The summer was at its height; it was the end of July; the weather was excellent. Oblomov hardly ever parted from Olga. On fine days he was in the park with her, in the noonday heat he accompanied her to the woods, where he sat at her feet among

262

the pine-trees, reading aloud; she had started another piece of embroidery – this time for him. In their hearts, too, it was hot summer: clouds sometimes scudded across their sky and passed away. If he had troubled dreams and doubt knocked at his heart, Olga kept watch over him like a guardian angel; she looked with her bright eyes into his face, discovered what was troubling him – and all was well again, and feeling flowed peacefully like a river reflecting the ever new patterns of the sky. Olga's views on life, love, and everything had grown still clearer and more definite. She looked about her with more confidence and was not worried about the future; her mind had developed and her character had grown in depth and poetic diversity, showed new propensities; it was consistent, clear, steady, and natural. She had a kind of persistence which not only overcame all the storms that lay in wait for her, but also Oblomov's laziness and apathy. If she decided that something should be done, it was done without delay. You heard of nothing else; and if you did not hear of it, you could see that she had only that one thing in mind, that she would not forget or give up or lose her head, but would take everything into account and get what she was out to get. Oblomov could not understand where she got her strength from nor how she could possibly know what to do and how to do it whatever circumstance might arise. 'It's because one of her eyebrows is never straight, but is raised a little, and there is a very thin and hardly perceptible line over it,' he thought. 'It's there – in that crease – that her stubbornness lies concealed.' However calm and contented her expression might be, this crease was never smoothed out and her eyebrows never lay level. But she was never overbearing in her ways and inclinations and she never exercised her strength crudely. Her stubbornness and determination did not make her less attractive as a woman. She did not want to be a lioness, to put a foolish admirer out of countenance by a sharp remark, or to surprise the whole drawing-room by the smartness of her wit, so that someone in a corner should cry, 'Bravo! bravo!' She even possessed the sort of timidity that is peculiar to many women: it is true, she did not tremble at the sight of a mouse or faint if a chair fell down, but she was afraid to walk too far from home, she turned aside if she saw a suspicious-looking peasant. She closed her window at night to make sure burglars did not climb in – all like a woman. Besides, she was so easily accessible to the feelings of pity and compassion. It was not difficult to make her cry; the way to her heart was easy to find. In love she was so tender, in her relations to everyone she showed so much kindness and affectionate attention – in short, she was a woman. There was sometimes a flash of sarcasm in her speech, but it was so brilliant and graceful, and it revealed so gentle and charming a mind, that one was only too glad to be its victim. On the other hand, she was not afraid of draughts and went lightly dressed at dusk – with no ill effect. She was brimming over with health, she had an excellent appetite, and knew how to prepare her favourite dishes herself. No doubt many other women are like that, too; but they do not know what to do in an emergency, and if they do, it is only what they have learnt or heard, and if they don't they immediately refer to the authority of a cousin or an aunt. ... Many do not even know what it is they want, and if they make up their minds about something they do it so listlessly that it is difficult to say whether they really want to do it or not. This is probably because their eyebrows are arched evenly and have been plucked with the fingers and because there is no crease on their foreheads.

A kind of secret relationship, invisible to others, had been established between Olga and Oblomov: every look, every insignificant word uttered in the presence of others, had a special meaning for them. They saw in everything a reference to love. Olga sometimes flushed crimson, in spite of her self-confidence, if someone told at table a love-story that was similar to her own; and as all love-stories are very much alike, she often had to blush. Oblomov, too, at the mention of it, would suddenly seize, in his confusion, such a fistful of biscuits that someone was quite sure to laugh. They had grown cautious and sensitive. Sometimes Olga did not tell her aunt that she had seen Oblomov, and he would say at home that he was going to town and walk to the park instead. But however clear-sighted and practical she was, Olga began to develop some strange, morbid symptoms, in spite of her good health. She was at times overcome by a restlessness which she could not explain and which worried her. Sometimes as she walked arm in arm with Oblomov in the noonday heat, she leaned lazily against his shoulder and walked on mechanically, in a kind of exhaustion, and was obstinately silent. Her cheerfulness deserted her; she looked tired and listless and often fixed her eyes on some point and had not the energy to turn them on some other object. She felt wretched, some weight pressed on her breast and perturbed her. She took off her cloak, her kerchief, but it did not help – she still felt something weighing her down, oppressing her. She would have liked to lie down under a tree and stay there for hours. Oblomov was at a loss what to do; he fanned her with a branch, but she stopped him with a gesture of impatience, and went on feeling wretched. Then she sighed suddenly, glanced round her with interest, looked at him, pressed his hand, smiled, and her cheerfulness returned, she laughed and was self-possessed once more.

One evening especially she had an attack of this restlessness, a kind of somnambulism of love, and revealed herself to Oblomov in a new light. It was hot and sultry; from the forest came the hollow rumble of a warm wind; the sky was overcast. It was growing darker and darker.

'It's going to rain,' said the baron, and went home.

Olga's aunt retired to her room. Olga went on playing the piano pensively, but stopped at last.

'I can't go on,' she said to Oblomov. 'My fingers are trembling. I feel stifled. Let's go into the garden.'

They walked for some time along the paths hand in hand. Her hands were moist and soft. They entered the park. The trees and bushes were merged into a gloomy mass; one could not see two paces ahead; only the winding, sandy paths showed white. Olga looked intently into the darkness and drew closer to Oblomov. They wandered about aimlessly in silence.

'I am afraid!' Olga said suddenly with a start as they groped their way down a narrow avenue between two black, impenetrable walls of trees.

'What of?' he asked. 'Don't be afraid, darling; I am with you.'

'I am afraid of you too!' she said in a whisper. 'Oh, but it is such a delightful fear! It makes my heart miss a beat. Give me your hand, feel how it beats!'

She trembled and looked round. 'See? See?' she whispered with a start, clutching at his shoulders with both hands. 'Don't you see someone flitting about in the darkness?'

She pressed closer to him.

'There's no one there,' he said, but a cold shiver ran down his spine.

'Darling,' she whispered, 'close my eyes quickly with something – tightly, please. Now I'm all right ... it's my nerves,' she added agitatedly. 'Look, there it is again! Who is it? Let us sit down. ...'

He felt his way to a seat and got her to sit down on it.

'Let us go back, Olga,' he entreated her. 'You're not well.'

She put her head on his shoulder.

'No,' she said, 'the air is fresher here. I feel so tight here – near the heart.'

She breathed hotly against his cheek. He touched her head – it was hot too. She breathed irregularly and often heaved a sigh.

'Don't you think we'd better go into the house?' Oblomov repeated anxiously. 'You ought to lie down.'

'No, no; please, leave me alone; don't disturb me,' she said languidly, almost inaudibly. 'Something's on fire here – here ...' she pointed to her chest.

'Do let us go back, please,' Oblomov hurried her.

'No, wait. This will pass. ...'

She squeezed his hand and now and then looked close into his eyes and was silent a long time. Presently she began to cry, quietly at first, then broke into sobs. He did not know what to do.

'For heaven's sake, Olga, let us hurry indoors,' he said in alarm.

'It's nothing,' she said, whispering. 'Don't disturb me. Let me have a good cry – my tears will make me feel better – it's just my nerves. ...'

He listened in the darkness to her heavy breathing, felt her warm tears on his hand, the convulsive pressure of her fingers. He did not stir or breathe. Her head lay on his shoulder and her breath burnt his cheek. He, too, was trembling, but he dared not touch her cheek with his lips. After some time she grew more composed and her breathing became more regular. She did not utter a sound. He wondered if she were asleep and was afraid to stir.

'Olga!' he called her in a whisper.

'What?' she replied also in a whisper, and sighed aloud. 'Now,' she said languidly, 'it's passed. I'm better. I can breathe freely.'

'Let us go,' he said.

'Let's,' she repeated reluctantly. 'My darling!' she whispered langourously squeezing his hand and, leaning against his shoulder, she walked home with unsteady steps.

He looked at her in the drawing-room. She seemed weak and was smiling a strange, unconscious smile as though she were in a trance. He made her sit down on the sofa, knelt before her and, deeply touched, kissed her hand a few times. She looked at him with the same smile, not attempting to take her hands away, and, as he turned to go, followed him to the door with her eyes.

In the doorway he turned round: she was still gazing at him, and there was the same look of exhaustion in her face and the same ardent smile as though she were not able to control it. ... He went away wondering. He had seen that smile somewhere: he remembered a picture of a woman with such a smile – only it was not Cordelia. ...

The next day he sent to inquire how Olga was. She was quite well, was the reply she sent back, and would he please come to dinner, and in the evening they were all going for a three-mile drive to see the fireworks. He could not believe it and went to see for himself. Olga was as fresh as a daisy: her eyes were bright and cheerful, her cheeks rosy, and her voice strong and melodious. But she was suddenly confused, and almost cried out, when Oblomov came up to her, and flushed crimson when he asked how she was feeling after last night.

'It was just a slight nervous upset,' she said hurriedly. 'Auntie says I ought to go to bed earlier. This has only happened to me lately and ...'

She did not finish and turned away as though asking him to spare her. But she did not know herself why she was confused. Why should the memory of that evening and her attack of nerves worry her so much? She felt ashamed of something and annoyed with someone. Was it with herself or with Oblomov? And at moments she could not help feeling that Oblomov had grown nearer and dearer to her, that she felt attracted to him to the point of tears, as though she had entered into a kind of mysterious relationship with him since the night before. She could not fall asleep for a long time, and in the morning she walked alone in agitation along the avenue, from the house to the park and from the park to the house, thinking hard, lost in conjectures, frowning, blushing, smiling at something, and still unable to decide what it was all about. 'Oh, Sonia,' she thought in annoyance, 'how lucky you are! You'd have decided at once!'

And Oblomov? Why had he been so mute and motionless with her the night before, though her breath was burning his cheek, her warm tears fell on his hand, and he had almost carried her home in his arms and overheard the indiscreet whisper of her heart? Would another man have acted like that? Other men looked so impudently – –

Though Oblomov had spent his youth among young people who knew everything, who had long ago solved all life's problems, who did not believe in anything, and who analysed everything in a manner both detached and wise, he still believed in friendship, love, and honour, and however much he was, or might still be, mistaken about people, and however much his heart bled because of it, his fundamental conception of goodness and his faith in it had never been shaken. He secretly worshipped the purity of a woman, acknowledged its rights and power, and was willing to make sacrifices for its sake. But he had not enough strength of character publicly to acknowledge the doctrine of goodness and respect for innocence. He drank in its fragrance in secret, but publicly he sometimes joined the chorus of the cynics, who dreaded being suspected of chastity and respect for it, adding his own frivolous words to their boisterous chorus. He never clearly grasped how much weight attaches to a good, true, and pure word thrown into the torrent of human speeches and how profoundly it alters its course; he did not realize that when said boldly and aloud, with courage and without a blush of false shame, it is not drowned in the hideous shouts of worldly satyrs, but sinks like a pearl in the gulf of public life, and always finds a shell for itself. Many people stop short before uttering a good word, flushing bright red with shame, while they utter a frivolous one boldly and aloud, without suspecting that, unfortunately, it will not be lost, either, but will leave a long trail of sometimes ineradicable evil behind it. Oblomov, however, never put his frivolous words into practice: there was not a single stain on his conscience, nor could he be reproached with cold and heartless cynicism that knows neither passion nor struggle. He could not bear to hear the daily stories of how one man had changed his horses and furniture and another his woman, and of how much money these changes had cost. He often suffered for a man who had lost his human dignity, grieved for a woman, a complete stranger to him, whose reputation was ruined, but he said nothing, afraid of public opinion. One had to guess all this: Olga did guess it.

Men laugh at such eccentric fellows, but women recognize them at once; pure and chaste women love them – from a feeling of sympathy; depraved ones seek intimacy with them – as a relief from their depravity.

Summer was drawing to a close. The mornings and evenings were growing dark and damp. Not only lilac, but lime blossom was over, the berries had been gathered. Oblomov and Olga saw each other every day. He had caught up with life – that is, he mastered all the facts he had neglected for years; he knew why the French ambassador had left Rome, why the English were sending troopships to the East, and he was interested in the new roads being made in France and Germany. But he gave no thought to the road from Oblomovka to the large village, he had not had the deed of trust witnessed in the courts, and had not answered Stolz's letter. The only subjects he mastered were those mentioned in the daily conversations at Olga's house, or read in the newspapers received there, and thanks to Olga's insistence he made a point of following current foreign literature. Everything else dissolved in pure love. In spite of the frequent changes in the rosy atmosphere, its main characteristic was a cloudless horizon. If Olga sometimes wondered about Oblomov and her love for him, if that love left her any free time or any free place in her heart, if not all her questions found a complete and ready answer in his mind, and his will did not respond to hers and he replied only by a long, passionate glance to her high spirits and bounding energy – if that happened, she sank into desolate brooding: something cold as a snake crept into her heart, wakened her from her day-dreams, and the warm, fairy-tale world of love was transformed into a grey autumn day. She wondered why she was dissatisfied, why her happiness was incomplete. What was lacking? What more did she want? Was it not her fate, her mission in life, to love Oblomov? That love was justified by his gentleness, by his pure faith in goodness, and above all by his tenderness, a tenderness she had never seen in a man's eyes. What did it matter if he did not always respond to her glance, if his voice sounded differently from what she had seemed to hear once – was it in her dreams or in reality? ... It was her imagination, her nerves: why listen to it and complicate matters unnecessarily? And, besides, if she wanted to escape this love – how was she to do it? The thing was done: she was already in love, and to discard love at will, like a dress, was impossible. 'You can't love twice in your life,' she thought. 'People say it is immoral.' That was how she was studying love, greeting every fresh step with a tear or a smile and pondering over it. It was afterwards that the concentrated expression appeared under which both tears and smiles were hidden and which alarmed Oblomov so much. But she never even hinted to Oblomov about her thoughts and struggles.

Oblomov did not study love; he gave himself up to the sweet drowsiness which he had once described in such glowing terms to Stolz. At times he began to believe in a life that was for ever cloudless, and once again he dreamt of Oblomovka, full of kind, friendly, and untroubled faces, of sitting on the verandah, of meditations that arise from perfect happiness. He sometimes indulged in these meditations even now, and twice without Olga's knowledge he even fell asleep in the woods while waiting for her. Then, suddenly, a cloud appeared unexpectedly. ...

One day they were returning slowly and silently from a walk, and just as they were about to cross the high road, they saw a cloud of dust coming towards them, followed by a carriage in which Sonia and her husband and another lady and gentleman were driving.

'Olga! Olga! Olga Sergeyevna!' they cried.

The carriage stopped. The ladies and gentlemen alighted, surrounded Olga, and began to exchange greetings and kisses. They all spoke together, and for some time did not notice Oblomov. Then they all looked at him suddenly, one gentleman through a lorgnette.

'Who is this?' Sonia asked quietly.

'Ilya Ilyich Oblomov,' Olga introduced him.

They all walked to Olga's house. Oblomov felt uncomfortable: he lagged behind the company and had already raised his foot over a fence to escape home through the rye when a look from Olga made him come back. He would not have minded if all these ladies and gentlemen had not looked at him so strangely. This, too, would not perhaps have mattered, for people had always looked at him like that before because of his sleepy and bored expression and his slovenly clothes. But the ladies and gentlemen looked in the same strange way at Olga, too, and their equivocal glances struck a chill into his heart; something seemed to gnaw at his heart, and the pain he felt was so excruciating that he could not bear it and went home, and was thoughtful and morose.

On the following day Olga's charming chatter and affectionate playfulness could not cheer him. In reply to her insistent questions, he had to plead a headache and submit patiently to having seventy-five-copecks' worth of eau-de-Cologne poured on his head. Then, the day after that when they came back home late, Olga's aunt looked somehow too wisely at them, especially at him, and then lowering her large, slightly puffy eyelids, thoughtfully sniffed her smelling-salts for a minute while her eyes seemed to be still looking at them. Oblomov felt unhappy, but he said nothing. He did not dare to confide his doubts to Olga, fearing to worry and alarm her, and, if the truth be told, he was also afraid for himself, afraid of disturbing their cloudless and unruffled world by so grave a question. For it was no longer a question whether or not it was a mistake on her part to have fallen in love with him, but whether the whole thing was not a mistake – those meetings of theirs in the woods alone and sometimes late in the evening.

'I dared to ask for a kiss,' he thought with horror, 'and that is already a criminal offence against the moral code, and not a small one either! There are many stages before it: pressure of the hand, declaration, letter. ... We've been through all that. But,' he thought, raising his head, 'my intentions are honourable, and I – –'

And suddenly the cloud vanished, and he saw before him Oblomovka, bright and festive, basking in the brilliant sunshine, with its green hills and silvery river; he was walking dreamily with Olga down a long avenue, his arm round her waist; or he was sitting in the summer-house with her, or on the verandah. ... Everyone bowed his head before her in adoration – in a word, everything was just as he had described it to Stolz.

'Yes, yes,' he thought in alarm again, 'but I ought to have started with that. The thrice repeated "I love you", the sprig of lilac, the declaration of love – all that ought to be the pledge of lifelong happiness, and never be repeated again, if the woman be pure. But what am I doing? What am I?' the question kept hammering in his head. 'I am a seducer, a lady-killer! All that is left for me to do is to follow the example of that dirty old rake with salacious eyes and a red nose, and stick a rose stolen from a woman in my buttonhole and whisper to my friends about my conquest so that – so that – – Oh Lord, where have I landed myself! That's where the abyss is! And Olga is not soaring high above it – she is at the bottom – why? why?'

He exhausted himself and cried like a child at the thought that the rainbow colours of his life had suddenly faded and that Olga was going to be sacrificed. His whole love was a crime, a blot on his conscience. Then his agitation subsided for a moment and he realized that there was a perfectly legal solution of his problem: to hold out his hand with a wedding ring to Olga. ...

'Yes, yes,' he murmured, trembling with joy, 'and her answer will be a look of shy consent. ... She won't utter a word; she will flush crimson and smile with all her heart, then her eyes will fill with tears. ...'

Tears and a smile, a silently held out hand, followed by lively, playful joy, a happy urgency in all her movements, a long, long conversation, an exchange of whispered confidences, and a secret agreement to merge two lives into one! A love, unseen by

271

anyone but themselves, would shine through every triviality, in every conversation about everyday affairs. And no one would dare to insult them with a look. ...

His face suddenly became stern and grave.

'Yes,' he said to himself, 'that's where the world of straight-forward, honourable, and lasting happiness is to be found! I felt ashamed to pluck these flowers, to rush about in the fragrance of love like a boy, to arrange assignations, walk in the moonlight, listening to the beats of a young girl's heart, to catch the excitement of her dream. ... Oh God!' He blushed to the roots of his hair. 'This very evening Olga shall know what stern duties are imposed by love; to-day I shall have my last meeting with her alone – to-day – –'

He put his hand to his heart. It was beating strongly and regularly, as an honest man's heart should. He was again upset at the thought of how grieved Olga would be when he told her that they must not meet; then he would tell her timidly of his intentions, but first he would find out what she thought and would enjoy her confusion. ... Then he saw in his mind's eye her shy consent, her smile, her tears, a silently held out hand, a long, mysterious whispering and kisses before the whole world.

12

HE RAN to look for Olga. He was told at her house that she had gone out; he went to the village – she was not there. He saw her walking up a hill in the distance, looking like an angel ascending the sky, so light was her step, so graceful her movements. He went after her, but she seemed scarcely to touch the grass with her feet, just as if she were really flying away. Half-way up the hill he began calling to her.

She waited for him, but as soon as he came within ten feet of her, she walked on, again leaving a big distance between them, then stopped once more and laughed. He stopped at last, certain that she would not escape him. She ran down a few paces to him, gave him her hand, and, laughing, dragged him after her. They entered the wood: he took off his hat, and she mopped his forehead with her handkerchief and began fanning his face with her parasol.

Olga was especially lively, talkative, and vivacious but, after a sudden outburst of affection, lapsed suddenly into thought.

'Guess what I was doing yesterday,' she asked when they sat down in the shade.

'Reading?'

She shook her head.

'Writing?'

'No.'

'Singing?'

'No. Telling fortunes!' she said. 'The countess's housekeeper came to see us yesterday. She can tell fortunes by cards and I asked her to tell mine.'

'Well, what did she tell you?'

'Nothing much. A journey, then a crowd of people, and a fair man everywhere, everywhere. ... I blushed all over when she said suddenly in Katya's presence that a king of diamonds was thinking about me. When she wanted to tell me whom I was thinking of, I mixed up the cards and ran away. You were thinking about me, weren't you?' she suddenly asked.

'Oh,' he said, 'if only I could think less of you!'

'And what about me?' she said thoughtfully. 'I seem to have forgotten that life can be different. When you were sulky last week and did not come for two days – you remember, you were cross – I suddenly changed and became terribly bad-tempered. I quarrelled with Katya as you do with Zakhar. I saw she was crying to herself and I wasn't at all sorry for her. I didn't answer Auntie, I didn't listen to what she said, I didn't do anything and didn't want to go anywhere. But as soon as you came I grew quite different suddenly. I made Katya a present of my lilac dress. ...'

'That is love!' he cried dramatically.

'What is? A lilac dress?'

'Everything! I can recognize myself in what you say. For me, too, life is not worth living without you. At night I keep dreaming of blossoming valleys. When I see you, I feel kind and active; when I don't, I am bored, I feel lazy, I want to lie down and not think of anything. ... Love, and never be ashamed of your love. ...'

He fell silent suddenly. 'What am I talking about? That's not what I came for!' he thought and began to clear his throat. He frowned.

'And what if I should suddenly die?' she asked.

'What an idea!' he said carelessly.

'Oh, yes,' she went on, 'I'll catch a cold and take to my bed with a high temperature. You will come here and not find me; you'll come to us and they will tell you that I am ill. The same thing next day. The shutters in my room will be closed. The doctor will shake his head. Katya will come out to you on tiptoe, in tears, and whisper: "She is ill, she is dying. ..."'

'Oh!' Oblomov cried suddenly.

She laughed. 'What will become of you then?' she asked, looking at his face.

'What will become of me? I'll go off my head or shoot myself, and then you'll get suddenly well again!'

'No, no, don't,' she said nervously. 'We are talking a lot of nonsense! Only you must never come to me when you're dead: I'm afraid of ghosts.'

He laughed and so did she.

'Goodness, what children we are!' she said, growing serious.

He cleared his throat again.

'Listen – I want to say something.'

'What?' she asked, turning round to him quickly.

He kept silent apprehensively.

'Go on,' she said, pulling him lightly by the sleeve.

'Oh, it's nothing,' he said, becoming frightened.

'Yes, you have something on your mind, haven't you?'

He was silent.

'If it's something dreadful, then you'd better not tell me!' she said. 'No, tell me!' she suddenly added again.

'But it's nothing – just nonsense.'

'No, no, I don't believe you: there is something; tell me!' she insisted, holding him by the lapels of his coat so closely that he had to keep turning his head from side to side so as not to kiss her.

He would not have turned it but for the fact that her stern 'Never!' still rang in his ears.

'Tell me!' she persisted.

'I can't – it's not necessary,' he pleaded.

'Why then did you preach to me that "confidence is the basis of mutual happiness"; that "not a single twist in one's heart should be hidden from a friend's eye"? Whose words are those?'

'All I wanted to say,' he began slowly, 'was that I love you so much, so much that if – –'

He hesitated.

'Well?' she asked impatiently.

'That if you fell in love with someone who could make you happier than I, then I – I'd swallow my grief in silence and give up my place to him.'

She let go of his coat suddenly.

'Why?' she asked in surprise. 'I can't understand it. I shouldn't give you up to anyone. I don't want you to be happy with another woman. This is a bit too clever. I don't understand it.'

Her glance wandered thoughtfully over the trees.

'Then you don't love me, do you?' she asked after a while.

'On the contrary, I love you so unselfishly that I'm ready to sacrifice myself for you.'

'But why? Who asked you to?'

'But I meant in case you fell in love with somebody else. ...'

'With somebody else! Are you mad? Why should I if I love you? Would you fall in love with another woman?'

'Why do you listen to me? I'm talking a lot of nonsense and you believe me. As a matter of fact, it wasn't that at all I wanted to say.'

'What did you want to say, then?'

'I wanted to say that I feel guilty before you, that I've felt guilty a long time. ...'

'What of? How?' she asked. 'Don't you love me? Was it a joke, perhaps? Tell me at once!'

'No, no, it isn't that!' he said in anguish. 'You see, what I mean is,' he began irresolutely. 'We meet – er – secretly. ...'

'Secretly? Why secretly? I tell Auntie almost every time that I've seen you.'

'Not every time, surely?' he asked anxiously.

'Why, what's wrong with that?'

'I'm sorry: I should have told you long ago that it isn't – done.'

'You did tell me.'

'Did I? Yes, of course I – er – I hinted at it. Well, I'm glad to say I've done my duty, then.'

He cheered up, glad that Olga had so lightly relieved him of his responsibility.

'Anything else?'

'Anything – er – no, that's all,' he replied.

'It isn't true,' Olga observed positively. 'There is something else. You haven't told me everything.'

'Well, you see,' he began, trying to assume a casual tone, 'I thought that – –'

He stopped, she waited.

'– we ought not to meet so often ...' He glanced at her timidly.

275

She was silent.

'Why not?' she asked after thinking it over for a short while.

'You see, I'm awfully worried – it's my conscience. We spend so much time alone. I – I grow excited, my heart beats fast and you too are – er – agitated. I can't help being afraid,' he concluded, speaking with difficulty.

'What of?'

'You are young and you don't know all the dangers, Olga. Sometimes a man loses his mastery over himself. He is possessed by some evil power, his heart is plunged into darkness, his eyes flash lightnings. He is no longer capable of thinking clearly: respect for purity and innocence is carried away by a whirlwind; he does not know what he is doing; he is overcome by passion, he can no longer control himself – and it is then that an abyss opens up at his feet.'

He shuddered.

'Well, what of it? Let it!' she said, looking at him open-eyed.

He said nothing; there was nothing more he could say.

She gazed at him for some time as though trying to read his mind in the lines of his forehead; she recalled his every word and look and, running over the whole history of their love, she got as far as the dark evening in the garden and suddenly blushed.

'You do talk a lot of nonsense, darling,' she said hurriedly, looking away. 'I never saw any lightnings in your eyes. You – you mostly look at me like – like my nanny Kuzminichna,' she added, laughing.

'You are joking, Olga, and I'm talking seriously and – and I haven't said everything yet.'

'What else?' she asked. 'What abyss are you talking about?'

He sighed.

'I mean that – that we ought not to meet – alone.'

'Why not?'

'Because it isn't nice.'

She thought it over.

'Yes,' she said thoughtfully, 'they say it isn't nice. But why?'

'What will people say when they know, when the story spreads – –'

'Who will say? I have no mother: she alone could have asked me why I saw you, and only in answer to her would I have cried and said that I wasn't doing anything wrong, nor you either. She'd have believed me. Who else is there?' she asked.

'Your aunt,' said Oblomov.

'My aunt?' Olga shook her head sadly. 'She would never ask. If I went away for good she would not go to look for me or ask me any questions, and I should never go back to tell her where I had been and what I had done. Who else is there?'

'Others – everybody. The other day Sonia looked at you and me and smiled, and all the ladies and gentlemen who were with her also smiled.'

He told her what an anxious time he had been through since then.

'While she looked at me,' he added, 'I didn't mind; but when she looked in the same way at you, a chill went through me.'

'Well?' she asked coldly.

'Well, I've been worried to death ever since, racking my brains how to prevent it from becoming public. I was anxious not to frighten you. I've long wanted to talk it over with you.'

'You need not have troubled,' she replied. 'I knew it without your telling me.'

'You knew it?' he asked in surprise.

'Of course. Sonia talked to me, tried to find out everything, taunted me, and even told me how I should behave with you.'

'And you never told me anything about it, Olga!' he reproached her.

'You never told me anything about your anxiety, either.'

'What did you say to her?' he asked.

'Nothing. What could I say? I just blushed.'

'Good Lord, so it has gone as far as that: you blush!' he cried in horror. 'How careless we are! What will come of it?'

She looked questioningly at him.

'I don't know,' she said shortly.

Oblomov had thought that by sharing his trouble with Olga he would set his own mind at rest and draw strength from her words and looks, but finding she had no clear and decisive answer, he suddenly lost courage. His face expressed irresolution, his eyes wandered dejectedly. Inwardly he was already in a feverish ferment. He had almost forgotten Olga: in his mind's eye he saw Sonia with her husband and the visitors; he heard their laughter and gossip. Olga, usually so resourceful, was silent, looked coldly at him and still more coldly said, 'I don't know.' He did not trouble, or did not know how, to find out the secret meaning of that 'I don't know'. He, too, was silent: without someone else's help his thoughts and intentions never matured and, like ripe apples, fell to the ground of themselves: they needed to be plucked.

Olga gazed at him for a few minutes, then put on her cloak, picked up the kerchief from a branch, and putting it round her head slowly, took her parasol.

'Where are you going? It's quite early!' he said, coming to himself suddenly.

'No, I'm afraid it's late. You're quite right,' she said, dejectedly and thoughtfully. 'We have gone too far and there is no way out: we must part as quickly as possible and forget the past. Good-bye,' she added, dryly and bitterly and, bending her head, walked down the path.

'Good heavens, Olga, what are you talking about! Not meet again? Why, I – – Olga!'

She was not listening and walked on, the dry sand crunching under her feet.

'Olga Sergeyevna!' he called.

She did not hear and walked on.

'For God's sake, come back!' he cried with tears in his voice. 'Even a criminal must be given a hearing. ... Good heavens, she can't be so heartless! There's woman for you!'

He sat down and buried his face in his hands. He could hear her footsteps no longer.

'She's gone!' he said, almost in terror, and raised his head.

Olga was before him.

He seized her hand joyfully.

'You haven't gone,' he said. 'You will not go, will you? Please, don't go. Remember, if you go away – I am a dead man!'

'And if I don't go away, I am a criminal and you, too – remember that, Ilya!'

'Oh, no – –'

'No? Why, if Sonia and her husband discover us together once more – I am ruined.'

He gave a start.

'Listen,' he began hurriedly in a faltering voice. 'I haven't said everything – –' and he stopped short.

What at home had seemed so simple, natural, and necessary to him, what pleased him so much that he regarded it as his happiness, suddenly appeared as a sort of abyss to him. He had not the courage to cross it. The step he had to take was bold and decisive.

'Someone's coming!' said Olga.

There was the sound of footsteps on a path.

'It couldn't be Sonia, could it?' asked Oblomov, looking petrified with terror.

Two men and a woman – complète strangers – went past. Oblomov breathed freely.

'Olga,' he began hurriedly, taking her by the hand, 'let's go over there, where there is no one. Let us sit down.'

He made her sit down on a bench, himself sitting on the grass at her feet.

'You flared up,' he said, 'went away, and I had not finished what I wanted to say, Olga.'

'And I'll go away again and I won't come back if you play with me again,' she said. 'You liked my tears once, and now perhaps you would like to see me at your feet and so little by little make me your slave, be capricious, moralize, weep, be frightened and frighten me, and then ask what we are to do. I'd like you to remember, sir,' she suddenly added proudly, getting up, 'that I've grown up a lot since I met you, and I know what the game you are playing is called, but – you will never see my tears any more!'

'I swear I am not playing with you,' he cried earnestly.

'So much the worse for you,' she remarked dryly. 'I have only one thing to say to all your apprehensions, warnings, and conundrums: till our meeting to-day I have loved you and did not know what I ought to do – now I know,' she concluded decisively, making ready to go, 'and I'm not going to ask your advice.'

'And I know too,' he said, retaining her by the hand and making her sit down again, and he stopped for a moment, plucking up courage to go on. 'Just imagine,' he began; 'my heart is full of one desire, my head of one thought, but my will and my tongue won't obey me: I want to speak and I can't utter the words. And yet it is so simple, so – – Help me, Olga!'

'I don't know what is in your mind, sir, do I?'

'Oh, for heaven's sake, please, without the *sir*: your proud glance is killing me, every word you say freezes me like ice. ...'

She laughed.

'You're crazy,' she said, putting her hand on his head.

'That's right, now I've received the gift of thought and speech! Olga,' he said, kneeling before her, 'will you marry me?'

She was silent and turned her face away.

'Olga, give me your hand,' he went on.

She did not give it. He took it and put it to his lips. She did not withdraw it. Her hand was warm, soft, and just a tiny bit moist. He tried to look into her face, but she turned away more and more.

'Silence?' he asked anxiously, kissing her hand.

'Is a sign of consent,' she finished the sentence for him softly, still not looking at him.

'What are you feeling now?' he asked, recalling his dream about the shy consent and the tears. 'What are you thinking?'

'The same as you,' she replied, continuing to look somewhere in the direction of the forest, only the heaving of her bosom showed that she was restraining herself.

'Has she tears in her eyes?' Oblomov wondered, but she was obstinately looking down.

'Are you calm?' he said, trying to draw her closer. 'Are you indifferent?'

'Not indifferent, but calm.'

'Why?'

'Because I foresaw it long ago and I've got used to the thought.'

'Long ago!' he repeated in surprise.

'Yes, from the moment I gave you the spray of lilac, I called you in my mind – –' She broke off.

'From that moment!'

He put out his arms wide to embrace her.

'The abyss is opening up, lightnings are flashing – take care!' she said slyly, cleverly avoiding his embrace and pushing away his hand with her parasol.

He recalled her stern 'Never!' and desisted.

'But you have never told me or showed me in any way – –' he said.

'We do not marry, but are given or taken in marriage.'

'From that moment – not really?' he said reflectively.

'Do you think that I would have been here alone with you if I had not known you?' she said proudly. 'Would I have sat in the summer-house with you in the evenings? Would I have listened to you and trusted you?'

'Then it's – –' he began, changing colour and letting go her hand.

A strange thought occurred to him. She was looking at him with serene pride and waited unwaveringly; and what he wanted at that moment was not pride and determination, but tears, passion, intoxicating happiness, if only for a moment – and then let life go on unruffled and calm for ever! And suddenly no violent tears of unexpected happiness and no shy consent! How was he to understand it? And the serpent of doubt awoke and stirred uneasily in his heart. Did she love him or was she merely anxious to marry him?

280

'But there is another road to happiness,' he said.

'Which?' she asked.

'Sometimes love does not wait and endure and calculate. ... A woman is all on fire, she trembles all over, she experiences at once such agonies and such joys that – –'

'I don't know what kind of road you mean.'

'A road upon which a woman sacrifices everything: her peace of mind, public opinion, respect, and finds her reward in love which takes the place of everything for her.'

'Need we walk along such a road?'

'No.'

'Would you have liked to look for happiness at the cost of my peace of mind and self-respect?'

'Oh no, no! I swear to God I never would,' he said warmly.

'Then why did you speak of it?'

'I – I don't know – –'

'But I do know: you were anxious to find out whether I would have sacrificed my peace of mind to you and gone with you along that road? Isn't that so?'

'Yes, I think you must be right. Well?'

'Never,' she said firmly. 'Not for anything in the world.'

He thought it over and then sighed.

'Yes,' he said, 'that is a terrible road, and a woman must love very much to go after a man on it – to face ruin and go on loving.'

He looked at her face questioningly: he saw nothing there: her face was calm and only the crease over her eyebrow stirred a little.

'Imagine,' he said, 'that Sonia, who is not worth your little finger, suddenly refused to recognize you in the street.'

Olga smiled and she looked as serene as ever. Oblomov, on the other hand, was too vain to resist the temptation to obtain some sacrifice from Olga and revel in it.

'Imagine that men did not lower their eyes with timid respect as they approached you, but looked at you with a bold and meaningful glance.'

He glanced at her: she was absorbed in pushing a pebble along the sand with her parasol.

'You would enter a drawing-room and several bonnets would stir with indignation. One of the women would go and sit farther away from you – and your pride would be the same as ever and you would know perfectly well that you were higher and better than they – –'

281

'Why are you telling me all these horrors?' she said calmly. 'I shall never go that way.'

'Never?' Oblomov asked dejectedly.

'Never!' she repeated.

'Yes,' he said thoughtfully, 'you would not have the strength to face shame. You might not be afraid of death: it is not the execution that is so terrible, but the preparations for it, the hourly tortures. You would not have been able to stand it. You would have pined away, wouldn't you?'

He kept peering into her face to see what she felt.

She looked cheerful: the picture of horror did not upset her; a light smile was playing on her lips.

'I don't want to pine away or die,' she said. 'It's all wrong; one can love all the more and yet not follow that road. ...'

'But why wouldn't you follow it,' he asked insistently, almost with vexation, 'if you are not afraid?'

'Because – people who follow it always end up eventually by – parting,' she said, 'and I – to part from you! ...'

She paused, put her hand on his shoulder, looked intently at him and, suddenly, flinging away her parasol, quickly and ardently threw her arms round his neck, kissed him, and, flushing crimson, pressed her face to his breast, adding softly:

'Never!'

He uttered a joyful cry and sank on the grass at her feet.

PART THREE

1

OBLOMOV walked home feeling deliriously happy. His blood coursed exultantly in his veins and his eyes were shining. It seemed to him that even his hair was ablaze. It was thus that he entered his room – and suddenly the radiance disappeared, and his eyes became fixed with unpleasant surprise on one place: Tarantyev was sitting in his chair.

'Why do you keep people waiting for hours?' Tarantyev asked sternly, giving him his hirsute hand. 'Where have you been gadding about? And that old devil of yours has got out of hand completely. I asked him for a bite to eat – there wasn't anything; I asked for vodka, and he refused to give me any, either.'

'I've been for a walk in the woods,' Oblomov said casually, still unable to recover from the shock of Tarantyev's visit, and at such a moment, too!

He had forgotten the gloomy surroundings in which he had lived for so many years and was no longer used to their stifling atmosphere. Tarantyev had in a twinkling brought him down, as it were, from heaven into a swamp. Oblomov kept asking himself painfully what Tarantyev had come for and how long he was going to stay. He suffered agonies at the thought that Tarantyev might stay to dinner and that he would be unable to go to the Ilyinskys'. He had to get rid of Tarantyev at any price – that was the only thing that mattered to him now. He waited gloomily and in silence for Tarantyev to speak.

'Why don't you go and have a look at your flat, old man?' asked Tarantyev.

'I don't need it any more,' said Oblomov. 'I – I am not going to move there.'

'Wha-at? Not move there?' Tarantyev cried menacingly. 'You've rented it and you're not going to move? And what about the agreement?'

'What agreement?'

'You've forgotten, have you? You signed an agreement for a year. Come on, let us have eight hundred roubles, and then you can go where you like. Four people were after that flat and they were all turned away. One of them would have taken it for three years.'

Oblomov only just remembered that on the very day of his moving to the country cottage Tarantyev brought him a paper which in his hurry he signed without reading. 'Good Lord, what have I done?' he thought.

'But I don't want the flat,' said Oblomov. 'I'm going abroad.'

'Abroad!' Tarantyev interrupted. 'With that German? You'll never do it, old man. ... You'll never go!'

'Why not? I've already got my passport. I can show you if you like. Bought a trunk too.'

'You won't go!' Tarantyev repeated indifferently. 'You'd better let me have the rent for six months in advance.'

'I have no money.'

'You can get it, can't you? Ivan Matveyevich, the landlady's brother, will stand no nonsense. He'll take out a summons at once: you won't be able to wriggle out of it then. Besides, I've paid him with my own money, so you'd better pay me.'

'Where did you get so much money?' asked Oblomov.

'It's none of your business. I've been repaid an old debt. Come on, let's have the money. That's what I've come for.'

'All right. I'll call one day this week and get a new tenant for the flat. I'm sorry, but I'm in a hurry now.'

He began buttoning his coat.

'And what sort of a flat do you want?' Tarantyev said. 'You won't find a better. You haven't seen it, have you?'

'I don't want to see it,' replied Oblomov. 'What do I want to move there for? It's too far – –'

'From what?' Tarantyev interrupted rudely.

But Oblomov did not say what it was far from.

'From the centre,' he added later.

'What centre? What do you want it for? To lie about?'

'No, I don't lie about any more.'

'Oh?'

'I don't. To-day – er – I – –'

'What?' Tarantyev interrupted.

'I am not dining at home.'

'Give me the money and then you can go to the devil!'

'What money?' Oblomov repeated impatiently. 'I'll call at the flat soon and talk it over with the landlady.'

'What landlady? What does she know? She's a woman! No, sir. You talk to her brother – then you'll see!'

'All right, I'll call and talk to him.'

'Will you? I don't think! Give me the money and go where you like.'

'I haven't any money. I shall have to borrow.'

'Well, in that case you'd better pay for my cab fare,' Tarantyev persisted. 'Three roubles.'

'Where is your cabby? And why so much as three roubles?'

'I've dismissed him. Why so much? Because he didn't want to bring me here. Not over the sand, he said. And there'll be another three roubles back!'

'You can go by bus from here for half a rouble,' said Oblomov. 'Here you are.'

He gave him four roubles. Tarantyev put them in his pocket, and then asked:

'What about dinner money?'

'What dinner?'

'I shall be late for dinner in town and I shall have to call at a pub on the way. Everything's terribly expensive here: they're sure to charge me five roubles at least!'

Oblomov took out another rouble and threw it to Tarantyev in silence. He did not sit down because he was anxious that his visitor should go as soon as possible; but Tarantyev did not go.

'Tell them to give me something to eat,' he said.

'But aren't you going to have your dinner at a pub?' Oblomov observed.

'Dinner – yes! But it's only just gone one.'

Oblomov told Zakhar to give him something to eat.

'There's nothing in the house, sir,' Zakhar said dryly, looking sullenly at Tarantyev. 'Nothing has been prepared. And when, sir,' he addressed Tarantyev, 'are you going to return the master's shirt and waistcoat?'

'What shirt and waistcoat?' Tarantyev asked. 'I returned them long ago.'

'When was that?' asked Zakhar.

'Why, my good man, I handed the things to you when you were moving, didn't I? You shoved them into some bundle, and now you ask for them.'

Zakhar was dumbfounded.

'Good Lord, sir,' he cried, addressing Oblomov, 'that's a scandal, that is!'

'Go on, tell me another,' Tarantyev replied. 'I suppose you sold them for drink and now you ask me for them.'

'No, sir, I have never in my life sold my master's things for drink,' Zakhar wheezed. 'Now you, sir – –'

'Stop it, Zakhar!' Oblomov interrupted him sternly.

'Didn't you take our broom and two of our cups?' Zakhar asked again.

'What broom?' Tarantyev thundered. 'Oh, you old rascal! Come on, you'd better give me a bite of something!'

'Do you hear how he swears at me, sir?' said Zakhar. 'There is no food in the house – not even any bread, and Anisya has gone out,' he declared firmly and went out of the room.

'Where do you have dinner?' asked Tarantyev. 'I must say it's funny all right – Oblomov goes for walks in the wood, doesn't dine at home – – When are you going to move to your flat? It'll be autumn soon. Come and have a look at it.'

'All right, all right. I will soon. ...'

'And don't forget to bring the money!'

'Yes, yes, yes!' Oblomov said impatiently.

'Well, do you want anything doing to your flat? They've stained the floors and painted the ceilings, doors, and windows – everything. It has cost more than a hundred roubles, old man.'

'Yes, yes, all right. ... Oh,' Oblomov suddenly remembered, 'there's one thing I was going to tell you. Could you, please, go to the courts for me – I have a deed of trust that has to be witnessed. ...'

'I am not your solicitor, am I?' Tarantyev said.

'I'll give you more for your dinner,' said Oblomov.

'The wear and tear of my boots will cost me more than you will give me.'

'Take a cab, I'll pay.'

'I'm sorry, but I can't go to the courts,' Tarantyev said gloomily.

'Oh? Why not?'

'I have enemies who bear me malice and are doing their best to ruin me.'

'Oh, very well, I'll go myself,' said Oblomov, picking up his cap.

'You see, when you move to the flat Ivan Matveyevich will do everything for you. He's a fine fellow, I tell you, not at all like some German upstart! A real, hundred-per-cent Russian official, has sat for thirty years on the same chair, runs his office, has money too, but never takes a cab. His coat is no better than mine; would never hurt a fly, speaks in a very low voice, never goes roaming abroad like your – –'

'Tarantyev,' Oblomov shouted, banging his fist on the table, 'don't talk of something you don't understand!'

Tarantyev opened his eyes wide at such unheard-of impudence on Oblomov's part and even forgot to be offended at being put below Stolz.

'So that's what you are like now, old man,' he muttered, taking up his hat. 'What energy!'

He stroked his hat with his sleeve, then looked at it and at Oblomov's hat that lay on the bookstand.

'You don't wear your hat,' he said, taking Oblomov's hat and trying it on. 'I see you have a cap. Lend it to me for the summer, old man.'

Oblomov, without uttering a word, removed his hat from Tarantyev's head and put it back on the bookcase. He then crossed his arms on his chest and waited for Tarantyev to go.

'Oh, to hell with you!' said Tarantyev, pushing his way clumsily through the door. 'You're a little – er – queer, old man. Wait till you've had a talk with Ivan Matveyevich, and see what happens if you don't bring the money.'

2

HE went away, and Oblomov sat down in the arm-chair, feeling thoroughly upset. He could not shake off the unpleasant impression left by Tarantyev's visit for a long time. At last he remembered his plans for the morning, and the hideous appearance of Tarantyev faded from his mind; a smile came back to his face. He stood before the looking-glass for some time, straightening his tie, smiling and looking to see if there was any trace of Olga's ardent kiss on his cheek.

'Two *nevers*,' he said softly, with joyful excitement, 'and what a difference between them! One has already faded and the other has blossomed out so gorgeously.'

Then he sank deeper and deeper into thought. He felt that the bright and cloudless festival of love had gone, that love was truly becoming a duty, that it was becoming intermingled with his whole life, forming an integral part of its ordinary functions and beginning to lose its rainbow colours. That morning, perhaps, he had caught sight of its last roseate ray, and in future it would no longer shine brightly, but warm his life invisibly; life would swallow it up, and it would be its powerful but hidden mainspring. And henceforth its manifestations would be so simple, so ordinary. The poetic period was over and stern reality was beginning: the courts, journey to Oblomovka, building the house, mortgaging the estate, constructing the road, never-ending business troubles with the peasants, getting the work on the estate organized – harvesting, threshing, casting up accounts, the agent's worried face, the noblemen's elections, court sessions. ... Only occasionally, at long intervals, would Olga's eyes shine upon him, the strains of *Casta diva* reach him, and after snatching a hasty kiss, he would have to hurry off to the fields, to the town, and then again to the agent and the click of the abacus. The arrival of visitors would bring little comfort to him: they would talk about how much spirit they had distilled, how many yards of cloth they had delivered to the Government. ... Oh dear, that wasn't what he had promised himself, was it? Was that life? And yet people lived as though this was all that life meant. Andrey, too, liked it!

But marriage – the wedding, why, that was, anyway, the poetry of life, that was a fully opened-up flower. He imagined how he would lead Olga to the altar: she would be wearing orange blossom on her head and a long veil. There would be whispers of wonderment in the crowd. She would give him her hand shyly, her bosom heaving gently, her head bowed with her usual graceful pride, and would not know how to look at the crowd. Now a smile would light up her face, now tears would appear in her eyes, or the crease over her eyebrow would stir thoughtfully. At home, after the guests had gone, she would throw herself on his chest, as she had to-day, still wearing her gorgeous wedding-dress. ...

'No,' he thought, 'I must run to Olga. I can't think and feel by myself. I'll tell everyone, the whole world – no, just her aunt, then the baron; I shall write to Stolz – he will be surprised! Then I'll tell Zakhar: he will fall at my feet and howl with joy. I shall give him twenty-five roubles. Anisya will come and try to kiss my hand: I'll give her ten roubles – then – then I shall shout for joy in a loud voice so that the whole world will hear and say: "Oblomov is happy, Oblomov is getting married!" Now I'll run to Olga – we shall sit and whisper together for hours, making our secret plans to merge our two lives into one!'

He ran off to Olga. She listened to his dreams with a smile, but as soon as he jumped up to run and tell her aunt, she knit her brows in a way that alarmed him.

'Not a word to anyone!' she said, putting a finger to her lips and begging him to speak lower so that her aunt should not hear in the next room. 'The time hasn't come yet!'

'Hasn't the time come now that everything has been decided between us?' he asked impatiently. 'What are we to do now? How are we to begin? We can't just sit and do nothing. We must think of our duties – serious life is beginning. ...'

'Yes, it is,' she agreed, looking searchingly at him.

'Well, so I'd like to take the first step – go to your aunt and – –'

'That's the last step.'

'Which is the first, then?'

'The first – to go to the courts: you have to write some document, haven't you?'

'Yes – to-morrow – –'

'Why not to-day?'

'To-day – to-day is a very special day, and I can't leave you, Olga, can I?'

'Very well, to-morrow. And then?'

'Then tell your aunt, write to Stolz.'

'No, then you must go to Oblomovka. ... Mr Stolz wrote to you what you had to do in the country, didn't he? I don't know what business you have there – building, is it?' she asked, looking into his face.

'Good Lord,' said Oblomov, 'if we are to listen to what Stolz says we'll never get as far as telling your aunt! He says that I must begin building the house, then construct the road, then open schools! ... You won't do that in a lifetime. Let's go there together, Olga, and then – –'

'But where shall we go to? Is there a house there?'

'No – the old house isn't good enough; I expect the front steps must have collapsed by now.'

'So where shall we go to?' she asked.

'We'll have to find a flat here.'

'For that you'll also have to go to town,' she observed. 'That's the second step.'

'Then – –' he began.

'I think you'd better take the two steps first and then – –'

'What's all this?' Oblomov thought mournfully. 'No whispering for hours, no secret plans to merge our two lives into one! Everything has turned out differently somehow. What a strange girl Olga is! She never stands still, she never indulges in romantic dreams even for a moment, just as though she'd never dreamed in her life, just as though she never felt the need of

289

giving herself up to day-dreaming! Go to the courts at once – look for a flat! Just like Andrey! They all seem to have conspired to be in a hurry to live!'

Next day he went to town, taking with him a piece of stamped paper to settle his business at the courts: he drove to town reluctantly, yawning and gazing about him. He did not know where exactly the courts were, and called first on Ivan Gerasimovich to ask in which department he had to witness the signature of the deed of trust. Ivan Gerasimovich was very glad to see Oblomov and would not let him go without lunch. Then he sent for a friend to find out from him how the business was to be done, for he himself had got out of touch with such things. The lunch and the consultation were over only by three o'clock. It was too late for the courts, and the following day was Saturday and the courts would be closed, so that it all had to be put off till Monday.

Oblomov went to his new flat in Vyborg. He spent a long time driving along narrow lanes with long wooden fences on either side. At last he found a policeman who told him that the house was in a different part of the suburb, and he pointed to a street where there were only fences and no houses, with grass growing in the road, which was full of ruts made of dried mud. Oblomov drove on, admiring the nettles by the fences and the rowan-berries peeping out from behind them. At last the policeman pointed to a little old house standing in a yard, adding: 'That's it, sir.' 'The house of the widow of the Collegiate Assessor Pshenitzyn', Oblomov read on the gate, and told the driver to drive into the yard.

The yard was the size of a room, so that the shaft of the carriage struck a corner and frightened a number of hens that scattered cackling in all directions, some even attempting to fly; a big black dog on a chain began to bark furiously, rushing to right and left and trying to reach the horses' muzzles. Oblomov sat in the carriage on a level with the windows, finding it rather hard to get out. In the windows, crowded with pots of mignonette and marigolds, several heads could be seen looking out. Oblomov managed to get out of the carriage; the dog barked more fiercely than ever. He walked up the front steps and ran into a wrinkled old woman wearing a *sarafan* tucked up at the waist.

'Who do you want?' she asked.

'The landlady, Mrs Pshenitzyn.'

The old woman bent her head in bewilderment.

'Are you sure it isn't Ivan Matveyevich you would like to see?'

she asked. 'I'm afraid he isn't at home. He hasn't come back from the office yet.'

'I want to see the landlady,' said Oblomov.

Meanwhile the hubbub in the house continued. Heads kept peeping out of windows; the door behind the old woman kept opening and closing and different people looked out. Oblomov turned round: in the yard two children, a boy and a girl, stood regarding him with curiosity. A sleepy peasant in a sheepskin appeared from somewhere and, screening his eyes from the sun, gazed lazily at Oblomov and the carriage. The dog kept up a low and abrupt barking and every time Oblomov moved or a horse stamped, it began jumping about on its chain and barking continuously. On the right, over the fence, Oblomov saw an endless kitchen garden planted with cabbages, and on the left, over the fence, he could see several trees and a green wooden summer-house.

'Do you want Agafya Matveyevna?' the old woman asked. 'Why?'

'Tell the landlady that I want to see her,' said Oblomov. 'I have taken rooms here.'

'So you are the new lodger, Mr Tarantyev's friend, are you? Wait, I'll tell her.'

She opened the door, and several heads drew back hastily and rushed away into the inner rooms. He managed to catch sight of a white-skinned, rather plump woman, with a bare neck and elbows and no cap on, who smiled at having been seen by a stranger. She, too, rushed away from the door.

'Please come in, sir,' said the old woman, coming back, and she led Oblomov through a small entrance hall into a fairly large room and asked him to wait. 'The lady of the house will be here presently,' she added.

'And the dog is still barking,' thought Oblomov, examining the room.

Suddenly his eyes lighted on familiar objects: the whole room was littered with his belongings. Tables covered in dust; chairs heaped in a pile on the bed; mattresses, crockery, cupboards – all thrown together in confusion.

'What on earth? Haven't they done anything about them – sorted them out, tidied them up?' he said. 'How disgusting!'

Suddenly a door creaked behind him, and the woman he had seen with the bare neck and elbows came into the room. She was about thirty. Her complexion was so fair and her face so plump that it seemed that the colour could not force its way through her cheeks. She had practically no eyebrows, and in their place she had two seemingly slightly swollen shiny patches with scanty fair hair on them. Her eyes were grey and as good-humoured as the whole expression of her face; her hands were white but coarse, with knotted blue veins standing out. She wore a close-fitting dress, and it was quite obvious that she used no artifice, not even an extra petticoat, to increase the size of her hips and make her waist look smaller. That was why even when she was dressed, as long as she wore no shawl she would with-out any danger to her modesty serve a sculptor or a painter as a model of a fine, well-developed bosom. In comparison with her smart shawl and Sunday bonnet, her dress looked old and worn.

She had not been expecting visitors, and when Oblomov asked to see her, she threw on her Sunday shawl over her ordinary everyday dress and covered her head with a bonnet. She came in timidly and stopped, looking shyly at Oblomov.

He got up and bowed.

'I have the pleasure of meeting Mrs Pshenitzyn, have I not?' he asked.

'Yes, sir,' she replied. 'Would you perhaps like to speak to my brother?' she asked hesitantly. 'I'm afraid he is at the office. He never comes home before five.'

'No, it was you I wanted to see,' Oblomov began when she had sat down on the sofa as far away from him as possible, looking at the ends of her shawl which covered her down to the ground like a horse-cloth. She hid her hands under the shawl too.

'I have rented rooms, but now, owing to certain circum-stances, I have to find a flat in another part of the town, so I have come to discuss the matter with you.'

She listened to him dully and fell into thought.

'I'm afraid my brother isn't in,' she said after a pause.

'But this house is yours, isn't it?' Oblomov said.

'Yes,' she replied briefly.

'Well, in that case you ought to be able to decide for yourself, oughtn't you?'

'But my brother isn't in, and he attends to everything,' she said monotonously, looking straight at Oblomov for the first time and then lowering her eyes to the shawl again.

'She has an ordinary but pleasant face,' Oblomov decided condescendingly. 'Must be a good woman!'

At that moment a little girl's head was thrust through the door. Agafya Matveyevna nodded to her sternly without being observed by Oblomov, and she disappeared.

'And in what Ministry does your brother work?'

'In some Government office.'

'Which one?'

'Where peasants are registered. I'm afraid I don't know what it's called.'

She smiled good-naturedly, and almost at once her face assumed its normal expression.

'Do you live here alone with your brother?' asked Oblomov.

'No, I have two children by my late husband, a boy aged eight and a girl aged six,' the landlady began talking readily enough and her face became more animated, 'and we have also our grandmother living with us; she's an invalid and can hardly walk, and she only goes to church; she used to go to the market with Akulina, but she has given it up since St Nicholas' day: her legs have begun to swell. And even in church she has to sit on the steps most of the time. That is all. Sometimes my sister-in-law stays with us and Mr Tarantyev.'

'And does Mr Tarantyev stay with you often?' Oblomov asked.

'He sometimes stays for a month. He is a great friend of my brother's. They are always together.'

And she fell silent, having exhausted all her supply of ideas and words.

'How quiet it is here!' said Oblomov. 'If it were not for the dog barking, one might think there was not a living soul here.'

She smiled in reply.

'Do you often go out?' asked Oblomov.

'Occasionally, in summer. The other day, on a Friday, we went to the Gunpowder Works.'

'Why, do many people go there?' asked Oblomov, gazing through an opening in the shawl at her high bosom, firm as a sofa cushion and never agitated.

'No, there weren't many this year. It rained in the morning, but it cleared up later. Usually there are lots of people there.'

'Where else do you go?'

'Hardly anywhere. My brother goes fishing with Mr Tarantyev and makes fish soup there, but we are always at home.'

'Not always, surely?'

'Yes, indeed. Last year we went to Kolpino, and sometimes we go to the woods here. It's my brother's name-day on June 24th, and all his colleagues from the office come to dinner.'

'Do you pay any visits?'

'My brother does, but the children and I only go on Easter

293

Sunday and at Christmas to dinner with my husband's relatives.'

There was nothing else to talk about.

'I see you have flowers. Do you like them?' he asked.

She smiled. 'No,' she said; 'I have no time for flowers. The children and Akulina have been to the count's garden and the gardener has given them these. The geraniums and the aloe have been here a long time – when my husband was still alive.'

At that moment Akulina suddenly burst into the room: a large cock was cackling and struggling desperately in her hands.

'Is this the cock I am to give to the shopkeeper, ma'am?' she asked.

'Really, Akulina, go away!' the landlady said, shamefacedly. 'Can't you see I have a visitor?'

'I only came to ask,' Akulina said, holding the cock by its feet head downwards. 'He offers seventy copecks for it.'

'Go back to the kitchen,' said Agafya Matveyevna. 'The grey speckled one, not that one,' she added hurriedly, and blushed with shame, hiding her hands under the shawl and looking down.

'Household cares!' said Oblomov.

'Yes. We have lots of hens and we sell eggs and chickens. The people from our street, in the summer cottages, and in the count's house, buy them from us,' she replied, looking at Oblomov much more boldly.

Her face assumed a business-like and thoughtful expression; even her vacant look disappeared when she talked about a subject she was familiar with. Any question that had nothing to do with what she was interested in, she answered with a smile and silence.

'You ought to have sorted it out,' Oblomov observed, pointing to the heap of his belongings.

'I wanted to, but my brother told me not to touch it,' she interrupted quickly, looking at Oblomov very boldly this time. ' "Goodness knows what he has in his cupboards and tables," he said, "if anything should be lost, he'll never leave us alone." '

She stopped and smiled.

'What a careful man your brother is,' Oblomov remarked.

She smiled faintly again and once more assumed her usual expression. Her smile was just a matter of form with her with which she disguised her ignorance of what to say or do in any given circumstance.

'I'm afraid I can't wait for him,' said Oblomov. 'Will you be so good as to tell him that, owing to a change in my circumstances, I no longer need the flat and therefore ask you to let it to somebody else? And I, for my part, will also try to find a tenant for you.'

She listened vacantly, blinking from time to time.

'Will you please tell him that so far as our agreement is concerned – –'

'But he isn't at home now,' she repeated. 'You'd better come again to-morrow: It's Saturday, and he does not go to the office.'

'I'm sorry, but I'm terribly busy – I haven't a moment to spare,' Oblomov excused himself. 'Be so good as to tell him that as the deposit will be yours and I would find you a tenant – –'

'My brother isn't at home,' she said monotonously. 'I don't know why he isn't back yet.' She looked out into the street. 'He usually walks past the windows and one can see him as he comes along, but he isn't here!'

'I'm afraid I must go,' said Oblomov.

'And what am I to tell my brother when he comes? When are you moving in?' she asked, getting up from the sofa.

'Tell him what I have asked you,' Oblomov said. 'Owing to my changed circumstances – –'

'You had better come to-morrow and talk to him yourself,' she repeated.

'I'm sorry, I can't come to-morrow.'

'Well, the day after to-morrow, then, on Sunday. We usually have vodka and snacks after Mass. And Mr Tarantyev comes, too.'

'Does he?'

'Yes, indeed, he does,' she said.

'I'm afraid the day after to-morrow I can't come either,' Oblomov pleaded impatiently.

'Next week, then,' she said. 'And when are you going to move in?' she asked. 'I'd have the floors scrubbed and the rooms dusted.'

'I'm not going to move in,' he said.

'You aren't? But what shall we do with your things?'

'Will you kindly tell your brother,' Oblomov began slowly, fixing his eyes straight on her bosom, 'that owing to changed circumstances – –'

'He's very late to-day, I'm afraid, I can't see him,' she said monotonously, looking at the fence which divided the yard from the street. 'I know his footsteps: I can recognize anyone walking along the wooden pavement. Not many people walk here. ...'

'So you will tell him what I said, won't you?' Oblomov said, bowing and walking to the door.

'I'm sure he'll be here himself in half an hour,' the landlady said with an agitation which was quite unusual for her, as though trying to detain Oblomov with her voice.

'I'm sorry, but I can't wait any longer,' he declared, opening the front door.

Seeing him on the steps, the dog began barking and trying to break its chain again. The driver, who had fallen asleep leaning on his elbow, began to back the horses; the hens again scattered in all directions in alarm; several heads peeped out of the windows.

'So I'll tell my brother that you called,' the landlady said anxiously when Oblomov had sat down in the carriage.

'Yes, and please tell him that because of changed circumstances I cannot keep the flat and that I'll pass it on to somebody else or perhaps he might look for – –'

'He usually comes home at this time,' she said, listening absent-mindedly to him. 'I'll tell him that you intend to call again.'

'Yes,' said Oblomov, 'I'll call again in a few days.'

The carriage drove out of the yard to the accompaniment of the desperate barking of the dog and went swaying over the dried-up mounds of mud in the unpaved street. A middle-aged man in a shabby overcoat appeared at the end of it, with a big paper parcel under his arm, a thick stick in his hands, and rubber shoes on his feet in spite of the dry, hot day. He walked quickly, looking from side to side and stepping as heavily as though he meant to break through the wooden pavement. Oblomov turned round to look at him, and saw that he turned in at the gate of Mrs Pshenitzyn's house.

'That, I suppose, is her brother coming back,' he concluded. 'But to hell with him! I'd have had to spend an hour talking to him, and I'm hungry, and it's so hot! Besides, Olga is waiting for me – another time.

'Go on, faster!' he said to the driver.

'And what about going in search of another flat?' he suddenly remembered, as he looked at the fences on either side of the road. 'I must go back to Morskaya or Konyushennaya – another time!' he decided.

'Faster, driver, faster!'

AT the end of August it began to rain, and smoke came out of the chimneys of the summer cottages that had stoves, and the people in those that had not went about with kerchiefs tied round their heads; at last, all the summer cottages were gradually deserted.

Oblomov had not been to town again, and one morning the Ilyinskys' furniture was carted and carried past his windows. Though to leave his flat, to dine out, and not lie down all day no longer seemed an heroic feat to him, he was now faced with the problem of how to spend the evenings. To remain alone in the country when the park and the woods were deserted and when Olga's windows were shuttered seemed utterly impossible to him. He walked through her empty rooms, walked round the park, came down the hill, and his heart was oppressed with sadness. He told Zakhar and Anisya to go to Vyborg, where he decided to stay until he found another flat, and himself went to town, had a quick dinner at a restaurant, and spent the evening at Olga's.

But autumn evenings in town were not like the long bright days and evenings in the park and the woods. In town he could not see her three times a day; there Katya did not run with a message to him, and he could not send Zakhar three miles with a note. In fact, all the flowering summer poem of their love seemed to have come to a stop, as though its subject-matter had run out. Sometimes they were silent for half an hour on end. Olga would be absorbed in her work, counting to herself the squares of the pattern with her needle, and he would be absorbed in a chaos of thoughts, living in a future that was far ahead of the present moment. Only at times, as he gazed intently at her, would he give a passionate start, or she would glance at him and smile, catching a glimpse of a tender look. He went to town and dined at Olga's three days in succession under the pretext that his rooms were not ready yet, that he was going to move during the week and could not settle down in his new flat before that. But on the fourth day he felt that it would be improper to call again, and after walking up and down the pavement before Olga's house for some time, he sighed and drove home. On the fifth day Olga told him to go to a certain shop where she would be and then walk back to her home with her while the carriage followed them. All this was awkward: they met people they knew, they exchanged greetings, and some of them stopped for a chat.

'Oh dear, how awful!' he said, perspiring with apprehension and the awkwardness of the situation.

Olga's aunt, too, looked at him with her large, languorous eyes, inhaling her smelling-salts thoughtfully, as though she had a headache. And what a long journey it was! Driving from Vyborg and back again in the evening took him three hours.

'Let us tell your aunt,' Oblomov insisted, 'then I can stay with you all day and no one will say anything.'

'But have you been to the courts?' Olga asked.

Oblomov was greatly tempted to say that he had been there and done everything, but he knew that Olga had only to look at him searchingly to discover the lie in his face. He sighed in reply.

'Oh, if you only knew how difficult it is!' he said.

'And have you spoken to your landlady's brother? Have you found a flat?' she asked afterwards, without raising her eyes.

'He's never at home in the morning, and in the evenings I am here,' said Oblomov, glad to have found some satisfactory excuse.

Now Olga sighed, but said nothing.

'I will most certainly speak to the landlady's brother to-morrow,' Oblomov tried to soothe her. 'It is Sunday to-morrow and he won't go to the office.'

'Until all this is settled,' Olga said reflectively, 'we can't tell Auntie and we must not see so much of each other.'

'Yes, yes – that's true,' he added hastily in alarm.

'You'd better dine with us on Sundays, our at home day, and then, say, on Wednesdays, alone,' she decided. 'And on other days we can meet at the theatre. I'll let you know when we are going and you to come.'

'Yes, that's true,' he said, glad that she took upon herself the arrangement of their future meetings.

'And if it's a fine day,' she concluded, 'I'll go for a walk in the Summer Gardens and you can come there. That will remind us of the park – the park!' she repeated with feeling.

He kissed her hand in silence and said good-bye to her till Sunday. She followed him with her eyes sadly, then sat down at the piano and became absorbed in the strains of the music. Her heart was weeping for something, and the notes, too, wept. She wanted to sing, but could not bring herself to.

When he got up on the following morning, Oblomov put on

the indoor coat he used to wear in the country cottage. He had parted with his dressing-gown long ago, having given orders to put it away in the wardrobe. Zakhar walked clumsily to the table with the coffee and rolls, holding the tray unsteadily in his hands as usual. Anisya, also as usual, thrust her head through the door to see whether Zakhar would carry the cups safely to the table and hid herself noiselessly as soon as Zakhar put down the tray on the table or rushed up to him quickly if he dropped something, so as to save the others from falling. When this happened Zakhar began to swear first at the things, then at his wife, making as if to hit her in the chest with his elbow.

'What excellent coffee! Who makes it?' Oblomov asked.

'The landlady herself, sir,' said Zakhar. 'She's been making it for the last five days. "You're putting in too much chicory and don't boil it enough – let me do it," she said.'

'Excellent,' Oblomov repeated, pouring himself another cup. 'Thank her.'

'Here she is herself,' said Zakhar, pointing to the half-open door of a side room. 'That must be their pantry, I expect. She works there. They keep sugar, tea, and coffee there as well as the crockery.'

Oblomov could see only the landlady's back, the back of her head, a bit of her white neck, and her bare elbows.

'Why is she moving her elbows about so rapidly there?' asked Oblomov.

'I'm sure I don't know, sir. Must be making lace, I expect.'

Oblomov watched her as she moved her elbows, bent her back, and straightened out again. When she bent down, he could see her clean petticoat and stockings, and her round, firm legs.

'A civil servant's widow, but she has elbows fit for a countess, and with dimples, too!' Oblomov thought.

At midday, Zakhar came to ask if he would like to taste their pie: the landlady had sent it to him with her compliments.

'It's Sunday, sir, and they're baking a pie to-day.'

'I can imagine the sort of pie it is,' Oblomov said carelessly. 'With carrots and onions!'

'No, sir,' Zakhar said, 'it's not worse than ours at Oblomovka – with chickens and fresh mushrooms.'

'Oh, that must be nice: bring me some! Who does the baking? That dirty peasant woman?'

'Not her!' Zakhar said scornfully. 'If it wasn't for her mistress, she wouldn't know how to mix the dough. She's always in

299

the kitchen, the landlady is. She and Anisya baked the pie, sir.'

Five minutes later a bare arm, scarcely covered with the shawl he had already seen, was thrust through the door of the side-room, holding a plate with a huge piece of steaming hot pie.

'Thank you very much,' Oblomov cried, accepting the pie, and glancing through the door, he fixed his eyes upon the enormous bosom and bare shoulders. The door was hastily closed.

'Wouldn't you like some vodka?' the voice asked.

'Thank you, I don't drink,' Oblomov said, still more affably. 'What kind have you?'

'Our own home-made one,' the voice said. 'We infuse it from currant leaves ourselves.'

'I've never drunk a currant-leaf liqueur,' said Oblomov. 'Please let me try it.'

The bare arm was thrust through the door again with a glass of vodka on a plate. Oblomov drank it and liked it very much.

'Thank you very much,' he said, trying to peep through the door, but the door was slammed to.

'Why don't you let me have a look at you and wish you good morning?' Oblomov reproached her.

The landlady smiled behind the door. 'I'm sorry, but I'm still wearing my everyday dress: I've been in the kitchen all the time, you see. I'll dress presently, and my brother will soon be coming from Mass,' she replied.

'Oh, *à propos* of your brother,' Oblomov observed. 'I'd like to have a talk with him. Tell him I want to see him, please.'

'All right, I'll tell him when he comes.'

'And who is it coughing?' Oblomov asked. 'What a dry cough!'

'It's Granny. She's been coughing for the last seven years.'

And the door was slammed to.

'How – how simple she is,' Oblomov thought. 'And there is something about her. And she is very clean, too!'

He had not met the landlady's brother yet. Every now and then early in the morning, when he was still in bed, he caught sight of a man with a large paper parcel under his arm rushing off on the other side of the fence and disappearing in the street; at five o'clock the same man with the paper parcel rushed past the windows and disappeared behind the front door. He was never heard in the house. And yet there could be no doubt, especially in the mornings, that the house was full of people: there was a clatter of knives in the kitchen; the peasant woman could be heard rinsing something in a corner of the yard; the caretaker was chopping wood or bringing the barrel of water; through the wall the children could be heard crying, or there came the sound of the old woman's dry, persistent cough.

Oblomov had the four best rooms in the house. The landlady and her family occupied the two back rooms, and her brother lived upstairs in the attic. Oblomov's study and bedroom looked out into the yard, the drawing-room faced the little garden, and the reception-room the big kitchen garden with the cabbages and potatoes. At the drawing-room windows the curtains were of faded chintz. Plain chairs, in imitation walnut, were placed along the walls; a card-table stood under the looking-glass; on the window-sills were pots of geranium and African marigold, and four cages with siskins and canaries hung in the windows.

The landlady's brother walked in on tiptoe and bowed three times in answer to Oblomov's greeting. His civil servant's uniform was buttoned to the top, so that it was impossible to say whether he wore a shirt under it or not; his tie was done up in a knot and the ends tucked in. He was a man of about forty with a straight tuft of hair on the forehead and two similar tufts over his temples, waving carelessly in the wind and resembling a dog's ears of medium size. His grey eyes never looked directly at an object, but first glanced at it stealthily and only then fixed themselves upon it. He seemed to be ashamed of his hands, and as he talked he tried to hide them behind his back, or put one behind his back and thrust the other in the breast of his coat. When giving some paper to his chief and explaining some point in it, he kept one hand behind his back and carefully pointed to some line or word with the middle finger of the other hand, which he held with his nail downwards, and, having shown it, at once withdrew his hand, perhaps because his fingers were rather thick and red and shook a little and he believed, with good reason, that it was not quite nice to display them too often.

'I believe, sir,' he said, throwing his double glance at Oblomov, 'that you were so good as to ask me to come and see you.'

'Yes,' Oblomov replied courteously, 'I wanted to talk to you about my flat. Please sit down.'

After the second invitation Ivan Matveyich ventured to sit down, leaning over with his entire body and thrusting his hands into his sleeves.

'I'm afraid I have to look for another flat,' said Oblomov, 'and I should therefore like to sub-let this one.'

'It is difficult to sub-let it now,' Ivan Matveyevich said, coughing into his hands and hiding them quickly in his sleeves.

'If you'd come to see me at the end of summer, there were lots of people after it.'

'I did call, but you were not in,' Oblomov interrupted.

'My sister told me,' the civil servant added. 'But don't worry about your flat: you'll be very comfortable here. The birds are not disturbing you, are they?'

'Which birds?'

'The hens, sir.'

Though Oblomov constantly heard from early morning the deep cackling of a broody hen and the chirping of chicks under his window, he paid no attention to it. Olga's image was before his mind's eye and he scarcely noticed what happened around him.

'No, I don't mind that,' he said. 'I thought you were talking about the canaries: they start twittering from early morning.'

'We will take them out,' Ivan Matveyevich answered.

'That doesn't matter, either,' Oblomov observed. 'But I'm afraid my circumstances make it impossible for me to stay.'

'Just as you like, sir,' Ivan Matveyevich replied. 'But if you don't find another tenant, what about our agreement? Will you pay compensation? You'll be sure to lose on it.'

'How much does it amount to?' asked Oblomov.

'I will bring the account.'

He brought the agreement and an abacus.

'Here we are, sir,' he said. 'The rent of the flat is eight hundred roubles, you've paid a hundred roubles deposit, which leaves seven hundred.'

'But, surely,' Oblomov interrupted him, 'you can't possibly demand a year's rent when I haven't been here a fortnight!'

'But why not, sir?' Ivan Matveyevich retorted gently and conscientiously. 'It would be unjust to expect my sister to suffer loss. She is a poor widow who lives by letting rooms and perhaps makes enough on her chickens and eggs to buy some clothes for the children.'

'But, good Lord, I just can't afford it,' Oblomov said. 'Just think, I haven't been here a fortnight. It's unfair. Why should I pay so much?'

'Just have a look, sir, at what it says in the agreement,' Ivan Matveyevich said, pointing to two lines with his middle finger and then hiding it in his sleeve. 'Read, please.'

' "Should I, Oblomov, wish to leave the flat before the expiration of the lease, I undertake to let it to another tenant on the same terms or, failing this, to compensate Mrs Pshenitzyn

302

by paying her a year's rent up to the first of June next year," '
Oblomov read. 'But how is that?' he said. 'That's unfair.'

'That's the law, sir,' observed Ivan Matveyevich. 'You signed
it yourself. Here is your signature.'

The finger again appeared under the signature and disappeared again.

'How much?' said Oblomov.

'Seven hundred roubles,' Ivan Matveyevich began clicking on
the abacus with the same finger, bending it quickly every time
and hiding it in his fist, 'and one hundred and fifty roubles for
the stables and the shed.'

And he clicked the beads of the abacus again.

'But really, sir, I have no horses – I don't keep any, so what
do I want stables and a shed for?' Oblomov retorted spiritedly.

'It's in the contract, sir,' Ivan Matveyevich observed, pointing to the line with a finger. 'Mr Tarantyev said you would keep
horses.'

'Mr Tarantyev was lying!' Oblomov said in vexation. 'Let
me have the agreement!'

'I can let you have a copy of it, sir; the agreement belongs to
my sister,' Ivan Matveyevich retorted mildly, taking the agreement. ' "In addition," ' Ivan Matveyevich read, ' "for kitchen
garden produce, such as cabbages, turnips, and other vegetables for one person, approximately two hundred and fifty
roubles. ..."'

And he was about to click the beads again.

'What kitchen garden? What cabbages? What are you talking about? I know nothing about it!' Oblomov rejoined almost
menacingly.

'It's here, sir! In the contract. Mr Tarantyev said that you
wanted it included. ...'

'So you're also settling without me what I am to have for my
table, are you? I don't want your cabbages and turnips,' Oblomov said, getting up.

Ivan Matveyevich, too, got up from his chair.

'Without you, sir? Why, here is your signature!' he retorted.

Again his thick finger shook over the signature and the whole
paper shook in his hand.

'How much do you make it in all?' Oblomov asked impatiently.

'For painting the doors and the ceiling, for altering the windows in the kitchen, and for new hinges for the doors – one
hundred and fifty-four roubles and twenty-eight copecks.'

'What? Have I got to pay for this too?' Oblomov asked in astonishment. 'The landlord always pays for that. No one moves into an undecorated flat.'

'Well, sir, it says in the agreement that you have to pay for it,' said Ivan Matveyevich, pointing from a distance to the appropriate clause. 'One thousand three hundred and fifty-four roubles and twenty-eight copecks altogether, sir!' he concluded gently, hiding both his hands with the agreement behind his back.

'But where am I to get it?' Oblomov said, pacing the room. 'I haven't any money. What do I want your cabbages and turnips for?'

'Just as you like, sir!' Ivan Matveyevich added quietly. 'But you needn't worry; you'll find it very comfortable here. As for the money, my sister can wait.'

'I'm sorry but I can't stay; I can't because of my circumstances. Do you hear?'

'Yes, sir, just as you like,' Ivan Matveyevich replied obediently, withdrawing a step.

'All right, I'll think it over and try to sub-let the flat,' said Oblomov, nodding to him.

'You'll find it's not as easy as you think, sir. However, just as you like,' Ivan Matveyevich concluded, and, bowing three times, left the room.

Oblomov took out his wallet and counted his money: there were only 305 roubles. He was dumbfounded.

'What have I done with my money?' Oblomov asked himself in astonishment, almost in terror. 'At the beginning of summer I received from the country one thousand two hundred roubles, and now there are only three hundred left!'

He began adding up, trying to remember all he had spent, and could remember only 250 roubles.

'Where has the money gone?' he said.

'Zakhar! Zakhar!'

'Yes, sir?'

'Where has all our money gone?' he asked. 'You see, we've none left!'

Zakhar began fumbling in his pockets, took out half-a-rouble and a ten-copeck piece and put them on the table.

'I'm very sorry, sir,' he said, 'I forgot to return it – been left over from the moving.'

'What are you shoving this small change under my nose for? Tell me what have we done with eight hundred roubles?'

'How should I know, sir? Do I know where you spend your money, what you pay the cabbies in fares?'

'Yes, the carriage did cost a lot,' Oblomov remembered, looking at Zakhar. 'You don't remember what we paid the cabby in the country?'

'Remember that, sir? Of course not. One day you told me to give him thirty roubles, so I remember that.'

'If only you had written it down!' Oblomov said reprovingly. 'It's bad to be illiterate.'

'I've spent all my life without knowing how to read or write, sir, and thank God I'm no worse than other people,' Zakhar said, looking sideways.

'Stolz is right about the need for schools in the country,' thought Oblomov.

'The Ilyinskys, sir,' Zakhar went on, 'had a footman who could read and write and he pinched their silver from the sideboard.'

'Did he now?' Oblomov thought apprehensively. 'Yes, indeed, servants who can read and write are all so immoral – spend all their time in public-houses with accordions, guzzling tea. ... No, it's much too soon to open schools!'

'Well, what other expenses did we have?' he asked.

'How do I know, sir? You gave Mr Tarantyev some money when he came to see you in the country.'

'So I did!' Oblomov cried, looking pleased at having been reminded of it. 'So that is thirty roubles to the cabby and I think another twenty-five to Tarantyev. What else?'

He looked questioningly and thoughtfully at Zakhar. Zakhar looked gloomily at him.

'Would Anisya remember, do you think?' asked Oblomov.

'That fool remember, sir?' Zakhar said contemptuously. 'What does a woman know?'

'I can't remember!' Oblomov concluded miserably. 'We haven't had any burglars, have we?'

'If we had had burglars, they would have taken everything,' said Zakhar, leaving the room.

Oblomov sat down in an arm-chair and pondered. 'Where am I to get the money?' he thought desperately. 'When will they send some from the country – and how much?'

He glanced at the clock: it was two – time to go to Olga's. This was the day he was to dine there. He cheered up gradually, ordered a cab, and drove to Morskaya Street.

4

HE told Olga that he had talked it over with the landlady's brother and added hastily that he hoped to be able to sub-let the flat in the course of the week. Olga went out with her aunt to pay a visit before dinner and he went to look at flats in the vicinity. He called at two houses; in one he found a vacant four-roomed flat at 4,000 roubles and in the other he was asked 6,000 roubles for a five-roomed one. 'Terrible! terrible!' he repeated, stopping his ears and running away from the astonished caretakers. Adding to these sums the thousand odd roubles he had to pay Mrs Pshenitzyn, he was so terrified that he could not add up the total and, quickening his pace, rushed back to Olga's. There was company there. Olga was very animated, talked, sang, and created a sensation. Only Oblomov listened absently, while she was talking and singing for him alone, because she did not want him to sit there looking crestfallen, but that everything in him, too, should be talking and singing.

'Come to the theatre to-morrow – we have a box,' she said.

'In the evening, through the mud, and all that way!' Oblomov thought, but, looking into her eyes, he answered her smile with a smile of consent.

'Book a stall for the season,' she added. 'The Mayevskys are coming next week. Auntie invited them to our box.'

And she looked into his eyes to see how pleased he was.

'Heavens,' he thought in horror, 'and I have only three hundred roubles left.'

'Ask the baron; he knows everyone, and book a seat for you to-morrow.'

And again she smiled, and looking at her he smiled too and, still smiling, asked the baron to book a seat for him, and the baron, also with a smile, undertook to do so.

'Now you will be in the stalls,' Olga added, 'and when you have finished your business, you will take your place in our box by right.'

And she smiled for the last time as she smiled when she was perfectly happy. Oh, how happy he suddenly felt when Olga slightly lifted the veil over the seductive vista, concealed in smiles as in flowers! He forgot all about the money, and it was only when on the following morning he saw Ivan Matveyevich with his parcel dash past his window that he remembered the

deed of trust and asked his landlady's brother to have it witnessed
at the courts. Ivan Matveyevich read it, declared that there
was one obscure point in it, and undertook to get it cleared up.
The document was copied out again, then witnessed and posted.
Oblomov told Olga triumphantly about it, and was pleased to
leave it at that for a long time. He was glad that there was no
need to look for a flat till he received an answer from the country and that in the meantime he would be getting something for
his money. 'One could live perfectly well here,' he thought, 'if
it were not so far from everything, for strict order reigns in the
house and it is run excellently.' And, indeed, the place was run
beautifully. Though he had his meals prepared separately, the
landlady kept an eye on his food too. He went into the kitchen one
day and found his landlady and Anisya almost in each other's
arms. If there is an affinity of souls, if kindred spirits recognize
each other from afar, it had never been more clearly proved than
in the sympathy Agafya Matveyevna and Anisya felt for each
other. They understood and appreciated one another at the first
glance, word and movement. By the way Anisya, rolling up her
sleeves and armed with a rag and a poker, brought into order a
kitchen that had not been in use for six months, and at a stroke
brushed away the dust from the shelves, the walls, and the
tables; by the wide sweep of her broom along the floor and the
benches, by the speed with which she removed the ashes from
the stove – Agafya Matveyevna appreciated the sort of treasure
Anisya was and what a great help she could be to her in the
house. Anisya, for her part, having only once observed how
Agafya Matveyevna reigned in her kitchen, how her hawk eyes
without eyebrows saw every clumsy movement of the slow Akulina; how she rapped out her orders to take something out, to
put in, to add salt, to warm up something, how at the market she would tell unerringly, at a glance, or at most by a
touch of a finger, the age of a chicken, how long a fish had
been out of water, when parsley or lettuce had been cut – gazed
at her with admiration and respectful fear, and decided that she,
Anisya, had missed her real vocation and that the true field of
her activities was not Oblomov's kitchen, where her constant
scurrying and her restless and nervous feverishness of movements were directed solely towards catching in the air a plate
or glass dropped by Zakhar, and where her experience and
subtlety of mind were suppressed by her husband's sullen
jealousy and coarse arrogance. The two women understood
each other and became inseparable. When Oblomov dined out,

307

Anisya spent her time in the landlady's kitchen, and out of love for the culinary art, darted from one corner to another, put pots in and took them out again, and almost at the same moment opened the cupboard, got out what was wanted, and slammed the door to again before Akulina had time to grasp what it was all about. Anisya's reward was dinner, six or more cups of coffee in the morning and the same number in the evening, and a long, frank conversation with the landlady and sometimes whispered confidences from her.

When Oblomov dined at home, the landlady helped Anisya, that is, indicated with a finger or a word whether or not it was time to take out the roast meat, whether red wine or some cream should be added to the sauce, and what was the right way of boiling the fish. ... And, dear me, how many useful household tips they obtained from each other, not only about the culinary art but also about linen, yarn, sewing, washing clothes, cleaning blond-lace and lace and gloves, removal of stains from various materials, as well as using all sorts of home-made medicines and herbs – everything, in fact, that an observant mind and lifelong experience had contributed to that particular sphere of life!

Oblomov got up about nine o'clock in the morning, occasionally catching sight through the trellis of the fence of the landlady's brother going to work with the paper parcel under his arm; then he applied himself to his coffee. The coffee was as excellent as ever, the cream was thick, the rolls rich and crisp. Then he lighted a cigar and listened attentively to the cackling of the broody hen, the chirping of the chicks, the trilling of the canaries and siskins. He did not order their removal.

'They remind me of the country, of Oblomovka,' he said.

Then he sat down to finish reading the books he had begun at his summer cottage, and sometimes casually lay down with a book on the sofa. There was perfect silence all around; only occasionally, perhaps a soldier or a small crowd of peasants with axes stuck in their belts walked down the street. Very rarely indeed a pedlar penetrated into this remote suburb and, stopping in front of the trellised fence, shouted for half an hour: 'Apples, Astrakhan water-melons,' so that you could not help buying something. Sometimes Masha, the landlady's little daughter, came in with a message from her mother to the effect that there were different varieties of mushrooms for sale and asked if he would like to order a barrel for himself; or he called in Vanya, the landlady's son, and asked him what he had been learning, and made him read and write to see how well he could do it. If the children forgot to close the door behind them, he caught sight of the landlady's bare neck and her elbows and back. She was always busy, always ironing something, pounding, polishing, no longer standing on ceremony with him and putting on her shawl when she noticed him looking at her through the half-open door; she merely smiled and went on pounding, ironing, and polishing on the large table. Sometimes he walked to the door with a book, looked in and talked to her.

'You're always busy!' he said to her once.

She smiled and went on carefully turning the handle of the coffee-mill, her elbow describing circles with such rapidity that Oblomov felt dizzy.

'You'll get tired,' he went on.

'No, I'm used to it,' she replied, rattling the coffee-mill.

'And what do you do when there is no work?'

'No work? Why, there is always something to do,' she said. 'In the morning there is dinner to cook, after dinner there is some sewing to do, and in the evening there is supper.'

'Do you have supper?'

'Why, of course we have supper. On Christmas Eve we go to vespers.'

'That's good,' Oblomov commended her. 'What church do you go to?'

'The Church of the Nativity; it's our parish church.'

'Do you read anything?'

She looked at him with a vacant expression and said nothing.

'Have you any books?' he asked.

'My brother has some, but he never reads. We get our newspapers from the inn, and my brother sometimes reads aloud – and Vanya, of course, has lots of books.'

'But don't you ever have a rest?'

'No, I never do!'

'Don't you go to the theatre?'

'My brother goes at Christmas.'

'And you?'

'Me? Why, I have no time. Who would get supper ready?' she asked, casting a sidelong glance at him.

'The cook could do without you.'

'Akulina!' she retorted in surprise. 'Good heavens, no! She could do nothing without me. The supper wouldn't be ready by the morning. I have all the keys.'

Silence. Oblomov gazed admiringly at her plump, round elbows.

'What lovely arms you have,' Oblomov said suddenly. 'One could paint them just as they are!'

She smiled and blushed a little.

'Sleeves are such a nuisance,' she remarked apologetically. 'Nowadays the dresses are made in such a way that one cannot help getting the sleeves dirty.'

She fell into silence. Oblomov did not speak either.

'Must finish grinding the coffee,' the landlady whispered to herself. 'Then I must break the sugar. Mustn't forget to send out for some cinnamon.'

'You ought to get married,' said Oblomov. 'You're such an excellent housewife.'

She smiled and began pouring the coffee into a big glass jar.

'Really,' Oblomov added.

'Who would marry me with my two children?' she replied, and began counting something in her mind. 'Two dozen,' she said thoughtfully. 'Will she be able to put it all in?'

And putting the jar into the cupboard, she rushed into the kitchen. Oblomov went back to his room and began reading.

'What a fresh and healthy woman, and what an excellent housewife! She really ought to get married,' he said to himself, and was lost in thoughts – of Olga.

On a fine day Oblomov put on his cap and took a stroll in the neighbourhood; after getting stuck in the mud in one place and having an unpleasant meeting with dogs in another, he returned home. At home the table was already laid and the food was so good and so well served. Sometimes a bare arm would be thrust through the door with the offer to try some of the landlady's pie on a plate.

'It's nice and quiet here,' Oblomov said as he drove off to the opera, 'but rather dull.'

One night, returning late from the theatre, he and the cabby knocked for almost an hour at the gate; the dog lost its voice with barking and jumping on the chain. He got chilled and angry and vowed that he would leave the very next day. But the next day and the day after and a whole week passed – and still he did not leave.

He missed Olga greatly on the days he could not see her, or hear her voice, or read in her eyes the same unchanging affection, love, and happiness. On the days he could see her, however, he lived as he had done in the summer, was enchanted by her singing or gazed into her eyes; and in the company of other people one look of hers, indifferent to all, but deep and significant for him, was enough for him. With the approach of winter, though, they found it more and more difficult to see each other alone. The Ilyinskys always had visitors, and for days together Oblomov did not succeed in saying two words to her. They exchanged glances. Her glances sometimes expressed weariness and impatience. She looked at all the visitors with a frown. Once or twice Oblomov felt rather bored, and one day after dinner he was about to pick up his hat.

'Where are you going?' Olga asked in surprise, coming suddenly upon him and taking hold of his hat.

'I'd like to go home.'

'Why?' she asked, raising one eyebrow higher than the other. 'What are you going to do?'

'Oh, I don't know – –' he said, hardly able to keep his eyes open.

'You don't think I'll let you, do you?' she asked, looking at him sternly first into one, then into the other eye. 'You're not thinking of going to sleep, are you?'

'Good Lord, sleep in the daytime!' Oblomov replied quickly. 'I'm just bored!'

And he let her take his hat from him.

'We're going to the theatre to-day,' she said.

'But we shall not be in the same box, shall we?' he added with a sigh.

'Does it matter? Is it nothing that we shall see each other, that you will come in during the interval, wait for me at the end, and offer me your arm to take me to the carriage? Mind you come!' she added imperiously. 'What's all this nonsense ?'

There was nothing to be done about it: he went to the theatre, yawned as though he were going to swallow the stage, scratched his head, and kept crossing and re-crossing his legs. 'Oh, if only it were all over and I could sit beside her, and not have to drag myself all the way here,' he thought. 'It's absurd that we should have to meet furtively and by chance after such a summer and that I should have to play the part of a lovesick boy. … To tell the truth, I wouldn't have gone to the theatre to-day had we been married: I've heard this opera six times already.'

In the interval he went to Olga's box, and could hardly squeeze his way in between two unknown elegantly dressed men. Five minutes later he slipped away and stopped in the crowd at the entrance to the stalls.

The next act had begun and people were hurrying to their seats. The two dandies from Olga's box were there too, but they did not see Oblomov.

'Who was the fellow in the Ilyinskys' box just now?' one of them asked the other.

'Oh,' the other one replied casually, 'someone by the name of Oblomov.'

'What is he?'

'He's – er – a landowner, a friend of Stolz's.'

'Oh!' the other cried significantly. 'A friend of Stolz's, is he? What is he doing here?'

'Goodness knows,' the other one replied, and they went to their seats.

But Oblomov was greatly disconcerted by this trifling conversation.

'Who was the *fellow – someone by the name of* Oblomov – what is he doing here? – goodness knows!' all this kept hammering in his brain. 'Someone – –! What am I doing here? Why, I am in love with Olga: I am her – –. However, so they are already asking what I am doing here – they have noticed me. Oh dear, I must do something!'

He no longer saw what was taking place on the stage, what knights and ladies appeared there; the orchestra thundered away, but he never heard it. He looked round to see how many people he knew in the theatre – there and there – they were everywhere, and all of them were asking: 'Who was the fellow in Olga's box?' and they all replied: 'Oh, someone called Oblomov!'

'Yes,' he thought, timidly and gloomily, 'I am just someone! People know me because I am a friend of Stolz's. Why am I at Olga's? Goodness knows! Those two dandies are looking at me and then at Olga's box!'

He looked at the box. Olga's binoculars were fixed on him.

'Goodness,' he thought, 'she doesn't take her eyes off me! What fascination can she have found in me? A fine treasure! Now she seems to be motioning to me to look at the stage – I believe those two dandies are looking at me and laughing – – Oh dear, oh dear!'

In his excitement he scratched his head again and once more crossed his legs. She had invited the dandies to tea after the theatre, promised to sing the *Cavatina*, and told him to come too.

'No, I'm not going there to-day again. I must settle this thing as soon as possible and then – – Why doesn't my agent send me an answer from the country? I should have left long ago, and become engaged to Olga before going. ... Oh, she's still looking at me! Oh, this is awful!'

He went home without waiting for the end of the opera. Gradually the impression of that evening at the opera was erased from his mind, and he once more looked at Olga with a tremor of happiness when he was alone with her, listened with suppressed tears of rapture to her singing when others were present, and on returning home lay down on the sofa – without Olga's knowledge – but he lay down not to sleep, not to lie there like a log, but to dream of her, play at happiness, and to contemplate with a thrill of excitement his peaceful life in his future home, where Olga would shine and everything near her would shine too. Looking into the future, he sometimes involuntarily and sometimes deliberately looked through the half-open door at the landlady's rapidly moving elbows.

One day there was perfect silence both at home and in nature: no rattling of carriages, no slamming of doors; in the entrance hall the clock was ticking away regularly and the canaries were singing; but that did not disturb the silence, merely adding a touch of life to it. Oblomov lay carelessly on the sofa, playing with his slipper, dropping it on the floor, throwing it up into the air, turning it over, and catching it with his foot when it fell. Zakhar came in and stopped in the doorway.

'What do you want?' Oblomov asked in a casual tone of voice.

Zakhar said nothing, looking not sideways, but almost straight at him.

'Well?' asked Oblomov, glancing at him in surprise. 'Is the pie ready?'

'Have you found a flat, sir?' Zakhar asked in his turn.

'Not yet. Why?'

'I haven't sorted everything out yet – crockery, clothes, trunks – it's all still in a heap in the box-room, sir. Ought I to sort it out?'

'Wait,' Oblomov said absent-mindedly, 'I'm waiting for a letter from the country.'

'So, I suppose, sir, your wedding will be after Christmas?' Zakhar added.

'What wedding?' Oblomov asked, getting up suddenly.

'Yours, of course!' Zakhar replied emphatically, as though the whole thing had long been settled. 'You are getting married, aren't you, sir?'

'I'm getting mar-ried? Who to?' Oblomov asked in horror, glaring at Zakhar in amazement.

'Why, sir, to the Ilyinsky young lady – –' Before Zakhar had time to utter the last word, Oblomov almost pounced on him.

313

'What are you talking about, you unhappy wretch?' Oblomov cried pathetically in a restrained voice, advancing closer and closer on Zakhar. 'Who has put this idea into your head?'

'I'm not an unhappy wretch, sir, I'm sure,' Zakhar said, retreating towards the door. 'Who told me? Why, the Ilyinsky servants told me in the summer.'

'Sh-sh-sh ...' Oblomov hissed at him, raising his finger and shaking it threateningly. 'Not another word!'

'I didn't invent it, did I?' Zakhar said.

'Not a word!' Oblomov repeated, looking sternly at him and pointing to the door.

Zakhar went out, heaving so loud a sigh that it could be heard all over the house.

Oblomov was staggered; he remained in the same position, gazing in horror at the spot where Zakhar had stood, then clasped his head in despair and sank into an arm-chair.

'The servants know!' the thought recurred again and again in his head. 'They are gossiping about it in kitchens and servants' halls! That is what it has come to! He had the cheek to ask me when the wedding would be. And her aunt still suspects nothing, and if she does suspect it is perhaps something else, something bad. ... Dear, dear, what will she think? And I? And Olga? Unhappy wretch, what have I done?' he said, turning over on the sofa and burying his face in a cushion. 'Wedding! This poetic moment in the life of lovers, this crown of happiness, is being discussed by footmen and coachmen, when nothing has been decided, when no reply has been received from the country, when I haven't a penny in my purse, when I haven't found a flat – –'

He began analysing the poetic moment, which suddenly lost all its glamour as soon as Zakhar had spoken of it. He became aware of the reverse side of the medal, and kept turning painfully from side to side, lay on his back, jumped up suddenly, took three turns round the room, and lay down again.

'There's going to be trouble,' Zakhar thought fearfully in the hall. 'What the devil made me say it?'

'How do they know?' Oblomov kept asking himself. 'Olga never breathed a word, and I never dared to utter my thoughts aloud, and in the servants' hall they have settled everything! That's what comes of *tête-à-tête* meetings, the poetry of sunrises and sunsets, passionate glances, and enchanting singing! Oh, those love-poems lead to no good! One must be married first, and then float in a roseate atmosphere – – Oh dear, oh dear, what shall I do? Run to her aunt, take Olga by the hand and say: "This is my fiancée!" But nothing is ready, no reply from the country, no money, no flat! Yes, first of all I must get the idea out of Zakhar's head, kill the rumours as one puts out a flame, so that they shouldn't spread, so that there shouldn't be either smoke or fire! Wedding! What is a wedding?'

He smiled, recalling his former poetic vision of the wedding: a long veil, orange blossom, the murmur of the crowd. ... But the colours were no longer the same: in the crowd he could see the coarse, dirty Zakhar and all Ilyinskys' house serfs, a number of carriages, the cold and curious eyes of strangers. ... And then he kept imagining all sorts of tiresome and dreadful things. ...

'I must get that idea out of Zakhar's head,' he decided, in a tumult of excitement one moment and painfully thoughtful the next. 'I must make him believe that it is utterly absurd.'

An hour later he called in Zakhar. Zakhar pretended not to hear and was about to steal quietly into the kitchen. He had opened one half of the door without making any noise, but he missed it and caught his shoulder against the other half so clumsily that both halves flew open with a bang.

'Zakhar!' Oblomov shouted imperiously.

'Yes, sir?' Zakhar replied from the passage.

'Come here!' said Oblomov.

'If you want me to bring you anything, sir, tell me what it is and I'll fetch it,' he replied.

'Come here!' Oblomov said slowly and insistently.

'Oh, I wish I was dead!' Zakhar wheezed, shuffling into the room. 'What do you want, sir?' he asked, getting stuck in the doorway.

'Come here!' Oblomov said in a solemn and mysterious voice, indicating a place so close to himself that Zakhar would have to sit almost on his master's knees.

'Where do you want me to come?' Zakhar protested, remaining stubbornly at the door. 'There's no room there, and I can hear from here just as well.'

'Come here when you're told!' Oblomov said sternly.

Zakhar took a step and stood still like a monument, looking out of the window at the wandering hens and turning a brush-like side-whisker to his master. His agitation had wrought a change in Oblomov in one hour. His face looked pinched and his eyes wandered uneasily.

'I'm in for it now!' thought Zakhar, looking gloomier and gloomier.

'How could you have asked your master such an absurd question?' asked Oblomov.

'He's off!' thought Zakhar, blinking in expectation of 'pathetic words'.

'I ask you: how could you have got such a preposterous idea into your head?' Oblomov repeated.

Zakhar said nothing.

'Do you hear, Zakhar? What right have you to think such things, let alone say them?'

'I think, sir, I'd better call Anisya,' Zakhar replied, taking a step towards the door.

'I want to speak to you and not to Anisya,' Oblomov replied. 'Why did you invent such a preposterous story?'

'I didn't invent it, sir,' said Zakhar. 'The Ilyinskys' servants told me.'

'And who told them?'

'I'm sure I don't know, sir. Katya told Semyon, Semyon told Nikita, Nikita told Vasilisa, Vasilisa told Anisya, and Anisya told me,' said Zakhar.

'Oh dear, all of them!' Oblomov cried in horror. 'It's all nonsense, absurdity, lies, slanders – do you hear?' Oblomov said, rapping his fist on the table. 'It cannot be!'

'Why not, sir?' Zakhar interrupted indifferently. 'It's an ordinary sort of thing – a wedding is! You're not the only one to get married – everyone does it.'

'Everyone!' Oblomov repeated. 'You certainly enjoy comparing me to other people! This cannot be! It isn't and it will never be! A wedding is an ordinary sort of thing – did you hear that? What is a wedding?'

Zakhar glanced at Oblomov, but seeing his master's furious eyes, at once looked at a corner, on the right.

'Listen, I'll explain to you what it is. "A wedding, a wedding," idle people will begin to say – women, children, in servants' halls, in shops, in the markets. A man ceases to be Ilya Ilyich or Pyotr Petrovich, and is called "the fiancé". The day before nobody would look at him, and the next day all are staring at him, as if he were a rogue or something. They won't leave him alone in the theatre or in the street. "There he is," they all whisper, "there!" And how many people come up to him during the day, each trying to look as stupid as possible, as you look just now' (Zakhar turned away quickly and looked at the yard), 'and to say something utterly preposterous. That's how it all starts. And, like a damned soul, you have got to drive every day to your fiancée first thing in the morning, always wearing pale-yellow gloves and brand-new clothes; you must never appear to be bored, you must never eat and drink properly, but live on air and bouquets! And this has to go on for three or four months! Do you see? Do you think I could do that?'

Oblomov stopped to see whether his description of the disadvantages of marriage had any effect on Zakhar.

'Shall I go now, sir?' Zakhar asked, turning to the door.

'No, wait! You're good at spreading false rumours, and you may as well know why they are false.'

'What's there for me to know?' said Zakhar, examining the walls.

'You've forgotten how much rushing about an engaged couple have to do. It wouldn't be you – would it now – who'd be running for me to the tailor, the cobbler, and the furniture shop? I couldn't be everywhere at once, could I? The whole town will know about it. "Have you heard? – Oblomov is getting married!" "No! Who to?" "Who is she? When's the wedding?",' Oblomov said in different voices. 'They'll be talking of nothing else. Why, I shall have a nervous breakdown because of it, and you can do nothing better than talk of a wedding!'

He glanced at Zakhar again.

'Shall I call Anisya, sir?' asked Zakhar.

'What do I want Anisya for? It was you and not Anisya who made this wild suggestion.'

'What have I done to deserve such punishment?' Zakhar whispered, heaving a sigh that raised his shoulders.

'And did you think of the expense of it?' Oblomov went on. 'Where am I to get the money? You saw how much money I had, didn't you?' Oblomov asked almost menacingly. 'And the flat? I have to pay a thousand roubles here, pay three thousand for a new flat, and goodness only knows how much for doing it up! Then there's the carriage, the cook, the living expenses! Where am I to get it all from?'

'How do other people with three hundred serfs get married?' Zakhar retorted, and was immediately sorry for it, for his master started so violently that he nearly jumped out of his chair.

'Are you talking of "other people" again? Take care!' he said, shaking his finger. 'Other people live in two, or – at most – in three rooms: the dining-room and the drawing-room are the same, and some people sleep there, too, the children in the next room. One maid does the work of the whole place. The mistress herself goes to market! Do you think Olga Sergeyevna will go to market?'

'Well, sir, I could go to the market, couldn't I?' Zakhar observed.

'Do you know how much Oblomovka brings in?' Oblomov asked. 'You've heard what the bailiff wrote, haven't you? The income is "about two thousand less"! And there's the road to be constructed, school to be opened, the house to be built. ... How could I think of a wedding? What are you talking about?'

Oblomov stopped. He was himself horrified at this terrible and comfortless prospect. The roses, the orange-blossom, the brilliant festivities, the whisper of admiration in the crowd – all had faded suddenly. He grew pale and sank into thought. Then he gradually recovered, looked round and saw Zakhar.

'What is it?' he asked gloomily.

'Why, sir, you told me to stand here!' said Zakhar.

'Go!' said Oblomov with an impatient wave of the hand.

Zakhar stepped over the threshold quickly.

'No, wait!' Oblomov stopped him suddenly.

'One minute it's go and the next wait!' Zakhar grumbled, holding on to the door.

'How did you dare to spread such ridiculous rumours about me?' Oblomov asked in an agitated whisper.

'But when did I spread them, sir? It wasn't me, sir, but the Ilyinsky servants who said that you had proposed – –'

'Sh-sh-sh!' Oblomov hissed, waving his hand menacingly. 'Not a word, do you hear? Never!'

'Yes, sir,' Zakhar replied timidly.

'So you won't spread this preposterous story abroad, will you?'

'No, sir,' Zakhar replied quietly, not grasping the meaning of half the words but knowing only that they were 'pathetic'.

'Remember, then, if you hear anyone talking about it, or if anyone should ask you, say the whole thing is nonsense and that there never was or could be anything of the sort!' Oblomov added in a whisper.

'Yes, sir,' Zakhar whispered almost inaudibly.

Oblomov looked round and shook a finger at Zakhar, who was blinking in alarm and tiptoeing towards the door.

'Who was the first to speak of it?' Oblomov asked, overtaking him.

318

'Katya told Semyon, Semyon told Nikita,' Zakhar whispered, 'Nikita told Vasilisa – –'

'And you told everybody!' Oblomov hissed menacingly. 'I'll show you how to spread slanders about your master! You'll see!'

'Why are you torturing me with your pathetic words, sir?' asked Zakhar. 'I'll call Anisya: she knows everything.'

'What does she know? Come on, out with it!'

Zakhar at once rushed through the door and walked into the kitchen with extraordinary rapidity.

'Leave your frying-pan and go to the master!' he said to Anisya, pointing with his thumb to the door.

Anisya gave the frying-pan to Akulina, unloosed the hem of her skirt, which she had tucked in at the waist, patted herself on the hips, and, wiping her nose with a forefinger, went in to the master. She calmed Oblomov in five minutes by telling him that no one had ever said anything about a wedding: she did not mind taking her oath on it and taking the icon down from the wall that this was the first time she had heard of it; she had heard something quite different: it was the baron who had made a proposal of marriage to the young lady. ...

'The baron!' Oblomov asked, jumping to his feet, and not only his heart, but also his hands and feet turned cold.

'That's nonsense too!' Anisya hastened to say, seeing that she had got herself out of the frying-pan into the fire. 'That was merely what Katya said to Semyon, Semyon to Marfa, and Nikita said that it would not be a bad thing if your master made an offer of marriage to our young lady. ...'

'What a fool that Nikita is!' observed Oblomov.

'Yes, sir, he certainly is a fool,' Anisya confirmed. 'He looks asleep when he sits behind the carriage. And Vasilisa did not believe him, either,' she went on, talking very fast. 'She told me on Assumption Day that the nurse herself had said to her that Miss Olga was not thinking of marrying and that it was hardly possible that our master would not have found a wife for himself if he had meant to marry, and that she had met Samoylo the other day and that he thought it a big joke: a wedding, indeed! And it didn't look like a wedding, but more like a funeral, that auntie kept having headaches, and Miss Olga cried and never uttered a word, and no trousseau being made; Miss Olga had hundreds of stockings that needed darning, and that last week they pawned their silver. ...'

'Pawned their silver? So they have no money, either!' Oblomov thought, raising his eyes to the walls in horror and fixing them on Anisya's nose, because there was nothing else he could fix them on. She seemed to be saying all this with her nose and not with her mouth.

'Mind, don't talk any more nonsense!' Oblomov said, shaking his finger at her.

'Talk, sir? Why, sir, I don't think about it, let alone talk,' Anisya rattled on, just as though she were chopping up sticks. 'Besides, sir, there's nothing to talk about, is there? It's the first time I've heard of it to-day, and that's the truth, may the Lord strike me dead if it isn't! I wasn't half surprised when you told me about it, sir. I was scared, that I was, trembled all over! Whoever heard of such a thing? What wedding? No one has dreamt of it. I never say a word to anyone; I'm always in the kitchen, I am. Haven't seen the Ilyinsky servants for a month, I'm sure I don't remember their names no more. And who is there to talk to here? With the landlady we talk of nothing except housekeeping, and with the granny one can't talk at all: she coughs and, besides, she's deaf too! Akulina is a fool, and the caretaker is a drunkard. There's only the children left, and you don't expect me to talk to them, do you, sir? And, besides, I've forgotten what Miss Olga looks like, I have. ...'

'All right, all right,' Oblomov said, waving her out of the room impatiently.

'How do you expect me to talk of something that doesn't exist, sir?' Anisya concluded as she was going out of the room. 'And if Nikita did say something of the kind, he is too big a fool to be taken any notice of. I'm sure it would never have occurred to me – slaving away all day long as I am, and I have other things to think of. Why, such a thing, indeed! There's the icon on the wall – –' With these words the speaking nose disappeared behind the door, but it went on talking for another minute behind the door.

'So that's what it is! Anisya too says that it is hardly possible,' Oblomov said in a whisper, clasping his hands. 'Happiness, happiness! How fragile you are, how uncertain! The veil, the wreath of orange-blossom, love, love! And where is the money? And what are we to live on? You, too, have to be bought, love, pure and lawful blessing!'

From that moment Oblomov's peace of mind and dreams were gone. He slept badly, ate little, and looked at everything absent-mindedly and morosely. He had wanted to frighten Zakhar, but had frightened himself more when he grasped the practical aspect of marriage and saw that it was not only a poetical but also a practical and official step to important and serious reality and a whole series of stern duties. His conversation with Zakhar turned out differently from what he had imagined. He recalled how solemnly he had intended to break the news to Zakhar, how Zakhar would have shouted with joy and fallen at his feet, how he would have given him twenty-five roubles and Anisya ten. ...

He remembered everything – his thrill of happiness, Olga's hand, her passionate kiss – and his heart sank: 'It's gone, faded away!' a voice inside him said.

'So what now?'

5

OBLOMOV did not know how he would face Olga, what she would say to him and what he would say to her, and decided not to go to see her on Wednesday, but to put off their meeting till Sunday, when there would be many visitors there and they would have no chance of talking alone. He did not want to tell her about the stupid stories of the servants so as not to worry her with what could not be remedied. Not to tell her would also be difficult, for he would not be able to pretend to her: she would be sure to get out of him everything he had hidden in the deepest recesses of his heart.

Having arrived at this decision, he calmed down a little and wrote another letter to the neighbour to whom he had entrusted the care of his affairs, in which he asked him to reply as soon as possible, adding that he hoped that his reply would be satisfactory. Then he began thinking how he could spend that long and unendurable day, which would otherwise have been filled with Olga's presence, the invisible communion of their souls, and her singing. And Zakhar suddenly had to worry him at such an inopportune moment! He decided to dine at Ivan Gerasimovich's so as to notice that unendurable day as little as possible. By Sunday he would be able to prepare himself and perhaps by then he would already have received the letter from the country.

The next day came. He was awakened by the furious barking of the dog and its desperate jumping on the chain. Someone had come into the yard and was asking for someone. The caretaker called Zakhar: Zakhar brought Oblomov a letter that had been posted in town.

'From the Ilyinsky young lady,' Zakhar said.

'How do you know?' Oblomov asked angrily. 'Nonsense!'

'You always used to get such letters from her in summer,' Zakhar persisted.

'Is she well?' Oblomov thought, opening the letter. 'What does it mean?'

'I don't want to wait for Wednesday' (wrote Olga) 'I miss you so much after so long a time that I will expect you to-morrow for certain at three o'clock in the Summer Gardens.'

That was all.

Again he became deeply perturbed; again he grew restless with anxiety at the thought of how he was going to talk to Olga and of how he would look at her.

'I can't do it – I don't know how to,' he said. 'I wish I could ask Stolz – –'

But he set his mind at rest with the thought that Olga would most probably come with her aunt or with Maria Semyonovna, who was so fond of her and could not admire her enough. He hoped that in their presence he would be able to disguise his embarrassment, and he prepared himself to be talkative and gallant. 'And at dinner time, too,' he thought as he set out, none too eagerly, for the Summer Gardens. 'What an hour to choose!' As soon as he entered the long avenue, he saw a veiled woman get up from a seat and walk towards him. He did not think it was Olga: alone! Impossible! She would never do a thing like that and, besides, would have no excuse for leaving home unchaperoned. However – it seemed to be her way of walking: her feet moved so lightly and rapidly that they did not seem to walk but to glide; her head and neck, too, were bent forward as though she were looking for something on the ground at her feet. Another man would have recognized her by her hat or dress, but he could never tell what dress or hat Olga was wearing even after spending a whole morning with her. There was hardly anybody in the garden; an elderly gentleman was walking very briskly, apparently taking his constitutional, and two – not ladies, but women, and a nurse with two children who looked blue with the cold. The leaves had fallen and one could see right through the bare branches; the crows on the trees cawed so unpleasantly. It was a bright and clear day, though, and warm, if one were wrapped up properly. The veiled woman was coming nearer and nearer. ...

'It is she!' said Oblomov, stopping in alarm and unable to believe his eyes.

'Is it you?' he asked, taking her hand. 'What's the matter?'

'I'm so glad you've come,' she said without answering his question. 'I thought you wouldn't come, and I was beginning to be afraid.'

'How did you get here? How did you manage it?' he asked, thrown into confusion.

'Please, don't! What does it matter? Why all these questions? It's so silly! I wanted to see you and I came – that's all!'

She pressed his hand warmly and looked at him gaily and light-heartedly, so openly and obviously enjoying the moment stolen from fate that he envied her for not sharing her playful mood. However troubled he was, he could not help forgetting himself for a moment when he saw her face showing no trace of the concentrated thought that could be discerned in the play of her eyebrows and in the crease on her forehead; this time she appeared to be without that wonderful maturity that so often disturbed him in her features. At that moment her face expressed such childlike confidence in their future happiness and in him. ... She was very charming.

'Oh, I'm so glad! I'm so glad!' she went on repeating, smiling and looking at him. 'I didn't think I'd see you to-day. I felt so terribly depressed yesterday – I don't know why, and I wrote to you. Are you glad?'

She looked at his face.

'Why are you so sullen to-day? Won't you tell me? Aren't you glad? I thought you'd be mad with joy, and you seem to be asleep. Wake up, sir, Olga is with you!'

She pushed him away a little reproachfully.

'Aren't you well? What is the matter with you?' she persisted.

'No, I'm well and happy,' he hastened to say, to make quite sure that she was not driven to wring the innermost secrets of his heart from him. 'I'm only worried about your coming alone – –'

'That's my worry,' she said impatiently. 'Would you have liked it better if I had come with my aunt?'

'Yes, I would, Olga.'

'Had I known I'd have asked her,' Olga interrupted in an injured voice, letting go his hand. 'I thought there was no greater happiness for you than being with me.'

'And so there isn't and there cannot be!' Oblomov replied. 'But how could you come alone – –'

'Let us not waste our time discussing it,' she said light-heartedly. 'Let's talk of something else. Listen. Oh, I was going to tell you something. ... I'm afraid I've forgotten. ...'

'Not how you came here alone?' he said, looking round anxiously.

'Oh no! Aren't you tired of repeating the same thing over and over again? What was I going to say? Oh, never mind. I'm sure to remember it later. Oh, how lovely it is here! The leaves have all fallen, *feuilles d'automne* – remember Victor Hugo? Look at the sunshine there – there's the Neva. ... Come, let's go to the Neva and take a boat. ...'

'Good Lord, what are you talking about? It's so cold, and I've only a quilted coat on.'

'I, too, have a quilted dress. What does it matter? Come along, let's go.'

She ran and dragged him after her. He resisted and grumbled. However, he had to get into a boat and go for a row on the river.

'How did you get here by yourself alone?' Oblomov kept asking anxiously.

'Shall I tell you?' she teased him roguishly when they got to the middle of the river. 'I can now: you won't run away from here, as you would have done there. ...'

'Why?' he asked fearfully.

'Are you coming to-morrow?' she asked instead of an answer.

'Oh dear,' thought Oblomov, 'she seems to have read in my thoughts that I did not mean to come.'

'Yes,' he said aloud.

'In the morning, for the whole day.'

He hesitated.

'Then I won't tell you,' she said.

'Yes, I'll come for the day.'

'Well, you see,' she began gravely, 'I asked you to come here to-day to tell you – –'

'What?' he asked in a panic.

'To come – to us to-morrow.'

'Oh, for goodness' sake!' he interrupted impatiently. 'But how did you get here?'

'Here?' she repeated absent-mindedly. 'How did I get here? Why, I just came. Wait – but why talk about it at all?'

She put her hand into the river and took a handful of water and threw it in his face. He screwed up his eyes and gave a start. She laughed.

'How cold the water is – my hand feels frozen! Goodness, how lovely it is here! Oh, I am so happy!' she went on, looking about her. 'Let's come again to-morrow, but straight from home.'

'Haven't you come straight from home now? Where have you come from then?' he asked hastily.

'From a shop,' she replied.

'What shop?'

'What shop? I told you in the garden – –'

'You didn't,' he cried impatiently.

'Didn't I? How strange! I've forgotten! I left home with a footman to go to the jeweller's – –'

'Well?'

'Well, that's all. What church is this?' she suddenly asked the boatman, pointing at a church in the far distance.

'Which one? That over there?' the boatman asked.

'The Smolny,' Oblomov said impatiently. 'Well, so you went to the shop and what did you do there?'

'Oh, there were lovely things there – I saw such a beautiful bracelet!'

'I'm not interested in bracelets,' Oblomov interrupted. 'What happened then?'

'That's all,' she added absent-mindedly, absorbed in looking about her.

'Where's the footman?' Oblomov pestered her.

'Gone home,' she replied curtly, examining a building on the opposite bank.

'And what about you?'

'Oh, how lovely it is over there! Couldn't we go there?' she asked, pointing with her parasol to the opposite bank. 'You live there, don't you?'

'Yes.'

'In which street? Show me!'

'But what about the footman?' Oblomov asked.

'Oh, nothing,' she replied in a casual tone of voice. 'I sent him for my bracelet. He went home and I came here.'

'But how could you do that?' said Oblomov, staring at her. He looked alarmed, and she, too, made an alarmed face.

'Talk seriously, Olga. Stop joking?'

'I'm not joking,' she said quietly. 'That's exactly what happened. I left my bracelet at home on purpose, and Auntie asked me to go to the jeweller's. You'd never have thought of anything like that!' she added with pride, as though she really had done something extraordinary.

'And if the footman comes back?' he asked.

'I asked them to tell him to wait for me because I had had to go to another shop – and I came here – –'

'And if your aunt asks you in which other shop you went?'

'I'll say I was at the dressmaker's.'

'And what if she asks the dressmaker?'

'And what if the Neva flows away into the sea, what if our boat capsizes, what if Morskaya Street and our house sink through the ground, and what if you suddenly fell out of love with me – –' she said, and threw some water in his face again.

'But the footman must have returned by now and is waiting,' he said, wiping his face. 'Boatman, back to the bank!'

'Don't, don't!' she told the boatman.

'To the bank! The footman has returned!' Oblomov insisted.

'Let him! Don't let's go back!'

But Oblomov insisted on having it his own way and walked hurriedly through the Summer Gardens with her, while she, for her part, walked slowly, leaning on his arm.

'Why are you in such a hurry?' she said. 'Wait, I'd like to be with you a little longer.'

She walked still more slowly, clinging to his shoulder and peering into his face, and he spoke gravely and boringly about duty and obligations. She listened absent-mindedly, with a languid smile, bending her head and looking down or peering into his face again and thinking of something else.

'Listen, Olga,' he said at last solemnly, 'at the risk of making you feel vexed with me and bringing your reproaches down on me, I must tell you definitely that we have gone too far. It is my duty, I – I think it incumbent upon me to tell you so.'

'Tell me what?' she asked with impatience.

'That we are doing wrong by meeting in secret.'

'You said so when we were in the country,' she said pensively.

'Yes, but at the time I was carried away: I pushed you away with one hand and held you back with the other. You were trustful and I – I seemed to deceive you. My feeling for you was still new then – –'

'And now it is no longer new and you are beginning to be bored.'

'Oh no, Olga! You're unjust. I say it was new, and that is why I had no time, why I would not come to my senses. My conscience worries me: you are young, you don't know the world and people, and, besides, you are so pure, your love is so sacred, that it never occurs to you what severe censure we are incurring by what we are doing – and I most of all.'

'But what are we doing?' she said, stopping.

'What do you mean? You are deceiving your aunt, leaving home secretly and meeting a man alone. ... Try admitting all this on Sunday before your visitors.'

'Why shouldn't I admit it?' she said calmly. 'I daresay I will.'

'And you will see,' he went on, 'that your aunt will faint, the ladies will rush out of the room, and the men will look at you boldly and knowingly.'

She fell into thought.

'But,' she countered, 'we are engaged, aren't we?'

'Yes, yes, dear Olga,' he said, pressing both her hands, 'and that is why we ought to be all the more careful and circumspect. I want to lead you down this very avenue proudly and before the eyes of all the world, and not by stealth; I want people to lower their eyes before you respectfully, and not look at you boldly and knowingly; I don't want anyone to suspect you, a proud girl, of having lost your head and, forgetting all shame and good breeding, being carried away and neglecting your duty – –'

'I haven't forgotten shame, or good breeding, or duty,' she replied proudly, taking her hand away from him.

'I know, I know, my innocent angel; but it isn't I who am saying this, it's what people and society will be saying, and they will never forgive you it. Do, for God's sake, understand what I want. I want you to be as pure and irreproachable in the eyes of the world as you are in reality.'

She walked on sunk in thought.

'Please understand why I am telling you this: you will be unhappy, and I alone shall be responsible for it. People will say that I seduced you, that I concealed the abyss from you on purpose. You are pure and safe with me, but how can you make people believe it? Who will believe you?'

'That's true,' she said, with a shudder. 'Listen,' she added resolutely. 'Let us tell Auntie everything and let her give us her blessing to-morrow. ...'

Oblomov turned pale.

'What's the matter?' she asked.

'Wait, Olga! Why be in such a hurry?' he hastened to say. His lips were trembling.

'But didn't you hurry me a fortnight ago?' she asked, looking coldly and attentively at him.

'I hadn't thought of all the preparations at the time, and there are so many of them!' he said, sighing. 'Let us wait for the letter from the country.'

'Why wait for the letter? Will this or that answer make you change your mind?' she asked, looking at him even more attentively.

'What an idea! Of course not! But I must take it into consideration, for we shall have to tell your aunt when our wedding is to be. It is not of love we shall be talking to her, but of all sorts of business matters for which I am not yet prepared.'

'We will talk about that when you get the letter, but meanwhile everyone will know that we are engaged and we shall be able to see each other every day. I'm awfully bored,' she added. 'The days seem to go on for ever; everybody notices it, they go on pestering me and hinting slyly at you.... Oh, I'm sick of it all!'

'Hinting at me?' Oblomov could hardly bring himself to say the words.

'Yes, thanks to Sonia.'

'You see? You see? You wouldn't listen to me then and were angry with me.'

'What is there to see? I don't see anything, except that you're a coward. I'm not afraid of their hints.'

'I'm not a coward, I'm merely careful. ... Well, for goodness' sake let's get out of here, Olga. Look, there's a carriage with some people we know. Oh dear, it throws me into a perspiration. ... Let's go, let's go,' he said fearfully, infecting her with his fear.

'Yes, come quick!' she said in a whisper, talking very fast.

And they almost ran along the avenue to the end of the gardens without uttering a word. Oblomov kept throwing terrified glances about him, and she bent her head very low and covered herself with her veil.

'To-morrow, then!' she said when they reached the shop where the footman was waiting for her.

'No, I'd rather come the day after to-morrow – or on Friday or Saturday,' he replied.

'Why?'

'Because, you see, Olga, I'm always wondering whether the letter will arrive.'

'Well, it might, of course. But to-morrow come just for dinner, do you hear?'

'Yes, yes, all right!' he added hastily, and she went into the shop.

'Dear me, how far things have gone! What a heavy weight has dropped on me all of a sudden! What am I going to do now? Sonia! Zakhar! Those dandies!'

6

HE did not notice that Zakhar served him a perfectly cold dinner, nor did he notice how after dinner he found himself in bed and fell fast asleep. The following day he was dismayed at the thought of going to see Olga. That was impossible! He imagined vividly how significantly they would all look at him. The hall porter, as it was, met him in a particularly kindly way. Semyon rushed headlong to fetch a glass of water whenever he asked for one. Katya and the nurse saw him off with a friendly smile. 'Her fiancé, her fiancé!' was written on all their faces, but he had not yet asked her aunt's consent, he hadn't a penny, and he did not know when he would have any, or what his income from the estate would be this year; there was no house in the country – some fiancé! He decided that until he received definite news from the country he would see Olga only on Sundays in the presence of witnesses. On the following morning he consequently did not think of getting ready to go to Olga's. He did not shave or dress, but lazily turned over the pages of some French journals he had brought from the Ilyinskys' the week before; he did not keep looking incessantly at the clock and did not frown because the hand did not move forward fast enough. Zakhar and Anisya thought that he would be dining out as usual and did not ask him what he would like for dinner. He scolded them sharply, declaring that he did not dine at the Ilyinskys' every Wednesday, that it was 'slander', that he sometimes dined at Ivan Gerasimovich's, and that in future he would always have his dinners at home, except on Sundays, and not every Sunday, either. Anisya immediately rushed off to the market to buy giblets for Oblomov's favourite soup. The landlady's children came in to see him: he corrected Vanya's sums and found two mistakes. He ruled Masha's copybook and wrote large As, then he listened to the singing of the canaries and looked through the half-open door at the landlady's rapidly moving elbows. Soon after one o'clock the landlady asked him from behind the door if he would like something to eat: she had been baking cheese-cakes. Cheese-cakes and a glass of currant vodka were placed before

329

him. Oblomov's agitation somewhat subsided, and he fell into a state of dull torpor in which he remained till dinner. After dinner, when lying down on the sofa he began nodding, overcome by drowsiness, the door leading into the landlady's rooms opened and Agafya Matveyevna appeared, with two pyramids of socks in each hand. She put them down on two chairs, and Oblomov jumped up and offered her the third one, but she did not sit down; it was not her habit: she was always on her feet, always busy and bustling about.

'I've been sorting out your socks to-day,' she said. 'Fifty-five pairs, and almost all need darning.'

'How kind you are!' Oblomov said, walking up to her and taking hold of her elbows playfully.

She smiled. 'Why should you trouble?' he said. 'It really makes me feel ashamed.'

'It's nothing,' she replied. 'It's my job to look after these things. You've got no one to sort them out, and I like doing it. Twenty pairs are no good at all: it's not worth while darning them.'

'Please don't trouble. Throw them all away. Why waste your time with this rubbish? I can buy new ones. ...'

'Why throw them away? These can all be mended,' and she began quickly to count the socks that could still be mended.

'But sit down, please,' he offered her a chair again. 'Why do you stand?'

'No, thank you very much, I really have no time,' she said, refusing the chair again. 'It's my washing day, and I have to get the clothes ready.'

'You're a real wonder, and not a housekeeper!' he said, fixing his gaze on her neck and bosom.

She smiled.

'So what shall I do?' she asked. 'Darn the socks or not? I'll order some wool. An old woman brings it to us from the country. It's not worth while buying it here: it's such poor stuff.'

'Yes, do by all means, since you are so kind,' said Oblomov. 'Only I really am ashamed to be giving you so much trouble.'

'Oh, don't worry about that. I've nothing else to do, have I? These I will re-foot myself, and those I'll give to Granny. My sister-in-law is coming to stay with us to-morrow, we shan't have anything to do in the evenings, and we'll mend them. My Masha is already learning to knit, only she keeps dropping the stitches: the needles are too big for her little hands.'

'Is Masha already beginning to knit?' asked Oblomov.

'Yes, indeed.'

'I don't know how to thank you,' said Oblomov. He looked at her with the same pleasure with which he had looked at her hot cheese-cakes that morning. 'I am very, very grateful to you and I will not remain in your debt, especially not in Masha's. I'll buy her silk frocks and dress her up like a little doll.'

'Why, you mustn't think of it! You've nothing to be grateful to me for. What does she want silk dresses for? She never has enough cotton ones: she wears things out so quickly, especially her shoes: we can't buy them fast enough in the market.'

She took up the socks and was about to leave the room.

'Why are you in such a hurry?' he said. 'Do sit down, I'm not busy.'

'Some other time, on a holiday; and you, please, come and have coffee with us. I'm sorry, but it's washing day and I must go and see if Akulina has begun.'

'Oh, well, I must not detain you,' said Oblomov, looking at her elbows and back.

'I also got your dressing-gown out of the box-room,' she went on. 'It can be washed and mended: such nice material! It's good for many more years!'

'There was no need for it. I'm not wearing it any more, I'm afraid; it's no use to me.'

'Well, never mind, let them wash it: perhaps you will wear it one day – when you are married!' she finished, smiling and shutting the door behind her.

His sleepiness suddenly left him. He pricked up his ears and opened his eyes wide.

'She, too, knows about it – everybody knows about it!' he said, sitting down on the chair he had offered the landlady. 'Oh, Zakhar, Zakhar!'

Again a flood of 'pathetic' words was let loose on Zakhar, again Anisya's nose was set in motion as she assured him that it was the first time she had heard the landlady speak about the wedding, that she never breathed a word about it in her talks with the landlady, that there was no question of any wedding, and, indeed, the whole thing was impossible. The whole thing, she opined, must have been invented by the common enemy of mankind, and as for her, she was ready to sink through the ground, and the landlady was also ready to take the icon off the wall and take an oath that she had never heard of the Ilyinsky young lady, and was thinking of someone else. ... Anisya went on and on, so that in the end he had to wave her out of the room. Next day Zakhar asked if he might go and see some of his friends in Gorokhovaya Street, but Oblomov told him off so effectively that he was glad to get out of the room.

'They don't know anything about it, so you must spread the slanderous story there. Stay at home!' Oblomov added sternly.

Wednesday passed. On Thursday Oblomov received another letter from Olga, asking what it all meant, what had happened, and why he had not come. She wrote that she had cried all the evening and hardly slept all night.

'She cries, she can't sleep, my angel!' Oblomov exclaimed. 'Lord, why does she love me? Why do I love her? Why did we meet? It's all Andrey's fault: he inoculated me with love as with a vaccine. And what sort of a life is it? All the time worries and anxieties! When at last am I to get rest and peaceful happiness?'

Sighing loudly, he lay down, got up, and even went out into the street, intent on trying to discover what was the right way to live a life which would be full and yet would go on quietly day after day, drop by drop, in mute contemplation of nature and slow, scarcely moving events of a peaceful busy family life. He did not want to think of it as a broad river, rushing along noisily with boiling waves, as Stolz thought of it.

'It is a disease,' Oblomov said, 'a fever, rushing over rapids, with burst dams and floods.'

He wrote to Olga that he had caught a slight cold in the Summer Gardens, had had to drink a decoction and stay indoors for two days, that it had now passed and he hoped to see her on Sunday. She wrote back praising him for having been careful, advising him to stay in on Sunday, too, if necessary, adding that she did not mind being bored for a week provided he took care of himself. The letter was brought by Nikita, the same Nikita who, according to Anisya, was chiefly responsible for the gossip. He brought some new books from Olga, who wanted Oblomov to read them and tell her when they met whether they were worth reading. She asked how he was, and after writing an answer, Oblomov gave it to Nikita, and having seen him off, he followed him with his eyes to the gate to make sure he did not stray into the kitchen and repeat the 'slanderous' story there or that Zakhar did not see him off into the street. He was glad of Olga's suggestion that he should take care and not come on Sunday, and he wrote to say that for a complete recovery it was really necessary for him to stay indoors for a few more days. On Sunday he paid a visit to the landlady, drank coffee, ate hot pie, and sent Zakhar across the river for ice-cream and sweets for the children at dinner. Zakhar returned across the river with some difficulty: the bridges had been removed, the Neva being on the point of freezing. Oblomov could not possibly go to Olga's on Wednesday, either. Of course, he could have rushed at once across the river, stayed for a few days at Ivan Gerasimovich's and visited Olga every day, even dined there. He had a quite legitimate excuse: the Neva had caught him while he was on the other side and he could not get across. Oblomov's first impulse was to do this, and he had already lowered his feet from his bed, but after a moment's reflection he slowly resumed his recumbent position, with a sigh and a preoccupied air. 'No, let the gossip die down and let the people who visit Olga's house forget me a little and meet me there again daily only after the official announcement of our engagement. It's a bore to wait,' he added with a sigh, taking up Olga's books, 'but it can't be helped.' He read some fifteen pages. Masha came to ask whether he would like to come and watch the river freezing over: everyone was going. He went and came back for tea. So the days passed. Oblomov was bored; he read, went for walks, and when he was at home he looked through the landlady's door to exchange a few words with her to pass the time. He even ground three pounds of coffee for her one day, and with such zeal that his forehead was covered in perspiration. He tried to give her a book to read. She read the title to herself, moving her lips slowly, and returned the book, declaring that she would borrow it at Christmas and make Vanya read it aloud, and then Granny would listen too, but she was too busy at present.

Meanwhile, a plank footway was laid across the Neva, and one day the dog's desperate barking and jumping on the chain announced Nikita's second visit, with a note inquiring after Oblomov's health, and a book. Oblomov, afraid that he might have to cross the river over the planks, hid from Nikita, writing to Olga that he had a small swelling in his throat, that he was still uncertain whether he ought to go out and that 'cruel fate deprived him of seeing his precious Olga for a few more days'. He gave strict orders to Zakhar not to talk to Nikita and again followed Olga's footman to the gate with his eyes, and shook a minatory finger at Anisya when she poked her nose out of the kitchen and wanted to ask Nikita something.

7

A week passed. Getting up in the morning, Oblomov first of all inquired anxiously whether the bridges had been put back.

'Not yet,' he was told, and he spent the day peacefully listening to the ticking of the clock, the rattling of the coffee mill, and the singing of the canaries. The chicks no longer chirped; they had long ago grown into middle-aged hens and were hiding in their hen-houses. He had not had time to read the books Olga had sent him: having read as far as the hundred and fifth page of one book, he put it away face downwards, and so it lay for several days. Instead he spent more time with the landlady's children. Vanya was such an intelligent boy, he memorized the capital cities of Europe in three lessons, and Oblomov promised to buy him a small globe as soon as he went to the other side of the river; and little Masha hemmed three handkerchiefs for him – badly, it is true, but how amusingly she worked with her tiny little hands, running to show him every inch of her work. He talked to his landlady incessantly every time he caught sight of her elbows through the half-open door. He could tell by the movements of her elbows what she was doing, whether she was sieving, grinding, or ironing. He even tried to talk to Granny, but she never could finish a conversation: she would stop half-way through a word, lean against a wall with her fist, bent double, and begin coughing, as though she were doing some hard work, then she would utter a groan, and that was the end of the conversation. The landlady's brother alone he never saw; he caught a glimpse of him rushing past the window with the large parcel, but he never heard anything of him in the house. Even when Oblomov accidentally entered the room where they were all having dinner, huddled together for lack of space, the landlady's brother quickly wiped his lips with his fingers and disappeared into his attic.

One morning, as soon as Oblomov woke up without a care in the world and began drinking his coffee, Zakhar suddenly announced that the bridges had been put back. Oblomov's heart missed a beat.

'It's Sunday to-morrow,' he said to himself. 'I'll have to go to Olga's, manfully endure all day the significant glances of all sorts of curious strangers, then tell her when I intend to talk to her aunt.'

And he was still in the position where he found it absolutely impossible to move an inch forward. He imagined vividly how their engagement would be announced, how all sorts of ladies and gentlemen would arrive the next day and the day after that, how he would suddenly become an object of curiosity, how his health would be drunk at the dinner specially given to celebrate his engagement to Olga. Then – as Olga's fiancé he would be expected to buy her a present.

'A present!' he said to himself in horror and burst out laughing bitterly. A present! And he had only 200 roubles in his pocket! Even if his money arrived, it would not be before Christmas, and perhaps later, after the corn had been sold, and when that would be, how much corn there was and what it would fetch – all that the letter would explain, and there was no letter. So what on earth was he to do? Farewell, his fortnight's rest! And amid these worries he saw Olga's beautiful face, her fluffy expressive eyebrows, her intelligent, grey-blue eyes, her sweet head, and her plait of hair, which was so long that it accentuated the noble proportions of her figure, from her head to her shoulders and waist. But no sooner did he begin to quiver with love than he was crushed by the thought: what was he to do, how was he to tackle the question of marriage, where was he to get the money, and what were they to live on afterwards? ...

'I will wait a little longer; perhaps the letter will come tomorrow or the day after,' and he began to calculate when his letter could have arrived in the country, how long his neighbour would take over his reply, and how long the answer would take to reach him. 'It must come in another three or at most four days – I'll go to Olga's a little later,' he decided, 'particularly as she can hardly be expected to know whether the bridges have been put back or not.'

'Katya, have the bridges been put back?' Olga asked her maid as soon as she woke that morning.

And this question was repeated every day. Oblomov did not suspect it.

'I don't know, miss. I haven't seen the coachman or the caretaker to-day, and Nikita does not know.'

'You never can answer my questions!' Olga said with displeasure, examining the chain round her neck as she lay in bed.

'I'll find out at once, miss. I didn't dare to go out, thinking that you would wake, or I'd have run down long ago.'

And Katya disappeared from the room. Olga opened the drawer of her bedside table and took out Oblomov's last note.

'He's ill, the poor darling,' she thought anxiously. 'He is alone there, he is bored. ... Oh dear, how much longer ...' She had not finished the sentence when Katya, all flushed, flew into the room.

'They were put back last night!' she cried joyfully, caught Olga, who had jumped out of bed, in her arms, threw her dressing-gown round her, and helped her into her tiny slippers. Olga quickly opened a box, took something out of it, and put it in Katya's hand. Katya kissed her hand. All this – her jumping out of bed, the coin dropped into Katya's hand and Katya's kiss – happened in one minute. 'Oh, to-morrow's Sunday: how lucky! He'll be coming!' thought Olga. She dressed quickly, had her breakfast, and went shopping with her aunt.

'Let's go to Mass at Smolny to-morrow, Auntie,' she begged.

Her aunt screwed up her eyes, thought it over, then said:

'Very well, only it's so far, my dear! Why do you want to go there in winter?'

Olga wanted to go there simply because Oblomov had pointed out the church to her from the river, and she wished to pray there – for him, that he should be well, that he should love her, that he should be happy with her, that – this uncertainty and indecision should end as soon as possible. Poor Olga!

Sunday came. Olga somehow contrived that the dinner should be to Oblomov's liking. She put on her white dress, concealed under the lace the bracelet he had given her, did her hair in the way he liked; she had arranged for the piano to be tuned the day before, and in the morning tried singing *Casta diva*. Her voice had not sounded so well since her return from the country. Then she waited.

The baron, who found her waiting for Oblomov, said that she looked again as pretty as in summer, but that she was a little thinner.

'The lack of country air and the slightly irregular mode of life have perceptibly affected you,' he said. 'What you need, my dear Olga, is the country and the air of the fields.'

He kissed her hand a few times, his dyed moustache leaving a little stain on her fingers.

'Yes, the country,' she replied wistfully, not to him but speaking into space to someone else.

'*A propos* of the country,' he added. 'Your lawsuit will be finished next month, and in April you will be able to leave for your estate. It is not big, but the situation is wonderful! You will be pleased. What a house! What a garden! There's a pavilion on a hill – you will love it! The view of the river – you don't remember it, do you? You were only five when your father left the estate and took you away.'

'Oh, how glad I shall be!' she said, and sank into thought.

'Now it's settled,' she decided, 'we'll go there, but he won't find out about it till – –'

'Next month, baron?' she asked quickly. 'Are you sure?'

'I'm as sure of that as I am of the fact that you are beautiful, and especially to-day,' he said, and went to her aunt.

Olga did not stir from her place, dreaming of the happiness that was so near, but she decided not to tell Oblomov her news and her plans for the future. She intended to watch to the end the change love wrought in Oblomov's lazy soul, to see how the great weight would lift from him, how he would not be able finally to resist the prospect of happiness, how he would receive a favourable reply from the country and, radiant with joy, would rush to her and put it at her feet, and how both of them would run to her aunt, and then – – Then she would suddenly tell him that she too had an estate, a garden, a pavilion, a view of the river and a house that was ready to live in, that they must go there first and then to Oblomovka. 'No,' she thought, 'I don't want a favourable reply, for he will put on airs and won't even feel glad that I have an estate of my own, a house, a garden. No, I'd rather he came looking upset by a disagreeable letter with the news that his estate was in a bad way and that he had to go there himself. He'd rush headlong off to Oblomovka, hastily make all the necessary arrangements, forget to see to a great many things, be unable to do many others, do everything just anyhow, rush back, and suddenly discover that it had not been necessary for him to go at all – that she had a house, a garden, and a pavilion with a view, that they had a place where they could live without bothering about his Oblomovka. ... No, no, she was not going to tell him; she would hold out to the end. Let him go to his estate, let him bestir himself, let him come to life – for her alone, in the name of their future happiness. Oh – no! Why should she send him to his estate? Why should they part? No – when, all dressed for the journey, he – pale and woebegone – came to say good-bye to her, she would tell him suddenly that there was no need for him to go till summer, that they would go together then. ...

So she dreamed on, and she ran to the baron and skilfully suggested to him that he should not reveal the news to anyone, absolutely not to *anyone*. By *anyone* she had only Oblomov in mind.

337

'Very well; why should I?' he agreed. 'Except perhaps to Mr Oblomov, if the subject should be mentioned. ...'

Olga restrained herself and said unconcernedly:

'No, please, don't tell him, either.'

'Oh, all right; you know your will is law so far as I'm concerned,' the baron added gallantly.

She was not without guile. If she wanted very much to look at Oblomov when other people were present, she would first look at two or three other people and only then at him. How much thought – and all for Oblomov. How many times had her cheeks begun to burn! How many times did she touch this or that key of the piano to see if it had not been tuned too high, or shifted the music from one place to another! And he did not come! What could it mean? Three o'clock. Four o'clock – he wasn't there! At half-past four she began visibly to wilt – her beauty was gone, her bloom faded, and she sat down at the table looking pale. No one seemed to have noticed anything, they were all eating the dishes which had been prepared for him, and talking cheerfully and unconcernedly. After dinner, in the evening – still he did not come. Till ten o'clock she fluctuated between hope and fear; at ten o'clock she went to her room. At first she vented on him all the bitterness that had accumulated in her heart; there was no word too sarcastic or too spiteful in her vocabulary for her to hurl it accusingly at his head. Then she felt suddenly as though her body were on fire and then turned cold as ice. 'He is ill, alone – he cannot even write,' it flashed through her head. This conviction took complete possession of her and kept her awake all night. She fell into a feverish slumber for a couple of hours, was delirious in the night, but got up in the morning calm and resolute, though pale.

On Monday morning the landlady looked into Oblomov's study and said:

'Some girl is asking for you.'

'Me? Impossible!' replied Oblomov. 'Where is she?'

'She's here. She came to our door by mistake. Shall I show her in?'

Oblomov had hardly time to make up his mind when Katya appeared before him. The landlady went out.

'Katya!' Oblomov cried in surprise. 'Is it you? What's the matter?'

'Miss Olga is outside,' Katya said in a whisper. 'She has sent me to ask – –'

Oblomov turned pale.

'Miss Olga!' he whispered in horror. 'It can't be true, Katya. You're joking, aren't you? Please, don't torture me!'

'It is true, sir. She's waiting in a hired carriage near the tea-shop. She wants to come here. She sent me to tell you to send Zakhar away. She'll be here in half an hour.'

'I'd better go and see her myself. She can't possibly come here, can she?' said Oblomov.

'You won't have time, sir. She may come in any minute. She thinks you're not well. Good-bye, I must run. My mistress is waiting for me – she's alone. ...'

And she went away.

Oblomov put on his boots, waistcoat, and tie with extra-ordinary rapidity and called Zakhar.

'Zakhar,' Oblomov said with feverish agitation, 'the other day you asked my permission to go and see your friends in Garokhavaya Street, didn't you? Well, you may go now!'

'I won't go, sir,' Zakhar replied emphatically.

'Oh yes, you will!' Oblomov persisted.

'I can't go visiting people on weekdays, can I? I won't go!' Zakhar said obstinately.

'Go and have a good time. Don't be obstinate when your master does you a favour and lets you off – go and see your friends!'

'I don't care about my friends, sir!'

'But don't you want to see them?'

'No, sir. They're all such rascals that every time I see them I never want to see them again!'

'Go – go for goodness' sake!' Oblomov kept repeating insist-ently, and the blood rushed to his face.

'No, sir,' Zakhar replied unconcernedly. 'I'll stay all day at home to-day, but on Sunday, sir, I'd be glad to go out.'

'You're going now – at once!' Oblomov hurried him agi-tatedly. 'You must – –'

'But why should I go all that way for nothing?'

'Well, just go for a walk for a couple of hours. Look at that sleepy face of yours – you want some fresh air!'

'There's nothing wrong with my face, sir,' Zakhar said, look-ing lazily out of the window. 'It's the right sort of face for the likes of me.'

'Goodness me,' Oblomov thought, mopping his brow, 'she's sure to be here any moment.'

'Please go for a walk, Zakhar, I beg you. Here, take twenty copecks and go and have a drink with one of your pals.'

'I'd rather sit down on the front steps, sir. I can't go for a walk in the frost, can I? I could sit down at the gate, of course. I don't mind doing that.'

'No,' Oblomov said quickly, 'you must go farther than the gate. Go to another street – to the left – over there, towards the park – across the river.'

'What's up?' Zakhar thought. 'Driving me out for a walk! It's never happened before!'

'I'd rather wait till Sunday, sir!'

'Are you going or not?' Oblomov said through clenched teeth, advancing upon Zakhar.

Zakhar disappeared and Oblomov called Anisya.

'Go to the market,' he said to her, 'and buy something for dinner.'

'But, sir, everything has been bought for dinner, and it'll soon be ready,' the nose began to expostulate.

'Shut up and listen!' Oblomov shouted so peremptorily that Anisya was frightened.

'Buy – well, some asparagus,' he said, trying to think of something to send her for.

'But, sir, asparagus is out of season – you will never find any there – –'

'Be off!' he shouted, and she ran off. 'Run there as fast as you can,' he shouted after her, 'and don't look round, and when coming back walk as slowly as possible and don't show your nose here for two hours.'

'That's a funny business and no mistake,' Zakhar said to Anisya, running across her at the gate. 'He has sent me for a walk and given me twenty copecks. Where does he think I can go walking?'

'He's your master and he has a right to tell you what to do,' the sharp-witted Anisya observed. 'You'd better go to Artemy, the count's coachman, and treat him to tea: he is always treating you, and I'll run down to the market.'

'What a funny idea, Artemy!' Zakhar said to the coachman. 'Master has told me to go for a walk and given me money for a drink. ...'

'Are you sure he's not intending to get drunk himself?' Artemy remarked wittily. 'He gave you something so that you shouldn't envy him. Come on!'

He winked at Zakhar and motioned with his head to a certain street.

'Come on,' Zakhar repeated, motioning towards the same

340

street. 'Dear, dear,' he wheezed to himself with a grin, 'fancy sending me out for a walk!'

They went away, but Anisya ran to the first crossroads, squatted down in a ditch behind a fence, and waited to see what happened.

Oblomov listened intently and waited. Someone took hold of the iron ring of the gate and at the same moment the dog began barking desperately and jumping on the chain.

'Damn the dog!' Oblomov muttered, grinding his teeth.

He snatched up his cap and rushed out to the front gate, opened it, and brought Olga to the front steps almost in his arms. She was alone. Katya was waiting for her in the carriage not far from the gate.

'Are you well? You're not in bed? What is the matter with you?' she asked quickly, without taking off her coat or hat and looking him up and down when she came into his study.

'I'm better now, my throat is – er – almost well,' he said, touching his throat and coughing a little.

'Why didn't you come yesterday?' she asked, casting so inquisitorial a glance at him that he could not utter a word.

'How could you do a thing like this, Olga?' he said in horror. 'Do you know what you are doing?'

'We'll discuss that later!' she interrupted him impatiently. 'I ask you, what's the meaning of your keeping away from me?'

He made no answer.

'You haven't got a stye, have you?' she asked.

He made no answer.

'You haven't been ill,' she said, knitting her brows. 'There was nothing wrong with your throat.'

'No, I haven't,' replied Oblomov in the voice of a schoolboy.

'You've deceived me!' she cried, looking at him in astonishment. 'Why?'

'I can explain everything, Olga.' He tried to justify himself. 'An important reason forced me to stay away from you for a fortnight – I was afraid of – –'

'Of – what?' she asked, sitting down and taking off her hat and coat.

He took both from her and put them on the sofa.

'Talk, gossip. ...'

'But you were not afraid of my spending sleepless nights, imagining all sorts of things and almost falling ill?' she said, looking searchingly at him.

'You don't know what's going on in me, Olga,' he said,

341

pointing to his head and heart. 'I'm worried to death; you don't know what's happened, do you?'

'What has happened?' she asked coldly.

'How far the rumours about you and me have spread! I did not want to worry you, and I was afraid to show myself at your place.'

He told her everything he had heard from Zakhar and Anisya, recalled the conversation of the dandies, and finished by saying that he had not been able to sleep ever since, and that in every glance he saw a question or a reproach or a sly hint at their meetings.

'But we have decided to tell Auntie this week,' she said. 'Then all these rumours will have to stop.'

'Yes, but I did not want to speak to your aunt this week, till I received my letter. I know that she will not ask me about my love, but about my estate, that she will want to know all the details, and I cannot explain anything to her till I've received an answer from my agent.'

She sighed.

'If I didn't know you,' she said thoughtfully, 'I don't know what I might have thought. You were afraid of worrying me by footmen's gossip, but you were not afraid of causing me all this anxiety! I simply can't understand you!'

'You see, I thought that their talk would upset you. Katya, Marfa, Semyon, and that fool Nikita, goodness only knows what they are saying – –'

'I've known for a long time what they are saying,' she said imperturbably.

'Who told you?'

'Katya and Nanny told me about it long ago. They asked me about you, congratulated me. ...'

'Congratulated you? Did they really?' he asked in horror. 'And what did you say?'

'Oh, nothing. I just thanked them. I gave Nurse a kerchief, and she promised to go on foot to St Sergius's shrine to offer up a prayer for me. I undertook to arrange Katya's marriage with a pastry-cook: she, too, is in love ...'

He looked at her with frightened and astonished eyes.

'You visited us every day, so it's natural that the servants should talk about it,' she added. 'They are always the first to talk. It was the same with Sonia: why does it frighten you so much?'

'So that's where the rumours came from!' he said in a drawn-out voice.

'They are not unfounded, are they? It's true, isn't it?'

'It is true,' Oblomov repeated, in a tone of voice that sounded neither like a denial nor like a question. 'Yes,' he added after a pause, 'you are quite right. But, you see, I don't want them to know about our meetings; that's why I am so afraid.'

'You are afraid – you tremble like a boy. ... I can't understand it! You are not stealing me, are you?'

He felt ill at ease; she looked attentively at him.

'Listen,' she said, 'there's some kind of a lie here somewhere, there's something wrong. Come here and tell me all you have on your mind. You could have stayed away for a couple of days or even for a week as a precaution, but you should have warned me, you should have written to me. You know I am no longer a child and I can't be so easily upset by some nonsense. What does it all mean?'

He pondered a little, kissed her hand, and sighed.

'This is what I think it is, Olga,' he said. 'All this time my imagination has been so frightened on your account by all these horrors, my mind has been so tortured by worries, my heart has been so sore with hopes that seemed to be on the point of fulfilment one moment and on the point of being shattered at another, and with expectations that my whole organism is shaken and has grown numb – it needs a rest even if it is only for a time – –'

'But why haven't I grown numb? Why do I seek a rest only beside you?'

'You are young and strong, you love me serenely and peacefully, while I – but you don't know how much I love you!' he said, sliding down to the floor and kissing her hands.

'No, I don't think I do – really. You are so strange that I don't know what to think. My mind misgives me and I lose hope – soon we shall cease to understand each other: if that happens, it will go badly with us.'

They were silent.

'What have you been doing all this time?' she asked, looking round the room for the first time. 'It isn't nice here – such low ceilings! The windows are small, the wallpaper old. ... What are your other rooms like?'

He rushed to show her his flat so as not to have to answer her questions about what he had been doing all that time. When she resumed her seat on the sofa, he again sat down on the rug at her feet.

'Well, what have you been doing this fortnight?' She repeated her question.

'Reading, writing, thinking of you.'

'Have you read my books? What are they like? I think I'll take them back.'

She picked up a book from the table and looked at the open page: it was covered with dust.

'You haven't been reading!' she said.

'No,' he replied.

She looked at the crumpled, embroidered cushions, at the untidiness of the room, the dusty windows, the writing-desk, turned over several dust-covered papers, touched the pen in the dry inkwell, and looked at him in amazement.

'What have you been doing?' she repeated. 'You haven't been reading or writing, have you?'

'I had so little time,' he began, faltering. 'When I get up in the morning they are tidying the rooms, they keep disturbing me, there follows the talk about dinner, the landlady's children come in and ask me to correct their sums, then there's dinner. After dinner – when is there time to read?'

'You slept after dinner,' she said in so positive a tone of voice that after a moment's hesitation, he replied softly:

'Yes.'

'But why?'

'So as not to notice the time: you were not with me, Olga, and life without you is dull and unbearable.'

He stopped short, and she looked sternly at him.

'Ilya,' she began earnestly, 'do you remember the day in the park when you told me that you felt alive again, when you assured me that I was the aim of your life and your ideal, when you took me by the hand and said that it was yours – do you remember how I gave you my consent?'

'How could I forget it? Hasn't it transformed my whole life? Don't you see how happy I am?'

'No, I don't. You have deceived me,' she said coldly. 'You're letting yourself go once more. ...'

'Deceived you? Aren't you ashamed to say that? I swear I'd throw myself into an abyss this very minute – –'

'Yes, indeed, if the abyss were here right at your feet at this moment,' she interrupted, 'but if it were put off for three days you would have changed your mind and got frightened, especially if Zakhar or Anisya began talking about it. That is not love.'

'Do you doubt my love?' he began warmly. 'Do you think that I am delaying out of fear for myself, and not for you?

Don't I guard your good name? Don't I watch over you like a mother so that no gossip should dare to touch you? Oh, Olga! Ask for proofs! I tell you again that if you could be happier with another man, I'd resign my rights to him without a murmur. If someone had to sacrifice his life for you, I'd be happy to die!' he concluded with tears in his eyes.

'But that's not necessary, no one asks you to! What do I need your life for? Just do what is necessary. It's an old trick of dishonest people to offer sacrifices which are unnecessary and which cannot be made so as to get out of making those that are necessary. You're not crafty – I know that, but – –'

'You don't know what these passions and anxieties have cost me!' he went on. 'I have had no other thought since I met you. And now, too, I repeat that you are my only aim, you alone. I shall die, I shall go mad if I have not got you beside me! I breathe, look, think, and feel only with you. Why are you surprised that I fall asleep and go to pieces on the days I don't see you? Nothing pleases me, I'm sick of everything, I'm just a machine: I walk about and do all sorts of things without noticing what I am doing. You are the fire and the force of this machine,' he declared, kneeling and straightening himself.

His eyes gleamed as they used to do in the park in summer. Pride and strength of will shone in them once more.

'I am ready to go at once where you tell me, to do what you wish. When you look at me, when you talk or sing, I feel that I am alive.'

Olga listened to these passionate effusions with thoughtful gravity.

'Listen, Ilya,' she said, 'I believe in your love and in my power over you. Why, then, do you frighten me by your indecision? Why do you make me doubt you? You say I am your aim – and you go towards it so slowly and timidly. And you have still far to go, for you must rise above me. I expect it of you! I have watched happy people in love,' she added with a sigh. 'Everything they do is full of energy and their rest is not like yours: they do not drop their heads, their eyes are always open, they seem hardly ever to sleep, they act! And you – no, I'm afraid it does not look as if love or I were your aim in life.'

She shook her head doubtfully.

'You are, my darling, you are!' he said, kissing her hands again excitedly as he lay at her feet. 'You alone! Heavens, what happiness!' he repeated as though in a delirium. 'And you imagine that it is possible to deceive you, to fall asleep after such an awakening, not to become a hero! You shall see – you and Andrey,' he went on, looking round with inspired eyes, 'to what heights the love of a woman like you can raise a man! Look, look at me. Have I not come back to life, am I not alive at this moment? Let us leave this place! Let's go, let's go! I can't stay here for another moment: I feel stifled, rotten!' he said, looking round him with undisguised disgust. 'Let me go on feeling like this the whole of to-day. ... Oh, if only the fire that burns in me now would go on burning to-morrow and always! But when you are away, it goes out and I sink! Now I am alive, I have come back from the dead. I think I – – Olga, Olga! You're the most beautiful thing in the world, you're first among all women, you – you – –'

He pressed his face to her hand and fell silent. He could not bring himself to utter another word. He pressed his hand to his heart to quiet his agitation, fixed his passionate, moist eyes on Olga, and remained motionless.

'He's tender, tender, tender!' Olga kept thinking, but with a sigh, and not as she used to think in the park, and she sank into deep thought.

'It's time I went,' she said affectionately as she recovered from her reverie.

He suddenly came to himself.

'Oh dear, are you here? At my place?' he said.

His inspired look disappeared, and instead he began looking round timidly. His tongue uttered no more ardent speeches. He grabbed her hat and coat hurriedly, and in his confusion he tried to put the coat on her head. She laughed.

'Don't be afraid for me,' she calmed him. 'Auntie has gone out for the whole day. At home Nurse alone knows that I am out, and Katya, of course. Please see me off.'

She allowed him to take her arm and, calmly and without the slightest excitement, in the proud consciousness of her innocence, crossed the yard to the accompaniment of the desperate barking of the dog, jumping on the chain, entered her carriage, and drove away. Heads were peering from the landlady's windows, and Anisya's head peeped out of the ditch from behind the fence round the corner. When the carriage had turned into another street, Anisya came back and said she had been all over the market and could find no asparagus.

Oblomov paced the room for a long time, too absorbed in his thoughts to hear that the carriage, which carried away his happiness and everything that was dear to him in life, had stopped crunching on the snow, his nervousness disappeared, his head and back straightened, the look of inspired radiance returned to his face, and his eyes were moist with happiness and emotion. A feeling of warmth, freshness, and high spirits spread through his body. And again, as many times before, he felt like being everywhere at once, far, far away: to go around with Stolz, accompanied by Olga; to go to the country, to the fields and woods; to shut himself up in his study and busy himself with his work; to travel to Rybinsk harbour, to construct the new road; to read the new book which had just been published and which everybody was talking about; to go to the opera – to-day. ... Yes, she had been to see him to-day, and he would go to see her and then – to the opera. What a full day it had been! How easy it was to breathe in the sort of atmosphere Olga lived in, in the rays of her virginal brilliance, her high spirits, and her young but subtle, deep, and sound intelligence! He felt as though he were not walking, but flying, as though he were being wafted about the room.

'Forward, forward!' Olga had said. 'Higher, higher, to that boundary where the power of grace and tenderness loses its rights and where man's kingdom begins!' How clearly she saw life! How easily she had found her way in that intricate book and had guessed instinctively his way in it too! Their two lives, like two rivers, must merge: he was to be her guide, her leader! She saw his powers, his abilities, she knew how much he could do, and was waiting submissively for him to assert his dominion over her. Wonderful Olga! A cool, brave, simple, but resolute woman, natural as life itself!

'How disgusting this place really is!' he said, looking round. 'And this angel descended into a swamp and sanctified it with her presence!'

He looked lovingly at the chair on which she had been sitting, and suddenly his eyes shone: beside the chair, on the floor, he saw a tiny glove.

'A pledge! Her hand: it's a portent! Oh!' he moaned passionately, pressing the glove to his lips.

The landlady thrust her head through the door to ask him if he would like to have a look at some linen: it had been brought for sale and he might like to buy some. But he thanked her dryly, without thinking of glancing at her elbows, said he was sorry, but he was very busy. Then he became absorbed in the recollections of the summer, went over all the details, remembered every tree, bush, and seat, every uttered word, and found it all more charming than it had been at the time when he was enjoying it. He seemed to have lost all control of himself. He sang, spoke kindly to Anisya, joked about her having no children, and promised to stand godfather to her first baby. He played so noisily with Masha that the landlady looked in and sent Masha away so that she should not interfere with their lodger's 'work'.

He spent the rest of the day indulging in even madder dreams: Olga was gay and sang, then there was more singing at the opera, then he had tea with them, and the conversation at the tea-table between him, the aunt, the baron, and Olga was so sincere and cordial that Oblomov felt absolutely a member of this small family. He need no longer live a solitary life: he had a home, his life was now built on firm foundations – he had warmth and light – and how lovely life was!

He slept little that night: he was reading the books Olga had sent him and read a volume and a half.

'To-morrow the letter from the country is sure to come,' he thought, and his heart beat fast – fast. 'At last!'

8

NEXT day Zakhar, while tidying the room, found a small glove on the writing-desk. He examined it for some time, grinned, and then gave it to Oblomov.

'I suppose, sir, the Ilyinsky young lady must have left it behind,' he said.

'You devil!' Oblomov thundered, snatching the glove from his hand. 'Nonsense! There was no Ilyinsky young lady! It was the dressmakers who came from the shop with some shirts for me. How dare you make up such stories?'

'What sort of devil am I, sir? I am making up stories, am I? You should hear what they are saying at the landlady's ...'

'What are they saying?' asked Oblomov.

'Why, sir, that the Ilyinsky young lady was here with her maid.'

'Good God!' Oblomov said in horror. 'How do they know that it was the Ilyinsky young lady? You or Anisya must have told them.'

At this moment Anisya thrust her head through the door.

'Aren't you ashamed to talk such nonsense, Zakhar?' she

said. 'Don't listen to him, sir. No one has been telling anyone, no one knows anything, I swear ...'

'All right, all right,' Zakhar wheezed at her, raising his elbow as though to hit her in the chest. 'Don't you poke your nose where you're not wanted!'

Anisya disappeared. Oblomov shook both fists at Zakhar, then quickly opened the door into the landlady's part of the house. Agafya Matveyevna was sitting on the floor sorting out some junk in an old trunk; all round her lay heaps of rags, cottonwool, old clothes, buttons, and bits of fur.

'I say,' Oblomov said kindly, but in an agitated voice, 'my servants talk all sorts of nonsense. Don't believe them, for goodness' sake.'

'I haven't heard anything,' said the landlady. 'What are they saying?'

'About yesterday's visit,' Oblomov went on. 'They say that some young lady came to see me. ...'

'It is none of our business what visitors our tenant may have, is it?' said the landlady.

'But, please, don't believe it: the whole thing is a slanderous story! I have had no visit from a young lady. It was the dress-maker who is making some shirts for me. She came to fit me. ...'

'Where have you ordered the shirts?' the landlady asked quickly. 'Who is making them for you?'

'In the French shop,' Oblomov muttered.

'Show me when they bring them. I know two girls who are excellent sempstresses. They stitch better than any French-woman. I saw their work myself; they brought it to show me. They are sewing for Count Metlinsky. No one could sew better. Your shirts, those you are wearing, can't be compared with those they make.'

'Thank you, I'll remember that. Only, for heaven's sake, don't think it was a young lady.'

'It's none of my business who comes to see my tenant, is it? Even if it was a young lady – –'

'No, no!' Oblomov denied it vehemently. 'Why, the young lady Zakhar is talking about is very tall and speaks in a low voice, and this one, the dressmaker, I mean, has a very high, clear voice – you must have heard her yourself, didn't you? She has a lovely voice. Please don't think – –'

'It's none of our business, is it?' the landlady said as he was about to go. 'So please don't forget to tell me when you want some shirts made: the girls I know stitch so wonderfully – they are called Lisaveta Nikolaevna and Maria Nikolaevna.'

'All right, I shan't forget, only, please, don't think – –'

He went out, then he dressed and drove to Olga's. On his return home in the evening, he found on his table a letter from his neighbour in the country. He rushed to the lamp, read the letter – and his heart sank.

'I should be greatly obliged,' the neighbour wrote, 'if you would transfer my power of attorney to some other person, for I have so great an accumulation of business that, to be quite frank, I cannot look after your estate as I should. It would be best for you to come here yourself, and better still to settle on your estate. It is a good estate, but it has been badly neglected. First of all, you must decide carefully which of your peasants are to pay an annual tax and which are to work your land three days a week. It is impossible to do that without you: the peasants have got out of hand, they take no notice of the new bailiff, and the old one is a rogue who must be carefully watched. It is impossible to tell you what your income amounts to. In the present rather confused state of affairs you will hardly receive more than three thousand, and that, too, only if you are on the spot. I have in mind the income from corn, for there is little hope of getting anything from the peasants who have to pay an annual tax: they have to be taken in hand and have their arrears sorted out – it will take three months to do that. The harvest was good and the price of corn high, and you ought to get the money in March or April, if you keep an eye on the sales yourself. But at the moment there is not a penny in cash. As for the road through Verkhlyovo and the bridge, I had no answer from you for so long that I decided to build the road with Odontsov and Belovodov from my estate to Nelki with the result that Oblomovka, I'm afraid, has been left a great distance away. In conclusion, I must ask you again to come here as soon as possible: in three months you will find out exactly what income to expect next year. By the way, we are having elections here: wouldn't you like to be a candidate for the post of district magistrate? Your house is in a very bad state of repair' (this was added at the end of the letter) 'I told the dairy-maid, the old coachman, and the two maids to move out of it into the cottage: it is dangerous to stay there any longer.'

A statement on the number of bushels harvested, threshed, stored, and for sale, and similar business details, was enclosed with the letter.

'Not a penny in cash, three months, must go myself, sort out the peasants' affairs, find out what income to expect, stand for elections' – all this crowded round Oblomov like so many phantoms. He felt as though he were in a forest at night when one seems to see a robber or a corpse or a wild beast in every bush. 'But the whole thing is disgraceful: I am not going to give in!' he kept repeating, trying to get better acquainted with these phantoms, just like a coward who tries to look at phantoms through half-closed eyes but only feels a chill at the heart and a weakness in the arms and legs. What had Oblomov been hoping for? He had thought that the letter would say definitely what his income would be and that, of course, it would be as much as possible, say, six or seven thousand; that the house was still in good repair, so that, if the worst came to the worst, he could still live there while the new one was being built; that, finally, his neighbour would send him three or four thousand – in short, that he would find in the letter the same laughter, high spirits, and love as in Olga's notes. He no longer walked on air in his room, he no longer joked with Anisya, or indulged in hopes of happiness – they had to be postponed for three months – no! in three months he would do no more than sort out his affairs, get to know his estate. As for the wedding – 'It's no use thinking of the wedding before a year,' he said timidly. 'Yes, yes, in a year's time – not before!' He still had to finish writing his plan, settle with the architect, then – then – he sighed. 'Borrow the money!' it flashed through his mind, but he rejected the idea. 'It's impossible! What if I can't repay it in time? If things go badly, the creditors will take out a summons, and the name of Oblomov, so far pure and untarnished – –' God forbid! For then it would be good-bye to his peace of mind, his pride – no, no! People who borrowed money rushed about, worked, lost their sleep, just as if they were possessed by a demon. Yes, a debt was a demon, a devil who could only be exorcised by money! There were, of course, clever fellows who lived all their lives at other people's expense; they grabbed right and left and did not care a damn! How they could sleep in peace, how they could eat their dinner was just beyond him. A debt! Its consequence was either the never-ending labour of a galley-slave or dishonour. To mortgage the estate? But was it not the same sort of debt, a debt that was irrevocable and that could not be set aside? He would have to pay every year – and for all he knew there would not be enough left to live on. To postpone his happiness for another year! Oblomov uttered a painful moan and sank down on his bed, but he rapidly recollected himself and got up. And what did Olga say? Had she not appealed to him as a man? Had she not trusted to his strength? She was waiting for him to go forward until he reached the height from which he would hold out his hand to her and lead her after him, show her the way! Yes, yes! But what was he to begin with? He thought it over carefully, then suddenly slapped his forehead and went to see his landlady.

'Is your brother at home?' he asked her.

'Yes, but he has gone to bed.'

'Will you please ask him to come in to see me to-morrow,' asked Oblomov. 'I should like to see him.'

9

THE landlady's brother came into the room in the same way as before, sat down on a chair, carefully hid his hands in his sleeves, and waited for what Oblomov had to say.

'I have received a very unpleasant letter from the country in reply to the deed of trust I sent – you remember, don't you?' said Oblomov. 'Will you read it, please?'

Ivan Matveyevich took the letter from the country, his eyes running quickly along the lines, while his hands trembled slightly. Having read it, he put the letter on the table and his hands behind his back.

'What do you think I ought to do now?' asked Oblomov.

'Your neighbour advises you to go there,' said Ivan Matveyevich. 'Well, sir, a thousand miles isn't such a very long journey. In another week the roads will be fit for sleighing, so, I suppose, you'd better go.'

'I dislike travelling intensely – I'm not used to it, you see, and I'd find it very difficult in winter in particular. I'd rather not go. Besides, it's very boring to be in the country by yourself.'

'Have you many peasants who pay you a tax?' asked Ivan Matveyevich.

'Well, I don't really know. You see, it's so long since I went to my estate.'

'You ought to know that, sir. You couldn't very well carry on without it, could you? For one thing, you could never find out what your income was.'

'Yes, I ought to,' Oblomov repeated, 'and my neighbour, too, writes so, but unfortunately it's winter. ...'

'And how much does the tax bring in?'

'The tax? I believe – er – I had a bit of paper here somewhere. Stolz drew it up for me, but I'm afraid I can't find it. Zakhar must have put it away somewhere. ... I'll show you it later – I believe it's thirty roubles per peasant.'

'What sort of peasants have you got?' Ivan Matveyevich asked. 'How do they live? How many of them work for you?'

'Look here,' Oblomov said, walking up to him and taking him trustfully by the lapels of his uniform, 'look here,' he repeated slowly, almost in a whisper. 'I don't know anything about the peasants who have to work for me; I don't know what agricultural labour is, or when a peasant is rich or poor; I don't know what a quarter of rye or oats means, or what it costs in different months, or how and when corn is harvested and sold; I don't know if I am rich or poor, if I shall have enough to eat in a year's time or be a beggar – I don't know anything!' he concluded dejectedly, letting go the lapels of Ivan Matveyevich's uniform, 'and therefore I'd be glad if you would speak to me and advise me as you would a child. ...'

'But, of course, sir, you ought to know, for if you don't, you won't be able to make head or tail of anything,' Ivan Matveyevich said with an obsequious smile, getting up and putting one hand behind his back and the other inside his coat. 'A landowner must know his estate and how to manage it,' he said edifyingly.

'But I don't know. Teach me if you can.'

'I'm afraid it isn't a subject I've had much experience in, sir. I shall have to consult those who have. And here, sir,' he went on, pointing with his middle finger, nail downwards, to the page of the letter, 'they tell you in the letter to stand for election. That's not such a bad idea, you know! You'd live there, serve as magistrate in the district court, and meanwhile learn all about farming.'

'I don't know what a district court is, what one is supposed to do there, and how one holds office there,' Oblomov said emphatically, but in an undertone, walking right up to Ivan Matveyevich's nose.

'You'll get used to it, sir. You've been a member of the Civil Service here, haven't you? Well, the work is the same everywhere, though the forms may differ slightly. Everywhere there are instructions, memoranda, records. ... Get a good clerk, and the rest will be easy. All you have to do is to sign your name. If you know how things are done in a Government office ...'

'I don't know how things are done in a Government office,' Oblomov declared monotonously.

Ivan Matveyevich threw his enigmatic glance at Oblomov and was silent.

'I expect, sir, you did nothing but read books,' he observed with the same obsequious smile.

'Books!' Oblomov retorted bitterly and stopped short.

He had not enough courage to bare his soul before a low-grade civil servant, and, besides, there was no need for him to do so.

'I haven't the faintest idea of books, either,' he thought uneasily, but he would not bring himself to utter the words and merely sighed mournfully.

'But you did do something, sir, didn't you?' Ivan Matveyevich added humbly, as though divining Oblomov's answer about the books. 'It's impossible not to – –'

'It is possible, sir, and I am the living proof of it. Who am I? What am I? Go and ask Zakhar, and he will tell you that I am a "gentleman". Yes, I am a gentleman and I can't do anything! Please do it for me, if you know how, and help me, if you can. Take anything you like for your trouble – that is what knowledge is for!'

He began pacing the room, while Ivan Matveyevich remained standing where he was, slightly turning his body in Oblomov's direction. Both of them were silent for some time.

'Where have you been educated?' asked Oblomov, stopping before him once more.

'I went to a secondary school, but my father took me away from the fifth form and got me a job in a Government office. I'm afraid my education doesn't amount to much. Reading, writing, grammar, arithmetic – I did not go beyond that. I got used to my work – more or less, and I am just managing to make ends meet. But your case is different, sir. You're a really educated man.'

'Yes, I suppose so,' Oblomov affirmed with a sigh. 'It's true I've studied higher mathematics, political economy, and law, but I haven't got the knack for business in spite of it. You see, though I have studied higher mathematics, I can't tell what my income amounts to. I returned to the country and did my best to find out how things were done there, I mean, in our house, on our estate, and all around. Well, it was not at all according to the laws I had learnt. I came here, thinking to make a career with the help of political economy. I was told, however, that my learning would come in useful in time, in my old age, perhaps, but that first I had to obtain a high rank in the Civil Service and to do that only one thing was needed – drawing up documents. So I just could not adapt myself to that kind of work and I became simply a gentleman, whereas you did adapt yourself. That's why I want you to tell me how to solve my problem.'

'I daresay I could, sir,' said Ivan Matveyevich at last. 'I daresay I could.'

Oblomov stopped before him, waiting to hear what he would say.

'You could entrust it all to an expert and transfer the deed of trust to him,' added Ivan Matveyevich.

'But where am I to find such a man?' asked Oblomov.

'A colleague of mine, Isay Fomich Zatyorty, who has a slight stammer, is such an experienced and business-like man. He was the manager of a big estate for three years, but the owner dismissed him because of his stammer. So he got a job at my office.'

'But can he be relied on?'

'Don't worry, he is as honest as they make 'em! He'd spend his own money to please the man who trusted him. He's been in our office for twelve years.'

'How could he go to the country, if he has to be at your office?'

'That's nothing. He could get leave for four months. If you make up your mind, I'll bring him here. He wouldn't go there for nothing, would he?'

'Of course not,' Oblomov agreed.

'You'll pay his travelling expenses and so much per day for his living allowance and then, when his work is done, a certain sum by arrangement. Don't worry, he'll go!'

'Thank you very much,' said Oblomov, holding out his hand. 'You've lifted a load off my mind. What is his name?'

'Isay Fomich Zatyorty,' Ivan Matveyevich repeated, hurriedly wiping his hand on the cuff of his other sleeve, taking Oblomov's hand for a moment and immediately hiding it in his sleeve again. 'I'll have a talk to him to-morrow, sir, and bring him along.'

'Yes, come to dinner and we'll talk it over. Thank you very much!' said Oblomov, seeing Ivan Matveyevich to the door.

10

IN the evening of the same day Ivan Matveyevich and Tarantyev were sitting in one of the rooms of the upper floor of a two-
storied house which, on one side, faced the street where Oblomov lived and, on the other, the quay. It was a so-called
'tavern', which always had two or three empty cabs waiting at
its front door, the cabmen staying on the ground floor and drinking tea out of their saucers. The upper floor was reserved for the
'gentlemen' of Vyborg.

Glasses of tea and a bottle of rum stood on a table before Ivan
Matveyevich and Tarantyev.

'Real Jamaica rum,' said Ivan Matveyevich, pouring some
into his glass with a shaking hand. 'Have some, old man.'

'You must admit it,' retorted Tarantyev, 'you owe me this
treat. You'd not have got such a tenant if you'd waited till the
house had rotted away.'

'True enough,' Ivan Matveyevich interrupted. 'And if our
business comes off and Zatyorty goes to the country, you'll get
your commission.'

'I'm afraid, old man, you're damned stingy,' said Tarantyev.
'One has to bargain with you. Fifty roubles for such a lodger!'

'I'm afraid he may be leaving – he's threatening to,' observed
Ivan Matveyevich.

'Don't talk nonsense – a man of experience like you, too!
Where will he go? He wouldn't be driven out even by force now.'

'And the wedding? I hear he's getting married.'

Tarantyev burst out laughing.

'He getting married! What do you bet that he won't?' he
replied. 'Why, he can't go to bed without Zakhar's help, and
you talk of marriage! Till now I've been giving him a helping
hand; if it hadn't been for me, old man, he would have died of
starvation or been clapped into jail. If the police inspector called
or his landlord asked him for something, he never knew what to
do – I had to do everything for him! He doesn't understand a
thing!'

'You're right. He told me he didn't know what they did in a
district court or in a Government department. He has no idea
what sort of peasants he has. What a fool! I nearly burst out
laughing.'

'And the agreement, the agreement we drew up!' Tarantyev

boasted. 'You're a past-master in drawing up documents, old man, I grant you that! It reminded me of my father. I wasn't bad at it, either, but I'm afraid I've lost the knack – aye, I've lost the knack! The moment I sit down at the table my eyes begin to water. He never bothered to read it, just signed it! Barns, stables, kitchen gardens, and all!'

'Yes, old man, while there are blockheads in Russia who sign papers without reading them, people like us can still manage to live. But for that life would have been terrible – things have grown so bad! In the old days it was different. What money have I made after twenty-five years in the Civil Service? Enough to live on in Vyborg without showing my nose anywhere else – plenty to eat, I'm not complaining! But, I'm afraid, a flat on Liteyny, carpets, a rich wife, and children who are admitted to the best houses – that's a dream of the past! I haven't got the right face for it, I'm told, and my fingers are red – Why do I drink? How can I help drinking? Just try! Worse than a footman – aye, to-day a footman doesn't wear boots like mine and changes his shirt every day. The trouble is, I haven't had the right education – the youngsters have got miles ahead of me: show off, read and talk French. ...'

'And have no idea of practical affairs,' added Tarantyev.

'That's where you're wrong, old man: they have, but it's different now. Everyone wants things to be as simple as possible and everyone is doing his best to trip us up. This is not the way to write, that's quite unnecessary, a waste of time – you could do it much more quickly – always tripping us up.'

'But the agreement is signed: they did not trip us up there, did they?' said Tarantyev.

'That, of course, is sacred. Let's drink, old man. He'll send Zatyorty to Oblomovka, and Zatyorty will gradually suck him dry: let his heirs get all that is left over. ...'

'Let them,' Tarantyev observed. 'And there aren't any real heirs, either: third cousins, some very distant relatives.'

'It's his marriage I'm afraid of!' said Ivan Matveyevich.

'Don't be afraid, I tell you. Mark my words!'

'No?' Ivan Matveyevich retorted gaily. 'You know,' he added in a whisper, 'he's casting sheep's eyes at my sister.'

'Not really?' Tarantyev said in astonishment.

'Mum's the word! I tell you I know what I'm talking about.'

'Well, old man,' Tarantyev said, hardly able to recover from his surprise, 'I'd never have dreamed of it! And what about her?'

'What about her? You know her, don't you?' he said, banging his fist on the table. 'She can't be expected to look after her interests, can she? A cow – that's what she is, a blamed cow: hit her or hug her, she goes on grinning like a horse at a nose-bagful of oats. Another woman in her place would – oh, well! But I'll keep an eye on them, I promise you – you realize what it may mean, don't you?'

11

'FOUR months! Another four months of constraint, secret meetings, suspicious faces, smiles!' thought Oblomov as he mounted the stairs to the Ilyinskys' flat. 'Good Lord, when will it end? And I'm sure Olga will hurry me: to-day, to-morrow. She is so insistent, so inexorable! It's difficult to convince her. ...'

Oblomov reached Olga's room without meeting anybody. Olga was sitting in her small sitting-room, next to her bedroom, absorbed in reading a book. He appeared before her so suddenly that she gave a start, then held out her hand affectionately and with a smile, but her eyes seemed to be still reading the book; she looked absent-minded.

'Are you alone?' he asked.

'Yes, Auntie has gone to Tsarskoye Selo. She wanted me to go with her. We shall be almost alone at dinner. Only Maria Semyonovna is coming; otherwise I should not have been able to receive you. You can't talk to Auntie to-day. What an awful bore it is! But to-morrow – –' she added and smiled. 'And what if I had gone to Tsarskoye Selo to-day?' she asked, jestingly.

He made no answer.

'Are you worried?' she asked.

'I had a letter from the country,' he said dully.

'Where is it? Have you got it on you?'

He gave her the letter.

'I can't read the writing,' she said, glancing at it.

He took the letter from her and read it aloud. She became thoughtful.

'What now?' she said after a pause.

'I consulted my landlady's brother,' Oblomov replied, 'and he recommended me as my agent a certain Isay Fomich Zatyorty: I'll give him the necessary instructions to settle everything.'

'A perfect stranger!' Olga objected in surprise. 'To collect the taxes, to look into the affairs of the peasants, to see to the sale of the corn. ...'

'He tells me Zatyorty is the soul of honour, he has been working in the same office with him for twelve years. ... The only thing is he stammers a little. ...'

'And what is your landlady's brother like? Do you know him?'

'No, but he seems to be such a practical, business-like man. Besides, I'm living in his house – he would be ashamed to cheat me!'

Olga said nothing and sat with her eyes fixed on the ground.

'You see, I should have to go there myself otherwise,' said Oblomov, 'and I must say I should not like to do that. I've lost the habit of travelling, especially in winter – in fact, I have never done it.'

She was still looking down, tapping the floor with the toe of her shoe.

'Even if I did go,' Oblomov went on, 'nothing would come of it, for I shan't get what I want. The peasants will cheat me, the bailiff will say what he pleases and I shall have to believe him, and he would give as much money as he liked. Oh, if only Andrey had been here: he'd have settled everything!' he added sadly.

Olga smiled, that is, she smiled only with her lips and not with her heart: there was bitterness in her heart. She began looking out of the window, screwing up one eye slightly and watching every carriage that passed.

'It seems Zatyorty managed a big estate once,' he went on, 'and the owner dismissed him only because he stammered. I'll let him have a deed of trust and give him the plans: he will arrange the purchase of the materials for building the house, collect the taxes from the peasants, sell the corn, bring the money, and then – – Oh, dear Olga,' he went on, kissing her hands, 'I'm so glad that I haven't got to leave you! I couldn't bear to part from you. To be alone without you in the country – oh, that would be awful! Only we must be very careful now.'

She looked at him with wide-open eyes and waited.

'Yes,' he began slowly, almost stammering, 'we mustn't see each other too often. Yesterday they again started talking about us at the landlady's and – and I don't want that. As soon as everything is settled and my agent sees about the building and brings the money – I mean, all this will be finished in about a year and – and we shan't have to part any more and – and we'll tell your aunt – and – and – –'

He looked up at Olga: she had fainted. Her head was bent sideways and her teeth showed from between her lips, which had turned blue. He didn't notice, while indulging in his dreams of their future happiness, that at the words: 'As soon as everything is settled, and my agent sees ...' Olga had turned pale and did not hear the end of the sentence.

'Olga! Good heavens, she has fainted!' he said and pulled at the bell.

'Your mistress has fainted,' he said to Katya, when she ran into the room. 'Water, quick! ... And the smelling salts!'

'Goodness, sir, she has been so happy all the morning! What's happened to her?' she whispered, bringing the smelling-salts from the aunt's table and bustling over Olga with a glass of water.

Olga came to, got up with the help of Katya and Oblomov and walked unsteadily to her bedroom.

'It'll pass,' she said weakly; 'it's just my nerves. I slept badly last night. I'll feel better presently and come back.'

Left to himself, Oblomov put his ear to the door, tried to look through the keyhole, but heard and saw nothing. Half an hour later he walked down the corridor to the maid's room and asked Katya how her mistress was.

'She's all right,' said Katya. 'She lay down and sent me away. I went in later and found her sitting in the arm-chair.'

Oblomov went back to the sitting-room, looked through the keyhole of Olga's bedroom again, but heard nothing. He tapped on the door with his finger – there was no reply. He sat down and pondered. He did a great deal of thinking in that hour and a half, there were a great many changes in his ideas, and he took many new decisions. At last he made up his mind to go to the country together with his agent, but first to get the consent of Olga's aunt to the announcement of their engagement, to ask Ivan Gerasimovich to find a flat and even to borrow some money – a little, to cover the expenses of the wedding. This loan he could repay out of the money he would get for the corn. Why, then, was he so dejected? Oh dear, how everything could change in a minute! In the country he and his agent would make all the necessary arrangements for the collection of the taxes, and, besides, he could write to Stolz, who would lend him some money and then come and get everything in Oblomovka ship-shape, make roads, build bridges, and open a school. ...

And he would be there with Olga! Lord, that was happiness! How was it he had never thought of it before? Suddenly he felt so light-hearted and gay; he began pacing the room, snapping his fingers and almost shouting with joy. He went up to Olga's door and called to her in a cheerful voice.

'Olga, Olga!' he cried, putting his lips to the keyhole. 'I've something to tell you! I'm sure you don't know what it is!'

He even decided not to leave her that day, until after her aunt returned. 'We'll tell her to-day and I'll go home as Olga's fiancé!'

The door opened quietly and Olga appeared: he looked at her and suddenly his heart sank. His joy vanished: Olga seemed to have aged. She was pale, but her eyes glittered; an intense inner life was hidden in her tightly closed lips and in every feature of her face, a life bound, as with ice, by her enforced calm and immobility. In her eyes he read a decision, but what kind of a decision he could not yet tell, though his heart pounded as it had never done before. Such moments he had not experienced in his life before.

'Listen, Olga. Please don't look at me like that – it frightens me!' he said. 'I've changed my mind, I'll have to arrange it all quite differently,' he went on, gradually lowering his voice, pausing and trying to grasp the meaning of the new expression of her eyes, lips, and eloquent eyebrows. 'I've decided to go to the country myself together with my agent – so that I – I could – –' he finished almost inaudibly.

She was silent, looking at him intently, like a phantom. He guessed vaguely the verdict that awaited him, and picked up his hat, but hesitated to ask: he was afraid of hearing the fatal decision against which there might be no appeal. At last he mastered himself.

'Have I understood you aright?' he asked her in a changed voice.

She slowly and gently bowed her head in assent. Though he had guessed her thought already, he turned pale and remained standing before her. She looked a little languid, but seemed as calm and immobile as a stone statue. It was the preternatural calm when a concentrated intention or a wounded feeling gives one the power of complete self-control, but only for one moment. She was like a wounded man who closes his wound with his hand so that he can say all that he has to say and then die.

'You won't hate me?' he asked.

'Whatever for?' she said weakly.

'For everything I've done to you.'

'What have you done?'

'I've loved you: that's an insult!'

She smiled pityingly.

'For having made a mistake,' he said, bowing his head. 'Perhaps you will forgive me if you recall that I warned you how ashamed you would be, how you would be sorry – –'

'I am not sorry. I feel so miserable, so miserable – –' she said, stopping short to take breath.

'I feel worse,' Oblomov replied, 'but I deserve it. Why should you torture yourself?'

'For my pride,' she said. 'I am punished, I had relied too much on my own powers – that was where I was mistaken, and not what you feared. It was not of youth and beauty that I dreamed; I had thought that I'd bring you back to life, that you could still live for me – whereas you died long ago. I had not foreseen that mistake, but kept waiting and hoping and – now!' she concluded with a sigh, barely able to speak.

She fell silent and then sat down.

'I can't stand: my legs tremble. A stone would have come to life from what I have done,' she went on in a languid voice. 'Now I won't do anything, I won't go anywhere, not even to the Summer Gardens: it's no use – you are dead! You agree with me, Ilya, don't you?' she added after a pause. 'You won't ever reproach me for having parted from you out of pride or caprice, will you?'

He shook his head.

'Are you convinced that there is nothing left for us – no hope at all?'

'Yes, he said, 'that's true, but,' he added irresolutely, 'perhaps in a year's time – –'

He had not the heart to deal a decisive blow to his happiness.

'Do you really think that in a year's time you would put your affairs and your life in order?' she asked. 'Think!'

He sighed and pondered, struggling with himself. She read the struggle in his face.

'Listen,' she said, 'I've been looking at my mother's portrait and, I believe, I obtained advice and strength from her eyes. If, like an honourable man, you will now – – Remember, Ilya, we're not children and we're not joking: it is a matter that concerns our whole life! Ask yourself conscientiously and tell me – I will believe you, I know you: would you be able to keep it up all your life? Would you be for me what I want you to be? You know me, you therefore understand what I want to say. If boldly and deliberately you say, 'yes,' I take back my decision: here is my hand, and let us go where you will – abroad, to the country, even to Vyborg!'

He said nothing.

'If you knew how I love you – –'

'What I want is not protestations of love but a brief answer,' she interrupted him almost dryly.

'Don't torture me, Olga!' he implored her disconsolately.

'Well, Ilya, am I right or not?'

'Yes,' he said, distinctly and resolutely, 'you are right.'

'In that case we had better part,' she decided, 'before anyone finds you here and sees how upset I am.'

But he still did not go.

'Even if we had married, what would have come of it?' she asked.

He made no answer.

'You would sink deeper and deeper into sleep every day, wouldn't you? And I? You see the sort of person I am, don't you? I shall never grow old or tire of life. And with you I should be living from day to day, waiting for Christmas, then for Shrovetide, go visiting, dancing, and not thinking of anything. We'd go to bed and thank God that the day had passed so quickly, and in the morning we'd wake up wishing that to-day would be like yesterday. That would be our future, wouldn't it? Is that life? I'd pine away and die – what for, Ilya? Would you be happy?'

He cast an agonizing look at the ceiling, wanted to move, to run away, but his legs would not obey him. He wanted to say something – his mouth was dry, his tongue would not move, his voice failed him. He held out his hand to her.

'So – –' he began in a faint voice, but broke off and finished his sentence with his eyes: 'Good-bye!'

She, too, wanted to say something, but could not; she held out her hand to him, but the hand dropped before it touched him; she, too, wanted to say 'good-bye', but her voice failed her in the middle of the word and broke off on a false note; a spasm passed over her face, she put her hand and head on his shoulder and burst into sobs. It was as though her weapons had been snatched out of her hands. The woman of intelligence was gone and in her place was simply a woman who was powerless against grief.

'Good-bye, good-bye,' the words escaped her between her sobs.

He was silent, listening in horror to her weeping and not daring to interfere with it. He did not feel any pity either for her or for himself; he was wretched himself. She sank into an armchair and, pressing her handkerchief to her face, leaned against the table and wept bitterly. Her tears flowed not as an irresistible hot stream released by a sudden and temporary pain, as in the park in summer, but coldly and cheerlessly, like autumn rain pitilessly watering the meadows.

'Olga,' he said at last, 'why do you torture yourself? You love me, you won't be able to bear the parting! Take me as I am, love whatever is good in me.'

She shook her head without raising it.

'No, no,' she made an effort to speak, 'don't be afraid for me and for my grief. I know myself: I will cry it out and then I will cry no more. And now, don't interrupt my tears – go away. ... No, wait, please! God is punishing me! Oh, it hurts me – it hurts me awfully – here, near my heart. ...'

Her sobs were renewed.

'And what if the pain doesn't stop,' he said, 'and your health suffers? Such tears are deadly. Olga, my darling, don't cry – forget it all. ...'

'No, let me cry! I am not crying about the future, but about the past,' she brought out with difficulty. 'It has "faded away", it has "gone". ... It isn't I who am crying, but my memories! The summer – the park – do you remember? I'm sorry for our avenue, the lilac. ... It has all grown into my heart: it hurts me to tear it out!' She shook her head in despair and sobbed, repeating: 'Oh, how it hurts – how it hurts!'

'What if you should die?' he suddenly cried in horror. 'Think, Olga – –'

'No,' she interrupted, raising her head and trying to look at him through her tears; 'I have only lately realized that I loved in you what I wanted you to have, what Stolz pointed out to me, what we both invented. I loved the Oblomov that might have been! You are gentle and honest – you are tender like – a dove; you hide your head under your wing – and you want nothing more; you are ready to spend all your life cooing under the roof. ... Well, I am not like that; that isn't enough for me; I want something else, but what it is I don't know! You cannot tell me, you cannot teach me what it is that I want, give it all to me so that I – – and as for tenderness – you can find it anywhere!'

Oblomov's legs gave way under him; he sat down in an arm-chair and wiped his hands and forehead with his handkerchief. It was a cruel thing to say, and it hurt him deeply: it seemed to have scorched him inwardly, while outwardly it was like the breath of ice-cold air. He smiled pitifully and painfully shame-facedly in reply, like a beggar reproached for his nakedness. He sat there with that helpless smile, weak with agitation and resentment; his eyes, from which the light seemed to have gone, said clearly: 'Yes, I am poor, pitiful, abject – hit me, hit me! ...'

Olga suddenly realized how harsh her words were; she rushed to him impetuously.

'Forgive me, my friend!' she said tenderly, with tears in her voice. 'I don't know what I am saying. I am mad! Forget everything. Let us be as before – let everything remain as it was. ...'

'No,' he said, getting up suddenly and rejecting her impulsive offer with a resolute gesture. 'It cannot remain as it was! Don't be upset because you've spoken the truth: I deserve it,' he added dejectedly.

'I am a dreamer, a visionary!' she said; 'I'm an awful character. Why are other women, why is Sonia so happy?' She wept. 'Go away!' she said, making up her mind and twisting her wet handkerchief again. 'I can't stand it. The past is too dear to me.' She again buried her face in her handkerchief, trying to stifle her sobs. 'Why has it all been ruined?' she asked suddenly, raising her head. 'Who laid a curse on you, Ilya? What have you done? You are kind, intelligent, tender, honourable, and – you are going to wrack and ruin! What has ruined you? There is no name for that evil. ...'

'There is,' he said in a hardly audible whisper.

She looked at him questioningly with her eyes full of tears.

'Oblomovitis!' he whispered; then he took her hand, wanted to kiss it and could not; he just pressed it tightly to his lips and hot tears fell on her fingers. He turned round without raising his head or showing her his face, and walked out of the room.

12

GOODNESS only knows where he wandered, what he did the whole day, but he returned home late at night. The landlady was the first to hear him knocking at the gate, and she woke Anisya and Zakhar, telling them that their master had come back.

Oblomov hardly noticed how Zakhar undressed him, took off his boots, and threw over his shoulders his – dressing-gown!

'What's this?' he asked, merely glancing at the dressing-gown.

'The landlady brought it to-day, sir,' said Zakhar. 'She washed and mended your dressing-gown.'

Oblomov remained sitting in the arm-chair. Everything around him had sunk into sleep and darkness. He sat leaning on his hand, without noticing the darkness and without hearing the clock strike. His mind was plunged into a chaos of vague, shapeless thoughts; they scudded along like clouds in the sky, without aim or connexion – he did not catch a single one. His heart was dead: life had ceased there for a time. The return to life and order, to the regular flow of the accumulated vital forces, which had been dammed up, took place slowly. The pressure was very severe, and Oblomov was not conscious of his body, of being tired, of having any needs. He could have lain like a stone for a whole day and night, or walked, or driven, or moved about like a machine. Man becomes resigned to his fate slowly and painfully, in which case his body gradually resumes all its normal functions, or he is crushed by grief, in which case he will rise no more – all depending on the intensity of the grief, and on the man himself. Oblomov did not remember where he was sitting or whether he was sitting at all: he watched the day break mechanically and without being aware of it; he could not tell whether or not he heard the old woman's dry cough, the caretaker chopping wood in the yard, the noise and clatter in the house; he saw and yet did not appear to notice the landlady and Akulina going to the market and the landlady's brother with his paper parcel darting past the fence. Neither the cocks, nor the barking of the dogs, nor the creaking of the gate could rouse him from his stupor. The cups rattled, the *samovar* began to hiss.

At last, soon after nine o'clock, Zakhar opened the door into the study with the tray, kicked the door, as usual, in order to shut it and, as usual, missed it, keeping the tray intact, however – he had grown expert at it from long practice, and, besides, he knew that Anisya was keeping an eye on him from behind the door and that if he dropped something she would at once rush to pick it up and put him to shame. His beard pressed into the tray which he hugged tightly, he reached the bed safely and was about to put the cups on the bedside table and waken his master, when he noticed that the bed had not been slept in and that the master was not in it! He gave a start and a cup flew on to the floor, followed by the sugar-basin. He tried to catch them in the air, the tray swayed, and the other things fell too. He succeeded in keeping only one spoon on the tray.

'What's all this?' he said, watching Anisya pick up lumps of sugar, broken pieces of the cup and the bread. 'Where is the master?'

The master was sitting in the arm-chair, looking terribly ill. Zakhar looked at him open-mouthed.

'Why did you sit in the chair all night, sir, instead of going to bed?' he asked.

Oblomov slowly turned his head, looked vacantly at Zakhar, at the spilt coffee, at the scattered sugar on the carpet.

'And why did you break the cup?' he said, and walked up to the window.

It was snowing heavily, the big flakes thickly covering the ground.

'Snow, snow, snow!' he kept repeating senselessly, looking at the snow which lay in a thick layer on the railings, the trellis fence, and the kitchen-garden. 'It has covered everything!' he whispered desperately, lay down on the bed and sank into a leaden, comfortless sleep.

It was past twelve o'clock when he was wakened by the creak of the landlady's door: a bare arm holding a plate was thrust through the door – on the plate lay a piece of steaming hot pie.

'It's Sunday to-day,' said a tender voice, 'and we've been baking a pie. Won't you have some?'

But he made no answer: he was in a high fever.

PART FOUR

1

A YEAR had passed since Oblomov's illness. The year had brought many changes in different parts of the world: here an insurrection had broken out, there it had been put down; here a world-famous luminary had set, there another one had risen; here the world had solved a new mystery of life, there houses and whole generations had been reduced to ashes. Where the old life lay shattered, the new one, like young verdure, began to show. ...

Though at the house of the widow Pshenitzyn, in Vyborg, days and nights passed peacefully without any sudden violent changes in its monotonous existence, and though the four seasons followed each other as regularly as ever, life did not stand still, but was constantly undergoing a change; but the change was slow and gradual as are the geological changes of our planet: in one place a mountain slowly crumbled away, in another the sea was washing up silt or receding from the shores and forming new land.

Oblomov had recovered. His agent, Zatyorty, had gone to the country and sent the full amount of the money received for the sale of corn, his fares, his living expenses, and his fee being paid out of it. As for the taxes, Zatyorty wrote that it was impossible to collect the money because the peasants were either ruined or had gone away to different places and their whereabouts were unknown – he was making energetic inquiries on the spot. There was no particular hurry so far as the road and the bridges were concerned, since the peasants preferred trudging over the hill and through the ravine to the large village where the market was held, to working on constructing a new road or building bridges. In short, the information and the money received were satisfactory, and, seeing no need for going himself to the country, Oblomov was reassured on that score till the next year.

The agent had also taken steps with regard to the building of the house: having estimated with the help of the provincial architect the quantity of the materials required, he left an order with the bailiff to begin carting timber early in spring and to build a shed for bricks, so that all that remained for Oblomov to do was to arrive in the spring and, with God's blessing, start building. By that time the taxes were to be collected and the estate mortgaged – there would be enough money therefore to cover expenses.

After his illness Oblomov was for a long time gloomy; he sat brooding for hours and sometimes did not answer Zakhar's questions, did not notice his dropping cups on the floor or his failing to dust the table, or, coming in with the pie on feast-days, the landlady would find him in tears. Then gradually dumb indifference took the place of deep grief. Oblomov gazed for hours at the snow falling and forming snowdrifts in the yard and in the street, covering the stacks of logs, the hen-houses, the kennel, the little garden, and the kitchen garden; he watched the posts of the fence being transformed into pyramids of snow and everything around dying and being wrapped in a shroud. He listened for hours to the rattling of the coffee-mill, the barking of the dog and its jumping on the chain, to Zakhar polishing boots, and the measured ticking of the clock. The landlady came into his room as before to ask if he would like to buy something or if he would have something to eat; the landlady's children ran in; he spoke to her with kindly unconcern, set lessons for the children, listened to their reading, and smiled rather listlessly and reluctantly at their childish prattle.

But the mountain gradually crumbled away, the sea receded from the shore or encroached upon it, and Oblomov was gradually resuming his normal life. Summer, autumn, and winter passed dully and listlessly, but Oblomov was again waiting for spring and dreamed about his departure for the country. In March fancy rolls in the shape of larks were baked, and in April the double windows were taken out in his rooms, and he was told that the ice on the Neva had broken up and that spring had come. He walked in the garden. Then vegetables were planted in the kitchen garden; the different feast-days came and went: Whitsuntide, Commemoration Thursday, and the first of May – all these were marked by the traditional birches and wreaths; they had their tea in the copse. At the beginning of summer they began talking in the house about the two great festivals to come: St John's Day, the name-day of the landlady's brother, and St Elijah's Day – Oblomov's name-day; these were the two important dates to bear in mind. When the landlady happened to buy or see in the market an excellent quarter of veal, or whenever her pies turned out to be particularly good, she said: 'Oh, if only I could find such veal or bake such a pie on St John's or St Elijah's Day!' They talked of St Elijah's Friday and the annual outing to the Powder Works, and of the festival at the Smolensk Cemetery at Kolpino. The deep clucking of the broody hen and the chirping of a new generation of chicks were heard under the windows again; chicken pies with fresh mushrooms and freshly salted cucumbers were served at dinner once more; soon strawberries and raspberries appeared on the table. 'Giblets aren't good now,' the landlady told Oblomov. 'Yesterday they asked seventy copecks for two lots of small ones, but there is fresh salmon – we could have cold fish and vegetable soup every day, if you like.' The meals in Mrs Pshenitzyn's house were so excellent not only because Agafya Matveyevna was such a model housewife or because that was her vocation, but also because her brother, Ivan Matveyevich Mukhoyarov, was a great epicure in affairs of gastronomy. He was more than careless about his clothes and linen: he wore a suit for years and was highly annoyed when he had to spend money on a new one; nor did he hang it up carefully, but threw it in a heap in the corner. He changed his underwear, like a labourer, only on Saturdays, but he spared no expense on food. In this he was guided to a certain extent by a principle he had enunciated at the time of his entry into the Civil Service: 'No one can see what's inside my belly and they won't tell tales about it; but a heavy watch-chain, a new frock-coat, and patent-leather boots – all this gives rise to unnecessary talk.' That was why the Pshenitzyns had first-class veal, amber-coloured sturgeon, and white hazel-grouse. Sometimes he went round the market or the shops himself, sniffing the air like a setter, and brought home under his coat the best capon, and he did not grudge four roubles for a turkey. He bought his wine from the wholesaler's and kept it under lock and key; no one ever saw anything but a decanter of vodka infused with black-currant leaves on the table; he drank the wine in his own attic room. When he went fishing with Tarantyev there was always a bottle of excellent Madeira hidden in his coat and when they had tea at the 'tavern', he brought his own rum.

The gradual silting up or raising of the sea-bed and the crumbling away of the mountain affected everybody and, incidentally, Anisya too: the mutual sympathy between Anisya and the landlady had turned into an indissoluble partnership, into one existence. Seeing how interested the landlady was in his affairs, Oblomov proposed to her once as a joke to take full charge of his board and save him from all trouble. Her face lit up with joy; she smiled quite vivaciously. How the field of her activity had widened: two households instead of one, or one – but how big! Besides, she acquired Anisya! The landlady had talked it over with her brother, and the next day everything from Oblomov's kitchen was removed to Mrs Pshenitzyn's; his silver and crockery were put into her sideboard, and Akulina was degraded from being a cook to looking after the poultry and the kitchen garden. Everything was done on a big scale: the buying of sugar, tea, and provisions, the pickling of cucumbers, the preserving of apples and cherries, jam-making – everything now assumed enormous proportions. Agafya Matveyevna seemed to have grown taller, Anisya spread out her arms like an eagle its wings, and everything went full speed ahead.

Oblomov dined with the family at three o'clock, with the exception of the landlady's brother, who dined separately later on, mostly in the kitchen, because he came back very late from the office. Tea and coffee were brought in to Oblomov by the landlady herself and not by Zakhar. The latter dusted the room if he was so disposed, and if he was not Anisya flew in like a whirlwind and, partly with her apron and partly with her bare arm, almost with her nose, flicked and blew away everything in a trice, pulled things straight, set them to rights, and disappeared; or else the landlady herself, when Oblomov went out into the garden, looked into his room, and finding it in disorder, shook her head, and muttering something under her breath, beat up the pillows, examined the pillow-cases, again whispered to herself that they needed changing, took them off, cleaned the windows, looked behind the sofa, and went out.

The gradual silting up of the sea-bed, the crumbling away of the mountain, and the occasional volcanic explosions had taken place mostly in Agafya Matveyevna's life, but no one, least of all herself, was aware of it. It became noticeable only as a result of its manifold, unexpected, and endless consequences.

Why had she not been herself for some time? Why was it that before, if the roast was over-done, the fish boiled too long, the vegetables not put into the soup, she sternly reprimanded Akulina, but with dignity and without losing her temper, and forgot all about it afterwards; but now if something of the kind happened she jumped up from the table, rushed into the kitchen, overwhelmed Akulina with bitter reproaches, and was sulky with Anisya, and the following day made quite sure herself that the vegetables were put into the soup and the fish was not boiled too long. It will be said that she was perhaps ashamed to be shown up before a stranger as incompetent in such a matter as housekeeping on which her vanity and activity were concentrated. Very well. But why was it that before, she could hardly keep her eyes open at eight o'clock in the evening, and after having put the children to bed and seen that the fire had been put out in the kitchen stove, the flues closed, and everything put away, she used to go to bed at nine, and a cannon could not have wakened her till six o'clock in the morning? But now, if Oblomov went to the theatre or stayed a little longer at Ivan Gerasimovich's and was late in coming home, she could not sleep, turned over from side to side, crossed herself, sighed, closed her eyes – but could not fall asleep in spite of everything! The moment there was a knocking in the street, she raised her head and sometimes even jumped out of bed, opened the little ventilating window and listened – was it he? If there was a knock at the gate, she threw on her skirt and rushed to the kitchen, roused Zahkar or Anisya and sent them to open the gate. It will be said perhaps that this merely showed that she was a conscientious housewife who did not like to have any disorder in her house and to have her lodger wait in the street at night till the drunken caretaker heard him and opened the gate and, last but not least, that she was afraid that any prolonged knocking might awaken the children. Very well. But why, when Oblomov fell ill, did she not let anyone into his room? Why did she cover the floor in it with felt and rugs, draw the curtains, and fly into a rage – she who was so kind and gentle – if Vanya or Masha uttered the least shout or laughed loudly? Why did she sit by his bedside all night, not trusting Zakhar and Anisya, without taking her eyes off him, till early Mass, and then, throwing on her coat and writing 'Ilya' in big letters on a piece of paper, run to the church, put the paper on the altar so that a prayer might be offered up for his recovery, and withdrawing to a corner, kneel down and lie for a long time with her face on the ground; then she hurried off to the market, and returning home fearfully, threw a glance at the door and asked Anisya in a whisper: 'Well, how is he?' It will be said that it was nothing more than pity and compassion, which are the predominant elements of a woman's heart. Very well. But why was it that when Oblomov, while convalescing from his illness, was gloomy all winter, hardly spoke to her, did not look into her room, was not interested in what she was doing, did not joke or laugh with her, she grew thin and cold and indifferent to everything: she might be grinding coffee and not know what she was doing, or she would put in such a lot of chicory that no one could drink it, but she could not taste the difference, as though she had no palate. If Akulina did not cook the fish properly and her brother grumbled and left the table, she did not seem to hear anything, just as though she had been turned to stone. Before, no one had ever seen her thoughtful, which, indeed, did not suit her at all, for she was a very active person who never missed anything, but now she sat motionless with the mortar on her knees, just as if she were asleep; then she would suddenly begin pounding with the pestle so loudly that the dog barked, thinking someone was knocking at the gate. But no sooner did Oblomov come to life, no sooner did he begin to smile kindly, no sooner did he start looking at her as before, looking into her room affectionately and joking, than she put on weight again, and she set to work again in her old active, cheerful, and gay manner, but with one little – though significant – difference: in the old days she used to be moving about all day, like a well-constructed machine, smoothly and regularly, she walked with a light step, spoke neither too loud nor too low; she ground coffee, chopped up a sugar loaf, sieved, sat down to her sewing, her needle moving as regularly as a pendulum; then she got up without bustle or fuss, stopped half-way to the kitchen, opened a cupboard, took something out, carried it away – all machine-like. But ever since Oblomov became a member of the family, she pounded and sieved differently. She had almost forgotten her lace. She would start sewing, settling comfortably in a chair, when Oblomov would suddenly shout to Zakhar to fetch his coffee – and in a trice she was in the kitchen, looking round her as keenly as though she were taking aim, seized a spoon, poured three spoonfuls of coffee out against the light to see if it was quite ready and if it had settled, and if there were not any dregs in it or any skin on the cream. If his favourite dish was being cooked, she watched the saucepan, lifted the lid, sniffed, tasted, then seized the pan herself and held it over the fire. If she grated almonds and pounded something for him, she did it with such enthusiasm and such vigour that she was thrown into a perspiration. All her household duties – pounding, ironing, sieving, etc., – had acquired a new vital significance; Oblomov's peace and comfort. Before, she regarded it as her duty; now, it became a delight. She began to live, in her fashion, a full and varied life. But she did not know what was happening to her; she never asked herself the question, but assumed this sweet burden absolutely, without resistance and without being swept off her feet, without trepidation, passion, vague forebodings, languor or the play and music of the nerves. It was as though she had suddenly gone over to another faith and begun professing it without wondering what kind of faith it was, what its dogmas were, but obeying its laws blindly. It seemed to have imposed itself upon her without her knowledge, and she seemed to have treated it as a cloud which she had neither tried to avoid nor run to meet; she fell in love with Oblomov as simply as though she had caught a cold or contracted an incurable fever. She never suspected anything herself: if she had been told, it would have been news to her and she would have smiled and blushed with shame. She accepted her duties towards Oblomov in silence, learned what every shirt of his looked like, counted the holes in his socks, knew with what foot he got out of bed, noticed when he was about to have a stye on his eye, knew what dish he liked best and how many helpings of it he had, whether he was cheerful or bored, whether he slept much or little, as though she had been doing so all her life, without asking herself why she did it or what Oblomov was to her, and why she should take so much trouble. Had she been asked if she loved him, she would again have smiled and said yes, but she would have given the same reply when Oblomov had lived no more than a week at her house. Why had she fallen in love with him and no one else? Why had she married without love and lived without falling in love till she was thirty, when it seemed to have come upon her suddenly? Though love is declared to be a capricious, unaccountable feeling that one contracts like an illness, it has, like everything else, causes and laws of its own. And if these laws have hitherto been so little studied, it is because a man, stricken with love, is hardly in a position to watch with scientific detachment how an impression steals into his soul, how it benumbs his senses as though with sleep, how at first he loses his sight, how and at which moment his pulse and then his heart begin beating faster, how he becomes suddenly compelled to declare his devotion till death, to desire to sacrifice himself, how his 'I' gradually disappears and becomes transformed into 'him' or 'her', how his intellect becomes extraordinarily dull or extraordinarily subtle, how his will is surrendered to that of another, how his head becomes bowed, his knees tremble, how the tears and the fever appear. ...

Agafya Matveyevna had not met many people like Oblomov before, and if she had it was from a distance, and she may have liked them, but they lived in a different sphere and she had no chance of getting to know them more intimately. Oblomov did not walk like her husband, the late Collegiate Secretary Pshenitzyn, with small, quick, business-like steps, he did not write endless documents, he did not shake with fear at being late at the office, he did not look at people as though begging them to saddle him and ride on his back, but he looked at everything and everybody openly and fearlessly, as though expecting them to obey him. His face was not coarse nor ruddy, but white and tender; his hands were hot like her brother's hands – they did not shake, they were not red, but white and small. When he sat down, crossed his legs, leaned his head on his hand, he did it all with such effortless ease, so calmly and so beautifully; he spoke in a way that was different from her brother and Tarantyev and not as her husband used to speak; a great deal of what he said she did not even understand, but she felt that it was clever, excellent, and extraordinary; and even the things she did understand he spoke differently from other people. He wore fine linen, he changed it every day, he washed with scented soap, he cleaned his fingernails – he was all so nice and so clean, there was no need for him to do anything – other people did everything for him: he had Zakhar and 300 other Zakhars! He was a gentleman: he dazzled, he scintillated! And, besides, he was so kind; he walked so softly, his movements were so exquisite; if he touched her hand, it was like velvet, and whenever her husband had touched her, it was like a blow! And he looked and talked so gently, with such kindness. ... She did not think all these things, nor was she consciously aware of it all, but if anyone had tried to analyse and explain the impression made on her mind by Oblomov's coming into her life, he would not be able to give any other explanation.

Oblomov understood what he meant to all of them in the house, from the landlady's brother down to the watchdog, which was now getting three times as many bones as before; but he did not understand how much he meant to them and what an unexpected conquest he had made of his landlady's heart. In her bustling solicitude for his meals, linen, and rooms he saw a manifestation of the main trait of her character he had noticed already during his first visit when Akulina suddenly brought into the room the fluttering cock and the landlady, though embarrassed by the cook's misplaced zeal, managed to tell her not to give the shopkeeper that cock but the grey one. Agafya Matveyevna herself was not only incapable of flirting with Oblomov and revealing to him by some sign what was going on inside her, but, as has already been said, she was never aware of it or understood it herself; she had, in fact, forgotten that a short time ago nothing of the sort had been happening to her, and her love only found expression in her absolute devotion to him. Oblomov was blind to the true nature of her attitude towards him, and he went on thinking that it was her character. Mrs Pshenitzyn's feeling, so normal, natural, and disinterested, remained a mystery to Oblomov, to the people around her, and to herself. It was, indeed, disinterested because she put up a candle in the church and had prayers said for his health because she wanted him to recover, and he knew nothing of it. She had sat by his bedside at night and left it at dawn, and nothing was said about it afterwards. His attitude towards her was much simpler: he saw in Agafya Matveyevna, with her regularly moving elbows, her watchful, solicitous eyes, her perpetual journeys from the cupboard to the kitchen, from the kitchen to the pantry, and from there to the cellar, her thorough knowledge of housekeeping and all home comforts, the embodied ideal of a life of boundless and inviolate repose, the picture of which had been ineradicably imprinted on his mind in childhood, under his father's roof. As in Oblomovka his father, his grandfather, the children, the grandchildren, and the visitors sat or lay about in idle repose, knowing that there were in the house unsleeping eyes that watched over them continually and never-weary hands that sewed their clothes, gave them food and drink, dressed them, put them to bed, and closed their eyes when they were dead, so here, too, Oblomov, sitting motionless on the sofa, saw something nimble and lively moving for his benefit, and that if the sun should not rise to-morrow, whirlwinds hide the sky, a hurricane blow from one end of the earth to the other, his soup and roast would be on his table, his linen would be fresh and clean, the cobwebs would be brushed off the walls, and he would not even know how it was all done; that before he had taken trouble to think what he would like, his wish would be divined and it would be put before him, not lazily and rudely by Zakhar's dirty hands, but with a cheerful and gentle glance, a smile of deep devotion, white hands, and bare elbows.

He was getting more and more friendly with his landlady every day: the thought of love never entered his head, that is, the sort of love he had recently experienced as if it were some sort of small-pox, measles, or fever, and which he shuddered at every time he recalled it. He was getting closer to Agafya Matveyevna just as one does to a fire which makes one feel warmer and which one cannot love. After dinner he gladly stayed in her room and smoked a pipe, watching her put away the silver in the dresser, take out the cups, pour out the coffee, and having washed and wiped one cup with meticulous care, pour out his coffee first of all, hand it to him, and look to see if he liked it. He gladly rested his eyes on her plump neck and round elbows, when the door of her room was opened, and even when it was not opened for a long time, he gently opened it himself with a foot, and joked with her and played with her children. But he did not miss her if the morning passed and he did not see her; instead of remaining with her after dinner, he often went to his room for two hours' sleep; but he knew that as soon as he woke his tea would be ready, nay, that it would be ready at the very moment he awoke. And, above all, it was all done without any fuss: he had no swelling in his heart, he never once had to ask himself anxiously whether he would see his landlady or not, what she would think, what he would say to her, how to reply to her question, how she would look at him – it was nothing, nothing of the kind. There were no yearnings, no sleepless nights, no sweet or bitter tears. He sat smoking, watching her sewing; sometimes he said something and sometimes he didn't, and yet he felt at peace with himself, he did not want anything, he did not feel like going anywhere, just as though everything he needed were there. Agafya Matveyevna made no demands on him, nor did she coax him to do anything. Neither did he have any ambitious desires or impulses, nor any aspirations for performing heroic deeds, nor any agonizing qualms of conscience about the way he was wasting his time and destroying his powers, about not doing anything, neither good nor evil, about being idle and vegetating and not living. It was as though some unseen power had placed him like a precious plant in the shade as a protection from the heat and under a roof to shelter him from the rain, and looked after him and cherished him.

'How deftly you move your needle past your nose, Agafya Matveyevna,' said Oblomov. 'You pick up the thread so quickly from underneath that I'm really afraid you might stitch your nose to your skirt.'

She smiled. 'Let me first finish stitching this seam,' she said, almost as though she were speaking to herself, 'and then we'll have supper.'

'And what is there for supper?'

'*Sauerkraut* and salmon,' she said. 'I'm afraid there isn't any sturgeon to be had anywhere. I've been to all the shops, and my brother asked for it, but there isn't any. Of course, if a live sturgeon is caught – a merchant from the Coaching Arcade had ordered one – I am promised a piece of it. Then there is veal and fried buckwheat-meal.'

'That's excellent! How nice of you to have remembered! I only hope Anisya won't forget.'

'And what am I here for? Can you hear it sizzling?' she replied, opening the kitchen door a little. 'It's being fried already!'

She finished sewing, bit off the thread, folded her work, and carried it to her bedroom.

And thus he drew nearer to her as to a warm fire, and once he drew very near, so that there was nearly a conflagration or, at any rate, a sudden blaze.

He was pacing his room and, turning to the landlady's door, he saw that her elbows were quite amazingly active.

'Always busy!' he said, going in to her. 'What is this?'

'I'm grinding cinnamon,' she replied, gazing into the mortar as though it were an abyss and clattering away mercilessly with the pestle.

'And what if I won't let you?' he asked, taking hold of her elbows and preventing her from pounding.

'Please, let me go! I must pound some sugar and pour out some wine for the pudding.'

He was still holding her by the elbows, and his face was close to the nape of her neck.

'Tell me what if I – fell in love with you?'

She smiled.

'Would you love me?' he asked again.

'Why not? God commanded us to love everyone.'

'And what if I kissed you?' he whispered, bending down so that his breath burnt her cheek.

'It isn't Easter week,' she said with a smile.

'Kiss me, please!'

'If, God willing, we live till Easter, we'll kiss each other then,' she said, without being surprised, alarmed, or embarrassed, but standing straight and still like a horse when its collar is put on.

He kissed her lightly on the neck.

'Please be careful, or I'll spill the cinnamon and there won't be any left for the pastry,' she observed.

'No matter,' he replied.

'Have you got another stain on your dressing-gown?' she asked solicitously, taking hold of the skirt of the dressing-gown.

'I believe it's oil.' She sniffed the stain. 'Where did you get it? It didn't drip from the icon lamp, did it?'

'I'm afraid I don't know where I can have acquired it.'

'You must have caught it in the door,' Agafya Matveyevna suddenly guessed. 'The hinges were greased yesterday – they all creaked. Take it off and let me have it at once, I'll take it out and wash the place: there will be nothing showing to-morrow.'

'Kind Agafya Matveyevna,' said Oblomov, lazily throwing the dressing-gown off his shoulders. 'Do you know what? Let's go and live in the country: that's the place for housekeeping! You've got everything there: mushrooms, fruit, jam, the poultry yard, the dairy – –'

'But why go there?' she concluded with a sigh. 'I've been born here, I've lived here all my life, and here I ought to die.'

He gazed at her with mild excitement, but his eyes did not shine or fill with tears, his spirit did not long for the heights or aspire to perform deeds of heroism. All he wanted was to sit on the sofa without taking his eyes off her elbows.

2

ST JOHN'S DAY was a great festive occasion. Ivan Matveyevich did not go to the office on the day before, he rushed about the town, each time bringing home a bag or a basket. Agafya Matveyevna had lived solely on coffee for three days, and only Oblomov had had a three-course dinner, the rest of the household living on anything that was available at any given hour of the day. On the eve of the great day Anisya did not go to bed at all. Zakhar alone slept enough for the two of them, regarding all these preparations almost with contempt.

'In Oblomovka,' he said to the two chefs who had been invited from the count's kitchen, 'we had such dinners cooked every holiday. There were five different kinds of sweet and more sauces than you could count! And they would be eating all day and the next day, too, and we would eat the left-overs for five days. And just as we would finish, new visitors would arrive, and the whole thing started all over again – and here it's only once a year!'

At dinner he served Oblomov first and refused point-blank to serve some gentleman with a large cross round his neck.

'Our master is a gentleman born and bred,' he said proudly, 'and these guests are a common lot!'

Tarantyev, who sat at the end of the table, he would not serve at all, or just threw as much food on the plate as he fancied! All Ivan Matveyevich's colleagues, about thirty of them, were present. An enormous trout, stuffed chickens, quail, ice-cream, and excellent wine – it was a feast worthy of the great annual occasion. At the end of it the guests embraced each other, praised up to the skies their host's good taste, and then sat down to play cards. Ivan Matveyevich bowed and thanked them, declaring that for the great pleasure of giving a dinner to his dear guests he had not been sorry to sacrifice a third of his yearly salary. The guests left towards morning, some in carriages and some on foot, but all hardly capable of standing up straight, and everything in the house grew quiet again until St Elijah's Day, Oblomov's name-day.

On that day the only people Oblomov had invited to his name-day dinner were Ivan Gerasimovich and Alexeyev, the silent and mild-mannered man who had, at the beginning of this story, invited Oblomov to accompany him to the First of May festival. Oblomov was determined not to be outshone by Ivan Matveyevich, and he did his best to impress his guests by the delicacy and daintiness of the dishes unknown in that part of the town. Instead of a rich pie there were pasties stuffed with air; oysters were served before soup; there were chickens in curling-papers stuffed with truffles, choice cuts of meat, the finest vegetables, English soup. In the middle of the table there was an enormous pineapple, surrounded by peaches, apricots, and cherries. There were flowers in vases on the table.

No sooner had they started on the soup and Tarantyev had cursed the pasties and the cook for the stupid notion of having no stuffing in them, than the dog began jumping on the chain and barking desperately. A carriage drove into the yard and somone asked for Oblomov. They all gaped in astonishment.

'Someone of my last year's friends must have remembered my name-day,' said Oblomov. 'Tell them I am not at home – not at home!' he said in a loud whisper to Zakhar.

They were having dinner in the summer-house in the garden. Zakhar rushed off to carry out his master's order and ran into Stolz on the path.

'Andrey Ivanych,' he wheezed joyfully.

'Andrey!' Oblomov addressed him in a loud voice and ran to embrace him.

'I'm just in time for dinner, I see,' said Stolz. 'May I join you? I'm famished. It took me hours to find you.'

'Come along, come along, sit down!' Oblomov said fussily, making him sit down next to him.

At Stolz's appearance, Tarantyev was the first to jump quickly over the fence into the kitchen garden; he was followed by Ivan Matveyevich, who hid behind the summer-house and then disappeared into his attic. The landlady also got up from her seat.

'I'm afraid I've disturbed you,' said Stolz, jumping up.

'Where are you off to? What for?' Oblomov shouted. 'Ivan Matveyevich! Mikhey Andreyich!'

He made the landlady sit down again, but he could not recall the landlady's brother or Tarantyev.

'Where have you sprung from? Are you staying here long?' Oblomov began firing questions at him.

Stolz had come for a fortnight on business and was then going to the country, to Kiev and all sorts of other places. He spoke little at table, but ate a lot; he evidently was really hungry. The others, it goes without saying, ate in silence. After dinner, when everything had been cleared away, Oblomov asked for champagne and soda-water to be left in the summer-house and remained alone with Stolz. They did not speak for a time. Stolz looked at Oblomov long and intently.

'Well, Ilya?' he said at last, but in so stern and questioning a voice that Oblomov dropped his eyes and made no answer.

'So that it's "never"?'

'What is "never"?' asked Oblomov, as though he did not understand.

'Have you forgotten? "Now or never!"'

'I'm not the same now – as I was then, Andrey,' he said at last. 'My affairs are in order, thank Heaven. I am not lying about idly, my plan is almost finished, I subscribe to the journals, I've read almost all the books you left. ...'

'But why didn't you go abroad?' asked Stolz.

'I was prevented from going abroad by – –' he stopped short.

'Olga?' said Stolz, looking significantly at him.

Oblomov flushed.

'What? Have you heard? Where is she now?' he asked quickly, glancing at Stolz.

Stolz went on looking at him without replying, and he seemed to look deep into his soul.

'I heard she'd gone abroad with her aunt,' said Oblomov, 'soon after – –'

'– she had realized her mistake,' Stolz finished the sentence for him.

'Why, do you know?' Oblomov said, overcome with confusion.

'Everything,' said Stolz, 'even about the spray of lilac. And aren't you ashamed, Ilya? Don't you feel sorry? Aren't you consumed with remorse and regret?'

'Don't speak of it – don't remind me of it!' Oblomov interrupted him hurriedly. 'I fell dangerously ill when I saw what a gulf lay between her and me, when I realized that I was not worthy of her. ... Oh, Andrey, if you love me, don't torture me, don't remind me of her. I pointed out her mistake to her long ago, but she refused to believe me – you see, I really am not very much to blame.'

'I am not blaming you, Ilya,' Stolz went on in a gentle and friendly tone of voice. 'I have read your letter. I am to blame most of all, then she, and you least of all.'

'How is she now?' Oblomov asked timidly.

'She? Why, she is overcome with grief, sheds floods of tears, and curses you. ...'

Alarm, sympathy, horror, remorse appeared on Oblomov's face with every word Stolz uttered.

'What are you saying, Andrey?' he said, getting up from his seat. 'Let us go to her at once, for God's sake! I'll go down on my knees and beg her to forgive me. ...'

'Sit still!' Stolz interrupted, laughing. 'She's in high spirits. Why, I believe she's really happy! She asked me to give you her regards. She wanted to write to you, but I advised her not to. I told her it might upset you.'

'Well, thank God,' Oblomov said, almost with tears. 'I'm so glad, Andrey! Let me embrace you and let's drink her health.'

They each drank a glass of champagne.

'But where is she now?'

'In Switzerland. In the autumn she and her aunt will go to her estate. That's why I am here now: I must get it all settled in the courts. The baron did not finish the business: he took it into his head to propose to Olga.'

'Did he? So it's true, is it?' said Oblomov. 'Well, and what did she do?'

'She refused him, naturally. He was hurt and left, and now I have to finish the business! It will be all settled next week. Well, and what about you? Why have you buried yourself in this God-forsaken hole?'

882

'It's peaceful here, Andrey. So quiet, no one interferes with you – –'

'In what?'

'In my work. ...'

'Why, this is Oblomovka all over again, only much worse,' said Stolz, looking round. 'Let's go to the country, Ilya.'

'To the country – well, why not? They'll be soon beginning to build my new house there. Only don't rush me, Andrey. Let me think it over first.'

'Again think it over! I know the way you think things over: just as you thought it over about going abroad two years ago. Let's go next week.'

'Next week? Why so suddenly?' Oblomov defended himself. 'You're ready for the journey, but I have to make ready. All my things are here. I can't leave them all, can I? I have nothing for the journey.'

'But you want nothing. What do you want? Tell me!'

Oblomov made no answer.

'I'm not feeling too well, Andrey,' he said. 'I am short of breath, I've been having styes again, first on one eye and then on the other, and my legs, too, are beginning to swell. And sometimes when I am fast asleep at night someone seems to strike me suddenly on the head or across the back, so that I jump up. ...'

'Listen, Ilya, I tell you seriously, you must change your way of life if you don't want to get dropsy or have a stroke. You can have no more hopes for a better future: if an angel like Olga could not carry you on her wings out of the bog in which you are stuck, I can do nothing. But to choose a small field of activity, put your small estate in order, settle the affairs of your peasants, build, plant – all this you can and must do. ... I won't leave you alone. Now it is not only your wishes I am carrying out, but also Olga's will: she is anxious – do you hear? – that you should not die altogether, that you should not bury yourself alive, and I promised her to dig you out of your grave.'

'She has not forgotten me yet!' Oblomov cried with emotion. 'Do I deserve it?'

'No, she hasn't forgotten you and, if you ask me, she never will: she is not that kind of a woman. She expects you to pay her a visit on her estate.'

'Not now, for goodness' sake, not now, Andrey! Let me forget. Oh, here there's still – –'

He pointed to his heart.

'What is there still? Not love, surely?' Stolz asked.

'No, shame and grief!' Oblomov replied with a sigh.

'All right, in that case let's go to your estate. You must get on with your building now. It's summer and precious time is being wasted.'

'No, I have an agent. He is there now, and I can go later when I am ready and have thought it over.'

He began boasting to Stolz how excellently he had settled his affairs without stirring from the house. His agent was collecting information about the runaway peasants and selling his corn at a good price. He had already sent him 1,500 roubles, and he would probably collect and send him the peasants' tax this year.

Stolz gasped with amazement at this tale.

'Why, you've been robbed all round!' he said. 'Fifteen hundred from three hundred peasants! Who's your agent? What kind of a man is he?'

'More than fifteen hundred,' Oblomov corrected him. 'I paid him his fee out of the money he received for the sale of corn.'

'How much?'

'I'm afraid I don't remember. But I'll show you. I have his accounts somewhere.'

'Well, Ilya, you really are dead – you're done for!' he concluded. 'Get dressed and come along to my place.'

Oblomov began to object, but Stolz took him away almost by force, wrote out a deed of trust in his own name, made Oblomov sign it, and told him that he would take Oblomovka on lease until Oblomov himself came to the country and got accustomed to farming.

'You will be getting three times as much,' he said, 'only I shan't be your tenant for long – I have my own affairs to manage. Let us go to the country now, or you can come after me. I shall be at Olga's estate: it's about three hundred miles from yours. I'll call at your place, too. Get rid of your agent, make all the necessary arrangements, and then you must come yourself. I won't leave you in peace.'

Oblomov sighed. 'Life!' he said.

'What about life?'

'It keeps disturbing you. Gives you no peace! I wish I could lie down and go to sleep – for ever!'

'What you mean is that you would like to put out the light and remain in darkness! Fine sort of life! Oh, Ilya, why don't you at least indulge in a little philosophy? Life will flash by like an instant, and you'd like to lie down and go to sleep! Let the flame go on burning! Oh, if only I could live for two or three hundred years!' he concluded. 'How much one could do then!'

'You are quite a different matter, Andrey!' replied Oblomov. 'You have wings: you don't live, you fly. You have gifts, ambition. You're not fat. You don't suffer from styes. You're not overcome by constant doubts. You're differently made, somehow.'

'Don't talk rubbish! Man has been created to arrange his own life and even to change his own nature, and you've grown a big belly and think that nature has sent you this burden! You had wings once, but you took them off.'

'Wings? Where are they?' Oblomov said gloomily. 'I don't know how to do anything.'

'You mean you don't want to know,' Stolz interrupted. 'A man who can't do something doesn't exist, I assure you.'

'Well, I can't,' said Oblomov.

'To listen to you one would think you couldn't write an official letter to the town council or a letter to your landlord, but you wrote a letter to Olga, didn't you? You didn't mix up *who* and *which* in it, did you? And you found excellent note-paper and ink from the English shop, and your handwriting, too, was legible, wasn't it?'

Oblomov blushed.

'When you needed it, the ideas and the language in which to express them came of themselves. Good enough for any novel! But when you don't need it, then you don't know how to do it, and your eyes do not see and your hands are too weak! You lost your ability for doing things in your childhood, in Oblomovka among your aunts and nannies. It all began with your inability to put on your socks and ended by your inability to live.'

'All this may be true, Andrey, but I'm afraid it can't be helped – what's done is done!' Oblomov said with a sigh, decisively.

'What do you mean – it's done!' Stolz retorted angrily. 'What nonsense! Listen to me and do what I tell you and it won't be done!'

But Stolz left for the country alone, and Oblomov stayed behind, promising to go there in the autumn.

'What shall I tell Olga?' Stolz asked Oblomov before he left.

Oblomov bowed his head and looked sad; then he sighed.

'Don't mention me to her,' he said at last, looking embarrassed. 'Tell her you've not seen or heard of me.'

'She won't believe it.'

'Well, tell her I'm done for, dead, lost. ...'

'She will cry and won't be comforted for a long time: why upset her?'

Oblomov pondered, greatly moved. His eyes were moist.

'Very well, then,' Stolz concluded, 'I'll tell her a lie and say that you are living on your memories of her and are looking for some serious aim in life. Note, please, that life itself and work constitute the aim of life – not woman; that was the mistake you both made. How pleased she will be!'

They said good-bye.

3

THE day after St Elijah's Day, Tarantyev and Ivan Matveyevich met again at the tavern in the evening.

'Tea!' Ivan Matveyevich gave his order gloomily, and when the waiter had brought tea and a bottle of rum he thrust the bottle back vexatiously. 'This isn't rum, it's more like old nails,' he said, and taking out his own bottle from the pocket of his overcoat, he uncorked it and let the waiter sniff at it. 'Don't you offer me any of your rum again,' he observed.

'Well, old man,' he said after the waiter had gone. 'Things don't look very bright, do they?'

'No,' Tarantyev replied furiously; 'the devil must have brought him! What a rogue that German is! Destroyed the deed of trust and got the estate on a lease! It's unheard of! He'll fleece the poor little sheep, I warrant you.'

'If he knows his business, old man, then I'm afraid there may be trouble. When he finds out that the taxes have been collected and it was we who received the money, he may take criminal proceedings against us.'

'Criminal proceedings, indeed! You're becoming scared, old man! It isn't the first time Zatyorty has put his paw in a land-owner's pocket. He knows how to steer clear of the law. You don't suppose he gives receipts to the peasants, do you? You can be sure there are no strangers about when he takes the money. The German will get into a temper and shout, and that will be the end of it. Criminal proceedings, my foot!'

'Do you think so?' Ivan Matveyevich said, brightening up. 'Well, in that case let's have a drink!'

He poured out some more rum for himself and Tarantyev.

'Well,' he said comfortingly, 'things are not as bad as they sometimes seem, especially after a drink.'

'In the meantime, old man,' Tarantyev went on, 'you'd better do this: make out some bills – any you like – for fuel or cabbage or whatever you please, since Oblomov has transferred the management of his household to your sister, and show it to him. And when Zatyorty arrives we shall say that all the taxes he collected went to meet the expenses.'

'But what if he should take the bills and show them to the German? The German will tot them up and then he might – –'

'Rubbish! He'll put them away somewhere, and the devil himself won't find them. By the time the German comes back, the whole thing will be forgotten.'

'Do you think so? Let's have a drink, old man,' said Ivan Matveyevich, pouring out a glass. 'It's a pity to dilute such fine stuff with tea. Have a sniff: three roubles. What do you say to a fine dish of salted cabbage soup and fish?'

'Not a bad idea.'

'Hey, waiter!'

'What a rogue,' Tarantyev began furiously again. 'Let me rent it, he says. Why, such a thing would never occur to us Russians! It's the sort of thing they do in Germany. Farms and leaseholds – it's the sort of thing they go in for there. You wait, he'll swindle him out of all his money by making him invest it in some shares.'

'Shares?' asked Ivan Matveyevich. 'What are they? I'm afraid I don't quite understand.'

'It's a German invention!' said Tarantyev spitefully. 'Some swindler, for instance, gets an idea of building fireproof houses and undertakes to build a town: he needs money, of course, so he starts selling papers at, say, five hundred roubles each, and a crowd of blockheads buy them and sell them to each other. If the business is reported to be doing well, the bits of paper rise in price; if it's doing badly, the whole thing goes bust. All you've got left is worthless bits of paper. Where is the town? you ask. Oh, they say, it's burnt down, or, there wasn't enough capital to finish building it, and the inventor has in the meantime run off with your money. That's what shares are! And the German will drag him into it, mark my words. It's a wonder he hasn't done it already. I have stood in the way, you see. Done all I could to save a neighbour from ruin!'

'Well, that's finished and done with, I'm afraid. We shan't

get any more taxes from Oblomovka,' Ivan Matveyevich said, as he got slightly drunk.

'Oh, to hell with him, old man! You've got plenty of money, haven't you?' Tarantyev replied, also slightly befuddled. 'Got an inexhaustible source – keep drawing from it and don't let up. Let's have a drink!'

'Not much of a source, old man. All you collect is one- and three-rouble notes all your life – –'

'But you've been collecting it for twenty years, old man, so what have you got to grumble about?'

'Twenty years, did you say?' Ivan Matveyevich answered thickly. 'You've forgotten that I've only been secretary for ten years. Before that there were only ten- and twenty-copeck pieces jingling in my pocket, and sometimes, I'm ashamed to say, I had to take a few coppers. What an awful life! Oh, old man, there are lucky people in the world who for a single word they whisper in someone's ear or a line they dictate, or simply for signing their name on a piece of paper, suddenly get such a swelling in their pocket as though a pillow had been placed there, so that they could sleep on it. Oh,' he cried dreamily, getting more and more drunk, 'if only I could do things like that! Never be seen by petitioners, who dare not come near me. Get into my carriage and shout, "To the club!" and at the club important chaps wearing stars shake hands with me. I play cards, but not for five-copeck stakes! And the dinners – the dinners I have. I'd be ashamed even to mention cabbage soup with fish – make a wry face with disgust. Spring chickens in winter; aye, get it specially ordered, I would, and wild strawberries in April! At home my wife would be wearing real lace, my children would have a governess, smartly dressed, their hair beautifully brushed. Oh dear, old man, there is a paradise, but our sins keep us out of it. Let's have a drink! Here they are, bringing our cabbage soup!'

'Don't grumble, old man; you've got plenty of money – plenty of money,' said Tarantyev, quite tipsy by now, with bloodshot eyes. 'Thirty-five thousand in silver – that's no joke, is it?'

'Quiet, quiet, old man,' Ivan Matveyevich interrupted. 'What about it? It's only thirty-five thousand. Think how long it will take me to make it up to fifty! And, besides, you won't be admitted to paradise even with fifty. If I get married, I'll have to live very carefully, count every rouble, forget about Jamaica rum – what sort of life is that?'

'But you must admit, old man, it's a comfortable sort of life –

a rouble from one fellow, two from another, and by the end of the day you've put away seven roubles. No bother, no one the wiser, no stigma, no smoke. While if you happen to put your name to some big affair once, you sometimes have to spend your whole life trying painfully to scratch it out. No, old man, you mustn't be unfair to yourself.'

Ivan Matveyevich was not listening; he had been thinking of something for some time.

'Listen, old man,' he suddenly began, opening his eyes wide and so pleased about something that he seemed to have become sober; 'but – no! I'm afraid I'd better not tell you – can't let such a glorious little bird out of my head – it's a real treasure, it is. ... Let's have a drink, old man, let's have a drink quick!'

'I won't drink before you tell me,' said Tarantyev, pushing away his glass.

'It's a very important business, old man,' Ivan Matveyevich whispered, glancing at the door.

'Well?' Tarantyev asked impatiently.

'It's a real find. You see, old man, it's the same as putting your name to a big affair, upon my word, it is!'

'What is it, for goodness' sake? Won't you tell me?'

'It's a gift – a gift!'

'Well?' Tarantyev egged him on.

'Wait a bit, I must think it over. Yes, it's as safe as houses, it's perfectly legal. All right, old man, I'll tell, but only because I need you; I couldn't very well carry it out without you. Otherwise – God's my witness – I shouldn't have told you for anything in the world. It's not the sort of thing you can very well confide to another soul.'

'Am I a stranger to you, old man? I believe I can claim to have been useful to you many times, as a witness and for making copies – remember? What a swine you are!'

'Look here, my dear fellow, hold your tongue, will you? I know the sort of chap you are – always letting the cat out of the bag!'

'Who the hell can hear us here?' Tarantyev said with annoyance. 'Have I ever forgotten myself? Why keep me in suspense? Come on, out with it!'

'Now, listen: Oblomov is a bit of a coward, and he has no idea how things are done. He lost his head over that agreement, and he did not know what to do with the deed of trust when he got it; he doesn't even remember the amount of the tax the peasants have to pay him. He told me himself that he did not know anything.'

'Well?' Tarantyev cried impatiently.

'Well, he's been going to my sister's rooms much too often. The other day he sat there till after midnight, and when he met me in the hall he pretended not to see me. So we'll just wait and see what's going to happen and – you'll have to take him aside and have a talk to him about it. Tell him that it isn't nice to bring dishonour on a family, that she is a widow, that people are talking about it, and that she'll find it impossible to get married again, that she had a proposal of marriage from a rich merchant, but now that he had heard that Oblomov was spend- the evenings with her, he is no longer anxious to carry on with his suit. ...'

'Well, what will happen is that he will get frightened, take to his bed and sigh, turning from side to side like a hog – that's all,' said Tarantyev. 'What do we get out of it? Where's your gift?'

'Don't be an ass! You tell him that I am going to lodge a complaint against him, that I have had him watched, that I have witnesses. ...'

'Well?'

'Well, if he gets thoroughly frightened, you can tell him that the whole thing can be settled in a friendly way by his sacrificing a small sum.'

'But where will he get the money?' asked Tarantyev. 'If he is frightened, he'll promise anything you like, even ten thousand.'

'You just give me a wink, I'll have an IOU ready – in my sister's name, to the effect that he, Oblomov, had borrowed ten thousand from widow So-and-so, to be repaid within – and so on.'

'What's the use of that, old man? I don't understand: the money will go to your sister and her children. What do we get out of it?'

'And my sister will give me an IOU for the same amount. I'll make her sign it.'

'But what if she doesn't? What if she refuses?'

'Who? My sister?'

And Ivan Matveyevich burst into a shrill laugh.

'She'll sign, old man, don't you worry. She'd sign her own death warrant without asking what it was. She'll just smile. She'll put down her name, Agafya Pshenitzyn, write it across the page crookedly, and never know what she has signed. You see, you and I will have nothing to do with it at all. My sister will have a claim against the Collegiate Secretary Oblomov, and I against the widow of the Collegiate Secretary Pshenitzyn. Let the German fly into a temper – it's all perfectly legal!' he said, raising his trembling hands. 'Let's have a drink, old man!'

'Perfectly legal!' Tarantyev cried delightedly. 'Let's have a drink!'

'And if it comes off without a hitch, we can have another try in two years' time. It's perfectly legal!'

'Perfectly legal!' Tarantyev cried again, nodding approvingly. 'Let's have another!'

'Another? I don't mind if I do.'

And they drank.

'The only thing I'm afraid of,' said Ivan Matveyevich, 'is that Oblomov may refuse and write first to the German. If he does that, we're sunk! We can't bring an action against him: she's a widow, after all, not a spinster.'

'Write?' said Tarantyev. 'Of course he'll write – in two years' time. And if he refuses, I'll tell him off properly!'

'No, no, heaven forbid! You'll spoil it all, old man. He'd say we forced him, he might even mention blows – and that would be a criminal offence. No, that won't do. What we could do, though, is to have a friendly collation with him first – he's very partial to currant vodka. As soon as he gets a little tipsy, you give me the wink and I'll come in with the IOU. He won't even look at the sum, and sign as he signed the agreement, and after it has been witnessed at the notary's it will be too late for him to do anything. Besides, a gentleman like him will be ashamed to admit that he signed it when he was not sober. It's perfectly legal!'

'Perfectly legal!' Tarantyev repeated.

'Let his heirs have Oblomovka then!'

'Aye, let them! Let's have a drink, old man!'

'To the health of all blockheads!' said Ivan Matveyevich. They drank.

4

WE must now go back a little to the time before Stolz's arrival on Oblomov's name-day and to another place, far from Vyborg. There the reader will meet people he knows, about whom Stolz did not tell Oblomov all he knew, either for some special reasons of his own or, perhaps, because Oblomov did not ask all there was to ask – also, no doubt, for special reasons of his own.

One day Stolz was walking down a boulevard in Paris, glancing absent-mindedly at the passers-by and the shop signboards without pausing to look at anything in particular. He had not had any letters from Russia for some time, neither from Kiev, nor from Odessa, nor from Petersburg. He was bored and, having posted three more letters, he was on his way home. Suddenly his eyes lighted on something with amazement and then assumed their usual expression. Two ladies crossed the boulevard and went into a shop. 'No, it can't be,' he thought. 'What an idea! I'd have known about it! It can't be them.' All the same, he went up to the shop window and examined the ladies through the glass. 'Can't see a thing! They are standing with their backs to the windows!' Stolz went into the shop and asked for something. One of the ladies turned to the light and he recognized Olga Ilyinsky – and did not recognize her! He was about to rush up to her, but stopped and began watching her narrowly. Good Lord, what a change! It was she and not she. The features were the same as hers, but she was pale, her eyes seemed a little hollow, there was no childish smile on her lips, no naïvety, no placidity. Some grave, sorrowful thought was hovering over her eyebrows, and her eyes said a great deal they had not known and had not said before. She did not look as she used to – frankly, calmly, and serenely – a cloud of sorrow or perplexity lay over her face.

He went up to her. Her eyebrows contracted a little; for a moment she looked at him in bewilderment, then she recognized him; her eyebrows parted and lay symmetrically, and her eyes shone with the light of a calm and deep, not an impulsive, joy. A brother would be happy if his favourite sister had been as glad to see him.

'Goodness, is it you?' she cried in a voice that penetrated to the very soul and that was joyful to the point of ecstasy.

Her aunt turned round quickly, and all three of them began speaking at once. He reproached them for not having written to him, and they made excuses. They had arrived in Paris only two days before and had been looking for him everywhere. At one address they were told that he had gone to Lyons, and they did not know what to do.

'But what made you come? And not a word to me!' he reproached them.

'We made up our minds so quickly,' said Olga's aunt, 'that we didn't want to write to you. Olga wanted to give you a surprise.'

He glanced at Olga: her face did not confirm her aunt's words. He looked at her more closely, but she was impervious, inaccessible to his scrutiny.

'What is the matter with her?' Stolz thought. 'I used to guess her thoughts at once, but now – what a change!'

'How you have grown up, Olga Sergeyevna!' he said aloud. 'I don't recognize you. And it's scarcely a year since we met. What have you been doing? Tell me!'

'Oh, nothing special,' she said, examining some material.

'How is your singing?' Stolz asked, continuing to study his new Olga and trying to read the unfamiliar expression on her face; but her expression flashed and disappeared like lightning.

'I haven't sung for ages,' she said in a casual tone of voice. 'For two months or more.'

'And how is Oblomov?' he asked suddenly. 'Is he alive? Does he write to you?'

At this point Olga might have betrayed her secret had not her aunt come to her rescue.

'Just fancy,' she said, walking out of the shop, 'he used to visit us every day, then he suddenly vanished. After we had made our arrangements for going abroad, I sent a message to him, but was told that he was ill and received no one; so we did not see him again.'

'Didn't you know anything, either?' Stolz asked Olga solicitously.

Olga was examining through her lorgnette a carriage that was driving past.

'He really had fallen ill,' she said, looking with feigned attention at the carriage. 'Look, Auntie, it's our travelling companions that have just driven past.'

'No, you must give me a full account of my Ilya,' Stolz insisted. 'What have you done to him? Why haven't you brought him with you?'

'*Mais ma tante vient de dire*,' she said.

'He's frightfully lazy,' the aunt observed, 'and so shy that as soon as three or four visitors arrived he went home. Just fancy, he booked a seat at the opera for the season and did not hear half the operas!'

'He did not hear Rubini,' Olga added.

Stolz shook his head and sighed.

'How is it you made up your minds to go abroad? Is it for long? What gave you the idea so suddenly?' Stolz asked.

'It's for her,' the aunt said, pointing to Olga. 'On the doctor's advice. Petersburg was having a distinctly bad effect on her health, and we went away for the winter, but haven't decided yet where to spend it – at Nice or in Switzerland.'

'Yes, you have certainly changed a lot,' Stolz said, looking closely at Olga and scrutinizing every line on her face.

The Ilyinskys spent six months in Paris; Stolz was their daily and only companion and guide. Olga's health began perceptibly to improve; her brooding gave way to calm and indifference, outwardly at any rate. It was impossible to say what was going on inside her, but she gradually became as friendly to Stolz as before, though she no longer burst into her former loud, child-like, silvery laughter, but only smiled with restraint when Stolz tried to amuse her. Sometimes she seemed to be annoyed at not being able to laugh. He at once realized that she was not to be amused any more: she often listened to some amusing sally of his with a frown between her unsymmetrically-lying eyebrows, looking silently at him, as though reproaching him for his frivolity, or impatient with him; or instead of replying to his joke, she would suddenly ask him some serious question and follow it up with so insistent a look that he felt ashamed of his insipid, empty talk. At times she seemed so weary of the daily senseless rushing about and chatter that Stolz had suddenly to discuss some subject which he seldom and reluctantly discussed with women. How much mental resourcefulness and thought he had to spend so that Olga's deep questioning eyes should grow bright and calm and should not seek for some answer from someone else. How upset he was when, as a result of a careless explanation, her look became dry and stern, her eyebrows contracted, and a shadow of silent but profound dissatisfaction fell over her face. And he had to spend the next two or three days in applying all the subtlety and even cunning of which he was capable, all his fervour and skill in dealing with women, in order to call forth, little by little and not without difficulty, a glimmer of serenity on her face and the gentleness of reconciliation in her eyes and her smile. Sometimes he returned home in the evening worn out by this struggle, and he was happy when he emerged from it victorious.

'Dear me, how mature she has grown! How this little girl has developed! Who was her teacher? Where did she take her lessons in life? From the baron? But he is so smooth you can learn nothing from his exquisitely turned phrases! Not from Ilya, surely?'

He could not understand Olga, and he ran to her again the next day; but this time he read her expression cautiously and with fear; he often felt baffled, and it was only his intelligence and knowledge of life that helped him to deal with the questions, doubts, demands, and everything else he divined in Olga's features. With the torch of experience in his hands, he ventured into the labyrinth of her mind and character, and each day he discovered new facts and new traits, but was still far from fathoming her, merely watching with amazement and alarm how her mind demanded its daily sustenance and how her soul never ceased asking for life and experience. Every day the life and activity of another person attached itself to Stolz's life and activity. Having surrounded Olga with flowers, books, music, and albums, Stolz stopped worrying in the belief that he had provided plenty of occupation for his friend's leisure hours, and he went to work, or to inspect some mine or some model farm, or into society to meet and exchange views with new or remarkable men; then he returned to her tired out, to sit by her piano and rest at the sound of her voice. And suddenly he found in her face new questions and in her eyes an insistent demand for an answer. Gradually, imperceptibly and involuntarily, he laid before her what he had seen that day and why. Sometimes she expressed a wish to see and learn for herself what he had seen and learnt. And he went over his work again: went with her to inspect a building or some place, or an engine, or to read some historical event inscribed on stones or walls. Gradually and imperceptibly he acquired the habit of thinking and feeling aloud in her presence; and one day he suddenly discovered, after subjecting himself to a stern self-examination, that he had someone to share his life with him, and that this had started on the day he met Olga. Almost unconsciously, as though talking to himself, he began to estimate aloud in her presence the value of some treasure he had acquired, and was amazed at himself and her; then he checked up carefully to see whether there was still a question left in her eyes, whether the gleam of satisfied thought was reflected in her face, and whether her eyes followed him as a conqueror. If that was so, he went home with pride, with tremulous emotion, and for hours at night he prepared himself for the next day. The most tedious and indispensable work did not seem dry to him, but merely indispensable: it entered deeper into the very foundation and texture of his life;

thoughts, observations, and events were not put away negligently and in silence into the archives of memory, but lent a brilliant colour to every day that passed. What a warm glow spread over Olga's pale face when, without waiting for her eager questioning glance, he hastened to throw down before her, with fervour and energy, fresh supplies and new material! And how perfectly happy he was when her mind, with the identical solicitude and charming obedience, hastened to catch his every word and every glance; both observed each other keenly: he looked at her to see whether there still was a question in her eyes, and she at him to see whether he had left anything unsaid or forgotten something or, worst of all, whether he had – heaven forbid! – omitted to open up for her some dark corner, which was still inaccessible to her, or to develop his thought completely. The more important and complicated the subject, the more thoroughly he expounded it to her, and the longer and more attentively her appreciative glance was fixed on him, and the warmer, deeper, and more affectionate it became.

'That child, Olga!' he thought in amazement. 'She is outgrowing me!'

He pondered over Olga as he had never pondered over anything.

In the spring they all went to Switzerland, Stolz having decided already in Paris that he could not live without Olga. Having settled this question, he began wondering whether Olga could live without him or not. But that question was not so easy to answer. He approached it slowly, circumspectly, cautiously, now groping his way, now advancing boldly, and thought that he had practically reached his goal whenever he caught sight of some unmistakable sign, glance, word, boredom, or joy: one more step, a hardly perceptible movement of Olga's eyebrows, a sigh, and to-morrow the mystery would be solved: she loved him! He could read in her face an almost childish confidence in him; she sometimes looked at him as she would not look at anyone, except perhaps at her mother, if she had a mother. She regarded his visits and the fact that he devoted all his leisure time to her and spent days trying to please her, not as a favour, as a flattering present of love, or as an act of gallantry, but simply as an obligation, as though he were her brother, her father, or even her husband: and that is a great deal, that is everything. She herself was so free and sincere with him in every word she uttered and every step she took that he could not help feeling that he exercised undisputed authority over her. He knew he possessed such an authority; she confirmed it every moment, told him that she believed him alone and could rely on him blindly in life as she could not rely on anyone in the whole world. He was, of course, proud of it, but then any elderly, intelligent, and experienced uncle could be proud of it, even the baron, if he had been a man of intelligence and character. But was that the sort of authority a man exercised over his beloved? That was the question! Did his authority have that seductive deception of love about it, that flattering blindness through which a woman is ready to be cruelly mistaken and be happy in her mistake? No, she submitted to him consciously. It is true her eyes glowed when he developed some idea or laid bare his soul to her; she gazed on him with radiant eyes, but he could always tell why she did it; sometimes she told him the reason herself. But in love merit is acquired blindly and without any conscious reason, and it is in this blindness and unconsciousness that happiness lies. If she was offended, he could see at once what offended her. He had never caught her unawares blushing suddenly, or being overcome with joy bordering on fear, or looking at him with a languishing or ardent glance; if anything of the kind had happened – if he thought she looked upset when he told her that he would be leaving for Italy in a few days and his heart missed a beat in one of those rare and precious moments – everything seemed suddenly to be hidden under a veil once more.

'What a pity,' she said naïvely and openly, 'I can't go there with you. I'd love to, but I expect you will tell me all about it and so well that I shall feel as though I'd been there myself.'

And the spell was broken by this openly expressed desire, which she did not conceal from anyone, and this vulgar and formal praise of his narrative powers. As soon as he gathered up all the threads and succeeded in weaving a most delicate network of lace and had only to fasten the last loop – steady now – one more moment and – she would suddenly once again grow calm, even, and sometimes actually cold. She would be sitting, carrying on with her work, listening to him in silence, raise her head from time to time, and look at him in such a questioning, curious, matter-of-fact way that he more than once threw down the book in vexation or, cutting short some explanation, jumped up from his seat and went away. If he turned round he would catch her surprised glance and he would feel ashamed, come back and invent some excuse. She listened to him with such unaffected simplicity and believed it. She did not doubt him in the least; there was not even the ghost of a sly smile on her lips.

'Does she love me or not?' he wondered. If she did love him, why was she so reserved and so cautious? If she did not, why was she so submissive and so anxious to anticipate his wishes? He had to go for a week to Paris and London, and came to tell her about it on the very day he was leaving, without any previous warning. If she gave a sudden start or changed colour, it was love, the mystery was solved, he was happy! But she just shook him firmly by the hand and looked grieved: he was in despair.

'I'll miss you awfully,' she said. 'I could cry, I feel like a real orphan. Auntie,' she added plaintively, 'look, Mr Stolz is going away!'

That was the last straw. 'Turned to her aunt!' he thought. 'That's the limit! I can see that she is sorry I am going, that she loves me, perhaps, but – this sort of love can be bought like shares on the exchange at the price of so much time, attention, and gallantry. ... I won't come back,' he thought sullenly. 'How do you like that? Olga – a little girl – why, she used to do everything I asked her! What's the matter with her?'

And he sank into deep thought.

What was the matter with her? There was one little thing he did not know: that she had loved, that, as far as she was capable, she had passed through the period of girlish lack of control, sudden blushes, badly concealed heartache, the feverish symptoms of love and its first ardour. Had he known this, he would have found out, if not whether she loved him or not, at any rate why it was so difficult to guess what was the matter with her.

In Switzerland they visited every place where tourists go, but more often they liked to stay in out-of-the-way and little-frequented spots. They, or at any rate Stolz, were so pre-occupied with their own affairs, that they were weary of travelling, which they regarded as of secondary importance. He went for walks with her in the mountains, looked at precipices and waterfalls, and she was in the foreground of every landscape. He would walk behind her up some narrow path, while her aunt remained sitting in the carriage below; he would watch her keenly and in secret, stopping when she reached the top and taking breath, and wonder how she would look at him, for it was at him that she looked first of all; there was no doubt in his mind about that by now. It would have been splendid: it made his heart feel warm and joyful, but then she would suddenly cast a glance over the landscape, and stand fascinated, lost in dreamy contemplation – and he was no longer there so far as she was concerned. The moment he stirred, reminded her of himself, or uttered a word, she gave a start and sometimes cried out: it was evident that she had forgotten whether he were beside her or far away – indeed, whether he existed at all. But afterwards, at home, at the window or on the balcony, she would speak to him alone for hours, describing her impressions at length till she had put it all into words; she spoke warmly and with enthusiasm, choosing her words and rapidly seizing some expression he suggested, and he would catch in her eyes a look of gratitude for his help. Or she would sit down in a large armchair, pale with fatigue, and only her eager and never-tired eyes would tell him that she wanted to listen to him.

She would listen to him without moving or uttering a word, and without missing a single detail. When he fell silent, she still listened, her eyes still questioned him, and in answer to this mute challenge, he went on talking with fresh force and fresh enthusiasm. It would have been splendid: he felt warm and joyful, and his heart beat fast; it meant that she lived in the present and that she wanted nothing more: her light, her inspiration, her reason was beside her. But she would suddenly get up looking tired, and those same questioning eyes of hers would ask him to go away, or she would grow hungry and eat with such an appetite.

All that would have been excellent: he was not a dreamer; he did not want violent passion any more than Oblomov, only for different reasons. He would have wished, however, that their feeling should flow in a smooth and broad stream, but not before it first boiled up hotter at the source, so that they could scoop it up and drink their fill of it and afterwards know all their lives where this spring of happiness flowed from.

'Does she or does she not love me?' he cried in an agony of suspense, nearly bursting into tears, nearly on the point of a nervous breakdown.

This question was becoming more and more an obsession with him, spreading like a flame, paralysing his intentions: it was becoming a question not of love, but of life and death. There was no room in his heart for anything else now. It was as though in these six months he had experienced all the agonies and torments of love against which he had so skilfully guarded in his relations with women. He felt that his robust constitution would break down if this strain on his mind, his will, and his nerves went on for many more months. He understood what he had so far failed to understand – how a man's powers are wasted in this secret struggle of the soul with passion, how incurable, though bloodless, wounds are inflicted upon the heart and give rise to cries of agony, and how even life may be lost. He lost some of his arrogant confidence in his own powers; he no longer joked light-heartedly when he heard stories of people going out of their minds, or pining away for all sorts of reasons, and among them – for love. He was frightened.

'I'm going to put an end to this,' he said. 'I'll find out what's at the back of her mind, as I used to before, and to-morrow – I shall either be happy or go away! I can't bear it any more!' he went on, looking at himself in the glass. 'I look like nothing on earth – enough!'

He went straight to his goal – that is, to Olga.

And what about Olga? Had she not noticed the state he was in or was she completely indifferent to it? She could not help noticing it: women less subtle than she know how to distinguish between friendly devotion and acts of kindness and the tender expression of another feeling. One could not accuse her of being a flirt, for she had a correct understanding of true undissembling and unconventional morality. She was above such vulgar weakness. It can only be assumed that, without having anything particular in mind, she liked the adoration, so full of passion and understanding, of a man like Stolz. Of course she liked it: this adoration made amends for her hurt feeling of self-respect and gradually put her back on the pedestal from which she had fallen; little by little her pride was revived. But what did she think would be the end of this adoration? It could not go on for ever expressing itself in the continual conflict between Stolz's inquiring mind and her obstinate silence. Did she, at any rate, realize that all this conflict was not in vain and that he would gain the suit on which he had spent so much will and determination? He was not spending all his fire and brilliance for nothing, was he? Would Oblomov's image and her old love dissolve in its rays? She did not understand anything of this, she had no clear conception of it, and she struggled desperately with these questions, with herself, and did not know how to escape from this confusion. What was she to do? She could not remain in a state of indecision: sooner or later this mute struggle and interplay of the feelings which were locked in their breasts would give way to words – what could she tell him about her past? How would she describe it and how would she describe her feeling for Stolz? If she loved Stolz, then what was her first love? Flirtation, frivolity, or worse? She blushed with shame and turned hot at

400

this thought. She would never accuse herself of that. But if that was her first pure love, what were her relations to Stolz? Again play, deception, subtle calculation to entice him into marriage so as to cover up the frivolity of her conduct? She turned cold and pale at the very thought of it. But if it was not play, or deception or calculation – so ... was it love again? But such a supposition made her feel utterly at a loss: a second love – eight or seven months after the first! Who would believe her? How could she mention it without causing surprise, perhaps – contempt! She dared not think of it. She had no right. She ransacked her memory: there was nothing there about a second love. She recalled the authoritative opinions of her aunts, old maids, all sorts of clever people, and, finally, writers, 'philosophers of love' – and on all sides she heard the inescapable verdict: 'A woman loves truly only once.' Oblomov, too, pronounced the same verdict. She recalled Sonia and wondered what she would have said about a second love, but visitors from Russia had told her that her friend was already engaged on her third. ...

No, she decided, she had no love for Stolz and, indeed, could not have! She had loved Oblomov, and that love had died and the flower of life had withered for ever! She had only friendship for Stolz, a friendship based on his brilliant qualities and his friendship for her, his attention, his confidence.

It was thus that she banished the thought, or even the possibility of love for her old friend. This was the reason why Stolz could not detect in her face or words any sign either of positive indifference or a momentary flash or even spark of feeling which overstepped by a hair's-breadth the limits of warm, cordial, but ordinary friendship. There was only one way she could have ended it once and for all: having noticed the first symptoms of love in Stolz, she ought to have gone away at once, and thus nipped it in the bud. But it was already too late: it had happened long ago, and, besides, she ought to have foreseen that his feeling would develop into passion; and he was not Oblomov: she could not run away anywhere from him. Even if it had been physically possible, it was morally impossible for her to go away. At first she enjoyed only the rights of their old friendship and, as before, found in Stolz either a playful, witty, and ironical companion or a true and profound observer of life and of everything that interested them. But the more frequently they met, the more intimate they grew spiritually and the more active his role became: from a mere observer of events he imperceptibly became their interpreter and her guide. Without her noticing it, he became her reason and conscience, and new rights made their appearance, new secret ties that entangled the whole of Olga's life, all except one cherished corner which she carefully hid from his observation and judgement. She had accepted this spiritual guardianship over her heart and mind, and saw that she had in her turn acquired an influence over him. They had exchanged rights; she had permitted this exchange to happen somehow without noticing it and without saying anything about it. How could she take it all away again now? And, besides, there was in it so much fun – pleasure – variety – life. What would she do if she were suddenly deprived of it? And, anyway, when the idea of running away occurred to her, it was too late; she had not the strength to do it. Each day she did not spend with him, every thought she did not confide in him and share with him, lost its colour and significance. 'Oh dear,' she thought, 'if only I could be his sister! What happiness it would be to possess a permanent claim on a man like that, not only on his mind, but also on his heart, to enjoy his presence openly and legitimately, without having to pay for it by heavy sacrifices, disappointments, and confessions of one's miserable past. And now – what am I? If he goes away, I not only have no right to keep him, but I ought to wish to part from him; and if I do make him stay, what am I to tell him? What right have I to wish to see and hear him every minute? Because I am bored, because I feel miserable, because he teaches me, amuses me, is useful and pleasant to me? That is a reason, of course, but not a right. And what do I give him in exchange? The right to admire me disinterestedly without daring to think of reciprocity when so many women would have thought themselves lucky – –'

She was unhappy and tried to find a way out of that situation, and saw no end to it, no purpose in it. All the future held for her was fear of his disappointment and of parting from him for ever. Sometimes it occurred to her to tell him everything and so bring to an end both his struggle and hers, but her courage failed her the moment she thought of it. She felt ashamed and unhappy. The strange thing was that since she had been inseparable from Stolz and he had taken possession of her life, she ceased to respect her past, and even began to be ashamed of it. If the baron, for instance, or anyone else had got to know about it, she would, of course, have felt embarrassed and uncomfortable, but she would not have tortured herself as much as she was doing now at the thought that Stolz might find out about it. She imagined with horror the expression of his face, how he would look at her, what he would say, and what he would think afterwards. She would suddenly appear so worthless to him, so weak and insignificant. No, no, not for anything in the world! She began observing herself, and she was horrified to discover that she was ashamed not only of her love affair, but also of its hero. ... And she was consumed with remorse for being ungrateful for the deep devotion of her former lover. Perhaps she would have grown used to her shame and made the best of it – what doesn't a person get used to? – if her friendship for Stolz had been free from any selfish thoughts and desires. But if she was successful in suppressing the artful and flattering whisper of her heart, she could not control the flight of her imagination: the shining image of this other love often appeared before her eyes; the dream of splendid happiness on the wide arena of many-sided life, with all its depths, sorrows, and delights – her happiness with Stolz and not in indolent drowsiness with Oblomov – grew more and more seductive. <u>It was then that she shed tears over her past and could not wash it away</u>. She recovered from her dream and sought refuge more than once behind the impenetrable wall of silence and friendly indifference that Stolz felt to be so unendurable. Then, forgetting herself, she was again carried away selflessly by the presence of her friend, and was charming, amiable, and trustful till the unlawful dream of happiness to which she had forfeited the right reminded her that the future was lost for her, that she had left her rosy dreams behind, and that the flower of life had withered. It is possible that, as the years passed, she would have become reconciled to her position and, like all old maids, would have renounced her dreams of the future and sunk into cold apathy or devoted herself to charitable works; but suddenly her unlawful dream assumed a more threatening aspect when from some words that escaped Stolz she realized that she had lost him as a friend and had acquired a passionate admirer. Friendship was lost in love.

She was pale on the morning she discovered it, she did not go out all day, she was agitated, she struggled with herself, wondering what she should do now and what her duty was – but could think of nothing. She merely cursed herself for not having overcome her shame and revealed her past to Stolz earlier, for now she had to overcome fear as well. At times, unable to bear the agony of her heartache any longer, she seemed to be filled with resolution and was ready to rush to him and tell him of her past love not in words but in sobs, convulsions, and fainting fits, so that he should see how great her repentance was. She heard how other women acted in similar cases. Sonia, for instance, told her fiancé about the lieutenant, that she had made a fool of him, that he was just a boy, that she purposely kept him waiting out in the frost till it pleased her to go to her carriage, and so on. Sonia would not have hesitated to say about Oblomov that she had made fun of him for amusement, that he was so ridiculous, that she could not possibly be in love with 'such a clumsy lout', that no one could possibly believe that. But such conduct might be excused by Sonia's husband and many others, but not by Stolz. Olga might have been able to put the whole thing in a better light by saying that she only wanted to draw Oblomov out of the abyss and, to do that, made use of a friendly flirtation – to revive a dying man and then leave him. But this would have been too sophisticated and forced and, in any case, false. No, no, there was no way out!

'Oh dear, what an awful mess I am in!' Olga thought in an agony of despair. 'To tell him! No, no! I don't want him ever to know about it, not for a long time! But not to tell him is no better than stealing. It's like deceiving him, like trying to ingratiate myself with him. O Lord, help me!' But there was no help.

However much she enjoyed Stolz's presence, there were times when she wished not to meet him again, to pass through his life as a hardly perceptible shadow, and not to darken his serene and rational existence by an illicit passion. She would grieve for her unhappy love, weep over her past, bury in her heart the memory of him, and then – then she would perhaps make 'a respectable match', of which there are so many, and become a good, intelligent, solicitous wife and mother, and would not live, but make the most of her life. Was it not what all women did?

But, unfortunately, it was not a question of her alone; someone else, too, was concerned in it, and he rested the last and ultimate hopes of his life on her.

'Why did I – love?' she asked herself in agony, recalling the morning in the park when Oblomov wanted to run away and she had thought that the book of her life would be closed for ever if he did. She had solved the question of love and life so boldly and so easily, everything had seemed so clear to her – and everything had got tangled up in a hopeless knot. She had tried to be too clever, she had thought it was enough to look simply at things and go straight ahead and life would spread out before her obediently like a carpet under her feet – and there she was! She had no one even to put the blame on: it was all her own fault.

Without suspecting what Stolz had come for, Olga got up light-heartedly from the sofa, put down her book, and went to meet him.

'I'm not disturbing you?' he asked, sitting down at the window of her room that overlooked the lake. 'You've been reading?'

'No, I had stopped,' she replied, speaking gently, trustfully, and friendlily. 'It's getting dark. I was expecting you!'

'So much the better,' he observed gravely, drawing up another chair to the window for her. 'I want to speak to you.'

She gave a start and turned numb. Then she sank mechanically into the chair and remained sitting in an agony of suspense with her head bowed and without raising her eyes. She wished she were a hundred miles away. At that moment her past flashed through her mind like lightning. 'The hour of reckoning has come. One can't play with life as one plays with dolls,' she seemed to hear a voice saying. 'Don't trifle with it, or you'll have to pay dearly for it.'

For several minutes neither of them spoke. He was evidently collecting his thoughts. Olga looked fearfully at his face that had grown thinner, his knit brows and compressed lips which expressed determination. 'Nemesis!' she thought, shuddering inwardly. Both seemed to be preparing for a duel.

'I suppose,' he said, looking questioningly at her, 'you've guessed what I want to talk to you about.'

He was sitting with his back to the wall so that his face was in shadow, while the light from the window fell straight upon her, and he could read what she had in mind.

'How am I to know?' she replied softly.

Confronted by this dangerous opponent, she no longer possessed the will-power, strength of character, penetration, and self-control she had always displayed with Oblomov. She realized that if she had so far been successful in concealing herself from Stolz's keen eyes and in carrying on the war against him, it was not due to her own powers, as in her struggle with Oblomov, but to Stolz's obstinate silence and his reserve. In the open field the odds were not in her favour; by her question she therefore merely wanted to gain an inch of ground and a minute of time so as to force the enemy to show his hand more clearly.

'You don't know?' he said ingenuously. 'All right, I'll tell you – –'

'No, don't!' she cried involuntarily.

She seized him by the hand and looked at him as though imploring for mercy.

'You see, I guessed that you knew!' he said. 'But why "don't"?' he added sadly afterwards.

She made no answer.

'If you had foreseen that I should declare myself one day, you must have known, of course, what your answer would be, mustn't you?'

'Yes, I have foreseen it and it made me so unhappy!' she said, leaning back in her chair and turning away from the light, offering up a silent prayer for the dusk to come to her aid so that he could not read the struggle of embarrassment and anguish in her face.

'Unhappy? That is a terrible word,' he said almost in a whisper. 'It is Dante's "Abandon all hope!" I have nothing more to say: it is all there! But I thank you for it, all the same,' he added with a deep sigh. 'I've come out of the confusion and the darkness, and I know at any rate what I have to do. My only salvation is to run away as soon as possible!'

He got up.

'No, for God's sake, no!' she cried imploringly, in alarm, rushing up to him and seizing him again by the hand. 'Have pity on me – what is to become of me?'

He sat down and so did she.

'But I love you, Olga,' he said, almost sternly. 'You've seen what has been happening to me in the last six months. What more do you want: complete triumph? Do you want me to waste away or go off my head? Thank you very much!'

She turned pale.

'You can go!' she said with the dignity of suppressed injury and deep sorrow she was unable to conceal.

'I am awfully sorry,' he apologized. 'Here we have already quarrelled without knowing what it is all about. I know that you cannot wish it, but you cannot enter into my position, and that is why you think that my impulse to run away is strange. A man sometimes unconsciously becomes an egoist.'

She shifted her position in the arm-chair, as though she were uncomfortable, but she said nothing.

'Well, suppose I did stay – how would it help matters?' he went on. 'You will, of course, offer me your friendship, but it is mine as it is. If I were to go away and return in a year or two, it would still be mine. Friendship is a good thing, Olga, when it is love between a young man and a young woman or the memory of love between old people. But heaven help us if it is friendship on one side and love on the other. I know that you are not

406

bored with me, but what do you think I feel when I am with you?'

'Well, if that's how you feel, you had better go!' she murmured in a hardly audible whisper.

'To stay?' he reflected aloud. 'To walk on the edge of a knife – some friendship!'

'And do you think it is better for me?' she retorted unexpectedly.

'What do you mean?' he asked quickly. 'You – you don't love ...'

'I don't know; I swear I don't! But if you – I mean, if there should be some change in my present life, what's going to happen to me?' she added sombrely, almost to herself.

'How am I to understand that? Explain yourself for God's sake!' he cried, drawing his chair nearer to her, taken aback by her words and the genuine, unfeigned tone of voice in which they were uttered.

He tried to make out her face. She was silent. She was deeply anxious to reassure him, to take back the word 'unhappy', or explain it differently from the way he understood it – she did not know herself, but she vaguely felt that both of them were labouring under a misapprehension, that they were in a false position, and that both were wretched because of it, and that only he, or she with his assistance, could bring order and clarity into the past and the present. But to do that she had to cross the gulf that separated her from him and tell him what had happened to her: how she prayed for and was afraid of – his verdict!

'I don't understand anything myself,' she said. 'I am more confused and more in the dark than you!'

'Listen; do you trust me?' he asked, taking her by the hand.

'Entirely, as my mother – you know that,' she replied weakly.

'In that case tell me what has happened to you since we parted. You're a closed book to me now, but before I could read your thoughts from your face. It seems to me this is the only way for us to understand each other. Do you agree?'

'Oh, yes, yes, I must do that – I must end it somehow,' she said, feeling wretched at the inevitable confession. 'Nemesis! Nemesis!' she thought, bowing her head.

She cast down her eyes and was silent. And he felt terrified at these simple words and still more at her silence.

'She is suffering! Oh, Lord, what could have happened to her?' he thought, turning cold and feeling that his hands and feet were trembling. He imagined something very dreadful. She was still silent and obviously struggling with herself.

'Well – Olga – –' he prompted her.

She was silent, except for again making some nervous movement he could not make out in the dark; he only heard the rustle of her silk dress.

'I am plucking up my courage,' she said at last. 'If only you knew how hard it was!' she added afterwards, turning away and trying to get the better of her fears. What she wanted was that Stolz should find everything out not from her, but by some miracle. Fortunately, it had grown darker and her face was already in shadow: only her voice could give her away, and she could not bring herself to speak, as though she could not make up her mind on which note to begin.

'Oh dear, how much I must be to blame, if I feel so ashamed, so miserable!' she thought agonizingly.

And not so long ago she was so confidently planning her own life and another one's and was so strong and intelligent! And now the time had come for her to tremble like a little girl! Shame for her past, poignant regret for the present and her false position, tortured her – it was unbearable!

'Let me help you – you – have loved?' Stolz brought himself to say with an effort – his own words hurt him so much.

She confirmed it by her silence. And once more he felt terrified.

'Who was it?' he asked, trying to speak firmly, though he felt that his lips quivered. 'It isn't a secret, is it?'

She felt even more dreadful. She wished she could give him another name, invent another story. For a moment she hesitated, but there was nothing for it: like a man who in a moment of extreme danger jumps off a steep bank or throws himself into the flames, she suddenly said:

'Oblomov!'

He was dumbfounded. For two minutes neither of them spoke.

'Oblomov!' he repeated in astonishment. 'It's not true!' he added emphatically, lowering his voice.

'It is true!' she said calmly.

'Oblomov!' he repeated. 'It's impossible!' he added confidently again. 'There's something wrong here: you did not understand yourself, Oblomov, or love!'

She was silent.

'That was not love; it was something else, I tell you!' he repeated insistently.

'Yes, I suppose you think I flirted with him, led him by the nose, made him unhappy, and – am now starting on you!' she said in a restrained voice in which, however, her feeling of resentment broke through.

'Dear Olga, please don't be angry. Don't speak like that: it isn't like you. You know I don't think anything of the kind. But I'm afraid the whole thing is beyond me. I can't understand how Oblomov – –'

'But he is worthy of your friendship, isn't he? You can't speak highly enough of him. Why, then, shouldn't he be worthy of love?' she declared in self-defence.

'I know,' he said, 'that love is less exacting than friendship. It is often blind, it cares nothing for merit – that is so. But something special is needed for love, sometimes just a trifle, something you cannot define or name and that my incomparable but clumsy Ilya has not got. That is why I am surprised. Listen,' he went on, speaking with great animation. 'We shall never get to the bottom of it – we shall never understand each other. Don't be ashamed of details, don't spare yourself for half an hour, tell me everything, and I'll tell you what it was, and perhaps also what it's going to be. I can't help feeling that there is something – wrong somewhere. Oh, if only it were true,' he added with enthusiasm. 'If it were Oblomov and no one else! Oblomov! Why, that means that you don't belong to the past, to love, that you are free. ... Tell me, please, tell me quickly!' he concluded in a calm, almost cheerful voice.

'Yes, oh yes!' she replied trustfully, glad that some of her chains had been taken off. 'All alone, I am going mad. If only you knew how wretched I was! I don't know whether I am to blame or not, whether I ought to be ashamed of my past or be sorry for it, whether to hope for the future or to despair. You have been talking of your sufferings, but you never suspected mine. Hear me out, then, but not with your intellect – I'm afraid of your intellect – better with your heart; perhaps it will realize that I have no mother, that I was completely at sea,' she added softly in a toneless voice. 'No,' she hastily corrected herself a moment later, 'do not spare me. If it was love, you'd better – go.' She paused for a minute. 'But come back later, when you don't feel anything but friendship for me again. But if it was frivolous coquetry, then punish me, run away from me as far as you can and forget me! Listen.'

In reply, he pressed both her hands warmly.

Olga's confession began, long and detailed. Distinctly, word

409

for word, she transferred from her mind into his all that had so long been gnawing at it, that had made her blush, that had once made her happy and moved her deeply until she suddenly fell into a slough of doubt and sorrow. She told of their walks, of the park, of her hopes, of Oblomov's renascence and of his fall, of the spray of lilac, even of the kiss. She only passed over in silence the sultry evening in the garden – probably because she still could not decide what had come over her then. At first only her embarrassed whisper could be heard, but as she went on with her story, her voice became clearer and more unconstrained; from a whisper it rose to an undertone, and then to full, deep notes. She finished calmly, just as though she were telling somebody else's story. She felt as though a curtain were being raised and the past, into which she had till that moment been afraid to look, slowly unfolded before her. Her eyes were opened to many things and she would have looked boldly at her companion if it had not been dark.

She finished and waited for the verdict. But dead silence was his answer. What did he have to say to it? She could not hear a word, not a movement, not a breath even, as though there were no one in the room with her. This muteness made her feel doubtful again. The silence continued. What did it mean? What verdict was being prepared for her by the most perspicacious and most lenient judge in the whole world? All the rest would condemn her without mercy, he alone could be her counsel, it was he she would have chosen – he would have understood it all, weighed it, and settled it in her favour better than she herself could have done. But he was silent: had she lost her case? She felt terrified again.

The door was opened and the two candles brought in by the maid lighted up their corner.

She threw a timid but eager and questioning glance at him. He had crossed his arms and was looking at her with such gentle, frank eyes, enjoying her confusion. A great weight lifted from her heart. She sighed with relief and nearly cried. Forbearance towards herself and confidence in him all at once returned to her. She was happy like a child that has been forgiven, soothed, and fondled.

'Is that all?' he asked softly.

'All!' she said.

'And his letter?'

She took the letter out of her case and gave it him. He went up to the candle, read it, and put it on the table. And his eyes turned on her again with an expression she had not seen in them for a long time. The old self-confident, slightly ironical, and infinitely kind friend who used to spoil her was standing before her. There was not a trace of suffering or doubt in his face. He took both her hands, kissed them, then pondered deeply. She, too, grew quiet and watched without blinking the movement of thought in his face.

Suddenly he got up.

'Good heavens, if I had known that it was a question of Oblomov, I shouldn't have suffered so!' he said, looking so kindly and trustfully at her as though she had not had that terrible past.

She felt so light-hearted, so festive. All her worries had gone. She saw clearly that it was before him alone she had been ashamed, and that he did not think of punishing her and running away. What did she care for the opinion of the whole world!

He was again self-possessed and cheerful; but this was not enough for her. She saw that she had been acquitted; but, as the accused, she wanted to hear the verdict. He picked up his hat.

'Where are you off to?' she asked.

'You are excited, and you must have a rest,' he said. 'We'll talk to-morrow.'

'Do you want me to lie awake all night?' she interrupted, keeping him back by the hand and making him resume his seat. 'You want to go without telling me what it – was, what I am now, and what – I am going to be. Have pity on me: who else will tell me? Who will punish me if I deserve it or – who will forgive me?' she added, looking at him with such tender affection that he threw down his hat and nearly threw himself at her feet.

'Angel – allow me to say – *my* angel!' he said. 'Don't torment yourself for nothing: there is no need to punish or pardon you. In fact, I have nothing to add to your story. What doubts can you have? You want to know what it was? You want me to tell you its name? You've known it long ago. Where is Oblomov's letter?'

He picked up the letter from the table.

'Listen,' he said, and he read : ' " Your present *I love you* is not real love, but the love you will feel in future. It is merely your unconscious need of love which, for lack of proper food, sometimes finds expression with women in caressing a child, in love for another woman, or simply in tears or fits of hysteria ... You have *made a mistake* " (Stolz read, emphasizing the words)

" the man before you is not the one you have been expecting and dreaming of. Wait – he will come, and then you will come to your senses and you will feel vexed and ashamed of your mistake" ... You see how true it is,' he said. 'You were vexed and ashamed of – your mistake. There is nothing to add to this. He was right and you did not believe him – that is all your guilt amounts to. You should have parted at the time but he could not resist your beauty, and you were touched by his – dove-like tenderness!' he added, not without a touch of irony.

'I did not believe him. I thought one's heart could not be mistaken.'

'Yes, it can, and sometimes very disastrously! But with you it never went as far as the heart,' he added. 'It was imagination and vanity on one side, and weakness on the other. And you were afraid that there would be no more sunshine in your life, that that pale ray had lit up your life and would be followed by eternal night.'

'What about my tears?' she said. 'Did they not come from my heart when I cried? I was not lying, I was sincere.'

'Dear me, women will shed tears about anything! You said yourself that you were sorry for the bunch of lilac and your favourite seat in the park. Add to that injured vanity, your failure as Oblomov's saviour, a certain degree of habit – and there you have lots of reasons for tears!'

'And our meetings and walks – are they mistakes, too? You remember I – I went to his flat,' she concluded in embarrassment, wishing, it seemed, to stifle those words herself.

She was trying to accuse herself only so as to make him defend her the more warmly, to appear more and more justified in his eyes.

'I can see from your account that during your last meetings you had nothing even to talk about. Your so-called "love" lacked all inner content – it could not have gone any farther. You had parted before your final separation, and you were faithful not to love but to its phantoms which you had yourself invented – that is the whole mystery.'

'And the kiss?' she whispered so softly that he guessed rather than heard it.

'Oh, that's awfully important,' he said with ironic severity, 'for that you ought to go – without your sweet at dinner.'

He was looking at her with ever-growing tenderness and affection.

'A joke is no condonation of such a mistake,' she retorted

412

sternly, offended by his indifference and casual tone. 'I should have felt happier if you had punished me by some harsh word and called my misdemeanour by its proper name.'

'I should not have joked if it were a question of someone else and not of Ilya,' he said by way of apology. 'If it had been somebody else your mistake might have ended in – disaster, but I know Oblomov.'

'Someone else, never!' she interrupted him, flaring up. 'I got to know him better than you do.'

'There you are!' he assented.

'But if – if he had changed, if he had come to life and listened to me and – don't you think I'd have loved him then? Could it have been a lie and a mistake even then?' she said, anxious to examine the position from every point of view so that there should be nothing whatever left unexplained.

'That is, if another man had been in his place,' Stolz interrupted. 'In that case, no doubt, your relationship would have grown into love, would have become consolidated, and then – – But that is another love-story and another hero, and it has nothing to do with us.'

She sighed as though throwing the last load off her mind. Both were silent.

'Oh, how lovely it is to – recover!' she said slowly, as though opening up like a flower, and turned on him a look of such deep gratitude, such warm and unparalleled friendship that in her glance he seemed to catch a glimpse of the spark he had been vainly seeking for almost a year.

A thrill of happiness went through him.

'No, it is I who am recovering,' he said, looking thoughtful. 'Oh, had I only known that the hero of your romance was Ilya! How much time was wasted, how much bad feeling bred! Why? Whatever for?' he kept on repeating almost with vexation.

But suddenly he seemed to recover from his vexation and came to himself after his heavy brooding. His forehead was smooth and his eyes were bright again.

'It seems it was inevitable, but,' he added with rapture, 'I am no longer worried now, I am – happy!'

'It's like a dream, as though nothing had happened,' she said pensively, barely audibly, amazed at her sudden regeneration. 'You have taken away not only the shame and remorse, but also the bitterness and the pain – everything. How did you do it?' she asked softly. 'But will it all pass – this mistake?'

'Why, I should think it has passed already!' he said, looking at her for the first time with eyes full of passion, and not concealing it. 'I mean, all that has been.'

'And what's going to be – will not be – a mistake, but the real thing?' she asked, hesitantly.

'It is written here,' he declared, picking up the letter again, ' "The man before you is not the one you've been waiting for and dreaming of: he will come and you will come to your senses," and, I may add, will fall in love, so much in love that not only a year but a whole lifetime will be too short for that love, but I do not know – with whom,' he concluded, looking intently at her.

She dropped her eyes and compressed her lips, but from under her eyelids a gleam of light broke through, and, though she tried hard, her lips could not control a smile. Then she looked at him and laughed so happily that tears came into her eyes.

'I've told you what has happened to you and what is going to happen,' he concluded, 'but you never gave me an answer to my question, which you did not let me finish. '

'But what can I say?' she said in embarrassment. 'And if I could, should I have the right to say what you want me to say and what – you deserve so much?' she added in a whisper, looking shyly at him.

He seemed once more to catch in her glance a spark of great affection; again he trembled with happiness.

'Don't hurry,' he added. 'Tell me what I deserve when your heart's mourning, your mourning of propriety, is over. This year, too, has taught me something. Now I want you to answer one question. Shall I go away or shall I stay?'

'Listen! You're flirting with me!' she cried gaily suddenly.

'Oh no,' he observed gravely. 'That is not the question I asked before. It has quite a different meaning now: if I stay, it will be as – what?'

She was suddenly embarrassed.

'You see, I am not flirting!' he laughed, pleased to have caught her. 'For after our talk to-night we shall have to treat each other differently: we are no longer the same people we were yesterday.'

'I don't know,' she whispered, still more embarrassed.

'May I give you a piece of advice?'

'Speak – I'll carry it out blindly!' she added, with almost passionate submissiveness.

'Marry me while you are waiting for *him* to come!'

'I daren't yet – –' she whispered, burying her face in her hand, excited but happy.

'Why don't you dare?' he asked, in a whisper, drawing her head down to him.

'But this past?' she whispered again, putting her head on his chest as though he were her mother.

He softly removed her hands from her face, kissed her head, and looked with pleasure at her embarrassed face and at the tears that started to her eyes and were again absorbed by them.

'It will wither like your lilac,' he concluded. 'You've had your lesson, now it's time to make use of it. Life is beginning: give your future to me and do not worry about anything – I vouch for it all. Let us go to your aunt.'

Stolz went home late. 'I have found what I was looking for,' he thought, gazing with a lover's eyes at the sky, the trees, the lake, and even the mist rising from the water. 'I've got it at last! So many years of patience, of craving for love, of economy of spiritual powers! How long I have waited – at last I have been rewarded. This is it – a man's greatest happiness!'

His happiness pushed all his other interests into the background: the office, his father's dog-cart, the chamois-leather gloves, the greasy accounts – the whole of his business life. The only thing that came back to his memory was his mother's fragrant room, Herz's variations, the prince's gallery, the blue eyes, the powdered chestnut hair – and Olga's tender voice rang through it all: in his mind he heard her singing. ...

'Olga – my wife!' he whispered, with a quiver of passion. 'Everything is found, there is nothing more to look for, there is nowhere further to go.'

And he walked home in a thoughtful daze of happiness, not noticing his way or the streets. ...

Olga followed him for some time with her eyes, then she opened the window and for several minutes breathed the cool air of the night; her agitation gradually died down and her breast rose and fell evenly. She gazed at the lake, into the far distance, and fell into such a serene and deep reverie that it seemed as though she were asleep. She wanted to catch what she was thinking and feeling, but could not. Her thoughts drifted along as evenly as waves, her blood flowed smoothly in her veins. She felt happy, but she could not tell where her happiness began or ended and what it was. She wondered why she felt so calm and peaceful, why she was so wonderfully happy, why her mind was so utterly at peace, while – –

'I am his fiancée,' she whispered.

'I am engaged!' a girl thinks with a proud tremor, having at

415

last reached the moment which sheds a radiance over the whole of her life, and looking down upon the dark path along which she walked alone and unnoticed only yesterday.

Why, then, did Olga feel no tremor? She, too, had walked along a lonely and inconspicuous path, and at the crossroads had met *him*, who gave her his hand and led her out, not into the dazzling sunlight, but, as it were, to a broad, overflowing river, to wide fields, and friendly, smiling hills. The brilliant light did not force her to screw up her eyes, her heart did not stand still, her imagination did not catch fire. Her eyes rested with quiet joy on the broad stream of life, on its vast fields and green hills. A shiver did not run down her spine, her eyes did not gleam with pride: it was only when she transferred her gaze from the fields and hills to the man who gave her his hand that she felt a tear slowly rolling down her cheek. ...

She still sat as though asleep – so quiet was the dream of her happiness: she did not stir, she hardly breathed. Sunk in a trance, her mental gaze was fixed on a blue still night, warm and fragrant and pervaded by a gently shimmering radiance. The phantom vision of happiness spread out its broad wings and sailed slowly, like a cloud in the sky, over her head. ...

In that dream she did not see herself wrapped in gauze and lace for a couple of hours and in everyday rags for the rest of her life. She did not dream of a festive board, of lights, or of merry shouts; she dreamed of happiness, but such ordinary and unadorned happiness that once more, without a tremor of pride, but with deep emotion, she whispered: 'I am his fiancée.'

5

DEAR me, how dull and gloomy everything was in Oblomov's flat about eighteen months after his name-day, when Stolz had inadvertently turned up to dinner. Oblomov himself had grown more fat and flabby; boredom had eaten itself into his eyes and looked out of them like some kind of disease. He would walk up and down the room, then lie down and gaze at the ceiling; he would pick up a book from the bookcase, skim through a few lines, yawn, and begin to drum with his fingers on the table. Zakhar had grown still more clumsy and slovenly; patches appeared on his elbows; he looked wretched and starved, as though he had not enough to eat, slept badly, and did the work of three men. Oblomov's dressing-gown was worn out and however carefully the holes in it were mended it kept giving way everywhere and not only along the seams: he should have got a new one long ago. The blanket on the bed was also worn out and patched here and there; the curtains at the windows were faded and, though clean, looked like rags.

Zakhar brought an old table-cloth, spread it over half of the table near Oblomov, then carefully with his tongue between his teeth, brought the tray with a decanter of vodka, put bread on the table and went out. The landlady's door opened and Agafya Matveyevna came in, carrying dexterously a frying-pan with a sizzling omelette. She, too, had changed terribly, and not to her advantage. She had grown thinner. She no longer had the plump, round cheeks which turned neither red nor pale; her scanty eyebrows were no longer shiny; her eyes were sunken. She wore an old cotton dress; her hands were sunburnt or rough with work, with the heat or the water, or both. Akulina was no longer in the house. Anisya had to do the work in the kitchen and in the vegetable garden; she had to look after the poultry, scrub the floors, and do the washing; as she could not manage it all by herself, Agafya Matveyevna had willy-nilly to do the work in the kitchen: she did little pounding, grating, and sieving, because they could afford but little coffee, cinnamon, and almonds, and she never even thought about lace. She had more often nowadays to chop onions, grate horse-radish, and similar condiments. There was a look of profound dejection on her face. But it was not about herself or her own coffee that she sighed; she was worried not because she had no opportunity to be busy and keep house on a big scale, to pound cinnamon, to put vanilla into the sauce, or boil thick cream, but because Oblomov had not tasted these things for over a year, because his coffee was not bought in large quantities from the best shops, but for ten copecks in the little shop round the corner; because his cream was not brought by a Finnish woman, but was supplied by the same little shop; because instead of a juicy chop, she was bringing him an omelette for lunch, fried with a tough piece of ham that had grown stale in the same little shop.

But what did it mean? It meant that for over a year the income from Oblomovka, sent punctually by Stolz, went in payment of the IOU given by Oblomov to the landlady.

The 'perfectly legal' transaction of the landlady's brother had been successful beyond expectation. At the first hint from Tarantyev at the 'disgraceful affair', Oblomov flushed and was thrown into confusion; then they came to an agreement, then all the three of them had a drink, and Oblomov signed an IOU which had to be met at the end of four years. A month later Agafya Matveyevna signed a similar IOU made out in her brother's name, without suspecting what it was and why she was signing it. Her brother told her that it was a document relating to the ownership of the house and asked her to write: 'This IOU so-and-so' (rank, name, and surname) 'has signed with her own hand.' The only objection she raised was that she would have so much to write, and she asked her brother to make Vanya write instead, because he wrote beautifully now and she might make a mess of it. But her brother insisted most firmly that she should do it herself, and she wrote it crookedly and slantingly and in big letters. She never heard of it again.

In signing the IOU, Oblomov partly comforted himself by the thought that the money would benefit Agafya Matveyevna's children, and on the following day, when his head had cleared, he recalled the affair with shame and tried to forget it, avoiding his landlady's brother; when Tarantyev brought up the subject, he threatened to leave the house immediately and go to the country. Afterwards, when he received the money from his estate, the landlady's brother came to see him and declared that he, Oblomov, might find it easier to start paying at once out of his income, for then the claim would be paid in three years, while if he waited for the time the payment fell due, his estate would have to be sold by auction, since Oblomov had not the necessary amount in cash and was not likely to have it. Oblomov realized into what clutches he had fallen when all the money sent by Stolz went to the payment of his debt and he had only a small sum left to live on. The landlady's brother was in a hurry to finish this voluntary arrangement with his debtor in about two years, fearing that something or other might happen to upset his plans, and that was why Oblomov suddenly found himself in difficulties. At first he did not notice it very much owing to his habit of never knowing how much money he had in his pocket; but Ivan Matveyevich took it into his head to become engaged to the daughter of some corn-chandler, and he rented a flat and moved out. Agafya Matveyevna's ambitious housekeeping plans were suddenly curtailed: sturgeon, snow-white veal, turkey made their appearance in another kitchen, in Ivan Matveyevich's new flat. There in the evenings the rooms were lit up, and his future relations, his colleagues, and Tarantyev gathered; everything had found its way there. Agafya Mat-

418

veyevna and Anisya were suddenly left with nothing to do, gaping in astonishment over their empty pots and pans. Agafya Matveyevna learnt for the first time that she possessed only a house, a kitchen garden, and chickens, and that neither cinnamon nor vanilla grew in her garden; she saw that the shop-keepers in the market gradually stopped bowing low to her and smiling and that these bows and smiles were now addressed to the tall, well-dressed new cook of her brother's.

Oblomov had given the landlady all the money her brother had left him to live on, and for three or four months she went on as before as if nothing had happened, ground pounds of coffee, pounded cinnamon, roasted veal and turkey, and went on doing it to the last day on which she spent her last seventy copecks and came to tell him that she had no more money left. He turned over three times on the sofa at the news, then looked into the drawer of his desk; he had not any either. He tried to remember where he had put it and could not; he fumbled on the table for some coppers and asked Zakhar, who replied that he had not the faintest idea. She went to see her brother and naïvely told him that there was no money in the house.

'And what did you and his lordship squander the thousand roubles I gave him for living expenses on?' he asked. 'Where am I to get the money from? You know I am going to be married. I can't provide for two families, and you and your gentleman had better cut your coat according to your cloth.'

'Why are you reproaching me with him?' she said. 'What has he done to you? He doesn't harm anyone. He keeps to himself. It wasn't I who enticed him to our house. You and Tarantyev did that.'

He gave her ten roubles and told her that he had no more. But having discussed the matter afterwards with Tarantyev at the 'tavern', he decided that it was impossible to abandon Oblomov and his sister in this way, for the news of it might reach Stolz, who would turn up unexpectedly, find out what was happening, and quite likely do something so that they would not have time to collect the debt in spite of its being 'perfectly legal'. He was a German and, therefore, a crafty old rascal!

He agreed to give her an additional fifty roubles a month, intending to recover that money from Oblomov's income three years hence; but he made it absolutely clear to his sister, and even declared his readiness to take an oath on it, that he would not let them have another farthing; he calculated how much they would have to spend on food, how they ought to cut down their expenses, and even told her what dishes she had to cook and when; having, finally, ascertained how much she could get for her chickens and cabbage, he declared that with all this she could live on the fat of the land.

For the first time in her life Agafya Matveyevna thought not of housekeeping but something else; for the first time she burst into tears, not because she was vexed with Akulina for breaking the crockery and not because her brother had scolded her for not doing the fish long enough; for the first time she was faced with the threat of privation, a threat directed not against her, but against Oblomov.

'How can a gentleman like him' she mused, 'start eating buttered turnips instead of asparagus, mutton instead of hazel-grouse, salted pike-perch and, perhaps, brawn from the little shop instead of Gatchina trout and amber-coloured sturgeon ...' The horror of it! She did not think it out to the end, but dressed hurriedly, took a cab, and went to see her husband's relatives – not at Easter or Christmas to a family dinner, but early in the morning, greatly worried, to tell them a strange tale and to ask them what she was to do and to get some money from them; they had plenty of money: they would give it to her at once when they knew it was for Oblomov. If she had wanted money for tea or coffee, for her children's clothes and shoes and other similar luxuries, she would never have dreamt of asking for it, but she wanted it for some pressing need: she simply had to have it to get asparagus for Oblomov, to buy hazel-grouse and French peas which he liked so much. ... But her relatives were surprised, gave her no money, but told her that if Oblomov had any gold or, perhaps, silver articles, or even furs, they could be pawned and that there were such nice people who would give him a third of their value and wait for repayment till he received his money from the country. This practical lesson would at any other time have been lost on the landlady and made no impression on her brilliant mind, however much one tried to explain the situation to her, but this time she grasped it with the wisdom of her heart, and having considered it carefully, pawned the pearls she had received as a dowry. The next day Oblomov, without suspecting anything, drank the currant vodka, following it up by some excellent smoked salmon, his favourite dish of giblets, and a fresh white hazel-hen. Agafya Matveyevna and the children had the servants' cabbage soup and porridge, and it was only to keep Oblomov company that she drank two cups of coffee. Soon after pawning her string of pearls she took out of a private chest her diamond necklace, then her silver, then her fur coat. ... When the money from the country came, Oblomov gave it all to her. She redeemed the pearls, paid the interest on the necklace, the silver, and the fur, and set about once more cooking asparagus and hazel-grouse for him, drinking coffee with him only for the sake of appearances. The string of pearls went back to the pawnbrokers. And so week after week and day after day she struggled along, worrying how to make ends meet, sold her shawl, sent her best dress to be sold, remaining in her cheap, short-sleeved, cotton dress, and covering her neck on Sundays with an old worn-out kerchief. That was why she had grown so thin, why her eyes looked sunken, and why she brought Oblomov his lunch herself. She even had the pluck to look pleased when Oblomov told her that Tarantyev, Alexeyev, or Ivan Gerasimovich would be coming to dinner the following day. The dinner was palatable and well served. She never put the host to shame. But how much agitation, running about, entreaties in shops, sleepless nights, and even tears this cost her! How deeply she found herself suddenly immersed in the troubles of life and how well she came to know its happy and unhappy days! But she loved this life: notwithstanding the great bitterness of her tears and anxieties, she would not have exchanged it for her former tranquil existence, when she had not known Oblomov, when she lorded it with dignity among the hissing and boiling saucepans, frying-pans and pots, and issued her orders to Akulina and the caretaker. She shuddered with horror when the thought of death suddenly occurred to her, though death would at one blow put an end to her never-drying tears, her constant rushing about by day, and her inability to close her eyes by night.

Oblomov had his lunch, heard Masha read French, spent some time in Agafya Matveyevna's room watching her mend Vanya's school tunic, turning it a dozen times this way and that, and at the same time rushing into the kitchen to have a look at the mutton roasting for dinner and to see whether it was time to make the fish soup.

'You shouldn't take so much trouble, really you shouldn't,' Oblomov said. 'Give it a rest!'

'Who's going to take trouble, if not I?' she said. 'As soon as I've put two patches here, I'll get the fish soup ready. What a naughty boy Vanya is, to be sure! Only last week I mended his coat, and now he's torn it again! What are you laughing at?' she turned to Vanya, who was sitting at the table in his shirt and trousers held up by one brace. 'If I don't mend it before morning, you will not be able to run out of the gate. I expect the boys must have torn it. You've been fighting, haven't you?'

'No, Mummie, it got torn by itself,' said Vanya.

'By itself, did it? You ought to be sitting at home and doing your homework and not running about in the streets. Next time Mr Oblomov says that you're not doing your French lessons properly, I'll take your shoes off as well: you'll have to do your homework then!'

'I don't like French.'

'Why not?' asked Oblomov.

'Oh, they've a lot of bad words in French.'

Agafya Matveyevna flushed. Oblomov burst out laughing. It was not the first time that the subject of 'bad words' had been raised.

'Be quiet, you naughty boy,' she said. 'Wipe your nose. can't you?'

Vanya sniffed, but did not wipe his nose.

'Wait till I get the money from the country – I'll have two coats made for him,' Oblomov interjected. 'A blue tunic and a school uniform next year: he'll be going to a secondary school next year.'

'Oh,' said Agafya Matveyevna, 'his old one will do very well yet. I shall need the money for housekeeping. We'll have to lay in a supply of salt beef and I'll make some jam for you. I must go and see if Anisya has brought the sour cream.'

She got up.

'What are we having for dinner to-day?' asked Oblomov.

'Fish soup, roast mutton, and curd dumplings.'

Oblomov said nothing.

Suddenly a carriage drew up, there was a knock at the gate followed by the barking and jumping of the dog. Oblomov went back to his room thinking someone had come to see the landlady: the butcher, the greengrocer, or some such person. Such a visit was usually accompanied by requests for money, a refusal by the landlady, threats by the shopkeepers, followed by entreaties and abuse, slamming of doors, banging of gates, and the desperate barking and jumping of the dog – an unpleasant scene altogether. But this time a carriage had driven up – what could it mean? Butchers and greengrocers did not drive about in carriages.

Suddenly the landlady rushed into his room in a panic.

'A visitor for you!' she said.

'Who? Tarantyev or Alexeyev?'

'No, no, the gentleman who came to dinner on your name-day.'

'Stolz?' Oblomov cried in alarm, looking round for a way of escape. 'What will he say when he sees. ... Tell him I'm not at home!' he added hurriedly, retreating to the landlady's room.

Anisya was just about to open the door for the visitor. Agafya Matveyevna had time to give her Oblomov's order. Stolz believed her, though he could not help expressing his surprise at Oblomov's not being in.

'Very well, tell your master that I'll be here in two hours and have dinner with him,' he said, and went to the public park in the vicinity.

'He'll come to dinner!' Anisya cried in alarm.

'He'll come to dinner!' Agafya Matveyevna repeated to Oblomov in a panic.

'You'll have to prepare another dinner,' Oblomov decided after a pause.

She gave him a look full of terror. All she had left was fifty copecks, and it was still ten days to the first of the month, when her brother gave her the money. She could get no more credit.

'We shan't have time,' she observed timidly. 'He'll have to be satisfied with what we have.'

'But he won't eat it. He hates fish soup, he doesn't even eat sturgeon soup. He never touches mutton, either.'

'I could get some tongue from the sausage shop,' she said as though with sudden inspiration. 'It's not far from here.'

'That's all right, do that. And get some vegetables, fresh kidney beans ...!'

'Kidney beans are eighty copecks a pound,' she was about to say, but didn't.

'Very well, I will,' she said, making up her mind definitely to get cabbage instead of the beans.

'Get a pound of Swiss cheese,' he commanded, having no idea of Agafya Matveyevna's means. 'And nothing more. I'll apologize and say we had not expected him. ... Oh yes, could you perhaps get some nice clear soup, too?'

She was about to leave the room.

'And the wine?' he suddenly remembered.

She answered with a new look of horror.

'You must send out for some Lafitte,' he concluded coolly.

6

Stolz arrived two hours later.

'What's the matter with you?' he asked. 'How changed you are! You look pale and bloated! Are you well?'

'No, Andrey, not at all well,' Oblomov said embracing him. 'My left leg keeps going dead.'

'Your room is in such an awful mess!' Stolz said, looking round. 'Why don't you throw away this dressing-gown of yours? Look at it! It's all in patches.'

'Habit, Andrey. I'd be sorry to part from it.'

'And the blankets, the curtains!' Stolz began. 'Is that also habit? Sorry to change these rags? Good Lord, man, can you really sleep in this bed? What *is* the matter with you?'

'Oh, nothing,' Oblomov said, looking embarrassed. 'As you know, I never was very particular about my rooms. ... Come, let's have dinner. Hey, Zakhar! Lay the table quick. Well, how are you? Are you staying here long? Where have you come from?'

'Guess what I'm doing and where I've come from?' Stolz asked. 'Why, I don't suppose you get any news from the outside world here, do you?'

Oblomov looked at him with interest, waiting to hear what he had to say.

'How is Olga?' he asked.

'Oh, so you haven't forgotten her, have you?' said Stolz. 'I did not think you would remember.'

'No, Andrey, I couldn't forget her, could I? That would have meant forgetting that I had been alive once, that I had been in paradise. ... And now here I am!' he sighed. 'But where is she?'

'She's looking after her estate.'

'With her aunt?' asked Oblomov.

'And with her husband.'

'Is she married?' Oblomov cried, staring at Stolz.

'Why are you so alarmed? Memories?' Stolz added softly, almost tenderly.

'Good heavens, no!' Oblomov cried, coming to himself. 'I wasn't alarmed, but surprised. I don't know why it startled me. How long has she been married? Is she happy? Tell me, please. I feel as though you had lifted a load off my mind. Though you assured me that she had forgiven me, I – well, you know, I felt uneasy! Something kept gnawing at me. ... Dear Andrey, how grateful I am to you!'

He was so genuinely pleased, he was so jumping about on the sofa, unable to keep still, that Stolz could not help admiring him and was even touched.

'What a good chap you are, Ilya,' he said. 'Your heart was worthy of her. I shall tell her everything.'

'No, no, don't tell her!' Oblomov interrupted. 'She'll think me unfeeling if she hears that I was glad to learn of her marriage.'

'But isn't gladness also a feeling, and an unselfish one too? You're only glad that she is happy.'

'That's true, that's true!' Oblomov interrupted. 'I don't know what I'm talking about. But who – who is the lucky man? I forgot to ask.'

'Who?' Stolz repeated. 'How slow you are, Ilya!'

Oblomov suddenly looked motionless at his friend: for a moment his face went rigid and the colour left his cheeks.

'It – it isn't you, is it?' he asked suddenly.

'Frightened again? What of?' Stolz said, laughing.

'Don't joke, Andrey, tell me the truth!' Oblomov cried agitatedly.

'Of course, I'm not joking. I've been married to Olga for over a year.'

Gradually the look of alarm disappeared from Oblomov's face, giving place to an expression of peaceful thoughtfulness; he did not raise his eyes, but his thoughtfulness was a minute later changed to a deep and quiet joy, and when he slowly looked up at Stolz, his eyes were full of tender emotion and tears.

'Dear Andrey!' said Oblomov, embracing his friend. 'Dear Olga – Sergeyevna,' he added, restraining his enthusiasm. 'God himself has blessed you! Oh dear, I'm so happy! Tell her – –'

'I'll tell her that I know of no other Oblomov!' Stolz interrupted him, deeply moved.

'No, tell her, remind her that we were brought together only for the sake of putting her on the right path and that I bless our meeting and bless her on her new path in life! What if it had been someone else?' he added in terror. 'But now,' he concluded gaily, 'I do not blush for the part I played, and I am not sorry for it. A heavy load has lifted from my soul; it's all clear there and I am happy. Dear Lord, I thank you!'

He again almost jumped about on the sofa with excitement: one moment he laughed and another he cried.

'Zakhar, champagne for dinner!' he cried, forgetting that he had not a farthing.

'I'll tell Olga everything, everything,' said Stolz. 'I understand now why she can't forget you. No, you were worthy of her: your heart is a well – deep!'

Zakhar thrust his head round the door.

'Please, sir, one moment!' he said, winking at his master.

'What do you want?' Oblomov asked impatiently. 'Go away!'

'I want some money, please!' Zakhar whispered.

Oblomov suddenly fell silent.

'Never mind,' he whispered into the door. 'Say you'd forgotten or that you hadn't time! Go now! No, come back!' he said aloud. 'Have you heard the news, Zakhar? Congratulate Mr Stolz: he is married.'

'Are you really, sir? I am glad, sir, to have lived to hear such joyful news. Accept my congratulations, Mr Stolz, sir! May you live happily for many years and have children in plenty. Dear me, this is great news indeed, sir!'

Zakhar bowed, smiled, grunted, and wheezed. Stolz took out a note and gave it him.

'Here,' he said, 'take it and buy yourself a coat; you look like a beggar.'

'Whom have you married, sir?' asked Zakhar, trying to catch Stolz's hand to kiss.

'Olga Sergeyevna – remember?' said Oblomov.

'The Ilyinsky young lady! Lord, what a nice young lady she is, sir! You were right to scold me that time, sir, old dog that I am! It was all my stupid fault, sir: I thought it was you. It was I who told the Ilyinsky servants about it, and not Nikita! Aye, that was slander, that was! Oh, dear me, dear me – –' he kept repeating, as he went out of the room.

'Olga invites you to stay at her house in the country. Your love has cooled down, so there is no danger: you won't be jealous. Let's go.'

Oblomov sighed. 'No, Andrey,' he said; 'it isn't love or jealousy I'm afraid of, but I won't go with you all the same.'

'What are you afraid of then?'

'I'm afraid of envying you: your happiness will be like a mirror in which I shall see my bitter and wasted life; for, you see, I won't live differently any more – I can't.'

'My dear Ilya, how can you talk like this? You'll have to live the same sort of life as those around you, whether you want to or not. You'll keep accounts, look after your estate, read, listen to music. You can't imagine how much her voice has improved! Remember *Casta diva*?'

Oblomov waved his hand to stop Stolz reminding him of it.

'Let's go, then!' Stolz insisted. 'It's her wish. She won't leave you alone. I may get tired of asking you, but not she. There is so much energy in her, so much vitality that quite often I find it hard to keep up with her myself. The past will again begin to stir in your soul. You will recall the park, the lilac, and you'll rouse yourself. ...'

'No, Andrey, no; don't remind me of it, don't try to rouse me, for God's sake,' Oblomov interrupted him earnestly. 'It doesn't comfort me, it hurts me. Memories are either the finest poetry when they are memories of actual happiness or a burning pain when they are associated with wounds that have scarcely healed. Let's talk of something else. Oh, yes, I forgot to thank you for all the trouble you are taking about my affairs and my estate. My friend, I cannot, I don't feel equal to it; you must look for my gratitude in your own heart, in your happiness – in Olga ... Sergeyevna, but I – I – cannot! I'm sorry I am giving you all this trouble. But it will soon be spring and I will most certainly go to Oblomovka. ...'

'But have you any idea what is happening in Oblomovka?' said Stolz. 'You won't recognize it! I haven't written to you because you don't answer letters. The bridge is built, and the house is finished, roof and all. But you must see about the interior decorations according to your own taste – I can't undertake that. The new manager is one of my own men and he is looking after everything. You've seen the accounts, haven't you?'

Oblomov made no answer.

'Haven't you read them?' Stolz asked. 'Where are they?'

'Wait, I'll find them after dinner. I must ask Zakhar.'

'Oh, Ilya, Ilya! I don't know whether to laugh or to cry.'

'We'll find them after dinner. Let's have dinner!'

Stolz frowned as he sat down to the table. He remembered Oblomov's name-day party: the oysters, the pineapples, the double-snipe; now he saw a coarse table-cloth, cruet-bottles stopped with bits of paper instead of corks, forks with broken handles, two large pieces of black bread on their plates. Oblomov had fish soup and he had barley broth and boiled chicken, followed by tough tongue and mutton. Red wine was served.

Stolz poured himself out half a glass, had a sip, put the glass back on the table, and did not touch it again. Oblomov drank two glasses of currant vodka, one after the other, and greedily attacked the mutton.

'The wine is no good at all,' said Stolz.

'I'm sorry,' said Oblomov. 'I'm afraid they were too busy to go over to the other side of the river for it. Won't you have some currant vodka? It's nice. Try it, Andrey.'

He poured himself out another glass and drank it. Stolz looked at him in surprise, but let it pass.

'Agafya Matveyevna makes it herself. She's a nice woman,' said Oblomov, slightly drunk. 'I must say I don't know how I shall be able to live in the country without her: you won't find such a housekeeper anywhere.'

Stolz listened to him with a slight frown.

'Who do you think does all the cooking? Anisya? No, sir!' Oblomov went on. 'Anisya looks after the poultry, weeds the cabbage patch, and scrubs the floors. Agafya Matveyevna does all this.'

Stolz did not eat the mutton or the curd dumplings; he put down his fork and watched with what appetite Oblomov ate it all.

'Now you won't see me wearing a shirt inside out,' Oblomov went on, sucking a bone with great relish. 'She examines everything and misses nothing – all my socks are darned – and she does it all herself. And the coffee she makes! You'll see for yourself when you have some after dinner.'

Stolz listened in silence with a worried expression.

'Now her brother has gone to live in a flat of his own – he took it into his head to get married – so, of course, things are not on such a big scale as before. In the old days she had not a free minute to herself. She used to be rushing about from morning till night, to the market, to the shopping arcade. ... Tell you what,' concluded Oblomov, having all but lost the use of his tongue, 'let me have two or three thousand and I'd have offered you something better than tongue and mutton – a whole sturgeon, trout, first-class fillet of beef. And Agafya Matveyevna would have worked wonders without a cook – yes, sir!'

He drank another glass of vodka.

'Do have a drink, Andrey; there's a good chap – lovely vodka! Olga Sergeyevna won't make you any vodka like this,' he said, speaking rather thickly. 'She can sing *Casta diva* but doesn't know how to make such vodka! Nor how to make a chicken-

and-mushroom pie! Such pies they used to make only in Oblo-movka and now here! And what's so splendid about it is that it isn't done by a man cook: you never know what his hands are like when he makes the pie, but Agafya Matveyevna is cleanliness itself.'

Stolz listened attentively, taking it all in.

'And her hands used to be white,' Oblomov, now well and truly befuddled, went on. 'So white you could not help wishing to kiss them! But now they're very rough, because, you see, she has to do everything herself. Starches my shirts herself !' Oblomov cried with feeling, almost with tears. 'Indeed, she does – seen it myself. I tell you many wives don't look after their husbands as she does after me – yes, sir! A nice creature, Agafya Matveyevna, a nice creature! Look here, Andrey, why not come to live here with Olga Sergeyevna? I mean, get yourself a summer cottage here. You'd love it! We'd have tea in the woods, go to the Gunpowder Works on St Elijah's Day, with a cart laden with provisions and a *samovar* following us. We'd lie down on the grass there – on a rug! Agafya Matveyevna would teach Olga Sergeyevna how to run a house, I promise you she would! Only, you see, things are rather tight now, her brother has moved out, and if *we* had three or four thousand, we'd get you such turkeys – –'

'But you're getting five thousand from me,' Stolz said suddenly. 'What do you do with it?'

'And my debt?' Oblomov blurted out suddenly.

Stolz jumped up from his seat.

'Your debt?' he repeated. 'What debt?'

And he looked at Oblomov like a stern teacher at a child trying to hide something from him.

Oblomov suddenly fell silent. Stolz sat down beside him on the sofa.

'Whom do you owe money to?' he asked.

Oblomov sobered down a little and came to his senses.

'I don't owe anything to anyone,' he said. 'I was lying.'

'Oh no, you're lying now, and clumsily too. What has been happening here, Ilya? What's the matter with you? Aha! So that's the meaning of the mutton and sour wine! You have no money! What do you do with it?'

'Well, as a matter of fact, I do owe my landlady – a little – for – er – my board,' Oblomov said.

'For mutton and tongue! Ilya, tell me, what's going on here? What kind of tale is this: the landlady's brother has moved, things have gone badly. ... There's something wrong here. How much do you owe?'

'Ten thousand on an IOU,' Oblomov whispered.

Stolz jumped to his feet and sat down again.

'Ten thousand? To the landlady? For your board?' he repeated in horror.

'Yes, I – er – got a lot on credit – I lived in great style, you know. ... Remember the pineapples and peaches, and – well, so I got into debt,' muttered Oblomov. 'But what's the use of talking about it?'

Stolz did not reply. He was thinking. 'The landlady's brother has gone, things have gone badly – that's so: everything looks so bare, poor, dirty! What sort of woman is this landlady? She looks after him, he speaks of her with ardour. ...'

Suddenly Stolz changed colour, having guessed the truth. He turned cold.

'Ilya,' he said, 'that woman – what is she to you?'

But Oblomov had put his head on the table and fallen into a doze.

'She robs him, takes everything from him – it's the sort of thing that happens every day, and I haven't thought of it till this very moment!' he reflected.

Stolz got up and opened the door leading to the landlady's room so quickly that, at the sight of him, Agafya Matveyevna in alarm dropped the spoon with which she was stirring the coffee.

'I'd like to have a talk with you, madam,' he said politely.

'Please step into the drawing-room,' she replied timidly. 'I'll come at once.'

Throwing a kerchief round her neck, she followed him into the drawing-room and sat down on the very edge of the sofa. She no longer had her shawl and she tried to hide her hands under the kerchief.

'Mr Oblomov has given you a bill of exchange, hasn't he?' he asked.

'No,' she replied with a look of dull surprise, 'he has not given me any bill.'

'Hasn't he?'

'I haven't seen any bill,' she repeated with the same expression of dull astonishment.

'A bill of exchange!' Stolz repeated.

She thought it over for a minute.

'I think,' she said, 'you'd better have a talk to my brother. I haven't seen any bill.'

'Is she a fool or a rogue?' Stolz thought.

'But he owes you money, doesn't he?' he asked.

She gave him a vacant look, then suddenly an expression of intelligence and even of anxiety came into her face. She remembered the pawned string of pearls, the silver, and the fur coat, and imagined that Stolz was referring to that debt, only she could not understand how he had got to know of it, for she had never breathed a word about it not only to Oblomov, but even to Anisya, whom she generally told about every penny she spent.

'How much does he owe you?' Stolz asked anxiously.

'Nothing at all. Not a penny.'

'She's concealing it from me, she is ashamed, the greedy creature, the usurer!' he thought. 'But I'll get to the truth.'

'And the ten thousand?' he said.

'What ten thousand?' she asked in anxious surprise.

'Mr Oblomov owes you ten thousand on an IOU – yes or no?' he asked.

'He owes me nothing. He owed the butcher since Lent twelve roubles and fifty copecks, but we paid it over a fortnight ago. We also paid the dairywoman for the cream – he owes nothing.'

'But have you no document from him?'

She looked blankly at him.

'You'd better have a talk to my brother,' she replied. 'He lives across the street in Zamykalov's house, just along here. There's a public-house in the basement.'

'No, ma'am, I'd rather have a talk with you,' he said decisively. 'Mr Oblomov says that he owes you money, and not your brother.'

'He does not owe me anything,' she replied, 'and as for my pawning silver, pearls, and a fur coat, I did it for myself. I bought shoes for Masha and myself, material for Vanya's shirts, and gave the rest to the greengrocer. I have not spent a penny of it on Mr Oblomov.'

He looked at her, listened and tried to grasp the meaning of her words. He alone, it seems, came near to guessing Agafya Matveyevna's secret, and the look of disdain, almost contempt he had cast at her when speaking to her was involuntarily replaced by one of interest and even sympathy. In the pawning of the pearls and silver he vaguely read the secret of her sacrifices, but he could not make up his mind whether they were made as a result of pure devotion or in expectation of blessings to come. He did not know whether he should feel glad or sad for Ilya. It was quite clear that he owed her nothing, and that this debt was some fraudulent trick of her brother's, but a great deal more had been revealed. ... What was the meaning of the pawning of the pearls and silver?

'So you have no claim on Mr Oblomov, have you?' he asked.

'You'd better talk it over with my brother,' she replied monotonously. 'He ought to be at home by now.'

'You say Mr Oblomov does not owe you anything?'

'Not a penny, I swear it's the truth!' she declared solemnly, looking at the icon and crossing herself.

'Are you ready to confirm it before witnesses?'

'Yes, before anyone. I'd say it at confession! As for my pawning the pearls and silver, it was for my own expenses.'

'Very good,' Stolz interrupted her. 'I'll be coming back to-morrow with two friends of mine. You will not refuse to say the same thing in their presence, will you?'

'I think you'd better have a talk to my brother,' she repeated. 'You see, I'm not dressed decently – I'm always in the kitchen. It wouldn't be nice for strangers to see me: they'll think ill of me.'

'Don't worry about that, and I shall see your brother to-morrow after you've signed a paper.'

'I'm afraid I'm quite unused to writing now.'

'You won't have to write much. Just two lines.'

'No, sir, I'd rather you spared me that. Why not let Vanya write? He writes beautifully.'

'No, you mustn't refuse,' he insisted. 'If you don't sign the paper it will mean that Mr Oblomov owes you ten thousand.'

'No, he doesn't owe me a penny,' she repeated. 'I swear he doesn't.'

'In that case you must sign the paper. Good-bye till-morrow.'

'To-morrow you'd better go and see my brother,' she said, seeing him off. 'He lives just there, at the corner, across the street.'

'No, and I'd ask you to say nothing to your brother till I come, or it will be very unpleasant for Mr Oblomov.'

'Then I won't say anything to him,' she said obediently.

7

ON the following day Agafya Matveyevna gave Stolz a written statement to the effect that she had no claim of any kind on Oblomov. With this statement Stolz suddenly appeared before her brother. That was a real bombshell for Ivan Matveyevich. He took out the IOU and pointed with the shaking finger of his right hand, which he held with the nail downwards, to Oblomov's signature and the attached notary's signature.

'It's the law, sir,' he said. 'I've nothing to do with it. I'm merely watching over my sister's interests. I have no idea what money Mr Oblomov had borrowed from her.'

'You have not heard the last of it!' Stolz threatened him as he drove off.

'It's perfectly legal,' Ivan Matveyevich pleaded, hiding his hands in his sleeves, 'and I've nothing to do with it!'

As soon as he came to his office on the following day, a messenger arrived from the General, who wanted to see him at once.

'The General?' all the clerks in the office repeated in horror. 'Whatever for? Does he want some document? Which one? Quick, quick! File the papers, draw up the schedules! What is it?'

In the evening Ivan Matveyevich came to the tavern greatly disconcerted. Tarantyev had been waiting for him there for hours.

'Well, what is it, old man?' he asked impatiently.

'What is it?' Ivan Matveyevich said monotonously. 'What do you think?'

'You were told off?'

'Told off!' Ivan Matveyevich mimicked him. 'I wish I'd been given a beating! And you're a nice one, too!' he cried, reproachfully. 'You didn't tell me what sort of German he was, did you?'

'But I told you he was a rascally fellow!'

'A rascally fellow, is it? We've seen plenty of rascals! Why didn't you tell me he had influence? Why, he's on familiar terms with the General, just as you are with me. Would I have had anything to do with him, if I'd known?'

'But,' Tarantyev retorted, 'it's perfectly legal!'

'Perfectly legal!' Ivan Matveyevich again mimicked him. 'Just try and say it there: why, your tongue will stick to the roof of your mouth. Do you know what the General asked me?'

'What?' Tarantyev asked curiously.

'Is it true that you and some other blackguard made the landowner Oblomov drunk and forced him to sign an IOU in your sister's name?'

'Did he actually say "and some other blackguard"?' asked Tarantyev.

'Yes, he did.'

'Who can that blackguard be?' Tarantyev asked again.

His friend looked at him.

'I don't expect you know, do you?' he said bitterly. 'It couldn't be you by any chance, could it?'

'Me? So I've got mixed up in it too?'

'You'd better thank the German and your country neighbour. The German, you see, has sniffed it all out, cross-questioned everybody. ...'

'You should have mentioned someone else, old man, and told them I had nothing to do with it.'

'Should I now? Why, what sort of a saint are you?'

'But what did you say when the General asked whether it was true that you and some other blackguard ...? That was when you should have tried to bluff him.'

'Bluff him? You can't bluff a fellow like that! You should have seen those green eyes of his! I tried my best to say that the whole thing was not true, that it was a slander, that I knew nothing about any Oblomov, and that it was all Tarantyev's fault, but I just couldn't get the words out of my mouth. I merely threw myself on his mercy.'

'Well, they're not going to prosecute you, are they?' Tarantyev asked hoarsely. 'Mind, I had nothing to do with it. Now, you, old man – –'

'You had nothing to do with it? No, sir, if we are in for it, you will be the first. Who was it persuaded Oblomov to drink? Who abused and threatened him?'

'But it was your idea,' said Tarantyev.

'Why, are you a minor, by any chance? I know nothing whatever about the whole business.'

'That's not fair, old man! Think how much money you had through me, and I've only had three hundred roubles.'

'You don't want me to take the whole blame on myself, do you? Clever, aren't you? No, sir, I know nothing about it. I was just asked by my sister to witness an IOU at a notary's, for, being a woman, she doesn't understand such things – that's all. You and Zatyorty were the witnesses, so it's your responsibility!'

'You should have had a good talk to your sister – how did she dare to go against her own brother?' said Tarantyev.

'My sister's a fool – what can I do with her?'

'What about her?'

'About her? She goes on crying and insisting that Oblomov owes her nothing and that she never gave him any money.'

'But you have an IOU from her,' said Tarantyev. 'You won't lose your money.'

Ivan Matveyevich took his sister's IOU out of his pocket, tore it up, and gave it to Tarantyev.

'Here, I'll make you a present of it, if you like,' he added. 'What can I take from her? Her house and the kitchen garden? I wouldn't get a thousand for it: it's all falling to pieces. And, anyway, what do you take me for – an infidel? Do you want me to let her go begging with her children?'

'So they are going to prosecute us, are they?' Tarantyev asked timidly. 'Well, old man, we'll have to do our best to get off as lightly as possible. You'll have to get me out of it, old man.'

'Who's going to prosecute you? There won't be any prosecution. The General, it is true, threatened to send me out of town, but the German interceded. He doesn't want to disgrace Oblomov.'

'You don't say so, old man! Ugh, what a weight off my mind! Let's have a drink!' said Tarantyev.

'Have a drink? Out of whose income, pray? Not yours, by any chance?'

'What about yours? I daresay you've collected your seven roubles to-day as usual.'

'Have I, indeed? I'm afraid it's good-bye to my income. I haven't finished telling you what the General said.'

'Why, what was it?' Tarantyev asked, getting suddenly frightened again.

'He told me to send in my resignation!'

'Good Lord!' Tarantyev said, staring at Ivan Matveyevich. 'Well,' he concluded furiously. 'I'll tell him off properly now!'

'All you can do is to tell people off!'

'I'll tell him what I think of him, whatever you say!' said Tarantyev. 'Still, perhaps you're right, and I'd better wait. I've just thought of something. Listen, old man.'

'Not again?' Ivan Matveyevich cried doubtfully.

'We could do an excellent piece of business, only it's a pity you've moved to another house.'

'What is that?'

'What is that!' Tarantyev said, looking at Ivan Matveyevich. 'Spy on Oblomov and your sister, see the sort of pies they are baking there, and – have your witnesses ready! The German himself won't be able to do anything then. And you're a free man now: if you bring an action against him – it's perfectly

435

legal! I daresay the German, too, will get cold feet and be glad to come to some arrangement.'

'I don't know, it might work!' said Ivan Matveyevich thoughtfully. 'You're not bad at thinking out new ideas, but you're no good at all for business, neither is Zatyorty. But I'll find some way. Wait a moment!' he said, getting excited. 'I'll show them! I'll send my cook round to my sister's kitchen: she'll make friends with Anisya and find out everything, and then – let's have a drink, old man!'

'Let's have a drink!' Tarantyev repeated. 'And then I'll give Oblomov a piece of my mind!'

Stolz tried to take Oblomov away to the country, but Oblomov asked him to let him remain only for a month, and he asked him so earnestly that Stolz could not help taking pity on his friend. Oblomov claimed that he needed that month to pay his accounts, to give up the flat, and to settle his affairs in Petersburg so that he need not return there. He had, besides, to buy everything he needed for his country house; finally, he wanted to find a good housekeeper, someone like Agafya Matveyevna, and he did not even despair of persuading her to sell her house and move to the country, to a job worthy of her – complicated housekeeping on quite a vast scale.

'Incidentally, about that landlady of yours,' Stolz interrupted him. 'I wanted to ask you, Ilya, what are your relations with her?'

Oblomov blushed suddenly.

'What do you mean?' he asked hurriedly.

'You know very well,' Stolz observed, 'or there wouldn't have been any reason for you to blush. Listen, Ilya, if a warning can be of any use, I ask you in the name of our friendship to be careful.'

'What of? Good heavens!' Oblomov, looking embarrassed, protested.

'You speak of her with such warmth that I am really beginning to think that you ...'

'Love her, did you want to say? Good heavens!' Oblomov interrupted with a forced laugh.

'Well, all the worse if there isn't anything spiritual about it, if it's only – –'

'Andrey, have you ever known me to do anything immoral?'

'Why did you blush, then?'

'Because you could have thought such a thing about me.'

Stolz shook his head doubtfully.

'Take care, Ilya, and don't fall into the pit. A common woman, filthy life, a stifling atmosphere, stupidity, coarseness – faugh!'

Oblomov was silent.

'Well, good-bye,' Stolz concluded. 'So I'll tell Olga we shall see you in summer, if not at our house, then at Oblomovka. Remember: she will not leave you alone.'

'Certainly, certainly,' Oblomov replied. 'You may even add that, if she lets me, I'll spend the winter with you.'

'We should be delighted!'

Stolz left the same day, and in the evening Tarantyev came to see Oblomov. He could not restrain himself from hauling him over the coals on account of Ivan Matveyevich. He omitted to take one thing into consideration, namely, that in the Ilyinskys' social circle Oblomov had lost the habit of associating with people like himself and that his putting up with rudeness and insolence had given way to disgust. That would have become apparent long ago, and, in fact, had partly shown itself when Oblomov lived at the summer cottage, but since then Tarantyev's visits had been less frequent, and they only met in the presence of other people, so that there had been no clashes between them.

'Good evening, old man!' Tarantyev said spitefully, without offering his hand to Oblomov.

'Good evening,' Oblomov replied coldly, looking out of the window.

'Well, have you seen off your benefactor?'

'I have. Why?'

'Some benefactor!' Tarantyev went on venomously.

'You don't like him, do you?'

'No, I'd have strung him up!' Tarantyev hissed with hatred.

'Would you really?'

'And you, too, on the same tree!'

'Whatever for?'

'Deal honestly with people: if you owe them money, pay up, and don't try to wriggle out of it. What have you done now?'

'Look here, Tarantyev; spare me your fairy-tales: I've listened to you long enough through laziness and carelessness. You see, I thought you had just a little bit of conscience, but you haven't. You and that cunning old rascal wanted to cheat me. Which of you is the worse I don't know, but you are both loathsome to me. A friend has saved me from that stupid affair ...'

'A nice friend!' Tarantyev said. 'I understand he has cheated you of your fiancée. A fine benefactor, I must say! Well, old man, you certainly are a fool!'

'None of your endearments, please!' Oblomov cut him short.

'I'll say what I like! You didn't want to have anything to do with me – you're ungrateful! I've found you a decent home here, I have found you a real treasure of a woman. Peace and comfort – it's me you have to thank for it, for it's me who got them for you, but you won't have anything to do with me. Found a benefactor, have you? A German! Rents your estate, does he? You wait: he'll skin you alive, make you buy shares. He'll make a beggar of you, mark my words! A fool, I tell you, that's what you are. More than a fool; you're a brute, an ungrateful brute!'

'Tarantyev!' Oblomov cried menacingly.

'What are you shouting for? I'll shout at the top of my voice for the whole world to hear that you are a fool and a brute!' Tarantyev shouted. 'Ivan Matveyevich and I waited hand and foot on you, looked after you, served you just as though we were your serfs, walked on tiptoe, tried to anticipate your every wish, and you went and discredited him before his superiors. Now he has lost his job and can't earn a living. That is a low-down trick! Now you must give him half your property. Let me have a bill of exchange in his name. You're not drunk now, but in full possession of your faculties; let me have it, I tell you. I won't go without it ...'

'What are you shouting like that for, Mr Tarantyev?' the landlady and Anisya said, looking in at the door. 'Two people in the street have stopped to listen.'

'I'll go on shouting,' bawled Tarantyev. 'I'll bring shame and disgrace on this stupid blockhead! Let that rogue of a German cheat you now that he is working hand in glove with your mistress. ...'

A loud slap resounded in the room. Tarantyev, struck on the cheek by Oblomov, fell silent instantly, sank on to a chair and rolled his stunned eyes in amazement.

'What's this? What's this – eh? What's all this?' he said, pale and breathless, holding his cheek. 'Dishonour? You'll pay for it! I'll send in a complaint to the Governor-General at once. You saw it, didn't you?'

'We didn't see anything!' the two women cried in one voice.

'Oh, so it's a plot, is it? A thieves' kitchen, is it? A gang of swindlers! Robbing, murdering. ...'

'Get out, you blackguard!' Oblomov cried, pale and trembling with rage. 'Clear out this minute or I'll kill you like a dog!'

He was looking round for a stick.

'Murder! Help!' shouted Tarantyev.

'Zakhar, throw this scoundrel out and see that he doesn't show his face here again!' Oblomov cried.

'Come along, sir,' said Zakhar, pointing to the icon and the door; 'here's God and there's the door.'

'I haven't come to see you, but my friend,' Tarantyev bawled.

'Good gracious, sir, I don't want to have anything to do with you, I'm sure,' Agafya Matveyevna said. 'You used to come to see my brother, not me. I'm sick and tired of you. You eat us out of house and home and abuse us into the bargain!'

'Oh, so that's it! Very well, your brother will show you what's what! And you will pay me for your insult! Where's my hat? To hell with you! Robbers, murderers!' he shouted as he walked across the yard. 'You'll pay me for your insult, you will!'

The dog jumped on the chain, barking at the top of its voice.

That was the last time Tarantyev and Oblomov ever saw each other.

8 Key - Big Picture

STOLZ did not come to Petersburg for several years. Only once did he pay a short visit to Oblomovka and Olga's estate. Oblomov received a letter from him in which Stolz tried to persuade him to go to the country and take charge of his estate, which was in good working order now; he and Olga were leaving for the south coast of the Crimea for two reasons: he had business in Odessa, and Olga was in delicate health since her confinement and hoped to benefit from a holiday in the Crimea. They settled in a quiet little spot on the seashore. Their house was small and modest. Its architecture and its interior decorations had a style of their own, which bore the imprint of the personal taste and thoughts of its owners. They had brought many things with them and had many more packages, cases, and cartloads sent them from Russia and abroad. A lover of comfort might perhaps have shrugged at the apparently discordant character of the furniture, old pictures, statues with broken arms and legs, engravings, sometimes rather bad but dear for sentimental reasons, and all sorts of knick-knacks. Only a connoisseur's eyes would light up eagerly at the sight of some of the pictures or a book yellow with age, old china, stones, and coins. But there was a breath of warm life among the furniture of different periods, the pictures, the bric-à-brac, which were of no significance to anybody, but which reminded them of some happy hour or some memorable occasion, and among the enormous number of books and sheets of music. There was something in it all that stimulated the mind and aesthetic feeling, something that made one aware of the unslumbering thought and the radiant beauty of human achievement as one was aware of the radiant and eternal beauty of nature all around. The tall desk which belonged to Andrey's father was also there, as well as the chamois-leather gloves. The oilskin cloak hung in the corner near the cupboard with minerals, shells, stuffed birds, samples of different kinds of clay, merchandise, and so on. The place of honour was occupied by an Erard grand piano, shining with gold and inlaid work. The cottage was covered from top to bottom with a network of vine, ivy, and myrtle. From one side of the balcony the sea could be seen, and from the other the road to the town. It was from that end that Olga watched for Andrey to return when he had been away from home on business, and, seeing him, she went downstairs, ran through a lovely flower-garden and a long poplar avenue, and flung herself on her husband's neck, her cheeks flushed with joy and her eyes sparkling, always with the same ardour of impatient happiness, in spite of the fact that it was not the first nor the second year of their marriage.

Stolz's views on love and marriage may have been odd and exaggerated, but they were, at any rate, his own. Here, too, he followed the free and, it seemed to him, simple road : but what a hard school of observation, patience, and labour he went through before he learnt to take these 'simple steps'! It was from his father that he inherited the habit of looking earnestly at everything in life, even at trifles ; he might perhaps have inherited from him also the pedantic severity with which Germans regard every step they take in life, including marriage.

Old Stolz's life was there for all to read, just as though it had been inscribed on a stone tablet, and there were no hidden implications in it. But his mother, with her songs and tender whispers, the diversified life in the prince's house, and later the university, books, and society had led Andrey away from the straight path marked out for him by his father; Russian life was drawing its own invisible patterns and transforming the insipid tablet into a broad and brilliant picture.

Andrey did not impose pedantic chains on his feelings and

even went so far as to give free rein to his day-dreams, trying only not to lose 'the ground under his feet', though when waking from them he could not refrain, either because of his German nature or for some other reason, from drawing some conclusion which had a direct bearing on some of life's problems. He was vigorous in body because he was vigorous in mind. He had been playful and full of mischief as a boy, and when not playing he was doing something under his father's supervision. He had no time to indulge in day-dreams. His imagination was not corrupted and his heart was not spoiled; his mother carefully watched over the virginal purity of both. As a youth he instinctively conserved his powers, and it was not long before he discovered that by keeping them fresh he also kept his cheerfulness and his vigour, and helped to form that manliness of character in which the soul must be steeled if it is not to capitulate before life, whatever it may be, and look upon it not as a heavy burden or a cross, but only as a duty, and wage battle with it worthily. He devoted much careful thought to the heart and its complicated laws. Observing consciously and unconsciously the effect of beauty on the imagination and then the transition of an impression into feeling, its symptoms, its play, and its result, he became more and more convinced, as he looked around and grew experienced, that love moved the world with the power of Archimedes' lever; that there is as much universal and irrefutable truth and goodness in it as there is falsehood and ugliness in its misuse and the failure to understand it. What is good? What is evil? What is the dividing line between them? At the question 'What is falsehood?' he saw in his imagination a motley procession of masks of the past and present. He contemplated with a smile, blushing and frowning in turn, the endless row of heroes and heroines of love: Don Quixotes in steel gauntlets, and the ladies of their dreams, remaining faithful to one another after fifty years of separation; the shepherds with their rosy faces and artless, bulging eyes, and their Chloes with lambs. Before his mind's eye marquesses appeared in powdered wigs and lace, with eyes twinkling with intelligence and dissolute smiles; they were followed by the Werthers who had shot, strangled, or hanged themselves; then by faded lovelorn maidens shedding endless tears and retiring into convents, and their mustachioed heroes with wild ardour in their eyes; by naïve and self-conscious Don Juans, the clever fellows who tremble at the least suspicion of love and secretly adore their housekeepers – all, all of them.

To answer the question 'What is truth?' he sought far and near, in his mind and with his eyes, examples of ordinary, honest, yet deep and indissoluble intimacy with a woman, but could not find it; and if he seemed to have found it, it only seemed so, and afterwards it was followed by disillusionment. This made him sink into melancholy thoughts and even give way to despair. 'It is clear,' he thought to himself, 'that this blessing has not been granted in all its fullness, or else those whose hearts have experienced the bright radiance of such a love are shy: they are timid and prefer to hide rather than argue with the clever people; perhaps they are sorry for them and forgive them in the name of their own happiness for trampling into the mud the flower that cannot take root in their shallow soil and grow into a tree that would spread its branches over the whole of their lives.'

He looked at marriage, at husbands, and in their attitude to their wives he always saw the riddle of the sphinx; there was something in it that was not understood, something that, somehow, remained unspoken; and yet those husbands did not puzzle their heads over complicated problems, but walked through married life with such even and deliberate steps as though they had nothing to solve and discover. 'Are they perhaps right? Perhaps there really is no need of anything else,' he thought, distrusting himself, as he saw how some men who went through love quickly as the ABC of marriage or as a form of gallantry, just as if they had made a bow on entering a drawing-room, and quickly applied themselves to more important matters! They fling the spring-time of life away impatiently; many of them, indeed, look askance at their wives for the rest of their lives as though unable to forgive themselves for having been foolish enough to fall in love with them. There are others whom love does not forsake for years, sometimes till old age, but the satyr's smile never forsakes them, either. ... Finally, most men enter into matrimony as they buy an estate and enjoy its substantial amenities: a wife keeps the house in excellent order – she is the housekeeper, the mother, the governess; they look upon love as a practical-minded farmer looks upon the beautiful surroundings of his estate; that is, he gets used to it at once and never notices it again.

'What is it, then?' he asked himself. 'An innate inability due to the laws of nature or lack of education and training? Where is the sympathy that never loses its natural charm, that never wears motley, that undergoes modifications but is never extinguished! What is the natural shade and colour of this ubiquitous and all-permeating blessing, of this sap of life?'

He cast a prophetic glance into the distant future, and there arose before him, as in a mist, the image of love and with it of a woman clothed in its colour and radiant with its light, an image so simple, but bright and pure. 'A dream, a dream!' he said with a smile, recovering from the idle excitement of his reverie. But the outline of this dream lived in his memory in spite of himself. At first this image appeared to him as the personification of the woman of the future; but when, after Olga had grown into womanhood, he saw in her not only the splendour of a fully developed beauty, but also a force ready to face life and eager to understand and fight life's battles – all the elements of his dream, there arose before him his old and almost forgotten image of love and he began to dream of Olga as its personification, and it seemed to him that in the far-distant future truth would manifest itself in their sympathy for each other – without growing shabby and without abuses of any kind. Without toying with the question of love and marriage and without confusing it with any considerations of money, connexions, and posts, Stolz, however, could not help wondering how to reconcile his external and hitherto indefatigable activity with his inner family life, how, in fact, he could transform himself from a traveller and business-man into a stay-at-home husband. If he was to settle down and put an end to his constant running about from one place to another, how would he fill his life at home? The bringing up and education of children and the direction of their life was not, of course, an easy or unimportant task, but that was still a long way off, and what was he going to do in the meantime? These questions had often troubled him, and he did not find his bachelor life a burden; nor had it occurred to him to put on the shackles of married life as soon as his heart began beating when he found himself in the presence of beauty. That was why he seemed to ignore Olga as a girl and admired her merely as a charming child of great promise. He would, casually and jokingly, throw some new bold idea or some acute observation of life into her eager and receptive mind, arousing in her, without realizing it, a lively understanding of events and a correct view of things; and then he would forget Olga and his casual lessons. And at times, seeing that she had quite original ideas and qualities of mind, that there was no falsehood in her, that she did not seek general admiration, that her feelings came and went simply and freely, that there was nothing second-hand in her, but everything

443

was her own, and that all this was so bold, so fresh, and so stable – he wondered where she had got it all and did not recognize his own fleeting lessons and remarks. Had he concentrated his attention on her at the time, he would have realized that she was going her own way almost alone, guarded from extremes by her aunt's superficial supervision, but not oppressed by the authority of numerous nurses, grandmothers, and aunts, with the traditions of their family and caste, of outworn manners, customs, and rules; that she was not being led against her will along a beaten track, but walked along a new path which she had to open up by her own intelligence, ideas, and feeling. Nature had not deprived her of any of it; her aunt did not rule despotically over her mind and will, and Olga divined and understood a great deal herself; she watched life carefully, listening – among other things – to her friend's words of advice. ... He did not take anything of this into consideration and merely expected a lot of her in the future, but in the far distant future, without ever thinking of her as his helpmate.

For a long time she would not let him guess what she really was either out of pride or shyness, and it was only after an agonizing struggle abroad that he saw with amazement into what a model of simplicity, strength, and naturalness this promising child he had almost forgotten had grown. It was then that the whole depth of her soul, which he might have filled but never succeeded in filling, was revealed to him.

At first he had long to struggle with the vivacity of her nature, to check the fever of youth, keep her impulses within definite bounds, and impart an even flow to their life, and that, too, only for a time. For as soon as he closed his eyes trustfully, an alarm was raised again, life was in full swing, some new question sprang from her restless mind and anxious heart: he had to calm her excited imagination, to soothe or rouse her pride. If she pondered over something, he hastened to give her the key to it. Belief in chance, mists and hallucinations disappeared from her life. A bright clear vista opened up before her and she could see in it, as in limpid water, every pebble, every crevice, and then the clean sandy bottom.

'I am happy,' she whispered, casting a glance of gratitude over her past life and, trying to see into the future, she recalled the girlish dream of happiness she had once dreamed in Switzerland, the wistful, blue night, and she saw that that dream, like a shadow, was haunting her life. 'Why should this have fallen to my lot?' she thought humbly. She pondered, and was sometimes afraid lest her happiness should end.

Years passed, but they did not tire of living. Peace came at
last, the emotional storms subsided; the ups and downs of life
no longer puzzled them; they put up with them cheerfully and
patiently, and yet life never flagged. Olga reached a true understanding of life. Two existences – Andrey's and hers – merged
into one; there could be no question of a riot of wild passions;
all was peace and harmony between them. It would seem that
they might have gone to sleep in this well-earned rest and be as
blissfully happy as people who live in some backwater, who
meet together three times a day, yawning over their familiar
conversation, falling into a dull slumber, languishing from morning till night because everything had already been thought,
said, and done over and over again and there was nothing more
to be said or done and because 'such is life'. Outwardly their life
was the same as other people's. They got up early, though not
at dawn; they liked to spend a long time over their breakfast,
and sometimes seemed to be lazily silent; then they each went
to their rooms or worked together, dined, drove to the fields,
had music – like everybody else, as Oblomov had dreamed. But
there was no drowsiness or depression about them; they spent
their days without being bored or apathetic; they never exchanged a dull word or look; their conversation never came to
an end and was sometimes heated. Their ringing voices resounded in the rooms and reached the garden, or tracing the pattern
of their dreams, they quietly communicated to each other the
first scarcely perceptible stirrings of thought, the barely audible
murmur of the soul. And their silence was sometimes the
thoughtful happiness of which Oblomov had dreamed, or the
solitary mental work over the endless material they provided
for each other. They often sank into silent amazement before
the eternally new and resplendent beauty of nature. Their sensitive souls could not get used to this beauty: the earth, the sky,
the sea – everything awakened their feelings – and they sat in
silence side by side and looked through the same eyes and with
one heart at this glory of creation and understood each other
without words. They did not meet the morning with indifference; they could not sink dully into the twilight of a warm,
starry, southern night. They were kept awake by the constant
excitement of the soul and the need to think together, to feel
and to talk! ... But what was the subject of these heated discussions, quiet conversations, readings, and long walks? Why,
everything! While they were still abroad, Stolz lost the habit of
reading and working alone: here, alone with Olga, he did not

even think alone. He could scarcely manage to keep pace with the agonizing rapidity of her thought and will.

The question of what he was going to do in his family circle was no longer urgent – it had solved itself. He had to initiate her even into his business life, for she felt stifled unless she took an active part in life. He did nothing without her knowledge or active participation, whether it was building, or something to do with her own or Oblomov's estate, or the company's business transactions. Not a single letter was posted without her reading it, not a single idea, and still less its realization, was kept from her; she knew everything, and everything interested her because it interested him. At first he did it because he found it impossible to hide anything from her: if he wrote a letter or conducted a conversation with an agent or contractor – it was done in her presence; later he continued this from habit, and at last it became a necessity for him too. Her remarks, advice, approval or disapproval were esteemed by him as a necessary check-up on his plans: he saw that she understood as well as he, that she thought and reasoned no worse than he. ... Zakhar resented such ability in his wife, and many men resent it – but Stolz was happy! And reading and learning – the perpetual nourishment of thought and its endless development! Olga was jealous of every book and article she was not shown and was seriously angry or offended if he did not think it worth while showing her something he considered too serious, boring, or incomprehensible to her; she called it pedantic, vulgar, retrograde, and scolded him for being 'an old German stick-in-the-mud'. They often had lively scenes about it. She was angry and he laughed, she grew angrier and made it up with him only when he stopped pulling her leg and shared his ideas, knowledge, and reading with her. The end of it was that she wanted to read about and to know everything he wanted to. He did not force technical terms on her in order to boast idiotically of a 'learned wife'. If she had uttered a single word or hinted at such a claim on his part, he would have blushed more than if she had replied with a blank look of ignorance to an elementary question that did not as yet form part of a woman's education. He merely wanted – and she doubly so – that there should be nothing inaccessible to her understanding, if not to her knowledge. He did not draw diagrams or figures for her, but discussed everything with her and read a great deal without pedantically avoiding economic theories or social or philosophical questions; he spoke with passion and enthusiasm and, as it were, drew for her an endless,

446

living picture of knowledge. Later on she forgot the details, but the general pattern was never erased from her impressionable mind, the colours did not fade, and the fire with which he lighted the world of knowledge he created for her was never extinguished. He was thrilled with pride and happiness when he noticed a spark of that fire shining in her eyes afterwards, how an echo of a thought he had imparted to her resounded in her speech, how it had entered into her consciousness and understanding, been transformed in her mind and appeared in her words no longer stern and dry but sparkling with womanly grace, and particularly if some fruitful drop from all he had discussed, read, and drawn for her, sank, like a pearl, into the translucent depths of her being. Like an artist and a thinker, he was weaving a rational existence for her, and never in his life – not at the time of his studies, nor in the hard days when he struggled with life, extricating himself from its coils and growing strong and hardening himself in the trials of manhood – had he been so engrossed as now in tending this unceasing, volcanic work of his wife's spirit.

'How happy I am!' Stolz said to himself, and dreamed in his own way, trying to guess what their future life would be like after the first years of their marriage.

In the distance a new image smiled at him, not of a selfish Olga, nor a passionately loving wife, nor a mother-nurse fading away in the end in a colourless existence no one wanted, but of something different, exalted, almost unheard of. ... He dreamed of a mother who created and took part in the social and spiritual life of a whole generation of happy people. ... He wondered fearfully if she would have enough will-power – and hastily helped her to subdue life, to acquire a reserve of courage for the battle of life – now, while they were still young and strong, while life spared them or its blows did not seem heavy and while grief was submerged in love. Their days had been darkened, but not for long. Business failures, the loss of a considerable amount of money – all that hardly affected them. It meant additional work and extra journeys, but was soon forgotten. The death of her aunt caused Olga bitter and genuine tears and cast a shadow on her life for about six months. The children's illnesses were a source of constant anxiety and lively apprehension, but as soon as the apprehension was gone, happiness returned. What worried him most was Olga's health: it took her a long time to recover from her confinements, and although she recovered, he still continued to feel anxious. He knew of no misfortune more terrible.

447

'How happy I am!' Olga, too, kept repeating softly, looking with pleasure upon her life, sinking into meditation at such moments – especially for some time past, three or four years after her marriage.

Man is a strange creature! The more complete her happiness was, the more pensive and even apprehensive she became. She began to watch herself carefully, and found that she was upset by the peacefulness of her life, by the way it seemed to stand still during the moments of happiness. She forced herself to shake off her pensive mood and quickened the pace of life, feverishly seeking noise, movement, cares, asking her husband to take her to town, trying going into society, but not for long. The bustle of society affected her but slightly, and she hurried back to her little home to get rid of some painful, unusual impression, and once more devoted herself entirely to the small cares of her household, staying in the nursery for hours, carrying out her duties of a mother and nurse, or spent hours reading with Andrey and talking with him about 'serious and dull' things, or read poetry and discussed a journey to Italy. She was afraid to sink into an apathy like Oblomov's. But however hard she tried to rid herself of those moments of periodic numbness and slumber of the soul, she was every now and then waylaid first by the dream of happiness, when she was once more surrounded by the blue night and bound in a drowsy spell, which was followed by an interval of brooding, like a rest from life, and then by – confusion, fear, longing, a sort of dull melancholy, and her restless head was filled with vague, hazy questions. Olga listened to them intently, trying in vain to find out what was wrong with her and unable to discover what her soul was seeking and demanding from time to time, and yet it was certainly seeking and longing for something and even – dreadful to say – seemed to miss something, as though a happy life were not enough, as though she had grown tired of it and were demanding some new experiences, peering farther and farther into the future.

'What is it?' she thought, horrified. 'Is there something else I need and ought to desire? Where am I to go? Nowhere. This is the end of the road. ... But is it? Have I completed the circle of life? Is this all – all?' she asked herself, leaving something unsaid – and – looking round anxiously to make sure that no one had overheard this whisper of her soul. ... Her eyes questioned the sky, the sea, the woods – there was no answer anywhere; there was nothing there but emptiness and darkness.

Nature said the same thing over and over again; she saw in it an uninterrupted and monotonous flow of life, without beginning or end. She knew whom to consult about her worries, and she might have found an answer; but what kind of answer? What if it was merely the dissatisfied muttering of a sterile mind or, worse still, the craving of an unwomanly heart that has not been created for sympathy alone? Heavens, she – his idol – was heartless and possessed a hard and never-contented mind! What would she become? Not a blue-stocking, surely? How she would fall in his estimation when he discovered these new, unwonted sufferings, which were, of course, known to him. She hid from him or pretended to be ill, and then her eyes, in spite of herself, lost their velvety softness and looked hot and dry, a heavy cloud lay on her face, and, try as she might, she could not force herself to smile or talk, and listened indifferently to the most exciting news of the political world and the most interesting explanation of some new scientific discovery or new creative work of art. And yet she did not want to cry, she felt no sudden excitement as when her nerves were on edge and her virginal powers were awakening and finding expression. No, that was not it!

'What is it, then?' she asked herself in despair, when she suddenly felt bored and indifferent to everything on a beautiful, quiet evening or sitting beside the cradle, or amidst her husband's endearments and speeches.... She suddenly stood stock-still and grew silent, then busied herself with a feigned liveliness to conceal her strange ailment, or said she had a headache and went to bed. But it was not easy for her to hide herself from Stolz's keen eyes: she knew it and prepared herself inwardly for the conversation that was to come with the same anxiety as she had once prepared herself for confessing her past. It came at last.

One evening they were taking a walk in the poplar avenue. She almost hung on his shoulder, hardly uttering a word. She was suffering from one of her mysterious attacks and replied curtly to whatever he said.

'The nurse says that little Olga was coughing in the night. Don't you think we ought to send for the doctor to-morrow?' he asked.

'I've given her a warm drink and will not let her go for a walk to-morrow, and then we shall see!' she replied monotonously.

They walked to the end of the avenue in silence.

'Why haven't you answered your friend Sonia's letter?' he asked. 'I kept waiting and nearly missed the post. It's her third letter you've left unanswered.'

'Yes, I want to forget her as quickly as possible,' she said, and fell silent.

'I gave Bichurin your regards,' Andrey began again. 'He's in love with you, you know, so I thought it might comfort him a little for his wheat not arriving in time.'

She smiled dryly.

'Yes, you've told me,' she said indifferently.

'What is it? Are you sleepy?' he asked.

Her heart missed a beat, as it did every time he began asking her questions that affected her closely.

'Not yet,' she answered with feigned cheerfulness. 'Why?'

'You're not feeling ill?' he asked again.

'No. What makes you think so?'

'Well, then, you must be bored!'

She pressed his shoulder tightly with both her hands.

'No, no!' she declared in an exaggeratedly cheerful voice, which certainly sounded rather bored.

He led her out of the avenue and turned her face to the moonlight.

'Look at me!' he said, gazing intently into her eyes. 'One might think that you were – unhappy! Your eyes are so strange to-day, and not only to-day – – What is the matter with you, Olga?'

He put his arm round her waist and took her back into the avenue.

'You know,' she said, trying to laugh, 'I'm famished!'

'Don't tell stories! I don't like it!' he added, with feigned severity.

'Unhappy!' she repeated, reproachfully, stopping him in the avenue. 'Yes, I am unhappy because – I am too happy!' she concluded in such a soft and tender voice that he kissed her.

She grew bolder. The assumption, though made light-heartedly and in jest, that she was unhappy, unexpectedly made her wish to speak frankly.

'I am not bored – I couldn't be, you know that perfectly well yourself – and I'm not ill, but – I can't help feeling sad – sometimes. There, you insufferable man, if you must know! Yes, I feel sad, and I don't know why!'

She put her head on his shoulder.

'I see! But why on earth?' he asked softly, bending over her.

'Don't know,' she repeated.

'But there must be a reason, if not in me, or in your surroundings, then in yourself. Sometimes such sadness is merely the first symptom of an illness ... are you well?'

'Yes, perhaps it is something like that,' she said earnestly, 'though I don't feel ill at all. You see how I eat, sleep, work, and go for walks. Then suddenly something comes over me – a sort of depression. I can't help feeling that something is lacking in my life. But no, don't listen to me! It's all nonsense!'

'Please go on,' he insisted. 'You say you feel there's something lacking in your life – what else?'

'Sometimes I seem to be afraid that things will change or come to an end – I don't know myself,' she went on. 'Or I'm worried by the silly thought – what else is going to happen? What is happiness? What is the meaning of life?' she said, speaking more and more softly, ashamed of these questions. 'All these joys, sorrows, nature,' she whispered, 'it all seems to make me long to go somewhere, and I become dissatisfied with everything. Oh dear, I'm so ashamed of all this foolishness – this day-dreaming. ... Don't take any notice, don't look,' she asked in an imploring voice, snuggling up to him. 'This melancholy fit of mine soon passes, and I feel gay and light-hearted again, as I do now!'

She pressed close to him timidly and tenderly, feeling really ashamed and as though asking forgiveness for her 'foolishness'.

Her husband questioned her a long time and it took a long time to tell him, as a patient does a doctor, the symptoms of her sadness, to put into words all the vague questions that worried her, to describe the confusion in her mind, and then – as soon as the mirage disappeared – everything she could remember and observe.

Stolz walked along the avenue in silence, his head bowed, pondering, anxious and perplexed by his wife's vague confession.

She peered into his eyes, but saw nothing, and when they reached the end of the avenue for the third time, she would not let him turn round, but herself now took him out into the moonlight and gazed questioningly into his eyes.

'What are you thinking of?' she asked shyly. 'You're laughing at my foolishness, aren't you? It is very silly, this sadness of mine, isn't it?'

He made no answer.

'Why are you silent?' she asked impatiently.

'You've been silent for a long time, although you knew, of course, that I've been watching you for some time, so let me be silent and think it over. You've set me no easy task.'

451

'Well, you'll be thinking now and I'll be worrying myself to death trying to guess what conclusion you've reached alone by yourself. I shouldn't have told you about it!' she added. 'You'd better say something. ...'

'What can I say to you?' he said thoughtfully; 'perhaps you're still suffering from strained nerves, in which case it is the doctor and not I who will decide what's wrong with you. We must send for him to-morrow. But if it isn't – –' He stopped short, pondering.

'What if it isn't? Tell me!' she persisted impatiently.

He walked on, still absorbed in his thoughts.

'Please!' she said, shaking him by the arm.

'Perhaps it's an over-active imagination, you're much too animated; or again, perhaps you've reached the age when – –' He finished in an undertone, speaking almost to himself.

'Please speak up, Andrey. I can't bear it when you mutter to yourself!' she complained. 'I have told him a lot of nonsense, and he hangs his head and mutters something under his breath! I honestly feel nervous here with you in the dark. ...'

'I don't know what to say – you feel depressed, you're worried by some sort of questions – I don't know what to make of it. We'll discuss it again later: you may be needing sea-bathing cure again. ...'

'You said to yourself – perhaps you've reached the age – what did you mean?' she asked.

'You see, I meant – –' he said slowly, expressing himself hesitantly, distrusting his own thoughts and, as it were, ashamed of his words. 'You see – there are moments – I mean, if it isn't a sign of a nervous breakdown, if there is absolutely nothing the matter with you, then perhaps you've reached the age of maturity when one stops growing – where there are no more riddles, and when it all becomes plain. ...'

'You mean I've grown old, don't you?' she interrupted him quickly. 'Don't you dare suggest it!' She shook a finger at him. 'I am still young and strong,' she added, drawing herself up.

He laughed. 'Don't be afraid,' he said; 'it seems to me you don't ever intend to grow old! No, that's not what I meant. In old age one's powers fail and stop struggling with life. No, your sadness and depression – if it is what I think it is – is rather a sign of strength. A lively, inquiring, and dissatisfied mind sometimes attempts to penetrate beyond the boundaries of life and, finding, of course, no answer, is plunged into melancholy and – temporary dissatisfaction with life. It is the melancholy of the

452

soul questioning life about its mysteries. Perhaps that is what's the matter with you. ... If that is so – it isn't foolishness.'

She sighed, but it seemed more like a sigh of relief that her apprehensions were over and that she had not fallen in the estimation of her husband, but quite the contrary. ...

'But I am happy, my mind is not idle, I am not day-dreaming, my life is full – what more do I want? Why all these questionings?' she said. 'It's a disease, an obsession!'

'Yes, perhaps it is an obsession for an ignorant, untrained, and weak mind. This melancholy and these questions have possibly driven many people mad; to some they appear as hideous apparitions, as a delirium of the mind.'

'My happiness is brimming over, I so want to live and – suddenly all is gall and wormwood. ...'

'Ah, that's what one has to pay for the Promethean fire! It isn't enough to suffer, you have to love this melancholy and respect your doubts and questionings: they represent the surfeit, the luxury of life, and mostly appear on the summits of happiness, when there are no coarse desires; people who are in need and sorrow are not bothered by them; thousands and thousands of people go through life without knowing anything about this fog of doubts and the anguish of questionings. ... But to those who have met them at the right moment, they are not an affliction, but welcome guests.'

'But it's impossible to manage them: they make you feel miserable and indifferent – to almost everything,' she added hesitantly.

'Not for long, though,' he said. 'Afterwards they make life all the fresher. They bring us to the abyss from which we can get no answer and then make us look upon life with greater love than ever ... they challenge forces that have been tried already to a fight with them, as though they did not want them to go to sleep. ...'

'To be worried by some fog, by phantoms,' she complained. 'All is so bright and sunny, and suddenly an ominous shadow falls upon life! Is there no remedy against it?'

'Of course there is! You must find strength in life, and if you can't, life becomes unbearable even without these questions.'

'What am I to do, then? Yield and be miserable?'

'Not at all,' he said; 'arm yourself with fortitude and go on your way in life patiently and perseveringly. You and I are not Titans,' he went on, putting his arm round her; 'we shall not

453

go, like Manfred and Faust, to struggle defiantly with formidable problems; we shall not accept their challenge, but bow our heads and humbly go through the difficult times, and then life and happiness will smile upon us once more and – –'

'But what if they never leave us alone and sadness troubles us more and more?' she asked.

'Well, what if it does? Let us accept it as a new element in life. But no, that does not happen; it cannot be so with us! This is not your sadness; it is the general ailment of mankind. One drop of it has fallen on you. All this is terrible when one has lost touch with life – when there's nothing to sustain one. But with us – I only hope this melancholy of yours is what I think it is and not the symptom of some illness – that would be worse, that would be a calamity which would leave me utterly defenceless and helpless. But do you really think that some vague sadness, doubts, or questionings could deprive us of our happiness, our – –'

He did not finish the sentence, and she threw herself into his arms like one possessed and, clasping her arms round his neck, like a bacchante, in a passionate embrace, remained motionless like that for a moment.

'Neither vague sadness, nor illness, nor – death!' she whispered rapturously, once again happy, calm, and gay. It seemed to her that she never loved him so passionately as at this moment.

'Take care that Fate does not overhear your complaint and take it for ingratitude,' he concluded with a superstitious observation, inspired by tender solicitude. 'She dislikes people who do not value her gifts. So far you were just getting to know life; you still have to test it. Wait till it gets going in good earnest, till sorrow and trouble come – and they will come – then you won't have time for these questionings. ... Husband your strength!' Stolz added softly, almost as though he were speaking to himself, in answer to her passionate outburst. There was a note of sadness in his words, as though he already saw 'the trouble and the sorrow' in the distance.

She was silent, struck suddenly by the sadness in his voice. She had infinite faith in him, and the sound of his voice inspired trust in her. She was infected by his thoughtfulness and became absorbed in herself. Leaning on him, she walked slowly and mechanically up and down the avenue, sunk in deep silence. Following her husband's example, she gazed apprehensively into the future where, as he said, trials, trouble, and sorrow awaited them. She was no longer dreaming of a blue night; another prospect opened up before her, one that was not translucent and festive, not life amid peace and plenty, alone with *him*. No, what she saw there was a series of privations and losses, bedewed with tears, unavoidable sacrifices, a life of fasting and forced renunciation, of fancies born in idleness, groans and lamentations caused by new feelings they had not experienced before; she dreamed of illness, business failures, her husband's death. ... She shuddered, she lost heart, but she gazed with courage and curiosity at that new aspect of life, examined it with horror and measured her strength against it. ... Love alone did not betray her in that dream; it kept guard faithfully over this new life, too; and yet it, too, was different! There were no ardent sighs, no bright rays, and no blue nights; as years passed, it all seemed child's play in comparison with that far-away love taken for its own by stern and uncompromising life. You heard no laughter and kisses there, nor pensive conversations, quivering with suppressed passion, in the summer-house among the flowers at the festival of nature and life. ... All that had 'withered and gone'. But that unfailing and indestructible love could be perceived in their faces as powerful as the life-force – at the time of common sorrow it shone in the slowly and silently exchanged glance of mutual suffering, and it could be felt in the infinite patience with which they met life's torments, in their restrained tears and stifled sobs. Other dreams, distant, but clear, definite, and menacing, quietly replaced Olga's vague sadness and questionings. ... Under the influence of the reassuring and calm words of her husband, and in the boundless trust she felt in him, Olga relaxed from her mysterious sadness, which only few people know, and the stern and prophetic dreams of the future, and she went cheerfully forward. The 'fog' gave place to a bright and sunny morning, with the cares of a mother and a housewife; she felt drawn now to the flower-garden and the fields and now to her husband's study. But no longer did she play about with life in careless abandon; instead she took heart of grace and, inspired by a secret thought, prepared herself, and waited. ... She was growing in grace. ... Andrey saw that his former ideal of woman and wife was unattainable, but he was happy even in the pale reflection of it in Olga: he had never expected even that. Meanwhile he, too, was faced for years, for almost his whole life, with the not inconsiderable task of maintaining his dignity as a man on the same high level in the eyes of a woman so proud and with so proper a regard for her own self-respect as

Olga, not out of vulgar jealousy, but so as to make sure that her life, which was clear as crystal, should not be darkened; and this might well happen if her faith in him were in the least shaken.

A great many women have no need of anything of the kind: once married, they resignedly accept their husband's good and bad qualities, reconcile themselves completely to the position and environment into which they have been placed, or as resignedly succumb to the first casual infatuation, finding it at once impossible or unnecessary to resist it. 'It is fate,' they say to themselves, 'passion – woman is a weak creature,' and so on. Even if the husband ranks above the crowd in intelligence, which is so irresistible an attraction in a man, such women pride themselves on their husband's superiority as though it were some expensive necklace, and even then only if his intellect remains blind to their pitiful female tricks. But if he dares to see through the petty comedy of their sly, worthless, and sometimes vicious existence, they find his intellect hard and cramping.

Olga did not know this logic of resignation to blind fate and could not understand women's cheap passions and infatuations. Having once recognized the worth in her chosen man and his claims on her, she believed in him and therefore loved him, and if she ceased to believe, she would cease to love, as had been the case with Oblomov. But at that time her steps were still unsteady and her will shaky; she was only just beginning to observe life closely and meditate on it, to become conscious of her mind and character and to gather her materials. The work of creative endeavour had not yet begun and she had not yet decided on her path in life. But now her faith in Andrey was not blind but conscious, and her ideal of masculine perfection was embodied in it. The more deeply and more consciously she believed in him, the harder he found it to remain on the same height and to be the hero not only of her mind and heart but also of her imagination. But her faith in him was so strong that she recognized no intermediary between herself and him or any other court of appeal than God. That was why she would not have put up with the slightest lowering in the qualities she acknowledged in him; any false note in his mind or character would have produced a shattering discord. The demolished edifice of her happiness would have buried her under its ruins, or had her strength been preserved, she would have looked for – – but no, women like her do not make the same mistake twice. After the collapse of such faith and such love, no rebirth is possible.

Stolz was profoundly happy in his full and exciting life, in which unfading spring was flowering, and he took care of it, tended and cherished it jealously, keenly, and energetically. He was horror-stricken only when he remembered that Olga had been within a hair's-breadth of destruction; that they had merely stumbled on their right path in life, and their two lives, now merged into one, might have diverged; that ignorance of the ways of life might have led to a disastrous mistake, that Oblomov – – He shuddered. Good heavens, Olga in the sort of life Oblomov had been preparing for her! Olga leading a day-to-day existence, a country lady, nursing her children, a housewife, and – nothing more! All her questionings, doubts, the whole excitement of her life, would have been frittered away in household cares, preparations for feast-days, visitors, family reunions, birthdays, christenings, and her husband's indolence and apathy! Marriage would have been a meaningless form, a means and not an end; it would have been merely a large and immutable framework for visits, entertainments of visitors, dinners and parties, empty chatter. How would she have endured such a life? At first she would have struggled, trying to find and solve the mystery of life, wept and suffered, and then she would have got used to it, grown fat and stupid, and spent her time eating and sleeping. No, it wouldn't have been so with her: she would have wept, suffered, pined away, and died in the arms of her loving, kind, and helpless husband. ... Poor Olga! And if the fire had not been extinguished and life had not come to an end, if her powers had held out and demanded freedom, if she had stretched forth her wings like a strong and keen-eyed eagle, checked for a moment by her weak arms, and flung herself on the high rock where she had seen an eagle who was stronger and more keen-eyed than she? ... Poor Ilya!

'Poor Ilya!' Andrey cried one day as he recalled the past.

At the sound of that name Olga suddenly dropped her hands and her embroidery into her lap, threw back her head, and sank into thought. His exclamation had brought back memories.

'How is he getting on?' she asked after a pause. 'Can't we find out?'

Andrey shrugged. 'One might think,' he said, 'that we were living at a time when there was no post, and when people who had gone their different ways regarded each other as lost and, indeed, lost all trace of each other.'

'You might write again to some of your friends: we should at least find out something.'

'We shouldn't find out anything that we don't know already: that he is alive and well and living in the same place – I know that without writing to my friends. As for how he is, how he is enduring his life, whether he is morally dead, or there still is a spark of life glowing in him – that no stranger could find out.'

'Please don't talk like that, Andrey: it frightens me and hurts me to hear you. I should like to know, and I'm afraid to find out.'

She was ready to cry.

'We shall be in Petersburg in the spring, and we shall find out for ourselves.'

'That isn't enough. We must do all we can.'

'Haven't I done so? Haven't I tried my best to persuade him, to do everything I could for him, arranged his affairs for him – if only he had shown the slightest sign of appreciation! He's ready to do anything when you see him, but as soon as you're out of sight it's good-bye – he's gone to sleep again! It's like trying to deal with a dipsomaniac!'

'But why do you let him out of your sight?' Olga said impatiently. 'He must be dealt with resolutely: put him in the carriage and take him away. Now that we are going to move to our estate, he'll be near us. We'll take him with us. ...'

'What trouble we have with him!' Andrey said, walking up and down the room. 'There's no end to it!'

'You don't find it a burden, do you?' said Olga. 'That is news! It's the first time I've heard you grumble about it.'

'I'm not grumbling,' replied Andrey. 'I'm just thinking aloud.'

'And why should you do that? You haven't come to the conclusion that it is a bore and a nuisance, have you?'

She looked searchingly at him. He shook his head.

'No, not a nuisance, but a waste of time. I can't help thinking that sometimes.'

'Don't say it, please!' she stopped him. 'I shall think of it all day again, as I did last week, and feel miserable. If your friendship for him is dead, you must try to do your best for him out of human feeling. If you grow tired, I'll go to him myself, and I shan't leave without him. I'm sure he will be moved by my entreaties. I can't help feeling that I shall cry bitterly if I find him broken-down or dead. Perhaps, my tears – –'

'Will bring him back to life, you think?' Andrey interposed.

'Well, if they don't bring him back to active life, they might at least make him look round him and change his way of living

458

for something better. He won't live in squalor, but near those who are his equals, with us. I only saw him for a moment that time, and he at once came to himself and was ashamed.'

'You don't love him still, do you?' Andrey asked, jestingly.

'No!' Olga replied in good earnest, thoughtfully, as though looking into the past. 'I don't love him still, but there is something in him that I love, something to which, I believe, I have remained faithful, and shall not change as other people do. ...'

'Oh? Who are those other people? You aren't thinking of me, are you? But you are mistaken. And if you want to know the truth, it is I who taught you to love him and nearly got you into trouble. But for me you would have passed him by without noticing him. It was I made you realize that he possessed no less intelligence than other people, only it was buried under a rubbish-heap and asleep in idleness. Shall I tell you why he is dear to you and what you still love in him?'

She nodded assent.

'Because he possesses something that is worth more than any amount of intelligence – an honest and faithful heart! It is the matchless treasure that he has carried through his life unharmed. People knocked him down, he grew indifferent and, at last, dropped asleep, crushed, disappointed, having lost the strength to live; but he has not lost his honesty and his faithfulness. His heart has never struck a single false note; there is no stain on his character. No well-dressed-up lie has ever deceived him and nothing will lure him from the true path. A regular ocean of evil and baseness may be surging round him, the entire world may be poisoned and turned upside down – Oblomov will never bow down to the idol of falsehood, and his soul will always be pure, noble, honest. ... His soul is translucent, clear as crystal. Such people are rare; there aren't many of them; they are like pearls in a crowd! His heart cannot be bribed; he can be relied on always and anywhere. It is to this you have remained faithful, and that is why nothing I do for him will ever be a burden to me. I have known lots of people possessing high qualities, but never have I met a heart more pure, more noble, and more simple. I have loved many people, but no one so warmly and so firmly as Oblomov. Once you know him, you cannot stop loving him. Isn't that so? Am I right?'

Olga was silent, her eyes fixed on her work. Andrey pondered.

'Is that all? What else is there? Oh,' he added gaily as he came to himself, 'I quite forgot his "dove-like tenderness" ...'

Olga laughed, quickly threw down her sewing, and, running

up to Andrey, flung her arms round his neck, gazed for a few minutes with shining eyes into his eyes, then, putting her head on her husband's shoulder, sank into thought. There rose in her mind Oblomov's gentle, dreamy face, his tender look, his submissiveness, then his pitiful, shamefaced smile with which he answered her reproach at parting – and she felt so unhappy, so sorry for him.

'You won't leave him?' she said with her arms still round her husband's neck. 'You won't abandon him, will you?'

'Never! Not unless a gulf opens suddenly, or a wall rises between us.'

She kissed her husband.

'Will you take me to him in Petersburg?'

He hesitated and was silent.

'Will you? Will you?' she asked, insisting on an answer.

'Listen, Olga,' he said, trying to free his neck from her embrace; 'we must first – –'

'No, say – yes! Promise, or I won't leave you alone!'

'All right,' he replied, 'only not the first, but the second time. I know very well what you will feel like if he – –'

'Don't say another word!' she interrupted. 'Yes, you will take me: together we shall do everything. Alone you won't be able to – you won't want to!'

'Perhaps you're right, only I'm afraid you will be upset, and perhaps for a long time,' he said, not altogether pleased that Olga had forced him to consent.

'Remember, then,' she concluded, resuming her seat, 'you will only give him up if "a gulf opens up or a wall rises between us." I won't forget those words.'

9

PEACE and quiet reigned over Vyborg, its unpaved streets, wooden pavements, meagre gardens, and ditches overgrown with nettles, where a goat with a frayed rope round its neck was busily grazing or drowsing dully beside a fence; at midday a clerk's elegant high heels clattered along the pavement, a muslin curtain in some window moved aside, and the wife of some civil servant peeped out from behind the geraniums; or a girl's fresh face suddenly appeared above the fence in some garden and at once disappeared again, followed by another girl's face, which also disappeared, then again the first appeared, and was followed by the second; then the shrieks and laughter of the girls on the swings could be heard.

All was quiet in Mrs Pshenitzyn's house. You walked into the small courtyard and you were in the midst of a living idyll: cocks and hens were thrown into a commotion and ran off to hide in the corners; the dog began jumping on its chain and barking at the top of its voice; Akulina stopped milking the cow, and the caretaker left off chopping wood, and both eyed the visitor with interest. 'Who do you want?' the caretaker asked, and on being given the name of Oblomov or the landlady, he pointed silently to the front steps and started chopping wood again. The visitor walked down a clean, sand-strewn path to the front steps, covered with a plain, clean carpet, pulled the brightly polished brass handle of the bell, and the door was opened by Anisya, the children, and sometimes by the landlady herself or Zakhar – Zakhar being always the last.

Everything in Mrs Pshenitzyn's house bore the stamp of such abundance and prosperity as was not to be seen there even when Marfa Matveyevna kept house for herself and her brother. The kitchen, the pantries, the sideboard were full of crockery, large and small, round and oval dishes, sauce-boats, cups, piles of plates, and iron, copper, and earthenware saucepans and pots. In the cupboards was kept Agafya Matveyevna's silver, redeemed long ago and never pawned since, side by side with Oblomov's silver. There were whole rows of enormous, tiny and paunchy teapots and several rows of china cups, plain and gilt, painted with mottoes, flaming hearts, and Chinamen; there were huge glass jars of coffee, cinnamon, and vanilla, crystal tea-caddies, cruets of oil and vinegar. Whole shelves were loaded with packets, bottles, boxes of household remedies, herbs, lotions, plasters, spirits, camphor, simple and fumigatory powders; there was also soap, material for cleaning lace, taking out stains, etc., etc. – everything, in fact, that a good housewife in the provinces keeps in her house. When Agafya Matveyevna suddenly opened the door of a cupboard full of all these articles, she was herself overcome by the bouquet of all these narcotic smells and had to turn her face away for a moment.

In the larder hams were suspended from the ceiling, so that mice could not get at them, as well as cheeses, sugar-loaves, cured fish, bags of dried mushrooms, and nuts bought from Finnish pedlars. On the floor stood cases of butter, huge, covered earthenware jugs of sour cream, baskets of eggs, and lots of other things. One would need the pen of a second Homer to describe fully and in detail all that had been accumulated in all the corners and on all the shelves of this small shrine of domestic life. The kitchen was the true scene of action of the great house-wife and her worthy assistant, Anisya. Everything they needed was in the house, and everything was handy and in its proper place; indeed, everywhere there was order and cleanliness – at least one might have said so had it not been for one corner in the house where no ray of light, nor breath of fresh air, nor Agafya Matveyevna's eye, nor Anisya's quick, all-sweeping hand, had ever penetrated. That was Zakhar's room or den. His room had no window, and the perpetual darkness helped to turn a human habitation into a dark hole. If Zakhar sometimes found there Agafya Matveyevna with all sorts of plans for improving and cleaning the place, he firmly declared that it was not a woman's business to decide when and how his brushes, blacking, and boots ought to be kept, that it was nobody's business why his clothes lay in a heap on the floor and his bed in the corner behind the stove was covered in dust, and that it was *he* and not she who wore the clothes and slept on the bed. As for the besom, some planks, two bricks, the bottom of a barrel, and two logs of wood which he kept in his room, he could not do without them in his work – though he did not explain why; furthermore, dust and spiders did not disturb him, and, in a word, since he never poked his nose into their kitchen, there was no reason why they should interfere with him. When he found Anisya there one day, he treated her with such scorn and threatened her with his elbow so seriously that she was afraid to look in any more. When the case was taken to a higher court and submitted to his master's decision, Oblomov went to have a look at Zakhar's room with the intention of taking all the necessary measures and seeing them strictly carried out, but thrusting his head through Zakhar's door and gazing for a moment at all that was there, he just spat and did not utter a word. 'Well, have you got what you wanted?' Zakhar said to Agafya Matveyevna and Anisya, who had come with Oblomov in the hope that his interest might lead to some change. Then he smiled in his own manner across his whole face so that his eyebrows and whiskers moved apart.

All the other rooms were bright, clean, and airy. The old faded curtains had gone and the windows and doors of the drawing-room and study were hung with green and blue draperies and muslin curtains with red festoons – all of it the work of

Agafya Matveyevna's hands. The pillows were white as snow and rose mountainously almost to the ceiling; the blankets were quilted and of silk. For weeks on end the landlady's room was crowded with several card-tables, opened up and placed end to end, on which Oblomov's quilts and dressing-gown were spread out. Agafya Matveyevna did the cutting out and quilting herself, pressing her firm bosom to the work, fastening her eyes and even her teeth upon it when she had to bite the thread off; she laboured with love, with indefatigable industry, comforting herself modestly with the thought that the dressing-gown and the quilted blankets would clothe, warm, caress, and delight the magnificent Oblomov. For days, as he lay on the sofa in his room, he admired the way her bare elbows moved to and fro in the wake of the needle and the cotton. As in the old days at Oblomovka, he more than once dozed off to the regular sound of the needle going in and out of the material and the snapping of the thread when bitten off.

'Do stop working, please; you'll be tired,' he besought her.

'The Lord loves work,' she answered, never taking her hands and eyes off her work.

His coffee was as carefully and nicely served and as well made as at the beginning, when he had moved into the house several years before. Giblet soup, macaroni and parmesan cheese, meat or fish pie, cold fish and vegetable soup, home-grown chicken – all this followed each other in strict rotation and introduced pleasant variety into the monotonous life of the little house. From morning till evening bright sunshine filled the house, streaming in at the windows on one side and then on the other, there being nothing to impede it, thanks to the kitchen gardens all round. The canaries trilled gaily; the geraniums and the hyacinths the children occasionally brought from the count's garden exuded a strong scent in the small room, blending pleasantly with the smoke of a pure Havana cigar and the cinnamon or vanilla which the landlady pounded, energetically moving her elbows. Oblomov lived, as it were, within a golden framework of life, in which, as in a diorama, the only things that changed were the usual phases of day and night and the seasons; there were no other changes, no serious accidents to convulse one's whole life, often stirring up a muddy and bitter sediment. Ever since Stolz had saved Oblomovka from the fraudulent debts of the landlady's brother, and Ivan Matveyevich and Tarantyev had completely disappeared, everything of a hostile nature had disappeared from Oblomov's life, too. He was now surrounded by simple, kind, and loving people who all conspired to do their best to make his life as comfortable as possible, to help him not to notice it, not to feel. Agafya Matveyevna was in the prime of her life. She lived feeling that her life was full as it had never been before; but, as before, she would never be able to express it in words or, rather, it never occurred to her to do so. She merely prayed that God would prolong Oblomov's life and save him from 'sorrow, wrath, and want', committing herself, her children, and her entire household to God's will. But, as though to make up for it, her face always wore the same expression of complete and perfect happiness, without desires and therefore rare, and, indeed, impossible for a person of a different temperament. She had put on weight; there was a feeling of content-ment about her ample bosom and shoulders, her eyes glowed with gentleness, and if there was an expression of solicitude in them, it concerned merely her household duties. She regained the calm and dignity with which she had ruled her house in the old days with obedient Anisya, Akulina, and the caretaker ready to take her orders. As before, she seemed to sail along rather than walk from the cupboard to the kitchen, and from the kitchen to the pantry, giving her orders in an unhurried, measured tone of voice, fully conscious of what she was doing.

Anisya had grown livelier than before because there was more work for her to do; she was always on the run, moving and bustling about, working, carrying out Agafya Matveyevna's orders. Her eyes had grown even brighter, and her nose, that speaking nose of hers, was thrust forward, glowing with cares, thoughts, and intentions, seeming to speak though her tongue was silent.

Both women were dressed in accordance with the dignity of their several positions and their duties. Agafya Matveyevna had now a big wardrobe with a row of silk dresses, cloaks, and fur coats; she ordered her bonnets on the other side of the river, almost in Liteyny Avenue; she bought her shoes not in the mar-ket but in one of the fashionable shopping arcades, and her hat – just think of it! – in Morskaya Street. Anisya, too, having fin-ished her work in the kitchen, put on a woollen dress, especially on Sundays. Akulina alone still walked about with her skirt tucked up at the waist, and the caretaker could not bring him-self to do without his sheepskin even in the summer holidays. Zakhar, too, was of course as bad as ever: he had made himself a jacket out of his grey frock-coat, and it was impossible to say what colour his trousers were or of what material his tie was made. He cleaned boots, then went to sleep, or sat at the gates, gazing dully at the few passers-by, or, finally, spent his time sitting at the nearest grocery shop, where he did the same things and in the same way as he had done before, first at Oblomovka and then in Gorokhovaya Street.

And Oblomov himself? Oblomov was the complete and natural reflection and expression of that repose, contentment, and serene calm that reigned all around him. Thinking about his way of living, subjecting it to a close scrutiny, and getting more and more used to it, he decided at last that he had nothing more to strive for, nothing more to seek, that he had attained the ideal of his life, though it were shorn of poetry and bereft of the brilliance with which his imagination had once endowed the plentiful and care-free life of a country squire on his own estate, among his peasants and house-serfs. He looked upon his present way of life as a continuation of the same Oblomov-like existence, except that he lived in a different place, and the times, too, were to a certain extent different. Here, too, as at Oblomovka, he managed to strike a good bargain with life, having obtained from it a guarantee of undisturbed peace. He triumphed inwardly at having escaped its annoying and agonizing demands and storms, which break from that part of the horizon where the lightnings of great joys flash and the sudden thunderclaps of great sorrows resound; where false hopes and magnificent phantoms of happiness are at play; where a man's own thought gnaws at his vitals and finally consumes him and passion kills; where man is engaged in a never-ceasing battle and leaves the battlefield shattered but still insatiate and discontented. Not having experienced the joys obtained by struggle, he mentally renounced them, and felt at peace with himself only in his forgotten corner of the world, where there was no struggle, no movement, and no life. And if his imagination caught fire again, if forgotten memories and unfulfilled dreams rose up before him, if his conscience began to prick him for having spent his life in one way and not in another – he slept badly, woke up, jumped out of bed, and sometimes wept disconsolate tears for his bright ideal of life that had now vanished for good, as one weeps for the dear departed with the bitter consciousness that one had not done enough for them while they were alive. Then he looked at his surroundings, tasted the ephemeral good things of life, and calmed down, gazing dreamily at the evening sun going down slowly and quietly in the fiery conflagration of the sunset; at last he decided that his life had not just turned out to be so

simple and uncomplicated, but had been created and meant to
be so in order to show that the ideally reposeful aspect of human
existence was possible. It fell to the lot of other people, he reflected, to express its troubled aspects and set in motion the
creative and destructive forces: everyone had his own fixed purpose in life! Such was the philosophy that the Plato of Oblomovka had worked out and that lulled him to sleep amidst the stern
demands of duty and the problems of human existence! He was
not born and educated to be a gladiator for the arena, but a
peaceful spectator of the battle; his timid and indolent spirit
could not have endured either the anxieties of happiness or the
blows inflicted by life – therefore he merely gave expression to
one particular aspect of it, and it was no use being sorry or trying to change it or to get more out of it. As years passed, he was
less and less disturbed by remorse and agitation, and settled
quietly and gradually into the plain and spacious coffin he had
made for his remaining span of life, like old hermits who, turning away from life, dig their own graves in the desert. He gave
up dreaming about the arrangement of his estate and moving
there with all his household. The manager engaged by Stolz sent
him regularly every Christmas a very considerable income, the
peasants brought corn and poultry, and the house flourished in
abundance and gaiety. Oblomov even acquired a carriage and
pair, but, with his habitual caution, the horses he bought were
so quiet that they only started at the third blow of the whip,
while at the first and second blow one horse staggered and
stepped aside, then the other horse staggered and stepped
aside, and only then, stretching out their necks, backs, and
tails, did they move together and trot off, nodding their heads.
They took Vanya to school on the other side of the Neva and
Agafya Matveyevna to do her shopping. At Shrovetide and
Easter the whole family and Oblomov went for a ride and to the
fair; occasionally they took a box at the theatre and went there,
also all together. In summer they went for a drive in the country, and on St Elijah's Day they drove to the Powder Works,
and life went on peacefully, one ordinary event following upon
another, bringing no destructive changes with it, if, that is, its
blows had never reached such peaceful corners. Unfortunately,
however, the thunderclap that shakes the foundations of mountains and vast aerial spaces reaches also the mousehole, less
loudly and strongly, perhaps, but still quite perceptibly. Oblomov ate heartily and with an appetite, as at Oblomovka, walked
and worked little and lazily, also as at Oblomovka. In spite of

his advancing years he drank wine and currant vodka with complete unconcern, and he slept for hours after dinner with even greater unconcern.

Suddenly all this was changed.

One day, when he had had his after-dinner nap, he wanted to get up from the sofa and could not; he wanted to say something, but his tongue would not obey him. Terrified, he just waved his hand, calling for help. Had he been living with Zakhar alone, he could have gone on telegraphing with his hand till the morning and in the end died, and have been discovered only on the following day; but the landlady's eye watched over him like Providence: it was her intuition rather than her intelligence that told her that there was something seriously wrong with Oblomov. And as soon as it had dawned on her, Anisya was sent off posthaste in a cab for a doctor, and Agafya Matveyevna put ice round his head and emptied her medicine cupboard of all its lotions and decoctions – of everything, in fact, that habit and hearsay prompted her to use in the emergency. Even Zakhar managed to put on one of his boots during that time and, forgetting all about his other boot, helped the doctor, Agafya Matveyevna, and Anisya to attend on his master.

Oblomov was brought round, bled, and then told that he had had a stroke and that he would have to lead quite a different kind of life in future. Vodka, beer, wine, and coffee were forbidden him, except on a few rare occasions, as well as meat and all rich and spicy food; instead he was ordered to take exercise every day and sleep in moderation only at night.

Without Agafya Matveyevna's constant supervision, nothing of this would ever have been carried out, but she knew how to introduce this regime by making the whole household submit to it, and by cunning and affection distracted Oblomov from being tempted by wine, rich fish pies, and after-dinner naps. The moment he dropped off, a chair fell in the room, without apparently any reason whatever, or some old and useless crockery was smashed noisily in the next room, or the children would raise a clamour enough to drive one out of the house. If that did not help, her gentle voice was heard calling him and asking him some question. The garden path was extended into the kitchen garden, and Oblomov walked on it for two hours every morning and evening. Agafya Matveyevna walked with him, or, if she could not, Vanya or Masha, or his old friend Alexeyev, meek, submissive, and always ready to comply with any request.

Here Oblomov was slowly walking down the path, leaning on

Vanya's shoulder. Vanya, almost a youth by now, wearing his school uniform, could hardly control his quick brisk steps and was trying hard to keep pace with Oblomov, who found it rather difficult to move one of his legs – an after-effect of the stroke.

'Let's go back to my room, Vanya, old man,' Oblomov said.

They set off towards the front door. Agafya Matveyevna met them on the doorstep.

'Where are you going so soon?' she asked, not letting them in.

'It isn't soon at all! We've walked twenty times up and down the path, and there's about one hundred and thirty yards from here to the fence, so we must have done well over a mile.'

'How many times have you walked?' she asked Vanya, who seemed to hesitate with his reply. 'Don't you dare lie to me!' she cried menacingly, looking into his eyes. 'I can tell at once. Remember Sunday; I won't let you go out.'

'Really, Mummy, we did walk – about twelve times!'

'Oh, you rascal,' said Oblomov; 'you kept tearing off the acacia leaves, but I counted every time ...'

'No, you'd better walk a little longer,' Agafya Matveyevna decided. 'The fish soup isn't ready yet, anyway,' and she slammed the door in their faces.

Oblomov had willy-nilly to count another eight times, and only then went in.

There he found the fish soup steaming on the big round table. Oblomov sat down in his usual place, alone on the sofa; to the right of him sat Agafya Matveyevna on a chair, to the left a child of about three on a small baby chair with a safety-catch. Masha, a girl of about thirteen by now, sat next to the child, then Vanya, and, finally, on that particular day, Alexeyev, who sat facing Oblomov.

'Let me give you another helping of fish: I've found such a fat one!' said Agafya Matveyevna, putting the fish on Oblomov's plate.

'A bit of pie would go down well with this,' said Oblomov.

'Dear me, I forgot all about it! I thought of it last night, but it went clean out of my mind!' Agafya Matveyevna said craftily. 'And I'm afraid I forgot to cook some cabbage for your cutlets, Ivan Alexeyevich,' she added, turning to Alexeyev. 'I hope you don't mind.'

That, too, was just a trick.

'It doesn't matter,' said Alexeyev; 'I can eat anything.'

'Why don't you have some ham with green peas or a beef-steak cooked for him?' asked Oblomov. 'He likes it.'

'I went to the shops myself, Ilya Ilyich, but I couldn't find any good beef. I had some cherry-juice jelly made for you, though,' she said, turning to Alexeyev; 'I know you like it.'

Fruit jelly could do no harm to Oblomov, and that was why Alexeyev, who was always ready to oblige, had to eat it and like it.

After dinner nothing and no one could prevent Oblomov from lying down. He usually lay down on the sofa in the dining-room, but only to rest for an hour. To make sure that he did not fall asleep, Agafya Matveyevna poured out coffee sitting on the sofa beside him, the children played on the carpet, and Oblomov had willy-nilly to take part in it.

'Don't tease Andrey,' he scolded Vanya, who had been teasing the little boy. 'He's going to cry any minute.'

'Masha, my dear, mind Andrey doesn't knock himself against the chair,' he warned solicitously, when the child crawled under a chair.

And Masha rushed to rescue her 'little brother', as she called him.

All was quiet for a moment while Agafya Matveyevna went to the kitchen to see if the coffee was ready. The children grew quiet. A sound of snoring was heard in the room, first gentle and as though on the sly, then louder, and when Agafya Matveyevna appeared with a steaming coffee-pot, she was met by a snoring as loud as in a coachman's shelter. She shook her head reproachfully at Alexeyev.

'I tried to wake him, but he paid no attention,' Alexeyev said in self-defence.

She quickly put the coffee-pot on the table, seized Andrey from the floor, and put him quietly on the sofa beside Oblomov. The child crawled up to him, reached his face, and grabbed him by the nose.

'What is it? Who's this? Eh?' Oblomov cried in alarm, waking up.

'You dozed off and little Andrey climbed on the sofa and wakened you,' Agafya Matveyevna said affectionately.

'I never dozed off,' Oblomov protested, taking the little boy in his arms. 'Do you think I did not hear him crawling up to me on his little arms? I hear everything. Oh, you naughty boy! So you've caught me by the nose, have you? I'll give you such a hiding! You just wait!' he said, fondling and caressing the child. He then put him down on the floor and heaved a loud sigh. 'Tell me something, Alexeyev,' he said.

'We've discussed everything, Ilya Ilyich. I've nothing more to tell you,' Alexeyev replied.

'Nothing more? Why, you always go about and meet people. Are you sure there isn't any news? You read the papers, don't you?'

'Yes, sir, I do sometimes – or other people read and talk and I listen. Yesterday at Alexey Spiridonovich's his son, a university student, read aloud.'

'What did he read?'

'About the English, who seem to have sent rifles and gunpowder somewhere. Alexey Spiridonovich said there was going to be a war.'

'Where did they send it to?'

'Oh, to Spain or India – I don't remember, but the ambassador was very much displeased.'

'What ambassador?' asked Oblomov.

'Sorry, I've clean forgotten!' said Alexeyev, raising his nose to the ceiling in an effort to remember.

'With whom is the war going to be?'

'With a Turkish pasha, I believe.'

'Well,' Oblomov said after a pause, 'what other news is there in politics?'

'They write that the earth is cooling down: one day it will be all frozen.'

'Will it indeed? But that is not politics, is it?' said Oblomov.

Alexeyev was completely put out.

'Dmitry Alexeyich,' he said apologetically, 'first mentioned politics and then went on reading without saying when he had come to an end with them. I know that after that he went on reading about literature.'

'What did he read about literature?' asked Oblomov.

'Well, he read that the best authors were Dmitriyev, Karamzin, Batyushkov, and Zhukovsky.'

'What about Pushkin?'

'Never mentioned him. I, too, wondered why he wasn't mentioned. Why, he was a genius!' said Alexeyev, pronouncing the *g* in genius hard.

There was a silence. Agafya Matveyevna brought her sewing and began plying her needle busily, glancing now and then at Oblomov and Alexeyev, and listening with her sharp ears for any commotion or noise in the house, to make sure Zakhar was not quarrelling with Anisya in the kitchen, that Akulina was washing up, that the gate in the yard had not creaked – that is, that the porter had not gone out to the 'tavern' for a drink.

Oblomov slowly sank into silence and a reverie: he was neither asleep nor awake, but let his thoughts roam at will light-heartedly, without concentrating them on anything, listening quietly to the regular beating of his heart and blinking from time to time like a man who was not looking at anything in particular. He fell into a vague, mysterious state, a sort of hallucination. There are rare and brief and dream-like moments when a man seems to be living over again something he has been through before at a different time and place. Whether he dreams of what is going on before him now, or has lived through it before and forgotten it, the fact remains that he sees the same people sitting beside him again as before and hears words that have already been uttered once: imagination is powerless to transport him there again and memory does not revive the past, and merely brings on a thoughtful mood. The same thing happened to Oblomov now. A stillness he had experienced some-where before descended upon him; he heard the ticking of a familiar clock, the snapping of a bitten-off thread; the familiar words were repeated once more, and the whisper: 'Dear me, I simply can't thread the needle: you try it, Masha, your eyes are sharper!' Lazily, mechanically, almost unconsciously he looked into Agafya Matveyevna's eyes, and out of the depths of his memory there arose a familiar image he had seen somewhere be-fore. He tried to think hard where and when he had heard it all … and he saw before him the big, dark drawing-room in his parents' house, lighted by a tallow candle, and his mother and her visitors sitting at a round table; they were sewing in silence; his father was walking up and down the room in silence. The present and the past had merged and intermingled. He dreamt that he had reached the promised land flowing with milk and honey, where people ate bread they had not earned and wore gold and silver garments. … He heard the stories of dreams and signs, the clatter of knives, and the rattle of crockery. He clung to his nurse and listened to her old shaky voice: 'Militrissa Kir-bityevna!' she said, pointing to Agafya Matveyevna. It seemed to him that the same cloud was sailing in the blue sky as then, the same breeze was blowing in at the window and playing with his hair; the Oblomovka turkey cock was strutting about and raising a great clamour under the window. Now a dog was bark-ing: a visitor must have arrived. Was it Andrey and his father who had come from Verkhlyovo? It was a great day for him. It really must be he: his footsteps were coming nearer and nearer, the door opened. ... 'Andrey!' he cried. Andrey was, indeed, standing before him, but no longer a boy – he was a middle-aged man.

Oblomov came to: before him stood the real Stolz, not a hallucination, but large as life.

Agafya Matveyevna quickly seized the baby, grabbed her sewing from the table, and took the children away; Alexeyev, too, disappeared. Stolz and Oblomov were left alone, looking silently and motionlessly at each other. Stolz seemed to pierce him with his gaze.

'Is it you, Andrey?' asked Oblomov in a voice that was almost inaudible with emotion, as a lover might ask his sweetheart after a long separation.

'It's me,' Andrey said softly. 'Are you all right?'

Oblomov embraced him and clung closely to him.

'Ah!' he said in reply in a drawn-out voice, putting into that *Ah* all the intensity of the sorrow and gladness that had lain hidden in his heart for a great many years and that had never, not perhaps since their parting, been released by anyone or anything.

They sat down and again looked intently at each other.

'Are you well?' asked Andrey.

'Yes, I'm all right now, thank God.'

'But you've been ill, have you?'

'Yes, Andrey; I had a stroke.'

'Really? Good Lord!' Andrey cried with alarm and sympathy. 'No after effects?'

'No, except that I can't use my left leg freely,' replied Oblomov.

'Oh, Ilya, Ilya! What is the matter with you? You've gone to seed completely. What have you been doing all this time? Do you realize we haven't seen each other for almost five years?'

Oblomov fetched a sigh.

'Why didn't you come to Oblomovka? Why didn't you write?'

'What shall I say to you, Andrey? You know me, so don't, please, ask me any more,' Oblomov said sadly.

'And all the time here in this flat?' Stolz said, looking round the room. 'You never moved?'

'No, I've lived here all the time. I'll never move now.'

'Do you really mean it? Never?'

'I really do mean it, Andrey.'

Stolz looked at him intently, fell into thought, and began pacing the room.

'And Olga Sergeyevna? Is she all right? Where is she? Does she still remember me?'

He broke off.

'She's all right, and she remembers you just as though you had parted only yesterday. I'll tell you presently where she is ...'

'And your children?'

'They are well too. But tell me, Ilya, are you serious about staying here? You see, I've come for you, to take you to us, to the country. ...'

'No, no!' Oblomov cried, lowering his voice and glancing apprehensively at the door, as though he were alarmed. 'No, please don't mention it – don't talk of it.'

'Why not? What is the matter with you?' Stolz began. 'You know me: I've set myself this task long ago, and I'm not going to give it up. Till now I've been prevented by all sorts of business, but now I am free. You must live with us, near us. That is what Olga and I have decided and that is what it is going to be. Thank God I have found you as you are and not worse. I hadn't hoped ... Come along, then! I'm quite ready to take you away by force! You must live differently – you know how ...'

Oblomov listened to this tirade with impatience.

'Please don't shout,' he begged. 'Speak softly ... there – –'

'What do you mean, "there"?'

'I mean, they may hear there and – and my landlady may think that I really want to go away.'

'What does it matter? Let her!'

'Oh, I can't possibly do that!' Oblomov interrupted. 'Listen, Andrey,' he added suddenly in a determined tone Stolz had never heard him use before; 'don't waste your time trying to persuade me: I shall stay here!'

Stolz looked at his friend in surprise. Oblomov met his look calmly and resolutely.

'You're done for, Ilya!' he said. 'This house, this woman – the whole of this way of living. ... It's impossible! Come on, let's go!'

He seized him by the sleeve and was dragging him towards the door.

'Why do you want to take me away? Where to?' said Oblomov, resisting him.

'Out of this pit, this bog, into the light, into the open, to a normal life!' Stolz insisted sternly, almost imperiously. 'Where are you? What has become of you? Come to your senses! Is this the sort of life you have been preparing yourself for – to sleep like a mole in its burrow? You'd better cast your mind back! ...'

'Don't remind me, don't disturb the past, for you will never bring it back,' Oblomov said, looking fully aware of what he was saying and determined to do as he thought fit. 'What do you want to do with me? I've broken completely with the world into which you are dragging me: you cannot weld together two halves that have come apart. I am attached to this hole with the most vulnerable part of my body – if you try to drag me away, I shall die!'

'But for goodness' sake, man, have a good look round where you are and in what company!'

'I know, I am aware of it. ... Oh, Andrey, I am aware of everything and I understand everything: I have for a long time been ashamed to live in the world! But I can't go on the same road as you even if I wanted to. Last time you were here it might perhaps have been possible, but now' – he dropped his eyes and paused for a moment – 'now it is too late. You go and don't wait for me. I am worthy of your friendship, God knows, but I'm not worth your trouble.'

'No, Ilya, you're hiding something from me. I tell you I'm determined to take you away just because I suspect you. Listen,' he said; 'put on some clothes and let's go to my place. Spend an evening with me. I've got lots to tell you: you don't know the exciting things that are happening in our part of the country now. You have not heard, have you?'

Oblomov looked questioningly at him.

'I forgot, you never see people: come along, I'll tell you everything. Do you know who is waiting for me in the carriage at the gate? I'll call her!'

'Olga!' Oblomov suddenly cried in alarm, and he even turned pale. 'For God's sake, don't let her come in here. Please, go away. Good-bye, good-bye, for God's sake!'

He was almost pushing Stolz out of the room; but Stolz did not move from his place.

'I can't go to her without you. I gave her my word – do you hear, Ilya? If not to-day, then to-morrow – you will only put it off, you won't drive me away. ... To-morrow or the day after – but we shall meet again!'

Oblomov was silent, bowing his head and not daring to look at Stolz.

'When is it to be? Olga is sure to ask me.'

'Oh, Andrey,' he said in a tender, beseeching voice, embracing him and putting his head on Stolz's shoulder, 'please leave me altogether – forget me – –'

'What, for ever?' Stolz asked in amazement, freeing himself from Oblomov's embrace and looking into his face.

'Yes,' whispered Oblomov.

Stolz stepped back from him.

'Is it you, Ilya?' he said reproachfully. 'You are pushing me away, and for her – for that woman! Good Lord,' he almost cried out, as though with sudden pain; 'this child I saw here just now – Ilya, Ilya! Run – run from here! Let's go this minute! How you have fallen! That woman – what is she to you?'

'She's my wife,' Oblomov said calmly.

Stolz was dumbfounded.

'And that child is my son! His name is Andrey, I called him after you!' Oblomov concluded his confession and breathed freely, having thrown off the burden of his secret.

It was now Stolz's turn to change colour. He looked round with bewildered almost senseless eyes. The 'gulf' suddenly 'opened up' before him and the 'stone wall' rose up and Oblomov did not seem to be there any longer, just as though he had vanished from his sight or sunk through the floor; he only felt that burning anguish a man feels when he hastens in excitement to meet a friend after a long separation and learns that the friend had long been dead.

'Done for!' he whispered mechanically. 'What am I going to tell Olga?'

Oblomov heard the last words and was going to say something, but could not. He held out both his arms to Andrey, they embraced firmly and in silence, as people embrace before a battle, before death. This embrace stifled their words, their tears, their feelings.

'Don't forget my Andrey!' were Oblomov's last words, which he uttered in a faint voice.

Andrey walked out of the house slowly and in silence, walked slowly and thoughtfully across the courtyard, and stepped into the carriage, while Oblomov sat down on the sofa and, leaning his elbows on the table, buried his face in his hands.

'No, I shall not forget your Andrey,' Stolz thought sadly as he walked across the yard. 'You're done for, Ilya: it is useless to tell you that your Oblomovka is no longer in the wilds, that its turn has come, and that the rays of sunshine have at last fallen upon it! I shall not tell you that in another four years there will be a railway station there, that your peasants will be working on the line, and that later on your corn will be carried by train to the quayside. And then – schools, education, and after that – but no! You will be frightened of the dawn of new happiness; it will hurt your eyes that are unaccustomed to the bright light. But I shall lead your Andrey to where you would not go, and I will carry out your youthful dreams together with him. Goodbye, old Oblomovka!' he said, looking back for the last time at the windows of the little house. 'You've had your day!'

'What's happening there?' Olga asked with a fast-beating heart.

'Nothing!' Andrey replied dryly and curtly.

'Is he alive and well?'

'Yes,' Andrey replied reluctantly.

'Why have you come back so soon? Why didn't you call me there or bring him here? Let me go to him!'

'You can't go to him!'

'What is happening there?' Olga asked in alarm. 'Has "the gulf opened up"? Are you going to tell me?'

He was silent.

'But what on earth is going on there?'

'Oblomovitis!' Andrey replied gloomily, and in spite of Olga's questions preserved a sullen silence till they got home.

10

FIVE years had passed. There had been many changes in Vyborg: the empty street leading to Mrs Pshenitzyn's house was full of newly built summer cottages, and among them rose a long brick Government building which prevented the sunshine from pouring in gaily through the windows of the peaceful refuge of tranquillity and indolence. The little house itself had become a little dilapidated and looked rather grimy and untidy, like a man who has not shaven and washed. The paint had peeled off, the rainpipes were broken in places, and there were, therefore, big puddles in the yard across which, as in the old days, a narrow plank was laid. When someone went in at the gate, the old black dog did not jump vigorously on the chain, but barked hoarsely and lazily without coming out of the kennel.

And the changes inside the house! Another woman was ruling over it and different children were playing about there. The red, drunken face of the rowdy Tarantyev appeared there again from time to time, and the gentle and meek Alexeyev was no longer to be seen there. Neither was Zakhar or Anisya to be seen: a new, fat woman cook was in charge of the kitchen, reluctantly and rudely carrying out the quiet orders of Agafya Matveyevna, and the same Akulina, the hem of her skirt tucked in at the waist, was washing troughs and earthenware jars; the same sleepy caretaker in the same sheepskin was idly spending the remaining years of his life in his dark hovel. Ivan Matveyevich's figure again darted past the trellised fence at the appointed hours of early morning and dinner-time with a big parcel under his arm and goloshes on his feet, in winter and summer.

What has become of Oblomov? Where is he? Where? His body is resting under a modest urn, surrounded by shrubs, in a lonely corner of the nearest graveyard. Branches of lilac, planted by a friendly hand, slumber over his grave, and the wormwood spreads its sharp scent in the still air. The angel of peace himself seems to be guarding his sleep. However keenly the loving eyes of his wife kept watch over every moment of his life, perpetual rest, perpetual stillness, and the indolent passage of time slowly brought the mechanism of life to a standstill. Oblomov passed away apparently without pain, without suffering, just like a clock that has stopped because it has not been wound up. No one witnessed his last moments or heard his last groan. He had another stroke a year after the first, and again he recovered from it, but then he grew weak and pale, ate little, hardly ever went out into the garden, and grew more and more taciturn and thoughtful; sometimes he even wept. He had a feeling that death was near, and he was afraid of it. He had several dizzy spells, but these passed off. One morning Agafya Matveyevna brought him his coffee as usual, and found him resting as gently in death as he had rested in sleep, except that his head had slipped off the pillow and his hand was convulsively pressed to his heart, where apparently a blood vessel had burst.

Agafya Matveyevna had been a widow for three years; during that time everything had gone back to what it had used to be before. Her brother had been dealing in Government contracts, but had gone bankrupt and managed in all sorts of devious ways to obtain his old job of secretary in the office 'where peasants were registered'; and again he walked to the office, bringing back fifty, twenty-five, and twenty copeck pieces to deposit them in his well-hidden box. Once more, as in the old days before Oblomov's arrival, they had the same plain and coarse, but rich and plentiful meals. The leading role in the house was now occupied by Ivan Matveyevich's wife, Irina Panteleyevna – that is, she reserved the right to get up late, drink coffee three times a day, change her dress three times a day, and see to one thing only in the house, namely, that her petticoats were starched as stiffly as possible. She did not concern herself with anything else, and Agafya Matveyevna was, as before, the live wire in the house: she looked after the kitchen and the meals, poured out tea and coffee for the whole family, mended their clothes, kept an eye on the washing, and the children, Akulina, and the caretaker. But why did she do that? Wasn't she Mrs Oblomov, a landowner? Couldn't she have lived by herself, independently and without being in need of anything or anybody? What could have made her assume the burden of other people's housekeeping, of looking after other people's children, and all those trifles to which a woman devotes herself either for love, for the sacred duty of family ties, or for the sake of a livelihood? Where were Zakhar and Anisya, her servants by every right? Where, finally, was the living pledge left her by her husband, little Andrey? Where are her children by her first marriage?

Her children are settled in life – that is to say, Vanya has finished his course of studies and has got a job in the Civil Service; Masha has married the superintendent of some Government office, and little Andrey is being brought up by Stolz and his wife, at their earnest request, and is being treated by them as a member of their family. Agafya Matveyevna never thought of little Andrey's future as in any way comparable to the future of her older children, though in her heart she unconsciously perhaps gave an equal place to them all. But little Andrey's education, manner of living, and future she considered to be altogether different from the lives of Vanya and Masha.

'Those two,' she said indifferently, 'are street arabs like myself. They were born for a hard life; but this one,' she added, almost with respect, fondling little Andrey, if not with timidity, then with care, 'is a little gentleman! See how fair his skin is – like a ripe peach! Such tiny hands and feet and hair like silk. He's the spit and image of his father!'

That was why she had agreed without protest, and even with a certain joy, to Stolz's proposal to bring up little Andrey with his own children, believing that his proper place was there, and not in her house, among 'the rabble', with her dirty nephews, her brother's children.

For about six months after Oblomov's death she lived with Zakhar and Anisya in the house, giving herself up to grief. She had trodden a path to her husband's grave and wept her eyes out, hardly ate or drank anything, and lived chiefly on tea; she scarcely closed her eyes at night and was completely worn out. She never complained to anyone about anything and as time passed she seemed to become more and more absorbed in herself, in her sorrow, and shut everyone out, even Anisya. Nobody knew what she really felt.

'Your mistress is still weeping for her husband,' the grocer said to the cook.

'Still sorrowing for her husband,' the churchwarden remarked, pointing her out to the woman who baked the host for the cemetery church, where the disconsolate widow came every week to weep and pray.

'She's still wasting away with grief,' they said in her brother's house.

One day the entire family of her brother's, the children, and even Tarantyev, suddenly descended upon her house under the pretext of offering condolences. They overwhelmed her with vulgar consolations and entreaties 'to spare herself for the sake of her children' – all that had been said to her fifteen years ago, when her first husband had died, and it had had the desired effect at that time; but now, for some reason it made her feel disgusted and wretched. She was relieved when they changed the subject and told her that now they could live together again and that it would be better for her because 'she would be wretched among her own people', and for them because no one could look after the house as well as she. She asked for time to think it over, and after grieving for another two months, she at last agreed to share the house with them. It was at that time that Stolz took little Andrey to live with him, and she was left alone.

Wearing a dark dress and with a black woollen shawl round her neck, she would walk from her room to the kitchen like a shadow, opened and closed cupboards as before, sewed, ironed lace, but slowly and without energy; she spoke, as it were, reluctantly, and in a low voice, and she no longer as before looked about her unconcernedly with eyes that never remained fixed in one place, but with an expression of concentration on her face and a hidden meaning in her eyes. This thought seemed to have imperceptibly settled on her face at the moment when she gazed intently and for a long time at her husband's dead face, and had never left her since. She moved about the house, did all that was necessary, but her mind was not on her work. Over her husband's dead body, and after she had lost him, she seemed suddenly to have grasped the whole meaning of her life and pondered over it – and ever since that thought lay brooding over her face like a shadow. Having sobbed out her intense grief, she concentrated on the sense of her loss: the rest was dead for her, except little Andrey. It was only when she saw him that she seemed to show signs of life and her features revived, her eyes filled with a joyful light and then with the tears of remembrance. She lost interest in all that happened around her: if her brother was angry because an extra rouble had been spent, or the roast was slightly burnt, or the fish was not quite as fresh as he liked; if her sister-in-law sulked because her petticoat had not been starched stiffly enough or her tea was weak or cold; if the cook was rude to her – Agafya Matveyevna did not notice anything, just as though they were not talking of her, and as though she never heard the sarcastic whisper: 'A lady, a landowner!' Her answer to it all was contained in the dignity of her sorrow and in her resigned silence. On the other hand, at Christmas or on Easter Sunday, or on the gay parties at Shrovetide, when everyone in the house was rejoicing, singing, eating, and drinking, she would suddenly burst into tears amid the general merry-making and hide herself in her room. Then she would withdraw into herself again and sometimes even look at her brother and his wife, as it were, with pride and pity. She realized that joy and laughter had gone out of her life, that God had breathed a soul into her and taken it away again, that the sun that had shone over her had set for ever. ... For ever, it is true; but her life, too, had gained a meaning for ever: for now she knew why she had lived and that she had not lived in vain.

She had loved so much and so utterly: she had loved Oblomov as a lover, as a husband, and as a born gentleman; but, as before, she could never tell this to anyone. And no one around her would have understood her. Where would she have found the right words? No such words were to be found in her brother's, Tarantyev's, or her sister-in-law's vocabulary, because they all lacked the ideas those words expressed; only Oblomov would have understood her, but she never told him, because at the time she did not understand it herself and did not know how to express it. As the years passed, she understood her past better and better and hid it more deeply within herself, becoming more taciturn and reserved. The seven years that had flown by like a moment shed their soft light over her whole life, and there was nothing more for her to desire, nowhere farther to go. Only when Stolz came to Petersburg for the winter, she ran to his house and looked eagerly at little Andrey, caressing him with timid tenderness; she would have liked to say something to Stolz, to thank him, to lay before him all that was pent up in her heart and was locked up there for ever – he would have understood her, but she did not know how to, and she merely rushed to Olga, pressed her lips to her hands, and burst into such a flood of scalding tears that Olga could not help weeping with her too, and Andrey, greatly agitated, hurried out of the room. They were all bound by the same feeling, the same memory of the crystal-clear soul of their dead friend. They tried to persuade her to go to the country with them and live with them, near little Andrey, but she always replied: 'Where one was born and bred, there one must die.' In vain did Stolz give her an account of his management of her estate and sent her the income due to her. She returned it all and asked him to keep it for little Andrey.

'It is his, not mine,' she repeated obstinately. 'He will need it, he is a gentleman, and I can manage without it.'

11

Two gentlemen were walking along the wooden pavements of Vyborg about twelve o'clock one day; a carriage slowly followed them. One of them was Stolz, and the other a friend of his, a writer, a stout man with an apathetic face and with pensive and, as it were, sleepy eyes. They came to a church; morning mass was over and people were pouring into the street, preceded by a large crowd of beggars of all sorts.

'I should like to know where the beggars come from,' said the writer, looking at the beggars.

'Where they come from? Why, from all sorts of nooks and crannies.'

'I don't mean that,' the writer answered. 'I should like to know how one becomes a beggar – how does one get to such a position? Does it happen suddenly or gradually? Is it true or false?'

'What do you want to know that for? Not going to write *Mystères de Petersbourg*, are you?'

'Maybe,' the writer replied, yawning lazily.

'Well, here's your chance: ask any one of them, and for a rouble he'll sell you the story of his life. You can write it down and sell it at a profit. Here's an old man who seems to be a most ordinary type of beggar. I say, old man, come here a moment, will you?'

The old man turned at the call, took off his hat and walked up to them.

'Kind sir,' he wheezed, 'help a poor old soldier, badly wounded in thirty battles – –'

'Zakhar!' Stolz cried in surprise. 'Is that you?'

Zakhar fell silent suddenly, then, screening his eyes from the sun with a hand, he looked intently at Stolz.

'I'm sorry, sir, I can't recognize you at all, I'm afraid – I'm quite blind, sir.'

'You haven't forgotten Stolz, your master's friend, have you?' Stolz said reproachfully.

'Why, Mr Stolz, sir! I must be as blind as a post, sir! I'm sorry, sir!'

He tried to catch Stolz's hand, and in his excitement missed it and kissed the skirt of his coat.

'Praise be to God, sir, for letting a miserable cur like me live to see such a joyful day,' he shouted, half crying and half laughing.

All his face, from forehead to chin, seemed to have been branded with purple. His nose had, besides, a bluish tint. He was quite bald; his whiskers were as big as before, but they were tangled into a thick mat, and each looked as though a lump of snow had been put in it. He wore a threadbare and completely faded overcoat, one side of which was torn off, a pair of old and worn goloshes on his bare feet, and in his hand he held a worn fur cap.

'The dear Lord, sir, has done me a real favour this morning on account of its being a feast-day, I suppose.'

'Why are you in such a state? Aren't you ashamed?'

'Good Lord, sir, what was I to do?' Zakhar began, heaving a deep sigh. 'I have to keep body and soul together, sir. Now, you see, sir, when Anisya was alive, I didn't knock about the streets, for I had enough to eat, but when she died during the cholera – God rest her soul – the mistress's brother refused to keep me – called me a parasite, he did, and Mr Tarantyev always tried to kick me from behind as I walked past him. Oh, sir, it wasn't much of a life, I can tell you. The names they called me, sir! Would you believe it, sir, things came to such a pass that I couldn't eat a bite – lost my appetite I have. If it wasn't for the mistress – God bless her! – I'd have perished long ago in the frost. She gives me some clothes for the winter and as much bread as I want, and she used to give me a corner on the stove, too, bless her heart, but they began nagging at her on my account, so I just walked out of the house, sir. Aye, sir, it'll be two years soon since I began leading this wretched life ...'

'Why didn't you take a job?' asked Stolz.

'Why, sir, you can't find jobs so easily nowadays. I had two situations, sir, but I didn't give satisfaction. It's all different now, not like it was in the good old days, sir. It's much worse. A footman must know how to read and write, and great noblemen, sir, haven't their entrance halls crammed with servants as they used to. All they want is one footman or at most two. They take their boots off themselves, seem to have invented some special machine for that,' Zakhar went on mournfully. 'It's a blooming shame and a disgrace, sir! There won't be any gentry left soon!'

He heaved a sigh.

'You see, sir, I got a job with one of them German merchants to sit in the hall. All went well till he sent me to wait at table. It's not really my line of business, sir, is it? I was carrying some crockery one day – Bohemian china, it was – and the floors were slippery, damn them! Well, sir, my feet suddenly slid apart and all the crockery – the whole blooming lot, sir, tray and all – crashed to the floor. Well, of course, sir, they gave me the sack. Another time an old countess liked the look of me. "You seem respectable," she says to me, and gave me the job of hall porter. It's a good old-fashioned sort of job, sir. All you have to do is to sit on a chair and look important, cross your legs, and just swing one foot slowly like, and if anyone comes you mustn't answer at once, but first you must give a growl and then let him in or kick him out, all according. And, of course, if important visitors come you must salute them with your staff, like that, sir!' Zakhar showed with his arm how to salute. 'It's a fine job, sir, and no mistake. But her ladyship was difficult to please – very difficult indeed! One day she looked into my room, saw a bug, and kicked up such an unholy row, sir, just as if I had invented bugs! What house is without bugs, sir? Anyway, another time she walked past me and thought that I smelt of vodka. Now, I ask you, sir! And she sacked me. ...'

'You certainly reek of vodka, and very strongly, too!' said Stolz.

'Aye, sir, I have a drop now and again to drown my sorrows; aye, sir, to drown my sorrows,' Zakhar wheezed, screwing up his face in bitter resentment of his fate. 'I tried being a cab-driver, too, sir. Hired myself out to a cab-owner, I did, but I had my feet frozen. Aye, sir, lost my strength, I have; getting old, that's the trouble! Got a real beast of a horse too. One day it rushed under a carriage and nearly threw me off my box. Another time I ran over an old woman and got dragged off to the police station. ...'

'There, that'll do! Now, listen; don't drink and don't knock about the streets, but come to me and I'll find some place for you in my house – you can come to the country with us – do you hear?'

'Yes, sir, but – –'

He heaved a sigh.

'You see, sir, I shouldn't like to go away from here – from his grave, I mean! Our dear master Ilya Ilyich,' he cried. 'I've said a prayer for him again to-day, God rest his soul! What a master the good Lord has taken away from me, sir. He just lived to make everybody happy – aye, he should have lived a hundred years, he should, sir,' Zakhar, said, whimpering and screwing up his face. 'Been to his grave to-day, I have, sir. Whenever I happen to be in them parts, sir, I goes straight to his grave. Sits there for hours, I does, with tears streaming from my eyes, sir. Sometimes I falls to thinking, it is very quiet all round, and suddenly I fancies he's calling me: "Zakhar! Zakhar!" Oh dear, it fairly gives me the creeps, so it does, sir! Aye, I shan't have another master like him – that's certain! And how he loved you, sir, the Lord bless his soul!'

'Well, come and have a look at little Andrey. I'll tell them to give you a meal and decent clothes, and then you can do as you like,' said Stolz, giving him some money.

'I'll come, sir; of course I'll come to have a look at the master's little boy! I expect he's grown up by now! Dear me, what a joyful day this has been! Yes, sir, I'll come; may the Lord keep you in good health and grant you many more years to live,' Zakhar growled, as the carriage drove away.

'Well, you've heard the story of this beggar, haven't you?' Stolz said to his friend.

'Who is this Ilya Ilyich he mentioned?' asked the writer.

'Oblomov: I've often spoken to you about him.'

'Yes, I remember the name, he was your friend and school-fellow. What became of him?'

'He's dead. He wasted his life!'

Stolz sighed and fell into thought.

'And he was as intelligent as anybody, his soul was pure and clear as crystal – noble, affectionate, and – he perished!'

'But why? What was the reason?'

'The reason – what a reason! Oblomovitis!' said Stolz.

'Oblomovitis?' the writer repeated in bewilderment. 'What's that?'

'I'll tell you in a moment: let me collect my thoughts and memories. And you write it down: someone may find it useful.'

And he told him what is written here.

FOR THE BEST IN PAPERBACKS, LOOK FOR THE 🐧

In every corner of the world, on every subject under the sun, Penguin represents quality and variety – the very best in publishing today.

For complete information about books available from Penguin – including Puffins, Penguin Classics and Arkana – and how to order them, write to us at the appropriate address below. Please note that for copyright reasons the selection of books varies from country to country.

In the United Kingdom: Please write to *Dept JC, Penguin Books Ltd, FREEPOST, West Drayton, Middlesex, UB7 0BR.*

If you have any difficulty in obtaining a title, please send your order with the correct money, plus ten per cent for postage and packaging, to *PO Box No 11, West Drayton, Middlesex*

In the United States: Please write to *Dept BA, Penguin, 299 Murray Hill Parkway, East Rutherford, New Jersey 07073*

In Canada: Please write to *Penguin Books Canada Ltd, 2801 John Street, Markham, Ontario L3R 1B4*

In Australia: Please write to the *Marketing Department, Penguin Books Australia Ltd, P.O. Box 257, Ringwood, Victoria 3134*

In New Zealand: Please write to the *Marketing Department, Penguin Books (NZ) Ltd, Private Bag, Takapuna, Auckland 9*

In India: Please write to *Penguin Overseas Ltd, 706 Eros Apartments, 56 Nehru Place, New Delhi, 110019*

In the Netherlands: Please write to *Penguin Books Netherlands B.V., Postbus 3507, NL–1001 AH, Amsterdam*

In West Germany: Please write to *Penguin Books Ltd, Friedrichstrasse 10–12, D–6000 Frankfurt/Main 1*

In Spain: Please write to *Alhambra Longman S.A., Fernandez de la Hoz 9, E–28010 Madrid*

In Italy: Please write to *Penguin Italia s.r.l., Via Como 4, I-20096 Pioltello (Milano)*

In France: Please write to *Penguin France S.A., 17 rue Lejeune, F-31000 Toulouse*

In Japan: Please write to *Longman Penguin Japan Co Ltd, Yamaguchi Building, 2–12–9 Kanda Jimbocho, Chiyoda-Ku, Tokyo 101*

FOR THE BEST IN PAPERBACKS, LOOK FOR THE 🐧

PENGUIN CLASSICS

Charles Dickens	**American Notes for General Circulation**
	Barnaby Rudge
	Bleak House
	The Christmas Books
	David Copperfield
	Dombey and Son
	Great Expectations
	Hard Times
	Little Dorrit
	Martin Chuzzlewit
	The Mystery of Edwin Drood
	Nicholas Nickleby
	The Old Curiosity Shop
	Oliver Twist
	Our Mutual Friend
	The Pickwick Papers
	Selected Short Fiction
	A Tale of Two Cities
Edward Gibbon	**The Decline and Fall of the Roman Empire**
George Gissing	**New Grub Street**
William Godwin	**Caleb Williams**
Edmund Gosse	**Father and Son**
Thomas Hardy	**The Distracted Preacher and Other Tales**
	Far From the Madding Crowd
	Jude the Obscure
	The Mayor of Casterbridge
	The Return of the Native
	Tess of the d'Urbervilles
	The Trumpet Major
	Under the Greenwood Tree
	The Woodlanders

FOR THE BEST IN PAPERBACKS, LOOK FOR THE 🐧

PENGUIN CLASSICS

Richard Jefferies	**Landscape with Figures**
Thomas Macaulay	**The History of England**
Henry Mayhew	**Selections from London Labour and The London Poor**
John Stuart Mill	**On Liberty**
William Morris	**News from Nowhere and Selected Writings and Designs**
Walter Pater	**Marius the Epicurean**
John Ruskin	**'Unto This Last' and Other Writings**
Sir Walter Scott	**Ivanhoe**
Robert Louis Stevenson	**Dr Jekyll and Mr Hyde**
William Makepeace Thackeray	**The History of Henry Esmond**
	Vanity Fair
Anthony Trollope	**Barchester Towers**
	Framley Parsonage
	Phineas Finn
	The Warden
Mrs Humphrey Ward	**Helbeck of Bannisdale**
Mary Wollstonecraft	**Vindication of the Rights of Woman**
Dorothy and William Wordsworth	**Home at Grasmere**

Honoré de Balzac	**The Black Sheep**
	The Chouans
	Cousin Bette
	Eugénie Grandet
	Lost Illusions
	Old Goriot
	Ursule Mirouet
Corneille	**The Cid/Cinna/The Theatrical Illusion**
Alphonse Daudet	**Letters from My Windmill**
René Descartes	**Discourse on Method and Other Writings**
Denis Diderot	**Jacques the Fatalist**
Gustave Flaubert	**Madame Bovary**
	Sentimental Education
	Three Tales
Marie de France	**Lais**
Jean Froissart	**The Chronicles**
Théophile Gautier	**Mademoiselle de Maupin**
Edmond and Jules de	
Goncourt	**Germinie Lacerteux**
La Fontaine	**Selected Fables**
Guy de Maupassant	**Bel-Ami**
	Pierre and Jean
	Selected Short Stories
	A Woman's Life

FOR THE BEST IN PAPERBACKS, LOOK FOR THE 🐧

PENGUIN CLASSICS

Pedro de Alarcón	**The Three-Cornered Hat and Other Stories**
Leopoldo Alas	**La Regenta**
Ludovico Ariosto	**Orlando Furioso**
Giovanni Boccaccio	**The Decameron**
Baldassar Castiglione	**The Book of the Courtier**
Benvenuto Cellini	**Autobiography**
Miguel de Cervantes	**Don Quixote**
	Exemplary Stories
Dante	**The Divine Comedy** (in 3 volumes)
	La Vita Nuova
Bernal Diaz	**The Conquest of New Spain**
Carlo Goldoni	**Four Comedies (The Venetian Twins/The Artful Widow/Mirandolina/The Superior Residence)**
Niccolò Machiavelli	**The Discourses**
	The Prince
Alessandro Manzoni	**The Betrothed**
Benito Pérez Galdós	**Fortunata and Jacinta**
Giorgio Vasari	**Lives of the Artists** (in 2 volumes)

and

Five Italian Renaissance Comedies (Machiavelli/**The Mandragola;**
   Ariosto/**Lena;** Aretino/**The Stablemaster;**
   Gl'Intronati/**The Deceived;** Guarini/**The Faithful Shepherd**)
The Jewish Poets of Spain
The Poem of the Cid
Two Spanish Picaresque Novels (Anon/**Lazarillo de Tormes;**
   de Quevedo/**The Swindler**)

PENGUIN CLASSICS

Carl von Clausewitz	**On War**
Friedrich Engels	**The Origins of the Family, Private Property and the State**
Wolfram von Eschenbach	**Parzival**
	Willehalm
Goethe	**Elective Affinities**
	Faust
	Italian Journey 1786–88
	The Sorrows of Young Werther
Jacob and Wilhelm Grimm	**Selected Tales**
E. T. A. Hoffmann	**Tales of Hoffmann**
Henrik Ibsen	**The Doll's House/The League of Youth/The Lady from the Sea**
	Ghosts/A Public Enemy/When We Dead Wake
	Hedda Gabler/The Pillars of the Community/The Wild Duck
	The Master Builder/Rosmersholm/Little Eyolf/ John Gabriel Borkman
	Peer Gynt
Søren Kierkegaard	**Fear and Trembling**
	The Sickness Unto Death
Friedrich Nietzsche	**Beyond Good and Evil**
	Ecce Homo
	A Nietzsche Reader
	Thus Spoke Zarathustra
	Twilight of the Idols and The Anti-Christ
Friedrich Schiller	**The Robbers and Wallenstein**
Arthur Schopenhauer	**Essays and Aphorisms**
Gottfried von Strassburg	**Tristan**
August Strindberg	**Inferno and From an Occult Diary**

Anton Chekhov	**The Duel and Other Stories**
	The Kiss and Other Stories
	Lady with Lapdog and Other Stories
	Plays (The Cherry Orchard/Ivanov/The Seagull/ Uncle Vanya/The Bear/The Proposal/A Jubilee/Three Sisters)
	The Party and Other Stories
Fyodor Dostoyevsky	**The Brothers Karamazov**
	Crime and Punishment
	The Devils
	The Gambler/Bobok/A Nasty Story
	The House of the Dead
	The Idiot
	Notes From Underground and **The Double**
Nikolai Gogol	**Dead Souls**
	Diary of a Madman and Other Stories
Maxim Gorky	**My Apprenticeship**
	My Childhood
	My Universities
Mikhail Lermontov	**A Hero of Our Time**
Alexander Pushkin	**Eugene Onegin**
Leo Tolstoy	**Anna Karenin**
	Childhood/Boyhood/Youth
	The Cossacks/The Death of Ivan Ilyich/Happy Ever After
	The Kreutzer Sonata and Other Stories
	Master and Man and Other Stories
	Resurrection
	The Sebastopol Sketches
	War and Peace
Ivan Turgenev	**Fathers and Sons**
	First Love
	A Month in the Country
	On the Eve
	Rudin